DESERVES
TO DIE

Books by Lisa Jackson

Stand-Alones

SEE HOW SHE DIES
FINAL SCREAM
RUNNING SCARED
WHISPERS
TWICE KISSED
UNSPOKEN
DEEP FREEZE
FATAL BURN
MOST LIKELY TO DIE
WICKED GAME
WICKED LIES
SOMETHING WICKED
SINISTER
WITHOUT MERCY
YOU DON'T WANT TO KNOW
CLOSE TO HOME

Anthony Paterno/Cahill Family Novels
IF SHE ONLY KNEW
ALMOST DEAD

Rick Bentz/Reuben Montoya Novels
HOT BLOODED
COLD BLOODED
SHIVER
ABSOLUTE FEAR
LOST SOULS
MALICE
DEVIOUS

Pierce Reed/Nikki Gillette Novels
THE NIGHT BEFORE
THE MORNING AFTER
TELL ME

Selena Alvarez/Regan Pescoli Novels
LEFT TO DIE
CHOSEN TO DIE
BORN TO DIE
AFRAID TO DIE
READY TO DIE
DESERVES TO DIE

Published by Kensington Publishing Corporation

LISA JACKSON

DESERVES TO DIE

KENSINGTON BOOKS

KENSINGTON BOOKS are published by

Kensington Publishing Corp.
119 West 40th Street
New York, NY 10019

Kensington and the K logo Reg. U.S. Pat. & TM Off.

ISBN 978-1-62953-154-0

Printed in the United States of America

DESERVES
TO DIE

Prologue

The Louisiana Bayou
October

She wasn't quite dead.

Though her eyes seemed fixed as they stared up at the night sky, her breathing was shallow, her heart still faintly beating as she lay, faceup on the tarp. She was still alive, but barely, only inches and seconds from meeting the grim reaper, which was a good thing, he thought. No longer could she taunt or ridicule anyone. No longer would she ever smirk again. Comatose, so near death that it would take little for her to cross over, she lay on the marshy bank of the bayou, an easy victim.

Crouching over her, he grinned at her ultimate vulnerability. If he wanted to, he could slice her throat and watch drips of blood accumulate over the grotesque smile he would carve into her white flesh.

He considered doing the deed with his knife, a slim switchblade that felt heavy in his pocket.

But no, she was close enough to death already and he had another, more intimate way of slicing her.

Something jumped into the murky water not ten feet away. A bullfrog maybe? It reminded him to get back to work; he didn't have much time. A full moon was rising, casting silvery shadows through the white-barked cypress, their roots exposed, Spanish moss draping over the dark water. Crickets chirped, fish jumped, and the water lapped gently in the isolated stretch of Louisiana.

Beads of sweat dotted his brow and ran down his face, creating salty tracks that passed over his lips and dropped onto her still body as he took her left hand in his, splaying her fingers easily. Antique diamonds winked in the pale moonlight, their brilliance seeming to mock him. Oh, what those icy stones had meant, the promises that had been vowed, the secrets they held.

A deep, smoldering rage ran through him as he eyed the stones. Using his free hand, he pulled a slim, automatic pocket knife from his pocket and clicked the blade open. It too reflected the moonlight. Without hesitation, he went to work, holding her fingers wide, then cutting quickly, nearly seamlessly slicing her finger off at the knuckle.

She didn't so much as flinch.

As her blood pumped, he yanked the ring from its ugly stump and felt a welling satisfaction at a job well done.

Straightening, he looked down at her, nearly a corpse, her gauzy dress filthy, her beautiful face condemned to death.

He held her finger in his open palm, the ring now his.

Exquisite diamonds.

So easily removed.

So easily pocketed.

Satisfied, he kicked the body off its mound, watching it roll down the short bank. With a soft splash, she slipped into the murky water to float for a second, catching the slow moving current, heading downstream and out of sight.

"Good riddance," he whispered.

He took in several deep breaths and wiped his brow before pocketing his treasure. As he turned back toward the dense foliage, he heard another sound over the chorus of crickets and bullfrogs, a quiet, ominous splash, the sound of a large reptile sliding into the water.

Perfect, he thought as the creature swam noiselessly under the water's surface. He smiled as he hurried to his hidden truck, knowing that she was already gator bait.

As if on cue, there was a loud splash, a frantic, sickening roiling of water, a flash of a white belly as the reptile rolled to make its kill, jagged teeth sinking into her skin, vise-like jaws gripping and pulling her under the water until the last bit of air escaped her lungs.

Then all went quiet for a second as the stillness of the bayou surrounded him and only the barest of ripples spread to the surrounding water. The chorus of insects, momentarily silenced, began again.

A fitting end, he thought. It served the cheating bitch right.

CHAPTER 1

Grizzly Falls, Montana
January

*T*his has to be the place.

Jessica Williams stared at the dilapidated cabin and her heart sank. Of course she'd been hoping for an isolated place to live, one without the prying eyes of nosy neighbors, but this little cottage went far beyond *rustic*, with its mossy roof, sagging porch, and rusted downspouts. At least the windows weren't boarded over, and there was a garage of sorts, but it was all piled under nearly a foot of snow. She doubted very strongly that there was any central heat within the building. If she'd expected a haven, she'd been sorely disappointed.

Too bad.

For the foreseeable future, this little eighty-year-old building nestled deep in the forested foothills of the Bitterroots was going to be home, whether she liked it or not.

"*Not*, is what I'm thinking," she said as she hopped from the cab of her ancient SUV, a Chevy that had over two hundred thousand miles on its odometer, and into the pristine snow. The air was crisp and cold, the snow crusted over and no longer falling. For the last fifty miles of her long journey the Tahoe's engine light had been blinking on and off and she'd ignored the warning, praying that she would get there before the damn thing overheated or gave out completely. Somehow, subsisting on energy bars, bags of Doritos, Red Bull, and bottled water, she'd arrived after nearly thirty-six hours on the road. She was tired to the marrow of her bones, but she couldn't stop. Not yet.

She glanced behind her vehicle to what could barely be called a lane where there was the merest break in the trees, just wide enough for her rig to pass. Twin ruts broke up the pristine mantle of snow, evidence that someone was occupying the cabin.

Jessica Williams, she reminded herself. *That's who lives here. That's my name now. Jessica Williams.* The name felt uncomfortable, like a scratchy coat that rubbed her bare skin, but it had to be worn.

Before she started unloading, she broke a path to the rotting porch and trudged up the two steps. Snow had blown across the porch, a couple inches piling near the door, dark dry leaves poking up through the thin layer.

She inserted her key into the lock. If it were rusted, which she half-expected, she'd be in trouble. *More trouble,* she reminded herself. She tried the key and it stuck, unmoving, in the lock. She rattled it. "Come on, come on," she muttered under breath that fogged in the air.

She'd rented this place online, and struck a simple deal with the out-of-state owner. She paid him up-front, in cash, no questions asked. She only hoped he held up his end of the bargain.

With a final twist, the lock gave and she was able to push the door open.

"Oh, man," she said, peering inside. She flipped a light switch near the door and nothing happened, so she headed back to her SUV. She found her flashlight and a roller bag that worked only so-so through the snow as she returned to the porch and the open door. Snapping on the flashlight, she swept its harsh beam over the interior that looked as if no one had been there for a decade. It smelled musty, the air thick with dust. She ran the beam across an old love seat with faded, lumpy cushions and a scarred wooden frame. A coffee table sat in front of it and a rocker, with most of its stuffing exposed, was situated by a river rock fireplace where she suspected birds might roost in the summer. Old nests were probably clogging the flue and that didn't begin to count the bats.

"Fixer Upper's Dream," she said aloud. The ad certainly hadn't lied about that, nor, probably, "A Hunter's Paradise." The terrain and the building were beyond rugged. From the looks of the cabin's interior, mice and other rodents had been the last house guests and she half-expected a raccoon or worse to be cowering in a kitchen cabinet.

On that she was proved wrong. There were no cabinets. Just a table near an antique wood-burning stove and an empty spot where a refrigerator, or maybe an icebox, had once stood. All the conveniences of home, which had been advertised, were sorely lacking. She'd asked for running water, electricity, a septic system, and cell phone access, if not the ability to connect to the Internet. It seemed she might have none of the basics.

"Great." She reminded herself that the most important aspect of the cabin, her tantamount request, was isolation, and that had been provided. "La-di-frickin'-dah," she said, then caught herself.

She tested the toilet. Of course it didn't flush, but once she twisted the valves underneath the tank, water began to flow. A good sign. She'd been afraid that the pipes had rusted through or were frozen. "Will wonders never cease?" She flushed again and water swirled down the stained fixture. It worked and when she tested the sink, water ran through the faucet, all of it ice cold.

Good enough for tonight.

She toured the rest of the cabin, which consisted of the kitchen, a bedroom, the bathroom, and a small loft tucked beneath a sloping roof. A back porch overlooked a small stream that ambled through the hemlocks and firs that lined its shores. It was nearly frozen over, just a trickle near the middle indicating that the water was still running some.

There were no visible signs of a furnace, nor duct work, just a kerosene space heater tucked into a gun closet, and of course the river rock fireplace with its charred and well-used firebox. "Home sweet home," she said as she walked through the interior and out the front door. She needed to unload the Tahoe, clean the place up if she could, dare start a fire and settle in for the night.

As she walked outside again, she noticed dusk was settling in, twilight casting deep shadows across the small clearing. A soft snow began to fall again and, of course, cover the tracks her rig had made when she'd turned off the county road twenty miles into the hills surrounding Grizzly Falls.

Good.

Surely I'll be safe here, she thought, her gaze scouring the woods. There was no way he could find her. Right? She'd covered her tracks completely. Again, she looked at the ruts her SUV had dug into the unbroken snow. If ever there were red arrows pointing to a target, those ruts were it. Worse yet, she felt as if she had been followed, though she'd seen no one in her rearview for miles.

Paranoia crept in with the night stealing across the snowy landscape. She always felt as if someone were only a step behind her, ready to pounce and slit her throat. Absently, she touched her neck and reminded herself that she had friends in Grizzly Falls, people she could trust.

And what good will they do, if he finds you? They can't save you, Jessica, *and you know it. No one can.*

Despair threatened her just as a stiff breeze kicked up, rattling the branches of trees and swirling around the thin walls of the cabin.

Get over yourself. The law in Grizzly Falls was supposed to be different from what she was used to, the sheriff a thinking man with deep convictions and an ability to sort fact from fiction.

Dan Grayson would help her.

He had to.

Setting her jaw and tamping down her fears, Jessica hauled in her sleeping bag, a pillow, a backpack, her empty thermos, and a single bottle of water, which, along with half a bag of jerky and a banana that was turning brown, would be her dinner. She eyed the living room, searching for any kind of hiding spot. There was a vent in the back corner of the firebox that allowed for the dropping of ashes and intake of air when opened. That would work for the items she wanted to keep safe but wouldn't need handy and also act as a decoy if the house were ransacked. In that little niche, she'd hide one set of fake identification documents, the ones she'd used in Denver. But that little hidey-hole wasn't enough, so she looked for other spots and decided her best bet was to pull off a section of the baseboard, tear out a hole in the wood wall, then replace the board. It was where she'd hide the other ID and money she wanted to stash. She spent the next hour at a spot at the edge of a built-in bookcase. Once she'd whittled out an area large enough, she stuffed her valuables inside and replaced the baseboard.

She thought of her weapons—a small switchblade that fit in her palm she'd keep with her, hidden inside the padding of her bra during the day and up her sleeve at night, and a gun. She'd carry it as well, in her SUV, under the seat, and at night, tucked beneath her head on a pillow. Not very imaginative, she knew, but the tiny pistol would be close enough to grab should an intruder burst in.

Her heart pounded at the thought.

Could she do it?

Pull a trigger?

Take a man's life?

Absolutely. In a flash, she remembered him, how cruel he was, how he'd enjoyed torturing her. She wouldn't think twice about blowing the bastard away.

After tucking the Kel-Tec P-32 under the pillow, she let out a slow breath and found her meager dinner.

Bon appetit! she thought as she peeled the banana and cracked open the bottle of water. Spreading her sleeping bag over the ancient love seat, she took a long swallow from the bottle, then checked her cell phone. So far, she had service. Maybe the Internet wasn't an impossibility. But not for tonight. No. After a double check to make certain she wasn't locking any creatures into the cabin with her, she threw the deadbolts, ate two bites of the banana and, lying on her makeshift bed with the wind keening down the mountainside, decided she'd never fall asleep.

Within two minutes, she was out like a light.

Detective Selena Alvarez sent up a prayer, one she'd learned in catechism, then added a personal request to God that he spare the life of Dan Grayson, who lay comatose in the hospital bed. Tubes and wires were attached to him, monitors tracking his vital signs, the room sterile and utilitarian. A tall man who barely fit on the hospital bed, Grayson was the sheriff of Pinewood County, one of the best men Alvarez had ever known, one she'd once fancied herself in love with. But the person lying under the crisp white sheets and slightly rumpled blankets was a shell of the man she remembered, the vibrant, slow-talking lawman whose eyes twinkled when he was amused and darkened dangerously when he was serious. His skin had a weird grayish tinge under the fluorescent lights, his gray mustache was untrimmed, his breathing labored.

She touched his fingers with the tips of her own, willing him to open his eyes, wishing he'd never stepped out of his cabin and been the target of a crazed assassin. The bastard who had wounded Grayson had been caught and was behind bars and awaiting trial for a variety of charges including murder and attempted murder.

"You hang in there." Her throat clogged and she chided herself as she was usually in control, her emotions under tight rein.

"A cold bitch," she'd heard in the lunchroom of the sheriff's office. It had come from Pete Watershed, a deputy who was quick with crude jokes and thought of himself as an expert when it came to the opposite sex.

"Ice water in her veins," Connors, the buffoon, had chimed in, sliding Alvarez a sly glance as if he hoped she'd overheard.

She had and had retorted with, "Better than carrying the double I-gene like you, for impotence and idiocy." Afterward, she'd kicked herself as she rarely let herself be goaded, had prided herself on keeping cool and collected. It was just that Connors was such a dick sometimes.

But the man before her in the hospital bed, Dan Grayson, was one of the best.

She glanced out the window to the still winter night. Snow was falling steadily, covering the parking lot and the scattering of cars parked beneath tall security lamps. She trusted Grayson was safe, but she wasn't certain he'd survive. Releasing a pent up sigh, she leaned forward and brushed a quick kiss against his cool cheek. Though she was in love with another man, one she hoped to marry, a part of her would always cherish this sheriff who had taught her humility, patience, and empathy.

She left the room quickly, nodding at the nurse on the night shift who opened the electronic doors. They parted and there, on the other side, waiting patiently, probably understanding how conflicted she was, stood Dylan O'Keefe, the man who had been in and out of her life for years and whom she loved.

"How is he?" O'Keefe asked, knowing full well how Alvarez felt about her boss. His eyes, a penetrating gray, were filled with concern.

"Not good." She flung herself into his arms as tears burned the back of her eyelids. "Not good."

Strong arms held her close. "Shh. He'll be fine," O'Keefe assured her and she took comfort in his lies. "He's strong. It takes more than a bullet or two to knock that cowboy down."

Squeezing her eyes shut, she wished to high heaven that she could believe him. And she had to. Despite all of her efforts to bring his assailant to justice, Dan Grayson still had to fight this battle on his own. She'd done all she could, even going off the rails and becoming a bit of a rogue cop—totally out of character for her—to arrest the man responsible for Grayson's injuries. But she couldn't help him now. He was fighting for his life and it was all down to the strength of his body and his will to live.

Sniffing, forcing back her own dread, she finally took a step back. "You're right. He is strong."

"Ready?"

She nodded and O'Keefe pressed the elevator call button. When a soft *ding* announced the car had arrived and the elevator's doors whispered open, they stepped inside, and once more, Alvarez silently prayed for Dan Grayson's life.

When Jessica woke up, she was disoriented, her bladder stretched to the breaking point, the darkness in the cabin complete. She found her phone in her pocket and first checked the time. Nearly five AM. She'd slept almost around the clock and had a crick in her neck to prove it.

But she'd survived.

At least one more night.

A quick glance through the window showed her that her footsteps were still visible, but quickly disappearing with the night's snowfall, as were the Chevy's tire tracks.

Good, though it really didn't matter. She couldn't stay hidden away. She had to go out today and would in the days after, as she needed to secure a job and fast. The cash she'd taken with her was running out and though her expenses were little, her dollars could only be stretched so far.

She relieved herself in the barely functioning toilet, then using her flashlight, followed its beam to the back porch where she'd seen a stack of wood the night before.

The split fir had been in its resting spot for years, judging by the nests of spiders within and the fact that it was dry as a bone. It would ignite easily. A small axe had been left, its blade stuck in a huge round of wood that had obviously been used as a chopping block. She carried in several large chunks and stacked them in the grate, checked the flue, opened the damper, then went back outside and, with her flashlight balanced on the porch rail, split some kindling.

Thank you, Grandpa, for showing me how to do this, she thought, conjuring up the old man with his bald, speckled pate, rimless glasses, and slight paunch. He'd been the one who had taken her hunting and camping, molding what he'd considered a pampered princess into a self-sufficient woman.

"Ya never can tell when you'll need to know how to shoot, or build a camp, or make a fire, Missy, so you'd best learn now," he'd told her. Smelling of chewing tobacco and a hint of Jack Daniels, he'd set about teaching her.

Of course he was long gone, but his memory and advice lingered. She set up one piece of fir, raised the axe, and brought it down swiftly. A bit of kindling split off. She repeated the process again and again until she'd made short work of three fir chunks and, despite the freezing temperatures and her fogging breath, was sweating profusely.

Once back in the cabin, she used her lighter and soon a fire was burning in the grate, smoke drawing through the chimney, heat emanating. There were still a couple hours of darkness, so she hoped to warm the little space and use the firelight as illumination. Once dawn broke, she would let the fire die so that no smoke was visible.

She made a list of essentials she'd need, then checked the online connection on her phone, which she used with a device she'd bought on the black market, along with a new identity.

"Jessica Williams." She eyed the driver's license from California and the social security number she'd been told wouldn't raise any red flags. Coupled with her disguise, she might just blend into the local Montana landscape for a while.

My life as a criminal, she thought, checking the help wanted area of a website dedicated to finding jobs in western Montana. She'd posted her resume two days earlier, indicating that she was moving to the area and only had a temporary address, so that anyone interested would have to contact her through the site. *So far, nothing,* she noted as she finished the rest of the banana.

She found the website for the Grizzly Falls newspaper and located the want ads where there were two opportunities to hire on as a waitress. Betsy's Bakery and the Midway Diner. She made note of them, then ate a couple bites of jerky and washed them down with her water.

Wasting no time, she cleaned up as best as she could with the cold tap water, changed her clothes, and examined her reflection in the cracked mirror on the medicine cabinet over the sink in the bathroom. Dawn was just breaking, light filtering through the falling snow and cloud cover.

Her features were still in shadow as she applied her makeup with the aid of the flashlight's harsh beam. Contacts to change her gold eyes a dark brown, tweezers to contour her arched eyebrows flat, a dull blond wig that hid her auburn hair, and removable appliances that made her jowly enough to match the padded body suit that seemed to add at least thirty pounds to her athletic frame.

Over it all, she dressed in too-tight jeans and a sweater under a jacket, then again, surveyed her image in the mirror. She was unrecognizable to anyone who knew her.

Maybe today she'd get lucky.

Lucky? Really?

Who would have ever thought she would end up here, the daughter of privilege, a woman who'd showed such promise, one with a damn master's degree, no less, and now on the run?

God help me.

For a split second, she was back in that swamp. In her mind's eye, she saw the glinting image of a blade, heard the lap of water, saw the blood flowing. . . . She felt the pain, the despair, the utter bleakness of that moment and remembered the fleeting feeling that if she just let go, if she finally gave up, she would be free.

But she'd fought.

And had miraculously survived.

So far.

Reaching up, she fingered the scar on her nape at her hairline, made sure the wig covered it and then headed for the door. She wasn't about to let *him* win.

Ever.

CHAPTER 2

The new guy was a prick.

At least in Detective Regan Pescoli's estimation.

She doubted she was alone in her viewpoint that Hooper Effin' Blackwater, until recently, commander of the criminal department, now acting sheriff, was a poor replacement for Dan Grayson.

Then again, Grayson's size twelve boots were damn hard to fill.

She crossed the department's parking lot and headed for the back door. It was cold as hell, the night still lingering enough that the street lamps were just winking off, the wind fierce enough to snap the flags and rattle the chains of the poles near the front of the building.

As she walked through the department's back door she shook the snow from her hair and brushed several melting flakes from the shoulders of her jacket before stomping whatever remained from her boots. Opening the vestibule door into the department, a wave of heat hit her full in the face, the old furnace rumbling as it worked overtime.

Already, the office was bustling with the sound of jangling phones, clicking and sputtering printers, and bits and pieces of conversation.

Unwinding her scarf, she headed past the lunchroom where some of the officers lingered, either before or after their shifts. A few straggling members from the night crew were gathering their things, having a last cup of coffee, and scanning the headlines of the latest edition of the newspaper. The morning workers were beating a path to the coffeepots already percolating on the counter, the rich aroma of some South American blend scenting the air.

Pescoli's stomach turned a little at the thought of coffee, a morning cup she once considered one of life's greatest pleasures. A cup of black coffee and a cigarette, what could be better? Now, of course, she indulged in neither, at least nothing with a jolt of caffeine in it. And zero nicotine.

A shame, really.

Sometimes being healthy and a role model to her children was a major pain in the ass.

Speaking of pains, she returned her thoughts back to the man in charge of the department, if only for the time being. The change didn't sit well, nor did sipping a caffeine-free Diet Coke. It just didn't hit the spot, but she dealt with it. She had to.

Because, surprise, surprise she was pregnant.

Again.

The baby was unplanned.

Again.

Would she never learn?

Bypassing the lunchroom, she nearly collided with Joelle Fisher, the department's receptionist and head cheerleader, at least in her own mind.

Bustling toward the cafeteria in pink, impossibly high heels that matched her suit and the little heart-shaped earrings dangling from her earlobes, Joelle caught herself before tripping. "Excuse me, Detective," she said a little sharply, her voice accented by the staccato rhythm of her footsteps. Balancing a huge white box that no doubt held dozens of cookies or cupcakes, she was, as always, in a hurry. Her platinum hair was piled into a high beehive, not a single strand waving as she moved with lightning speed toward the lunchroom.

It was Joelle's mission to ensure every member of the force was filled to the brim with whatever holiday goodies were in season. From her great-great-great-grandmother's recipe for fruitcake at Christmas, to the "witch's tarts" she created for Halloween, Joelle ensured that each officer of the Pinewood Sheriff's Department had his or her sweet tooth satisfied and blood sugar levels elevated.

Maybe all those sweets were a good thing. She had to be around sixty, but she appeared a full decade younger, despite her nod to 1960s fashion.

"I'm . . . I'm not drunk," a loud voice insisted from around the corner. "Ya hear me? Damn Breathalyzer is broke, I tell ya! Issus . . . it's who? Ten in the morning?"

"A little after eight, Ivor." Deputy Kayan Rule's voice was firm. "Time to sober up."

"But I am . . . I am sh . . . sober. I'm tellin' ya."

"You've told me a lot of things. Let's go." Just as Pescoli reached her office she caught a glimpse of Rule, a tall black man who looked more like an NBA power forward than a county road deputy, shepherding a cuffed and unhappy Ivor Hicks to the drunk tank.

"Bastard!" Hicks said angrily.

Pescoli had no love for the man or any member of his family; in fact she had a personal, deep-seated loathing for Ivor's son, but she tried not to think about that particular nut job. Nonetheless, her skin crawled as Ivor was shepherded along the hallways.

"You'll get yours," Ivor predicted with some kind of sanctimonious malice, the joy being his ability to predict Rule's dire future. From behind thick, owlish glasses, he glared at the deputy. "Mark my words. That son of a bitch, Crytor? He'll get you, y'know. Damn general of that pod, he'll come for you like he did for me. And he'll plant a damn invisible chip in you, too!"

"He'll have to stand in line. I've got lots of folks out to get me," Rule said and tossed Pescoli a *what're-ya-gonna-do* look. Then he guided tipsy Ivor Hicks, still ranting about the leader of the army of reptilian aliens he'd believed had abducted him, around a corner at the end of the hall. Ivor was convinced that the extraterrestrials had done a vast array of medical experiments on him years before and that his memories of the terrifying event had nothing to do with his fondness for whiskey.

Just a normal day at the office.

As they passed out of sight, Pescoli stepped into her office and stripped off her jacket and scarf. Outside it was freezing, a raging storm from Canada passing through, but inside the building, the heat was almost stifling. The temperature was set above seventy and in Pescoli's current state, the department felt like a sauna. She was sweating by the time she kicked out her desk chair and sat at her computer.

God, she thought, logging onto her e-mail, *I'd kill for a Diet Coke* with *caffeine.* But it was not to be. She was going to have to opt for decaf coffee, instant, no less.

Waiting for the screen to come up, she made her way back to the lunchroom and found the carafe marked HOT WATER and poured a cup. It steamed as she returned to her desk. She didn't want any of her coworkers to note that she'd switched from "high-octane" to "unleaded" because she hadn't shared her secret with anyone, including Nate Santana, her fiancé and the father of her unborn child. He had no children of his own, and she wasn't sure how he would react to the news. She trusted him, loved him, and had agreed to marry him, though she'd been reluctant as she'd walked down the aisle twice before, once to Joe Strand, her son Jeremy's father. A cop like her, he had died in the line of duty. Theirs had been a rocky, if passionate union. The same could be said for husband number two, Luke "Lucky" Pescoli, a sexy trucker who had swept her off her usually grounded feet. She'd married him on the fly and the results were their daughter Bianca and a divorce. Lucky had remarried Michelle soon afterward who was, in Pescoli's biased opinion, a life-sized, walking, talking Barbie doll, barely older than her stepson Jeremy and a whole heck-of-a lot smarter than she let on.

As she carried her mug back to her desk, Pescoli heard Blackwater on the phone, but she didn't peer into the sheriff's office as she passed, not like she used to when Grayson was there. She couldn't stomach the thought of Blackwater leaning back in Grayson's chair, feet on the desk, receiver to his ear as he kiss-assed the higher ups; or, more likely, sitting ramrod stiff in the chair and doing isometric exercises as he restructured the department.

Maddening.

Once seated at her desk again, she shoved aside a stack of papers, then added freeze-dried decaf coffee crystals to the steaming water in her mug and stirred with a spoon she kept handy in the top drawer. She caught a glimpse of one of the pictures she kept on her desk and felt a tug on her heart. The shot was of Jeremy at nine, his smile stretched wide, his teeth still a little too big for his face, his hair mussed. He was standing on a flat rock near the banks of a stream and proudly holding his catch, a glistening rainbow trout.

Her heart squeezed. The years since then had flown by and he was nearly an adult who, despite her protests, was going to follow in his parents' footsteps and become a cop.

Lord help us, she thought, though the truth was that her son had saved her life recently, and it seemed, in so doing, had finally crossed the threshold into manhood.

After taking a sip of her coffee, she felt an instant souring in her gut. From the coffee? Or Blackwater, whose voice still carried down the hall. Irritated, she rolled her chair to the door to shut it and thought, again, of the new life growing inside her.

Pregnant.

And pushing forty.

Now *that* had been a surprise. She had near-grown kids already. Jeremy was almost out the door . . . well, that had yet to be seen, but he'd made a few futile attempts in the past. Bianca was in the last years of high school and deep into teenage angst.

So *now* a baby?

Starting all over again with diapers, sleepless nights, shifting schedules, and juggling a full-time job?

She wasn't ambivalent about the baby, not really. She just knew how much work and chaos a baby brought into the home, especially a home that wasn't exactly picture-perfect already. And she wasn't married. Not that being unwed and pregnant was such a big deal these days, but Santana was already pushing for them to tie the knot.

She had the ring to prove it, even if the band with its diamond was currently tucked into a corner of the top drawer of her bureau. She'd had it on briefly, but with everything that had happened recently, she didn't feel like bandying it about quite yet.

She took another sip of the coffee, found it too bitter, and put the half-drunk cup aside on her already cluttered desk.

A sharp rap on her door sounded, then Alvarez stuck her head inside. "Busy?" she asked as Pescoli swiveled in her chair. "Or do you have a minute?"

"Something up?"

Alvarez shook her head and slipped into the tiny room, leaving the door open a crack. "I just wanted to see if you'd gone to visit Grayson."

"Not for a few days. I was going to drop by the hospital after work. Wanna go with?"

"I was there last night." Alvarez was grim as she shook her head.

"And?"

"Not good."

"It's only been—"

"I know. But I expected him to, I don't know, come around by now." Compressing her lips together, Alvarez gave her head a quick shake as if dispelling an unwanted picture in her mind. Though it had been Pescoli who'd found him lying in a pool of blood at his cabin, Alvarez had been the most shaken up by the attack on their boss.

"They're moving him out of ICU, into a private room," she added. "That's what one of the nurses told me before I went in to see him."

"I thought he was going to be transferred to Seattle, a neurological unit specializing in brain trauma or something."

"That plan's been scrapped and I don't know why," Alvarez said, obviously frustrated. "The doctors seem to think he's stable enough that he doesn't need round-the-clock observation, that he'll get better with time, but I don't know."

"He'll be okay."

Alvarez looked up sharply. "How do you know? Everyone keeps saying that, but really, it's just words." Her mouth was pinched, her eyes flashing.

"I . . . well, you're right. I don't really know, but that's a good sign, isn't it? That he's being transferred out of intensive care. Come on, Alvarez, have a little faith."

"You, the self-professed agnostic? You're telling *me* to have faith?"

"I'm just saying that if anyone can pull through, it's Dan Grayson. He's a big, strapping man and . . ." Pescoli let her voice trail off. "One of the good guys."

"Yeah—"

"Detectives?" Hooper Blackwater's voice preceded him as he took the time to stick his head into Pescoli's office.

Pescoli looked up at him.

"Reports?" His eyebrows raised, a nonverbal reminder that there was work to be done that bugged the hell out of her. "The Haskins suicide? Armstead domestic dispute?"

"Both done," Alvarez said.

"Good. E-mail them to me." With a quick, sharp nod, he was off, boots ringing as he strode down the hall, probably searching for his next Red Bull or a spot where he could drop and do twenty quick push-ups. Just because he could.

"I can't stand that guy," Pescoli said under her breath.

"I know," Alvarez said. "And he knows. For that matter, we all know." Her dark eyes were without reproach, though, as if she silently agreed. "Maybe you shouldn't make it so obvious."

Pescoli didn't respond. She knew she was being bitchy, but she didn't really care.

"Try it," Alvarez suggested, her professional mask slipping back into place. "I'll catch you later." She was out of Pescoli's office quickly.

Once more, Pescoli rolled her desk chair to the door and pushed it firmly shut, a practice that was new to her. Since Blackwater had grabbed the reins of the department, she felt she needed privacy, at least for now and the foreseeable future.

She wasn't kidding herself. Grayson, if he ever returned, was a long way off from regaining his rightful place as sheriff. She and the whole damn office were stuck with Blackwater, the go-getter who let everyone know it.

"Shit," she whispered.

Grayson, forever with his black lab Sturgis at his heels, his Stetson squarely on his head, was soft-spoken and thoughtful, yet quietly firm. A tall, rangy man who looked more cowboy than lawman, a sheriff elected by the people of Pinewood County, his quiet command was effective. He had strong opinions and all hell could break out when he was angry, but for the most part, he was in control and steady, a rock-solid force Pescoli could depend upon.

Blackwater was all action—fast-paced and guns blazing as if he had to prove himself. He made sure that everyone who worked for him knew he was an ex-Marine who had served two tours in Afghanistan. Pescoli had heard that he ran every morning, three miles minimum in all kinds of weather, and three days a week he spent hours in the gym, boxing and lifting weights to reduce his stress and stay in Marine-proud shape. At work, he downed Red Bull, Rock Star, or Monster energy drinks the way an alcoholic tossed back martinis. Part Native American, he appeared perpetually tanned, his eyes an intense brown bordering on black, his nearly six-foot physique all compact muscle.

Pescoli admitted to herself that he was handsome enough, if that mattered, with a slightly Roman nose that looked as if it had been broken at least once, bladed cheekbones, and black hair without a trace of gray, cut short, again, a reminder of his military background. Blackwater was smart, too, Pescoli allowed, and had the law degree to prove it. He attacked each problem head-on with the ferocity of a wounded bear, no excuses, and had already made it clear that he expected every member of his staff to do the same.

It wasn't his work ethic that got under her skin. It was his style that rankled. All his terse sentences, orders, and damn meetings indicated that he'd come to not only play but to stay.

Pescoli had been toying with the idea of quitting, or at the very least, cutting back her hours to part-time, and her pregnancy had only reinforced her plans. However, there was that little matter of making sure Grayson's would-be assassin spent the rest of his life behind bars. She wasn't going to do anything until she was certain that son of a bitch never walked free again.

She'd have to suck it up for a while. Yes, the entire atmosphere in the department had changed and it bothered her, but so what? A lot bothered her these days.

Deal with it, she told herself as she clicked on her mouse and focused her attention on her e-mails. She sure as hell didn't want to be late with any damn reports.

Her life had become a pathetic good news–bad news joke, Jessica thought as she drove past the snow-crusted fields of a farm on the outskirts of Grizzly Falls.

The good news? She'd landed the job at the Midway Diner.

The bad news? Dan Grayson, the man she had thought just might be her savior, was in the hospital fighting for his life, so her plans to enlist his help would have to be put on hold. Indefinitely. Her spirits were low; she'd counted on the even-tempered sheriff's help. Her plans would have to change.

Taking a corner a little too fast, she felt her wheels slip on the icy road and eased off the gas. The tires gripped the road anew and her SUV straightened. The radio was blasting over the rumble of the engine and the clock on her dash indicated it was a few minutes after midnight.

Fiddling with the Chevy's finicky heater, she considered her options. With the temperature having dropped below freezing, the heater was blowing lukewarm air, its rattle nearly drowning out a country song about the pain of love lost that filled the interior. Snapping off the radio, she noticed the defroster was fighting a losing battle with the condensation that was crawling inward over her viewing angle. She gave the glass a swipe with an extra sweatshirt that was lying on the passenger seat, and squinted, trying to find the turn off to the long lane that wound to her cabin. "Home," she reminded herself.

Snowflakes danced, swirling as they were caught in the headlights' glare, piling along the fencerows and frosting the branches of the evergreens that rose in the foothills.

She could continue to lie low, retaining her disguise while keeping her ear to the ground, or she could bolt again, heading farther west or north. Or, she could seek her own revenge, try to turn the tables on the bastard from whom she was running, lure him in, and then destroy him. The thought of taking another human life had always repulsed her, but she'd never been so scared before, had never been fighting for her own existence. She'd always had the luxury of naiveté. If she came face-to-face with him again, she had no doubt she could shoot him dead or plunge a knife deep into his black heart and give the blade a little twist.

"Sick bastard," she whispered.

As the wipers of the old Tahoe slapped snow from the windshield, leaving streaks upon the glass, she checked her rearview mirror for the hundredth time.

No one was following her.

No menacing pickup's headlights appeared over the last rise. Still, she could sense her pursuer.

Letting her breath out slowly, she noticed an old No Hunting sign posted on the massive trunk of a giant hemlock that caught in the headlights. She was close. The engine groaned a little as the incline grew steeper, and less than a quarter mile up the hill, she spied the spot where the trees parted a bit and the old lane ambled off the county road. Of course, there were tracks from her Tahoe, enough to be visible despite the snowfall, but so far, he hadn't appeared.

Had she finally lost him?

Most likely not. Several months had passed from the moment she'd stared up at the moon and gasped for air as she'd lain on the soft banks of the bayou. It was there she'd fought the battle of deciding whether to live or die.

Life had won out, and she'd started her journey of two thousand miles down a desperately crooked path that had finally ended up in the wilds of western Montana.

Was she safe?

She doubted it.

He was nothing if not dogged and deadly.

Shivering a little, she nosed her Tahoe through the stands of hemlock and fir to the tiny clearing where her cabin, after a call to the owner, was finally equipped with electricity and hot water. There was still no furnace, but she'd picked up a used space heater at a secondhand shop, along with a few other essentials.

House Beautiful the old cottage was not, but at least it was functioning, the utilities in the owner's name and billed to him. She parked near the garage, locked her SUV, and made her way inside where the smell of wood smoke and last night's microwave popcorn greeted her. On a makeshift coffee table was the local paper, where she'd first learned of the attack on Dan Grayson and his subsequent hospitalization. There was a new sheriff in town, if only temporarily, a man by the name of Hooper Blackwater who was rumored to be a strict, by-the-book officer of the law, a person she was pretty certain she couldn't approach.

So who, then, would help her?

The simple answer was Cade Grayson, Dan's brother, the man from whom she'd heard about the sheriff. But she wasn't about to go running to that rangy cowboy, at least not right away. Unfortunately, he was the man who had started all her trouble and as such would only be her last resort.

CHAPTER 3

Troy Ryder rolled into Grizzly Falls, Montana on a wing and a prayer. His old Dodge truck was wheezing by the time he pulled into a service station and mini-mart where he filled up his tank, added antifreeze to the radiator, and bought a prewrapped ham and cheese sandwich, bag of chips, and two bottles of beer.

He'd spied a motel on his way into town, one of those long, low buildings with a shared porch, empty parking lot, and a sign proudly announcing FREE WI-FI AND CABLE TELEVISION right next to the VACANCY sign. Good enough. His back ached a bit, his stomach was growling, and he needed to settle in for at least a few hours to study the lay of the land and figure out if Anne-Marie had landed there.

It seemed unlikely, but then stranger things had happened.

Hell, didn't he know it?

He drove back to the motel. After locking his old pickup, he crossed the icy lot and pushed open a glass door to a small, brightly lit reception area that smelled of bitter, overcooked coffee and a hint of cigarette smoke. A second after he approached the counter, a heavyset woman of fifty or so appeared through an open doorway leading to the inner sanctum of the River View Motel. Wearing a uniform that was on the tight side, she took one look at Troy and smiled widely enough to show off a gold crown on one of her molars. "What can I do ya for?"

"Lookin' for a room."

"That we got. How many nights?"

"Just one to start with." After all, he wasn't certain that Anne-Marie had stopped here. "Then, we'll see."

"Got a double-double or a king. What's your pleasure?"

"One bed'll do. 'Round back, if you've got a room there."

"You're in luck," she said, then her eyebrows drew together as her hands clicked over the keyboard of a computer that looked as if it had been built before the turn of the millennium. "Well, I mean, if you call room thirteen lucky. It's the only one that's ready on the back side, where, you know, you get a river view. You're not superstitious, are you?"

"Not much." He filled out the required paperwork, listened to her drone on about the beauty of that part of the country, then snagged the key from her hand and returned to his truck where he drove to the far side of the building and parked in front of room thirteen, an end unit with what only an optimist could describe as a "view" of the river. Not that he cared. He hauled his gear inside, flipped on the lights, and closed the door.

A big bed that looked as if it sagged in the middle, a television on a stand, two night tables with matching lamps, and one chair positioned near the window were the extent of the furniture.

Good enough.

The place was showing its age. The carpet near the door was discolored, the comforter on the bed fading a little, the smell of disinfectant not quite masking a lingering odor of cigarettes, but all in all, it would do.

After cracking open a beer and taking a long swallow, he took a short shower, then changed into fresh clothes and went to work. One way or another, he was going to find Anne-Marie Calderone and haul her tight little ass back to New Orleans.

Alvarez was right.

Okay, she was right *again*, Pescoli thought as she drove down a winding lane that led to the partially built home where she and Santana were planning to live once they were married. Two days earlier, her partner had informed her that Dan Grayson was being moved from ICU and sure enough, when Pescoli had gone to visit him, the sheriff was in a private room, hooked up to all kinds of monitors, not too far from the hub of a nurse's station.

She had expected him to be recovering a lot faster than he was, but she told herself to be patient. So he hadn't woken from his coma, that didn't mean anything. If it were a problem, certainly the doctors and nursing staff would do something. And Grayson's family, his two brothers, Cade and Big Zed, had been at the hospital, along with Hattie, their deceased brother's wife, every day since the assassination attempt.

At least, she thought as she drove around the edge of an icy pond, *Grayson's attacker had been rendered harmless.* Injured during his capture, he was in custody, a bullet lodged against his spinal cord, his ability to walk in question. Though still under doctor's care, the son of a bitch who'd nearly taken her boss's life was no longer a threat.

No armed guard needed to be posted at the hospital any longer.

As she drove along the lane, she tried to be positive. She wasn't certain how she felt about moving as she already owned her own little cabin in the hills, a place that was finally paid off and the home where she'd raised her kids. It wasn't much to look at, but it was cozy, and she'd been proud that she'd been able to pay it off early by doubling up her payments whenever she was able, and finally claim it as her own.

She caught a glimpse of the lake on which the new cabin was built. It would be roomier than her little house, everything within it new enough that she wouldn't have to rely on her questionable plumbing and electrical skills, and it would provide a fresh start with no reminders of the other husbands she'd been married to. She and Santana planned to start their life together there. *It sounds perfect,* she thought as the house erected on the shores of the icy lake came into view.

And yet . . .

She didn't know if she was making the right choice. Jeremy had graduated from high school a couple years earlier and Bianca had one more year, so wouldn't it be smarter to wait?

"No time like the present." Santana's advice echoed through her mind as she cruised along the lake's snowy shores. *"May as well let the kids claim their rooms and feel like they are a part of this."*

That made sense, she supposed, or at least it had until she'd realized there was a new baby on the way, another child who would need his or her own room eventually. She seemed to be involved in revolving door parenting—as one kid was leaving a new one was coming to take his place.

The house came into view and she swallowed hard, wondering if she would ever think of it as home, *her* home. Two stories of raw cedar with a pitched roof covered in snow. With a gray stone fireplace, the house was nestled in the trees on the shore of the lake, picture-perfect. The garage was attached by a short, windowed breezeway and had private stairs that led to an area overhead where Santana planned to make his office. Considering everything, she wondered if Jeremy might tag the spot as his own, insisting the baby needed its own room as much as he needed his own privacy.

"Not gonna happen," she said under her breath, then decided she was borrowing trouble. Besides, Jeremy was working, taking classes, planning to enroll full-time spring term, and finally appeared to be on a path going forward. He'd been through his own trauma the last few weeks but wouldn't hear of her trying to help him in any way. She didn't want to do anything that would impede his progress, like maybe telling him he was going to have another sibling soon . . .

But she was getting ahead of herself, far ahead of herself, she decided as she pulled into the parking area and cut the engine.

Nikita, Santana's husky, appeared in the open doorway to the main house and gave a quick bark before bounding through the snow to greet her with his back end wiggling wildly.

"Hey, Detective!"

She looked up to see Santana standing on the upper floor deck, off the bedroom, looking every bit as sexy as the first time she'd met him, in a bar no less. Wearing a faded shirt that stretched across his shoulders, he folded his arms over his chest and leaned a shoulder against the frame of the French doors as he stared down at her. One side of his mouth drew into a lazy smile. "About time you showed up."

"Always the bastard," she threw out at him, trying to hide her own amusement.

His grin widened, showing off white teeth against his bronzed skin. Like Blackwater, he had more than a trace of Native American blood in his veins, visible in his high, bladed cheekbones, ink-black hair and dark eyes, the kind of eyes that seemed to sear to her soul, eyes that were twinkling with that sexy kind of mischief that she found impossible to ignore.

What had started out as a white-hot attraction and equally hot affair hadn't flamed out as she'd expected. No, she thought, petting Nikita's furry head before heading into the house, that first spark of interest had burned through all her barriers to the engagement and, she hoped, marital bliss.

"Third time's the charm," she told herself as, with the dog on her heels, she walked through the open door and found her way up the stairs that would remain open, offering a view through the glass walls of the living room to the lake visible between each free floating step.

The staircase had been designed before she had any inkling that she would get pregnant, or that in the not-so-distant future a toddler would be trying to climb up and down the steps. At that thought, she paused, imagining a child with Santana's dark hair running through the hallways.

She almost smiled and decided the staircase would need to be boxed in, at least for the next few years.

Sooner, rather than later, she'd have to break the news to Santana.

But not today.

She just wasn't in the mood.

Eli O'Halleran couldn't believe his good luck. Though his father, Trace, had always taken him with him when there were chores to be done around the farm, until today he had never said, "Yeah, son, come with me. You can be the lead dog on this one. Let's see if we can find any other holes in the fence."

"All right!" Eli had said, thrilled. Within a matter of minutes, he'd ignored his breakfast, run to the barn and, with his dad's help, saddled and bridled Jetfire, his black gelding.

While his dad was still cinching his bay mare's saddle, Eli rode Jet through the barn's big roller door and into a back paddock. Both dogs, Dad's shepherd and Bonzi, Kacey's dog, which was at least part pit bull and probably yellow lab, were milling around, anxious to be a part of the action.

"Hold up!" Trace called, but Eli kept going through a series of corrals as the snow fell, all the while feeling like a real cowboy, though he was not quite nine years old.

"Come on," he urged the horse as they reached the open gate to the final field. Glancing over his shoulder, he caught a glimpse of his father leading Mocha from the barn and swinging into the saddle. The dogs, of course, had already escaped the barn and were sniffing and running in the fallen snow, while a cold wind was blowing, snowflakes falling from the gray Montana sky.

"Eli!" his father called, just as Eli leaned forward, eased up on the reins and let the horse go.

Jet surged forward, speeding into a full gallop and tearing down the long, tractor lane covered in snow. Eli's hat blew off, but he didn't care, loving the feel of the wind slapping his face and blowing his hair as he caught sight of the dogs bounding through the drifts and giving chase. Jetfire, after being cooped up in the barn, was eager to run. As Eli hung on, Jet tore up the field, a black blur streaking toward the foothills.

Breathless, Eli didn't care that his dad would probably be mad at him for taking off. It just felt right.

The ground sloped up to a small rise and the gelding ran eagerly upward, breathing hard, racing toward the crest. Eli clung like a burr, his nose running and feeling numb in the cold.

On the far side, the ground dropped off, sloping downward to the creek where the fence separated O'Halleran land from that of the federal government. It was where the problem had started, his dad had told him, a broken spot in the fence where five calves had found the break and gotten through. The strays had been rounded up, and the major hole in the fence had been repaired, but they were just making sure there weren't any more areas where those idiot cows could get through.

The truth was that Trace was tired of being cooped up, too. Otherwise, why would he have decided to survey the fence line in the middle of a near blizzard? It didn't matter, though. Eli was just glad to be out of the house as there was no school.

Plowing through the snow, kicking up powdery clods, Jet crested the hill and raced downward to the meandering brook that cut like a sidewinder back and forth beneath the fence. The field gave way to woods that, on the government side of the property, covered the foothills of the Bitterroots.

Nearing the creek, Eli pulled back on the reins and Jetfire slowed easily, cantering down to a walk just as his dad and Mocha appeared over the rise behind them.

"Didn't you hear me?" Trace demanded as he reined his horse to a stop once they'd reached the corner of the property. He held the reins with one gloved hand and in the other, Eli's stocking cap.

"Sorry," Eli mumbled, though he really wasn't. For the first time, he felt a jab of the cold piercing his jacket.

Trace glared at his son for a second, then let out a sigh. "No harm, no foul, I guess." He still wasn't smiling. "Believe it or not, I was your age once. Broke my arm, being bucked from Rocky. That was my horse at the time."

Eli knew better than to say "I know," even though he'd heard the story before.

Leaning forward, Trace handed Eli his hat. "Think you lost something."

"Thanks." Eli pulled the hat down over his ears as they were starting to freeze, but he didn't dare complain. After all, he'd begged to be a part of this. But as snowflakes slid under the collar of his jacket and the wind blew bitter cold, he was starting to second-guess himself. Not that he would admit it.

"You still want to do this?" his father asked.

Though much of Eli's enthusiasm had faded, he wasn't going to admit it. Nodding, he swiped the back of his gloved hand under his running nose.

His father raised one eyebrow, then gave a quick nod. "Okay, then. You ride up ahead and I'll follow. We'll see if there are any more breaches."

Eli did as he was told, riding along the fence line, growing colder by the second, while his father, more thorough as he scrutinized the wire from atop his mount, lagged behind.

Sometimes being a cowboy really sucks, Eli realized belatedly, his gaze trained on the wire mesh that cut a straight line through the thickets of hemlock, fir, and maple. The stream, nearly frozen, wandered back and forth, a thin trickle in the middle gurgling softly.

Another blast of wind rattled the branches of the surrounding trees and he shivered, tired of the adventure. He just wanted to return to the house, so he urged Jetfire forward through the icy woods. The sooner the job was done, the sooner he could go back inside.

Though he'd begged his father to let him come, Eli began to wish he'd never said a word, just stayed in his pajamas and played on his iPad until breakfast was ready, because inside the house there was a hot fire, a warm cup of hot cocoa, and Kacey, his soon-to-be stepmom. She would be getting ready to go to the clinic where she worked. But instead of being seated at the table, sipping hot chocolate and eating peanut butter toast while watching television, he was out in the cold.

Jetfire stepped quickly through the drifts and Eli swept another quick glance over his shoulder to make certain that his dad was following on the rangy bay. Sure enough, he saw Trace easing his horse through a stand of pines about twenty yards behind him. The two dogs were following, Bonzi with his head lifted as if he were testing the air, Sarge farther behind, exploring a bend in the creek.

Eli wished his dad would hurry.

Through the veil of snow, man and rider were partially obscured, blending into the wintry landscape, appearing almost ghostly. Even the dogs seemed to disappear.

Eli waved at his father, but Trace didn't notice, his concentration and gaze steady on the fence as he appeared and disappeared in the wind-fueled flurries. It worried Eli a little that he was so far ahead of his dad, but he reminded himself to be cowboy-tough. He had a job to do. Once more, Trace and the bay vanished for a second and Eli wondered what he'd do if his father didn't reappear, if he became lost somehow.

But that was nutty.

He knew where he was and his dad was right behind him. Squinting, Eli searched the grove. But no. He couldn't see his father. Nor the dogs.

About to call out to him, Eli caught a glimpse of the bay stepping through the trees again, a phantom horse, barely visible just like in the cartoons he watched or the video games he played.

Feeling a little better, he leaned over the saddle horn, shifting his weight, urging Jetfire forward. Man, it was cold. Too cold. The sooner he found the dumb hole in the wire mesh, the sooner he could go back inside. Jetfire picked up the pace, threading through a copse of saplings as Eli peered through the shifting snowflakes. The fence crossed the stream again as it cut through the trees, heading in a crooked path to the river a few miles to the west.

The fence looked a little different, not as much ice building up over the wire, no snow sticking to the posts. Maybe the cattle had rubbed up against it when searching for a way through. After all, he was near a deeper part of the stream. A particularly stubborn calf with just enough curiosity and no darned brains could wade in and, if he tried hard enough, maybe duck under the wire where the fence spanned the creek. There was no guard there, no floating cattle panel that moved with the current. Squinting through the snowfall, Eli encouraged Jetfire forward, closer to the creek, but the horse snorted and balked.

"Come on," Eli insisted, giving Jetfire a nudge with his knees, urging the gelding to walk closer to the creek.

Instead, Jetfire started backing up.

"Hey!" Eli said sharply. "Let's go!"

But the gelding was having none of it. Tossing his head and snorting, Jet shied away from a thicket of maples.

Eli took a firmer grasp on the reins. "What's got into you?"

From somewhere nearby, a dog growled low and warning, the sound causing the hairs on the back of Eli's neck to lift. Jet reared up.

Eli fought the reins. "Whoa. Stop!"

Bonzi appeared, his caramel-colored coat dappled with snow, his lips snarling, showing teeth. His eyes were trained on the creek, just beyond the brush. As Jet shied, the hairs on the back of the dog's thick neck raised. Tail stiff, he snarled and barked, his eyes focused on a bend in the creek.

What was it? A wildcat or puma? Maybe a wolf?

Shivering inwardly, Eli followed the dog's gaze with his own.

"Trouble?" his father shouted from somewhere not far behind.

The last thing he wanted was his dad to think he couldn't handle his horse. Eli's gaze scoured the wintry banks of the creek, searching the exposed rocks and tangled, snow-covered roots. "No," he said, shaking his head, "It's just—"

His words died in his throat.

His stomach dropped.

Fear cold as an Arctic blast cut through him as he saw what the dog had sensed. Ten feet ahead in a deep pool, a woman's arm stretched out of the water, fingers wide as if supplicating the heavens.

Eli yanked hard on the reins as he stared at the hand. Reaching upward, one finger severed, the hand seemed to be grasping into the empty air for help.

"Oh . . . Oh . . . God . . ." he whispered, horrified. The horse, feeling his fear, minced in a tight circle, tossing up snow.

Eli forced himself to look harder. There, under a thin layer of ice, lay a woman. She was staring straight up, the current below her rippling around her, feathering her long brown hair, causing her blouse to billow around her midriff. Set in a death mask, her face was a grayish hue, and beneath the glaze of ice, her eyes were wide and fixed, seeming to stare straight into his soul.

"Eli?"

His father's voice barely registered. He felt as if he might be sick. "No . . . oh . . ." His insides turned to water. "Dad!"

Screaming before he could stop himself, Eli nearly toppled out of the saddle as Jetfire, nostrils distended, reared, then spun and took off at a full gallop, racing through the trees and across the pastureland, his hooves throwing up clods of snow. Over the rush of wind in his ears, Eli heard his father shout and the dogs begin to howl and bark, but all he could do was hang on to the reins and saddle horn as the horse tore up the rise toward the house. The world went by in a blur of white, but all Eli saw, indelibly etched in his brain forever, was that mutilated hand reaching for the sky.

CHAPTER 4

You're a chicken.

That irritating voice inside Pescoli's head wouldn't leave her alone, even though she'd tried to immerse herself in the autopsy report she'd found on her desk this morning.

She'd had the perfect opportunity to tell Santana about the baby after he'd met her at the top of the stairs, kissed the damn breath from her lungs, and for the first time in their new house, made love to her right on the hard subfloor of their master bedroom. Okay, there *had* been a sleeping bag, but still. . . . The sex had been intense, maybe even a little rough, but filled with the passion she found exhilarating. Afterward, as she'd snuggled up against him, both their naked bodies shining with sweat, she should have screwed up her courage and let him know that he was going to be a father later this year. But she hadn't, content to hold him tight, feel his strength, and listen to his heartbeat as she stared through the open French doors and watched the nightfall.

Every time she moved in her desk chair, her rump ached and she was reminded of Santana and how animal their union had been. Their lovemaking had always been that way—playful and utterly primal. And yet, before, during, or even after, she hadn't uttered a word about the pregnancy.

With an effort, she focused on the autopsy of a man in his late forties, who may or may not have been the victim of a homicide. Derrick "Deeter" Clemson had died of wounds he'd received after a fall off a cliff. The question was whether he'd made a mistake and his death was accidental, if he'd leaped intentionally down nearly one hundred feet of timberland, or if he'd been helped in the fall by his bride of six months. The autopsy report didn't give any clear answers, and she was slightly distracted by the noise filtering through her doorway, that of Blackwater on the telephone in Grayson's office.

She hadn't shut her door yet and could hear Blackwater. Undoubtedly at his desk down the hall, he was having a one-sided phone conversation with someone it sounded like he was trying to impress. Either someone higher in the department or a reporter, she guessed. Maybe even that cockroach Manny Douglas, of the *Mountain Reporter* or, worse yet, Nia Del Ray from KMJC in Missoula.

Blackwater was making noises as if he were about to hang up, so she rolled her desk chair to close her door. She didn't need him poking his head in again and giving her another gung ho speech.

Her hand had just come off the knob when the door was flung open and Selena Alvarez burst in, her expression grim, her jaw set. "Let's roll," she said without preamble. "Looks like we've got a DB at the O'Halleran ranch."

"Dead body?" Pescoli rolled her chair back to her desk, got to her feet, and reached for her jacket and sidearm. "Who?"

"Jane Doe."

"What happened?" Sliding her arms through her jacket's sleeves, she was on Alvarez's heels as they walked crisply down the hall toward the doors leading to the parking lot. Blackwater, whose door was ajar, looked up as they passed, but was already punching out numbers on his phone for his next call.

"No one knows. Trace O'Halleran and his kid were checking the fence line and found her dead in a deep spot of the creek that runs through their property."

"What is it with that place?" Pescoli asked, digging in her jacket pocket for her keys. "Don't those people ever get a break?" She was thinking of the last shootout that had occurred on the ranch where O'Halleran and the local GP in town, Kacey Lambert, had been targets of one of the many madmen who seemed to have discovered their part of Montana. Once a sleepy little town set in the Bitterroots, Grizzly Falls seemed to attract psychos like magnets.

"I guess lightning really does strike twice," Alvarez said as they walked through the back door.

A gust of wind hit Pescoli full in the face. Ducking her head against the weather, she touched the remote for her keyless lock and her Jeep beeped from the spot in the parking lot where she'd parked it not an hour earlier. By the time Pescoli had settled behind the steering wheel, Alvarez was buckled in and already on the phone, talking to the deputy who'd first taken the call and was on the scene. Pescoli fired the engine, snapped on the heater and backed out of the parking spot as the police band crackled. She hit the wipers and lights, then nosed her Jeep into the sludge of traffic that seemed crippled by the storm.

Lights flashing, she eased around slower vehicles, then pushed the speed limit. She was used to the storms and worsening driving conditions in winter and had little patience for those who weren't.

As a van from a local church pulled over to let her pass, she hit the gas and sped through the outskirts of town, her Jeep whipping along a road that skimmed the edge of Boxer Bluff, which offered a view of the Grizzly River and the falls for which the town had been named.

From the corner of her eye, she saw Alvarez click off her phone, letting the edge rest against her chin for a second as if she were lost in thought. "Anything?"

"A crime scene unit is on the way, might beat us there. O'Halleran's kid Eli was out riding the fence line with his father, as I said. They weren't side by side and the boy saw the victim first. His horse spooked or something and he took off. O'Halleran was riding to the spot where the commotion occurred, spied the woman, and pulled her from the stream, tried to revive her, but she was dead, the body nearly frozen."

"ID?"

"None. But she was dressed. Only mark on her is a missing ring finger. Left hand."

"What? Missing? You mean, like a birth defect? Or?"

"Severed. Recently."

"Oh, Jesus."

"Yeah, it doesn't sound like she was just out walking, fell and hit her head, and drowned."

Pescoli glared through the windshield where her wipers were

doing battle with snow that had been falling for hours. "I'm amazed O'Halleran and his kid were out in this."

"Ranchers. Just about as crazy as cops, I guess."

Pescoli harrumphed. "They can't let the weather beat them, either." She turned onto the county road that cut through snowy fields where drifts piled against the fences and icicles hung from the few mailboxes that guarded long lanes leading to farmhouses surrounded by barns and outbuildings.

The O'Halleran place was no different. The big, square two-story farmhouse set upon a small rise far off the road was barely visible through the falling snow. A county-issued Jeep with its lights flashing was parked near the garage.

As Pescoli slowed at the end of the drive, they were met by a deputy for the department. Pete Watershed was tall and good-looking, something he'd never quite forgotten. She didn't like him much. That whole lady-killer attitude rankled her, and his jokes, sometimes with a misogynist twist or teetering on bigotry, put her off. Not that she was a prude, but she could do without the slightly sexual remarks. Watershed tended to push it. If he weren't a good cop, dedicated and all business when on duty, she would have been in his face more than she already was.

"What have we got?" she asked, the wind rushing in when she rolled down the window.

"DB found in the creek out back," he said, pointing to the area behind the house. "You can drive down there. Just follow the tracks. I'll come with." Leaving his partner in the other vehicle, he climbed into the back seat and pointed out the makeshift road. "This is the lane O'Halleran uses for his tractor and hay baler and other equipment," Watershed explained.

She drove through a series of paddocks where the gates had been left open and followed the tire tracks that wound their way onto a huge field where the pristine blanket of snow had been broken into a thick trail of tire tracks running along one fence.

"This butts up to government land," Watershed explained. "O'Halleran and his kid were out checking for holes in the fence." As the Jeep powered through six to eight inches of snow, he went on to tell the same story Alvarez had relayed earlier, finishing with, "So once the kid spooked and took off for the house on his horse,

O'Halleran investigated and found the woman, obviously dead. Still, he pulled her from the water and checked for a pulse, listened to her lungs, but she'd been in there a while, her body half frozen. You'll see."

"And the missing finger?" Alvarez asked.

"Ring finger, left hand. Not found. So far. Sliced off pretty cleanly at the first knuckle. Don't know if it was pre- or postmortem."

"Lovely," Alvarez said. "A finger fetish?"

"Just a freak," Pescoli said as they reached the end of the field near a meandering brook bordered by stands of trees. Officers were already on the job, a tarp laid out across which a partially clothed body of a woman lay. Her skin was blue, her hair wet, the finger missing, but Pescoli noted there were earrings visible in her earlobes. "O'Halleran didn't see anything out of the ordinary?"

Watershed shook his head. "Nope. And no tracks have been found around the area. Don't know if she was killed here, or brought here and the body dumped. Could have come from the federal land. There's an access road about a mile west."

Pescoli asked, "What about the neighbors?"

"Haven't talked to them yet."

"Let's do it," Pescoli said, scanning the area. "She had to get here somehow." Squinting through the falling snow, she added, "Not much chance of finding any trace." The frigid weather was working against them, but then it always did.

"You don't know what we'll find." Alvarez was always more optimistic than she, a woman who believed that with today's technology, anything was possible.

At the edge of the trees, parked helter-skelter, were a rescue vehicle from the fire department, another department-issued Jeep, a crime scene van and a banged-up pickup with two dogs locked in the cab, their noses pressed to the window. Officers dressed in heavy outerwear were already scouring the creek bed and surrounding area. Crime scene tape stretched from one sapling to the next, roping off the area that was to be searched.

Pescoli parked the Jeep close to the rescue van. "O'Halleran here?"

"Yeah, out talking to Cabral," Watershed said as Pescoli cut the engine.

She noticed the rancher standing near another deputy, Rosetta

Cabral, new to the force, all of twenty-four years old. Just a girl in Pescoli's opinion, though she was a college graduate, divorced, and a single mother of a two-year-old. Cabral was blessed with the same gung ho fire as Blackwater and was currently engaging Trace O'Halleran in conversation.

"The kid?" Pescoli asked.

"In the Jeep with Beaumont." Watershed nodded toward the other Pinewood County vehicle. "Came back down here with his mom after he ran back to the house. She's a doctor, you know. Drove like mad down here in that truck," he said, hitching his chin toward the beat-up Chevy. "Brought the kid with her 'cause she wasn't sure what was going on. She thought that maybe she could save the Jane Doe, but nah, it was . . . too late."

They climbed out and trudged between the vehicles to the tarp where a woman, maybe thirty or thirty-five, lay stretched onto a tarp, another sheet of plastic tented so that the body was protected and couldn't be viewed from the vehicle where the O'Halleran boy was keeping warm.

"We got statements from everyone?" Pescoli asked, and Watershed nodded.

Mikhail Slatkin, a forensic scientist, was kneeling on the edge of the tarp, examining the body as they waited for someone from the coroner's office to arrive. Over six feet and rawboned, the son of Russian immigrants, he was one of the best forensic scientists Pescoli had ever worked with.

"What happened to her?" she asked, studying the victim.

She'd been short, around five-two, Pescoli guessed, with long brownish hair on the curly side that was stiff and riddled with tiny ice crystals. The woman's face was heart-shaped, with a straight little nose and blue eyes that were fixed, seeming to stare blindly upward. Neatly plucked eyebrows and thin cheeks lay above cold, blue lips. She was wearing a dress, gray and fitted, earrings that looked like diamond studs, and fingers and toes that were polished a matching cranberry hue. Unbroken fingernails, neatly manicured, suggested there had been no struggle. Well, except for the ring finger of her left hand, most of which was missing.

What's up with that? The killer's trophy? Or an accident that had sent her running here? Pescoli regarded the wooded foothills where snow was covering the ground, boulders and snags protruding from the thick white blanket, the nearly frozen stream softly gurgling as it wound between the trees.

Slatkin glanced up, his blue eyes finding her gaze. "Don't know yet. Maybe drowned. Or could be head trauma. Got a few bruises." He frowned thoughtfully, eyeing the woman's slim throat. "Possible strangulation." His thick eyebrows drew together over his cold-reddened face. "Won't know until the autopsy."

Nodding, Pescoli stared down at the dead woman and wondered what had happened to her. How had she ended up in this creek? Had she made it under her own power, or had someone left her here? And why here? She glanced around the stretch of ranch land where field met forest. Why had this place been chosen as either the killing ground or dumping spot? Eyeing the creek, she saw that it was deep enough for a body to submerge, despite the encroaching ice. Where was the woman's coat or jacket? Her shoes? Her purse and, especially, her finger?

What kind of whacked-up freak would cut off the finger?

Of course, Pescoli reminded herself, *we don't know one hundred percent that the woman has been murdered*.

The missing finger certainly suggested that something violent had gone down, maybe even some kind of accident. She had learned over the years not to make quick assumptions, though oftentimes her gut instinct proved right. Until all the facts were in, however, she wouldn't make a final decision.

Once more, she looked at the left hand where a finger had been severed, the bone and flesh visible. Her stomach turned a bit and she drew her eyes away for a second, nausea building.

She'd never been queasy at a crime scene, except years before . . . Oh, God. Another roll of her guts, and saliva gathered in her mouth. *For the love of—*

At that moment, she knew she was going to be sick. She turned away, took a few steps from the creek, and just managed to get behind a fir tree before she upchucked into the snow. She hadn't thrown up at a crime scene since . . . she was pregnant with Bianca. Morning sickness. *Perfect.*

"Hey!" Alvarez said. "You okay?"

Pescoli heaved once more, then straightened, a sour taste in her mouth. "Fine," she lied, running her tongue over her teeth.

"Jesus, Pescoli! Look what you're doing to the crime scene," Watershed admonished. "It's not like you haven't seen a dead body before."

She didn't dignify his remark with an answer. To Alvarez, she said, "I'll talk to O'Halleran. You take the boy. See what he has to say. Maybe he saw something he doesn't realize might help."

Alvarez was already on her way to the idling car where an officer was staying with Eli O'Halleran, and Pescoli walked over to where Trace O'Halleran was deep in conversation with Cabral.

Nurse Amy Blanchette was dead tired. Thankfully, her shift was nearly over. In five minutes, come hell or high water, or even a damn plague, she was "outta here." Northern General Hospital wasn't her idea of a dream place to work, but since Johns Hopkins and the Mayo Clinic didn't seem to be calling, she'd stick it out and collect her paycheck, at least until she could figure out if she was going to stay in Montana near her parents, who lived in Hamilton, or venture out into the much bigger world. God, she'd love to get out of the miserable weather and try somewhere a little warmer, or exotic, or at least, somewhere that had a little more mystique. A place by the ocean, maybe.

LA sounded good. Or maybe San Antonio or somewhere in Florida. Anywhere she didn't have to wake up to piles of snow and freezing temperatures would be nice. Better still, a hospital where she didn't work with her damn ex-fiancé, who'd decided to bail six months into the engagement. Thankfully, she'd only lost her heart, not her life savings on a wedding. But even though she tried desperately to work opposing hours, she ran into Dr. Dylan Stone—yes, he sounded like he was one of those fake doctors on an old soap opera— too often. The fact that he was dating a handful of her coworkers made her working environment all the more caustic. By summer, she swore, she'd have that job elsewhere.

She had a few more minutes of her ten-hour workday to get through. A few nurses and orderlies on her shift were starting to leave while the nurses for the next ten hours were arriving. The hub was a little chaotic with the switch. Nurses who were leaving exchanged patient information, a few jokes, and a little bit of gossip with the nurses coming on duty. Worse yet, the flu had not only infected several patients on the wing, but the staff as well, devastating some of the teams. Her floor in particular was short-handed and the staff was forced to depend upon recruits from other areas of the hospital, sometimes working for the first time with newbies. Just today, Amy had shared her area of the wing with a couple orderlies, two doctors, and a nurse she'd previously never met.

But it was about over.

"One more patient," she reminded herself as she responded to the call light for room 212. The patient, Reina Gehrig, was a real pain in the butt. Amy wasn't one bit sorry that she would be able to pawn the older woman off on Mona Vickers, the nurse scheduled to take over Amy's patients. Mrs. Gehrig in particular, seemed to believe she was the only patient in the entire hospital.

Most definitely a pain in the backside.

Forcing a smile, Amy slipped into the room where Reina Gehrig was propped in her hospital bed, television tuned to a game show, her head swiveling expectantly as the door opened.

"How're you doing?" Amy asked, turning off the call light.

"Oh, not so good, I'm afraid," the small woman said. She was a frail thing with a lined, narrow face and a halo of thin white curls that didn't quite hide the pink of her scalp.

She's lonely, Amy thought and felt a little ashamed for thinking badly of her.

Barely a hundred pounds, with hazel eyes that snapped behind the folds of her eyelids and thick glasses, Reina said solemnly, "I think there's something wrong."

"Well, that won't do." Amy gave the woman a smile. "Tell me, how do you feel? Rate your pain." She indicated the chart that hung on the wall that showed caricatures of faces in varying expressions of discomfort.

" 'Bout an eight, maybe a nine, I'd say," the patient said. "And it doesn't just hurt in my leg, but all over." Frowning a little, she added, "I think I might be coming down with something. The flu's going around this year, you know. And my neighbor Elsa, she caught it. Nasty stuff."

"Hmm. Well, we can't have that," Amy said. "Let me check your vitals again."

The patient's chin suddenly thrust out. "I need to see Doctor Lambert."

"She didn't do your surgery." Amy checked Mrs. Gehrig's temperature, blood pressure, and pulse again, noting that everything was in the normal range, right where it should be. "Dr. Bellingham says you can go home tomorrow."

"Oh, I don't think so. I'd feel a lot better if Dr. Lambert had a look at me." Mrs. Gehrig was nodding in her bed as if agreeing with herself. Her thin hands, with veins visible, plucked at the edge of the sheet covering her.

"I'll let her know," Amy promised, " and mark it on your char—"

"Room two-o-six STAT!" Polly, another floor nurse, poked her head into the room as she passed the open doorway just as Amy heard the Code Blue announcement from the speakers in the hallway.

"What?" Mrs. Gehrig was confused.

Amy was already reversing toward the door. "I'll be back."

"No, please—" Mrs. Gehrig's face folded on itself in disappointment. "Wait! Where are you going? I need—" The rest of her request was cut off as Amy rushed toward the room a few doors down.

"Mr. Donnerly's coding!" Polly called to her as they entered 206.

Already, the room was bustling with staff members. The patient had recently had heart surgery and had been improving enough to be released from ICU to his private room. One nurse was handling his chest compressions while another had a bag valve mask in place over the patient's mouth and nose. A doctor was giving orders as the defibrillator cart was rolled quickly inside and another locking cart with narrow drawers for medications followed. Amy stood at the ready should she be required to administer the epinephrine or whatever other drug the doc ordered.

"How long?" the doctor asked.

"Coded under two minutes ago," a floor nurse who had been attending Benson Donnerly said as the rest of the team continued working.

"Pulse?" the doctor asked and another nurse pressed against the patient's neck, checking the patient's carotid artery.

"No pulse."

"Code Blue!" another page called over the loudspeaker, adding to the tension.

We're here already, Amy thought, refusing to be distracted in case she was needed.

"Code Blue! Room two-twenty!"

"What?" The doctor turned his head.

"Has to be wrong," Polly said, surprised.

"Double-check," he said, nodding at Amy, who quickly slipped out of the room and caught up to two nurses headed rapidly down the hallway.

"Let's go," Reba, a tall RN with a single braid falling down her back said to Amy. She was hurrying, the braid swinging side to side as she tried to keep up with Brad King, a male nurse with a trimmed beard and long, athletic stride.

Avoiding an orderly heading in the opposite direction, Amy hurried to fall into step with Reba. "Wait," she said, trying and failing to keep up. "The patient who's coding is in two-o-six." She hooked her thumb in the direction of Mr. Donnerly's room.

"Yesterday's news," Brad said over his shoulder as he broke into a jog and Reba followed suit. "We've got another patient coding."

Two cardiac arrests on the same floor at the same time? It happened, of course, but very infrequently. "But—Hold up." Amy was processing what the senior nurse had said. "Two-o-six?" she repeated, hoping she'd misunderstood. "Isn't that the sheriff's room?"

"That's right," Brad confirmed as he pushed open the door of the room where the patient lay unmoving, his chest no longer rising and falling, his pallor weak, his eyes closed.

Oh, no.

His heart monitor was visible from the doorway and the green line moving across the screen remained level, not so much as bumping the slightest as a piercing sound that should have been softly beeping was a steady, ominous warning.

Brad moved to the patient's side and started compressions on his chest as Reba found the bag valve mask to force air into the patient's lungs.

"Make sure the doc knows that we've got a second cardiac arrest. We need a defib cart ASAP!" Brad was still working over his patient as he barked at Amy.

"The cart's in Mr. Donnerly's room—"

"Order another one."

"There's only one on the floor."

"Then get one from another floor. STAT!" he ordered as he worked over the patient who, so far, wasn't responding. His heart monitor showed a flat green line, its high-pitched whine piercing. "For Christ's sake, move it!"

Amy was already turning into the hallway to get more help, but her own heart was pounding double-time at the thought of losing this patient, who just happened to be the sheriff of Pinewood County.

CHAPTER 5

Hearing the sound of another vehicle approaching, Pescoli looked up and squinted through the curtain of falling snow. She and Alvarez were about to leave the O'Halleran ranch as they'd already taken statements and looked around as much as they could in the frigid conditions. The victim's body had been taken to the morgue, the emergency workers had left, and the O'Hallerans had returned to their house. A guard was still posted near the front gate and the crime scene team was still finishing up gathering trace evidence, but her work was done.

A Jeep emerged, twin headlights cutting through the gloom, big tires kicking up snow. The driver parked next to the crime scene van, cut the engine, and emerged swiftly. Blackwell.

"Just what we need," Pescoli said under her breath. Half expecting to see the KMJC news van following in his wake, she glanced to the ruts cut into the snow where half a dozen or more vehicles had come and gone, mashing the snow beneath dozens of tires.

But Blackwater was alone, no entourage of reporters following.

A first. Well, that wasn't really the truth, but she wasn't in the best of moods after losing her breakfast and dealing with the bitter cold as, potentially, another nutcase of a killer was making his presence known in this part of the Bitterroots.

Blackwater's expression was grim as he strode through the powder to her vehicle.

"We're just about done here. Wrapping things up," Pescoli told him.

"Good. I need to talk to the both of you. In person." A muscle worked in his jaw.

"Something up?" Pescoli asked as Alvarez's eyes narrowed a fraction.

He hesitated, glanced at the woods for a second, then forced his gaze back to the two detectives standing before him. "Bad news," he said,

Pescoli felt her back muscles tighten. "What?"

Beside her, Alvarez drew a sharp breath as if she guessed what was coming.

"It's the sheriff," he said solemnly, the corners of his mouth twisting downward. "He didn't make it."

"What?" Pescoli exploded. "What the hell are you talking about?"

"I'm sorry."

"Oh, God." Alvarez leaned hard against the front panel of Pescoli's Jeep, her knees buckling. Her face had washed of all color and she was shaking her head. Even as she did, she made the sign of the cross over her chest.

"No!" Pescoli stared down Blackwater and fervently shook her head. "Not Dan Grayson. There must be some mistake."

"I wish there was." Blackwater seemed sincere, holding back his own emotions. "Grayson's heart stopped. A Code Blue was issued, and as I understand it, the team was there in seconds, trying to get him going again. Spent nearly forty minutes trying to get a pulse—defibrillation, epinephrine, whatever it is they do to bring someone back, but it was over. They couldn't revive him." He glanced from Pescoli who'd gone numb with disbelief to Alvarez who turned her head away, probably to hide her tears.

"What the hell happened?" Pescoli demanded, gesturing angrily. "He was getting better. Stable, that's what the hospital and his damn doctor said. They even moved him out of ICU because he'd improved, right?" She didn't wait for an answer. "He was shot in the head, not the heart, for Christ's sake! His heart was fine. Strong." She swung back to look at Alvarez for confirmation, but her partner didn't respond. To Blackwater, she snapped again, "What the hell happened?"

"The hospital is checking. Could be that the injuries he sustained were too much for him and his heart just stopped," Blackwater said without his usual bluster. To his credit, he seemed genuinely disconsolate. "I don't know. No one does. Yet. He'd been through a lot."

"Through a lot and out the other side!" Pescoli insisted, though the truth, like the steadily falling snow, was cold and bleak as it settled over her. "Oh . . . oh Jesus," she finally said in a rush as she started to believe what Blackwater was saying.

"I came out to tell you myself, so you wouldn't hear it on the police band or the news or from someone else."

Alvarez let out a soft moan.

"They told us he would be all right," Pescoli said. "And those bastards lied." Turning to Alvarez, she said, "Let's go."

"Where?" her partner asked and even as she did, she seemed to stiffen her spine, to gain control, her mask of always cool detachment slipping back into place.

"To the hospital to get some damn answers. To find out what went on, why they lost him." As she said the words, the full truth hit her like a ton of bricks. Grayson was gone. Forever. She'd been there when he'd been shot and in her mind's eye, it was Christmas morning once more and she watched in horror as the bullets from a hidden assassin's rifle had struck the tall man with kind eyes and a thick moustache.

Grayson's body had spun with the first bullet, his ever-present Stetson flying off his head, the split kindling he'd been carrying flying end over end to land on the snow-covered earth. With the second shot, his head had snapped back and he'd fallen to the snowy ground and lay inert. Pescoli, who had been driving to his house to ask about cutting back her hours, never got the chance.

She'd been the first responder, viewed his blood, prayed like she'd never prayed before and then had sworn vengeance on his assailant, that coward who had hidden in the snowdrifts with a high-powered rifle aimed straight at Dan Grayson.

"Son of a bitch!" she said angrily and kicked one of the Jeep's tires in fury.

"You're not going anywhere," Blackwater said. "You've got a new case to investigate with the Jane Doe found right here, so I suggest you start." He frowned. "Hell, I know this is a blow for the two of you and the whole department. That's why I came out, but that doesn't mean we still don't have jobs to do." Snow was collecting on the brim of his hat and shoulders of his jacket. Though there was a trace of compassion in his eyes, he remained rigid, ever in charge. "The

Missoula police are on the scene and the hospital is double-checking every procedure, all of his vital signs records, every report and notation. Of course, there will be an autopsy."

"Fuck the autopsy!" Pescoli said, her anger exploding. "I'm going to the hospital, whether you like it or not!"

"Detective," he warned.

But Pescoli was already around the Jeep and behind the wheel.

Alvarez slid into the passenger seat. "Let's go," she said in an out-of-character display of disobeying her commanding officer.

"What?" Hattie Grayson dropped the jar of jam she'd been holding. The small container shattered on her kitchen floor, shards of glass flying, sticky strawberry jam spraying in thick clumps. "No. Not Dan. Not Dan!"

She stared into the tortured gaze of Dan's brother Cade, who had just driven over to give her the news that cracked her world in two. Disregarding the spilled jam and shards of glass, she fell into his arms. Tears welled and she felt as if they'd started in the center of her soul. She'd known Dan all her life, been married to Bart, one of his brothers, and had half-fancied herself in love with him before reuniting with Cade. The Grayson brothers—all four of them, including Big Zed—had been the center of her universe.

Now two of the brothers were gone. Bart's death had been ruled a suicide, though she was certain that he'd been killed. Dan had been murdered by a maniac as well, someone he should never have trusted.

"I don't want to believe it."

"Me neither."

"The bastard who did this—"

"Will pay."

That much was true. Dan's assailant was already captured and behind bars, fighting his own injuries.

Still, the rage at the man who'd snatched Dan's life away burned deep. "I hope he rots in hell."

Cade's strong arms folded her tight against him. "I know."

Thank God he didn't say "it will be all right" or any other platitude, because deep in Hattie's heart, she knew that it would never be. With Dan Grayson's easygoing strides no longer walking the earth, the planet would be an emptier, colder place. He'd been so good to her, to her twin daughters, to everyone in Grizzly Falls. At least she had time to pull herself together before she told her girls. Mallory and McKenzie would be as devastated as she was. A coldness settled over her and she shivered in Cade's embrace.

"First Bart, now Dan," she whispered, drinking in the smell of the man holding her so close. The scents of leather and horses clung to him and filled her nostrils. "I don't want to believe this, Cade. I just . . . I just can't. There's got to be a mistake."

"I wish, darlin'," he said, his own voice rough, his warm breath ruffling her hair. His jaw was scratchy with beard-stubble, his eyes a deep, somber gray, all of the carefree, bad-boy attitude gone. He squeezed her a little more tightly and his voice cracked as he said, "God, don't I wish."

The hospital was remarkably calm, Alvarez thought, almost as if the whole world surrounding Grizzly Falls hadn't changed drastically with the passing of Sheriff Dan Grayson. Yes, there was a news camera crew outside. Nia Del Ray, a reporter for KMJC, was standing near the sign at the entrance of Northern General Hospital, snow catching on her short black hair as she was probably reporting on Grayson's demise, unless some other story had trumped his, which Alvarez doubted.

Inside the wide hallways, the floors gleamed under bright lights, conversation hummed, and people went about their work as if nothing monumental had just gone down within the hospital's walls. Near a placard that listed those who had donated to the hospital, she and Pescoli stepped around a woman with a cast on her leg, being wheeled down the hallway by the orderly, after which they nearly ran into an elderly man who had suddenly stopped for no apparent reason.

"Sorry," he apologized, blinking as if he'd been in a daze.

They moved past him to the elevators. "You know what this means, don't you?" Pescoli said, slapping the call button just as the doors to one of the cars opened and a group of three women emerged.

"Tell me." Alvarez walked into the car.

Once they were inside and the elevator doors had whispered shut, Pescoli pounded her fist on the button for the second floor. "That the son of a bitch who took down Grayson just lost his GET OUT

OF JAIL card forever. No more *attempted* in the charge. He's going down for murder."

The doors opened and they stepped into the wide hallway, again brightly lit and complete with alcoves, benches and chairs, and a wide nurse's station at the center of it all.

They walked up to the desk and a woman seated at a computer looked up. Pescoli showed her badge and said, "Detective Regan Pescoli, Pinewood County Sheriff's Department. This is my partner Detective Alvarez. We have some questions about . . . about the sheriff . . . Dan Grayson . . . and what happened to him. We'd like to talk to the supervisor of the floor and his doctor, whoever was in charge of his care."

Alvarez's gaze shifted to Pescoli, whose green eyes shifted in hue with the light.

Under the glare of the hospital's illumination they were a light jade color and hard as stone. Athletic and tall, with sharp features and a penetrating gaze, she was intimidating. An ex-basketball player, Pescoli wasn't afraid to get into anyone's face and bore more than her share of battle scars as a no-nonsense police officer and single mother. She was glaring at the small, nervous-looking nurse behind the desk as if the poor woman was a hardened criminal.

"I'll get Rinalda, uh, Mrs. Dash. She's in charge," the girl behind the desk said.

Before either of the detectives could thank her, a booming female voice carried up the hall. "Is there a problem, Stephanie?"

In her peripheral vision, Alvarez caught a glimpse of a slim woman quickly approaching. Tall, African-American with close-cropped hair and an expression that was as stern as Pescoli's, she stopped at the desk. "I'm Rinalda Dash." With her height, she actually looked down at Pescoli. "What can I help you with?"

Again, Pescoli flashed her badge and introduced them both. "We're here about Dan Grayson, who was your patient. We'd like to know what happened."

"We all would," Nurse Dash said solemnly. "And we're looking into it as we do with all unexpected deaths. There's a place where we can talk more privately," she said, indicating a small niche near a bank of windows. Complete with a square of carpet, a coffee table, bench, fake ficus tree, and two side chairs, the spot offered little privacy, but it would have to do.

To the nurse behind the desk, the supervisor said, "Stephanie, page Dr. Zingler, please. See if he's still in the building. I'm sure the detectives would like to speak to him, as well." She gave Pescoli a patient but firm smile as she led them into the alcove. "Believe me, we will find out what exactly caused the sheriff's death."

Blackwater held a meeting in the conference room, which not only opened from the hallway but from his office as well. Everyone who worked for the department and currently not on the road was required to attend. One person in each department was to man the phones and he expected the meeting to be short, but he owed it to the officers, those who had worked under Dan Grayson, to explain the situation as best he knew it. He stood before the deputies, secretaries, volunteers, detectives, and various officers and met all of their solemn gazes with his own.

"This is a bleak day for the Pinewood County Sheriff's Department," he began at the podium. "A difficult time for all of us, most of you more than me, as you had the honor of working with Sheriff Dan Grayson much longer than I did. We all respected him. He was a man who walked tall among men, a fair and just man, a man with a steely determination balanced by his compassion and quick wit. He would want, no, he would expect, all of us to continue working here for the good of Pinewood County, to protect and serve its citizens, and so we shall.

"That doesn't mean that I, as the acting sheriff, will not expend every effort to find out what happened at the hospital, and if there were extenuating circumstances regarding his death. I promise each and every one of you that the person responsible for sending Dan Grayson to Northern General Hospital will be tried and convicted for his crimes. The district attorney is already updating the charges against the suspect." He glanced around the room, letting his words settle, then added, "The best way we can honor Dan Grayson's memory and years of service is to continue with our jobs as officers of the law. Sheriff Grayson would have expected as much, and so do I. We have cases that require our immediate and undivided attention and I expect each and every one of you to give a hundred percent in ferreting out those responsible for the crimes under our jurisdiction and bringing them to justice."

He paused for effect. "For an as yet undetermined amount of

time, I'm lowering all of the building's flags to half mast. Everyone, please, keep the sheriff's memory alive by continuing to provide the citizens of Pinewood County with your best service. Thank you."

He thought about saying more, even including a quick prayer, but decided short and to the point was all that was necessary. Each officer would grieve on his or her own terms. Hopefully, the meeting would provide some closure until a funeral could be arranged and business could go on as usual.

It wasn't that he was just a hard-ass. He believed that the work of the department couldn't be interrupted for anything, even a commander's death. He would back off a bit, allow a few tears and conversations, let those who were closest to Grayson have a few days to grab hold of their emotions, but he had a department to run and a sicko on the horizon, if the body discovered on the O'Halleran ranch was any indication.

That case bothered him in its brutality, but he knew that it would also raise the community's awareness of him as the sheriff. It was an opportunity to show that he was up to the task, and was also a test of his mettle and skills. The Jane Doe whose body had been found in that near-frozen creek could be his ticket to the kind of fame he needed to be elected sheriff.

As he strode to his office, the one so recently occupied by Grayson, he considered that there could be an outside chance that a perfectly sound explanation existed as to why a healthy-looking thirtyish woman had ended up dead in a near-frozen pool of a creek, her ring finger recently severed. *Not much of a chance*, he thought, *but one that had to be explored.*

Walking into his office, he ignored the feeling that he was stepping into another man's boots. More than one, if he were honest with himself. Yes, Grayson had worked here. Yes, he was beloved by the staff and citizens, but he wasn't the first exalted leader, nor would he be the last. The long row of eight-by-ten photos in the lobby proved the point of how many had gone before Dan Grayson. The empty wall invited those who would follow.

Blackwater settled into a chair that was too big for him in more ways than he wanted to consider. He only hoped that he could finish out Grayson's term and be elected to sheriff on his own merit, so that one day his own picture would grace the wall of the lobby.

Of course, in order for that to happen, he had to prove himself.

Show the citizens of Pinewood County that he was the logical choice for sheriff.

He thought about the detectives on his staff and wondered how long he'd be able to deceive them. Alvarez with her master's degree in psychology. A beautiful Hispanic woman with jet-black hair, full lips, and dark, suspicious eyes, she did little to enhance her looks, but she took her job seriously. She was dedicated, he'd give her that. A natural Type-A who worked out in the gym, she kept her body tight and her mind sharp, and usually reined in her emotions. Called an "ice princess" or "bitch with a heart of stone" behind her back, she was harder on herself than anyone else was.

Blackwater related to her, knew she was a good cop, and that she played by the rules. With the news about Grayson, she'd fallen completely out of character, though he supposed it was understandable given her staunch belief in him and her loyalty. But she'd defied his orders to join her partner.

That one. Pescoli. She was as out of control as her partner was in. Married a couple times, with kids who gave her fits, she was a wild card. A good cop, yes, but she relied on gut instinct and adrenaline, more than Blackwater liked. He had little doubt that she'd take him on if given half a chance. Wearing one's emotions on one's sleeve was never a good idea in his opinion, and for a cop, it was worse.

She was a rogue. Period. Didn't respect the rules one iota.

He leaned back in his chair and glanced through the door he'd left ajar. Pescoli's office was just down the hall, which was perfect.

Because he planned to watch her like a hawk.

CHAPTER 6

"Sheriff Grayson is dead? He . . . he . . . passed away?" Jessica repeated, stunned as she loaded the order for table five—three coffees and a tea—onto her tray in the kitchen of the Midway Diner.

"That's what everyone's saying." Misty, a tall, leggy redhead, frowned down at the platters warming under the lights on the counter ready for pickup. She was at least five foot ten. With her hair twisted into a knot on the top of her head, she probably brushed six feet. "Hey! Armando!" she shouted at the cook manning the grill where burgers and strips of bacon were sizzling. Her lips, colored the exact shade of her hair and fingernails, were pursed in disgust. "I said, 'no onions' on one of these burgers."

"*Sì*," he said, pointing to the middle platter. "No onions."

Misty picked up the top half of the bun and surveyed the patty. "Okay. Sorry. My bad."

"*Sì*. Next time, maybe you check first," Armando grumbled as he plucked one of the dual baskets from the deep fryer and gave the pale French fries within a quick shake before letting the basket descend into the boiling grease again.

Satisfied that her order was complete, Misty picked up the three platters and, as if they'd never been interrupted, went on with her gossiping. "I had two deputies in from the sheriff's department at table nine earlier today and they were talking all about it. How some of the people on the force are really upset and speculating about what will happen to the department." She headed for the swinging doors complete with portholes that separated the kitchen from the dining area but kept talking. "Sounded to me that nobody really likes the new guy, but he was promoted from the higher-ups, or something. I couldn't really hear everything. It was busy and the woman at table eleven was a real piece of work, complaining about every darned thing. Anyway, what I got out of it is that Grayson died. Maybe a heart attack. Maybe not. No one knows." She pushed the doors open with her shoulder and spun around as she entered the dining area.

Misty was a gossip, one of those people who practically licked her lips when she heard something "juicy" about someone else, and she had no qualms about embellishing that bit of information and passing it quickly along. Jessica had figured that out from the moment she walked through the back door, tied on an apron, introduced herself, and said she was ready to work. She thought back to that first day.

"I'm Misty," the older woman introduced herself. Smelling of a recent cigarette, she was sorting coffee cups and glassware that had been left in the dishwasher. "You'll be sorry you ever decided to take a job here, let me tell you. The boss, Nell, is a real piece of work, always thinks the employees are stealing her blind, got her nose in the damn till every hour or so. And Armando can't cook his way out of a paper bag."

"I heard that." The sour-faced cook was slicing onions, working quickly and efficiently with a butcher's knife not six feet away from where Misty had been complaining.

Jessica, as always, felt her stomach curdle as she caught a glimpse of the long blade glinting under the harsh overhead lights.

"Good. You should hear it. You know it's true," Misty said, unrepentant.

"*Perra,*" he muttered, his knife making a quick tattoo with the rapid fire motion.

Jessica said, "You know, I make it a policy not to insult anyone with a weapon in his hands."

"Meh." Unconcerned, Misty lifted a shoulder.

"*Idiota!*" Flashing Misty a condemning look, Armando turned so that his back was to her, effectively shunning her as he concentrated on his work and muttered something unintelligible under his breath.

Undaunted by the cook's disregard for her, Misty continued with her litany of complaints. "Marlon. He's the busboy? Always late. Considers himself some kind of Romeo and is out tomcatting, so he can never get here on time. A real pain in the ass, let me tell you." To emphasize the fact, she rattled the silverware tray, then started wrapping table knives, forks, and spoons into paper napkins, creating individual settings and stacking them neatly near the glassware. "Besides all that, the tips are lousy and this"—she pointed to the dishware she'd carefully prepared—"is not my job." With a glance over her shoulder to the back door, where a boy who looked as if he'd just rolled out of bed was striding through, she pasted on a false smile and said, "Good morning, Casanova."

"What's good about it?" he countered.

"Well, now that I think about it, nothing. But you owe me half an hour's wages!" She quit stacking the silverware to glare at him, one hand on a hip.

"So I owe you. Sue me." The kid, like Armando, seemed inured to Misty's barbs and went about rummaging in the linen closet near the back door, where he found a clean apron and began cinching it over his black jeans and once-white shirt. His hair, a bristly brown, had been gelled into unruly stiff peaks, his face clean shaven, his build that of a middleweight wrestler, not an ounce of fat on him.

"Yeah, you owe me all right," Misty agreed. "The way I figure it, you're up to about a year's salary, but I won't hold my breath. You can finish with the silverware and you'd better hop to. We're opening the doors in fifteen and you know the regulars, they don't like to wait."

"Yeah, yeah." He dismissed her, but had taken over the duties of organizing the flatware and dishes.

Satisfied, Misty whispered to Jessica, "He's hopeless," then pushed through the swinging doors to the dining area where tables were scattered between a long L-shaped counter and the windows. Behind the counter was a walkway with a scarred floor covered with rubber mats. Along one wall was a narrow ledge that housed the coffee and milkshake machines, the soda dispenser, tubs for dishes, and rows of condiments like soldiers beside them.

Misty's waitressing lessons began then. "Okay, so let's start with the coffee since the customers that are already driving here will expect it to be ready. Fresh every day. Every hour. You think you can handle that?" She was teasing. Sort of, but she thought she was the only person capable of running the diner. "We need two pots of regular brewed and ready to go by the time we open the doors, oops, in less than twelve minutes." She eyed the big schoolhouse clock positioned near the door. "I always have a pot of decaf ready, too, for the wimps who want to start their day with 'unleaded,' for whatever reason. Then I check the pots every fifteen minutes during the rush. Marlon is supposed to be on top of it, but I don't trust him. He's too busy flirting with the customers or checking his cell phone for his next hot date. If Nell gets here and finds the coffeepots empty, there will be hell to pay, but Marlon doesn't care. 'Cause he's Nell's nephew. Doesn't think he'll ever be fired. Punk kid. Once the crush is over, like I said, every hour."

Jessica watched Misty measure coffee into the pots.

"Gotta be careful here. Don't put too much in, y'know. We're famous for our weak coffee, but if I make it any stronger, Nell's all over me. Cuts into profits, y'know."

"I think I can handle this." Jessica started filling the basket for the decaf. "But if it's so miserable, why do you stay?"

"Good question." Misty took an empty glass pot and carried it to a nearby sink for a refill. As she shut off the water, she pretended to think for a second. "Must be because I'm a masochist."

As she carried her tray into the dining area, Jessica couldn't help but think about Dan Grayson and the fact that he'd died. She'd been prepared to talk to him, to confess, and when she'd discovered that he was hospitalized, she'd decided that she'd have to deal with Cade instead because she couldn't spill her guts to just anyone. It was more imperative than ever that she ask Cade for direction. A once-upon-a-time lover, Cade Grayson was one of the few people in the world she could trust. Well, at least she hoped so. Truth to tell, she and he hadn't parted on the best of terms.

Cade would be deep into mourning and, if she bared her soul to him, she would take a chance that he wouldn't believe her, wouldn't trust her, or give her the benefit of the doubt.

But who else?

At least Cade was a person who could understand deception, even twisting the law a bit.

He was her last chance.

That is, if she decided to stay in Grizzly Falls.

But what else could she do?

Run, she supposed as she pinned a smile on her face and started distributing the coffee and tea to her customers seated at table five. "Your orders should be up in a minute," she told them.

"Oh, could I please get a little honey for my tea?" the round-faced woman at the table asked.

"Sure. No problem." Jessica turned back to the counter where the packets of condiments were kept and vowed to herself that she was done running, that she was through looking over her shoulder and always having one foot out the door.

Finding the honey packets, she grabbed several and as she carried them back to the table, prayed she could keep that promise to herself.

"What happened?" Jeremy, who had been staring into the refrigerator, swung the door closed as Pescoli walked into her house and Cisco, her dog, went into his usual frenetic routine. The little terrier mix was dancing circles at her feet as she unzipped her jacket and left her boots on the patch of linoleum by the back door. From the living room, the television was tuned to a reality show.

"Bad day," she said, and bent down to pet the excited yapping dog. Cisco's tail was wagging in a blur, and he licked Pescoli's cheek as if he hadn't seen her in years rather than hours. Sturgis, Dan Grayson's black lab, climbed out of his bed and stood at her feet as well, his tail moving side to side, his dark eyes looking up at hers as if he understood. "I'm sorry," she said, scratching him behind his ears. "Oh, buddy." Her voice cracked. "I've got bad news." Sturgis's long tail slowed and he stared straight into her eyes as if he understood. Her heart fractured and she felt near to tears.

Hormones, she told herself . . . *and grief.* Sniffling, she straightened and found her son staring at her.

"Then it's true," Jeremy said. "About the sheriff?"

"Yeah, it's true." She cleared her throat. Willed her tears away. "He passed today."

"Shit. I mean . . . damn . . ."

She didn't bother saying anything about his language.

"I can't believe it!"

She nodded in silent understanding.

Jeremy's expression grew dark and he swore again, under his breath. Then he leaned hard against the counter where the remains of breakfast—two empty bowls and a half-eaten piece of toast left on a napkin—had spent the day.

"That bastard really killed him?" His jaw was set, reminding Pescoli of her first husband, Joe Strand, Jeremy's father. As her son matured, he looked more and more like his dad and the funny thing was he even displayed some of Joe's mannerisms, though he'd never really known his father, surely couldn't remember him. They shared the same build, though Jeremy topped his father's six-foot frame by about two inches and his features were still slightly softer than she remembered Joe's were, but the way he threw a ball, or looked over his shoulder? Pure Joe Strand. That part didn't bother her. No. The bad news, at least in her opinion, was that Jeremy had decided to follow in his father's footsteps by becoming a cop. Just like his dad. Even though his father had lost his life in the line of duty.

Don't blame Joe. You're on the force, too. A cop's life is all your son has ever known.

Some of the blame definitely rested on her shoulders.

Though Pescoli loved the fact that he was enrolled in school again and was thrilled that he finally seemed to have some direction, she hated the idea of him becoming a member of the police force after seeing what the dedication to protecting and serving had done to their own family.

How often had she rued her vocation? Yeah, she loved being a cop, but she'd be a fool if she didn't admit that the stress and long hours of her job hadn't taken their toll on parenting her kids.

And now there's going to be another one. Oh, Lord.

"But didn't you say he was improving?" Jeremy asked. "How could this happen?"

"I guess he was more fragile than anyone, the doctors included, realized. The doc in charge, Zingler, he's double-checking everything," she said but didn't add that what really bothered her was that there were two patients who had flatlined about the same time. The first, just seconds before Grayson, happened to a patient named Donnerly who had over thirty years on Grayson. But he'd survived.

Of course, he hadn't suffered the same kind of attack as the sheriff, but Pescoli couldn't help but wonder if the heart stoppages had happened in the reverse order, if Grayson flatlining had been the first emergency, would the hospital staff have been quicker to respond? Would he have survived? It just didn't sit well with her.

"So, what happens now?" Jeremy wanted to know.

"I'm not sure," she admitted. "It's not good down at the station. Morale is at an all-time low, and that's saying something." She hung up her jacket on the hall tree and noticed the snow on her boots was already melting, making puddles. "Everyone's upset. Even Joelle isn't interested in decorating for Valentine's Day, which is probably a good thing, because Blackwater definitely isn't into it." She scowled remembering his recent edict about keeping the offices spotless and professional at all times. That would be a trick considering the drunks, suspects, informants, criminals, and general scum of the earth who were dragged through the hallways of the Pinewood County Sheriff's Department on a daily basis. "Hopefully he's only temporary."

"You don't like him because he's taking Grayson's job," Jeremy pointed out.

"That's not it. Well, not *all* of it."

"I don't think he's all that bad."

She glared at her son as if he'd uttered sacrilege, which he had. "You're only there part-time. *Very* part-time. As a volunteer. You don't really work for him."

"Yet." Jeremy caught his mother eyeing the dirty dishes on the breakfast bar and actually picked up the two bowls and placed them into the sink with the stack of ever-mounting pots, pans, and plates. Of course, he couldn't quite seem to find the dishwasher, but, Pescoli reminded herself, *baby steps*.

Not that long ago, her son was adrift, playing video games all day, smoking weed on the side, and chewing tobacco. Things were improving. He was growing up. Yeah, he still chewed. And of course, he continued to play video games, but even that had slowed down a bit and she thought his pot smoking had abated. Thinking about it, she unconsciously crossed her fingers.

As far as she could tell, Jeremy's general "hanging out" with some of his suspect friends had tapered off and his steady girlfriend of the past few years had moved away, thank God. It had only been a few weeks, but without Heidi Brewster as a distraction, Jeremy already seemed more focused.

His job at Corky's Gas and Go coupled with volunteering at the station kept him busy and he was talking about moving out with a friend. Again. So far, he'd bounced back after a couple half-assed attempts at living on his own. She'd already suggested that he move into the room over the garage in Santana's new home, but Jeremy had balked. Residing in any building attached to his mother's place of residence obviously didn't qualify as "moving out."

Considering her own rebellious history as a teen, she wasn't about to argue.

He saved your life.

That much was true. If it hadn't been for Jeremy taking aim at Grayson's killer during an attack, she wouldn't be alive.

"Give Blackwater a chance," Jeremy suggested, opening the refrigerator door and hanging on it again, as if somehow the contents within had changed in the last five minutes. "I think he's a good guy."

"We'll see." She wasn't convinced.

He discovered a previously overlooked slab of pie that had to be a week old and pulled it from the depths. "Since we can't have Grayson back," he said soberly.

She nodded, swallowed, then checked her watch. "So where's your sister?"

"At Lana's. Studying," he added dryly.

"Ahh. Well, you know, they could be."

He grabbed a fork that had been left near the sink, then carried the pie into the living room and plopped onto the worn couch. "They *could* be," he allowed. Both dogs, hoping he might drop a bit of food, followed at a brisk trot and positioned themselves at his feet, their ears cocked, their eyes beseeching.

"You know something I should?" Pescoli asked, following him into the living room.

"Just a gut feeling. Kinda like your cop instinct."

"Does she need a ride?"

"What she needs is a car."

"So she tells me. Every day." She found her cell phone to text her daughter.

"Lucky says she can have one. He'll buy it for her."

"And the insurance? And the gas?" Pescoli hated the fact that her ex could offer up extravagant gifts with no strings attached and, when they didn't work out, leave her to pick up the pieces and deal with the fallout.

"That, you'll have to talk to him about."

When hell freezes over, she thought darkly, relieved to feel something other than grief, if even for a moment, as she texted Bianca. Briefly, she considered having a beer, then immediately banished the thought. A "cold one" after work, one of life's pleasures, was out the window for around seven or eight more months.

"Have the dogs been fed?" she asked.

"Do they look like they've eaten?" Taking a huge bite of chocolate and whipped cream, he found the television's remote and switched stations.

"Hey, guys!" She found the opened bag of dog food in the pantry, scooped kibblets into two metal bowls and turned to find both animals waiting expectantly. "Hungry?"

Cisco spun in tight little circles while Sturgis swept the floor with his tail.

"Here ya go." As she fed the dogs, she received an incoming text from Bianca saying she had a ride and would be home within the hour.

Good. In time for dinner, whatever the hell that was going to be. Spaghetti out of a jar? Tuna casserole or cheese sandwiches and tomato soup from a can? Something Bianca would eat. She was beyond finicky and Pescoli was keeping an eye on her because she was obsessed with her weight, her body, and wearing the tiny bikini her stepmother had bought her for Christmas. At her stepmother's encouragement, Bianca was talking about becoming a model, so there were all kinds of comments about nutrition and exercise, carbs and fat, calories and workouts falling from her daughter's lips. Eating healthy would be great, but the operative word was eating, not starving. Working out, again, a great idea, but not to the point of passing out. Pescoli wished Michelle, a smart enough woman who was fixated by her own looks, would just leave her daughter alone and quit putting weird ideas into her head. As a teenager, Bianca already had enough of those.

So what could she whip up in the kitchen that her daughter

would find palatable? Nothing she'd already considered and, anyway, the thought of cooking made her already queasy stomach turn over. Maybe takeout, she thought, opening the drawer where they kept pencils, note pads, out-of-date telephone books, and menus for their favorite restaurants in Grizzly Falls. She'd just pulled out the menu for Wild Will's when her cell phone bleeped and she saw Santana's name and picture on the screen.

"Hey," she greeted him.

"I just heard about the sheriff." Santana's voice was grim.

"Yeah. Not good."

"You okay?" he asked.

"Not great," she admitted. "But I'll be fine."

"You sure?"

"Yeah." That was a lie.

"I'm coming over."

"No. Don't. Look, Santana, uh, I need to deal with the kids first." He hesitated and she sensed he thought she was shutting him out. "Seriously. I'm fine. The kids will be, too, but we have to deal."

Again silence.

"I need you to understand," she said.

"Okay. But, I'm here."

"I know. I . . . thank you."

"Tomorrow?"

"Yeah, I'll call. It's crazy at the station. Weird. I . . . just give me a little space to sort this all out."

"I always do," he said and she squeezed her eyes shut so she wouldn't shed a tear.

She hung up quickly. Afraid he might tell her he loved her and want to talk about their upcoming wedding. She just felt too raw and uncertain. It wasn't that she didn't love him. She did. Totally. But it was hard for her to be vulnerable, and uttering those three little words could break the dam of her emotions. "I'm sorry," she whispered as if he could hear her and was so glad he couldn't.

Jeremy called from the living room, "Hey, Mom. Maybe you wanna see this."

Still holding the menu, she walked from the kitchen and saw Hooper Blackwater's image on the screen. In full uniform, standing ramrod straight in front of the half-masted flags that were snapping in the wind, snow blowing around him, he was a somber and solid officer of the law. Looking directly into the camera's lens, he vowed to prosecute Dan Grayson's killer to the maximum extent of the law.

"This is what I was talking about," she said, glaring at the screen. "It's called grandstanding." She slid a look at her son. "And for the record? I don't like it."

CHAPTER 7

Talk about doom and gloom. The sheriff's office couldn't have been more somber if it were draped in black and a funeral dirge was playing throughout the hallways. Everyone was grim, feeling Grayson's loss, going about their business in whispered tones, not smiling, just getting through the day. Joelle had toned it down to a long charcoal-colored dress with a lighter gray sweater. Though she still wore three-inch heels, their clip was decidedly less sharp as she made her way down the hallway. Now that he'd spoken to the press and made his position clear, Blackwater had even holed himself into his office.

Pescoli hated the department's vibe as well as the empty feeling that had stayed with her throughout the night and followed after her like a shadow. She tried burying herself in work, but found herself distracted.

When Alvarez stuck her head into the office, Pescoli looked up, rolled back her chair, and said, "Come on, let's go," before her partner could utter a word. "I'll drive." She yanked her keys from her purse.

"Where?"

"To the morgue." Pescoli was already standing and reaching for her jacket and sidearm. "I can't stand this place another second."

"Okay."

"Maybe the ME can tell us about our Jane Doe. Any luck IDing her yet?"

Alvarez stepped out of the doorway to let Pescoli pass. "I talked to Taj in Missing Persons and so far no reports of anyone resembling our victim have been filed."

Pescoli's bad mood didn't get any better. As she waited for Alvarez to grab her own jacket, scarf, and gloves, she wondered about the woman found in the frozen creek. Though it wasn't conclusive that foul play had occurred, it seemed likely.

Once Alvarez slipped her cell phone into her pocket, they were on the move again, working their way to the back door, skirting a few solemn-faced officers walking in the other direction.

"It's personal," Alvarez said as she pushed open the door to the outside and a gust of frigid air swept inside. "If our vic was killed, I mean."

Squinting against the snow flurries, Pescoli shot a look at her partner. "I'm betting a year's salary that she didn't slice off her own finger, find a way to the O'Halleran ranch, and fling herself into the creek to commit suicide." They reached the Jeep just as Pescoli hit the button twice to unlock all the doors. Across the snow-covered roof, she added, "That's not how it's usually done. And an accident? With a recently lopped off finger?" She opened the driver's door and got behind the wheel.

"I'm just saying all the evidence isn't in yet."

"Sometimes evidence only proves what you already know." Pescoli started out of the lot, but waited for a snowplow to pass. Moving slowly, it piled a berm of snow and clods to the side of the road, impeding the driveways of the surrounding businesses but freeing up the street.

Rather than follow the slow-moving plow, she turned in the wrong direction for a few blocks, then circled back and headed for the main road leading to Missoula, and the basement of the very hospital where Dan Grayson had drawn his last, weak breath. "So *if* our Jane Doe's a homicide victim, why do you think it was personal?"

"The ring finger. That makes a statement."

"Could be we have a nutcase who collects fingers," Pescoli said.

"And possibly rings? Wedding rings? Engagement rings? What's the significance there?" Alvarez was thinking hard, absently rubbing her chin between her finger and thumb.

"Maybe just the handiest finger."

Alvarez splayed the fingers of her left hand in front of her. "Nope. One of the hardest to lop off. It's significant."

"So we've got ourselves another psycho. You know, we've been getting more than our share."

"Uh-huh." She was still staring at her hand and seemed lost in thought. "And why the creek? Was she taken there? Drowned?" Her lips compressed as Pescoli slowed for a light. "I'm getting a bad feeling about this one."

Pescoli actually laughed. "Like Grace Perchant?"

Alvarez shot her a pissy look.

Grace was one of the local nut jobs. She swore she held conversations with ghosts, could commune with spirits from the other side of life, poor trapped souls who hadn't completely passed. She also owned a couple wolf hybrids and had come into town with them in tow to warn some of the citizens about their murky futures. It was a little unsettling.

"More like you and your gut instincts."

The light changed and Pescoli held herself back from pointing out that Alvarez had always dismissed her sometimes unscientific approach to a case. "Here we go," she said, spying a coffee kiosk, then making a quick turn to pull behind a dirty red Jetta that was just pulling out. As she found her wallet, she asked Alvarez, "Want anything?"

"Sure. Tea. Hot. Some morning blend. Whatever they have."

"Got it." Pescoli turned to face the girl who was standing within the kiosk, waiting. Quickly rolling down her window, Pescoli repeated Alvarez's request and added a decaf latte for herself.

As the barista turned away, Alvarez asked, "What happened to black coffee?"

"I'm hungry this morning. Thought a latte would take care of it."

"A *decaf* latte," Alvarez reminded her. "Aren't you the same woman who drinks yesterday's Diet Coke when you find it in your Jeep's cup holder and orders double or triple espresso shots if your morning gears aren't revved?"

"Sometimes."

"All times. 'Coffee and a cigarette—a working woman's breakfast,' to quote you not so long ago."

"A loooong time ago," Pescoli disagreed as cash and cups were exchanged. "I'm jazzed enough today, okay?" She handed Alvarez her cup and placed her latte into the drink holder of the console.

Alvarez took an experimental sip. "Just wondered if you were feeling okay. Or coming down with something, considering that you lost your lunch."

"Weird that, huh? Guess all the changes in the department have gotten to me." Pescoli cringed inwardly, uncomfortable using Grayson's death as an excuse. But it was true enough, and she wasn't willing to admit to Alvarez just yet that she was pregnant. *First,* she told herself, *I have to give Santana the news.* She owed him that much. Then, when she felt the time was right, she'd explain it all to her partner.

But not now.

Though the snow was still coming down, it seemed lighter, the windshield wipers keeping up with the flakes. The interior of the Jeep smelled of coffee, the police band crackled.

"The department's never going to be the same," Pescoli observed, keeping emotion out of her voice with an effort as they drove past snow-crusted fields. "I mean, without Grayson."

Alvarez sighed, frowning into her cup as she obviously struggled with a wave of grief. Then, as if she'd convinced herself that she had to face the inevitable, she took a deep breath and said, "We'll all just have to adjust. It'll be difficult, but that's the way it is."

"It sucks."

"Amen."

Pescoli drove onto a curving bridge, a semi heading in the opposite direction. "I was thinking about cutting back on my hours anyway and since we've got Grayson's killer in custody, I'll probably put in a request. See what happens."

"Today?"

"Probably in the summer," she said.

Alvarez was looking through the passenger window. She nodded as if she'd expected this conversation. "You sure that's what you want?"

"My kids need me."

"Okay, but they're nearly grown."

"Then there's Santana."

"You're marrying him. Is that a reason to be semiretired? You're not even forty, for God's sake."

"I'm not talking retirement. Just cutting back a little."

"What're you going to do? Take up knitting? Join a wine club? Try out new Crock-Pot recipes?"

"Give me a break."

"Then what? Racquetball? Save mankind by joining some cause for world peace?"

Pescoli actually laughed. "Yeah, that's it."

"You'd miss it. Whether you know it or not, Pescoli, you live for this. Being a cop's in your blood."

"Now you sound like some B movie from the seventies."

"I'm serious, damn it."

"So that's it? You think we're destined to be together, riding in these Jeeps in the snow and ice, chasing bad guys, risking our lives and bowing to the likes of Hooper Blackwater?" She finally took a sip of her latte and scowled. "Jesus! People really drink this stuff?" The milky-sweet coffee hit her stomach and seemed to curdle. Dropping the cup back into its holder she added, "I don't need working eighty hours plus some weeks in my life."

Alvarez sent her a sharp look. "This is *all* about Blackwater and we both know it." When Pescoli didn't respond, she added tautly, "I don't like the new sheriff either, but he's what we're stuck with. For now. You're not the only one missing Dan Grayson."

Pescoli should have left it alone, but she was too raw, too bothered. "Yeah, well, I didn't fancy myself in love with him, either," she snapped and saw her partner's lips tighten. "What the hell was that all about?"

"Nothing."

"Oh, come on." She hit the gas and sped around a tractor inching down the highway, the driver huddled against the elements in a thick jacket and hat with ear flaps. "Jesus. Why the hell would you pull your John Deere out in this weather?" she grumbled.

Alvarez, obviously stung, didn't answer. She pulled her cell phone from her pocket and turned her attention to her e-mail and texts, scanning them quickly "Got reports from the O'Halleran neighbors. The Zukovs, Ed and Tilly, who live on one side of the O'Halleran spread. They told the deputy they saw nothing, were inside all day because of the blizzard."

"Smart."

"Same with the Foxxes, who are on the other side of the Zukovs. The husband ventured out to his barn, but took care of his cattle and that was it. Haven't heard from the ranch across the road or the one on the other side of the O'Hallerans yet." She tucked her phone into her pocket.

"I'm thinking whoever did it came in from the back," Pescoli said.

"A team checked the nearest access road."

"Tracks?" She felt a little ray of hope.

"Some. Maybe hunters."

"In this?" Pescoli said, staring out the windshield.

"Or cross-country skiers or snowshoers. People don't necessarily stay inside just because it's cold or snowing."

"Then they're idiots."

Alvarez gave her a long look. "What's going on with you?"

Oh, shit. She'd hoped that since the conversation had turned to the case at hand it wouldn't circle back to her. "What do you mean?"

"Don't play dumb. You're even more out of sorts than usual."

"Nice," she said, gripping the wheel more tightly as the farmland gave way to the outskirts of Missoula, but she silently admitted Alvarez had a point. Pescoli's emotions were all over the place. Since there wasn't much she could do about them, she shut up. Alvarez again buried herself in the information flowing through her phone and they drove the short distance to the hospital in uncomfortable silence.

Each lost in her own thoughts, they parked, hurried inside, and took the elevator down to the morgue. Pescoli tried not to dwell on the fact that Dan Grayson had given up his tenuous grip on the world, because, like it or not, that part of her life was over.

Ryder's breakfast consisted of black coffee from the machine in the motel's lobby and a burrito of sorts from a vending machine in the mini-mart located at the intersection half a block from the River View's front entrance. Even with the addition of hot sauce from a couple free packets he'd gotten at the store, the meal was tasteless, but he didn't much care. Along with the burrito, he'd picked up a newspaper, a bag of chips, a packet of jerky, and a six-pack of Bud, which he'd tucked into the tiny insulated cabinet the River View's management had optimistically dubbed a refrigerator.

Despite the fact that the bed had sloped decidedly toward the center of a sagging mattress, he'd slept like a rock. "The sleep of innocents," his grandmother had said, though, in his case, that assessment was far from the truth. He'd learned to catch his winks wherever he could, whether it be wrapped in a thin sleeping bag on some ridge under the stars, or in his truck in broad daylight, after he'd spent a night huddled in his pickup on a stakeout swilling strong coffee and holding his bladder until it felt like it would burst. Either way, he'd learned to drop off and catch whatever sleep he could. So the River View's sagging mattress hadn't bothered him any more than the meal of processed mystery meat—beef, if the label on the plastic-wrapped burrito was to be believed—trapped inside a tortilla that was probably several weeks past its pull date.

"So where are you?" he asked aloud as he pulled several ziplock bags from his duffel and laid them on the table that sufficed as a desk in the room. From each bag, he pulled out pictures, eight by tens, all in black and white, which had been taken of different-looking women, but whom, he believed, all were one and the same: Anne-Marie Calderone, the object of his search.

If he was right, and he'd bet his truck that he was on the money, she'd taken a crooked path from New Orleans to Grizzly Falls, Montana.

She'd become a master of disguise. Each photo was different; her style of dress, her hair color and cut, the shape of her body, whether she wore glasses or not, the curve and thickness of her eyebrows and lips. In one case where he thought she was wearing a short blond wig, she appeared seven months pregnant. In another, her bare leg was exposed by a short skirt and a tattoo was visible on her calf. In still another, her eyes appeared dark, almost black, though through the gray filter it was hard to determine the shade. Makeup accentuated her high cheekbones, or an appliance stuffed beneath her cheeks sometimes stole them from her. Her teeth were never the same, sometimes crooked, sometimes straight, but always longer or wider or with odd, gaze-catching overlaps than usually graced her smile. He found one where she'd placed a mole above her lip, and another where her fingernails were impossibly long, still another where her hair was stringy and dull. There were all kinds of distractions to catch the eye so that the viewer wouldn't take in the whole picture of her face and be able to say for certain that she was the woman in the first photograph, the one in color, of the real woman.

Picking up that photo, he studied the details of Anne-Marie's oval face—straight, aquiline nose dusted with fine freckles, naturally arched eyebrows, wide gold eyes, and full lips that, he remembered, stretched into a sexy and secretive smile. Her teeth were straight, incisors a little longer than the others, and the glint in those incredible eyes had caused more than one male heart to beat a little faster. A natural athlete, her hips were slim, her breasts small, her legs long.

She was far more clever than he'd given her credit for. Twice, he'd nearly caught her and just as many times she'd given him the slip.

"No more," he vowed as he found his iPad where he'd stored most of his notes on her. The pictures were on the device as well as his phone, but he liked the photographs as they were easier to pocket and pull out when necessary if he came across someone who might have run into her. They were easier to give to the person rather than let anyone handle his phone with all of its stored data.

Also, it seemed more likely to him that if he were "her brother," or "her cousin" or "a friend," all claims he'd made while tracking her down, that he would have an old photo. Bringing out a gallery of different shots stored on a computer file might be off-putting.

He checked his notes again. Her connection to Grizzly Falls was frail at best. Then again, when it came to the chameleon that was Anne-Marie Calderone, what he knew about her was about as solid as quicksand, the lies soft and shifting, hiding the solid footing of the truth.

His jaw grew tense at the thought of how she'd duped him.

All too easily.

Because he hadn't been thinking with his head when he was around her.

He felt the same cold fire burn through him as he gathered up her pictures and stuffed them back into the plastic bags.

Time to get moving.

He didn't know where she was. But he knew where to start looking for her.

Cade Grayson.

He shouldn't be too hard to find. Grayson was an ex-rodeo rider. Hard drinking. Womanizing. Trouble. The kind of man Anne-Marie had found irresistible. So of course, she'd come to seek him out.

From what Ryder had read in the local newspaper, Cade was one of two surviving brothers of Dan Grayson, recent sheriff of Pinewood County and the victim of a homicide. Cade and Zedediah still owned and maintained the Grayson ranch outside town, the place their ancestors had claimed as a homestead.

It seemed the likely place for Anne-Marie to show up. Ryder grabbed his heavy jacket and tucked his pistol and knife within. In a small case, he put the iPad, night-vision goggles, some various spy equipment, and his camera with all of its lenses.

After double-checking that everything, including the packs of chips and jerky, were in place, he zipped up the case and tossed on his jacket.

As he locked the door of the shabby room behind him, he thought of her again. How she'd once been. Without the makeup and disguises. Stripped bare. A natural beauty, a woman of privilege, smarter than most people knew.

He threw open the door of his truck, tossed in his gear, climbed inside, and fired the engine, her visage with him still. He'd trained himself not to think too much about her but sometimes he couldn't help himself. All his practiced self-control slid away and the door of his memories cracked open. When that happened, as it did as he backed out of the icy parking spot, he couldn't help but remember her naked body, shining with perspiration, flesh warm and smooth, eyes a smoldering shade as she stared up at him, almost daring him to give in to her.

She had been as erotically sensual and emotionally dangerous a woman as he'd ever met; a deadly combination he'd been unable to resist.

It wasn't a big surprise that he'd decided to hunt her down, he thought, driving out of the lot and joining a slim stream of traffic heading toward the town of Grizzly Falls.

It was the least she deserved.

Usually nothing about the morgue got to Pescoli. She could deal with the sight of a dead body, blood, and organs, and the cooler temperature in the room hardly registered. The clinical aspect of it was a comfort, if anything, and the smell, though unpleasant, wasn't a big deal. Even watching the pathologists work, examining and weighing organs while making notes on computers, was more interesting than troubling to her. She'd been there enough times, most often to collect the fingerprints off dead bodies. Nothing about the tiled room with its refrigerated coffin-like drawers, scales, stainless steel tables with sinks, or mutilated bodies really ever bothered her. She figured the dead were dead. Unfeeling.

It was her job to find out why, and if a crime had been committed, to bring the lowlife who'd perpetrated said crime to justice. Knowing the trauma a victim had gone through burrowed under her skin and increased her determination to nail the son of a bitch who'd committed the crime. Her emotions were often volatile, while her partner exuded a cool, almost icy detachment, but Pescoli wasn't particularly sensitive to the nuances. She just did her job.

At the moment, her senses were all out of whack. The smell alone was awful, that dead, sickly-sweet odor seeming to cling to her nostrils as she viewed the dead body of their Jane Doe lying faceup, her skin a grayish tone, her hair pushed away from her face, her eyes wide open and seeming to stare straight up at the huge body lift suspended over her gurney. Also, Pescoli couldn't help but let her gaze wander to the refrigerated drawers. Morbidly, she wondered if Dan Grayson's body was lying within one.

Her lungs constricted for a moment, but she told herself there was no reason to speculate. Forcing her gaze back to the victim, she tried to concentrate on the case.

Obviously, Jane hadn't been autopsied yet, no Y slice cut into her torso, no thin line sawed across her forehead and into her skull.

"I assume the autopsy has been scheduled?" asked Alvarez. She was standing at the side of the gurney. Her gaze had moved from the vic to the forensic pathologist who had pulled Jane from her resting spot in the refrigerated drawers lining one wall.

"Tomorrow, right after lunch."

Pescoli's already queasy stomach turned. "Ugh."

Alvarez glanced up at her quickly, obviously wondering at the comment that just slipped out.

Dr. Esmeralda Kendrick didn't even look up. She was one of those women who was all business. Somewhere in her early thirties, she could have been pretty, but made no effort, at least not for work. Pescoli appreciated that. Everything about Dr. Kendrick was professional. Her manner, her speech, her body language. As usual, her blondish hair was scraped back into a no-nonsense ponytail. She wore no makeup, not even a trace of lipstick, and her blue eyes, behind huge glasses, were serious. Though barely five-three, she managed to appear commanding. She wore scrubs, tennis shoes, a lab coat, and the air of someone who was very busy and didn't like to be interrupted.

The little bit of a tattoo, a shamrock it seemed, peeked from beneath her ponytail, so Pescoli guessed that Dr. Kendrick might not be as straightlaced and cold away from the morgue as she was while doing her job. Maybe.

"You've got her personal effects?" Pescoli asked her.

She nodded. "Not much. Just her clothes that have been examined and are laid out and drying, and a pair of earrings. Look like diamonds. Could be cubic z. Not sure yet. Nothing else."

Pescoli glanced down at the fingers. "Fingernail scrapings?"

"Done at the scene. And an officer came and took prints when the body was brought in," Kendrick said, looking toward the door which led to an underground parking area where bodies could be brought in discreetly. Across the wide room and through another doorway was a hallway that led to a viewing area, waiting room. Farther along was the staff area, much like the lunchroom at the station.

In the sterile-looking examination room, the feel was decidedly different. An operating room without the intensity, as no anesthesia was being forced into lungs to keep the patient under during surgery, no anxious relatives relegated to a waiting area to hear the outcome of the procedures, no life being saved. No, the lives here had already been lost, sometimes violently.

Pescoli eyed the surroundings, computer monitors, metal cabinets for equipment, scales, and three long stainless steel tables equipped with faucets, hoses, and gutters, the kind that reminded her of working in the cannery as a youth, where the detritus from the berries on the belt merged with the water running in the gutter to unknown drains, or as the gossip mill insisted, was used in wine making. Sticks, bees, rotten fruit, even a snake once, were pushed into the ever present stream of water flushing out the berries to be canned and sold in markets across the country.

The difference was that in the morgue the gutters were primarily for blood.

Observing the dead usually wasn't a big deal, just part of her job, until today, when the smell kept causing her stomach to roil uneasily and she'd had to fight to keep the nausea at bay.

"So what do we know about her?" Pescoli asked.

"We'll X-ray the body, look for anything out of the ordinary in the results, of course. There's not much in the form of distinguishing marks, other than a scar on her right forearm, probably from an accident when she was a kid, and a small tattoo of a flower—a daisy—on her ankle.

"She may have drowned," Dr. Kendrick said, her eyebrows pulling together thoughtfully. "Again, we won't be certain until we examine her lungs. There is a little bruising at her throat, but I can't be certain that the hyoid was crushed. We do know that she wasn't sexually assaulted, she wasn't pregnant, and the only serious and outward sign of trauma is her ring finger, which was sliced off cleanly and neatly."

Pescoli's gaze went to the hand in question where the stump was visible, then, once more, she looked at the woman's face. Serene in death. *Who are you?* she wondered. *And what the hell happened?*

CHAPTER 8

Jessica adjusted the padding around her waist, hips, and torso and stared at her reflection in the mirror she'd purchased at a thrift shop and mounted on the bathroom door. The suit wasn't comfortable, but necessary, she knew, hiding her otherwise slim frame. She'd already donned the dark contacts and wig, then eyed her reflection in the mirror. Not bad. She added a little more makeup, far more than she ever wore, changing the contour of her lips and eyes, then slid a mouthpiece over her natural teeth, changing her smile before pushing a pair of glasses onto the bridge of her nose. From a distance, the transformation would hide her identity. Close up, if anyone really knew her and was on to her disguises, she might not be able to get away with denying who she really was.

Hopefully, she wouldn't have to; not until she talked to Cade and decided upon her next move. She struggled into her uniform, a gold-colored dress with a front zipper, gingham trim, and red piping, like something waitresses wore in a 1950s diner, something Nell Jaffe had decided would attract customers. Slowly, she was converting the bland interior of the diner into a copy of something straight out of *American Graffiti*, a movie she outwardly adored.

After locking the cabin, Jessica drove into town and kept one eye on the rearview mirror. So far, she thought she was safe. But she wasn't going to let her guard down. She'd been in Grizzly Falls only a few days so she was still on pins and needles, fearing that, at any moment, she would run into him again, that he would find her. Her stomach twisted at the thought and her chest became tight, feelings she battled by breathing slowly and relaxing her muscles, even stretching her fingers rather than holding on to the steering wheel in a death grip.

The falling snow had abated and the plows had been at work, ruts being replaced by smooth roads where pavement was visible in some spots. Even the diner's lot had been partially cleared. After parking in the rear of the restaurant, she grabbed her backpack and hurried inside where the furnace was working overtime and already the smells of warm coffee and sizzling bacon greeted her.

Near the storage closet where fresh linens were kept, she yanked off her boots and stepped into the shoes she'd brought in her backpack, then exchanged her jacket for an apron and started sorting silverware. She was scheduled to work through the noon crush, then have some time off before dinner. Nell had asked her to return as two other waitresses were out sick. Nell had pulled a face and made quotes with her long fingers as she'd mentioned the flu, but as they were shorthanded, Jessica was fine with it. The more work, the better, though she'd probably have to put off tracking down Cade Grayson.

"Leave that for Marlon," Misty advised as she swept through the swinging doors and caught Jessica wrapping napkins around sets of knives, spoons, and forks. "Coffee's already on and, okay, the first of the local yokels who need their caffeine fix should be here in . . . uh"—she glanced down at her watch—"eleven minutes. Hear that, Armando? Kip Cranston will be pounding on the door soon. He'll want the usual."

"Already got it going," Armando said, not even looking over his shoulder as he tossed some onions onto the grill. They sizzled and filled the kitchen with their sweet aroma. Jessica's stomach growled and she realized she'd forgotten to eat her usual container of yogurt.

"Toast ready?" Misty called. "You know Kip likes rye and Jimmy is always looking for a stack of pancakes. And Patch wants his sausage cooked all the way through, no pink."

"*Sì.* I told you! I got this." Armando flung the words over his shoulder then turned away and muttered something in Spanish under his breath.

None of it, Jessica suspected, was good.

"I'm unlocking the door." Misty found the keys in a drawer and tucked them into her pocket.

"*Sì, sì.* I heard you. *Dios! ¿Te crees que soy sordo?*"

"No, I don't think you're deaf," Misty replied, her lips pursing, her eyes, with their iridescent lilac lids, narrowing. "Just stubborn."

"Like the bull. *El toro*. Yes?" With a snort, Armando returned to his work.

Over his mutterings, the roar of the fan, and the popping grease, Jessica heard the thrum of heavy bass and loud rumble of exhaust pipes announcing that Marlon, in his tricked-out Honda, had arrived.

"The Dashing Dishwasher has decided to make an appearance," Misty said before heading into the dining area. "Now, it's officially showtime."

Jessica followed her inside and sure enough, a group of men in their sixties and seventies were huddled under the portico. As Misty unlocked the door and pulled it open, they walked briskly inside. With red faces, stocking caps, bulky jackets, and gloved hands in their pockets, they streamed to the two tables that she had already pushed together.

" 'Bout time you opened the damn doors," a grizzled old fellow said good-naturedly. "I was like to freeze, and Ed there, he claimed he'd have to go warm up in the cab of his truck where he keeps a bottle of Jack handy."

"No need for extreme measures," she said, falling into an easy banter. "Coffee all around, except for you, Syd? You want decaf."

"Yeah," a short guy said, showing a wide girth matched by a grin that stretched from one side of his bearded face to the other. "Not what I want, but I'd better if I don't want my ticker to start racing."

"You got it." Misty flitted around the table like the pro she was, juggling two pots of hot coffee while the regulars turned up the cups on their tables indicating they'd like a little morning jolt. She poured and chatted while a couple showed up and took a table by the window, away from the crowd in the middle of the room where the group of eight was talking, several conversations buzzing at once.

As Jessica brought water and tea for her table, she heard snippets of gossip. Dan Grayson's name was mentioned several times but there was another topic of interest, a woman's body found in a creek on a ranch several miles out of town. She told herself not to make more of it than it was, that it had nothing to do with her, but as she brought an order of a farmer's breakfast and a veggie omelet to a middle-aged couple near the door, she heard the word *mutilation*.

Her heart stopped for a fraction of a second.

"What do you mean *mutilation*?" the woman asked as she found Jessica hovering near the table. In her mid-seventies, she turned her face upward and lifted a hand, catching Jessica's full attention. "Oh, dear, sorry to bother you, but could you get us a fresh bottle of catsup? This one"—she indicated the small, full bottle resting near the napkin holder and salt and pepper—"is a little, well, you know. It's got a little bit of gunk around the lid."

Jessica picked up the offensive glass bottle though she saw nothing other than fresh red catsup within. "Certainly."

"And could I bother you for another knife? I see a spot on this one's blade." Smiling, the woman held up the flatware in question and yes, there was a bit of a water stain on the stainless steel.

"No problem. I'll be right back."

"Wait! Please bring some hot water, would you be a dear? My tea's already gone cold." Her smile was beneficent, but a little malicious gleam shone in her eyes, as she narrowed her gaze on Jessica through rimless glasses. "If you wouldn't mind."

"Not at all." Jessica was off and the woman turned to her husband again.

"Harry?" she said, catching his attention. "I asked you what you mean by *mutilation*?"

Though he answered, Jessica couldn't hear the conversation, whispered as it was. When she returned with the requested items, the woman ended her conversation quickly, then eyeballed the new knife and bottle skeptically.

She took a sip of her tea after Jessica poured hot water into her cup and teabag, then let out a satisfied sigh. "Aaah. Much better," she intoned, finally sated, probably just because she was able to get someone to do her bidding.

Jessica had the sneaking suspicion that the little errands she ran for the fussy woman were more for the old lady's amusement than from any real need, but she kept her thoughts to herself and tried not to panic over the bits of information she'd overhead. A dead body had been found? It was a woman? There was mutilation? Oh. God. Jessica's stomach clenched and she nearly stumbled as she was carrying water glasses to a booth where a man and a woman in uniform had taken a seat.

Pull yourself together.

Fortunately, as they were at one of her tables, she was able to overhear their conversation, or at least snippets of it, as she waited on them. What she hadn't expected when she placed the ice water on the table was that the man was wearing a badge marked SHERIFF.

"Coffee?" she asked, reading his name. BLACKWATER. The man she'd heard was taking over Grayson's position, at least until the next election.

"Black," Blackwater said, his eyes cool, his expression without the hint of a smile.

"Sure," said his compatriot, a woman whose name tag read DEPUTY DELANIE WINGER. "With sugar."

Nodding, Jessica slid menus onto the table, then, her knees trembling a bit, motioned to the whiteboard hanging near the swinging doors. "We've got some interesting specials today," she said by rote, though she felt the sheriff's gaze upon her. "Marionberry waffles, a BLT with a fried egg, and a peanut butter and chocolate smoothie. I'll give you a few minutes." She was sweating nervously, her hands nearly shaking under his piercing glare, almost as if he could see through her disguise. *Impossible.* She'd never met Blackwater, nor the deputy he was talking to.

Servicing the other tables near the booth where they were seated, she heard bits of "shop talk", but nothing more than general information.

"Waiting on the autopsy," the sheriff told his colleague. "No, nothing yet from Missing Persons . . ." and "checking other jurisdictions."

That conversation, Jessica figured, was about the woman they'd discovered.

Then, very seriously, he said, ". . . a shame . . . yep, a good man . . . irreplaceable, but I've got to try." Words for Dan Grayson.

There was other talk about what she assumed were open cases, but she couldn't hear much as they spoke in low tones, and became quiet as she served a breakfast burrito to the deputy and a spinach and egg white omelet to the sheriff.

"Refills?" she asked on a second go-around when they were nearly finished.

The deputy said "Yes," and Blackwater nodded, so she started pouring the coffee.

Crash! The clatter of silverware rang through the building and Jessica jerked, slopping hot coffee as a stream of angry, rapid-fire Spanish emanated through the pass-through to the kitchen.

"Sorry . . . oh, I'm so sorry," she said, seeing that she'd sloshed coffee onto Blackwater's wrist.

"It's fine," he said shortly.

"I'll get a towel."

His eyes turned on her and she quickly withdrew her hand. What the hell had she been thinking? She never touched a customer, and especially not a cop.

"Sorry," she repeated and turned away, carrying the coffee back and retrieving a clean towel from the linen storage inside the kitchen where Marlon was busily picking up knives, forks, and spoons, then loading them into the dishwasher haphazardly.

Armando shook his head over the grill. *"Por el amor de Dios. ¡Qué idiota!"*

Breathing fire, Misty flew through the swinging doors, her mouth set in a red bow of disgust. "What the hell do you think you're doing?" she demanded of the busboy.

As Misty unleashed the reaming out, Jessica hurried back to the dining area where a few of the patrons were craning their necks toward the kitchen and Blackwater was reaching for his jacket.

"It's fine," he told her as she offered up the towel.

"No no no. I'm so sorry."

For the briefest of seconds, his eyes, dark as obsidian, seemed to look through her facade, past her disguise. In the brightly lit diner, she sensed that he could see deeper into her soul, which was absolutely ludicrous. It was all she could do not to take a step backward.

"Of course, your breakfast . . . both of your meals," she added with a quick look at the younger deputy, "will be comped. I'm really sorry."

To her surprise, he flashed her a smile, white teeth against darker skin. "I think I'll live."

In an instant, the awkward moment had dissipated as if it hadn't existed and Jessica told herself that she was jumping at shadows, reading more into the situation than there was,

Blackwater, even though she slid the plastic receipt holder back into the pocket of her apron, left enough money on the table to cover the cost of both meals and include a decent tip. "Accidents happen," he said and shrugged into his jacket.

"Miss?" a man in another booth said, flagging her down and holding up his coffee cup for a refill.

"Be right there." To the sheriff, she said, "Thanks for coming in," and turned her attention to the man in the baseball cap with the empty cup.

From the corner of her eye, she saw Blackwater give her another once-over as he held the door open for his deputy, and that look chilled her to the bone.

As acting Sheriff, Hooper Blackwater had a lot of responsibilities. No problem. He easily shouldered most tasks assigned him. In fact, he welcomed them. *The more the better*, he thought as he drove his Jeep along the older section of Grizzly Falls, where the town sprawled upon the shores of the river as it had for well over a hundred years. Traffic moved slowly past the storefronts with their western "Old Montana" flair. He noticed the county courthouse, an ancient brick building where he'd often given testimony, and nestled beside it, a bank building that had the appearance of the Hollywood stereotype of buildings robbed in old black-and-white movies set in the late 1800s.

Ahead of him, in her own vehicle, Deputy Winger was heading toward her assignment as one of the road deputies who patrolled the county. She was one of the few people in the department he completely trusted, and so he'd initiated their breakfast meeting, which, he reminded himself, was *not* a "date." One thing was certain, he wasn't going to mix business and pleasure again. The women on his staff were off-limits. Period.

He'd made that mistake once already and wasn't about to do it again. Besides, aside from Deputy Winger, he didn't trust anyone working for him. It wasn't that the other men and women on the force weren't good officers. Just the contrary was true. But nearly every one of them was so loyal to Sheriff Grayson that they weren't as yet swayed to the inevitable fact that he was the right man to step into the job as acting sheriff.

I'll have to change that, he thought, pausing at the railroad tracks as a long freight train barreled through the town, blocking his route up the steep hillside. He watched the cars hurtle past, just on the other side of the crossing's flashing arm, and tapped his fingers on the steering wheel. An ambitious man by nature, he looked upon

Grayson's passing as a tragedy, but an opportunity, as well. Not that he would have ever wished his predecessor ill will or an early death. But since Grayson had passed on, Blackwater wasn't a man to let a chance like this slip through his fingers.

He believed in the old adage his great-grandmother had conveyed to him when he was very young. "Where there's a will, there's a way," she'd told him on more than one occasion and he'd used that saying as his personal credo from the time he'd entered school and sensed that he was different from his peers. He'd been able, from an early age, to know when someone was lying or hiding something, even if that person was adept at concealing their feelings. It was an ability that had served him well in his job. That waitress at the diner, Jessica, according to the pin on her uniform, had definitely been afraid of revealing something about herself. He'd known it as if she'd suddenly announced it to the world. When she'd recognized he was "the law", she'd been all thumbs, as evidenced by the coffee splatters on his clothes.

The last rail car shot by in a clatter of steel on steel, the train heading underneath a tunnel on the south end of town. As he half listened to the crackling police band, Blackwater watched the signal's flashing blade lift slowly. He eased onto the gas while on the opposite side a girl in an older Ford Mustang was looking down, no doubt paying attention to her phone and unaware the signal bar had lifted. On the road behind her, the irritated driver of a huge Suburban laid on the horn, startling the girl. She hit the gas and the Mustang lurched forward, the woman in the Suburban scowling darkly as she followed close on the blue car's bumper.

Road rage. Never good. A part of him wanted to pull over both drivers, one for possibly texting, the other for tailgating, but he had other fish to fry, specifically solving the cases that would help him be elected at the end of Grayson's term. He snapped on his wipers as the snow began to fall again. He was probably ambitious to a fault, but so what? Even though this job had just fallen into his lap, he wasn't going to let it go. In his thirty-eight years, he'd already learned that real opportunity knocked only once on a man's door, and sometimes passed by a person's house altogether.

The engine strained a little as the hills steepened, the road slicing into the hillside and skimming the top of the ridge.

Blackwater had been a poor kid growing up. His dad had loved baseball, alcohol, and other women more than he did his family and had bailed on his wife and kids when Hooper was a sophomore in high school. From that point on, he'd been the "man of the house", and he'd reveled in the responsibility . . . and yes, power. And he wanted the power that came with the job of sheriff.

He drove his Jeep into the lot for the station, and with a sense of rightful ownership, parked in the space marked SHERIFF. First up on his to-do list was make certain Grayson's killer was prosecuted to the full extent of the law, convicted, and locked away forever. He had limited control on that one. His department could only provide testimony and evidence to convict, but he'd been in talks with the DA ever since hearing the news of Grayson's death and that office was definitely on the same page. A couple other potential homicides would keep his staff busy and the public concerned, and that didn't begin to touch the normal crimes involving robbery, drugs, domestic violence, and such. Yeah, the department would be busy.

He loved it.

As he yanked his keys from the ignition, just for a second, he thought of the waitress again. Along with her anxiety at slopping hot coffee on him and the fact that he was a lawman, he'd sensed there was bone deep terror that she was definitely trying to conceal. He'd been left with the feeling that covering things up and hiding were all a very integral part of who she was. A mystery, the waitress.

Not your problem. You have more than enough to deal with.

After locking his Jeep, he jogged through the lightly falling snow, past the poles where the flags were drooping at half-mast, to the front door. It was cold, but he found the change of the seasons invigorating, the winters bracing after spending so much of his life in the Southwest. Inside, the bright lights and gleaming floors didn't match the somber atmosphere. Even Joelle, usually bubbly to the point of being ridiculous, was subdued, her demeanor sober as she looked up and told him that several reporters had already stopped by for interviews.

"Not this morning," he said. "Maybe a press conference, later. If necessary."

He started to turn away, but she held up a beringed finger. "Sheriff, I mean . . . Sir, I was thinking," she said.

He noted that the black stones of her ring matched her earrings, part of her mourning attire, he presumed.

"Maybe we should dim the lights for the rest of the week, make a little shrine here, beneath Sheriff Grayson's picture"—she motioned to the wall where the past sheriffs were displayed—"and, you know, have a moment of silence every day?"

"No."

"But—"

"This is the sheriff's department. Our business is the public's and we'll remain open at full staff, with the lights on. No shrine. I've got the flags at half-mast and we'll run the department with a skeleton staff for the funeral so any and all officers who want to go can attend. Sheriff Grayson will get a full-blown law enforcement funeral, motorcade, three volley salute, the whole nine yards, but the department will remain open, uncompromised, ready to handle any and all calls and emergencies. We owe that to Sheriff Grayson's honor."

Though her lips were pursed in disapproval, she didn't argue, just nodded tightly and turned to a ringing phone.

If Blackwater had to be a hard-ass as commander to keep the county safe and well protected, so be it.

Noting that the offices seemed quieter than usual, he walked briskly along the hallway to the office marked SHERIFF. No doubt about it, he felt a twinge of satisfaction as he hung his jacket on the hall tree near the door. This, he sensed, was where he belonged.

CHAPTER 9

The last thing Pescoli needed was Hattie Grayson seated across her desk bringing up the same damn topic she had in the past. When it came to the subject of her ex-husband's death, the woman was a broken record. Worse, she'd come in with Cade Grayson who, rather than take a seat, decided to stand, leaning against the file cabinets, looking enough like his brother to give Pescoli a weird sense of deja vu.

"So you don't think it's odd that two of the brothers are dead?" Hattie asked, her eyes red-rimmed, her face drawn. She'd been close to her brother-in-law and had, according to the local rumor mill, dated not only Cade, but Dan, too, before marrying Bart, or some such nonsense. The timeline seemed skewed to Pescoli, not that she cared. She did know that Dan, in the past couple years, had spent a lot of time with Hattie and her daughters. Then Cade had returned, and Hattie had turned her attention to Dan's younger, wilder brother. It seemed, them being together, that Hattie and Cade were a couple.

Pescoli gave a mental shrug. What did it matter? Considering her own love life, she wasn't going to judge Hattie on hers. But the obsession about Dan and Bart's deaths being connected was nonsense. Bart had committed suicide; Dan had been shot by an assailant.

"I think it's tragic that we lost the sheriff and that his brother died before him," Pescoli said neutrally.

"Bart did *not* kill himself," Hattie insisted, as she had ever since her ex, supposedly despondent over their split, had walked into the family's barn, tossed a rope over a crossbeam, and hung himself.

"I know that's what you think, but his death was ruled a suicide." There it was. The bone of contention.

"He wouldn't do that to . . . to the girls," she insisted, then more softly, "or to me."

"We know who killed the sheriff," Pescoli reminded the distraught woman seated on the edge of one of the visitors chairs positioned near her desk. The detective's gaze moved to that of Cade Grayson to include him in the conversation. "There's no argument. That man's behind bars. He'll be prosecuted and convicted."

"Are you sure?" Hattie asked.

Dear Jesus, yes! I saw Dan go down, I witnessed him take the bullets. And I was there when the son of a bitch who killed him was arrested. I almost lost my own damn life to that psycho. Though her emotions were roiling, she managed to keep her voice calm. "Of course."

Hattie squeezed her eyes shut and held up her hands, fingers spread wide as if she knew she'd stepped over the line. "Yes, I know that you got Dan's killer, but you told me you'd look into Bart's death again. Reopen the case." Blinking rapidly, she swiped under her eyes with a finger.

Pescoli located a box of tissues under an unruly stack of papers. Nudging it around two near-empty cups of decaf to the far side of the desk, she said to Cade, "You think someone killed Bart, too?"

"Don't know." His jaw slid to one side and Pescoli remembered that Cade had been the unlucky person who had found his brother's body hanging from a crossbeam in the barn.

"Could be." A couple years younger, Cade looked a bit like Dan with his long, lean body, square jaw, and intense eyes. The Grayson genes were strong enough that a family resemblance was noticeable, though he was a couple inches shorter than the sheriff had been, and, from all reports, a lot more of a hellion in his youth. He'd ridden the rodeo circuit, only recently returning to Grizzly Falls. "Bart was having his problems," Cade said, his gaze drifting to Hattie for a second. "We all know that."

Hattie's face grew more ashen.

"But she's right," Cade said, hitching his chin toward his ex-sister-in-law. "Bart loved those girls and it seems unlikely that he would take himself out, denying McKenzie and Mallory from knowing their dad."

Pescoli felt trapped. "Look, I said I'd look through the files, and I will. But I didn't mention reopening the case."

"Semantics," Hattie said.

"More than that. A major difference." Pescoli wanted to make certain they understood her position.

"Just, please." Hattie swallowed and plucked a tissue from the box to wipe her eyes. Too late. Mascara was already beginning to streak her cheeks. Clearing her throat and standing, she said, "I know you were a good friend to Dan, and your partner Selena . . . she and Dan were close."

Pescoli waved a dismissive hand indicating that she didn't understand but accepted Alvarez's romantic fantasies about their boss.

"Dan would want whoever killed Bart to be brought to justice," Hattie said determinedly.

That much was true. Pescoli reminded, "If he was murdered, but—"

"He was murdered!" Hattie leaned over the edge of the desk so that she could meet the doubt in Pescoli's gaze with her own conviction.

Pescoli rose from her chair and said firmly, "We don't know that."

"That's because when he died, everyone just assumed the worst," Hattie stated. "So, you're right, we don't know, but it's your job to find out."

"His death was investigated at the time. Even his brother—"

"Dan was never satisfied about the outcome," Cade put in, straightening. They were all standing in the room, regarding each other tensely.

Hattie lifted her chin. "If it makes you feel any better, Detective, don't do this for me. Do it for Dan." With that she walked away, her sharp footsteps echoing along the hallway.

Cade said, "She's serious about this, you know. And Dan wasn't happy with the outcome of the investigation, though, of course, he wasn't sheriff at the time. I know you weren't involved then, either, but if you've got the time, I'd appreciate it."

Something in his eyes reminded Pescoli of his older brother. For a second, she imagined the sheriff standing in front of her. But then Cade squared his hat onto his head and followed after Hattie.

Pescoli looked at the case files stacked on the corner of her desk. Deeter Clemson's fall to his death, Jimbo and Gail Amstead's domestic violence case where each had ended up in the hospital, Ralph Haskins's suicide, as well as the new, deceased Jane Doe. Throw her personal life into the mix, and she really didn't have time to dig into a long-closed suicide just because the ex-wife and beneficiary of the life insurance policy wanted her to. As Pescoli understood it, the insurance company had balked at paying the benefits to Hattie and her twin daughters as it was determined that Bart had taken his own life.

Pescoli really shouldn't bother with Bart Grayson's death. The case had been investigated and closed, but Hattie's final words echoed through her mind. *If it makes you feel any better, Detective, don't do this for me. Do it for Dan.*

"Oh, hell," she muttered and knew that she'd dig through the case file. Just a cursory look, then maybe her guilty conscience would be assuaged.

Then again, probably not.

Ryder gassed up his truck at a station-convenience store with the unlikely name of Corky's Gas and Go. *Sounds bad any way you cut it,* he thought as he replaced the nozzle and, hands deep in his pockets, dodged a minivan and a Prius parked beneath the broad canopy covering several pumps. A fuel truck had pulled around back, ready to refill the underground tanks, and a woman in a long coat and boots nearly ran him down as she pushed open the glass door to the market about the time he was walking in.

"Watch where you're going," she said as she hurried outside.

Ignoring her, he walked past her to where the heater was cranked to the max, a wall of hot air meeting him as he strode down the aisles to the back case and grabbed a beer and a couple bottles of water as the H_2O that flowed from the tap of his room at the River View wasn't exactly pristine.

A girl in her early twenties was manning the register in a tank top; it was that warm inside. "Hire anyone yet?" he asked, motioning toward the HELP WANTED poster taped to the glass just inside the door.

"Nuh-uh. Don't think so." She rang up his purchases. "You get gas?"

"Pump six. Any applicants?"

"Corky, he's the owner, just put up the sign this mornin'. It's still pretty early."

"What's it for?"

"You interested?"

"Maybe."

"Well, you have to take a drug test and submit to a background check." She rolled her eyes, indicating that was a pain. "Then, you start helping out at the pumps. Some people don't like to pump their own, y'know?" Another eye roll. "Corky's a stickler," she said.

Ryder decided Anne-Marie wouldn't take a chance on a background check. No, she'd find a job where the owners of the establishment weren't as conscientious as Corky.

Of course, there was always Grayson.

Ryder could go right to the source.

But he didn't want to spook her and there was more than a little bad blood between Cade and himself. And there was that little problem about Cade just losing his brother. The man might be hair-trigger touchy and who knew how it would go down if Ryder just showed up and Grayson was harboring Anne-Marie. If she caught wind that he was on to her, no doubt she'd bolt again.

For now, Ryder needed the element of surprise, so he had to be careful.

He bought a couple maps of the area that he'd study then keep in his truck, as the Internet service was often spotty, especially when he was driving in the hills. Besides, sometimes he got a better feel for the land with an old fashioned map rather than wireless Internet service. Climbing into his truck, he drove through town again.

Three times already he thought he'd caught a glimpse of Anne-Marie in the small town, and three times he'd been wrong. He'd gone through Craigsist, the want ads, and any Internet Web site that listed houses, rooms, and apartments to rent. He'd scoured through ads from a few weeks earlier, but had come up with nothing. At the same time, he'd gone through the motions of checking listings for job opportunities, marking off those that he thought would require background checks.

In the past, he'd always been one step and three or four weeks behind her, nipping at her heels, only to reach the town in which she'd landed to realize, after a week or two, that she'd taken off again. It always took a while to discover her next move.

This time, though, he believed he'd gotten the jump on her.

Of course, he'd missed her by several days in Denver, but had gotten lucky and found a bar where she'd poured drinks for six weeks before getting spooked. Wanda, one of her coworkers, had recognized her, even caught her adjusting a dental appliance and had figured out she was on the run. "Anne-Marie? Huh. I knew her as Stacey."

"Not Heather Brown?" That was the name she'd used in Omaha.

Wanda had shaken her head. "She's Stacey Donahue. She go by somethin' else, too?"

"Yeah." *A lot of something elses,* he'd thought

"That happens a lot, y'know. People changin' their names and runnin' from their pasts. Husbands, ex-boyfriends . . ." She'd skewered Ryder with a suspicious glare, then shrugged as if she'd determined he wasn't dangerous. "As I said, happens all the time."

Ryder had then interviewed all the workers at the establishment and discovered no one had really known where she lived. He'd ended up in a confab with Wanda and a couple other employees.

"Rented a room, I think. Somewhere not too far because she walked to work most days," Wanda offered. "I think she said she had family in San Bernardino that she was hoping to see . . . that was it, right? No, wait, maybe it was San Jose, oh, hell all those towns in California sound the same to me. Donella, you knew her better. Where did Stacey say she had family. San Jose?"

"I didn't know her that well," Donella denied, giving a quick shake of her head, her ponytail wagging. "I thought she said . . . San Jacinto. Maybe."

"No, that ain't it." Wanda let out a frustrated sigh. "All I know was it wasn't San Diego or San Francisco, but it started with San . . . wait, or maybe Santa. There's a lot of those, too."

"Talk to Tanisha," Donella declared. "She's the one who talked to her the most."

He'd thanked them, then, hours later, had shown up for Tanisha's night. The place was rockin' by then, a band coming on at nine, but he hadn't been thinking it would make any difference as Anne-Marie had told everyone she worked with a different story about heading out to somewhere in California, or Las Vegas, or Phoenix. Diversions to hide her true destination.

However, Tanisha, who happened to be one of the bartenders, had given him his first real clue.

"Yeah, I talked to her, but she kept to herself," she confided in a smoky voice that hinted at too many cigarettes. A short, black woman with a hard stare if a customer was getting too rowdy, she added,

"Said she was from Texas somewhere. Maybe Houston. I can't really remember."

Encouraged, Ryder had stuck around, ordering drinks and placing healthy tips in the jar on the counter.

Finally, Tanisha remembered. "You know, she did say something once about looking up an old boyfriend. When I asked her who he was, she clammed up and said she'd thought better of it. Didn't say his name, but I think he was some kind of cowboy. But y'know, we're in Colorado. Everybody's a cowboy here." She'd laughed then.

But Ryder had known Anne-Marie must have been talking about Cade Grayson. "Did Stacey ever talk about Montana?"

Tanisha was polishing the long wooden bar with a cloth and a man at the far end raised a finger, indicating he'd like another drink. Ryder had been impatient, wishing he had the bartender's attention all to himself, but then she said, "Y'know, that's about the one damn place in these United States she didn't mention."

Bingo.

He'd then canvassed the area and found a rooming house where the landlady who, for a little cash, admitted that her last tenant, a woman she "never trusted," had moved on and told her to forward any mail to a post office box in LA. Ryder hadn't taken that bait. He'd been fooled by Anne-Marie too many times. Instead, he'd followed the only clue that had made any sense to him—that she was going to hook up with an old boyfriend. Maybe that had been her plan all along, to go to Cade, or maybe it was a move out of desperation. Whatever the case, one-time rodeo rider Cade Grayson was Anne-Marie's ex-boyfriend and a bona fide son of a bitch.

And he'd returned right to his hometown of Grizzly Falls, Montana.

CHAPTER 10

Seated across the table from Santana in a booth at Wild Will's, Pescoli frowned at the screen of her cell phone.

"Bad news?" he asked, taking a swallow of beer as he eyed her.

The restaurant was crowded and noisy, most of the tables filled. Waitresses and busboys flitted through the cavernous dining area decorated with rough plank walls, wagon wheel chandeliers, and the heads of game animals mounted on the walls beneath the rafters.

"Depends on your perspective, I guess," she said and managed a perturbed smile.

They'd left on bad terms the other night when he'd called to offer his condolences about Grayson, and true to form, she'd been a stone-cold bitch, icing him out and pushing him away. Sometimes she wondered why he put up with her. They'd met in the parking lot after a brief phone call where Santana had suggested they have dinner at the familiar restaurant on the banks of the Grizzly River, just under the falls.

They hadn't met in person since Dan Grayson's death, only spoken on the phone. Seeing Santana again had brought tears to her eyes. Standing by his truck, he'd opened his arms wide and she'd stepped into them, letting him pull her close. He'd whispered, "God, Regan, I'm sorry."

She'd felt like a heel for how she'd treated him and had let herself be wrapped in the warmth of his embrace. He'd smelled earthy, of leather and horses and a bit of musk. With the snow beginning to fall around them and the rush of the river tumbling over the falls in her ears, she'd closed her eyes and forced herself not to cry.

"I am, too," she'd admitted. "Not just for Grayson, but for the other night. You wanted to come over and I . . . was dealing with a lot."

"I know," he'd said, but he hadn't told her that her behavior was okay, because it hadn't been.

But he did allow her to be herself and she knew he would never try to change her. Santana, more than anyone, understood how devastated she'd been with the loss of Grayson, that she had witnessed the horror of the sheriff being shot, and that she'd woken up screaming in the middle of the night, reliving the experience. She hoped the nightmares would cease or at least abate soon. Always before, whether it had been dealing with her grief after Joe had been killed or handling the aftermath of her own terror at the hands of a psychotic killer, she'd spent several weeks, even months reliving the horror in her dreams. With time and effort, she had shed the need to replay the awful scenes in her subconscious.

She only hoped the same would happen this time.

"So?" he said, nodding at the phone. "Work?"

With a quick shake of her head, she said, "Bianca's a no-show. Again." Pescoli didn't want to think what that might mean. "Third time this week." She glanced down at the text one more time. At Lana's. Homework. Be home later. A frowning emoticon followed the word *homework*.

She couldn't help feeling that she was being played. Never before had one girlfriend taken up so much of Bianca's time. Pescoli had considered this new friendship a good thing, as Lana was a more studious girl than those Bianca usually hung out with, the more boy-crazy crowd. However, she was second-guessing her daughter.

When she'd told Bianca about Grayson, her daughter's face had clouded briefly. "I heard. Lana's mom said something and Michelle called. It's too bad." Then she'd gone to her room.

Too bad?

It was a helluva lot more than that.

Irritated, Pescoli tapped the edge of her phone on the table then slid it into her pocket.

"You think she's lying," Santana stated.

"Not think. Know. Just don't know why."

"Maybe you're being too much of a detective."

Pescoli gave him a look. "I was a teenager once, you know. Not *that* long ago. So were you."

His mouth quirked and his eyes glittered. "I remember."

"So."

"Maybe you should have a beer."

"Not tonight. I need to be clearheaded."

"To deal with your daughter?"

"Amen. She's sharp. And then, unfortunately, I have to catch up on some work. At home."

"Then you definitely need a beer."

"Rain check," she said and he lifted a shoulder, cool with whatever she wanted. God, she loved him. She did want to spend the rest of her life with him though she hadn't yet slipped the engagement ring back on her finger. Santana had asked her about that, too, and she'd answered truthfully that she hadn't wanted to deal with all of the questions at the department, or the ribbing from her coworkers, especially after Grayson had been attacked. Those who had noticed her engagement ring had been few, and no one seemed aware that she wasn't wearing it anymore, or at least they weren't saying anything. She'd assured Santana that she wasn't backing out. She wanted to marry him. She just needed to do things her way.

He asked, "What about Jeremy? He coming?"

"Legitimate excuse. He's working."

"Then I guess it's just you and me." Santana's smile stretched wider and the twinkle in his eye turned a little wicked as the waitress brought a loaf of sourdough bread to their table and asked for their orders. "Ladies first."

"The stew and a house salad," Pescoli said, then Santana ordered the special—chicken fried steak and mashed potatoes with country gravy. All of it sounded like heaven.

"You could come to my place after this," he suggested once they were alone again.

"You mean 'our' place?" She sliced off a chunk of the bread.

"Not really ours until you move in."

"I don't think I'll do that until you, er, we have heat and running water. Furniture, too."

"Fair enough."

As she slathered the bread with butter and held it up to him, a peace offering of sorts, he shook his head and said, "I thought you were going to cut back on your hours."

"I was, but now we've got this new case."

"There's always going to be one, you know."

"Yeah." She bit into the bread.

"Maybe you need a long vacation away from everything for a while. See how it goes."

She almost choked. That's exactly what was going to happen, whether she wanted it to or not. Pregnancy leave.

Something in her expression must have showed because he became deadly serious. "You'd tell me if we weren't okay, right?"

She reached over and clasped his hand. "We're okay," she assured him.

He heard the sincerity in her voice and nodded.

By the end of her second shift, Jessica hadn't learned a lot more about the dead woman found on the O'Halleran ranch. She'd heard plenty of gossip, just snippets from customers that had peppered into the conversations about work, family, kids, school, friends, or grandkids. One item was about a preacher approaching retirement age who was leaving his wife for a young parishioner. There was also a missing dog, an apparent suicide, and a homicide investigation of a man who was either pushed, or fell, from a mountain trail around these parts. The biggest news stories by far rippling through the dining area over the clink of flatware and the endless loop of songs from the fifties and sixties was the county losing Dan Grayson as its sheriff and the discovery of the body of an unknown woman found in a creek winding through the O'Halleran ranch.

Unfortunately, Jessica heard nothing substantive about the dead woman and though she told herself it was just coincidence—a woman's body found in a deep pool of a local creek—she couldn't help the tide of panic that rose within her.

He's here, she'd thought frantically. *He's here somewhere in Grizzly Falls.*

By sheer will, she'd forced herself to remain calm as the hours wore on. Even if he really had found a way to chase her to Grizzly Falls, she hadn't sensed anyone following her. So far. Several times during the day, she'd scanned the dining area, but he hadn't been inside the diner, she was sure of it.

Yet, she reminded herself.

She considered her options. *Slim and none.*

Except for Cade.

God help her that her fate was dependent on the cowboy who had put her in danger in the first place. It was pure hell to think she needed to depend on him.

At the end of her shift, Jessica glanced outside to the parking lot in front of the diner. Empty of vehicles, the security lamps casting blue pools of light over the snow-covered asphalt, the area looked a little surreal. Again snow was falling, softening the edges of ruts made by earlier vehicles. From inside the diner, with its bright lights and wide bank of windows, she felt as if she were in a fish bowl, that anyone hiding in the shadows could watch her every move undetected. Feeling a sudden chill, she told herself she was imagining things. She was safe. For now.

Nonetheless she squinted, trying to peer through the veil of snow.

"Hey, hit the switch for the sign that says we're open. Just turn it off, so we can go home. It's that one there, the one with the piece of black tape on it. Yeah, over there." Misty was shouting her orders from behind the counter and waggling a finger toward a toggle switch near the door. "Then flip the sign on the door for the morons who can't figure it out even when the neon goes dark."

"Got it." Jessica pushed on the switch, then twirled the two-sided hanging placard on the door so that it read COME IN, WE'RE OPEN to anyone looking at it from the interior and SORRY, WE'RE CLOSED to potential customers peering through the glass.

Misty slapped at another switch near the doors to the kitchen and half the interior lights turned off. "That should do it," she said, one hand on the swinging doors. "You'd think people would understand that when we're closed, we're goddamn closed." She was in a bit of a snit as the last customer had come in fifteen minutes before closing, idled over her meal, texting and playing some game on her phone before asking for a doggy bag and leaving half an hour after the restaurant was supposed to close.

Nell was a stickler for attending to each person who walked through the door and so, though the doors had been locked, the customer was not hurried out the door.

A bare fifteen minutes since the customer had left, almost forgetting the leftovers she'd asked to be bagged, the floors had been quickly mopped, chairs squared around each table, booths brushed off, each station cleaned. All the tables were sparkling, coffee mugs turned face down on the Formica surfaces, condiments refilled and standing at the ready for the morning crowd that was due to arrive within eight hours.

With one last glance through the windows, Jessica started untying her apron as she walked through the swinging door to the kitchen.

Armando and Marlon were long gone and Nell was in the office with the door shut, where, as each night, she was counting the day's receipts and balancing the cash register.

Connie, one of the teenaged bus girls, was swabbing the kitchen floor with a mop that had seen better days, while sterile glasses were still steaming in the open dishwasher. The warm room smelled of pine-cleaner that didn't quite mask the lingering odors of deep-fryer grease and coffee.

"I can't believe this," Misty said, digging through the purse she'd retrieved from her locker area. Shaking her head, she crumpled the empty cigarette pack she'd located and tossed it into the trash. "Anyone got a ciggy?"

As Jessica shook her head, Connie gave a quick nod, reached into her pocket, and withdrew a pack of Marlboro Lights. To Jessica, she said, "I'm eighteen, okay?"

"I owe ya," Misty said, shaking out a filter tip, then flipping the pack back to the girl, who slipped the pack quickly into her pocket.

Jessica tossed her dirty apron into a bin with other laundry and unlocked her locker to grab her purse.

Misty, still clutching the cigarette, was shrugging into her jacket.

Jessica asked, "So did you hear anything about the woman who was found in the creek?"

"Just bits and pieces, same as you." Misty zipped up the jacket. "I did catch it on the news as I passed by the office. Nell had it on. It was that woman from the station in Montana. Oh, God, what's her name? Nia Something-Or-Other, not that it matters. All I heard was that they haven't IDed her yet. Kinda sounds like they suspect foul play and I don't blame them. You wouldn't believe the nutcases that have blown through here lately." Her lips, faded now as most of her makeup had worn off, twisted downward. "Not too long ago, Grizzly Falls was a sleepy little town, no trouble other than a drunk getting into a fight or shootin' up the WELCOME TO GRIZZLY FALLS sign. Now, though, it seems we get more than our share of psychos. And I'm not talking about our local weirdos like Grace Perchant. She's the gal who owns wolf-dogs and thinks she talks to ghosts." Misty shook her head. "Or that idiot Ivor Hicks who still claims he was taken in some kind of spaceship or something and experimented on by lizard people. No, those are our usual Grizzly Falls oddballs. That's not what I'm talkin' about. Nuh-uh."

Connie stopped mopping for a moment and nodded to Jessica, letting her know she should listen up.

Misty went on. "Just a little while back some lunatic killed women and then displayed them in the snow or some other fucked-up thing. Damn serial killer, that one was. And he wasn't the first. Right, Connie?"

"Sure thing." Slightly heavy, Connie was sweating as she leaned on her mop. "My mom is thinking about moving away and she's lived here all her life. But she had faith in Sheriff Grayson. He always caught the nutcases. Now—" She shrugged, indicating who knew what the future might bring, then carried her mop and pail to the back door.

Misty jabbed the unlit cigarette between her pale lips. "The trouble is, the way things are going, another psycho's probably coming down the pike."

Jessica's gut tightened. "You think that the woman found on the ranch is the victim of a serial killer?"

"Maybe. Who knows? Around here you have to go there, whether you want to believe it or not."

Connie opened the back door and threw the dirty water from her bucket into an area that, beneath the snow, was graveled.

"Watch out! We don't want that to freeze and end up being slippery as snot," Misty said. "The last thing I need is to break my leg, or wrench my damn back."

Connie said, "I tossed the water right where you told me to. Not in the damn parking lot or near the steps. It's in the effin' garden. Your idea."

"Last summer it was, when the temperature was in the eighties." Misty caught the girl's angry glare and lifted a hand. "Yeah, okay. Sorry. It's fine."

"I know it's fine." Connie peeled off her apron and stalked to her locker.

As the locker door slammed, Misty and Jessica walked outside together and Jessica asked the question that had been nagging at her ever since she'd heard the first whisper of a rumor about the victim. "Did you hear that the woman they found on the O'Halleran ranch was mutilated?"

Misty was clicking her lighter to the end of her cigarette. "Mutilated? Shit, no." Positively stricken, she drew in hard on her filter tip. "Oh, Jesus." She shook her head as snowflakes caught in her hair. "I didn't hear that, but I was too busy to pay much attention. You sure about that?"

"No. Just something I overhead."

"Well, I hope to heaven it's not true. Mutilated, how?"

"I don't know."

"Who was talking about it? That new sheriff? I saw you waiting on him. He should be careful about talking in public. That is, if he wants to get elected."

"No," Jessica said quickly, remembering the intense look he'd sent her way. "It was the woman who came in about the same time, the one who asked me for a million additions."

Misty's eyes narrowed through the smoke. "Oh, God, that's right. Lois Zenner, she was with her husband. Such a pain. Left you one dollar for a tip, right?" she asked. "One lousy buck. Well, she's a gossip and a prig and tight as ever, but she does have a niece who works at the department, I think. An underling, but usually Lois's gossip is right on."

Jessica's heart stilled. *That information had come out of the department?*

"But mutilated? Christ, what is the world coming to? The sickos sure find us, don't they?" Misty walked to her car and slid inside as Jessica made her way to her own vehicle. If she were lucky, she could get home and still catch the late-night news.

This has nothing to do with me.

But as she drove away, trying to deny that he had found her again and convince herself that he wasn't nearby, she couldn't stop her heart from beating a little faster, nor could she keep her fingers from nervously clenching the wheel. At the first stoplight, she slowed, let the car idle, and eyed the surrounding area nervously. The town was quiet, no one on the streets, no other sets of headlights behind her, no taillights in front. The traffic light blinked an eerie red upon the powdery streets and every muscle in her body was tense.

He's not here, she told herself, turning on the radio. Stepping on the gas, listening to Adele's voice, she wondered if she'd ever feel safe again.

Of course not. Until he's locked up or dead, you'll always be looking over your shoulder. You'll never have peace. You know what you have to do, don't you? Either find a way to send him to prison forever, or kill the son of a bitch.

That thought was unsettling and she checked the rearview mirror often on her drive home. No one followed her, at least no one that she could pinpoint in her mirrors. No tracks of any kind had broken through the snow to her cabin, it seemed, since she'd left.

Good. She let out a breath and walked inside, found the cabin just as she'd left it. "There's no place like home," she said, and wished she had a dog or a cat or even a parakeet. Something living to greet her, something she could talk to. Maybe a dog. One that would guard the place and put up a ruckus if anyone was lurking outside, one that could smell if an intruder had been inside. She warmed to the idea. Maybe.

After locking the door, Jessica threw her keys onto the scarred coffee table and tried to shake off her case of nerves. She turned on the television, then as it started glowing, the volume low, she double-checked the tiny rooms in the cabin to make certain she was alone. Once she knew the place was secure and the stained shades were drawn, she stoked the fire and space heater, then quickly stripped out of her uniform, body suit, wig, and contacts.

Earlier, she'd cleaned the phone booth-sized shower with liberal amounts of bleach and Pine-Sol though some stains refused to fade. She didn't care. The tiles were disinfected. She was bone tired and felt the diner's grease clinging to her skin. She stepped under a weak spray of lukewarm water, then lathered her body and her hair. For a second, she remembered another shower where the hot steam fogged the glass and the wide stall was equipped with multiple sprays and glistening tiles.

"A long time ago," she said aloud. "Another lifetime." She rinsed off and cranked hard on the handle. Old pipes groaned as she threw her one towel around her and dried off quickly. Shivering, she reminded herself that giving up creature comforts was a necessity. For now. Until she figured out what to do.

She threw on a pair of sweats, then combed out her hair. When she looked into the mirror, her face washed of makeup, her body no longer laden with extra padding or a wig, dental appliances, contacts, or glasses, she caught a glimpse of her younger self and remembered the woman she'd thought she'd be. She felt a pang in her heart as she remembered her dreams of a career, a marriage, and a family—all dust in the wind—foolish fantasies from a privileged girl who'd naively thought she could be anything she wanted to be, do anything she wanted to do, that success was dependent only on her desire.

That's where she'd made her mistake, thinking her wants and needs were so damn important.

Now, of course, she knew better.

She walked back to the living room. The television caught the local stations, so she watched while searching the Web, hoping for more information about the body that had been found. She sat on the edge of the couch, her gaze flicking back and forth between the bubble screen of the TV and the laptop's flat monitor. She was nervous about the discovery but wouldn't have thought that much about it except for that whispered word *mutilation*, one that caused warning bells to clang wildly in her head. Was he back? Was the dead woman a means to frighten her?

It's not about you. Remember that. A woman is dead. Killed, possibly. Murdered. It's just gossip, after all. Unproven. A rumor. Nothing to get upset about.

What are the chances that he's followed you all the way from New Orleans? You've covered your tracks. Relax.

And yet, she couldn't stop the paranoia that had been chasing her for months. Even now, she walked the perimeter of the small rooms, checking door locks and window latches, then peering through the blinds and the falling snow expecting a dark figure to shift in the shadows or the reflection of eyes to catch in the light.

Shuddering, she walked back to the fire and stoked the flames again, hearing the soft crunch as a log fell apart and sparks glowed brightly. She carried the poker with her to the couch and kept it nearby, within reach if she couldn't reach the pistol for some reason.

Until this madness ended, she would be forever looking over her shoulder, hiding, worrying that he was out there, bird-dogging her, waiting to strike.

That was the worst part, knowing that he enjoyed her terror, that he got off on it.

No more, she thought, dragging the sleeping bag around her. *No more.*

CHAPTER 11

Pescoli sipped decaf coffee and avoided the lunchroom where there was talk of Grayson's funeral.

Another two days had passed and Joelle had come alive again, taking the bull by the horns and making plans for the service. It was something to do, to keep her busy. Blackwater was involved as well, along with some higher-ups, but Joelle was coordinating with the family—Grayson's brothers and two ex-wives. He had no children, but had kept up friendly relations with his first wife, Cara, married to Nolan Banks with whom she had a daughter and a couple of stepkids. Dan Grayson had also been divorced from his second wife, Akina, to whom he'd been wed briefly. She, too, had remarried and had children.

The kicker was that Cara Grayson Banks was a half sister to Hattie Grayson. They shared the same mother, and it seemed, the same fascination with the Grayson brothers.

It was all a little incestuous in Pescoli's estimation.

She turned her attention to the new case involving the unidentified victim and searched the incoming reports. Jane Doe's fingerprints weren't registering, at least not according to the information Pescoli had received. AFIS had reported back on the nine prints that were taken, but the victim's identity remained a mystery. She was not a known criminal with a record and her prints hadn't been recorded for any government job, either.

"Great," Pescoli said, tapping the eraser end of her pencil against the desk. Feeling a pang of hunger, she realized she was suddenly starving, despite upchucking in the bathroom before she'd driven to work. That was the trouble. She was either unable to think because she was battling nausea in the morning or so suddenly hungry in the afternoon that eating became priority number one. As if reading her thoughts, her stomach rumbled, and she said, "Quiet," as if the baby, or her insides, could hear her. Ridiculous. The baby was probably about the size of a kidney bean. She knew. She'd checked on one of those Web sites dedicated to pregnancy, something she'd not been able to do with either of her earlier pregnancies.

Things had changed a lot in the past sixteen plus years, she decided as she found a protein bar in her desk drawer and unwrapped it quickly. Macadamia and white chocolate and billed as "healthy" when she doubted it was all that different from the Snickers candy bar she'd hidden deeper inside that same drawer, for "an emergency."

Taking a bite, she let out a contented sigh. *I hope you're satisfied now,* she thought, mentally communicating with the minuscule baby growing inside her. A part of her was worried sick about having a child this late in life, another part was a little giddy at the idea. Three children with three different men. Who woulda thunk? Not exactly brilliant family planning nor how she'd expected her life to play out twenty-odd years ago when she was desperately in love with Joe Strand. But there it was. And damn it, the new little addition to her unconventional family would be worth every gray hair she would undoubtedly grow.

She just had to convince her existing near-grown teenagers of the fact. She tossed her pencil onto the desk and noted that the ring on her finger caught the light. She'd finally decided to wear the diamond Santana had given her. She was going to get some guff from her coworkers. *So what?* She was engaged and that was that. She'd show the kids tonight, not that it would be a big surprise; they'd already had many discussions about moving into the new house and the very real possibility of their mother remarrying.

With one foot out the door, ready to move out and get on with his life, Jeremy hadn't said too much, but Bianca had thrown a hissy fit, taking the opportunity to turn the whole thing around so that Pescoli's involvement with Santana was all about her. Pescoli thought about that drama-infused argument at the dinner table.

* * *

"You're only marrying him because Dad's married to Michelle!" Bianca charged.

"My relationship with Santana has nothing to do with that."

"Oh, come on, Mom. You've been jealous of Michelle from the minute she and Dad started seeing each other." Bianca reached up and fiddled with the rubber band holding her hair on the top of her head in a curly, seemingly careless knot that Pescoli figured took a minimum of fifteen minutes to create.

"Jealous?" she repeated with a derisive snort as Jeremy had reached for the bowl of spaghetti on the table and spooned out a second huge portion. "I don't think so."

That, of course, had been a lie. Any bit of envy she felt for his second wife at the time Lucky had taken up with her had rapidly disappeared. The more she knew Michelle, the less she cared. As for him, Pescoli realized how lucky it was that they'd split. Not that he still didn't have the ability to push all of her buttons. As long as they were parents, they would always have to deal with each other whether she liked it or not, so she tried to get along with him, even though most of the time she would have preferred to hit him alongside the head with a two-by-four. Not to do any permanent damage. Just hard enough to get his attention.

"Lay off Mom, Bianca." Jeremy defended her as he pronged two meatballs with a long fork and dumped them unceremoniously onto the mound of pasta on his plate. At their feet, Cisco whined for a treat while Sturgis regarded them from his dog bed in the living room. "She's entitled to her own life, you know." From a pitcher on the table, he poured a liberal amount of sauce over his plate while Bianca pursed her lips, her eyes flashing rebelliously as she picked at her dinner.

"Like you have it all figured out," she muttered.

"More than you." Jeremy had forked a huge wad of saucy pasta into his mouth, then met her churlish stare with his own as he'd chewed.

"You're an animal, y' know?" she declared.

He shrugged.

"Enough," Pescoli intervened. "This is dinner time. Family time."

Bianca's head snapped up so fast that her over-sized bun wobbled. "Right. The three of us." Using her fork, she made a circular motion to include them all. "We don't need any more."

"Tell me that when you want to get married. Or have a kid," Pescoli rejoined, thinking of the baby again. "Or Jeremy does. Families evolve, Bianca. That's why we count Michelle as part of ours. And now Santana will be."

"Awesome," Bianca said sarcastically. "So what if Jeremy and Heidi get married? Huh? What about that kind of evolution? Will she be part of the family?"

"They're broken up and Heidi's in California," Pescoli said.

"Like that means anything," Bianca muttered.

Pescoli's gaze flew to Jeremy, who was suddenly paying his undivided attention to slicing a meatball. "Right, Jeremy? You and Heidi aren't together anymore."

"We're friends," he mumbled, not meeting his mother's eyes. "She's in California," was his unsatisfactory answer.

Pescoli saw Bianca's smirk and wondered what she'd missed.

Thinking her mother wasn't looking, Bianca slid part of a meatball from her plate toward the floor where Cisco gobbled it up. "Heidi's thinking about coming back to Montana to go to college after she graduates high school in San Leandro."

"Is that true?" Pescoli asked as Sturgis stretched out of his bed and wandered over to the dining area.

Jeremy dropped his fork and glared at his sister. "Maybe."

"Hasn't she applied to University of Montana?" Bianca put in sweetly.

Pescoli's stomach lurched. "Jer?"

Jeremy snapped, "Pre-applied."

"What does that mean?" Pescoli asked.

"It's an option. That's all. She's still got family here. One of her sisters is going there." Jeremy tried hard to act as if nothing was the least bit out of place,

Pescoli tried to sort out what it all meant. She'd hoped that Heidi Brewster was out of her son's life. Beautiful and manipulative, Heidi had twisted Jeremy around her little finger for the past several years. When the decision was made to move from Montana to California, Pescoli had prayed that the two teenagers' fascination with each other would fade away.

"Why didn't I know about this?" she asked, only vaguely aware that Sturgis had seated himself next to her chair.

Jeremy turned to face her. "Because I knew you'd freak, Mom, and it looks like I was right."

"I'm not freaking."

"Don't worry," Bianca interjected. "Jeremy and Heidi aren't married . . . yet. They just can't stand to be away from each other. Besides, it's not really a big deal. Families evolve, you know."

Pescoli had wanted to wipe the "gotcha" grin off her daughter's face and send her to her room. Instead, she'd forced herself to remain calm. "Glad you understand. So, Santana and I are getting married and we're all going to move to the new house. Better start thinking about what you want to pack. And please, don't feed Cisco from the table. It makes him worse. Look, even Sturgis is getting into the act." At the mention of his name, Sturgis wagged his tail.

Like the lingering scents of garlic and tomato sauce from last night's dinner, the argument still hung in the air. This morning, Pescoli had left the house before either kid had bothered to get up and thrown herself into her work rather than dwell on the problems with her ever-growing family.

Heidi Brewster? Her daughter-in-law? *No way.* Angry at the thought, she bit into the energy bar. As she plopped the last bit into her mouth, she heard rapid footsteps in the hallway and Alvarez nearly slid into her office.

Pescoli looked up sharply.

"Taj might have something," Alvarez said. "Possible ID on our Jane Doe."

"About damn time." Pescoli tossed the wrapper into the trash can near her desk and was out of her chair in one swift motion. They needed a break on this one.

In the missing persons department, Taj Nyak was waiting for them. She stood on the other side of a long counter covered in some kind of wood veneer that was popular in the 1970s. An exotic looking African-American woman with features that hinted at some Asian ancestry in her genealogical mix, she flashed them a quick smile. "That was quick."

Alvarez asked, "What've you got?"

Taj turned her computer screen around so that they could see the image thereon, a clear picture of a female who appeared identical to the woman they'd seen in the morgue the day before, the woman found on the creek at the O'Halleran ranch.

"Ladies," Taj said, "meet Sheree Cantnor."

I know how to handle death, Alvarez thought as she sat in the interrogation room.

Dealing with those who had died was all a part of her job. She made her living trying to find justice for the dead. Death was business as usual except in the case of those near to her. Dan Grayson's death had leveled her, made her question her decision to be a cop, caused her to lose sleep at night. There were no platitudes nor soft words of encouragement that would assuage the pain she felt when she thought of the sheriff and how cruelly and needlessly he'd died. She'd toyed with quitting or transferring to another department, but she'd made this part of Montana her home, had a biological son with whom she'd recently been reunited, and had finally found a steady partner in Dylan O'Keefe, a man who had been in and out of her life for years.

He was back, and she felt centered for the first time in memory. Though the hole in her heart was painful, she had decided she would heal, given enough time and enough work. She worked as a cop because she loved it, and as she eyed the man seated in the interrogation room, she remembered why.

Heat flowed through the air duct overhead, whispering into the room little more than a cubicle. It was warm. Stuffy. A camera mounted in a ceiling corner recorded her conversation with Douglas Pollard, the man who had reported Sheree Cantnor missing. Slouched in the molded plastic chair on the other side of the table, he was sweating, dark circles evident beneath his sleeves, dots of perspiration dotting his high forehead.

Was he sweating from the heat?

Or a case of nerves?

Probably a little of both.

Though he had reported Sheree Cantnor missing, it wasn't inconceivable that he had killed her. Most violent crimes were committed by someone close, a "loved" one, and so Alvarez handled him carefully and wasn't going to take his story or his alibi at face value. It happened often enough that the person who murdered the victim, after he or she had come up with a solid alibi, was the one who also reported that their loved one hadn't come home. It was a tactic to throw off the police and to show innocence, but most of the time, it didn't work.

"So you and Sheree Cantnor were engaged?" Alvarez was seated at a table across from the distraught man. He was tall with a soft look about him, twenty-six years old with reddish-blond hair that was already starting to recede despite his efforts to comb it forward. His jaw was unshaven, at least for the past few days, and his eyes were a sad brown that matched his uniform. He drove a truck for a local delivery company.

"*Are* engaged. We are engaged." He frowned. "Do you know something?"

No reason to beat around the bush. "You probably heard that we found a body," Alvarez said quietly, then pushed a folder across the table.

He eyed it skeptically, not touching it, as if he expected something to jump out at him.

"We'd like you to tell us if you recognize the woman in the picture."

Biting his lip, he reached forward to flip the folder open. Two pictures of the woman in the morgue were visible. One of her face, the second of the daisy tattoo on her ankle. Pollard's color drained and his chin wobbled. Squeezing his eyes shut, he shook his head and pushed the folder away. "No . . . no."

Alvarez suspected his denial was that she was gone, not her identity, so she asked gently, "Is this your fiancée, Mr. Pollard?"

"Yes," he choked out. "It can't be true." He shuddered and when he opened his eyes, they glistened with tears. "Who did this? Huh? Who the fuck did this?"

"That's what we're trying to find out."

"We?" he repeated.

"My partner, me. Everyone in the department."

He glanced nervously at the mirror, behind which, everyone knew, was a darkened viewing room where Pescoli, the DA, and Blackwater were standing. "What do you want to know?"

"Let's start with when was the last time you saw Sheree?"

"Two days ago. In the morning. Before work." He closed his eyes and screwed up his face. "We fought."

Alvarez's ears perked up. "What about?"

"A stupid argument. Nothing really. She wanted to go visit her family. This week. Just pack up and go, but I couldn't. My job isn't that flexible. She wasn't happy about it as Janine, that's her sister, is due to deliver twins. Any minute." He paused and sighed. "She might even have had 'em by now. Anyway, we got into it and Sheree wanted to talk more, but I left. I was already late for work. We didn't . . . we didn't talk or text all day, which is weird for us, and when I got home, she wasn't there. No big deal, but then . . . she never came home that night and I figured she was just showing me how mad she was."

"She's done this before?"

"Once. Before we were engaged. About a year and a half ago."

"Can you tell me about it?"

He paused again, took in a deep breath, and launched into his story.

He and Sheree Cantnor were high school sweethearts who had grown up together in Utah, but had moved to Grizzly Falls when he'd been transferred to Missoula. They'd been excited for the move, ready to make a fresh start, away from their parents and siblings who inhabited Salt Lake City and the surrounding towns. He'd given her a ring about a year ago on Valentine's Day, and they'd moved the following June after she'd graduated from BYU in Provo. She'd found a job working as a receptionist and bookkeeper for a local insurance agency and they lived in an apartment on Boxer Bluff, located on the hillside. Their one bedroom unit had a peekaboo view of the river. Sheree's job was in a strip mall within walking distance from the apartments.

"She wanted it close by so she could walk to work," he said. "We have a cat and . . . and Sheree likes to get away from the office, you know, get a little exercise, eat lunch at home and play with Boomer. . . ." His voice lost all power as the weight of what was happening, that he'd lost his fiancée, settled over him. "Who would do this? Who?"

"Did your fiancée have any enemies?"

"None. Sweetest girl to walk God's earth." He slumped farther in his chair and eyed the folder as if it were malevolent.

"But you fought."

"Not that often. We . . . we're happy. Planned on getting married around Christmas time. In Salt Lake . . . Oh, Jesus." He seemed about to break down completely so Alvarez nudged a box of tissues closer to him, but he ignored them. "I want to see her," he announced suddenly, his face mottled and red.

"Mr. Pollard—"

"I want to see her," he insisted. "This . . . this could all be wrong." He motioned to the pictures and shook his head. "This woman. She could be like Sheree's twin."

"She had a twin?" Alvarez asked.

"No, no, but like a dead-ringer. And that tattoo. It's stock. Not a big deal." He rubbed a hand over his jaw, scraping the whiskers beginning to show on his jaw. Again he stated emphatically, "I want to see her." He was grasping at straws.

"I have a few more questions," Alvarez began, but he cut her off.

"Don't you get it? I *have* to see her. To be sure." His jaw was firm.

Alvarez saw that he was set on his plan, hoping that there had been a mistake, an error in the photography, a mix-up in the morgue, some ridiculous idea she knew she couldn't dislodge.

She said, "One more thing, then we'll take a break and drive to the morgue."

"What?"

"You said you and Sheree were engaged."

"That's right."

"Did you give her a ring?"

"Of course I gave her a ring. A *diamond* ring. Why? Why are you asking about it? Was the ring stolen?" His mouth dropped open. "Man, that thing cost a fortune. I'm still paying on it." He looked miserable.

"Did it fit her?"

"Yes."

"It wasn't too big? And might fall off?"

"No, of course not. I went to a jeweler and had it sized. It fit perfectly."

"What about her earrings?"

"I don't know. She had lots of pairs."

"Diamond studs."

"Well . . . cubic zirconia. She bought 'em herself. They're not valu-able—" He cut himself off and held up both hands. "Doesn't matter. I don't give a damn about her jewelry. I need to see her. I have to." He stood then as if it were decided.

Alvarez got to her feet and glanced to the mirror, a signal to Pescoli as she ushered Pollard out the door.

CHAPTER 12

Pollard stared through the window separating him from the viewing room where the draped body had been wheeled. An attendant pulled the sheet from the victim's face and he got a clear view. His knees buckled and he leaned against the glass as Pescoli grabbed him by the arm. "It's her," he choked out in a bewildered voice.

With Alvarez's help, Pescoli guided him to one of the two chairs placed against one wall. He nearly fell onto the worn seat and dropped his face into his hands. "No no no," he said, then looked up. "Who would do this? Why, oh, God, why?"

"That's what we're trying to find out." Alvarez had found a box of tissues and handed it to him.

He fumbled for a tissue—the last one—and started wiping frantically at his eyes as his head wagged back and forth. "But she was the sweetest, the most loving, the perfect girl." His voice cracked and he buried his face in his open hands again. "Why would anyone hurt her?"

"We're going to need your help to find out," Alvarez told him.

"Mr. Pollard, do you have anyone to stay with you?" Pescoli asked. "A relative? Close friend."

"No. Sheree, she . . . she's . . . she was . . . my . . ." His voice drifted away, and he seemed lost in thought for a few seconds. When he finally blinked and returned to the moment, he said, "I just can't believe this."

Alvarez glanced at the window where the attendant was waiting near the body. With a quick nod she indicated that they were done viewing and the attendant covered the dead woman's face again and rolled the gurney though wide double doors that opened automatically upon her approach. "We'll head back to the station now."

Pollard struggled to his feet and without another glance at the window and the empty room beyond, shuffled behind them, walking as if he were closer to a hundred years old than thirty.

The drive back was almost silent as Pollard, in the rear seat, was alone with his thoughts. Neither Alvarez nor Pescoli wanted to interrupt his newfound struggle with loss and grief.

"Her parents," he said, once they were back at the sheriff's office and he was following Alvarez inside. "I'll have to call them. And her sisters . . . she's got five, you know . . . no brothers." Shuddering against the cold or his own despair, he walked to the office where both detectives showed him back into the interrogation room. Seated in the chair he'd occupied earlier, he was less reticent to talk and he readily wrote down the names of her relatives and friends as well as the cities where they lived. He was fixated on the task, in fact.

Pescoli had seen it before, a way to stave off the terrible truth that a loved one was dead.

"I just don't know all the addresses, but I have their phone numbers." Pollard added those from his contact list and said, "She didn't make a lot of friends here, y'know. Just people from work. Her boss, Alan Gilbert. He's a dick. Had the hots for her. And then Marianne Spelling, no Sprattler. Oh, I don't know her last name, something that starts with an *S*, I think. She and Vickie and Sheree, they all worked in the same room, but different cubicles, you know. They'd all go out for a drink or girl talk or whatever, every now and again. It wasn't really all that often, maybe four times since we moved here, usually like during Monday Night Football. Sheree doesn't drink that much." Pollard wrote down a couple other names of people they knew, from the church they attended sporadically, and the wife of a guy he worked with. "We went out a couple times, to dinner, but Sheree didn't like Angie much. Thought she was stuck on herself or something, but Bob, he's a good guy."

He drew a breath and shuddered.

"Tell me about the engagement ring," Alvarez urged as he finished with the list of people Sheree had known.

"I told you it's a diamond. My grandmother's."

"I thought you said you were paying on it."

"I took out a loan to buy it from my mother. She inherited it and decided that she'd probably sell it before she died and split the money between me and my brother and sisters. I told her I wanted it. I'm the youngest and my sisters already had their own rings. My brother really didn't want it. So Mom had it appraised and it came to about twenty grand. I had some money, but I had to take out a loan on my car for the rest. It was worth it, though," he added. "I surprised Sheree with it last February. Put it in a box of chocolates. She almost bit into it," he admitted, smiling before the tiny grin wobbled and he had to clear his throat.

"Do you have a picture of the ring?"

"Oh, yeah. I insured it. It's valuable." He scrabbled in his pocket for his phone, brought up the picture gallery and spying a photo of himself with Sheree, quickly found another shot of a left hand with the engagement ring visible. "Two karats," he said proudly. "And those, the smaller stones flanking the diamond? Rubies. It's an antique, you know. Sheree, she loves . . . loved it." Before he could dissolve into tears again, he asked, "You think someone killed her to rob her?"

"We don't know," Alvarez answered truthfully.

"Why wouldn't she just give it to him?" he asked. "I mean, if it was her life . . ."

"We don't know what happened," Pescoli said. "We're trying to figure that out, so any help you can give us will help."

"But I can't. Everybody loved Sheree."

"No one was unhappy that you were engaged?" Alvarez asked.

"No." He gave a quick shake of his head as if dislodging an unwanted idea.

"Maybe you had an ex-girlfriend who didn't like it."

"Sheree and I started dating when I was sixteen and she was fifteen. We . . . we were each other's firsts."

"Can you send the picture of the ring to me?" Alvarez asked, offering up her e-mail address.

"I can do it now." He typed onto the keypad of his phone, then said, "There."

"Thanks. We'll need to go over to your place, take your computer and anything of hers that might be of interest."

"Okay." His shoulders drooped wearily.

Two hours later, Pollard had finished calling Sheree's relatives and

Alvarez had coordinated information with the office so that bank, insurance, cell phone, and tax records could be accessed. Pescoli and Alvarez had not only examined the victim's living space and taken her personal computer and iPad but her fiancé's electronic gear, as well. Pollard had offered up passwords and given them Sheree's cell phone number, which he'd admitted to calling "about a hundred times" when she hadn't come home.

They were young and unmarried. There were no life insurance policies, even though she worked for an insurance agency. Just hadn't gotten to it yet, he claimed. Sheree didn't own a car, and she was a renter, so there were no other assets besides her missing ring.

As the detectives were leaving, Alvarez said to Pollard, "We're sorry for your loss."

He looked about to break down again, then stiffened his spine. "Just get the motherfucker bag who did this." He turned and walked into the apartment alone.

Next, the detectives went to Sheree Cantnor's place of business. Armed with a warrant, they approached the twenty-something behind a wide wooden desk and asked for her boss. Pescoli's eye followed a blue carpet that ran behind the receptionist and through a room bristling with cubicles. A one-sided conversation was emanating from the only office, where shades were drawn over the glass walls, but the door was ajar.

"Wait a second, Len," said the male voice inside the shaded box. "I'll call you back. I think I may have a situation I have to deal with here. No . . . no . . . give me five. No big deal."

Seconds later, hitching up his ill-fitting slacks, a man who was as wide as he was tall sauntered out of the office. "I'm Alan Gilbert," he stated, obviously the "dick" that Pollard had mentioned. Also the namesake for the Alan Gilbert Insurance Agency. He was balding and, as if to compensate, had grown a thick, neatly trimmed beard that was just beginning to fleck with gray. Frowning from behind slim glasses, he said, "Can I help you?"

"Detectives Selena Alvarez and Regan Pescoli. We're looking into the disappearance and possible homicide of Sheree Cantnor."

Behind Pescoli a woman gasped.

"Homicide?" Gilbert blinked rapidly. "Oh, holy . . . Sheree didn't show up a few days ago and we've been calling . . ." He looked as if he might actually swoon.

"We'd like to check out her work space and speak to everyone who worked with her," Alvarez said.

"What? Now? Oh . . ."

"We have a warrant," Pescoli said, handing him the document. She asked for someone to box up Sheree's personal things. "We'll also need access to her computer."

He glanced at it unseeingly, still processing. "Yes, yes. Of . . . of course. Uh, there's a conference room in the back." He waved limply at a glassed-in area behind a row of cubicles.

Pescoli glanced at it and saw four different women's heads stretched over their soundproof half walls. Every face showed shock, from the girl barely out of her teens and still wearing braces, to an older woman with a phone headset buried deep in her neat, gray curls.

"I, uh, I have to leave at three," he said, rubbing his broad forehead as if that would help him think. "This way." He walked along a path toward the conference room at the far end, passing by an empty cubicle. "This . . . this is Sheree's."

The small, boxed-in desk was neat with pencils and pens in a cup inscribed with *DOUG AND SHEREE, NOW AND FOREVER* and a date, presumably of their engagement as they weren't yet married. Pictures of Doug adorned the cloth-covered walls along with a few of them as a couple, a calendar, and various notes and memorabilia.

"I'll be right with you," Pescoli said, stopping to look through Sheree's work space and gather what she thought might aid in the investigation. As she sorted through the personal belongings, she heard one woman softly crying and two others whispering. Sheree, it seemed, had made more friends than her fiancé knew.

By the time Pescoli met Alvarez and Gilbert in the conference room with a faux-wood table, Alvarez had already set up. A recorder was in place, a notepad at her side, and she was asking Gilbert basic questions about Sheree—how long she'd been with the agency, what kind of an employee she'd been, any odd behavior, who were her friends, and who were not.

The interview took less than thirty minutes and the same was true for the women who worked with her, all who happened to be present. After the interviews, in which the detectives learned again that everyone was convinced Sheree didn't have an enemy in the world, they crossed the parking lot to Pescoli's Jeep. Daylight had faded and dusk had begun to creep through the snowy streets. Street lights had winked on, adding a bluish illumination to the coming night, and traffic rushed by, wheels humming, engines purring, most vehicles pushing the posted speed limit of thirty miles an hour.

Once inside the car, Pescoli jabbed her keys into the ignition and threw Alvarez a disappointed look. She suddenly craved a cigarette. "We've got nothing," she said, feeling a little defeated.

"It's early. We haven't begun to dig yet. So the work place was a bust. Maybe there's something on her calendar or on her computer."

Pescoli shook her head, started the SUV, and backed out of the parking slot. She felt her stomach rumble. "Let's grab some coffee. Maybe something to eat. I'm starved."

"Fine."

Pescoli took a detour to the lower level of town located on the banks of the river, then drove to Joltz, her favorite coffee shop, with not only a walk-up but a drive-up window. A blond barista took their orders. Decaf coffee and a raspberry scone for her and just a cup of jasmine tea for Alvarez.

"I got this," Pescoli offered before her partner could dig into her wallet. As the Jeep idled beneath a wide awning covering the order pick-up area, she dug into a space meant for sunglasses where she'd wedged a change purse along with a spare set of shades. She pulled out a couple bills, then rolled the window down as the barista appeared again. Despite the shelter of the roof, a blast of cold wind managed to sneak into the car as Pescoli handed the blonde some cash in exchange for the drinks and a white paper bag presumably holding her scone. "Keep the change," she told the barista, then rolled the window up quickly and handed Alvarez her cup. "God, it's cold."

"Montana. In winter." Alvarez pulled the tab from the top of her cup and tested a sip as Pescoli took a long swallow.

She dropped her cup into its holder and eased the Jeep onto the street. "Yeah, but you know we could still do this same job in Phoenix or San Diego or El Paso or somewhere warmer."

"You'd hate Phoenix."

"Why?"

"Too dry. Too many people. Not your style. San Diego's crowded, too close to the border. El Paso?" Alvarez's eyebrows raised a fraction. "Really?"

"Maybe."

"For sure."

Pescoli rolled to a stop at the light and took another drink, the warm coffee taking off a bit of the chill as the police band crackled.

"So," Alvarez said as Pescoli turned onto the road that wound along the face of Boxer Bluff, the Jeep's wheels bouncing a little over the railroad tracks. "You're wearing your ring again."

"I'm getting married." Pescoli had put the ring on again, but she wished she hadn't.

"What's going on?"

"Oh, I don't know. . . ." Pescoli sighed. "I was talking to my kids and they're less than enthusiastic, but I'm going to marry Santana, crazy as that may be. My third time, and all. I just didn't want to talk about it, so I took the ring off."

"Okay."

"I don't mean with you," Pescoli assured her. "Just everybody else. And with Grayson's death, I just . . ."

"I know. I do," Alvarez said solemnly. "It's so damn hard."

"You got that right. Jeremy's okay with it. He's planning to move out, anyway." As they reached the station, Pescoli waited for a flatbed heading in the opposite direction to pass, then pulled into the parking lot and nosed into an empty slot, her tires slipping into the ruts from an earlier vehicle. "Bianca isn't a fan of the idea. She's made that abundantly clear."

"She'll come around."

"Hope you're right." Cutting the engine and pocketing her keys, Pescoli thought of her daughter's issues. Bianca's preoccupation with her looks, how she was trying to "diet" to fit into the bikini good old Michelle had given her for Christmas, that she was obsessive about her weight. Not good signs.

Luke and Michelle planned to take Jeremy and Bianca on a trip to Arizona or California or somewhere warm enough to sunbathe for spring break. Hence, all of Bianca's concerns about being "bikini ready." There was even talk of a spa treatment before the trip that included manicures, pedicures, facials, and waxing.

"Have you set the date yet?"

"No." Pescoli found the bag with her scone in it, dropped it into her purse, grabbed her coffee cup, and opened the door. Again, the winter weather billowed inside. *San Diego can't be* that *crowded,* she thought. As she slammed the door shut and headed into the building, she said, "It'll be a small thing, though. The wedding. Maybe just the two of us, maybe my kids. We haven't even discussed it. But I've already been to this rodeo a couple times, so it'll be low key."

"Got it." Once they were inside, Alvarez added, "I'll start with the victim's family and associates, friends, enemies—"

"She didn't have any. Remember?"

"Right."

They exchanged a look.

"I'll take the ring," Pescoli said. "It's pretty distinctive, so maybe we'll get lucky and find it in a pawn shop."

"No one has to cut off a finger to get a ring to pawn."

"Yeah, well, we're dealing with a sick bastard."

"Amen," Alvarez said. "I'll fill Blackwater in."

"Good." The less Pescoli had to deal with the new sheriff, the better. She started for her office. Halfway down the hallway, she heard the distinctive clip of mincing footsteps and a few seconds later, Joelle called out, "Detective." Pescoli glanced over her shoulder and caught the receptionist waving frantically to flag her down.

With an inward sigh, Pescoli waited in the hallway while Joelle, black leather heels tapping, ebony earrings swinging in rhythm, approached. "There's going to be a memo later, of course, but I thought you, being as you were so close, should know the memorial service for the sheriff will be a week from Saturday. I know it's a long time away, but because of all the officers from other jurisdictions who might want to attend, the family thought it would be best to wait. That way all the final tests will be performed on the body and"—she took in a deep breath, collected herself—"the service will be held at the Pinewood Center. As I said, there'll be more information on the interoffice memo via e-mail."

"The family?"

Joelle flicked a hand. "Cade and Zedediah, but of course Hattie had a hand in the decisions, too." She looked about to launch into the gossip about Hattie being married to Bart Grayson while supposedly involved with either Cade or Dan, depending on the year, but seemed to think better of it. Her polished lips, in a shade of pale pink, were pursed in disapproval as she clicked back down the hallway in her black heels. With Joelle, there really wasn't any need for e-mail or interoffice memos or even telephones. She spread the word more effectively than any technology. "Sergeant," she was calling as she tip-tapped along the hallway, her sweater billowing like a black cape behind her.

Pescoli stepped into her office, slung her jacket and holster over the hall tree, kicked out her chair, and nearly devoured the scone, which had, she guessed from its dry consistency, been sitting in the case at least one day, maybe two.

She was opening her e-mail, looking over the reports, hoping for a full autopsy on Sheree Cantnor, when she heard footsteps and a familiar voice outside the door to her office.

"You requested this?"

She looked up to find Jeremy standing in the doorway. He was carrying a worn cardboard box with a case file sticker attached that read GRAYSON, BARTHOLOMEW, a case number and dates of the investigation.

"Hi," she said, always a little surprised to see her son, whose hours at the department were few and far between. It hadn't been that many years ago that she'd been afraid he would make a wrong turn and end up working on the other side of the law. "Sure. Just set it there in the corner." She pointed to a space between the filing cabinet and her desk. Then, as he turned to go, added, "Hey, Jer, got a sec?"

He looked pained. "I guess."

"Close the door, would you?" she asked, waggling her finger at the door to the hallway.

Pushing the door shut, he leaned against it. "What?"

"I, uh, I wanted to apologize for last night."

"For what?"

Seriously? Is he that clueless? Maybe. "For what I said about you and Heidi. You've grown up in the past six months or so, seem to know what you want. If you're seeing Heidi, I'm not going to fight it. Your decision."

"It's not a big thing, Mom. I like her, yeah, and you know, we plan to go out when she comes back here or if I go visit her, but that's about it." His face was serious. "She's been through a lot, too. Her folks are splitting up and her sisters are all in college. It's just her and her mom. In a new town."

"I know," Pescoli said. "She's probably grown up a lot, too."

"Yeah, I guess. She's talking about moving out and getting married and—"

Pescoli felt the blood drain from her face just about the same time her stomach did a slow, nauseous flip.

"Oh, not to me, Mom. I mean, I don't think so. But someday she wants to—hey!"

She retched. Unable to stop herself, she grabbed the garbage pail beneath her desk, bent over, and upchucked all over the wrappers and trash already in there.

"Gross." Jeremy gazed at his mother in horror.

"Sorry," she said after spitting a couple times. She grabbed a cold cup of coffee and washed the bile out of her mouth, drinking the foul-tasting concoction down.

"What's wrong with you? I didn't say I was getting married."

"No, no, that's not it," she assured him and almost laughed aloud. "I haven't felt well all morning."

"Have you got the flu?"

"Something I ate, probably." She sensed the blood returning to her face. "I feel better now."

"But"—he motioned to the garbage pail—"God, it stinks."

"Maybe you should clean it up. Isn't that part of your job description?"

"Are you kidding?"

"You think you can look at dead bodies, blood spatter, go to an accident with people barely alive, mangled in their smashed cars, but you can't clean up a little puke?" She was shaking her head. "Better get used to it, Jer. Sometimes deputies have drunks throw up all over them, or do worse in their squad cars, defecating and all."

"I know, Mom, but, this is *my mother's* vomit!"

She did laugh at his obvious disgust. "Not in your job description?"

"No!"

"Okay, okay. I'll handle it. *This* time."

"*Any*time."

Her grin stretched wider. "I was just yanking your chain."

"Geez, Mom, *not* funny!" Swiftly, before she could change her mind, he opened the door and nearly sprang through.

She eyed the mess in her trash can. He was right. The sour odor of vomit reeked, causing her stomach to roil again. She had no choice but to haul the trash to the women's restroom and clean up the mess as best she could.

She spent most of the rest of the afternoon on the phone, calling the local pawn shops and faxing or e-mailing photos of the missing ring, hoping to get a hit. She was only partway through the list that Doug Pollard had provided of people who knew Sheree, when the calls from Utah started coming in. A torrent of them. She spoke with Sheree's distraught parents and three of her five sisters, even a cousin. The family itself was immense and the upshot was no one had left the Salt Lake City-Provo area, nor spoken to Sheree, in the last week before her disappearance. Of course, they all told Pescoli the same thing—Sheree had no enemies, no one even the least disgruntled with her as far as anyone knew. Sheree, it seemed, was an "angel," which was usually the case when someone came to a violent and unexpected end. Less usual were the remarks about Doug and how great he was. Theirs was a perfect match, except, of course, for the parents wishing they'd gotten married before they started living together, but even that ultimate sin was forgiven as Doug was so devoted, such a "good guy."

"Nobody's that great," Pescoli said under her breath before pushing back her chair and checking her e-mail again. Two of the four pawn shops within a sixty mile radius had responded. Neither one had Sheree Cantnor's missing engagement ring.

Maybe it had been fenced. Or kept for a trophy by the killer. Or was still in Sheree's attacker's pocket a thousand miles from Grizzly Falls. *It's early yet,* she told herself. If the maniac who'd done this had his wits about him, he'd wait, but if he needed money fast, for instance in order to score drugs, then he might try to get cash for the ring ASAP.

Then why leave the earrings? Did he know they weren't valuable? And why hack off her finger instead of just yanking the ring off?

Because robbery isn't the motive.

Alvarez was right. It was personal somehow. Cutting off the finger was making a statement to the victim or someone else.

Pescoli glanced down at her own engagement ring and twisted it a little, thinking hard. The earrings bothered her, but she told herself that they were just lucky the sicko hadn't sliced off the woman's ears and stolen them along with the fake diamond studs. Would he have known they were of little value? How? Not unless he was an expert or Sheree, or someone else, had told him so.

Despite the fact that Sheree was "beloved by all," Pescoli wondered who might hate her so much that they wanted to torture her before killing her. Or, had the severing of the digit been postmortem? The case was troubling, that was for sure.

From the corner of her eye, she caught a glimpse of the case file Jeremy had hauled down on Bart Grayson. "Later," she said to the box of notes and evidence reports. Hattie's wild theories about some connection between the Grayson brothers' deaths would just have to wait.

Pescoli had enough on her plate, personally and professionally, to last a couple lifetimes.

CHAPTER 13

Ryder sat in his truck, not running the heater, staring through the windshield and falling snow at the Midway Diner across the street. He'd parked in the shadows, avoiding the pools of light from the street lamps, and every once in a while he turned on the engine long enough to clear the snow from the glass.

It had taken him a few days to find her, but he'd done his homework, whittled down his options by focusing on job opportunities that didn't require too much of a background check, and rooms for rent around the area. He'd also checked out Cade Grayson, who was already involved with another woman, one who had been married to his brother Bart, a victim of a suicide. Ryder wasn't really surprised. Cade Grayson was a love 'em and leave 'em kind of guy, though taking up with his dead brother's wife seemed low, even for the likes of him. So far, it seemed Anne-Marie wasn't in the picture.

Yet.

After learning that this particular restaurant had advertised for a waitress about a week earlier and the job had been filled, Ryder started watching the place. Just today, he'd caught a glimpse of the new hire through the windows. The pudgy waitress with the blond hair and full lips didn't look much like the woman he'd known in New Orleans.

His jaw slid to the side and he had to give her mental kudos for the transformation. The new woman appeared matronly, at least ten, maybe fifteen years older than Anne-Marie Calderone.

Then again she was a mistress of disguise, something he'd

learned the hard way. It had been a slow realization on his part that the woman he was with was more fantasy than reality, but by then, he'd been caught in the pure heat of her, willing to let inaccuracies slide, uncaring that the facts didn't add up.

Idiot, he thought and flicked a glance at the rearview mirror, catching sight of his own gaze. Troubled hazel eyes glared back at him.

The restaurant was closing down. He could tell as the final patrons were leaving, the parking lot thinning out.

Lights were dimming in the diner, and the Sorry, We're Closed sign was visible. Ten minutes passed. He flipped on the wipers again, then cut the engine. Another five minutes and then he saw her, the woman he thought was Anne-Marie, as she headed to an SUV, an older model Chevy Tahoe. He watched her climb inside. The headlights flashed on, the engine sparked to life.

He waited as she drove out of the parking lot, then pulled out when another car was between them, following a couple blocks behind.

The streets of the godforsaken little town were nearly empty, only a few cars moving cautiously around corners or along the storefronts. He didn't bother with headlights until he was certain that, if she had been looking in her rearview, she wouldn't notice him joining traffic about the same time. He kept his truck behind the car between them, a Volkswagen Beetle that had seen better days. When the Bug turned a corner and only the snowy street stretched between their vehicles, he lagged back until she, too, turned off, heading out of town away from the businesses and through a residential district with widely spaced houses on large lots. At one stoplight, two vehicles turned onto the street behind her, pulling between them. One was a bulky delivery truck and he couldn't see around it for a time, but it turned onto a side street. The other was a smaller compact that didn't block his view and he could easily keep her in his sights.

Eventually the compact turned onto a residential street but Anne-Marie kept on, leaving the residential district and turning onto a county road that wound its way past farms with large snow-covered fields and into the hills where the farmland gave way to wooded foothills.

He smiled to himself. For once, rather than hide in the throng of a city where she could get lost in a crowd, Anne-Marie had chosen isolation. Her mistake. Though he had to slow down and make certain the curtain of snow between them hid his vehicle, sometimes losing sight of her, it was still better that she was away from prying eyes.

Few cars drove in the opposite direction, nor did he see a glimpse of headlights in his side mirrors. The snowfall became thicker, visibility lessening. As he crested a rise, he caught a glimpse of red taillights, burning brighter for a second, then the road dipped again and they disappeared. When he reached that next hillock, the lights were nowhere to be seen. He hit the gas and drove a little faster, hoping to close the distance, to catch another glimpse of her. As he rounded a corner, he expected to see a hint of red through the thick snow, but there was nothing. Just curves and bends making it difficult to speed in that section of the forest. Gritting his teeth, he pressed down on the accelerator, feeling his tires slip a little as the truck rounded the sharper curves. Still, no hint of her Tahoe.

He drove another four miles, but had the sinking sensation that she'd gotten away.

"Damn it," he muttered, traveling another mile even faster, his tires struggling for purchase. Finally, he realized he'd lost her. He ground his teeth. Rather than drive endlessly on the road, he turned around in a wide spot in the road and with the wipers flicking off the snow, retraced his tracks. No cars met him on the way back. The woods were dense, only a few lanes veering off the main road. He slowed when he thought he'd come near the spot where he'd seen her brake lights flash, squinting into the darkness, searching the snow pack.

The ditches on the sides of the road were buried, brush barely visible in the mounds of icy white powder. There were no mailboxes. He'd thought he'd lost her for good when he noticed a drift and then another, realizing that they were actually ruts in the snow, fresh tire tracks, with only a trace of fresh snow covering them.

Bingo, he thought but kept driving, making note of the landmarks, a split tree across the road, the snag knifing upward, and a huge boulder about a hundred feet closer. He also pressed the button on his odometer so he could track the distance to his room at the River View, then he made a note of the location on his GPS and cell phone. He'd come back once he was sure that she was at work. There was no reason to confront her now.

Not until he was certain that she was, indeed, Anne-Marie.

He had work to do.

"I really have to go," Pescoli said. She was lying in Santana's arms, his naked body spooned against hers in the downy folds of a sleeping bag in the master bedroom of their new, unfinished house. The musky scent of their recent lovemaking still hung in the air and perspiration was evaporating on her skin.

He gazed out the French doors to the night beyond. It was peaceful there. Serene. Snow falling, the lake a mirror, the world and all its problems seeming far away. "I'd argue with you, but I've tried that before."

"And?"

"I'm not saying you're mule-headed . . ."

"But," she prodded.

He chuckled deep in his chest, kissed the back of her head.

"So you *are* saying it."

"Maybe."

Twisting in the bag so that she faced him, she said, "So . . . there's something I need to tell you."

"Shoot."

His eyes, dark with the night, held hers. Unflinching. His lips had twisted into that sexy smile that had a way of burrowing into her heart.

"I'm pregnant." She let the words hang in the air and the silence was suddenly deafening.

He was still as stone. "You're kidding."

"As serious as I've been about anything in my life." Clearing her throat, she added, "I haven't been to the doctor yet, but I took an in-home test a while back and then, of course, three more. They all turned out positive. We're going to have a baby."

His gaze searched her face and she knew he still didn't believe her. They'd been lovers for years and had always been careful. Though they'd never discussed children, the unspoken understanding was that they weren't going to be parents, at least for the present. All that had changed, of course. For a second, he didn't say a word. She was aware she was holding her breath and her heart clutched.

Finally, he said tautly, "You mean it?"

"I wouldn't make this kind of bad joke. I'm having a baby; it's a fact. I know it's not ideal, but it happened. I didn't plan it, but I realize some people aren't cut out to be parents and—"

"Whoa. Wait a sec. Give me a minute to catch up. Okay?" He was staring at her in wonder. "You're for real?"

"Yes. For real. Near as I can tell, I'm due late summer, or probably early fall."

"I thought you didn't want any more kids." He pulled her into a sitting position, the sleeping bag falling open.

"I don't know how I feel. My kids are nearly grown and though it's been great, it's also been a pain and now . . . just when they're about out of the house . . . to start all over? With diapers and breast feeding and late night feedings, and then toilet training and preschool and bratty friends and snooty mothers, most of whom are fifteen years younger than me?" She shivered and pulled the sleeping bag over her bare shoulders.

He froze. "Are you saying you don't want the baby?"

"No, no, of course not! But you and I never discussed kids. You had a hard enough time getting me to say I'd marry you, and now we're talking about sleepless nights and colic and teething and bottles, then baby food. It's been so long since I've been through it, it's probably all changed."

A slow smile was spreading across his jaw, his teeth white against his skin in the half-light, his arms surrounding her more tightly. "You're sure?"

"Four pregnancy tests. *Four*. I wasn't going to tell you until I was certain."

He suddenly grabbed her shoulders and kissed her again. Hard this time. "This," he said once he lifted his head, "is the best damn news I've ever had."

"Really?"

"Yes."

She held him at arm's length. "Honestly? I just want to make sure. If you don't see yourself as a father, if this isn't what you had planned for your life . . . Raising kids is a major responsibility, and I—"

"What do I look like?" He was grinning like a fool.

Her heart soared. "Happy?"

"Very happy. God, Pescoli, I'm stoked. What do I have to do to show you, run outside naked, whooping in the snow?"

"That I'd like to see," she said.

He kissed her, his arms wrapping around her shoulders and dragging her close. Sighing, she let her worries slide away.

"We need to get married," he said. "Soon."

"Don't worry, my father's not around and I don't even know if he ever owned a shotgun. It's not as if this is the first time this happened. You'd think by now that I would know how to keep this from happening."

"You do."

"What?" She hit his chest.

"I'm just saying that at some level we both wanted this without saying so, and we became less vigilant. And I'm glad. I love you," he added gently.

"Hmmm," she said, mollified. "Wait until I'm eight months pregnant and big as a whale or when we're at a soccer game for Little Santana and they think I'm the kid's grandma."

"Football, and you'll be the sexiest damn old lady rooting on the sidelines."

"Nice," she mocked.

"I've always had a thing for older women."

"You're digging yourself a deeper and deeper hole, you know."

"Why don't we elope?" he suggested. "This weekend."

"Nope. I still have to tell my kids. Once you have your own, you'll understand. I hope. And I don't want to leave until after Grayson's funeral. That's a week from tomorrow."

"Immediately after, then. Las Vegas. No arguing."

"This isn't my first rodeo, you know. The first couple times I said 'I do' didn't turn out all that great."

"Third time's a charm."

"What an optimist." But she was smiling.

"Come on, Regan. Take a chance on me. On us. You've already said, 'yes,' and are wearing the ring again—glad to see it—so let's just do this thing." He was so sincere, her heart nearly melted.

"It's a matter of timing, that's all." She thought about the cases that were outstanding, especially Sheree Cantnor's murder, then decided she, too, deserved a life. After all, she was going to be a mother again. "Just let me get through the funeral and take care of a few things, including telling my kids, then . . . then it's a go." She said the words and felt a little trill of excitement. Or was it trepidation?

"I'm holding you to it." His grin was a devilish slash of white.

"All right, Santana," she finally agreed and he gathered her close. Nose to nose, they smiled at each other in the darkness.

The next morning, Ryder waited in the snow flurries outside the Midway Diner until he saw the Tahoe drive into the customer lot at the front of the building. The SUV bounced a little at the curb where the snow was piled high, then disappeared beyond the building to the employee parking area around back. It was early, not quite six and still dark outside, but he recognized Anne-Marie through the glass as she appeared inside the restaurant a few minutes later. Her wig was in place as was the extra padding, hiding her figure enough that she had a little trouble tying her apron around her thickened waist.

Itching to move, to sneak to her vehicle and plant a small GPS device, he forced himself to wait. He'd seen the owner, two waitresses, and a couple of cooks show up, then finally another girl who worked as a busboy. Usually a kid in a souped-up Accord was the last to arrive and Ryder wanted them all inside before he started near the Tahoe.

A few minutes later, he heard the sound of after-factory exhaust pipes ripping through the winter air as the kid wheeled into the lot, his car nearly taking flight over the berm of ice and snow, the bass from his radio so loud it throbbed.

That should be it, Ryder thought. He gave the kid five minutes to get into the parking lot. Still, he had to be careful. The security lamp was illuminated and with all of the snow, the darkness was incomplete. Nonetheless, once he caught a visual of the Honda's driver tying on an apron and working at the service counter, Ryder climbed out of his truck. Staying to the shadows, he walked down a side street, then through an alley, and landed at the Dumpster behind the restaurant.

The back door was closed, thankfully. With one eye on the building, he slipped between the parked cars and tucked the tiny device on the undercarriage of Anne-Marie's SUV.

Headlights flashed, the beams washing over the Dumpster.

He froze, his heartbeat accelerating. For a second, he thought he'd missed an employee and would get caught.

Crap. How would he explain himself?

Fortunately, the beams disappeared quickly and he realized that the flash of illumination was from a vehicle turning into the front lot, a customer who'd shown up before the diner was open.

About to leave, he took a step toward the alley when the back door of the diner opened suddenly.

Ryder ducked down, hiding behind the Dumpster, certain he'd been seen. *Damn!*

Footsteps trudged through the snow.

"Shit, fuck, damn! Goddamn bitch," a male voice growled as the lid of the trash bin creaked open. Then, a falsetto voice, "Marlon, take out the garbage. Marlon, get your butt in here. Marlon, do this. Marlon do that!" *Thud.* Something landed on the metal bottom, then the lid slammed down so forcefully it clanged and the entire Dumpster shuddered. "Fuckin' goddamn bitch," he said again.

Ryder didn't so much as move a muscle. Getting found out wouldn't be good.

"Wish I could throw your scrawny ass out with the trash!"

Noiselessly, barely breathing, Ryder waited, listening hard as snow collected on his shoulders and hat. He heard Marlon's heavy footsteps thump through the snow and fade away, then the sound of the back door creaking open to slam shut again. He held fast, mentally counting to thirty before he peeked over the top edge of the Dumpster to assure himself he was alone.

The parking area was empty and all of Midway Diner's employees appeared to be inside. Quietly, he made his way through the alley and eventually to his truck parked in the shadows.

Inside the cab, he took a deep breath as he watched another car drive into the lot. He stared at the diner's front windows, waiting for another visual of the woman he presumed was Anne-Marie. As a pickup signaled to turn into the diner's parking area, Ryder witnessed the blond waitress flipping the COME IN, WE'RE OPEN sign as the early birds, dressed in heavy jackets, boots, and caps, jonesing for their morning cup of joe, started bustling inside.

Time to make tracks.

For the next few hours, the diner would be busy with the morning rush and he'd have time to hook up equipment at the cabin in which he assumed she resided. He drove out of town and into the hills, his own GPS as his guide, until he saw the snag and boulder and on the other side of the road, a lane with obvious tire tracks. He kept going, drove to the next opening in the trees where a broken down gate with a faded PRIVATE PROPERTY, NO TRESPASSING sign had been posted. He made short work of the gate, breaking the rusted lock and pushing the creaking metal gate inward. Ignoring the warning, he drove through. There were no tracks on the snowy land, so he drove cautiously through the opening in the trees, but, of course, he had no idea how far it wound or where the residence, if there was one, was located. Also, he would be guessing that the cottage or cabin or whatever Anne-Marie was using as a hideout was about the same distance from the main road. He hoped that was the case or otherwise he would lose valuable time searching for the place.

Less than an eighth of a mile in, the trees parted to a clearing where a house had once stood. It was a shambles—the roof collapsed, charred boards visible through the snow, a river rock chimney standing but losing stones. One wall with a broken window was still upright, though listing, and the remains of a staircase, about five steps, climbed upward to end abruptly, leading nowhere. Obviously, a fire had destroyed the cabin, the singed branches of a few nearby trees in evidence. Over the rubble, snow had drifted, softening the angles, muting the blackened boards.

Ryder wasted no time. From the bed of his truck, he grabbed his cross-country skis and snapped them on to his boots. Then he clipped his snowshoes to his backpack and slid his arms through the straps. The pack held electronic gear as well as other items he might need.

As dawn broke, a gray light stealing through the trees, snow forever falling, he started moving through the trees, gliding on his skis while using the compass on his phone to make sure he was heading in the right direction. The snow was thick enough to make skiing easy and soon he came upon a fence that was in the same condition as the gate and house, totally broken down and neglected. Without any difficulty, he skied through a wide gap in the mesh. Avoiding fallen trees and sliding over a frozen stream, he wound his way toward where he thought Anne-Marie's new residence might be. It took awhile. He had to double back once but finally caught a glimpse of a cabin through the trees. Carefully, he skied to the secondary row of evergreens surrounding the building and eyed it. No smoke trailed from the chimney, but the snow was mashed in the front of the cabin, multiple sets of tracks making ruts in the snow. The curtains were drawn, but it seemed as if no one was inside. He traded the cross-countries for his snowshoes and, after breaking off a low hanging hemlock branch, he trekked across the shortest expanse of cleared area to the back of house. After dumping his backpack onto the porch, he worked quickly, using a pick to open the lock, then took off his boots, and in his stocking feet, let himself inside.

The cabin was crude. Just the barest of essentials.

Quite a come down for the princess.

The ancient cottage had none of the creature comforts she was used to. Located in this frigid section of the Bitterroots, her new, if temporary, residence was a far cry from the manicured lawns, graceful verandas and wide, magnolia flanked porches of her New Orleans home. No fancy paddle-fans that moved the warm, sultry air of Louisiana, no white pillars or brick facades of the genteel Southern manor she was familiar with.

Nuh-uh. Just bare bones, and crappy bare bones at that.

No time for comparisons, he reminded himself, so he went to work. Quickly. Efficiently. The first order of business was to rule out that she'd set up her own security system. With a trained eye, he searched for any electronic equipment but found nothing. Next, he unfolded a small plastic sheet onto which he put all the pieces of his electronic equipment so that none would get lost. Then, he went about setting up tiny cameras and recorders, hiding them expertly. His training in the Special Forces served him well. Lastly, he hid the wireless transmitter. Military grade, it would broadcast to his receiver in his room at the River View.

Less than an hour after he'd arrived, he packed up his tools, walked out of the cabin, and relocked the door behind him. He stepped into his boots and after making certain the porch looked undisturbed, backed out within his original footsteps, using the hemlock branch to sweep them away. But if she returned in the next few hours, and there wasn't enough time for the snowfall to obliterate the tracks, Anne-Marie would realize someone had been at her cabin and she'd bolt again. However, he was betting on the snowfall and her shift at the diner keeping her busy until long after his tracks had disappeared. His plan was far from foolproof, but it was the best he had.

At the edge of the woods, he traded his snowshoes for skis and again whisked away his tracks with the branch until he was a hundred yards or so into the forest. Then he took off, skiing rapidly next to his own ruts and reaching his truck quickly. He threw his gear into the bed of his Dodge, turned the pickup around, and drove to the main road where he stopped to relatch the gate. Thankfully no one drove by as he was securing the place, and he only hoped that Anne-Marie didn't miss her turn-off and happen to drive past this lane as she might notice that the snow had been disturbed.

If so, she'd run like a rabbit.

But this time, he'd be right on her tail.

CHAPTER 14

"You're getting married? Like, *soon?*" Jeremy asked, dumbstruck. He was pulling a carton of orange juice out of the refrigerator.

"In the next couple weeks."

"Why?" Bianca had come out of her room at her mother's request and was as shell-shocked as her brother. "You can't."

"Why not?"

"But . . . but . . . is *he* going to live *here?* Because I'm not moving!" Her little face was set and she tossed her dark curls away from her face. Blue eyes thinned suspiciously. "Why *now?*"

Here came the lie. At least a partial lie. "Because life is short. That really came home to roost this past week or so."

Jeremy let the refrigerator door close. "Because of Sheriff Grayson." He took a big swallow from the carton.

"Glass, please," Pescoli said automatically.

"Don't talk about that. Too depressing," Bianca said with a shudder. She was dressed in skinny jeans and a sweater that hung off one shoulder, showing the strap of her black bra.

"It is depressing," Pescoli agreed.

"You're getting married and he's moving in here?" Bianca flounced into a kitchen chair. "This sucks."

"No one's moving anywhere yet. Santana and I haven't even talked about that part yet. We just decided the other night. We're planning on going to Vegas in a week or so. Depending."

"Are we, like, invited?" Bianca asked, her ears perking up at the mention of Sin City.

"I haven't got that far yet."

"It's your wedding, Mom!" her daughter declared.

"My *third* wedding. Not to put too fine a point on it."

"Well, it wasn't like I could go to either one of the first two be-cause I wasn't born yet," Bianca said. "Jeremy got to be there when you married Dad."

"He was a toddler," Pescoli said at the same time Jeremy drawled, "Like I remember it."

Bianca lifted a shoulder and had to adjust the wide neck of her sweater. "Maybe it would, you know, make it suck less, if we were there."

"I'm not going to be blackmailed into this," Pescoli said. "If I de-cide it's the right thing to do, then we'll work it out. As I said, we'll all move in together once the new house is ready." She thought of the construction. "It'll be awhile yet. At least a month, maybe two, but probably three. It's not as if you haven't been expecting this. Haven't I been telling you to go through your things and start thinking about moving? How far have we gotten with that?"

"I'm *not* moving there." Jeremy finished off the juice and crushed the carton in one hand. "I'll get my own place."

"Good. I'll live with you," Bianca announced.

"Yeah, right," Pescoli said dryly.

"I'm almost seventeen!"

"Precisely."

"You just don't care what I want," Bianca huffed.

Refusing to be baited, Pescoli nodded. "That's right. I've never put your needs before mine in the last sixteen years."

"You don't understand!"

"Probably not."

"Do you know you're like . . . impossible?" Bianca charged, so angry she was nearly spitting, "It really doesn't matter because I'm moving in with Dad and Michelle. *They* want me."

Pescoli just looked at her daughter. They'd had this argument be-fore. Dozens of times, Bianca had angrily threatened to move out and live with Lucky and his second wife. Though the hot argument always ripped out Pescoli's heart, she'd learned to play it cool and keep her reactions to a minimum. "I think you should give living with Santana and me a chance. You could love it."

Bianca rolled her eyes. "Mom, I don't like him and I never will, okay? So don't get this super romantic idea that we're going to live like some big loving, *blended* family."

Pescoli slid a look at her son, who was leaning against the breakfast bar that separated the kitchen from the eating area. "I thought you might want to live in the apartment over the garage. Well, it's not really an apartment with all the bells and whistles, but it's big, kind of a bonus room with its own bath. If you wanted, you could take in a microwave and minifridge. It even has its own separate entrance."

Jeremy asked, "That's cool with Santana?"

"It will be."

"I thought you said it was going to be his office."

Pescoli lifted a shoulder because she wasn't really certain. "We can move things around. Besides, it wouldn't be forever."

"If Jer doesn't want it, I'll take it," Bianca said, seizing what she perceived as a prime opportunity to assert her independence.

"How would that work? You'd commute from Lucky and Michelle's?" Pescoli asked.

Bianca glared at her mother. "I'd live there, as you well know. In the apartment over the garage."

Pescoli shook her head. "But not for a few years."

"That's just not fair!" Bianca actually stomped a bare foot and marched back to her room, slamming her door behind her.

"Sixteen going on twelve," Pescoli muttered.

"Give her a break," Jeremy said, opening the refrigerator again and finding some deli meat. He sniffed it, deigned it good enough to eat, and slapped it on a slice of bread that he'd left on the counter. "It's not easy, you know."

"I know. It's not easy for me, either, but it's going to happen. I want it to happen."

"Okay." Jeremy dug deeper into the fridge and pulled out a jar of mayo. He quickly slathered one slice of bread, then squirted a thick dollop of some kind of hot sauce onto the meat. "It'll be cool."

She eyed her son as he grabbed a butcher knife from the block near the stove and sliced his sandwich into two thick halves. "Yeah?"

"Uh-huh."

"Wish I could believe you," she said on a sigh.

"You can."

"What, are you suddenly clairvoyant?"

"Yeah, me and what's her name? The nutcase who talks to ghosts."

"Grace Perchant, and we don't call her a nutcase."

"Since when?" He eyed his mother, almost daring her to argue.

"Plate!" she yelled and he rolled his eyes, but pulled a plate from the already-opened cupboard and transferred the sloppy sandwich onto it. "What about some vegetables on that."

"Mom . . ."

She lifted her hands in surrender. She knew she was one of the worst offenders when it came to nutrition, although that was going to have to change, too.

"Give Bianca some space. Y'know? She'll come around." He picked up a thick, dripping half. "If she doesn't and moves in with Lucky and Michelle, who cares? It's not the end of the world. Isn't that what you always say?" He smiled as he threw her words back at her, then took an impossibly large bite.

She didn't argue, because he was right, even though it burned her to think of Michelle parenting her daughter. But she'd given her kids a lot to swallow, so she bit her tongue. She figured it was time to let the news of her impending marriage settle in and Jeremy and Bianca find a way to deal with it.

Jessica's feet throbbed, her back ached, and she was fighting the pounding in her head as she drove along the mountain road to her newfound home. Working a double shift was well worth it in tips, but her body was rebelling. She envisioned a magnolia scented bath, thick towels, luxurious shampoo, and the open doors to a shaded veranda where a pitcher of iced tea was waiting.

In another lifetime.

She checked the rearview of her Tahoe, but the street was empty aside from the ever-falling snow. Would it never let up? Enough of the icy flakes had fallen and piled by her drive that it was nearly impossible to see her tracks and she almost missed the turn-off. Again.

One last look in the mirror, then she cranked on the wheel and guided her Chevy through the trees to the clearing and the little ramshackle cabin. Wearily, she locked the SUV and unlocked the house that was dark and nearly as cold inside as out. Closing the door behind her, she stood in the living room for a second, listening. She left the rooms in darkness for a second, hearing the drip of a faucet and the whistle of the outside air as it swirled down the chimney and rattled the window panes. Normal sounds. Noises she'd gotten used to.

She snapped on the lights, one room after another, checking to see that the house was still secure, assuring herself that she was, at least for the moment, safe.

So why did she have the nagging feeling that something wasn't right? That there was a disturbance in the air?

Because nothing is right. Nothing has been for a long time. Why else would you be on the run, hiding out in this isolated cabin? How long are you going to keep running?

As she'd dragged herself from the banks of that muddy river months before, she'd told herself that she just needed a little time to pull herself together, to go back and face the music, to end this.

Before he found her.

God, what a mess. Yanking off the wig, she dropped it onto the couch, then clicked her dental appliance from her mouth. Stretching the muscles of her face, she unpinned her hair and shook it free, then started working on the dress and padding. When she was naked, her clothes folded, she took a quick shower, never really getting rid of the chill as the water was lukewarm at best.

She toweled off and pulled on fresh underwear and sweats. Tomorrow, in between her shifts, she'd need to drive into town to the Laundromat she'd used once before to clean her uniforms and to take care of other errands.

Then, she determined, she would finally look up Cade Grayson. From the gossip in the restaurant she'd pieced together that the sheriff's funeral was still a week in the future and she couldn't wait any longer. Not when she felt as if she still wasn't safe.

You're paranoid.

He won't find you here. He can't. . . .

But she wasn't convinced. There were still rumors about the corpse of the woman found on the O'Halleran farm, a woman named Sheree Cantnor, being mutilated in some way. That in and of itself wasn't enough to convince her that he'd found her, but then she knew him and also knew what he was capable of. For the love of God, she'd fancied herself in love with him once upon a time. Even gone so far as to marry him.

Naive fool. He'd never loved her, had only been after her money, but still believed he'd possessed her. That she had no longer wanted him, had no longer wanted to be one of his possessions, had brought out his rage, the depth of his depravity and cruelty.

Her stomach quivered at the thought.

She had trouble believing that he would go so far as to murder an innocent woman. The idea was beyond far-fetched. Surely he wouldn't kill someone else just to terrorize her. No no no. That didn't make any sense.

It's not about you. That woman, Sheree Cantnor, is the one who suffered. Don't turn this around.

Still, Jessica's skin crawled and she felt unseen eyes upon her, as if he were watching her. She double-checked the locks and latches, making certain any possible way into the cabin was secure. She adjusted the shades and curtains, blocking out the chance that anyone could see into the small rooms.

You can't keep running. You can't go on hiding. You have to go to the police.

And tell them what? They'll only think you're crazy. Even you doubt your own sanity at times. They will not keep you safe. No one can.

Disgusted, she flopped back onto the poor excuse of a couch.

Somehow, someway, the madness had to stop.

This place is no-damn-where.

Calypso Pope drove through the frigid streets of Grizzly Falls and wished she'd never taken the detour off the freeway. On her way to Missoula, her coffee had kicked in and not only was she a little hyped up on caffeine, her bladder was stretched to its fullest, which was such a pain. She drove past the brick courthouse and noted that the buildings along the waterfront were at least a hundred years old and the parking spaces weren't only narrow, but nearly nonexistent. It seemed everyone in the hick town must be out for the night.

"Come on, come on, come *on!*" she muttered, shutting off the radio in irritation as the song she'd been listening to faded out into a cluster of static. She considered heading back to the main artery into town when she spied a neon sign for a restaurant called, oh so quaintly, Wild Wills. "Ugh."

She saw a parking spot on the street. Unfortunately, so did the driver of a huge Hummer or whatever they were called, some long-ass rig that hung out into the street and nearly swiped the cars on either side of him.

"Bastard," she muttered under her breath, circling the block to come upon a street that led to the edge of the river, an alley almost, and two blocks down found an area under a bridge that was posted *NO PARKING.*

Oh, hell. Who cares? She'd just run into the damn restaurant, use the bathroom, and get something to go, if that. Maybe another coffee.

She nearly slipped getting out of her Mercedes and had to catch herself. Swearing silently, she tucked her purse under her arm, remotely locked the car, and hurried carefully along the dimly lit alley to Wild Wills.

Once inside, she nearly peed herself when she came face-to-face with a huge grizzly bear, standing upright, its long teeth pulled back in a snarl, its glass eyes glittering angrily. It was stuffed and dressed in a ridiculous Cupid outfit complete with glittery wings and a quiver filled with arrows that had red hearts rather than feathers stuck into the shafts. Worse yet, the huge creature was swaddled in a pink diaper and a bow had been propped into one clawed paw.

Whose dim idea was that? "Your bathroom?" she asked a tall girl with a ponytail and a sour expression who was standing at the hostess station.

"It's just for customers."

"I plan on being one. And, if you don't want me to pee all over your floor in front of that ridiculous creature"—Calypso jabbed a long finger at the bear—"you'll point me in the direction." At that moment, she saw the sign with the little cut out woman in the dress indicating the women's room. She didn't bother explaining further and barreled down the short hallway, with the pissy-faced hostess calling after her.

"Hey! Wait!"

Calypso ignored her. *Please don't let it be occupied,* she thought, pushing against the broad panels. She breathed a sigh of relief as the door swung inward and, just in time, she dashed into one of the two empty stalls. "Thank-you, God," she whispered as she yanked down her jeans and thong in one swift movement, then relieved herself.

She almost sighed in ecstasy as the sensation was as close to orgasmic as she'd ever want to feel in a public restroom.

Once she'd cleaned up and regained some of her dignity, she walked back into the foyer where the damn bear seemed to be leering at her.

"As I said before, I'm a customer, and now I'd like dinner," she said with a haughty lift of her chin.

"Right this way." The hostess led her to a table in a cavernous room where stuffed animals abounded. A moose head and a stalking puma graced one wall; antelope and deer faces glared down at her from another. A porcupine was balanced on a shelf to her right, while wagon wheel chandeliers and paddle fans hung from the wide expanse of ceiling.

"This place is beyond rustic and weird as hell," she observed, sliding into a booth. She was relieved to see that no family with a raft of little children was seated anywhere near her. "I mean, seriously, dead, dusty stuffed animals don't exactly spark one's appetite."

"People seem to like them," the hostess said as she slid a menu onto the table.

"No one from PETA, I bet."

The girl looked lost. "From where?"

"Never mind."

"Would you like to hear the specials?"

"Sure," Calypso said and slid her reading glasses out of her purse to scan the menu quickly while half-listening as the girl mentioned something about monkfish and wild trout and . . . *God, did she actually say* reindeer? A shiver ran through Calypso.

Scowling as she read the menu, she was about to say something about the taxidermy and putting dead animals on display being so nineteenth century and totally un-PC, but the hostess had disappeared. "How rude," she muttered under her breath, then checked her cell phone, searching for a message from that jerk Reggie.

Another girl, one with a smile plastered to her young face which indicated she, at least, had learned the valuable lesson about customers and tips, slid a water glass onto her table. "Did Tiffany tell you about the specials?" she asked.

"If Tiffany was that sour-faced hostess, then, yes, she did, but I'm not interested in reindeer for God's sake. What's wrong with you people?" Calypso asked, setting her phone down after one last peek. "And this," she indicated the menu with a flip of her wrist to point at the plastic-covered sheets. "You're a little heavy here on the meat, aren't you?" She gazed over the half lenses of her glasses. "I mean, do you have anything remotely vegetarian or whole grain or healthy? Or gluten-free? Something that won't send my cholesterol into the stratosphere?"

The girl opened her mouth, closed it, and finally said, "All . . . all of our entrees are—"

"Oh, forget it. Just get me a cup of coffee. Black. Wait. Is it Starbucks?"

"No. I'm sorry, we use—"

"Doesn't matter," Calypso said, sighing through her nose. "Just bring me some skim milk with it. None of that powdered shi—stuff, okay? That's nothing but chemicals, and I won't drink it. I'm talking real milk. Make sure it's not one percent!" She thought about ordering her usual, a house salad with balsamic vinegar dressing, but it didn't sound appealing in the least, despite her need to always diet. Oh, what she wouldn't do for a slight case of bulimia, slight being the operative word.

She glanced around the room at the stuffed beasts again, noticing a long-whiskered bobcat posed on a ledge as if ready to pounce on a ring-necked pheasant. *Oh, God, soooo barbaric!* Then she saw the slowly spinning pie case located on the counter and her stomach nearly rumbled. Chocolate. Strawberry. Key lime. She couldn't resist. "And a piece of the lemon meringue pie." She needed to indulge. Just a little. "Oh. Wait. Is it fresh? Made with real lemons?"

"Baked this morning," the smiling waitress said. Her name tag read TERI with one *R*.

"Organic, though? Yes?"

"I-I don't know."

Well, at least the twit was honest. Calypso pursed her lips, then reminded herself not to, that she was just begging for those nasty little wrinkles around her mouth. That was the main reason she'd given up smoking. God, she missed that guilty little pleasure. She caught the waitress staring at her. "Oh, okay. The pie will do, I suppose."

"Nothing else?"

"Just the coffee. With skim? Remember?" Then Calypso pointed at her watch. "And I'm in a bit of a hurry."

The girl hurried off and Calypso leaned against the back of the booth to close her eyes for a second. She was fighting a headache again and knew she should eat something more substantial, but really, was that even possible in this den of death? The weird meats that were on the menu, rabbit and pheasant and bison, were probably laced with salmonella or E. coli or God knew what else. She probably shouldn't have any more coffee considering that it was the overwhelming urge to relieve herself that had brought her to this place. Usually, though, she had a bladder of steel and she needed to stay awake for the rest of the drive. It was already pushing eleven. That's why the dining area was shutting down, she realized, though there were still a few straggling customers scattered within the restaurant, most of them lingering over a drink or a cup of coffee and the remains of their meals.

She probably should find a room for the night. She'd been driving for hours as it was and it really didn't matter if she landed in Spokane later tonight or early in the morning, but the thought of searching out a decent, clean, safe hotel in this little burg was daunting. She checked her cell phone for local hotels. *Decent* hotels. Or even damn motels. Maybe she could make it as far as Missoula and then—

"Here ya go." The waitress was back with a cup of coffee, tiny pitcher of milk, and a thick wedge of lemon pie topped with three inches of meringue that Calypso would have loved to plunge her face into as she was suddenly starving.

"Anything else?"

"Not right now," Calypso said and the girl, grin intact, stepped backward, leaving her with a few minutes of heaven as she poured the skim milk slowly into her cup, took a sip and then dug into the scrumptious dessert. "Mmm." She couldn't help sighing, then caught herself as a text message came in. Reggie.

She felt a warming jolt of satisfaction, but thought, *No thanks.*

Reginald Larue didn't know it yet, but they were o-v-e-r.

His text, a sloppy apology for standing her up twice in one week, pissed her off, so she deleted it and turned her phone off so that she could concentrate on the pie. "Sorry, my ass," she said under her breath then put Reggie—*oh, excuse me. Reginald A. Larue III*—where he belonged. Completely out of her mind.

Well, almost.

There was a part of her that wanted to see him grovel, to twist and turn in utter despair over losing her, crawl on his knees to beg her forgiveness. Not that she'd give him another chance. No-effin'-way. She was thirty-six for Christ's sake and though she ignored the tick, tick, tick of her biological clock, she still wanted to get married and have someone else take care of her. She couldn't keep up this pace forever. Yes, she was a corporate attorney and a damn good one, but smart as she was, she wasn't into working sixteen hours out of twenty-four. She'd hoped, actually planned, to find Mr. Right in law school or in the firm she joined in Seattle, but so far it hadn't worked out that way.

She glanced down at her left hand where her grandmother's engagement ring with its huge diamond glittered under the cheesy wagon-wheel lights. She always wore the ring when she was out and, the funny thing was, it didn't appear to discourage men from hitting on her in bars. In fact, sometimes it seemed as if she posed a challenge.

That's how she'd met stupid, two-timing Reggie. Figured. He was probably stepping out on someone else when he'd tried to pick her up. She'd played hard to get until she'd checked him out and found that he was set to inherit a fortune from oil wells. But she knew he would never settle down with one woman, and when she got married, that lucky son of a bitch who claimed her as his bride had god-damn better be faithful. Or she'd have to cut off his balls.

She blinked and realized that she'd been daydreaming again. She'd nearly finished her pie without even savoring every bite. All because of Reggie. She studied the last morsel but pushed her plate aside, then finished her coffee in one gulp. She lifted her hand and signed to the smiley-faced waitress that she wanted her check, then sent a lingering look at the last bit of pie. But no. She always left at least one bite on her plate, no matter how hungry she thought she was. It was a matter of mind over matter.

"Would you like anything else?" Teri asked.

"No. Just the check. I think I mentioned I'm in a hurry."

The girl whipped out the folder with a piece of paper and a pen inside and Calypso handed her a credit card with a mere glance at the bill.

Two minutes later the transaction was finished, and Calypso was heading outside to the wintry streets of Grizzly Falls once more. *Pathetic town,* she thought, winding her scarf more tightly around her neck as the snow fell. She headed back the way she'd come and for the first time since parking illegally hoped beyond hope that her car hadn't been towed. The sidewalk was uneven, her boots slipping a little as she walked, head bent against an icy wind that chilled her to the bone.

Maybe a hotel wasn't such a bad idea after all. Cinching the belt of her wool coat a little tighter, she tried not to notice that the trail of mashed down snow was a little eerie, the back side of the ancient buildings dark, the loading bays empty. Only a few lights from apartments on the upper stories were visible. One streetlight hadn't illuminated and another was fading slowly in and out as if it were soon to die. No other pedestrians were out at this time of night, not even some idiot walking his dog in the damn snow.

Jesus, it's cold.

Following a wrought-iron fence that separated the pedestrian path and the sheer drop-off to the river below, she shivered against a wind that drove icy snow pellets right into her face, stinging her cheeks.

That decided it. She would find a place to stay, a motel close to the freeway. Hadn't she seen one on the way into this funky little town? A Holiday Inn or Motel 6? She'd backtrack in her car, follow the route she'd taken into town, find that motel, grab a room, then take off early in the morning after a hot shower, a few hours rest, and a cup of crappy motel coffee. That would be the smart thing to do.

Another bitter gust.

"God, it's cold." *And nerve-wracking.*

Even the tread of the pathway she was following was beginning to be covered with a thick layer of snow. Worse yet, between the whoosh of the wind and the rushing sound of the damn falls, she couldn't hear anything. Not really a surprise as her aching ears felt as if they were nearly frozen solid. It was as if she were the only person in the arctic world.

Just get to the damn car.

She stepped a little quicker, though she reminded herself there was nothing to be freaked out about. *So I'm alone? So it's weirdly dark? So what?*

Squinting against the harsh wind, she caught a glimpse of her Mercedes parked where she'd left it under the bridge.

Things were looking up.

She hit the unlock button on her remote key and her car's headlights flashed, though, if the lock had dinged, she couldn't hear it. Didn't matter. She just had a few more feet and—

Thump! Thump! Thump!

Her heart nearly stopped.

What was that? What the hell was that?
Footsteps?
Looking over her shoulder, she saw nothing but swirling snow.
Get over yourself!
She was nearly at the bridge.
Thump! Thump!
Adrenaline pumped through her blood and she broke into a jog.
For the love of Christ!
Just a few more steps!
Bam!
Someone torpedoed her from the back!

Her feet slid wildly in the snow and she fell forward, desperately trying to keep her balance.

Impossible. He was too heavy.

His weight slammed her forward. Down she went.

Crack!

Her knees slammed into the icy pavement, pain jarring through her body, her purse and keys sailing into the darkness.

No. Oh, God no!

This couldn't be happening. "Get off me!"

A gloved hand clamped over her mouth and she bit hard, struggling, kicking, fighting the weight upon her back. *Oh, Jesus, he's so heavy!* He drove her face into the snow. Pain ripped through her and she had trouble breathing.

No way! No way was she going to let this fucker harm her!

Wrenching her body, she struggled. Where the hell was another pedestrian, or a business owner locking up or a goddamn *cop*? Her lungs were burning and she thought she might pass out. *No no no!* Twisting, she tried to get a glimpse of him, but all she saw was a huge figure dressed in black, snow dancing around him, his body pinning her mercilessly. "Bastard!" she tried to scream, but her voice was muffled.

"Let me go!" she yelled. Again her plea was only a muted mumble. Fear spurted through her. This jerk wad wasn't giving up. *Oh, God, is he going to kill me? Shit, no!* She struggled, but his thumb pinched her nostrils together, his body pressing her flatter onto the path. Her lungs were beginning to burn. She whipped around, trying to force air through her nasal passage, but it was impossible. *No no no!*

Panic took over, but she was losing strength, her flailing arms more sluggish. It occurred to her that she might actually perish in this godforsaken town with a psycho squeezing the life out of her.

She fought valiantly until the blackness pulled her deep, her arms and legs becoming sluggish and clumsy, not obeying her mind. Her eyes rolled upward and she was vaguely aware of her body growing limp, her appendages useless. The last thing she remembered was being rolled onto her back and seeing the monster above her. In one hand he held something . . . a knife? Before she could make one last attempt to struggle, he grabbed her by the throat again and slowly, deliberately squeezed and squeezed and squeezed.

CHAPTER 15

"We might have caught a break," Alvarez said to Pescoli the minute she walked into her office. Her hair was pulled back into a knot at her nape, gold hoops dangling from her earlobes, and she was carrying two steaming cups. "Decaf." She set that one on the corner of Pescoli's desk.

"Thanks. What break?"

"The autopsy report is back. You've got a copy in your e-mail. Strangulation. Hyoid bone crushed. Not much water or foam in the airways." Alvarez took a sip from her cup. "She was definitely killed first, then tossed into the stream."

Pescoli hung up her jacket and unwound the scarf at her neck. "Not a surprise. And not exactly a 'break.'"

"There's something else."

"Yeah?" she picked up her cup, took a sip, found the coffee hot even if it didn't have a kick.

"Half a mile downstream on the Barstow property, the farmer found a shoe nearly covered by snow. Wedged between some roots."

"You think it's our victim's?"

"Woman's red heel. Covered with prints."

Pescoli was interested. "Sheree Cantnor's?"

"All except one partial which has been run with no hits. But it's something. There's a crew out scouring the area, hoping to find the other shoe, her purse, phone." She rolled a palm upward. "Whatever."

"Maybe a finger and a ring."

"Those, I think he kept."

Pescoli agreed. "Trophies."

"Uh-huh."

She took another sip of the decaf and heard Blackwater walk into his office. *His* office. Not Dan Grayson's. Funny how she'd started thinking in those terms already, funny and sad. "We got anything else?"

"Not really. I did find out that despite Doug Pollard's insistence that he and Sheree were high school sweethearts and their life was all hearts, flowers, and romance, there was an instance where she took up with another guy for a while. She and Doug had their one breakup, I guess. Then that guy landed in prison."

Pescoli looked up sharply, but Alvarez shook her head. "For a B and E. The guy's still doing time in Utah. I double-checked."

Breaking and entering was a far cry from homicide and the guy was incarcerated to boot. "So we're back to the unknown assailant." Pescoli sighed.

"Looks like." Alvarez started walking out of the office but stopped short.

Blackwater filled the hallway just outside the door. His face was set and hard, lips compressed. "Got a call from a deputy at the waterfront. They're pulling a body out of the river, just below the old bridge. A woman." His dark gaze moved from Alvarez to Pescoli. "Looks like you two are up."

"Suicide?" Pescoli asked. Every once in a while, someone took a leap from the bridge, in summer kids who dared each other jumped or dived into the river under the falls despite the postings, and sometimes, when someone decided to end it all, they took that same plunge.

"Unknown." He backed up a step as Alvarez made her way into the hall. "Maybe. Units are already in place, but it sounds like we've already got a crowd, people stopping to rubberneck. Check it out. Report back to me."

A phone rang nearby and Blackwater marched to his office.

"He should have a field day with this," Pescoli said to Alvarez, who was still standing in the hall. "Big splash, you know. Pardon the pun." Pescoli kicked out her chair and reached for her jacket again. "No rest for the wicked. Meet you at the Jeep? I'll drive."

"Yep." Alvarez disappeared into her office to get her coat and within minutes they were in Pescoli's vehicle and heading down the road that cut across the face of Boxer Bluff to the lower part of town. The snow had quit falling, but nearly ten inches had piled up overnight, so the plows were out and traffic was a snarl. They followed a school bus over the tracks before they turned onto the street that bisected the older area of Grizzly Falls. Despite the fact that she'd turned on the flashers and hit the siren, they had trouble making headway due to the traffic snarls. She pulled into the courthouse and parked in a spot reserved for a judge.

"You're going to hear about that," Alvarez said.

"Yeah." They walked the three blocks and threaded their way through the crowd. A television news crew was already on the scene despite the clog of vehicles and pedestrians. Traffic was being detoured around from the old arched bridge, constructed before nineteen hundred. Access to the river's crossing had been cordoned off, two miles farther downstream.

Alvarez showed her badge to an officer as they reached the perimeter of the area beneath the bridge and he motioned them through. Several vehicles were parked along the alley.

Probably from workers who had arrived before the police, Pescoli thought, *or had been left overnight by someone who had consumed one or two too many at one of the nearby taverns.*

There were other cars in the parking lots that serviced the rear entrances of the buildings positioned on the main street—a couple city cop cars, along with those from employees who had already started their shifts. From the back doors of those businesses a number of people were loitering, some smoking, all watching the action as it unfolded. An ambulance had gotten through and it stood by, lights flashing.

"What've we got?" Alvarez asked Jan Spitzer, the deputy who was obviously in charge.

Short, a little pudgy and smart as a whip, Spitzer looked tired, as if she'd put in her shift and was well into overtime. "Female. Caucasian. Already fished out. Thirty-five or so, looks like. Not long in the water. No decomp and, you know, the river's close to freezing over, so the body would be, too, but no fish or whatever had started taking nibbles."

Pescoli looked up to the underside of the bridge, where in warmer weather birds and bats probably roosted. "ID?"

"None on her."

"Distinguishing marks?" Alvarez asked.

"Surgical scar on her abdomen, another on the inside of her left arm, and a couple tattoos—a tramp stamp of hearts and butterflies. You know, the usual. And some kind of tiny hummingbird on her right shoulder, but that's not what's interesting." Spitzer glanced at Pescoli. "Our Jane Doe is missing a finger."

Pescoli's stomach dropped.

Spitzer continued. "Ring finger. Left hand. Sliced clean off."

"Shit." Pescoli exchanged glances with her partner. "So, it's another psycho?"

How many could one town the size of Grizzly Falls have?

Alvarez said, "Let's see."

"Right this way, ladies." Spitzer walked them over to the ME's van where a body bag, blocked from the crowd's view by the bulky vehicle, lay atop a gurney. As Spitzer unzipped the heavy bag, Pescoli felt her queasy stomach give a lurch and she fought a rising tide of nausea.

With a flip of the flap, the dead woman was exposed, supine, fully clothed, water collecting around her.

Pescoli forced back the urge to retch as she stared at the victim. Where there had been makeup were now only smudges. She was thin with a square face and her skin was tinged the bluish-gray hue of death. Her blue eyes were open and seeming to stare upward, her short, streaked hair wet and flattened to her head.

"Doesn't look much like Sheree Cantnor," Alvarez said as if she'd read Pescoli's thoughts.

The victim's hands were already bagged. Hopefully there had been a struggle and there was DNA evidence lodged beneath her nails.

"Any obvious areas where the attack occurred?" Pescoli asked as she looked toward the distant mountains, inhaling and exhaling slowly. Thankfully, her stomach was settling down.

"Near the bridge, it looks like. We found a couple tubes of lipstick and a case for eyeglasses by that section of fence." She pointed to an area not quite under the bridge's span, where snow had drifted near the tall pickets.

"Who called it in?" Pescoli asked.

"Over there." Spitzer, whose walkie-talkie began to crackle, pointed to a sheriff's cruiser.

For the first time, Pescoli and Alvarez saw Grace Perchant, the nutcase who claimed to talk with ghosts and predict the future among her many talents. Pale as a corpse herself, Grace was dressed in a long white coat, gloves, and tan boots. Her graying blond hair was anchored by a knit cap but whispered around her face. At her side were a pair of dogs, both half-wolf, one black, the other silvery gray. On slack leashes, each animal watched the approaching detectives with intelligent, if wary, eyes.

"Hello, Grace," Pescoli said. "Mind if we ask you a few questions?"

"Not at all." Grace gave some unspoken command and both dogs sat, obviously more relaxed.

"You found the body?"

"Yes. I was taking the dogs out. Sometimes we come down here, walk across the bridge. Sheena and Bane love the river, so this morning, just before dawn, I parked across the river, and we walked over the bridge. I didn't notice anything on the way over, probably because I was on the far side of the span. Then, we walked into town and around several blocks down here." She motioned behind her, past the buildings and their loading zones to indicate part of the city between the river and the high cliffs of Boxer Bluff.

"I wanted to take the steps up to the overlook," she said, mentioning a concrete staircase of nearly a thousand steps that wound up the hillside to a point above the river where one could get a bird's eye view of Grizzly Falls. "But it was so cold, we just went a few blocks down here and headed back. The dogs were a little whiny, they both kept trying to look over the railing and then I felt it. You know, a disturbance."

"Disturbance?" Pescoli repeated.

Both detectives had dealt with Grace numerous times in the past. With her dire predictions, she was a frequent visitor to the sheriff's department. Was she accurate in foretelling the future? Probably about fifty percent of the time. But she had made personal predictions about Pescoli and Alvarez that had been surprisingly on the mark—chillingly so. Neither detective could completely discount the self-proclaimed psychic's abilities.

"When I was returning to the car and recrossing the bridge, I was on the other side of the road, on the falls' side of the span. The dogs began acting up. You know, pulling at their leashes and whining, noses into the wind. Bane"—she indicated the bigger dog with the lighter coat—"was all over the railing, trying to get over. I looked then and noticed something floating down by the rocks. It wasn't quite light yet, but I thought it was a body and called 9-1-1." She shrugged, her pale green eyes unreadable.

There was something about the woman that made Pescoli uneasy. Maybe it was Grace's infinite calm despite her predictions of disaster and death, or maybe the aura of peace that she insisted surrounded her. Or maybe it was the fact that she lived alone with two wolf-dogs in the middle of the forest.

You live with two dogs, she reminded herself. *You're often alone now that your kids are always looking for ways to escape. You live and breathe your job and are as isolated as she is in many ways. Yet, you're not weird. Right?*

"I waited," Grace was saying, "And now, here we are."

And where is that? Pescoli wondered, staring at the arch of the bridge backlit by the rising sun, then watching as the body bag was loaded into the ME's van. *Just where the hell is that?*

The buzz in the diner was all about the body that had been pulled from the river this morning, customers chattering and gossiping, bits of information floating in the din of the dining room. Over the clatter of forks, rattle of ice cubes, and gurgle of the espresso machine, the conversation was centered on a second body found in so short a time.

"It just never seems to end," Misty confided to Jessica when both were at the serving counter, picking up orders. "Hey, Armando, this omelet's supposed to come with guac!"

"*Sì, sì!*" he snapped, irritated. He found a dish of guacamole and placed it on the platter. "Where is Denise? I cannot do this by myself!"

Denise Burns was a fry cook sous-chef. And she was over an hour late.

"She called Nell. Got caught in that mess of traffic near the bridge." Misty surveyed her two platters, then pulled them from the counter. To Jessica, she said, "We've already had one psycho this season and now this."

"You think there's a madman running around?" Jessica asked, eyeing a platter that Armando slid onto the counter. "Wheat toast," she said to the head cook, "not sourdough."

"*Dios!* I cannot work like this!" Armando grumbled just as Denise, in a gust of cold air, walked through the back door.

"Sorry, sorry, sorry!" she said, holding up her hands as if she expected Armando to open fire. "It's impossible to get through town right now. The damn bridge I usually use is closed and all the roads are backed up." She was stripping off her jacket as she came inside and threw her purse, scarf, and phone into her locker. It banged shut as she reappeared, wrapping an apron around her slim waist. "Bring me up to speed," she said to Armando as she twisted her hair into a net and began washing her hands.

After slapping a stack of wheat toast onto the counter, he began reading off the orders to her, rapid-fire.

Jessica carried her platters to a table near the windows where a mother of three kids under six was trying to convince her three-year-old daughter to eat "one more bite" of a barely touched waffle. The baby was picking at Cheerios on the high chair tray, and the third child, around five, was plucking the blueberries out of his pancakes.

"Sorry for the delay," Jessica said, finally delivering the parents their breakfasts.

The mom said, "No problem," though it sounded as if it really was a major inconvenience. The dad didn't look up from his cell phone.

"Can I get you anything else?"

"Catsup," the mother said as her husband eyed his small screen.

"The body they pulled out of the river today was a woman," he told his wife. "There's talk that she might've been murdered."

Jessica's heart lurched.

"We moved here to get away from all of that, George!" the mom hissed. "Isn't that what you said? If we leave the city, life will be safer. Slower paced?"

"Who gots murdered?" the three-year-old asked.

"Nobody. I mean nobody we know." The mom shushed her.

Jessica moved out of earshot, wending her way through the tables, telling herself this latest murder had nothing to do with her. Nothing. It was just partial stories, bad information, gossip.

But throughout the morning shift and into lunchtime she heard more and more about the woman found in the Grizzly River, supposedly first seen by a woman who owned wolves and cast spells, a witch of sorts, if the gossip could be believed. Table after table of patrons speculated about the identity of the woman and if, as Misty had mentioned earlier, another madman was in their midst.

Around ten, a big man came into the diner and though Jessica was certain she'd never seen him before, there was something familiar about him. Within minutes, she realized he was Zedediah, "Big Zed," Grayson, Cade and the fallen sheriff's brother. She steeled herself, wondering if Cade would join the large man, but thankfully that wasn't the case. He was seated in Misty's section, so she didn't have to deal with him.

Others did, however, including Nell, who deigned to come out of the office to offer condolences. She'd been tallying receipts from the day before, balancing them with the payments received. "So sorry for your loss."

"Oh, Zed, a shame about Dan. Such a good man," a seventyish woman with a red beret pinned to her shiny gray hair offered up, her friend nodding solemnly.

"We're gonna miss Dan. Helluva man," a farmer-type put in.

"The town will never be the same," declared another man in a suit.

And so it went for the hour that Zed occupied his chair. He was alone, an unread newspaper spread on the table. He scooped up his paper as soon as he was finished eating, squared his hat onto his large head and, after paying his bill, strode quickly out of the building.

Misty sidled over to Jessica and confided, "That's one of the dead sheriff's brothers. You know, there's a strange thing about him. He doesn't quite seem to fit with the others. Dan was a handsome man, as was his brother Bart, the one who offed himself in the barn. You heard about that?"

Jessica nodded, though she didn't admit she'd heard about the suicide from Cade, years before. Luckily, Misty didn't ask.

"Well, that Bart, he was a looker, too. And Cade . . ." Misty made a big show of fanning herself. "Hot, let me tell you. That cowboy can park his boots under my bed any day of the week. *Any* day. But Zed," she said, watching through the window as the big man made his way to a huge king cab. "He's different. Not just in size being that he's a head taller and got seventy pounds or so on his brothers, but he keeps more to himself. Not as friendly. Almost . . . oh, I don't know, darker somehow. Someone you wouldn't want to meet at night in a deserted alley, you know what I mean?"

Jessica watched Zed put his truck into gear and drive off.

"Oh, maybe I'm all wet. I mean, Zed's done nothing to make me think there's anything wrong with him. It's just that he's so damn different from his brothers." Misty shrugged. "But it takes all kinds, now, doesn't it? Say, would you cover for me for a minute? I need to take five." She was already reaching for the pack of cigarettes in her apron pocket and heading for the back door before Jessica could agree.

Near noon, Jessica learned that Sheriff Blackwater had held a press conference. According to the customers who had smart phones and Nell, who caught it on the office TV, he'd stood on the steps of the department and made a public statement. She'd been too busy to watch the report, but from what she could gather from the customers who'd caught the news, the acting sheriff's speech had been short and concise without any room for questions. The sheriff's department wasn't giving out much information other than that the woman's death was being investigated as a homicide. Her name wasn't being released, pending notification of next of kin.

Jessica went cold inside.

Another woman fished out of a body of water.

Talk of mutilation.

Has he followed me?

She nearly dropped a tray of drinks, she was so distracted.

Quicksilver memories slid through her brain—seeing him for the first time at her parents' home near the river, the smell of magnolia in the air, spring air clear, the cloudless sky a cerulean blue, the murmur of guests as they'd wandered the grounds. His gaze had found hers and she'd sensed then that he was a rogue, a handsome man whose civility was probably only skin deep, that there was more to him to explore.

He'd wooed her easily, his laughter infectious, his kisses promising so much more, his hands on her body exciting and a little rough, but she'd wanted something that would crack the veneer of her family's genteel and oh, so fake civility.

The summer had swept by in dark moonlight nights, hours of pent-up passion, and quick decisions that, in hindsight, had proved deadly—a wedding on the broad lawn under a hot August sun. Sultry air and thick clouds, a storm brewing that had been, as she looked upon it now, a warning she hadn't heeded.

"Jessica?" Misty's harsh voice broke into her reverie. "I think table seven might want those." She nodded her head at the tray of burgers Jessica had been holding, the one that shook in her trembling hands. "Hey, you all right?"

"Fine," she said, swiftly returning to the harsh lights and noisy din of the diner. She didn't bother to explain. Couldn't. She just set about her work, listening hard to the bits of conversation that buzzed through the diner and telling herself that she couldn't take a chance any longer. Whether the woman who had been found under the falls was the victim of his cruelty or not, it was time to take action.

CHAPTER 16

Pescoli eyed her ring, the diamond glittering brightly under the failing fluorescent tubes humming above Blackwater's head in the meeting room attached to his office. Blackwater was presiding over a hastily convened gathering and she'd taken her usual chair, the spot where she'd sat so many times while Grayson had spoken to them. A small group had been called in for a briefing and discussion of the case uppermost on the minds of the citizens of Grizzly Falls. The windowless room felt close.

"Okay, looks like we've got ourselves a serial killer," Blackwater said, standing at the head of the long cafeteria-style table where everyone else was seated.

"Another one," Brett Gage interjected. As the chief criminal detective, he oversaw all cases, and, like Dan Grayson who had been his boss, he gave those under him free rein. At forty, he was only slightly older than Pescoli. A runner who was in great shape, a father of two who had completed four or five marathons—maybe more than that.

"Yes, another one." Blackwater nodded curtly. "And that's not making the mayor very happy. She called this morning and reminded me of the fact that our little corner of the state seems to be a hotbed for homicide. I couldn't argue. She's worried about a mass exodus of citizens and I don't blame her. When we actually confirm that these two victims were killed here in Grizzly Falls by the same person, all hell will break out."

"Again," Gage said, and Blackwater sent him a quick, hard look. Everyone in the department knew that Gage was angling for the vacant under-sheriff job and, apparently, he was determined to make his mark at this meeting. Politics. In the middle of a homicide investigation.

"Right, again. My point." Blackwater wasn't backing down. "So, it's early, I know, but what have we got?"

Alvarez, seated next to Pescoli, said, "We're a little ahead of the game on this one. We know the victim died last night. Sometime between ten and two is the best guess, taking into account the temperature of the water. This makes sense as so far, no one saw or heard anything."

"In the middle of town? Before the bars closed?" Blackwater asked.

"I said, 'so far,' " Alvarez repeated. "Deputies are still checking with the establishments open last night. We also think we might have an ID. There were several cars left down by the waterfront, but one, a late model Mercedes, has Washington plates and is the only vehicle not registered to a local. We checked with Washington DMV. The car is registered to a Calypso April Pope."

"Seriously?" Pete Watershed said, chewing his Nicorette gum with a vengeance. He was the only deputy in the room, called in for some reason only Blackwater understood. "Calypso? Who would name a kid that? Calypso April Pope? Jesus!"

Pescoli shot him an *oh-just-shut-up* look which he ignored.

Alvarez barely missed a beat. "That's the name on her license and the picture looks like our victim."

"Calypso danced her last dance," Watershed said.

Blackwater glared, reminding him, "You're here by invitation. And next time?" His face was set in disapproval, his irritation palpable. "Lose the gum."

Watershed's jaw quit moving and he swallowed hard, his chosen way to dispose of the gum, as Blackwater explained, "Deputy Watershed thought he saw the victim's car earlier, pushing the speed limit around ten last night, but he'd already pulled someone else over for DUI, so . . ."

That cleared up the reason for Watershed's appearance. It wasn't a major connection, but something. Still the deputy, handsome and always thinking he was God's gift to women, bugged Pescoli. She'd been on the butt end of his jokes one too many times.

Alvarez said, "We're trying to find out more about Ms. Pope. So far, no missing persons report has been filed. We're attempting to find any connection between victim one and victim two, assuming they were both killed by the same person."

The meeting went on with plans to call in the Washington State Patrol and, of course, inform the FBI, as it appeared as if they had a serial killer on their hands. There was discussion about procedure and autopsy reports and other details of the crime before the short meeting was adjourned with Blackwater saying, "Let's find this guy. If we can do it without the feds, all the better." Before anyone could protest, he held up a hand. "Hey, if we need them, yeah, work with them. They have access to manpower, equipment, you name it. The important thing is to get our man." With that he scraped his chair back and everyone filed out of the room.

Pescoli was two steps down the hallway when Watershed caught up with her. "So, are congratulations in order?"

"What?" she looked up sharply, her mind zeroing in on her pregnancy.

"Noticed the ring," he said, nodding to it.

She braced herself. Watershed and his ilk were the reasons she'd taken the ring off for a while.

"You gettin' married again?" he asked.

"Yeah."

"To Santana? Jesus, Pescoli, don't you ever learn? A cop, a trucker, and now what? Some goddamn horse whisperer dude? You know, your track record is—"

"My business. Keep your nose out of it and shove it up your ass where it feels at home," she snapped.

"Wow. Touchy."

"Yeah, I am, so maybe you should back off a bit. It's legal for me to carry a firearm, remember."

"Someone's having a bad day. That time of the month?"

If you only knew, she thought angrily. Why did stupid guys always go *there*? She jabbed a finger at his chest. "If you haven't noticed, dickhead, things aren't all that great around here. Not only have we lost one of the best lawmen in the history of the state, but since he's been gone, two women have been killed and we've probably got a brand new sicko running around. Keep your adolescent remarks to yourself and stay out of my way."

"Sheeeit," he said as Joelle came clipping down the hallway, her eyebrows raised over the tops of her reading glasses at the exchange.

"Children, children, children," she chided.

Pescoli growled under her breath, stormed into her office, and started to slam the door, but Alvarez caught it, holding it open. "Why do you let him get to you?" she asked. "He's just a loser who loves baiting women. Don't go there."

"I usually don't."

"Stress of getting married again? Because this stuff"—Alvarez motioned to the piles of paperwork on the desk—"is always here, at some level."

"I guess it is the idea of walking down the aisle again," Pescoli lied. "But Watershed's right, damn it. I'm not all that great at picking husbands." She dropped into her desk chair. "But I'm right, too. It's none of his damn business what I do."

"Amen."

"What a tool." She scowled at the door, then determined she was going to shake it off. "Let's get to work."

Rather than drive all the way home, Jessica peeled off her work clothes in the small bathroom at the Midway Diner after her shift ended at two. She wasn't due back to work until four-thirty, for the early-bird dinner crowd, so she decided to make good on her vow to become proactive.

After changing into jeans and a sweater, then replacing her work shoes with boots, she found her jacket, threw it on, and made her way to her SUV where frost had collected on the windshield. The sun was actually out, beams glistening on the snow, the sky a clear, Montana blue, the day so bright she had to slip a pair of sunglasses onto the bridge of her nose. If circumstances had been different, she might have felt lighthearted; as it was, a deep sense of dread clung to her.

She made one stop at the cleaners located in a strip mall on the outskirts of town. A smiling girl in braces worked behind the counter. After counting and gathering up Jessica's uniforms, she promised to have them ready the next day. "No problem."

Jessica left and slid behind the wheel of her Tahoe again, steeling herself. Facing Cade wouldn't be easy, but lately, what had been?

"Nothing," she whispered as she waited for a slow stream of traffic, four cars behind an older Cadillac that inched through the streets, as if it were rolling through glue.

Finally, she was able to turn down a side street before making her way to the county road leading out of town. Now that she had made her decision to face Cade again, she pushed the speed limit, afraid she might chicken out.

It wasn't all that hard to locate the Grayson ranch. Nearly everyone who had come into the diner had talked about the sheriff's death and how hard it was on a family that had been in the area for generations. Misty, always a fountain of gossip and information, had told her where the Grayson spread was located and Jessica had double-checked on the Internet and the white pages.

As the sunlight bounced off snow-covered fields, she followed the directions on her GPS to the address where an old mailbox confirmed that she'd found the Grayson homestead.

"Here goes nothing," she whispered as she cranked on the wheel and eased her SUV along the long lane that had, at one point, been cleared of snow, piles of the white stuff lining the drive, tracks visible in a newly-fallen layer. Jessica's heart was thudding, her stomach in knots as she considered how Cade would react to seeing her as they hadn't parted on the best of terms. "Too bad," she reminded herself.

Wide fields flanked the lane as it rose to the heart of the ranch where a sprawling ranch house had a three hundred and sixty degree view of the surrounding property. Half a dozen outbuildings had sprouted around the residence, but Jessica zeroed in on a garage, the doors open, one bay empty, another filled with a pickup that was facing outward. Thankfully, Big Zed was gone, or at least his truck was. She needed to talk to Cade alone.

"Now or never," she said, eyeing the rearview mirror and catching the reflection of her oversized shades in the glass as she parked near a path winding to the front door. She cut the engine in a parking area where the snow had been mashed by various vehicles and pocketed her keys.

She hiked her way toward the three front steps that had been cleared of snow, and climbed them to a broad porch where a dying wreath was mounted upon a massive door.

She rapped loudly. Three sharp knocks. From inside, a dog began barking wildly as if his sudden rash of loud woofs made up for the fact that he'd been asleep at the switch, not hearing that a stranger had arrived.

"Shad. Enough!" a male voice, Cade's voice, ordered.

Jessica's heart fluttered. *Oh, dear God, what am I doing?*

The door opened suddenly and Cade, in faded jeans and a flannel shirt that he used as a jacket over a black T-shirt, stood on the other side. He was unshaven and his hair was rumpled, uncombed. He had that outdoorsy *I-don't-give-a-damn* look that she'd always found far too sexy, but she ignored it. Whatever they'd once had, that white-hot spark of years ago, had been extinguished by lies. Her lies.

"Yes?" he said.

A speckled hound, his gait uneven, rushed out. Rather than snarl and growl, it wiggled and wormed around her feet, begging to be petted as he balanced himself on three legs.

"Hello, Cade," she said and saw his eyes darken for a second before she leaned down and gave the dog a couple pats on the head. To the animal, she said, "I'm guessing you're Shad."

"You know me?" Cade asked.

"Yeah, I do." Straightening, she pulled her sunglasses from her face.

"You sure? Oh. Jesus! Wait a second." Cade's face hardened. "You look like—"

"I know." She yanked out her dental appliance, the one that changed the shape of her teeth, and the other that plumped her cheeks. As he stared, she next removed her wig, letting down her hair.

"For the love of Christ." His eyebrows slammed together. "Anne-Marie?"

"In the flesh." She patted her stomach. "Well, more than just flesh. I'm wearing a little extra, you know, to complete the look."

"Holy shit." Dumbstruck, he filled the doorway, a tall, rangy man who was glaring at her as if she were Satan incarnate.

"Can I come in?"

He hesitated.

"It's important, Cade. You know it is. Otherwise, I wouldn't be here."

His jaw slid to the side and his gaze narrowed suspiciously. "Okay," he finally agreed, stepping back and swinging the door wide. "But what the hell's going on? What's with the getup?" The dog streaked back into the house and before she could follow, he said, "Wait. Don't tell me. You're in a little bit of trouble again."

"More than a little," she admitted as he closed the door behind

her and she remembered all too vividly what it felt like to kiss this
love 'em and leave 'em cowboy. "This time, Cade," she admitted, "it's
a matter of life and death."

"You can talk to Teri, she's the waitress who served her," Sandi,
the owner of Wild Wills said when Pescoli and Alvarez showed up at
the restaurant.

One of the deputies who had helped canvas the area had shown
Calypso Pope's picture to Sandi and she'd remembered one of her
last customers from the night before. The detectives were following
up, trying to figure out anything they could about the victim.

"I know she's dead, and I'm sorry, but let me tell you, that
woman," Sandi said, standing at the hostess podium, "was a real pain
in the butt. Came in late, almost closing, and didn't like Grizz." She
pointed to the mascot of the establishment, the huge stuffed grizzly
bear that, with the changing holidays, was dressed in appropriate or
not-so-appropriate attire, depending on how one viewed it.

Pescoli had seen Grizz wearing an angel costume for Christmas, a
red, white, and blue Uncle Sam outfit for Independence Day, and a
Pilgrim hat and collar for Thanksgiving. At his place of honor in the
vestibule, Grizz currently was dressed as Cupid in honor of Valentine's Day, his snarl at odds with the cute little sparkling wings
strapped to his broad, shaggy back.

"Odd to think she didn't see the humor," she said.

"A real sourpuss. Tried to go all organic and vegan, which is fine,
but not here. This is Grizzly Falls, Montana, and it's wild out here."
Sandi, a known animal lover who had three rescue dogs and two cats
at last count, was clearly deeply irked. "It's not as if I killed all these
animals, for God's sake. They came with the place when you-know-
who and I originally bought it." You-know-who was Sandi's ex-husband;
he who could not be named, apparently. They'd been through a bitter
divorce and Sandi had ended up with the restaurant, only to make it
thrive under her management. "She ended up with her nose in her
iPhone—a lot of that going around these days—and ordered just pie
and coffee, and left a miserable tip."

Pescoli asked, "Was she with anyone?"

"Nope. Alone. I saw, you know, 'cause I'm always close. As far as I
could tell, she didn't speak to anyone."

"We'd like to talk with Teri. Is she here?"

"Just came on an hour ago. You can use the office if you want some privacy."

Sandi led them into a crowded office with a desk and one chair, files piled to the high ceiling. She cleared off a stack of invoices and then found Teri. Wary, it turned out she was unable to tell them any more than Sandi had. Calypso Pope had arrived close to eleven and left at eleven thirty-two, according to the credit card receipt she'd signed.

"Lousy tipper," the waitress grumbled, almost as if getting killed served Calypso Pope right for being so cheap. Then she heard herself and straightened as if caught in some nefarious act. "Not that I would wish anyone dead."

"Was she wearing a ring?" Pescoli asked.

"Oh, yeah, one with *major* diamonds. But no wedding band. Just like an engagement ring."

"You noticed there wasn't a second ring?" Alvarez asked.

"Oh, yeah." Teri's head was bopping up and down. "I pay attention. Me and my boyfriend, we've been looking at rings 'cause we're coming up on our one year anniversary, and I think it's time."

"How old are you?" Pescoli asked.

"Nineteen."

"Give it a year or two," she said and saw the girl's eyes cloud. "Sorry. None of my business. Anything else you can tell us about the woman?"

"Other than that she was in a real bad mood? I don't know if that's her normal personality or not, but if it is, she really needs an attitude adjustment. That's what my dad always tells my mom when she's in one of her bitch moods. Oops." She placed her fingers over her lips. "Sorry. That just slipped out."

"No problem," Pescoli said, thinking of the language she'd heard from her own kids.

They ran some more questions but didn't learn anything more as no one else in the place had been on duty or remembered the one customer.

As they walked back to the Jeep, Alvarez found her sunglasses and slipped them on. "We're already waiting for the security cameras from the buildings along the river. Maybe we'll catch a break and one of them will show something."

"Or the Spokane PD will find something in her home," Pescoli thought aloud as they knew the victim's address, but she wasn't holding her breath. So far, they knew little about the woman other than where she lived. They'd found no connection between the two victims, other than they'd both been killed and had their ring fingers, complete with diamond rings, sliced off their left hands.

"This guy got a thing against engagement?" Alvarez thought aloud as they crossed the street and got into Pescoli's rig.

"Or marriage. But that's half the male population."

"And then there's the missing fingers."

"What the hell do you think he does with those?" Pescoli asked.

"Hmmm . . ." Alvarez shook her head in disgust. As they reached the base of Boxer Buff her cell phone went off. "Alvarez," she answered. "Yeah . . . where? You're sure?"

Pescoli glanced over at her partner.

Yeah . . . okay. We'll be right there." Alvarez hung up and said, "We got lucky."

"What?"

"Calypso Pope's purse. Found by a teenager on the rocks near the falls. All her ID intact. Credit cards, too, or so it seems on first inspection. No cash. Anyway, he turned it in at the station. It's at the lab already and they're processing it, checking for trace evidence, fingerprints."

"Needle in a haystack."

"Maybe, but it's something."

"Yeah."

"Lars Bender, the kid who found it, claims there wasn't a dime in it," Alvarez said. "He's already asking about a reward."

"Figures." Pescoli cranked on the wheel and turned up the hill behind a tow truck with a crumpled mid-sized sedan on its bed. "You never go wrong being disappointed in human nature."

With his gaze on the GPS monitor, Ryder followed the woman he was certain was Anne-Marie Calderone. He drove a mile or two behind her outside of town, past a smattering of houses on the fringe of Grizzly Falls, and into the rolling hills of farmland. The road was getting chewed up from traffic, but the pastures that spread beyond the fences were still covered in a white, pristine mantle, sunlight bouncing off the icy crystals of snow so that he was forced to squint and finally find an old pair of sunglasses he kept in the glove box.

Slipping on the polarized lenses, he kept driving, meeting a few other vehicles, checking his mileage and finally guessing where she was heading. Sure enough, he passed a long driveway and saw from the small monitor's screen that she'd turned into the lane. No surprise the oversized mailbox had the name GRAYSON written across it.

Some things never change.

He told himself it didn't matter, but he couldn't help wondering why she'd decided to go to Cade Grayson. Was he the real reason she'd taken this winding path from Louisiana to Montana? The end piece of her game? Ryder drove past the place and turned around about a mile up the road. Then he waited, wondering what she was doing, thinking that after meeting with Grayson she might take off again.

He'd have some time, though. She hadn't packed up.

Yet.

He'd been watching, feeling every bit the voyeur as he'd sat in his dive of a motel room, sipping beer and staring at the monitor of one of his laptops, the one that had been hooked up as a receiver to the wireless transmitter he'd left on her property. The second one he used for research and communication.

He'd nearly collected enough evidence, and after today, it would be time to execute phase two of his plan.

His lips twisted a little at that thought.

Seeing Anne-Marie face-to-face for the first time in months would give him a small degree of satisfaction. But then telling her what he was going to do with her, that was going to be difficult because like it or not, he still felt a connection to her, that same old attraction that hadn't quite let go, despite everything.

She deserves what she's getting he told himself. *It's only right that it comes at my hand. This will all be over soon.* He took heart that once the job was finished, he could forget about Anne-Marie Calderone forever.

Never in a million years would Cade have expected Anne-Marie to be standing on his doorstep, on the ranch in Montana. "A long way from New Orleans," he said, rubbing his chin and eyeing her from across the room. He'd offered her a seat in the living room that didn't get used much and was still filled with memorabilia and furniture from the days over a decade earlier when his mother had still been alive.

"I know. Cade, I'm sorry about your brother."

She appeared sincere, but he didn't trust his instincts around her. They'd always been off a bit. She'd come to his home in a disguise, and he couldn't read her eyes as they'd been darkened with contact lenses. She was still wearing some kind of padding. Her body didn't fit her head now that she'd removed whatever it was that had changed the contour of her cheeks and the look of her teeth. That she'd shown up out of the blue with no word for years, her beauty intently played down, wasn't a good sign.

"I doubt you came all the way up here to give me your condolences."

"No," she admitted, clearly nervous. She glanced away for a second, and he wondered if she was concocting her story, trying to think of a way to make it plausible. "That's not why I'm here."

"You said it was life or death."

"I think so, yes." Though she was nodding as she balanced on the edge of the dusty couch, she didn't seem so sure of herself. It was as if she were suddenly second-guessing her arrival on his doorstep.

He decided that was just desserts. He owed her nothing.

"Look, Cade," she said, one hand nervously plucking at a bit of fabric on the couch. "Years ago, you said if I was ever in trouble . . . you know, with the law, that I could count on your brother, that . . . he would help."

"You came up here to talk with Dan?"

"Yes," she admitted weakly, "and then, well, I heard that he'd passed."

"Killed," Cade corrected. "He was murdered in cold blood. A bastard he knew and trusted laid in wait and pulled the goddamn trigger. That's what happened."

"I'm sorry."

"So you said." He closed his eyes for a second and tried like hell to tamp down the rage that overtook him every time he thought of his brother's death. That the son of a bitch who'd taken Dan's life was still alive pissed him off. Forcing his eyes open, he stared at her and asked, "What is it?"

"I think," she started as if unsure of herself, "he's followed me here. I think he might be behind the attacks on the other women who were killed. I don't know, but . . ." She let out her breath slowly.

"Who?" he asked, but he felt it, that chill of premonition that warned him that bad news was coming his way.

"My husband," she whispered softly. "I think he followed me here."

CHAPTER 17

"Your husband?" Cade repeated, his expression guarded, suspicion visible in his eyes as Shad settled into a dog bed near the fireplace.

Too late, Jessica realized she'd made a big mistake in going there, in hoping he might be able to help her. But she was in too deep to backtrack. "I've been hiding from him."

"Here? In Grizzly Falls?"

"Yes. That's why I'm dressed like this." She made a sweeping gesture to include her whole body. "When I drove here, I didn't know about Dan, about what had happened to him. I was just desperate. You'd said once that if I were ever in serious trouble that your brother was someone I could trust, a fair officer of the law. And I thought, hoped, that I could explain to him what happened and . . . and that he would believe me and trust me and help me."

"You think your husband is out to kill you?" Cade asked dubiously.

"I know he is," she said, shivering inwardly. "He tried once, thought he'd gotten rid of me, but I managed to survive. And now he has to make sure."

He regarded her suspiciously. "You have family."

"Who have disowned me."

"And why is that?"

She didn't answer. Didn't have to. They both knew why. "Look, Cade, even if I contacted them and told them my story, they wouldn't believe me. Because . . . because . . ."

"Because you've cried wolf one too many times."

"Essentially." She was nodding. "Yeah, that's about it."

"Let's just tell it like it is. You're a liar, Anne-Marie. You lied to your family, you lied to me, hell, you probably lied to your damn husband. Christ, I *know* you did. So now you're on the run and you wind up here and you expect me . . . *me* . . . to believe you and do what? Take you in? Hide you out from some *imagined* threat? Start something up again."

"No!"

Obviously, he wasn't buying it. "Jesus H. Christ. You're unbelievable. And you can take that literally."

"I'm telling you the truth."

"That's the trouble with compulsive liars; they start believing their own shit."

"Cade. Trust me, I'm not—"

"Trust you?" he threw back at her. "That's a laugh. You expect *me* to trust *you.*" He was angry, his jaw hard, but it wasn't the raw, passionate fury she'd witnessed in him before. No, this was cold and deep, the kind of wrath that has had time to burrow and fester. It was obvious he wasn't buying her desperate pleas and she knew that he had good reason.

"I made a mistake coming here."

"You got that right," he said, his glare cutting through her. "I don't know what you're involved in and I don't care. If you seriously believe someone is out to kill you, whether it's your husband or someone else, then you need to go to the police. Immediately. No matter how wild a tale you spin, they'll look into it."

"I'd planned to, but then—"

"I know. Dan died. Jesus, don't you know I'm painfully aware of that fact," he said.

She shrank back. "I didn't mean—"

He waved off her apology. "Whatever it is you think you're involved in, it has nothing to do with me." A muscle worked in his jaw as if he were trying and failing to rein in his anger. "Just go down to the station and tell your tale. They'll ask you some questions and that'll be it. Maybe they can sort out what's real and what's all in your head."

"I'm not making this up." She was on her feet. "You think I drove all the way from New Orleans to seek you out because of some convoluted, sick fantasy? Have you noticed women are being *killed*?"

"I don't really see how they're connected to you. Did you know them? The first girl's been IDed, some woman from Utah, I think, and the second one"—he shrugged—"I haven't heard."

"You're the only person I knew in Grizzly Falls before I came here. But I think he followed me somehow."

"As I said, tell it to the police. I don't know the new sheriff or much about him, but someone thought he was fit for the job, so go and tell him your tale."

"I don't think that's a good idea," Anne-Marie said.

"Why not?"

She remembered the acting sheriff, how when she'd spilled coffee on him, he'd turned his attention on her like a laser.

"If you're serious about this. If you really think that you being here in Montana has cost two women their lives, you have to go to the police. It's your moral obligation."

She felt her back go up. "Moral obligation? You're a fine one to lecture me on morals."

"I wasn't the one who was married," he said.

She saw in his eyes that he was daring her to tread farther, into dangerous emotional territory which, she knew, would be unwise. "Okay. I get it," she said, deciding it was time to leave just as she heard the muted rumble of an engine. Shad was on his three feet in an instant, howling and barking and running into the kitchen.

She glanced through the window and saw a massive pickup had pulled into the empty bay of the garage. Zed's truck. Her heart sank as she watched the Grayson brother climb out of his king cab.

"I should leave," she said, reaching up to twist and pin her hair onto her head. Quickly she donned her wig again, uncaring that it wasn't on perfectly. Then, she slid her sunglasses onto the bridge of her nose. She started for the front door but looked over her shoulder. "I know it's a lot to ask. And God knows you don't owe me any favors, but please . . . don't give me away until I talk to the police."

"You're going there?"

"I will . . . just not right now." She drew in a long breath.

"When?" he asked as she noticed Big Zed squinting at her car as he walked toward the back of the house.

"This week."

"And if you don't?"

"You won't have to worry about me. I'll be gone and . . . and he'll follow."

"To kill again," he said, lifting an eyebrow. "That's what you're trying to get me to believe."

She let out a nearly inaudible sigh and opened the door. "Believe whatever you want, Cade." She heard another door open and didn't wait any longer. She didn't want to explain herself to Zed or anyone else, yet.

She followed her earlier tracks across the front yard to her car and wondered if Cade were watching her or if Zed was asking questions. Well, so be it.

She should never have shown her hand, never have driven there and tried to drag Cade into it.

Her hopes for help from anyone named Grayson had died with the sheriff.

It was time to come up with Plan B.

"Who was that?" Zed asked as he walked into the house and found Cade staring out the living room window.

"No one."

"Like hell."

"Okay. Someone I knew a long time ago." He watched Anne-Marie drive off and thought, *Good riddance.* It surprised him that she'd tracked him down, but it didn't surprise him that she'd shown up with some wild-ass story. She'd always been slightly off, one wheel not quite on the track. Yes, she'd been his lover and he still remembered how passionate she was in the bedroom, but he also recalled what a crazy and bona fide liar she was. The kind of woman best left alone. He didn't know why she was in Grizzly Falls, but if it was to start something up again, he'd shut her down. Fast. It was over, and for the first time in his life, he wasn't interested. He was with Hattie and had her daughters to consider. He'd be a fool to risk losing his family, and he wasn't about to do it with Anne-Marie Calderone.

"A woman." There was a sneer in Zed's voice.

Cade turned and faced his older brother. "Yep."

"Women are always getting you into trouble."

That much was true. Sex had always been Cade's downfall. He liked women. All women. Lots of women. And he'd never been one to shy away from danger, especially if it involved a slightly over the top woman, the operative word being *slightly*. At least that's how he'd reacted until recently, but Anne-Marie had been trouble from the get-go. He'd wondered then, as he wondered now, if she was missing a few vital screws. She'd always been attractive and sexy, but mentally a little unbalanced. And there was the lying thing; he hadn't been kidding when he'd called her compulsive. It was as if she just couldn't stop.

"She's just a friend."

"No such thing. Not with you."

"Believe me," Cade said.

"So how do you know that waitress from the diner?" Zed asked. To Cade's look, he said, "That's who it was. I saw her there."

For a reason Cade couldn't name, he felt suddenly protective of a woman he'd sworn to abhor. "Long story. Long time ago. Long over."

Zed's eyes thinned and he took a look out the window, but Anne-Marie's car had disappeared. "Okay," he said as if he didn't quite believe Cade, but was willing to move on. "I was just at the funeral home. Everything's a go for the service."

Cade grunted. He didn't want to think about Anne-Marie, true enough, but he also didn't want to dwell on the fact that the brother he'd looked up to was gone. "Can you handle the night's feeding?" he asked Zed.

"S'pose. Where you goin'?"

"Into town to have dinner with Hattie and the girls." The darkness in his soul dissolved a little when he thought of Mallory and McKenzie, the twins he'd recently found out were not sired by his brother Bart, but by Cade himself. Had it changed how he felt about them? Not much. Since Bart's death he'd thought of the girls as his, anyway. The new biological information had been a shock, but not an unpleasant one. Truth be known, it was a possibility he'd considered a couple times but had tossed aside while his brother had been alive.

"Hattie." Zed snorted again. "She's no good, y'know. I don't know what your deal is, or was, with the waitress from the diner, but it sure as hell has to be a lot less complicated than the thing you've got going with Bart's wife."

"Ex-wife."

"Or maybe even an excuse. The reason she was his ex might well be because of you."

Every muscle in Cade's body clenched. He was super-sensitive in that area. Hell, maybe they both were. "Let's not go there, Zed. We've already lost two brothers. Now it's just you and me."

"And Hattie."

And your whores, the one-night stands that don't encumber you. "And Hattie," Cade said, thinking of the woman he loved. Theirs was a complicated relationship and always had been.

"So why the fuck don't you just up and marry her? That's where this is all heading, isn't it? To make it legal? That little thing you had going with your brother's wife."

Cade grabbed a piece of Zed's work shirt in his fist and yanked. "I never touched Hattie while she was married and you know it."

"I don't know a damn thing," Zed said, his eyes blazing, his lips barely moving.

"That's the first thing you said that's right."

Zed punched him. Hard. In the ribs.

"Jesus!" Cade's fingers released and he fell backward, barely catching himself.

Zed, his face red, warned, "Don't you ever put your hands on me again."

"Then stop all this shit-talking about Hattie, you got that? She's the mother of my kids."

"That's the goddamn problem," Zed growled. His hands balled into fists and he looked as if he were about to launch at Cade as they had when they were young bucks, always fighting. Kicking, punching, knocking holes in the walls, the four boys had all possessed hot tempers and become the hellions of town, much to their mother's dismay. Though they'd grown out of their testosterone-charged teen years, that sibling rivalry always simmered just beneath the surface. They'd fight like hell for each other in public, then turn brother against brother when they were home, either fueled by alcohol or spurred by jealousy over a woman.

"You don't want to take me on, Zed," Cade warned.

"Don't I?"

"You're bigger, but I'm smarter."

"Fuck you!" Zed lunged and Cade rolled deftly away as the big man landed face-first into their mother's couch in the very spot Anne-Marie had so recently vacated. The sofa skidded into the wall with the window, panes rattling, a lamp teetering on an end table, to fall and crash, its bulb shattering, the shade ripping. Shad, who had been on a nearby chair, let out a startled yip, then began barking and hopping around on his three legs.

"Told ya."

"You got lucky."

"Luck had nothing to do with it," Cade said but felt little satisfaction in the statement. Zed was a pain, yeah, but he was the only damn brother he had left. "Just be sure to feed the damn cattle and horses, would ya? And Shad, too."

As Zed struggled to his feet, Cade walked into the kitchen to the anteroom near the back door where his boots sat under a bench and his jacket hung on a peg. There was no use arguing with Zed when he was in one of his dark moods, which seemed to be all the time. Not that Cade could blame him much. Ever since a sniper had taken shots at Dan, Cade too had been tough to live with.

Gingerly, he shrugged into his jacket, his ribs aching. Jesus, were they cracked? That would be a helluva thing. The fights with Zed had been increasing lately though it was the first time they'd gotten physical.

Not a good sign.

Maybe it would be best for everyone concerned if he moved out, found a place, tried living with Hattie and the girls. It wouldn't be so bad. Hattie had admitted her mother, who'd been diagnosed with cancer, was losing that hard-fought battle. Hattie could use a little help with the girls. Yeah, that part would be more than all right. But, he wasn't ready for marriage yet. They had too many things to iron out, but there was a chance, someday in the not too distant future, he might be ready to finally settle down.

Then again, maybe not.

The darkness was complete.

Whichever way she looked, she saw no one, heard nothing. But he was here. She sensed his presence.

Creeaak!

A door opened and she whipped around, her gaze scouring the blackness. No shaft of light appeared. There was no indication from which direction the sound had come.

Think, Jessica, think. You know this place. You know him! You can escape.

She started moving, inching backward, afraid that at any second she might stumble and fall, and he would pounce on her.

Her throat was dry as dust in fear. The night, so black and cold, seemed to wrap around her, its talons piercing her skin, an icy fear infusing her blood.

There was no way out. No walls, no windows, no doorway that she could sense. Backward, step by step, bracing herself for the inevitable—

Bam!

The gun went off though no flash of light burst from its muzzle. Anne-Marie stumbled backward, farther into the darkness.

Bang! Another hit! She felt no pain, but when she clutched her stomach, then lifted her hand, she saw the blood. Dark red stains running down her palm.

Why? she mouthed, staring at her attacker. *Why?*

"Because you deserve it," he sneered, his voice deep and accusing. "Because of what you did."

"I'm sorry!" she cried, staring into the void.

"I loved you, Stacey. That's what you go by now, isn't it? Stacey Donahue."

"Y-yes, I'm Stacey," she admitted, though that didn't sound right. *No, wait!* "You've got the wrong person," she said desperately. "I'm Jessica. Jessica Williams. Yes, Jessica Williams!"

"Are you?" he said, toying with her. "Last I heard you were Stacey Donahue."

"No! You're wrong."

"While you were in Colorado," he reminded her. "Denver."

She was confused, still stumbling backward, her skin crawling as she felt him getting closer. "I'm . . . I'm from Louisiana," she said, then realized her mistake. "I mean Nebraska!" Oh, God was that right? She couldn't remember.

"Anne-Marie is from New Orleans." His voice was cold. Empty. And he was getting closer. Squinting, she tried to see him, even just a glimmer of his shadow, or the glow of his eyes, or *any*thing, but she saw nothing but blackness.

"I'm Jessica. Jessica Williams. I live in Montana. Yes. That's right. I'm Jessica and I live in Montana—"

"Not for long."

Oh, God, he was going to kill her!

The bullet into her gut wasn't enough. And then she saw it. Rising silver in a slow arc, a knife with a glinting blade.

"No!"

Recoiling, she stumbled and fell backward, tumbling and flailing. Trying to get her grip, she descended into the darkness. Downward, farther and farther until she splashed into the water, piercing the surface of a slow moving river. The water covered her and she began kicking, trying to swim to the surface, but the harder she struggled, the farther down she slid, the water sucking her into a slow-turning but deadly whirlpool. Downward she spun, trying to scream, to breathe, as the vicious eddy funneled far from the surface. In the darkness, she spied a plume, blood red and swirling around her, enveloping. Thrashing, she tried to breathe, couldn't suck in any air, gasped wildly. Desperately she fought.

Bang!

She shot upward, throwing off her pillow and sitting straight up in bed. Her tiny pistol tumbled to the floor and landed with a sharp thud. For a second, she didn't know where she was, couldn't find her bearings. Her heart was drumming and she was breathing hard from the feeling of suffocation, her own damn pillow having covered her face.

Oh, Lord. She dropped her face into her hands and tried to cast off the dream, the fear, the feeling of desperation.

It had been so real. No, so surreal, but she was still cold, the flesh on her arms rising in tiny goose pimples despite her sweatshirt. She pulled the sleeping bag over her shoulders for warmth.

Bang!

She nearly shrieked, scrambled on the floor for her gun, then realized the noise was the wind buffeting the cabin, its gusts causing something, probably a tree limb, to pound against the roof. In her dream, the rush of the wind whistling down the chimney had been the sound of the river and the thud of that branch had become the report of a gun, nothing more.

She let out her breath slowly, then threw off the covers and walked to the window where she peered outside to the darkness beyond.

Is this how you want to live the rest of your life?

Alone?

Isolated?

In fear?

Always looking over your shoulder?

Forever thinking you're being chased?

Almost believing that others are harmed because of your damn sins?

"No," she said aloud, squinting through the dirty glass. Outside, the snow-laden branches were moving with the stiff breeze, the whiteness of the ground in stark contrast to the black, unforgiving sky.

It had to end.

She could no longer live in fear.

With a shiver, she remembered the fights, the shattered dishes, the balled fists, the pain she'd endured far too long. Trusting that he would be able to control his temper, that he loved her, that he truly was sorry after each of their fights, she'd stayed with him, never reporting what had happened. Because of the shame. Because she'd stupidly believed that no one would believe her. Who would take *her* word—a spoiled woman who had her own emotional issues—against a man well regarded in the community, a smooth talker and outwardly, a do-gooder whose rage few had witnessed? Outwardly cool and in control, his demeanor had changed behind closed doors, just little things at first and then . . . oh, God, and then . . .

If I could only go home, she thought for the millionth time.

But she'd burned those bridges long ago. For all intents and purposes, she was dead to Talbert and Jeanette Favier, all because of *him*.

Well, not entirely, her wayward mind reminded her. *You carry your own burden here. You are far from blameless. Cade Grayson is proof enough of that. And he's not the only one. Some of your heartache and your fear can be placed on your own damn shoulders.*

With no one to turn to and no one to trust, she'd run.

Away from her home. Away from wealth. Away from privilege.

Her family didn't believe her then; they wouldn't now.

She was painfully aware of that horrid little fact.

Nonetheless, the running, which had seemed her only option a few months back, had to stop.

"Tomorrow," she whispered. After her morning shift. Then she realized that it would be Friday come morning and she'd be working most of the day. No, she needed a clear head to come clean with the police.

Saturday was the funeral for Dan Grayson.

Sunday was another full day at work and she didn't want to try and track down the sheriff or the appropriate detective over the weekend.

Excuses, excuses, her mind chided and she wondered if she'd chicken out altogether. Cade's assessment of her hadn't been that far off. But he was right. If innocent women were dying because of her, then she had to go to the police.

If not, she still needed help in straightening out the whole mess. Just because the cops in New Orleans were dirty didn't mean the same held true in this little town. Most officers of the law were heroes and worked for the common good: To protect and serve. Just because Dan Grayson was no longer the sheriff didn't mean that the man who'd taken his place wouldn't be just as good, nor that he wouldn't uphold the law.

And therein lies the problem, yes? Because you are guilty, aren't you? It's not as if you're pure as the driven snow.

She felt that same sense of doom nip at her heels again, the one that had been chasing her since leaving Louisiana. God, she'd made a mess of things.

No matter what the consequences, she would try to face the music and right her wrongs, if possible.

On Monday.

Come hell or high water, she'd march into the Pinewood Sheriff's Department and tell her story.

If she didn't turn tail and run again. Crossing her fingers, she told herself she needed to do it. Before anyone else ended up dead.

CHAPTER 18

Alvarez stood and stretched, using her desk chair for support. She hadn't been to the gym for the better part of a week, nor had she had time for her usual daily run. That would have to change as all of her muscles were tight and her brain was clogged with dozens of questions about the murdered women. Fortunately, the other active cases had been closed.

Ralph Haskins had taken his life. He'd left a good-bye note blaming his mother for his depression and his wife for their bankruptcy. The position of his Magnum as it had fallen from his hand as he'd collapsed after putting a bullet in his brain, and the fact that gunshot residue was all over his hands, had made the case pretty cut and dried. End of story.

She raised an arm over her head and stretched as if she were reaching for the overhead light fixture. Then she did the same with her other arm before rotating her neck and finally, leaning over from her hips, allowing her arms to fall free.

The latest domestic abuse accusation in a long series had been dropped. Again. Jimbo Amstead's wife, Gail, had changed her mind for the fourth time in half as many years. Though the DA wanted to prosecute the bastard for "slapping the bitch around" as he'd told a friend, bragging after a few too many at the Black Horse Saloon, that good ol' boy refused to testify, said he'd probably been mistaken, heard wrong in the loud bar. Besides, he'd been drunk at the time. Since Gail Amstead refused to speak ill of her husband, even though she was recovering from her sixth black eye in three years, the DA was powerless to prosecute. Gail swore she'd been mistaken about the fight and had run into a door once again.

"You know how many times I've 'run into a door' in my lifetime?" Pescoli had asked Alvarez when they'd heard the decision. "Exactly zero." She'd slid her partner a look. "How about you?"

"The same."

"So in our combined seventy plus years, not one door and yet Gail, who's not quite fifty, has done it three times that she's reported. In the last couple years or so. Either she's a damn klutz, or lives in a house with attacking woodwork, or . . . she's a liar and lives with a bastard who beats the shit out of her. Take your pick."

Alvarez's mouth had been a thin line. She had so wanted to nail Jimbo to the wall. Big, with a swagger and yellowed teeth from too many years of chewing tobacco, the guy leered at every woman he passed, then beat the one woman who had agreed to be his wife.

Alvarez would have loved to see him wearing a prison suit for the rest of his life.

She finished stretching, checked her e-mail and concentrated on the most pressing case, that of the homicide victims who had been strangled, then mutilated. The autopsy on Calypso Pope had been given top priority, and damn if she hadn't died the same way Sheree Cantnor had. Strangled, then tossed into a body of water, though it seemed Sheree had been strangled somewhere else, probably snagged while walking home for lunch or dinner, and left in the creek that wound through the O'Halleran property. They had come up with no further evidence after the one shoe. Odd that. What had happened to the other?

She was about to walk to Pescoli's office when Joelle, clicking briskly down the hall, showed a middle-aged woman into the room. In one arm, the woman clutched her purse so close against her body it seemed as if she expected it to be snatched out of her arms right there in the station. The fingers of her other hand were curled around the upper arm of a pimply-faced boy of about fourteen. Grasping his arm so tightly as to crush the fabric of his ski jacket in her iron grip, she looked as if she could spit nails.

"Detective Alvarez?" Joelle said, silver crosses swinging from her earlobes. "This is Mrs. Bender and her son, Lars. They would like to speak to you if you have the time."

"Lars Bender?" Alvarez said, recognizing the name of the kid who'd located Calypso Pope's purse on the rocks below Grizzly Falls. As Joelle made her way out of the tight office, Alvarez asked the boy, "You found the purse belonging to Ms. Pope?"

Scrawny in his oversized jacket, the kid didn't meet her eyes but gave a short nod.

"Answer her. Where are your manners?" his mother asked impatiently. "I'm Elaine, by the way," she said extending her hand across the desk, then retrieving it quickly.

"Please, have a seat." Alvarez settled back into her chair as mother and son sat down across from her.

"Lars has something to tell you." The severity of Elaine's expression was matched by the harsh lines of her haircut, which probably was supposed to bring a youthful hipness to dull brown locks that were beginning to gray. Stick-straight, her hair was whacked sharply at the point of her chin. Straight cut bangs ended nearly an inch above round owlish glasses that only emphasized the sharp angles of a face that looked as if it was fixed in a perpetual state of being perturbed.

"What is it, Lars?" Alvarez asked.

"Go on. Tell her!" Elaine said as she dug into the prized purse and came out with a ziplock bag holding a cell phone.

"I found it," the boy said.

"Where?" the mother prodded, handing the bag over to Alvarez as if it might burn her fingers. "Where did you find it, Lars?"

"In the bag," the kid mumbled, looking down at his hands.

"The purse we turned in earlier, the one from that woman who was killed," Elaine explained in clipped words. "That's the bag he was talking about. I didn't find anything else, but he found it and went through it first and he kept that phone." She jabbed a long, accusing finger at the smart phone. "He was going to sell it or something. Lars is acting out, you know. Because his dad and I split up, like it was my fault." Lips pursed even further, she added, "Jeff, that's his father, had an affair. Wants to marry this . . . this *woman*. Met her in the church where he's a part-time youth minister. It's no wonder that Lars is on the wrong path."

She sent a pointed look to her son. "What kind of an example is that? A youth minister!" She let out a shaky breath and shivered, her severely chopped hair shaking in her rage. "I don't know if Lars took anything else. He says not. But he came up with a new video game this morning," She flung her son another condemning glare. "How'd you pay for that, huh?"

He shrugged.

"Answer me, Lars!"

"Money from Christmas!" he spat out. "From *Dad!* Geez."

Mrs. Bender rolled her eyes and looked across the desk to Alvarez as if silently saying, *Do you see what I have to deal with?*

Alvarez focused on the son. "Okay. Lars, why don't you tell me everything about finding the purse? Was there anything else in it or around it?"

"No." He caught a warning glance from his mother. "No."

"God hears everything," she reminded him. "He sees *every*thing."

Lars swallowed, his prominent Adam's apple bobbing nervously. "Okay, maybe there were a couple bucks inside." His head actually seemed to shrink into his neck.

"A couple?" his mother sneered. "How much is a couple?"

"I dunno. Sixty . . . maybe eighty."

"Oh my God!" His mother's hands fell onto her lap. To Alvarez, she said, "Can you believe it?" Before Alvarez could answer, Elaine turned on her son again. "So, what was it, Lars? How much did you steal? And from a dead woman!"

Lars's head snapped up. "I didn't know she was dead! Not then!"

She wasn't derailed. "So, was it sixty or eighty, or maybe a hundred?"

"Eighty," the kid answered quickly.

Alvarez suspected he'd shaved the amount and that Lars was smart enough to hide the extent of his theft, giving his mother a large enough amount to make it believable, but less than what he'd really pocketed.

"You'll have to tell your father and work off the debt. You'll pay the family back or if they don't want it, give it to the church, after you tell Preacher Miller what you've done. You can start by shoveling the snow off the walkway, which you should do for free anyway!" She folded her hands over the long skirt that covered her legs. "There are lots of projects Lars can tackle. We can't stay in the house, anyway. It's much too expensive now that I'm a single mother."

Before Mrs. Bender could launch into another diatribe about the sins of her ex, Alvarez cut her off. "Let me ask Lars a few questions," she suggested, then turned to the boy. "Tell me about finding the purse and this phone. Other than picking it up, did you touch it? Use it?"

He looked absolutely miserable. "Maybe."

"Answer her with the truth!" his mother almost screeched.

Alvarez held up a hand. "Please, Mrs. Bender."

The detective had a teenaged son who lived with his adoptive parents. Even though she'd just recently reconnected with Gabe, she understood that the boy was far from perfect and had already had a brush or two with the law. The same, it seemed, held true for Lars, but thoughtless teenaged stunts were not always a precursor to a life of crime.

"Let Lars speak."

The kid did. The fingers of one hand working over the fist of another, he answered her questions one by one. She found out that he'd swiped the phone and the cash out of the purse. He'd found nothing else inside or around the bag and seen nothing that would help. Yes, he'd made a call or two on the phone, tried to download an app, but was unable without Calypso Pope's user ID and password, and he'd gone on the Internet where he'd entered some chat rooms and surfed a bit.

By the time his mother had marshaled him out of the office, Alvarez had learned little, but since she knew the approximate time of death, and when the purse had presumably been lost, she would be able to figure out who was the last person Calypso called or texted.

Grabbing her jacket, she walked to Pescoli's office where she found her partner at her desk reading an old case file, the box on the floor open, the lid propped against the wall.

"What's that?"

"I told you about Hattie Grayson and her insistence that Bart's death wasn't a suicide."

Alvarez asked, "Don't you have enough to do?"

Pescoli snorted. "I should have never told Hattie I'd look into it, but I did, and now I can't just ignore the file or she'll be calling every day." She set the file on her messy desk.

How Pescoli could ever find anything on a work surface cluttered with notes, cups, pens, and papers Alvarez didn't understand.

"I imagine I'll run into Hattie at the funeral on Saturday, and she'll be asking me about Bart's suicide and make some ridiculous connection to Dan's murder. I thought I'd better read over the old reports, you know, get my ducks in a row." Pescoli rolled back her chair. "Anything new?"

Alvarez held up the cell phone in its plastic bag. "The kid who found it seems to have a little bit of larceny in his blood and his God-fearing mother is having nothing of it."

"Good thing," Pescoli said.

"Yeah, I'm glad to have the phone, but the mother—" Alvarez shook her head. "Let's just call Elaine Bender a piece of work and leave it at that." She brought her partner up to speed as Pescoli donned a pair of gloves and took out the phone.

She looked into the recent activity, the calls and texts and e-mail connections that had gone in and out, and said, "Looks like we'd better check out someone named Reggie."

Jessica's shift was over at nine that night. Dead tired, her lower back aching from hours on her feet, her brain was exhausted from the mental strain of a double-shift and not sleeping due to her wild dreams. She'd been dragging all day.

Misty had even seen fit to comment, "Not our usual Miss Merry Sunshine today, are we?"

Jessica had wanted to tell her to shove it, but had held her tongue.

She was tired, cranky, and hungry. She hadn't been able to choke down any of the leftovers that had been congealing on the counter for the better part of the evening. They'd consisted of an order of fries proclaimed "too salty" by a customer, and a wilted salad that had been topped by French dressing when the patron had insisted she'd said, "dressing on the side." As was the custom at the Midway Diner, orders that were returned to the kitchen weren't immediately thrown out, but left for the staff, should they be interested, before they were tossed into the trash.

"Waste not, want not," Nell had professed to them enough times that it had become a standing joke behind the boss's back. The trouble was that Marlon took Nell's suggestion to heart and somehow, in between clearing and resetting tables, washing dishes, and even swabbing the floors for spills, he was able to inhale anything that was placed in the return area of the counter. Hamburgers, chicken strips,

Diet Cokes that were supposed to have been the real thing and desserts that were just "too rich" or "not what I thought" or "really, I said coconut cream, not banana," somehow got gobbled up while he was on the job. So all that was left were the unappealing cold fries and wilted lettuce.

She didn't waste any time leaving and was glad Misty and Marlon were handling the few stragglers who might wander in. She just wanted to get home.

As if that cold, dark cabin could ever be considered anything close to what she would think of as her home.

Inside the Tahoe, she flipped on the engine and the wipers as desultory flakes of snow were drifting from the heavens. Her stomach rumbled and though it seemed ridiculous after working around food in a diner for most of the day, she decided to stop at the local pizza parlor that she'd spied earlier in the week.

Within ten minutes, she was pulling into a parking spot on the street one block away from Dino's Italian Pizzeria. She hurried inside and the sharp smells of tomato sauce and oregano hit her in a warm, welcoming wave. The crowd was thinning out, and it didn't take long to reach the counter and order a small pizza to go. As she waited, she sat at a table in the corner and watched people coming and going, attacked by more than one pang of desperation. Here were people, all involved in their personal lives—teenagers goofing around with friends, even blowing the papers off straws at each other; a frazzled mother trying to corral three stair-step toddlers all of whom made a beeline to the ice cream counter; other tweens playing video games in an arcade; a twentysomething couple who held hands as they decided on what kind of pizza to order. Everyday people. Ordinary lives. With the common stresses and worries of normal living.

No one running for his or her life.

No one concerned that a crazed husband was intent on killing her.

"Pizza to go for Williams," a teenager behind the counter called and she was out of her chair in an instant. She collected her order and carried the box outside. Snow was still threatening, a few solitary flakes drifting from the sky, catching in the lamplight. Cars rolled by on the quiet streets and she couldn't shake the feeling that someone was watching her.

Don't be a fool. No one's followed you.

But she kept up her pace and sensed her heartbeat beginning to increase, her pulse pounding. Last night's dream crawled through her brain in a frightening memory that she struggled to shake off.

The street was deserted, nothing to worry about, not a soul on the icy sidewalks, no car moving slowly along the snowy asphalt.

You're fine. Nothing to worry about.

A figure rounded the corner in front of her and she nearly jumped out of her skin.

But it was nothing, just a woman walking her dogs. Jessica let out her breath slowly and was about to step into the street when the woman called her name. "You're Jessica," she said in a voice that was cold as the night.

Jessica hesitated. The knife in her bra would be hard to reach because of her coat, and the pistol was tucked under the seat of the SUV. "Yes," she said. "Do I know you?"

"I've seen you," the woman said, advancing slowly in her long, white hooded coat. Her dogs were large and shaggy, their heads lowered, their gold eyes looking upward to hers. Though not on leashes, they kept pace with their mistress, noiselessly moving forward, staying close to her side. "You visited my dreams, Anne-Marie. You worry me."

"What did you say?" Jessica stopped. Aside from Cade, no one in this town knew her real name. "I'm sorry, you're mistaken."

"Am I?" The woman was so serene, almost ghostly.

Realization flashed. She must be Grace Perchant with her wolf-dogs and claims of talking with the dead.

"You're in danger." Still Grace approached.

"From whom? Or what?" Jessica asked, poised for flight. Where the hell were all the people? It wasn't *that* late. Why wasn't someone coming out of Dino's or the pub down the street?

The woman closed the distance between them. Under the lamp-light, Jessica saw that her eyes were light green and piercing, her pale blond hair mixed with gray, strands blowing around her face where it escaped her hood. Her skin was so white it appeared almost bloodless.

"From him," the odd woman clarified in that same emotionless voice.

"Who?"

"You know, Anne-Marie." The pale woman seemed so certain of herself.

"I don't know what you're talking about," Jessica lied.

Grace's lips twisted into a disbelieving smile, but she didn't argue. Instead, in a voice without inflection, she said, "You're no longer safe. Trust no one."

"Lady—" Jessica began in protest.

Grace struck as quickly as a snake, her hand streaking forward, her fingers wrapping over Jessica's forearm.

Jessica gasped and dropped the box holding her pizza. "Let go of me!"

"No one," Grace repeated then released her grasp.

Neither dog so much as glanced at the cardboard container though the lid had popped open, pizza slices jumbling together.

Freak, Jessica thought. *Weirdo!* Her pulse raced, fear and adrenaline pumping through her blood as she picked up the ruined pizza.

She glanced back as Grace added, "Remember. Not a soul."

Jessica stood up, shaken. "Okay."

To the dogs, Grace ordered softly, "Sheena. Bane. Come." Then she walked across the street and disappeared into the darkness of an alley.

Her appetite gone, Jessica hurried to her vehicle. She tossed the box onto the passenger seat. *How did that woman know my name and what the hell was she prattling on about danger? How could she know? How the hell could she know?*

Fingers shaking, nerves stretched to the breaking point, Jessica hustled into the driver's seat and started the Chevy. The smell of pepperoni, garlic, and onion was nearly overpowering.

Now, of course, she saw others on the street—two guys hanging out by the pub, smoking near the doorway; the couple she'd seen in the pizzeria huddling close together as they made their way to a sedan parked just around the corner from Dino's; a Prius cruising past in electric mode. Where had they been during her exchange with Grace?

She started to pull onto the street and was rewarded with a blast of a loud horn. She jumped, hit the brakes, and watched as a Jeep painted in camouflage nearly clipped her. The driver with a shaved head and a furious glare looked across the passenger seat and flipped up his palm as if to say, *Stupid woman driver! Watch out!*

Once the Jeep had passed, she pulled out and drove, checking her rearview mirror every five seconds, trying not to be rattled, telling herself that no one was following her. Yet, despite all her internal pep talks, the weird woman's warning echoed through her brain.

Trust no one.

CHAPTER 19

"I found her." Lying on his bed in his room at the River View, his cell phone pressed against his ear, Ryder stared at his computer monitor. The grainy black and white image was clear enough to observe Anne-Marie as she slept restlessly on the old couch in her cabin. He watched as "Jessica," or, really, Anne-Marie, tossed and turned, her pistol tucked under her pillow, her sleep broken and tortured. He felt more than one niggle of guilt for observing her every move, but he reminded himself it was just a job, nothing more.

At least, that's the level to which it had dissolved.

"You're sure it's her?" the voice on the other end asked, the slight Louisianan accent discernible.

"Oh, yeah." Shifting, the back of his head moving against the stacked pillows, Ryder nodded as if the SOB on the other end of the wireless connection could actually see him.

"Why haven't you finished the job?"

Good question. "I had to be certain. Now I am."

"Then get to it."

"I will, when the time is right. She should have a day or two off work."

"She works?" A sneer in the voice.

"She's a waitress."

"My, my." A clucking of the tongue. "How the mighty have fallen." Satisfaction oozed through the phone.

Ryder wondered again why he'd ever agreed to do this job. The answer was stone-cold simple. He'd wanted to chase her down. He wanted to face her. He wanted her to know that it was he who had found her.

"So what's the problem?"

"As I said, I'm waiting for her to not be expected at her job so I can get a head start before anyone gets wise and realizes she's missing."

"Won't they just think she took off? No one really knows her."

"I can't take a chance. The extra twenty-four, maybe forty-eight hours, will give me a head start."

"I don't understand." Obvious irritation came through the phone.

"We don't need any interference from the police," Ryder pointed out.

A pause.

He could almost hear the gears turning in the head nearly a thousand miles away.

"Just don't screw this up."

"I won't."

"Good. Because it's been a while. I've been patient. Either she's been extremely elusive or you've fucked up. Or maybe a little of both."

"I said I'd handle it." Ryder's eyes focused on the screen where Anne-Marie was still sleeping. He was reminded of waking up next to her, the smell of her hair mixed with the odor of recent sex causing him to second-guess his need to run her to the ground.

Again.

He witnessed her shift again. One arm stretched over her head, her eyebrows drew together, and his guts wrenched.

"Just end this," he was advised, then the connection was severed.

The woman on the screen opened her eyes wide, startled, instantly awake as if through some invisible cosmic connection, she'd heard the conversation and was ready to bolt.

"You'd better get down here," Alvarez said as Pescoli groggily answered her cell. She'd spent the night with Santana in the new house again, the sun already up and shining, beams streaming through the windows.

"Why?" she asked, sitting up and pulling the sleeping bag over her naked breasts as she tried to shake the cobwebs from her brain. Beside her, a disturbed Santana rolled closer to her, one arm circling her waist.

Alvarez said, "Could be a break. The lab found a print on Calypso Pope's bag and get this. It looks like it matches the partial found on Sheree Cantnor's shoe."

As if the missing digit and ring weren't enough to tie the two victims together, but at least it was physical evidence.

"I'm on my way." Pescoli pushed her mussed hair from her eyes as she reached for her clothes.

Santana opened a bleary eye.

"Gotta run," she explained, yanking on her underwear and jeans, then reaching for her bra. "Possible big break in the case."

He didn't argue, didn't so much as mention that it was the weekend as he'd learned long ago that Pescoli's work took precedence over her free time. "What about today?"

"How 'bout I meet you at the funeral?" she suggested. "I'll go with Alvarez and the officers from the station, and you and I can hook up with the kids then. Jeremy is supposed to pick up Bianca at Luke's place and they'll peel off after the service."

"Works for me," Santana said, for once not trying to lure her back into the bed, which was really just sleeping bags thrown on the floor. He flung off the covers, got to his feet, and walked naked to the French doors where he looked through the clear panes to the grounds and lake. "Good day."

Pulling her sweater over her head, she said, "For a funeral?"

"For anything."

She forced her arms down the sleeves and pulled her hair through the cowl neckline. She glanced at Santana. He was looking away from her and she sighed inwardly. The sight of his wide, muscular shoulders and smooth back that narrowed into a slim waist and taut buttocks, the cheeks of which might have had a few marks from her fingernails, made her blush a little at the memory of their lovemaking. She imagined their hungry, primal sex would last until her pregnancy got in the way or until it became routine. Stolen as their time alone was, the kissing and touching and stripping of clothes was almost frantic, their desire heightened by so much time spent apart.

Would it change once they were married?

Probably. It always did.

But for some, that physical connection never completely abated, and they kept their desire hot while their emotional bond deepened.

Maybe this time, she thought, searching for a missing boot, *I'll get lucky.* She certainly hoped so. "I'll call you later if there's a change in plans," she said, zipping up her boots and reaching for her jacket, which had been tossed carelessly over a ladder that stood near the top of the stairs.

"Do," he said. "Hey, wait! You're forgetting something."

"What?" She smiled, certain that he was going to give her a kiss. To her surprise he scooped up the cell phone she'd dropped into the folds of the sleeping bag when she'd hung up.

"This."

"Oh." She extended her palm.

He dropped it into her outstretched hand and, slightly disappointed, she turned toward the stairs.

Strong fingers clasped over her wrist and he spun her back against him. "And this." He kissed her then. Hard. Determined. His tongue slid past her teeth as she responded, opening her mouth and leaning into him. Memories of the night before and their heated lovemaking in the cold room flooded her head. Her heart cracked a little and she realized just how much she loved this man, the cowboy who worked with horses that she swore she'd never fall for. What an idiot she'd been, and probably still was.

When he finally lifted his head, a cocksure smile twisting his lips, she said, "That's better."

"Not better," he returned as she started down the plywood steps. "The best."

"If you say so."

"I *know* so."

"Egomaniac," she called up the unfinished staircase and hurried outside where the sun was blazing, the snow a shimmering white, and her Jeep damn near frozen solid.

Montana in winter.

Glorious.

"What the hell's wrong with you?" Alvarez demanded an hour later as Pescoli suddenly rushed to the bathroom from Alvarez's office where the two partners had been going over new information on the case.

Upon her return, Alvarez eyed her closely. "You coming down with something?"

Pescoli, white faced, shook her head. "Santana and I celebrated a little too much last night," she lied.

"What about the other times? All of a sudden you can't view dead bodies without losing your lunch? Is it the flu? What—"

"I'm pregnant, okay?" Pescoli said through her teeth. She went to Alvarez's office door and pushed it shut.

"Holy moly." Alvarez stared at her.

"I know. My kids are grown. I could be a grandmother in a few years. I'm only telling you because we spend so much time together. I haven't even confided in my kids yet. So far, just Santana knows. Now, you. It wasn't planned. I wasn't convinced that I'd even have another baby. Not with Santana. Not with anyone. My kids . . . are going to be dumbstruck. Worse than even you are."

Alvarez shook her head. "Wow. You're sure?"

"I took a bunch of in-home tests and they all turned out positive. I'm late, and feeling like crap, emotional as hell and tossing my cookies in the morning, so yeah, I'm pregnant. I go to the doctor next week."

"Well . . . congratulations."

"Thanks. You'll keep this to yourself?"

"Of course."

"Good."

"No wonder you've been all over Blackwater."

"What do you mean?" Pescoli bristled.

"You're pregnant. Emotional. Grayson's death, and Blackwater stepping in. You're not handling it well."

"Like you are?"

"I don't like Blackwater, but I *deal* with him. He's the boss, and unless I think he's handling things all wrong or crooked or neglectful, I'll keep dealing with him. Do I miss Dan Grayson? You bet. Do I wish he was still alive, still running this department? Every damn day. But that's not the way it is, and me having my own personal snit fit about it isn't going to change it."

"I haven't been having snit fits," Pescoli snapped.

"I just gave you a pass for being pregnant. Let's leave it at that."

"Snit fits . . ." she muttered.

Alvarez almost laughed. "Are you going to stay on the force? You were thinking about cutting back, but now . . . ?"

"I don't know. I'm still dealing with the news," Pescoli admitted. "I just told Santana this week, and as I said, my kids are still in the dark. Santana wants to move up the wedding to like, yesterday, but"—she turned both palms upward, toward the ceiling—"there's a lot to figure out and it's not like I'm not buried here."

"You have to have a life. We *both* have to have lives."

"I was going to talk my hours over with Grayson when . . ." Closing her eyes for a second, she drew in a long breath. "Well, you know. Anyway, we've got this case we need to figure out."

Alvarez nodded.

"Let's just get through today. It's going to be a rough one, right?"

It was a rhetorical question that didn't require an answer. A funeral was never easy. This one, not only for a fallen officer but for a mentor as well, would be especially tough. Grayson had been an officer who had epitomized everything Alvarez believed was the essence of a true lawman. He had also been the person she'd fallen for, the one who had taught her to trust again. And that was the truth of it . . . until Dylan O'Keefe had reentered her life and shown her what real love could be. Nonetheless, the service was going to be emotionally ravaging. Already, she felt that awful pang deep in her heart again, the one reserved for Sheriff Dan Grayson.

She took a deep breath and put the conversation back on track. "We should get an answer from AFIS soon about the prints, if the killer is in the system." The Automated Fingerprint Identification System was usually fairly quick. Now that they had a full print, there might be a match in the database that held millions of prints on file.

Pescoli said, "Let's hope." There was a chance that the prints only matched each other, that the culprit had never been printed, and therefore couldn't be identified. If so, they were back to square one.

"I got hold of Reggie," Alvarez told her. "Actually Reginald Larue the Third. He lives in Spokane and admitted to dating Calypso. Nearly fell into a million pieces when I mentioned that we found a body we think could be hers. Couldn't get off the phone fast enough and is even now on his way to ID the body. He sounded shocked and very upset. He claims both of her parents are already dead and she has no siblings. No kids, no ex-husband, at least that she told him about. As far as he knows, he's the closest thing to family she has."

"What about a job?"

"She was a consultant. An engineer. Worked with road crews. Again, on her own. A one woman show."

"The Teflon woman. No one sticks to her."

"At least according to Reggie. I checked the call log and text log on her phone. He was the last one who tried to contact her at two twenty-three in the morning. That's when the last text was sent, all of them more and more pleading, asking her to call him and forgive him. Here they are, printed out." Alvarez slid the pages to Pescoli. "I double-checked with his cell phone carrier. His phone was in Spokane when he sent them. I thought there was a chance he might be trying to call or text her after she was dead to throw us off, but the phone, at least, was in Spokane, or so it seems. I can't say that he was actually there."

"No alibi?"

"He's got one and it's pretty interesting. A woman."

"Another woman was with him that night?" Pescoli asked. "As in *all* night?"

"So they both claim."

"But now he's in a million pieces about Calypso?"

"Seemed real, but I'll find out. I'm meeting him at the morgue before the funeral. There's enough time for questions, I think."

"Should be interesting," Pescoli said.

They discussed the case a little while longer, then each went their separate ways. Pescoli was all about getting her kids ready for the sad event while Alvarez returned to her condo to meet Dylan. He would be her rock during the service.

At least with him at her side, she could get through the event without completely falling apart . . . she hoped. Usually, she was the cool, level-headed detective and kept her emotions under tight rein.

Dan Grayson's death had changed all that.

CHAPTER 20

Pescoli had dreaded this day from the minute she heard the sheriff had died.

She was dressed in full uniform, Sturgis with her. The idea had been Joelle Fisher's, and for once, Pescoli had agreed with the receptionist that Sturgis's presence would be fitting as the dog had been constantly at Grayson's side, in or out of the office. Sturgis was part of the department, too, and he always behaved himself.

With a quick look around the crowded auditorium of Pinewood Center, she located her children standing together in the center of one section of chairs. Santana wasn't with them, but that was no surprise as they weren't yet a family. In fact, she wondered if there ever would be a time where they existed cohesively . . . and doubted it. She finally found him amidst the standing room only throng, near enough to the wide set of double doors at the back to satisfy the fire marshal.

She moved to the section reserved for law enforcement, where she and her fellow officers would stand during the service.

Though there had been a hum of conversation rising to the tall ceiling before the funeral got underway, a hush fell over the mourners as Blackwater approached the podium and introduced himself. Without any fanfare, he gave the opening remarks about the dedication and service of Dan Grayson. He was sincere and true, without any self-promotion and his remarks were surprisingly spot-on without the usual aggrandizing of the dead's accomplishments. No flowery phrases. No inordinate sentimentality. He called Grayson a straight shooter who was respected by his peers and those who worked for him, and stated that the sheriff was embraced by the community that had elected him. Blackwater summed up by saying that Sheriff Daniel Grayson would be missed by those he worked with and those he worked for, and that the community had lost an honest, kind, and dedicated officer of the law.

Pescoli grudgingly had to admit Grayson would have approved of the acting sheriff's remarks.

Flanked by flags of the United States and the State of Montana, a huge picture of the sheriff hung from a wall of navy-blue draping in the front of the hall. In the headshot, Grayson wasn't smiling, his stern expression offering none of the warmth that had epitomized the man. His sense of humor, his calm hand in running the department, the love he had for the dog at her side weren't evident.

Considering Pescoli's emotional state, it was probably a good thing. She, like so many others jammed into the large room, remembered him for the level-headed and kind man he was.

Officers from other jurisdictions as well as the Pinewood County Sheriff's Department, the city of Grizzly Falls' Police Department, and the Montana State Police were in attendance. Friends and family, townspeople, and neighbors filled the large hall to overflowing.

As she listened to the eulogy given by the chaplain, Pescoli caught glimpses of the wives and husbands of the officers, as well as Trace O'Halleran and Dr. Kacey Lambert along with Grace Perchant and Ivor Hicks. For once, Hicks was quiet, not causing a scene. She hoped he could maintain as much for the duration of the service.

Pescoli noticed Manny Douglas, the reporter for the local paper, taking notes. *God, the guy has no couth.*

Sandi from Wild Wills was in attendance, as was the owner of Dino's, the local pizza parlor. Pescoli recognized the local veterinarian and the pharmacist. There were several hundred people she didn't know along with more than a sprinkling of familiar faces.

The Grayson family was seated front and center, everyone dressed in black, each member grim-faced. Dan's brothers Cade and big Zed were seated with Hattie, Bart's ex-wife. She was fighting a losing battle with tears, a tissue wadded in her fist. Her girls were also part of the group.

Nearby, both of Dan's ex-wives, neither of which Pescoli cared much for, sat ramrod straight. Akina Bellows, seated next to her current husband, Rick, remained dry-eyed, but sober. Their one-year-old daughter, squirming slightly, was seated on Akina's lap.

Dan Grayson's first wife, Cara, a petite woman who was related to Hattie—Pescoli frowned. *Maybe a half sister or something?*—sat stiffly next to her husband, Nolan Banks. Their daughter, Allison, who was a little younger than Bianca, sat between her father and brothers and was fiddling with her cell phone despite what appeared to be several reprimands from her father. Nolan's jaw tightened and finally he rolled his palm toward the ceiling and wiggled his fingers, silently indicating she should hand over the phone. The girl, ever-petulant, slid the offensive cell into a small clutch purse.

Pescoli suspected Allison was her own kind of trouble. Ezekiel and Isaiah, Nolan's sons from a previous marriage, were leaning forward, elbows on their knees. Both boys, around college age, looked uncomfortable as they whispered and pulled at their collars and ties.

It seemed as if everyone in town had come to pay their respects. The chairs were all full, mourners spilling out into the hallway and anteroom.

After the chaplain, Cade and Zed approached the podium. While Zed didn't say a word, Cade offered up some anecdotes about Dan Grayson, the man and the brother. Cade's voice broke as he admitted he'd looked up to Dan, who had often been his ideal and sometimes even a father figure. Dan could get mad enough, but he'd always been able to see the clear path and had helped his hellion of a brother find his way, too.

After a prayer, there was a solo of "Amazing Grace" by Frannie Hendrickson, who led a choir at the Methodist church on Sundays and was known for her purple wig and karaoke renditions at the Tin Roof Saloon in Missoula on Saturday nights. Today, her hair was black, as were her dress and heels, her voice a clear and pure soprano that rose to the rafters.

Once again, Pescoli felt teary. She patted Sturgis's head and the damn dog licked her hand, then leaned against her. At that moment, she knew that she'd keep the black lab until his dying day. Until then, she'd thought one of Dan's brothers might want the dog, but it no longer mattered. Sturgis was hers and would be a living reminder of the sheriff. She caught Santana's eye just before the last prayer and he gave her an encouraging smile and small wink that somehow made her heart swell despite her sadness. Her throat clogged at how suddenly grateful she was to be marrying him.

With the back of one finger she swiped away her tears and mentally reminded herself to toughen up, that if the chaplain were to be believed, Dan Grayson was in "a better place." She wasn't certain about that, but it was a nice idea and she liked to think it was true even if she didn't quite believe it.

Once the service had concluded with another quiet prayer, the flag-draped coffin was wheeled out of the hall by the pallbearers—Grayson's brothers and four officers from the department.

Pescoli, the dog in tow, left the hall and found her kids outside. They were standing close together, talking, their breath visible in the air as they waited by Jeremy's pickup, which was parked in the side lot. She and Sturgis made their way to the truck.

"Thanks for coming. It means a lot to me."

" 'Course," Jeremy said. He'd even dressed for the occasion in a long-sleeved striped shirt and slacks that could've stood a pressing, but hey, a vast improvement over his sweats or jeans and sloppy football jersey. He'd found an old suit coat of his father's that was a little short in the sleeves and slightly faded, but at least he'd taken the time to appear presentable. Bianca, starting to think of herself as a fashionista, was dressed in a short charcoal gray dress with matching leggings and a black coat that hit her at the knees, just an inch above her boots.

"Are you coming to the cemetery?" Pescoli asked them.

"No," Bianca said quickly.

"Yes, we are," Jeremy disagreed. He shot his sister a look that suggested she not argue.

"I don't see why." Bianca started to go into her petulant routine.

"Because Mom worked for him, and so did I and like, duh"—Jeremy motioned toward Sturgis—"we've got his dog." He was firm as he strode to the driver's side of his truck. "We're going, Bianca. Get in."

Bianca's shoulders slumped as if she were an eight-year-old being punished and sent to her room.

Pescoli said, "I think it's a good idea. Respectful. Dan Grayson was good to all of us."

"Let's go," Jeremy yelled from behind the wheel and fired the engine before slamming his door shut.

"Great," Bianca grumbled but climbed into her brother's rig as Pescoli made her way to her own Jeep.

Santana was waiting for her. "Trouble in paradise?" he asked, hitching his chin toward Jeremy's truck as it wheeled out of the lot.

"Nothing serious." She didn't want to go into it.

Santana picked up on it. "You want to ride to the cemetery together?"

"Yes. Please. That would be great." It felt good to let someone else take charge, if only for a little while. "But there's three of us," she said, indicating Sturgis.

Santana's dark eyes sparkled in the sun. "I'm used to that. Come on." He walked her to the passenger side. She handed him her keys and slid into the Jeep. Sturgis hopped inside.

They drove to the cemetery in a long procession and Pescoli stared out the window. Once they were through the city with its plowed streets and piles of graying snow, they passed by broad fields spangled beneath the bright sun. The cemetery was located on a hill outside the city limits that angled softly upward and offered a view of the valley and the town sprawled below. Tombstones half buried in snow sprouted from the frozen ground and two roads bisected the graves. Ahead was a fresh plot—dark earth turned over in the snow, an oblong hole in the ground surrounded by several floral sprays, a small tent, and fake grass.

Fewer people had made the trek to the cemetery, though a bevy of vehicles were parked and mourners trudged through six inches of frigid powder to stand at Dan Grayson's final resting spot. The chaplain said a few more words and led another prayer. The Grayson family sat in a sober group near the grave.

Pescoli's stomach knotted at the finality of it all. When the guns were fired in salute, she fought a fresh spate of tears. Sturgis didn't so much as whimper as the rifles blasted and afterward the dog, head down, followed Pescoli obediently to Santana's truck.

It was over.

For everyone.

Sheriff Dan Grayson had been laid to rest.

Jessica woke Sunday morning feeling tired all over, and at work, the diner was a madhouse. While Saturday had been a little slow, the crowd had returned for Sunday breakfast, brunch, lunch, and then later for dinner.

Nell was beside herself, delighted that the receipts were keeping the register busy. "This is just what we needed," she said, grinning.

Misty was quick on her feet, and obviously thrilled with the tips. "Maybe I will take that winter vacation to Puerto Vallarta after all. My cousin's got a place down there, ya know. Always asking me to come down, but the airfare's out of my league. However, with a couple more days like this, I can see myself sitting on a beach and sipping a margarita from some hottie in a Speedo."

Armando rolled his eyes and muttered something in Spanish under his breath. He and Denise had worked harder than ever getting the orders cooked and plated at a breakneck pace. Though Denise was handling the extra work effortlessly, Armando was at his rope's end, griping that they were running out of staples and that too many of the orders came in with changes. Jessica, grateful for the fast pace, didn't have time to think about the fact that she'd promised herself to go to the sheriff's office the next morning.

But as the shift wound down and the last customers drifted out of the diner, her stomach once again knotted. Could she go through with it?

It was a little before eleven when Misty said, "You run on home. I'll close."

Jessica nodded. She was dead tired and told herself to get a decent night's sleep, then face the music. When she drove out of the lot, she found the city streets nearly deserted, the town of Grizzly Falls seemingly folded in on itself and closed up for the cold winter's night.

She told herself again that she wasn't being followed, that the headlights she'd seen in her rearview mirror weren't zeroed in on her. As she had before, she considered all of her options. She could wait for the bastard to find her, stand her ground, and try to blow him away herself, but then she'd end up in a trial and possibly prison or the mental hospital. Again.

No, thank-you.

Fleeing or turning herself in to the police were her options.

If she ran again, she was only putting off the inevitable. Buying a little frantic time. Putting more people in danger. Again, she'd pass.

That left going to the police, telling them her story, and hoping they would believe her, trust her, go against all the evidence.

She turned onto the county road and the streetlights gave way to darkness. No car seemed to be following her and the more distance she put between herself and Grizzly Falls, the more she told herself to relax. She had only one more night on the run, then, come morning, her life would take another turn and change.

Forever.

"So be it," she said, the beams from her headlights cutting through the deep night. A few snowflakes drifted lazily from the night sky to catch in the light. As she left the city behind she should have felt calm, but instead, she was still uneasy. Restless. She fiddled with the radio and heard an old Johnny Cash song on a country station that kept cutting out. She thought of her family and a bitter taste rose in her throat. Would they come to Montana? Would she be sent to Louisiana where she would face them again through iron bars or through thick glass where they could only speak through phones mounted in the walls? Or would they abandon her?

Did she even care? Those ties had been severed a while back, their frayed ends unable to be stitched back together.

She had, of course, not only betrayed and embarrassed them, she'd renounced them publicly, a sin for which she would never be forgiven. Her mother and father lived by a very stiff and archaic set of standards. A public life that was, to all who looked at it, picture-perfect. No cracks to be seen. But once the doors were closed, their private life was very different and very guarded.

She'd known the rules growing up.

She'd not only broken them, she'd done so in a very public way.

She remembered the day she'd first confronted her mother.

Outside on a lounge chair, her mother was reading a paperback. Wearing a sundress and dark glasses, she'd positioned herself on the porch in the shade of the overhanging oak tree, leaving only her legs exposed to the sunlight.

Though it was barely nine in the morning, the summer heat was sweltering, the day sultry, almost sticky, a haze in the blue Louisiana sky. An Olympic-sized pool, her father's prized possession, abutted the veranda of her parents' home outside New Orleans. It shimmered as it stretched far into the tended backyard.

"Mom?" Anne-Marie called, gathering her nerves.

Jeanette looked up and set her paperback onto her lap. A glass of sweet tea was sweating on the small table beside the lounge chair. A smaller glass of ice and a clear liquid, most likely gin, sat near a pack of long cigarettes by the ashtray and a lighter. Paddle fans, as always, were softly whirling overhead. Butterflies with orange and black wings flitted through the heavily blossomed bougainvillea flanking the yard.

"This is a surprise." Jeanette smiled, but Anne-Marie knew it was false. Jeanette Favier had never been a warm person.

"I have something to tell you."

"Oh." Nothing more. Just the hint of disappointment from dealing with a daughter who had continually disappointed and bothered her.

"It's about . . . him."

"Again?" Her mother sighed, her smile falling away. "Why you have such a problem with your husband, I'll never understand. Marriage isn't easy, and given your . . . condition, you're lucky he wanted you."

"My condition. You mean because I was a little wild?" Anne-Marie challenged.

Her mother sighed through her nose. "Your brothers were 'a little wild,' but you pushed the boundaries, got yourself in that accident and—" She stopped. "Oh, well."

"Go ahead. Say it. I've never been the same since. Isn't that what you were going to tell me? You blame me for falling off a damn horse and hitting my head and think that's the cause of every bad thing that's happened to me since."

"You were in a coma for days, but of course, you don't remember that. When you finally woke up"—Jeanette shook slightly—"you were . . . different."

"With a condition."

"You went from bad to worse. I'd thought . . . no, I'd hoped . . . when you finally decided to get married that you would settle down, make a decent life for yourself. But that's not the way it ever is with you."

"He's not the man I thought he was."

"No one is. We all have girlhood dreams of white knights and thunderous steeds and chivalrous men who pledge their lives to us, but in the end, they are all just men." Jeanette let out a long breath and shook her head. "Have you forgotten the 'for better or worse' part of your vows?"

"He hit me, Mom."

Jeanette looked up sharply. "Oh, Anne-Marie," she said as if she didn't believe her, as if Anne-Marie were spinning another lie.

"I'm serious, Mom," she insisted and witnessed the cords in her mother's neck tightening, the way they always did when Jeanette was forced to deal with her wayward, rule-breaking daughter's problems.

"Okay. So he shoved you," she finally said, finding a way to make the statement more palatable. "Why don't you just, you know, keep quiet about it?" Jeanette Favier's type of motherly advice. "That's what we do, you know." She reached for her cigarettes, then her fingers scrabbled over the glass top of the table, nearly knocking over her iced tea before she clenched the soft pack.

Anne-Marie stood her ground. "He beat me!" she repeated, her fists clenching at her sides. "That's assault, Mom."

"Hush!" Her mother sat up quickly, then glanced furtively over her shoulder toward the inside of the huge plantation-style home. "For the love of God, Anne-Marie, keep your voice down. The cleaning people are here and your father's in his study." She pointed overhead to the area in the general direction of Talbert Favier's private office.

"You don't care that he hit me?"

"Of course I care." Jeanette tried to shake a cigarette out of the crumpled pack.

"You should, because he hit me over and over again. I thought . . . I thought he would crack my ribs."

"But he didn't, did he?" Jeanette managed to shake out a cigarette and light up despite the fact that it was slightly bent. Her hands were trembling.

Anne-Marie stared down at her mother. "Not yet. But he will."

"No, no. You don't know that."

"He's going to really hurt me."

"Now, look, Anne-Marie," Jeanette said, sighing in a cloud of smoke. "This is not good. But you knew he had a temper before you married him."

"Not like this. I didn't know he was violent."

Lifting up her sunglasses, Jeanette squinted at her daughter through a thin tendril of smoke. "So what do you want to do?"

"Go to the police."

"What? Oh, Lord!" She shook her head at the thought, then set her cigarette in the ashtray. "No way. You have to leave the police out of it."

"He beat me, Mother. What part of that don't you get?" To prove her point, Anne-Marie took off her own shades to display the red in her eye, the bruise surrounding her eye socket.

"Oh . . . oh, dear." Jeanette winced.

Not stopping with the damage to her face, Anne-Marie lifted her T-shirt to show the black, blue, and sickly green discoloration across her abdomen.

Her mother sucked in a swift breath. "I'm so, so sorry." In an act so foreign to her mother that Anne-Marie was stunned, Jeanette grabbed a towel draped over a nearby chair and dipped one corner into the pool. "Sit," she said, indicating the end of the chaise and then, smelling of smoke and her signature perfume, she gently dabbed at her daughter's injuries.

Anne-Marie sucked in her breath as her mother touched her face, pressing the cold towel against her cheek.

"I think you'll live," Jeanette pronounced.

"This time."

"It's not that bad." She took her time folding the towel.

"He attacked me, Mother. Beat me. Then raped me." Anne-Marie was trembling inside, the memory of the vicious attack fresh and brutal. She needed her mother to understand, to be her champion.

"Oh, darling," her mother said softly.

For an instant, Anne-Marie believed Jeanette's hard exterior had cracked with empathy and love for her only daughter, but that hopeful impression was short-lived as the older woman asked gently, "Whatever did you do to provoke him so?"

"What? Didn't you hear me? He assaulted me, gave me these." Once more, Anne-Marie lifted her T-shirt to display her bruises. She hurt inside, was as emotionally beat-up as she was physically. But it was at the hands of her own damn mother, the woman whom she'd hoped would believe her and protect her.

"Oh, I heard you, sweetheart," Jeanette said as she leaned over the table and took a final puff of her cigarette before putting it out in a series of nervous taps until the filter tip was mashed in the ashtray. Then she turned to grab her daughter by the shoulders. "I know you're sore. It's obvious, but . . . but your husband's a good man, maybe a little rough around the edges in private, but you just have to try to please him."

"How can you say that?" Anne-Marie nearly screamed. "These aren't the dark ages for God's sake! Mother, listen to yourself. Do you really think I should stay with a man who does this to me?" She held her T-shirt higher, where bite marks were visible on her breasts over the top of her bra.

"Honey." Her mother picked up the towel again, and, looking as if she really had no idea what to do, tried to dab at the contusion on Anne-Marie's cheek again.

Anne-Marie dropped the hem of her T-shirt and grabbed her mother's wrist, stopping her. "He's an animal," she hissed. So angry she was nearly spitting, she shoved her face close to her mother's so that their noses nearly touched. She saw the tiny imperfections in the older woman's face, the pores that were a little larger on her nostrils and the telltale web of red lines running across her nose to her cheeks. Minuscule threads lurking beneath the surface, they were evidence of far too many gin and tonics by the pool that were stubbornly resisting an ever-thickening layer of makeup.

Anne-Marie said, "I will not be used as a human punching bag."

Jeanette backed up. "You married the man."

"I didn't know."

"Listen to me, Anne-Marie. There is no divorce in our family. You might see that as archaic, but that's the way it is. Your father is an elder in the church, a respected businessman. And your grandfather's a preacher. Do you hear me? My father preached from the Good Book. Your brothers have problems with their wives and kids and they're working it out. You haven't been easy, my dear. Not at all. Not with the craziness you spew. But," she said and then repeated, "but . . . we are proud, genteel people, expected to set an example for the community."

"You would sacrifice me? For the sake of . . . what? Some ridiculous and antiquated notion of what a marriage is? Your precious reputation?"

Slap!

Her mother's palm struck fast and hard, leaving a red mark over Anne-Marie's already bruised cheek. "Sacrifice is a part of life, a path to heaven. And marriage is sacred. Don't you ever forget it. And as for divorce? In this family, it's out of the question." She yanked her arm back.

Anne-Marie let it go. "You can't tell me what to do. I'm a grown woman."

"Then act like one." Disgusted, Jeanette added tautly, "Do your duty, Anne-Marie."

"Are you kidding?"

"You're a wife. His wife. Your choice. And, let's face it, you haven't been a very good one, have you?"

Anne-Marie didn't answer.

"I didn't think so." With a frown, Jeanette said, "Look into a mirror. Think about what you've done. You're not the victim here."

"He hit me."

"Then deal with it. But, please, don't come running to me!" She started for the inside of the house.

"I'm divorcing the son of a bitch."

Her mother hesitated at the French doors leading to the kitchen. With one hand on the doorknob, she glanced over her shoulder. "Then you're divorcing all of us, Anne-Marie. You won't be welcome here again."

Anne-Marie's stomach tightened and she'd fought the urge to run to her mother and beg her forgiveness, but she stood firm.

"I trust you can show yourself out," were the last words her mother said to her.

CHAPTER 21

Jessica shoved thoughts of her family aside as she drove through the night. They would not be any help. Never had been. Even her grandmother on her mother's side, Marcella, who had adored her only granddaughter, wouldn't come to her aid.

Not any longer.

That, of course, was her own fault. The effect of stealing from someone who loved and trusted her.

Would the police be able to protect her?

She doubted it. She had too many strikes against her—a mental patient as well as a thief and a known liar. No, she didn't really believe the cops would help her, at least not the cops in New Orleans. She'd pinned her hopes on Dan Grayson. But even if he'd still been alive, chances were he wouldn't have come to her rescue, either.

"Face it," she said to the disguised woman in the mirror, "you're on your own."

Then again, hadn't she always been?

The snow began to fall a little more heavily, collecting on the windshield, and she remembered the storm that had been predicted, a blizzard moving south from Canada, the biggest of the winter. *Great,* she thought sarcastically. Just what she needed. She flipped on the wipers and from the corner of her eye, caught a flash of headlights shining through the night, a vehicle somewhere behind her.

You're not the only one who lives out here, she reminded herself.

"But almost," she said, her gloved hands tightening over the steering wheel. Again, she looked back. Again she saw lights.

She swallowed hard and wondered where the hell all of her bravado had gone. It was as if her courage had dissolved in the time, over a year, since that conversation with her mother.

It's nothing. Don't be paranoid. Get a damn grip.

Her heart was pounding like crazy. Despite the cold, her fingers began to sweat in her gloves as she clenched the wheel.

Another look in the mirror.

The lights had disappeared.

Probably turned off at that last junction. She let out her breath.

It was nothing. See? *For God's sake pull yourself together. You have to keep a level head.*

She saw the lane leading to her cabin and started to turn in when two eyes caught in the headlights. "Oh, God!" She slammed on the brakes and the SUV skidded, back end fishtailing as the deer leaped nimbly into the surrounding trees.

She sat for a second, waiting for her rollicking heart to return to normal as snow drifted down, falling steadily, piling on the ground.

It was a damn deer. Nothing more.

She pressed on the gas pedal. Wheels spinning, she whispered, "Come on, come on," as the back end slid some more. Finally, the front wheels caught, the Tahoe lurched forward, and she drove along the ruts to the cabin, a tiny dark abode in the middle of nowhere.

She'd been foolish to come to Grizzly Falls, she realized, propelled by fear and confusion and, yes, paranoia. But, come the daylight, she would make things right.

The rest of the drive down the winding length of the lane was uneventful. She parked, hurried into the cabin, then went through her usual routine of replacing firewood, then stoking the flames, and double-checking all the locks on the doors and latches on the windows before making certain that every curtain or shade was pulled tight.

After twisting on the shower to get the warm water running, she took off the pieces of her disguise. She hung her wig and padding on a hook behind the bathroom door then secured her dental appliance in a ziplock plastic bag that she left on the counter. Cold to the bone, she showered quickly, then dried off, tossing her towel over a hook near the window. She cracked the window just enough to clear the room of what little steam had collected. Shivering, she pulled on her sweats, grabbed her uniform and underclothes, then hurried back to the living room where the fire was burning more brightly, some heat emanating from the grate.

Yeah, this place is miserable, she thought. Hardly a haven.

By habit, she folded her work clothes then placed them on the table at one end of her makeshift bed. Finally, she settled in by the fire and turned on her computer to catch up on the day's news and watch some mind-numbing television. Currently, she found no more information about the two women who had been killed in Grizzly Falls and she prayed that they hadn't been targeted because of her.

No way.

That was impossible, right?

Creeeaaak.

Her heart stilled as she listened.

Had she been mistaken, or had a floorboard squeaked somewhere in her house?

Waiting, not moving a muscle, she listened hard.

Nothing.

There's no one here. No one. You know it.

But there had been a noise. She was sure of it. And it sounded as if it had emanated from *inside* the house.

Swallowing back her fear, she stayed motionless, her ears straining as she listened, but she heard nothing other than the sound of dry tinder popping and moss hissing as they caught fire, the sound of the wind outside the cabin, and the damn drip of the bathroom faucet.

Get over yourself.

Still, she held her breath, then slowly retrieved her tiny pistol and, moving slowly, carefully went through the house to investigate. Cautiously she moved through the small rooms. Over the internal clamoring of her heart, she listened for any sound that was out of the ordinary while searching the nooks and crannies, every shadow, for someone or something that was trapped inside.

An animal. That's it. A squirrel or rat or rabbit. Or God forbid, a skunk might have found its way inside. Right? Or do they hibernate? She didn't really know. Just hoped that whatever it was, it wasn't human.

Her throat was dry as sand.

Fear pulsed through her.

The living area was clear, no one inside. The kitchen alcove was empty, too, and cold, a bit of air seeping from the area around the window over the sink. On bare feet, she made her way to the back door and lifted the shade where she could peek outside to the small porch.

The snow was falling faster. The predicted blizzard had arrived. She worried her lower lip and wondered if she'd be trapped, her plans of telling her wild tale to the police thwarted.

You're not backing out of this. Too many times you've turned tail and run. Tomorrow, come hell or high water . . .

She forcibly steeled herself. For months, she'd been a coward, but no longer. She had a four-wheel-drive vehicle and would make it to the police station . . . if she got through this last, lonely night.

Trying to see through the thickening veil of snow, she saw no one. Nothing sinister seemed to be peering from the shadows. Narrowing her eyes, she studied each of the trees closest to the house and the back of the old garage and the small pump house. She waited, anticipating movement, but nothing moved other than the flurries of snow that swirled past frantically, the wind increasing.

Give it up, Anne-Marie or Jessica or whoever it is you're calling yourself now.

Her fingers clutched fiercely over the pistol's grip, because something didn't seem right outside. Everything looked peaceful, even serene and yet . . . what was it?

Then she knew. It wasn't that she saw anyone, but the snow behind the house seemed uneven rather than smooth. Were those footprints on the landscape, large impressions in the icy powder that she hadn't created?

She looked harder, but, of course, she couldn't be certain as it was so dark, and really, who would be skulking around the cabin? Who knew she was there?

No one.

Well, besides Cade. And maybe Big Zed as he had to have seen her SUV parked in the driveway, but they wouldn't be a problem. No one would come. And it was her last night in the cabin.

She hoped.

Staring into the night, she saw no movement other than the sway of branches and swirl of snow. The impressions she thought were footprints could have been caused by the irregular terrain behind the house—dirt clods or boulders or brush. Surely there was no clear trail, no path that someone had broken in the snow, no clear print on the thin snow of the back step. No, no, she was just letting her wild imagination get the better of her.

Still convincing herself that she was safe, that no one was lurking in the frigid shadows outside, she backed away from the door, letting the shade drop. She moved silently to the bathroom, slowly pushing open the door a bit with the muzzle of the gun so that the weak light of the living area could permeate the darkness. She started to step inside and—

No!

Her heart jolted at the sight of a dark figure in the reflection of the cracked mirror.

She bit back a scream, stepped back, and pointed her pistol at the doorway. "Drop your weapon!" she ordered, taking another step back, gun aimed, ready to fire.

Nothing.

No movement.

No response.

"Drop your weapon! Step out! Hands over your head!"

Again no response.

Just the keen of the wind and somewhere a branch banging against the side of the house.

"I mean it. I'll shoot!"

She was breathing hard, nearly hyperventilating. The gun beginning to wobble. She considered firing a warning shot, but was afraid of the ricochet. "Come out. Now!"

Damn. He wasn't responding. In fact, he hadn't so much as moved a muscle.

Cautiously, her finger on the trigger, she moved forward to the side of the door in case he should jump into the bathroom and start firing.

But that wasn't his style, was it?

"Who the hell are you?" she cried and then, ever so cautiously looked into the bathroom, to the mirror.

He was still in the same position. Crouching. Hiding halfway behind the door. His eyes were guarded, but his hair was visible. She swung her straight arm around the edge of the door. "I said 'Drop!' " she cried.

Not a whisper.

Trembling, she repeated, "I said—" But the command died in her throat and she felt all the strength seep out of her. "For the love of God."

As she looked more closely, first in the mirror, and then around the door to the wall itself, she realized she wasn't looking at some sinister cloaked figure ready to do her bodily harm. The "figure" wasn't a person at all. What she'd seen in the distorted image of the broken mirror was her own disguise, the padding and wig suspended from a hook in the wall behind the door. Just where she'd left it not an hour earlier.

"Idiot," she muttered, leaning against the vanity. Her knees were jelly and she felt herself flush in embarrassment. What was wrong with her? She was letting her paranoia get the better of her.

You keep this up and you'll end up in the mental hospital again. Is that what you want? For God's sake, get a damn grip, would ya?

She studied her image in the cracked mirror and thought it was ironically symbolic that her face was disfigured and warped.

So so true.

As her heart rate eventually slowed, she collected her wits and yanked the window shut tight, latching it securely.

Why would anyone, even a maniac as malicious as her husband, harm an innocent person? She'd leaped to the wrong conclusion. Again.

Still, she felt as if someone were watching her, following her, tracking her. The feeling never left her. From the moment she awoke, all through her days at the diner, on the road, and even in the cabin, it was the same. She glanced around the room and wondered about bugs—the kind with tiny microphones and itsy little cameras—and even her own computer. It had a camera in it. Could someone even now, be looking through—

Stop it! No one's been here. No one's planting listening devices, for God's sake. You don't even talk to anyone. And as for cameras—really? Why would anyone on God's green earth go to all that trouble? Why not just come in and kill you in your sleep? Get over your crazy self!

Whether there was reason or not, she did a quick sweep with her flashlight of the obvious places, and double-checked her stashes that she'd hidden to make certain her money and fake licenses and passports that had cost her so much were in place. Using the cash she'd stolen, she'd purchased them from a sketchy friend of a sketchy friend of a sketchy friend. She and the contact had met twice, once in an alley behind a crowded bar in the wee hours and the second time when she'd actually been handed the perfect-appearing documents on the waterfront of the slow-moving Mississippi in New Orleans in the dead of night. With the noise and lights of the French Quarter not far away, they'd made the exchange. Being that close to the river alone had made her skin crawl, and dealing with the skinny sharp-nosed man who didn't hide the fact that he was carrying a weapon, had been nerve-wracking. The pictures on her ID were far from perfect, of course, but so far, she hadn't been asked to show her driver's license anywhere. That would change when she told her story, of course.

Oh, God, she hoped the officer she connected with would believe her.

Don't freak out. You're safe. You'll go into the sheriff's department in the morning and demand protection, explain yourself. Everything will be fine.

That of course was a lie, but she swallowed back her fear, forced her heartbeat to slow, and found a way to become calm again. Tomorrow, come what may, she would be done running.

The fire crackled and hissed. Warmth radiated through the small room. She closed her eyes on the couch and touched the underside of her pillow, making certain the pistol was back where she'd placed it.

As nervous as she was, she felt too wound up to fall asleep and the minutes ticked by in the dark. She heard the wind screaming through the mountains and that damn limb bang against the house. The drip in the faucet, too, was audible, but it had become a part of her environment and eventually, as the fire began to die, exhaustion finally took over and she drifted off.

She didn't know how long she'd slept, but awoke slowly. *Today is the day,* her mind nagged, but she pulled the sleeping bag tighter around her to fend off the cold. She didn't open her eyes, didn't want to wake up. Not yet. Who knew what the day would bring? After all, it wasn't as if she'd gotten a full night's rest. It had been late when she'd fallen asleep and her recurring nightmare of drowning in blood had been peppered with the noises of the cabin. Images of glowing eyes watching her as she'd frantically tried to swim had been accompanied by a keening laughter and the steady clap of her attacker's hands. The wind screaming, the window panes rattling, the pounding of the branch against the house all added to her unrest. She'd even half-woken once, certain she wasn't alone, that someone was near enough that she felt his warm breath against her neck, but after blinking her eyes open and seeing nothing, she'd rolled over and settled back into fretful sleep.

Hours later, her back aching from her uncomfortable position on the old couch, a crick in her neck, Jessica rolled over without opening her eyes. It felt as if she hadn't slept a wink. Thankfully, she had a couple days off so she could sleep in.

And put off the inevitable? Isn't that what you're doing? Get up! Get going! Face the damn music. It's time to get on with the rest of your life.

"No," she said aloud and shivered, pulling up the sleeping bag as the temperature in the cabin had fallen overnight. She needed to get up and stoke the fire. Try to make herself presentable. Get her story straight.

What story? For once you'd better tell the truth.

That thought was foreign. Unappealing.

"Oh, God," she whispered. Throwing off the covers, she opened her eyes.

The cabin was nearly dark, of course, though she discerned from the bits of gray light filtering through the shades or cracks in the curtains that dawn had broken. *Good.* It was time to stoke the fire and get moving, face the damn music.

Finally, the waiting, and, oh God, the running, were nearly over.

She flung her legs off the couch and, stretching her arms over her head, yawned as she tried to wake up. Rotating the tightness from her neck, she felt it—that sizzling, heart-stopping sensation that something wasn't right.

Don't be silly.

Then she heard a scrape of leather against old floorboards.

Instinctively she rolled off the couch, her arm shooting forward under the pillow, her fingers searching for the hard steel of her pistol.

Nothing.

What? No!

"It's not there," a deep voice said.

Turning to look over her shoulder, she saw him then, the huge dark figure standing against the door.

Oh, God!

He'd found her.

CHAPTER 22

Pescoli had half-expected the atmosphere around the department to be different after Grayson's funeral, but when she got to work on Monday it didn't feel that way. Stomping snow from her boots, she felt a wall of heat greet her along with that same sense of somberness. Everyone who'd worked for Grayson may have gotten some closure from the ceremony, but it was going to take a while until it was business as usual again.

Winter had returned full force, a mother of a storm blowing in from Canada that had dumped nearly a foot of snow in the area and wasn't done yet. The wind was gusting and brutal, the temperature plunging to below freezing. Currently, most of the roads were clogged, some closed, maintenance crews working overtime. Deputies from the department had been called in early to deal with traffic snarls. Parts of the county were reporting electrical outages. Frozen pipes might be next, and the homeless population needed more shelter.

All that along with their current whack job—one who liked fingers and rings and dead women.

Pescoli, who had always claimed to have hated all the folderol over celebrations from New Year's to Christmas, found she missed the lightheartedness of Joelle's attempts to decorate the office, or at least her chance to poke fun at it. It was going to take a while until denial slowly morphed into reality and people got back into routine.

She had gotten up early and it was still predawn outside, not her norm by a long shot. She'd been unable to sleep, so she'd come to the station earlier than usual, ready to get back to the job, even though she was working for a man she didn't much like.

As she unwound her scarf, she told herself it was time for a personal attitude adjustment. She didn't like Blackwater, and she was pretty sure he didn't like her. So what? It was a time to get along, at least as long as she was employed in the department. Considering her current state—engaged, pregnant, the mother of teenagers who still needed her words of wisdom and guidance—it might be time to pack it in.

But not quite yet.

She still needed to find who'd killed Sheree Cantnor and Calypso Pope. That part—solving the mysteries of homicides, catching the culprits, and slamming their asses behind bars—she would miss. As for the particular freak they were currently chasing, she wanted him behind bars and fast. She and Alvarez needed to wrap it up.

Unzipping her outer coat as she walked by Blackwater's office, she caught a glimpse of him on the floor doing a slow, determined set of push-ups. "Detective?" he called before she could move past. "I'd like to have a word."

She paused. Backed up a step. Stood in the open doorway.

"Glad you're in early."

His face was away from her and as far as she could tell he hadn't even looked in her direction, which was a little disconcerting. She hadn't spoken, wasn't usually in before eight, and didn't think her footsteps were all that unique, yet there was no doubt he'd known it was she who was passing by his door.

"Come on in." He lifted one arm, still balancing himself off the floor with the other as he waved her inside.

Was he showing off? For her? She could have told him it wasn't going to work.

She stepped inside the small room that had once held a dog bed and hat rack. Both were gone, as were all of Grayson's personal belongings. Then again, his memorabilia had been missing for a while because Blackwater wasn't the first person to claim this office after Grayson had been shot; another man had sat in his chair, wielding his own brand of distorted power for a very short period.

"What can I do for you?" she asked him.

Dressed in uniform, his sleeves rolled up, his body straight as a board, not so much as breaking a sweat, Blackwater did three more slow, perfect push-ups, holding his body rigidly off the floor.

"You look busy," she said, looking longingly toward her office door.

"Nope. Finished. For now." In one swift, athletic motion he hopped to his feet and straightened, his face only slightly flushed. "Have a seat," he said, and she thought better of arguing, even though she was still wearing her jacket and hadn't even spent a second at her desk. "I'd like your take on the Cantnor and Pope homicides. Bring me up to speed."

"I thought Alvarez talked to you." Pescoli was pretty sure Blackwater had all the information they did.

"She did. As did Gage. But I'd like to hear what you think." He was staring at her intently, almost as if he were trying to read her mind.

So, he wants a recitation. Fine. "Well, I think we've got ourselves another nutcase." She perched stiffly on the chair she'd occupied so often when Grayson was alive.

Some kind of classical music was playing softly, Blackwater's computer was at the ready, the monitor glowing with the logo for the department on display, and every book, file, pen, or note pad was placed neatly on the desk or the surrounding cases, his awards mounted precisely on the walls. The whole "neat as a pin" feel gave Pescoli a bad feeling—kind of like Alvarez's office on steroids. It was all part and parcel of Blackwater's consistent military style.

"I think the murders are linked. That's the obvious conclusion, and I think it's the right one. We've got one sick jerk-off who gets his jollies by slicing off the victim's ring finger. I've got no real idea who's behind the deeds yet." She almost lost her train of thought, he was staring at her so intently, but she went through all the facts again as they knew them, finally returning to, "The big connection so far is the missing fingers and rings, and that fingerprint. We only hope we'll come up with a hit and be able to ID whoever picked up Sheree Cantnor's shoe and Calypso Pope's bag."

His eyebrows pinched together. "Not one suspect so far?"

He knew that, too, but apparently wanted her to reiterate. "No. At least not until we identify the print found on Cantnor's shoe and Pope's bag. Or, if our killer is dumb enough to try and pawn the rings and give himself away."

Blackwater picked a pencil out of the holder and leaning back in his chair, fiddled with it. "Odd case."

"We get our share around here."

"And then some," he agreed.

"Must be the water, or the hard winters. Makes people crazy."

He didn't so much as crack a smile. So much for a little levity.

"You got anything else?" he asked.

"We're still looking for a connection between the two women, old schools or boyfriends or friends, even friends of friends, but as near as we can tell at this point, the two victims didn't know each other."

"Random?"

"Or possibly each woman knew the killer, but not each other. If this were a TV show, it would turn out that the female victims happened to share the same bad-boy lover who maybe went to prison and hired some lunatic to off them or something like that. So far, we haven't been lucky enough to find any connection between the victims and Montana's version of a modern day Jerry Brudos."

When Blackwater didn't immediately respond, she elucidated. "The guy in Oregon who had a fetish for shoes and cut off body parts and kept 'em in the freezer. Back in the sixties, I think. My folks told me about it. Our guy has a thing for fingers and rings."

Listening, Blackwater asked, "You think the killer will strike again? Here?" He pointed to the office floor, but she knew he meant in the general area of Grizzly Falls.

"I would have said 'probably not' after the first victim. I mean, who knew what was going on? I thought the Cantnor woman's killer might just be a pissed off ex-boyfriend. But after Pope that doesn't make as much sense now. Maybe he's setting up for another kill, or maybe he was just passing through, did his business here, twice that we know of, then moved on. For all we know, there could be more bodies of earlier victims that have been killed and dumped somewhere else, and not yet discovered."

"He could have had other victims. Cases before ours."

"We're double-checking that, as well as the names of all of the women who've gone missing in the past month."

"Do you think he's moved on?" Blackwater asked.

Pescoli slowly shook her head. "Just a gut feeling, but no. Our doer seems to know the area pretty well. Either that, or he's been extremely fortunate, as we can't find a link between the women, and we have no video footage or pictures of anyone near the victims in their last moments. Somehow, he avoided any cameras on that stretch of the waterfront when he attacked Calypso Pope. The same goes for Sheree Cantnor, yet these days everyone has a camera phone in their purse or pocket. People are always taking pictures and posting them on social media sites. And most businesses keep security cameras running twenty-four seven. So, how's our guy been so lucky unless he's really aware of the area?"

As if realizing he was fiddling with the pencil, Blackwater replaced it. "Why the rings? The fingers?"

"Trophies? You know, to relive the moment. Again, like our friend Brudos. Or maybe some kind of personal statement about the rings, or marriage? Maybe both?" She shook her head. "Hard to know what kind of psychosis the doer's dealing with."

"You think he's insane?"

"Without a doubt, but, hey, I'm not giving the killer a defense. I'm just saying he's not what most of us would call normal."

Blackwater nodded. "Rings with fingers. A weird fetish."

"Name a fetish that isn't abnormal," she suggested and realized that for the first time since Blackwater had taken over they seemed to be on the same page.

His phone rang and he ended the meeting abruptly with, "Okay. Just wanted your thoughts. Keep me posted."

"Will do." She rose, then couldn't help herself from asking, "So, what's with the push-ups?"

"Keeps the blood flowing. Any kind of exercise. I do something every two hours, makes my brain clearer."

"Oh."

"You should try it."

"I should," she said equably.

He actually smiled, seeing through her. "And Pescoli?"

"Hmmm?"

"Just for the record, I know what happened. Out in the woods that day when you'd chased down Grayson's killer."

"Oh, yeah?" *Where is this going?*

"I'm glad your son saved your life and shot the son of a bitch who was trying to kill you." His hand was poised over the phone which was on its third ring, but his gaze was locked with hers.

Surprised, she said, "Umm. Me, too."

"You're lucky." Then he added, "Jeremy's a good kid." Blackwater actually flashed a quick smile, straight white teeth against bronzed skin. "And fortunately a damn good shot."

"Thanks," she said, then started down the hall to her office. She still wasn't fond of the man, but it seemed like he was at least trying harder. Unless he was just blowing hot air up her skirt because he sensed she neither trusted nor liked him. He was smart enough to pull that off, she knew.

As she reached the door to her office, she heard him answer, "Sheriff Blackwater," and the muscles in the back of her neck clenched. She had to remind herself to get over it. The office was his. Whether she trusted him or not, he was her boss. Until someone else was elected, or she quit, she'd just have to deal with him.

End of story.

Her hand searched frantically beneath the pillow, but her damn gun was missing!

Terrified, Anne Marie sat bolt upright, her eyes narrowing, her mind racing. It was a dream. That was it. A very real nightmare.

"I've got it." His voice was a raspy whisper over the wind screaming outside.

She blinked. Knew it was no dream. It was happening. *He'd* found her. Somehow. Someway. Her heart pounded, her courage flagged, and she wanted to melt into the couch.

You're still alive. He's got the gun, but you're still alive. Maybe he doesn't want to kill you . . .

And then she knew. Not kill. Torture. Maim.

Fight, damn it. Don't give up.

How had he found her? How had he broken in and she not heard? How the hell had he plucked the gun from under her head without her waking? She licked suddenly dry lips and remembered her dreams, the hot breath against her neck, the waking and thinking someone was inside, then convincing herself otherwise. Had he been right beside her? Within touching distance? If so, why hadn't he just killed her then, if that was his intent?

Her insides curdled at the thought of him watching her sleep while she lay unaware. While her heart was hammering wildly, she tried to think, to plot out her escape. But there was nowhere to run in the storm. If she tried to leave, he'd catch her fast. Still, her gaze slid to the window, so near the door where he stood, blocking any chance of escape. If she flung herself over the back of the couch and tried to make it across the room and through the kitchen to the back door, no doubt he would be on her in less than a second.

No no no! Even if she was able to run outside, how far would she get barefoot in the snow, in the raging wind and driving storm?

Unless she made it to her SUV.

She could drive to the sheriff's office. . . . Wait! Her phone! If she could somehow get away from him and call 9-1-1, she might have a chance.

A very slim one.

Or she could try to reason with him.

Oh, yeah. Right. Like that had ever worked.

"What are you doing here?" she finally demanded when she had her wits about her. Fear had driven any lingering vestige of sleep from her mind. As her eyes adjusted to the dim light, she tried to see him more clearly, still in the same position at the door. She tried to make out his features, to read his expression.

"Come on, Anne-Marie," he said, his voice a little clearer, his faint Texas drawl perceptible. "Is that any way to greet your husband?"

CHAPTER 23

Grabbing a cup of decaf from the carafe in the lunchroom, Pescoli settled down at her desk. Though it was still early, the department was starting to come alive. Officers, talking, laughing, and shaking off the cold, were drifting into the building with the change of shifts. Phones rang and a common printer positioned off the hallway near Joelle's desk hummed and clacked while the beast of a furnace wheezed as if it was on its last breath.

She sipped her weak-ass coffee and scanned her e-mail. Though she wouldn't admit it to Blackwater, she'd spent a lot of her free time on Sunday going over the Bart Grayson suicide file, as much for Dan as for Hattie. She felt it was an exercise in futility, but it had seemed fitting somehow, almost cathartic. With her kids at Luke's for the weekend, and Santana working on the new house, she'd put in some serious hours reviewing the years-old case and had tried to look at it with a new eye. But she'd found no hard evidence in the old reports that indicated Bartholomew Grayson had died by anything other than his own hand. Even though there was no suicide note left at the scene, nor message found in his belongings, nor conversation with a close friend or family member about taking his life, it still added up to the same conclusion. Friends and family alike had admitted how despondent Bart had been over the breakup of his marriage to Hattie. Apart from his widow, they, like the authorities, believed he'd ended it all. He'd died from suffocation by hanging himself in the barn, which was where his brother Cade had found him.

Bart Grayson's death had been a tragedy, of course. Unfortunate.

And probably preventable. He'd been a young, strapping man with two kids who, it seemed, had so much to live for.

Pescoli was certain everyone in the Grayson family, Dan included, had beat themselves up for not seeing the signs of Bart's depression. No one had been aware of how deep his despair had run.

Still, the bare facts of the case all pointed to the man taking his own life.

She would have to call Hattie and tell her as much. No doubt Bart's ex-wife still wouldn't accept the truth. In Pescoli's opinion, Hattie had been grappling with guilt ever since hearing the sad news about her ex and it was probably the root cause of her obsession with proving the suicide was really a murder. She fervently believed Bart would never willingly leave his daughters, that his love for them would have stopped him from taking his own life.

Pescoli wondered about the whole tangled web of Hattie Dorsey and the Grayson brothers. As rumor had it, Hattie's love for Bart hadn't exactly trumped her interest in the other men in his family. Then there was Cara, Dan's first ex-wife, whom Pescoli had learned at the funeral was Hattie's half sister. That was the family connection. It was all so intertwined, but hey, who was she to judge? Hattie had always had a fascination with all things Grayson.

Another aspect of the case was the insurance money. Bart had taken out two substantial policies with Hattie Grayson and her daughters listed as the beneficiaries. As it was, those benefits had never been paid, not because Bart had changed them, nor because he and Hattie had been divorced at the time of his death, but because Bart had taken his own life, thereby nullifying the payment. The insurance companies had been within their legal rights to refuse to pay. The upshot was that Hattie and her daughters had inherited Bart's portion of the Grayson ranch, but they'd been cut out of several hundred thousand dollars that would have been theirs if Bart's death was declared a murder.

Therein lay the problem. Hattie Grayson was not a rich woman and could really use the money. A single mom, she worked in her own catering business in order to support her children, no doubt struggling at times to make ends meet. She could probably sell her part of the Grayson ranch to the remaining brothers, but she hadn't done that yet.

Money, in the form of insurance benefits, could be another reason beyond basic guilt that Bart's ex and beneficiary was so stubbornly insistent that he hadn't killed himself.

"The facts are the facts," Pescoli said to herself, satisfied that Bart Grayson's death was neither a mystery nor a homicide. The man took his own life.

She replaced the reports in the box Jeremy had brought in a few days earlier, then unzipped her bag to retrieve a banana.

God, she was hungry. Always, it seemed. So she'd eat, then, not half an hour later, puke.

Taking her first bite, she heard quick footsteps in the hallway and half-expected Joelle to appear. Instead, Alvarez nearly slid as she rounded the sharp corner into Pescoli's office.

"Guess what?" Alvarez said.

"Not in the mood for twenty-questions."

Alvarez actually flashed a smile, the first Pescoli had witnessed since Dan Grayson had been shot, and she was energized for the first time in weeks. "We got a hit."

"A hit?" Pescoli repeated, and for a second or two, she forgot the hunger pangs that had been so overpowering only seconds before. "On the fingerprint?"

"Yeah." Dark eyes sparking, Alvarez nodded. "It's from a missing person from New Orleans."

"New Orleans?"

"Yep. A missing heiress who was disowned by her family. They filed the report, uncertain if she were alive or dead, but, I'd say from the prints we found, she's very much alive. And deadly. Her name is Anne-Marie Calderone."

"How do you know this already? It's barely eight in the damn morning."

"It's earlier in New Orleans, so I've been in contact with them already. Been here since five."

"Good God," Pescoli said, aghast.

"Look, I couldn't sleep. O'Keefe's not here. The animals wanted to get up early, so the dog and I tried to go for a run, but it was too nasty. Nearly impossible, so I gave it up. Anyway, I had too much on my mind to sleep in," she admitted. "Like you, right? You're in earlier than usual."

"Not at five friggin' a.m."

Alvarez's smile faded a bit, and she glanced over her shoulder to the open doorway as if she thought someone might overhear. "It's weird, you know," she admitted over the rumbling of the furnace and the hard tread in the hallway as two deputies passed by the open door. "I thought that after the funeral, I'd be able to put everything in perspective. Get back to business here and make sure my personal life was on track, kind of sort things out, but . . ." She shrugged, her black hair shining nearly blue under the fluorescent fixtures on the ceiling.

Pescoli nodded. Sometimes it was eerie how Alvarez's thoughts echoed her own feelings. "At least we have a lead now. Though, I gotta admit, I didn't figure the killer for a woman. The strangulation and then the pre- or postmortem mutilation? It just seems too brutal, too physical."

"Women can be violent," Alvarez countered, though she, too, sounded a little dubious.

"I know, I know, but . . . it's hard for me to get my head around it."

"Well, that's the way it's looking."

"How was she careless enough to leave a print at each crime scene? Who the hell is Anne-Marie Calderone?"

"You're *not* my husband," Anne-Marie said, her fear bleeding into anger at the realization that the man standing in front of her had the nerve, the unmitigated gall to hold her at gunpoint and say he was her husband when they both knew it wasn't true. He wasn't the maniac she'd expected, the butcher from whom she'd been running. The man by the door was Troy-damn-Ryder.

"And whose fault is that?" he drawled in the damnably sexy West Texas drawl she'd once found so intriguing.

She decided to duck that particular, painful question. "What the hell are you doing here?" she demanded, her heart trip-hammering. A million emotions, none of them good, swirled inside her.

Troy was no killer. Or not that she knew of. Okay, he was rough around the edges and the law had never been something he'd worried about too much, but he wasn't the brutal psychopath she'd thought was chasing her down, the person she'd thought had killed at least two women as some kind of warning to her. How could she have been so foolish to think those poor women who had been murdered had anything to do with her? Was she that much of an egomaniac? If she could jump to such conclusions, maybe she really was ready for the loony bin again, just as her husband had claimed.

And this damn cowboy in front of her, the one she'd tried, and failed, to marry . . . *what is he doing here?*

In the shadowy interior of her cabin, she struggled to see his features, to read his expression, but failed.

"Isn't that what husbands do when their wives just take off? Track them down?"

"But you're not my husband," she repeated. "You know you're not my husband."

"Oh, yeah, that's right. When you said 'I do' at that little chapel in Vegas, you were still married."

That much was true. "I didn't know," she said, but even as the words passed her lips, they sounded lame.

"How could you not know?"

"It was an assumption on my part. A mistake. We've been over this." She felt the chill of his gaze cutting through the dark atmosphere, and for a second, she regretted what she'd done, how she'd led him on, not that she'd meant to. "You know I thought my ex had signed the papers and—"

"He wasn't your ex."

"Okay, okay. Not officially."

"Not legally," Ryder bit out, irritated. "Kind of important."

"Oh, forget it." She threw up her hands in surrender. "Saying I'm sorry now doesn't cut it. I know that. I screwed up."

"Big time."

"*Yes.* Yes." When he didn't respond, she said, "I can't believe that you hunted me down, in this . . . in this damn blizzard in Montana to steal my gun and argue about the past. You *scared* me." It felt like a dream, a remnant of the terrors that had invaded her brain during the night and made her think she'd woken up when she was really still asleep, everything taking on a weird twist. But that was only wishful thinking. She was very much awake, beyond alert, and she was in the cold, dark, smelly cabin with the wild-ass cowboy she'd fallen for so hard that she, like him, had ignored the details of the law.

"I get it that you're pissed. You should be. But that was over a year ago and . . . and since when are you such a stickler for legalities?"

'When it comes to my damn wife." He strode closer to her. "You're impossible, you know."

"I'm not the one pointing a gun at the person I once swore I loved." Folding her arms over her chest, she squinted up at him, trying to see his features, read the expression in his eyes. "But why? Why go to all these lengths? I thought we understood each other."

He muttered furiously under his breath, but just said, "I came to get you."

For the briefest of instants, her heart tripped, a tiny bit of hope soared, but she tamped it down quickly. She wasn't that foolish anymore. She didn't trust him blindly. Nor did he trust her. And then, there was the matter of the weapon. "Well, okay, but most men who come for a woman, don't hold her at gunpoint."

"It probably happens more often than you think. I never understood until now. But I didn't come here to patch things up."

"You couldn't," she said, cringing inwardly at the bit of a lie. The truth was, she'd never completely gotten over him. Not one hundred percent. There was a part of her, a tiny very feminine part of her, that still fantasized about him, but she tamped that emotion down, wishing she could kill it.

"Just for the record, this"—he moved his hand, displaying her pistol—"is a pathetic excuse for a gun."

"Thank-you so much. That's so helpful," she shot out, then wished she'd held her tongue. That was the trouble with Ryder. Her blood ran hot around him, her emotions volatile. "It might be small, but you're still aiming it at me."

"You're lucky I don't just pull the trigger."

"You didn't come all this way just to shoot me. You could have done that and been halfway back to Louisiana by now."

"Well, darlin', at least you're starting to get it."

"What?"

"It's time to go. The reason that I'm pointing this gun at you is because I want you to grab your things and get moving. I figured you might not be all that keen on the idea, so your pistol came in handy. So, get up. Now."

* * *

"I'm just not buying it," Pescoli said from her desk chair. She was still processing the information her partner had given her and trying to see a woman as their doer. "I know a lot of women who have jewelry envy. They're all about who has the biggest rock as some kind of validation of love or something. Even my daughter went crazy over my ring when she first saw it. But I've never heard of one who would kill for a ring by cutting the damn finger off."

"Women kill," Alvarez said. "If it isn't for a justifiable cause like protecting their children, then it's over a man. Usually a loser of a man."

"Yeah, that's true," Pescoli admitted.

"You ever watch *Judge Judy*?"

"No. You do? You have time for reality TV in the middle of the day?"

"I record it."

That surprised Pescoli as she'd pegged Alvarez as a workaholic.

"O'Keefe got me started on it, and once in a while I tune in. If the litigants are complaining about loans and gifts or rent and broken leases, it's usually some woman all up in arms that her friend slept with her boyfriend or husband or whatever. The weird thing is that to a one, they blame the other woman as if it was all that woman's fault and their poor, dumb husband couldn't resist. That he was just the patsy in the Jezebel's lurid, malicious trap, and that's why he couldn't keep it in his pants."

"No one on *Judge Judy* is a killer," Pescoli pointed out.

"I'm just saying it's not impossible. We've run in our share of women who've killed. You know it."

"But to cut off a finger—"

"What about those women who kill a pregnant woman and cut open her uterus because they want the baby or have somehow convinced themselves that the baby inside is really theirs?"

"Those women are mentally deranged." Pescoli fought an overpowering need to place her hands protectively over her own midsection and failed.

"Sorry," Alvarez said, pulling herself up short. "But our killer's mentally deranged, too. Taking a finger wouldn't be past a woman. That's all I'm saying."

Pescoli glanced at the autopsy report on Calypso Pope, a copy of which lay atop another file on her desk. "A crushed hyoid bone. In both cases. That takes strength."

"Strength, but not necessarily size. And know-how. Maybe martial arts?"

Pescoli tossed the remains of her banana in the trash. "So you think this Anne-Marie Calderone is our killer?"

"That's the avenue I'm taking."

"Doesn't it seem a little too obvious? To leave a print on the one piece of evidence that's located? There's not a second shoe, and that's the only print on Pope's Mercedes. Lots of other prints all over that car," she corrected herself. She was thinking aloud. "The Cantnor woman's purse wasn't located, but the second victim's bag was found fairly easily and it had that identifying print."

"But any way you look at it, this woman is at the top of the suspect list. Right now, she's all we've got. She's obviously involved, we just don't know how. I've got a call in to the New Orleans PD and Zoller is checking all the newspaper and police databases, looking for information about Calderone." Sage Zoller was a junior detective with the department. Tiny and fit, she ran marathons, mentored at-risk teens and was a techno wiz kid. A dynamo. "She'll report back to us."

"Good."

At that moment, Alvarez's cell phone rang. She answered, "Detective Alvarez," then held up a finger. "Thanks for calling back, Detective Montoya. We've got a situation up here—a couple homicides—and we found the same fingerprint at both scenes. Looks like it belongs to Anne-Marie Calderone. I was hoping you could supply me with a little more information about her as she's just become a person of interest up here."

She nodded at Pescoli and headed out of the office.

Pescoli rolled her chair closer to the desk, where she brought up the basic information on Anne-Marie Favier Calderone from New Orleans. The woman's driver's license picture and information appeared on the screen and though, more often than not, the photo taken at the DMV was usually pretty damn bad, this woman was stunning with her large eyes, easy smile, and oval face. Her hair was a deep brown with red highlights, shoulder-length and thick, her height and weight consistent with someone who kept herself in shape.

Pescoli stared long and hard at the photo. Was she looking into the face of a cold-blooded killer? A woman who took satisfaction, even joy, in cutting off fingers and diamonds?

She found herself playing with her own ring and stopped. This was insane. Or was it?

"No way," she said aloud, but, of course, she couldn't argue the facts. Anne Marie Calderone was connected to the dead women. Pescoli just had to figure out how.

CHAPTER 24

Shivering, the cold of the morning seeping into her bones, Anne-Marie said, "I'm not going back to New Orleans." She stared pointedly at the man in shadow. "Gun or no gun." But she did climb off the couch, her bare feet touching the floor. "Come on in. You don't have to guard the damn door. Where do you think I'm going in this?"

As if to add emphasis to her words, the wind squealed around the house and the damn limb started banging against the exterior wall again. Ignoring him, she walked the few steps to the fireplace and went to work, grabbing chunks of split wood she'd hauled inside the night before, prodding at the charred logs with the poker, searching for an ember glowing red beneath the ash. When she had success, she blew on the coals so that they burned brighter, a flame sparking against the moss and dry hemlock as the wood caught fire.

Settling back on her heels, she watched as the flames began to grow, crackling as they devoured the fuel. Her fingers tightened over the poker still in her right hand. She didn't want to harm Ryder, but she wasn't going back to Louisiana with him. No way. She never wanted to see her family again and there was a chance that *he* would find her there. Now that she felt a new security, that she realized it was Ryder who had been following her rather than the monster who had tossed her into the Mississippi, she could finally feel some sort of relief and believe that she did have a chance for a new life for herself. A life without any ties to the past and that included Troy Ryder.

"Drop it," he ordered.

Still crouching near the grate, she looked over her shoulder to see that he still had the gun pointed at her. For the love of God, did he really think she believed for a second that he would shoot her? She didn't let go of the poker, but stared at him over her shoulder. He was still near the door, about eight feet from her. If she sprang and swung, she might be able to hit him hard. She needed to take his advantage away and somehow, remove his gun. She had the poker, and her little switchblade was hidden in the folds of the clothes she'd piled near the couch.

Maybe there was some way to disarm him, gain the upper hand. As the fire burned brighter and hotter, the room lightened. Finally she saw his face, no longer in complete shadow and her heart twisted again. His was a rugged visage. His features were oversized—his jaw strong, big eyes deep in his sockets, a nose that had been broken a couple times, a hard line of a mouth, and a square jaw covered in a couple of days' worth of stubble.

"I said, 'drop it,' Anne-Marie. Don't even think about it."

Her grip tightened.

"Jesus, are you serious? You think you're going to get the better of me with a poker?"

"You won't shoot me. I'm not going back to New Orleans. Not ever." The fire popped then and her muscles jumped. Then, as if he'd been reading her thoughts all along, she saw him reach into his pocket with his free hand only to withdraw a stick of some kind . . .

Click! Her switchblade snapped open in his hand, its spring-loaded blade suddenly reflecting the shifting light from the fire.

"How—?" Inadvertently, her gaze slid to the stack of folded clothes where she was certain she'd hidden the deadly knife. She didn't finish the sentence. Her mind spinning, she wondered how the hell he'd known she had it, how he'd found it as well as the gun. She'd assumed he'd guessed she had hidden a weapon under her pillow, but the knife from her clothes? Had he rifled through her things while looking for the pistol and found the switchblade first, then continued his stealthy search while she'd been restlessly sleeping unaware or had he . . .

"You *spied* on me?" she charged, astounded, her mind taking hold of the idea and churning wildly. "You were in here before and planted devices and *spied* on me?" That was a big leap, a major vault, but he didn't immediately deny it. She remembered feeling as if she were being watched, that though the shades had been drawn, the doors locked tightly, that there had been hidden eyes following her every move. "What is wrong with you?"

"I had to make certain that Jessica Williams was really Anne-Marie Calderone. And that my leads were right, that Jessica was also the same person as Stacey Donahue in Denver and Heather Brown earlier on."

Dear God, how long had he been following her? He knew *all of it*.

"I wasn't going to barge in on the wrong person, so I had to make sure."

She shook her head, disbelieving, not even understanding how he, a damn half-broke rodeo rider, could understand about high tech electronics. It suddenly occurred to her that because their romance had been so white-hot and rushed and she'd decided to marry him after knowing him only a few weeks, there was much more to the cowboy from somewhere in West Texas than met the eye. She hadn't known him and his secrets any better than he'd known her and the lies that were the bones of her past.

But now she wanted to.

"Who *are* you?"

After hanging up from Detective Montoya, Alvarez coordinated the information he'd given her with what was known about the crimes in Montana. Zoller had e-mailed some information on Anne-Marie Calderone and was checking to see if there had been any similar killings in the last year in other parts of the country. So far, the department hadn't heard of women who had been murdered, the ring fingers of their left hands severed, nor had they found any other crimes where the Calderone woman's fingerprints had shown up.

But, she told herself, *it is still early.*

The Pinewood Sheriff Department might be on the track of one of the most deadly female serial killers in history.

I'm getting ahead of myself, she thought, leaning back in her desk chair and taking a sip of her tea that she'd gotten from the break room. It was stone-cold, the tea bag still steeping in it, the orange-spice so strong she nearly gagged. Setting her cup aside, she concentrated on her computer screen, reminding herself that most likely there were no other identical crimes anywhere close by or she would have already found mention of it. Because of computers and communication systems, like crimes were more quickly identified.

She glanced at her e-mail, searching for more reports and heard a text come into her cell phone. One look and she smiled.

The short missive was from Gabriel, her biological son with whom she'd recently reconnected. **No school!!!** Along with the two words he'd attached a winking smiley face.

She quickly texted back, **Have fun. See you soon.**

Her heart swelled at the thought of him, the teenager who'd been raised by Aggie and Dave Reeve. Aggie was Dylan O'Keefe's cousin and not all that happy that her son had discovered his birth mother, but the two women were working things out. Alvarez kept her distance as she didn't want to intimidate the woman who had spent all of Gabe's life caring for him, raising him, teaching him right from wrong.

She added a smiley face to her text despite the fact that she loathed all the emoticons. *But when in teenaged Rome . . .* She hit SEND.

She turned her attention back to the matter at hand—running Anne-Marie Calderone to the ground. Whether the woman who'd left her fingerprint on the belongings recovered from the victims was the actual killer or an accessory, or something else, she had some explaining to do. Some serious explaining.

Taking a swing at him wouldn't help, so Anne-Marie let loose of the poker, stood, and dusted her hands.

"Who am *I?*" Ryder repeated. "I'm not the one with myriad disguises, a series of fake IDs, and multiple aliases."

"But you were spying on me. I don't remember you being some kind of techno geek who could bug rooms. Where the hell are they?" she demanded and turned around in a tight circle, searching in the dark corners, the lamps, wherever.

"You never bothered to find out that I was in the Special Forces and specialized in communications, did you?" When she looked at him as if he were mad, he admitted, "Afghanistan. Nothing I really want to dwell on."

"Was this pre- or post-cowboy?"

"Between," he admitted, snapping the switchblade closed and putting it, along with her gun, into a pocket.

Now that it was light, she could see that pocket was already bulging. "Wait a minute. You have your own damn gun?"

He smiled then. That reckless, roguish smile she'd found so irresistible. "You didn't think I'd come in here unarmed."

"But you stole my gun."

"Didn't feel like having you use it on me."

"I wouldn't have . . . well, if I'd known it was you, anyway."

Apparently satisfied that she wasn't going to flee or attack him, he started stripping small microphones and cameras from the tiniest of places around the room—a crack in the fireplace, a dark corner of the bookcase, even the damn wood box.

"Really?" she said, watching in disbelief and suddenly feeling bare and vulnerable, all of her worst fears coming to the fore. He'd been observing her every move, whether she'd been awake or asleep. He'd seen her break down or flop in despair or rail at the heavens. "I can't believe you would do all this—"

"Believe," he said without emotion.

She was trying to make sense of it all but couldn't. She'd thought, once they'd broken up, she would never see him again. He'd been so furious with her that she'd thought he might strangle her. He'd said as much. "Go to hell, Anne-Marie," he'd said, "and don't look over your shoulder."

So, why would he be there now, dissecting her life . . . no, injecting himself back into it . . . trying to force her to retrace her steps and return to a city she'd sworn she'd never set foot in again?

"I don't understand why you want me to go back to New Orleans," she said.

"I've actually got a couple reasons," he admitted. "The first is that after you and your husband disappeared—"

"Me and my husband?" she interrupted.

"Yes, after—"

"He left, too?" The dread that had temporarily abated came flooding back.

"You know that."

"No." She shook her head and swallowed with difficulty. Dear God, she was back to where she'd started. "Why would he leave?"

"You two had a major fight. The neighbors heard it."

Her knees went suddenly weak at the memory and cold terror slipped through her veins. She dropped back onto the mussed sleeping bag covering the couch.

"My name came up," Ryder said.

Of course. Oh. Sweet. Jesus.

"So, you both go missing and guess who's left holding the emotional bag? Yours truly."

"But you had nothing to do with it."

"As I tried to explain, but the police had a different idea. A guy by the name of Detective Montoya? He's pretty sure that somehow I'm involved in both disappearances."

"What? No!" She couldn't believe it. "But that's insane."

"Insanity to you and me. *Motive* to the police. The theory is that I might have been so damn pissed about the affair blowing up in my face the way it did, that I went into a jealous rage and got rid of you both."

"You're lying."

"That's your department, darlin'." Ryder's voice was cold. "The police are grasping at straws, and I told them that. But my alibi of being on the road that night didn't hold any water with them. That hotheaded homicide detective? Montoya? He's a real piece of work and he never quite believed my story. The only good news was that he didn't have a body, not even one . . . with two people missing, so they couldn't build a case against me. Not that he isn't trying. So, it would be a big favor to me, if you'd go prove that you're not dead."

"That still leaves my husband," she whispered.

"Your problem. Not mine."

"Oh, God," she whispered, believing Ryder's story, knowing she'd left a mess behind her when she'd worked so hard to disappear. And the mess kept following her. The only good news was that she was more convinced than ever that the two women who'd been recently killed around Grizzly Falls had nothing to do with her.

"So pack up because we're leaving."

"There's a storm outside," she reminded.

"Always a storm of one kind or another, always a road block." He cast a glance in her direction. "We'll take our chances."

"That's nuts."

"All relative, especially where you're concerned." He pocketed yet another camera, then walked into the kitchen and small bath.

He'd even seen her showering or on the toilet or . . . "You're a pervert, Ryder," she yelled, but her eyes were on the front door. She only needed her keys and she could race to the Tahoe and peel out of there. Or—*Crap!* Why hadn't she thought of it before? Her cell phone. It was . . .

In the pile of clothes where her switchblade had been hidden. She quickly tossed her jeans and sweater aside, but, of course, the tiny phone wasn't where she'd left it. Her keys . . . no, they were gone, too.

"Son of a bitch," she hissed just as he returned from the bathroom. "You really are a bastard, aren't you?" She was standing in the middle of the living room, trying to come up with some kind of option because no matter what he thought, she was not returning to Louisiana.

"You know, I try my level best."

At the news of a potential suspect in the Cantnor and Pope homicides, Blackwater wanted an up-to-the-minute report on everything the department knew about the new suspect. If the lead panned out, he would order a BOLO—Be On The Lookout—bulletin for the woman.

He called in Alvarez and Pescoli, Zoller, the junior detective in charge of the Internet research, Deputy Winger as he trusted her advice, and Brett Gage, the chief criminal deputy.

Joelle Fisher, of course, couldn't let a meeting go without bringing in a tray with two kinds of coffee, cups along with napkins, creamers and sweeteners.

Blackwater finally understood that, especially with the receptionist, there was a certain amount of decorum that had to be followed, tradition, if you will. He could appreciate Joelle's single-mindedness when it came to a task, but worrying over who drank decaf or avoided artificial sweeteners or that the platter had a damn paper doily covering it, weren't his top priorities. He wished Joelle would dial it back, just a notch or two, and he'd said as much.

She'd complied, but he sensed it was only temporary. Decorations and baked goods, celebrations of all kinds were part of her DNA, just like her throwback beehive hairstyle.

"Thank-you," he said as she left the meeting room, each step reverberating quickly against the tile floor.

"Let's get to it," he said as the invitees took spots around the table.

Other than Gage, no one bothered filling a cup. Alvarez and Zoller each had electronic notebooks, Gage and Pescoli notepads and pens. Blackwater had both at his fingertips. "I know about the prints and the connection, but what do we know about this person, Anne-Marie Calderone? You talked to someone in New Orleans, right?"

"Detective Montoya, yes," Alvarez said, taking the lead in the discussion and passing out two pages, one with the picture from the suspect's Louisiana driver's license, the other a sheet of facts about the woman in question. "Anne-Marie Favier Calderone. She's thirty years old and, according to Montoya, been missing for several months. He's sending us the files and a timeline, but the long and the short of it is that she was married to Bruce Calderone, a medical doctor who, until recently, worked at a private hospital in New Orleans. Once connected to the Catholic church, it's now run by lay people. He was a surgeon."

"Was?" Blackwater interrupted, feeling his eyebrows slam together.

"He seemed to have disappeared, as well. Both he and his wife. From the interviews Montoya did with friends and family, it appears the marriage wasn't stable, with accusations of affairs on both sides. Though there were never any charges filed, there were rumors of abuse."

Alvarez continued on, saying that Anne-Marie Favier had grown up a daughter of privilege. The Faviers had once had family money, at least during Anne-Marie's youth. According to her parents' sworn statements, she was headstrong and brilliant but a little unbalanced. In high school, she spent three months in a mental hospital for undisclosed issues. Montoya had said the records were sealed as she'd been a minor at the time. Later, she'd not only finished a four year program but also held an MA in philosophy from Tulane University.

The trouble started after her marriage to Bruce Calderone, a medical student whom she'd helped through school. There followed breakups and reconciliations, even some long separations, which included the last one. She and Calderone had been separated and she'd filed for divorce. She'd signed, but Calderone had balked.

She'd ignored that little fact when she'd married her latest fling, a cowboy by the name of Troy Ryder in a tiny chapel in Las Vegas. When that relationship apparently soured, she returned to New Orleans sans the new groom, but when Calderone learned about the second marriage he'd blown a gasket. Though, again, not reported to the police at the time, the neighbors had heard screaming and yelling which ended abruptly around ten or ten-thirty. The next day, they were gone. Both of them. All of their worldly possessions left behind. It was, according to Montoya, as if they'd each just fallen off the face of the earth.

No cars taken, no credit cards used, no cell phones answered or turned on so the cops could locate them.

"That's basically it, except for one interesting fact," Alvarez said. "Though Anne-Marie wasn't close to either of her parents, she was adored by her grandmother. The grandfather died years earlier, but the weekend Anne-Marie and her husband went missing, the grandmother was robbed. She claimed she had fifty thousand dollars in her safe and no one, other than her granddaughter and her daughter, knew the combination, though they of course could have told others. Montoya thinks the mother is in the clear and that leaves Anne-Marie."

"She would steal from the one person she loved?" Pescoli asked.

Alvarez paused. "Maybe she was desperate. According to her parents, Montoya notes, that despite all of her education, their daughter never made any serious money or pursued a career in her field of interest. She held odd jobs all through school. Worked as a clerk or a waitress even after she graduated."

"While her husband finished medical school?" Blackwater asked.

Alvarez studied her screen. "Uh-huh. What little Anne-Marie made, coupled with his student loans, kept them afloat."

Blackwater asked, "Either of them ever steal before?"

"Neither had a criminal record. So if they had, they were never caught. But if they had the grandmother's cash to finance their disappearance, and maybe new identities, it could explain why we can't find either one of them."

He rubbed his chin and shook his head as he thought. "They hated each other, so it's unlikely they were on the run together, and if he had a thriving medical practice—"

"Not thriving." Alvarez shook her head. "In fact, Dr. Calderone not only worked at the hospital but was a partner in a clinic. The business was going bankrupt, though his partners think he was not only syphoning off money but prescription drugs, as well. After he disappeared, a couple women came forward and reported that he'd been inappropriate with them. They're suing his practice as well as him personally, and as such, his wife."

"Because she had money?"

"Her family had money, *at one time*, but according to the New Orleans PD, Mr. and Mrs. Talbert Favier are teetering on the verge of bankruptcy. It's kind of a case of everyone believing everyone else had huge piles of dough stashed somewhere, but the Faviers had invested in real estate and their own business and it was all hit hard during the recession. The only person with any money left is Grandma Favier."

Blackwater frowned at the flat image of the woman who seemed to be staring up at him from her driver's license photo. "Do we have any more pictures?"

"Montoya's sending them through e-mail." Alvarez checked her iPad. "Oh, here we go. Let me hook this up." She spent a few seconds connecting her device to a large monitor on the wall and clicked through a series of images of a beautiful woman in her twenties, laughing and mugging for the camera. "Some of these are from her Facebook account. No activity of course since they disappeared. Nothing on any social media platforms. And here." She flipped through another series. "This is the husband, Bruce Calderone."

They all leaned forward to look at the picture. Calderone was a big man with even teeth and an easy smile. He was dressed in a lab coat.

"And one more. Anne Marie Calderone's love interest. Troy Ryder." Another image filled the screen, a man of thirty odd years with tanned skin, crow's feet, and eyes set deep in his skull.

Blackwater looked from Alvarez to Pescoli, who'd let her partner do all the talking. Pescoli's mouth was stubbornly set as if she didn't agree with what was going on.

He glanced back at the picture. "So, now we've got a love triangle, a robbed grandmother, two missing people from New Orleans, and our two dead victims with the severed fingers dumped here in Grizzly Falls." He glanced around the table. "Am I missing anything else?"

"Just one more thing," Alvarez said. "There was talk about her being involved at one time with Cade Grayson."

"Another boyfriend?"

"Long before Ryder. Cade's a person who could be her connection to Grizzly Falls, maybe why she ended up here."

"That woman really gets around," Gage observed.

"Two boyfriends, one husband," Pescoli said. "Not so much getting around."

"More like two husbands, one boyfriend," Gage rejoined. "She seems to have a little trouble with her marriage vows."

"Lot of that going around," Pescoli said.

Blackwater interrupted. "Someone needs to talk to him. See if Grayson's seen her."

Alvarez said, "Already on it."

"Good. Now, is there anything else?"

Gage shrugged and Alvarez shook her head. Zoller and Winger were both busily taking notes. He focused on Pescoli. "What do you think, Detective?"

"Fingerprint or no fingerprint, I have trouble believing our doer's a woman."

Blackwater felt impatient, but whether he liked the rogue detective or not, he grudgingly respected her gut instincts.

"I think it's damn convenient that we have her prints, no, make that *print*, singular. One at each scene," Pescoli went on. "Doesn't anyone else find that convenient?"

Gage gave another shrug. "Maybe odd."

Blackwater regarded Pescoli for a moment, then said, "Since we can't find hide nor hair of Mr. or Mrs. Calderone, maybe we should be looking for Ryder. Unless he's hiding, too, and they're all involved in this thing together, which I don't believe, there should be records of him. Credit card receipts and cell phone records?"

"Montoya's already on it," Alvarez said, reading from her device. "Looks like he was recently in Denver, but he did buy gas in Casper, Wyoming and Billings, Montana and finally, a few days ago, made a purchase right here in Grizzly Falls at Corky's Gas and Go."

Blackwater said, "And I assume we have a make and model of his vehicle?"

Alvarez glanced up from her computer while Winger broke down and poured herself a cup of coffee. "We do."

"Then I suggest you start at the gas station with pictures of Ryder. Take the others as well, just in case he's traveling with either of them, then check the local motels. He probably doesn't think anyone's looking for him, so he might be registered under his own name. Let's bird-dog him." Blackwater felt a warm spot deep in his gut. Maybe this case would break under his watch, the culprits of a scandalous crime spree that stretched from the deep South to Grizzly Falls brought to justice. "Don't forget Cade Grayson. The two on the run might be in disguise, so let's work with the computer guys, do some enhancements, Photoshop a little, play with the images." He grinned at his team. That's right, *his* team. "Who knows, the missing Calderones might be hiding in plain sight right under our noses."

CHAPTER 25

Anne-Marie was through being bullied. She jabbed an angry finger straight at Ryder. "I'm never going back to Louisiana, but I was willing to turn myself in here."

"Because of Cade Grayson?"

She'd picked up her jeans and was reaching for her sweater but stopped to look at him in surprise.

"I knew about him. And when your coworkers in Denver mentioned you were hooking up with an old boyfriend, he came to mind."

"What happened between Cade and me was a long time ago."

"But you came here."

"I was going to meet with his brother. Dan was the sheriff. Cade had sworn he was fair and would look at all sides of an issue. I knew I had to turn myself in, that I couldn't keep running, but I didn't trust anyone in New Orleans. My father golfs with judges and lawyers and . . . and he thought I'd made a big mistake. That no matter what, I should stick with Bruce. He would rather believe I was lying." She bristled at that thought, that her own parents had sided with the man who had beaten her.

"So, what made you finally run?" Ryder asked, a tenderness in his voice.

It made her heart soften though she knew it was stupid. He didn't care for her, possibly never had. After the whole bigamy thing, he could never trust or think kindly of her again. Yet there was a note in his words that pierced beneath the shield she'd built around her heart.

She sat on one arm of the couch and pulled on her jeans. The fire was burning bright and finally casting some heat into the room. "We'd had one of our classic fights. The last one, I'd hoped. It was on the phone and I'd decided, once and for all, it was over. I was strong enough to leave him forever.

"I'd never moved back into the house once you and I . . . well, ever since Las Vegas. I didn't love him. Probably never had. I was done. I wanted out. If I never saw him again, that would have been fine. I knew he'd never forgive me, but I made a major mistake. I still had things at his house where I used to live, and so . . . I knew he was working at his office, so I went back to our townhouse intent on loading up the rest of my things and leaving town."

She clenched her teeth at the memory, and heard once again in her mind, the downstairs door opening when she'd been on the upper floor in the master bedroom.

She had already stripped out the closet. Her clothes were strewn across the king-sized bed she'd come to hate. Barely able to breathe, she prayed he had just come home for a quick bite, that he hadn't seen her car parked out back.

And then she heard his footsteps on the stairs, his tread swift and determined as he mounted the steps to the second floor. She cowered in the closet, but it was no use. He threw open the bedroom door, looked at the mess on the bed, and zeroed in on the closet. As he opened the door, a shaft of light pierced the messy interior where she was hiding between his suits and shirts.

"What do you think you're doing?" he roared, though her intent was painfully obvious. "Leaving? Leaving me? You think you can do that? Leave me for some cheap cowboy? Steal away like a common whore in the middle of the night?" His face, the contours of which she'd once found so handsome, twisted in rage. Nostrils flared, skin flushed, cords in his neck pronounced, he grabbed her by the hair and pulled her forcibly from the interior of the closet.

She swung at him hard, connected with his ribs, and then saw the hypodermic needle in his free hand. Oh God, she thought, he knew she'd returned and was ready for her.

She felt the jab of the needle in her arm and, as the room began to swim, saw him pick up the rings she'd put on the night stand—the engagement ring and wedding band that he'd given her—that she shouldn't have ever let him see again.

"Are you fucking kidding me? This isn't over until I say it's over." The diamonds winked in his hand and then he closed his fist around the clear stones. His lips were curled in rage.

Still swinging her arms and flailing wildly, she gratefully passed out at that moment.

Anne-Marie shook her head. From that point, she remembered nothing at all until she became groggily aware. It all came back.

She felt cold air on her bare skin and a dull throb in her hand, something slick beneath her, the smell of dank earth in her nostrils. Before she could fully revive, she was kicked hard, sent spinning and rolling. The plastic tarp whipped from under her body as she careened down a berm and splashed into the murky water where she woke with the first gulp of silty water.

She knew she had to play dead, to let the slow-moving current carry her on its path. She caught glimpses of moonlight through scudding clouds, saw the ghostly roots of cypress trees rising above the water line, and knew she wasn't alone in the sluggish water, that alligators waited, hunting. Yet she managed to slip slowly downriver, around a wide curve, and deeper into the woods, undisturbed.

She eased her way to the bank, praying that she didn't disturb a nest of gators or step on a snake as she dragged her naked body out of the water by grabbing on to a thick, bleached root. She made her way through the soupy ground to a shack that was boarded over. She broke through a small window and found clothing three sizes too large, but dry. She quickly dressed and stumbled out to the road.

She made her way to the outskirts of New Orleans, hitching a ride with some teenagers high on marijuana.

"Anne-Marie?"

She heard and snapped back to reality and the dilapidated cabin where Ryder was still waiting for an answer. There was more to her story, of course. The most pivotal part that she hated to think about.

He was standing by the fire, warming the backs of his legs.

"I ran because he beat me, Ryder. That's why I ran." She closed her eyes at the admission, and though she knew she shouldn't be ashamed, it was difficult to admit the hateful truth. How could someone who'd sworn to love her, to protect her, had vowed to be her husband for all their lives, been able to raise his hand to her, to beat her with a viciousness that could only be described as hatred?

"I put up with it for a while, believed him when he claimed to love me, begged me to come back, and promised that he would never hurt me again. He cried, and I wanted to believe him. At least in the beginning." She saw the unasked questions in Ryder's eyes, listened to them ricochet off the walls of her brain because she'd asked herself the same things—*Why did you stay? Why didn't you walk away the first time? Why didn't you call the police? Why in the world did you let it happen more than one damn time?*

"You didn't tell me any of this."

"I didn't want you to know." She couldn't read what he was thinking, so she just went on. "I finally realized that he would never change so we split up. He wasn't happy about it, but I was through being his punching bag. It wasn't about love, it was about ownership. I was his, and though he really didn't want me anymore, he sure as hell didn't want anyone else to have me." Her fists clenched at the memory. "So, I filed for divorce, met you . . . and it felt so good to laugh again, to fall in love, to . . . oh, hell, I don't know . . . to *live* again without fear. I wanted it to work out with you and me. Wanted it so much."

She blinked back tears. Refused to cry. She knew that she'd thrown herself into her affair with Ryder far too fast and her enthusiasm had more to do with breaking free of her old life than of starting a new one with him. She hadn't really known him and had kidded herself about finding true love with a happy-ever-after ending.

Forcing her balled fists to unclench, she said, "I thought he'd sign the divorce papers, but I should have known better. Bruce Calderone doesn't lose. Especially to his wife. My leaving meant that I'd won. At least to him. I was naive enough to think that with time, he'd cool off, see that our marriage was a big mistake from the get-go. I convinced myself that he would calm down and accept that we shouldn't be together."

Ryder was frowning hard, but he let her continue without comment.

"I made the mistake of returning to the house after we'd been separated for over a year to pick up some of my things. And . . . and he beat me within an inch of my life."

Ryder's jaw slid to one side, a muscle working under his temple. "So, what happened to him?"

"Don't know. Don't care."

"He's still your husband."

Her insides shriveled at the thought. She didn't want to think about it anymore. Something Ryder had mentioned earlier still bothered her. "You said that there were two reasons you wanted to haul me back to Louisiana, the first being to clear your name as that detective down there . . . what's his name?"

"Montoya."

"He thought you were involved in my disappearance." She pulled her sweater from the pile of clothes she'd gathered on her lap and drew it over her head. "What was the second?"

Ryder was still standing by the fireplace. He'd scarcely moved a muscle.

"What's the other reason?" she asked again. "You've made it abundantly clear that it isn't because you missed my company."

He was quiet, as if he didn't want to admit to his reasons.

Though she'd sworn she didn't care, she felt a niggle of disappointment. She'd kidded herself that he was different, that he wasn't interested in her because of her looks, or her charm, or the fact that her family had money and someday she would inherit a small fortune. No, Troy Ryder had been different from the others, more into her as a person than anyone, including Bruce Calderone and Cade Grayson, had been.

She saw he wasn't all that different, after all. And then, like a tidal wave that's drawn far out to sea only to turn, she realized the truth in a crashing, drowning blow. "Let me guess," she said, hating the thought. "You're here because you think I have money."

"Close." His jaw was hard.

"You think my family will pay for me? You're going to hold me for ransom?"

"Gettin' warmer," he said but didn't seem to have any pride in his statement. And the drawl she'd once found so endearing actually grated.

"What the hell is that supposed to mean?"

"It's not a ransom," he said shortly. It was clear he was having some difficulty explaining himself.

Why would he chase her down, then spend these last months searching for her? Then she knew. "It's a bounty. My damn family offered you money to bring me home and you accepted." She let out a disgusted sigh and folded her arms across her chest, staring at him. "How disappointing."

That actually looked like it penetrated, but she wasn't going to let her romantic side believe something that wasn't true any longer. "I can't believe they even care," she said bitterly. "How much am I worth, if I dare ask?"

It took him a moment or two, but then he bit out, "One hundred thousand dollars."

"Cade Grayson's still not answering," Alvarez said from the passenger seat of Pescoli's Jeep after calling twice. She'd left two messages for him to call her back.

"He might not have his phone with him." Pescoli was driving, her wipers slapping off the snow. "He doesn't seem the type to keep his cell with him twenty-four seven, and I don't see him texting." She turned off of the road leading down Boxer Bluff. "He's probably pretty busy with his livestock in a storm like this. It's not a picnic. If we have to, we'll drive out there."

Alvarez said dryly, "Conditions couldn't be better."

Ever since the meeting at the station less than half an hour earlier, Pescoli had been anxious, more anxious than usual. Her fingers tapped on the steering wheel as she followed three cars all creeping through town. Her mind was on the case, running through the newfound information about Anne-Marie Calderone. She felt a sense of urgency, as if time were her enemy and she had to keep moving—which was damn difficult as traffic was crawling more than ever, just inching along.

"Why don't these people stay home?" she muttered when the lead car finally pulled into the parking lot of a pharmacy. The guy, ninety if he was a day, cruised slowly into a handicapped spot, his front tires running against the berm in front of the sidewalk.

"People still need their meds."

"Then they should learn to drive in the frickin' snow."

Alvarez shot her a look and Pescoli gripped the wheel a little harder. She was tired, cranky, hungry, and had no use for anyone out driving in the bad weather who didn't know how. No, strike that. She had no use for anyone driving and getting in her way.

Finally, the gas station mini-mart came into view. At the first entrance, she pulled into the parking area of Corky's Gas and Go, the very station where her son worked off and on, and wheeled into an empty parking space. "Let's do this," she said, and she and Alvarez climbed from the vehicle.

Inside, a girl in her early twenties with huge eyes rimmed thickly in mascara was manning the cash register. The detectives flashed their badges, introduced themselves, showed a picture of Troy Ryder, and asked if she'd seen him.

"Oh, yeah," the clerk said, nodding her head so rapidly the twist of hair that had been pinned on her crown threatened to slide off. "He came in last week, I think it was, bought a few things, gas and beer, maybe. He saw the Help Wanted sign in the window and was, like, asking about a job."

"A job," Alvarez repeated. Bells rang indicating another car had pulled into the pumps.

"Yeah. He, um, got turned off when I told him Corky, that's the boss, insists on background checks and drug tests." The clerk pulled a face. "Funny thing, y'know. He didn't look like a druggie." She lifted a shoulder. "But then everyone smokes weed these days. Oh. Sorry," she added quickly, having forgotten she was talking to cops. "Not me. I don't. I couldn't. Corky would fire me. Corky, he's not into that. Not just for the liability. He just don't like any drug stuff. Won't even sell papers for rolling your own."

Good for him, Pescoli thought, wondering how her son had held a job here because she suspected that Jeremy, if not a habitual user, had dabbled with weed more than a time or two. However, it seemed he'd grown out of that phase of his life, or somehow managed to hide it from her.

"Do you remember this guy's vehicle?" Alvarez asked, pointing to the picture of Ryder.

"Beat up old pickup, maybe? It had out of state plates, I think. I kinda noticed that because sometimes it gets a little boooring around here, if ya know what I mean. But it didn't have any special marks or bumper stickers or anything on it, that I noticed. It was kinda like the type everyone else around here drives." She glanced out the plate glass window as a man in ski gear filled the tank of his sedan.

She slid her gaze back to the picture of Ryder on the counter. "With him though it fit, y'know. He looked like a cowboy type. Well, again, like everyone else around here." She rolled her expressive, mascara-laden eyes and then thought of something. "Wait a minute." Her gaze zeroed in on Pescoli. "Aren't you Jeremy's mom? Jeremy Strand? I think I read about you in the paper awhile back. He, like, saved your life, shot a guy who was trying to kill you."

Pescoli nodded. She was proud of Jeremy, how responsible he'd become, and she did owe him her life.

"Tell him 'hi,' from Jodi," the girl said as a big bear of a man walked into the convenience store, a gust of freezing wind and snow following after him. "Brrr. It's soooo cold."

"Do you remember anything else about the guy in the picture?" Alvarez asked.

Jodi shook her head and the top knot wobbled precariously again. "He was in here for, like, half a second."

She was about to turn her attention to the next person in line when Pescoli said, "Hold on a sec." She took two steps to the candy counter and returned with an oversized package of Peanut M&M's. "I'll take these. You want anything?" she asked Alvarez and when her partner declined, paid for the bag. "I don't need a receipt."

Jodi rang up the sale, then turned her attention to the older man with the silvery stubble, rimless glasses, and a baseball cap with a John Deere logo. He was fishing in his back pocket for his wallet so that he could pay for gas, a pack of Rolos, and some chewing tobacco.

"For my grandson," he said, half-flirting with the clerk.

"Oh, I like Rolos, too," the girl said as Alvarez opened the door and Pescoli opened her bag of candy with her teeth.

"The Rolos? Those are for me." The old geezer winked at Jodi and started pulling bills from a slot in the well-used wallet. "The tobacco? That's for Josh."

Perfect, Pescoli thought as the bag popped open and peanuts threatened to spill out every which way. She managed to corral them and thought, *Way to go, Gramps. Get the kid hooked. Great idea.*

Maybe it was a joke, the old guy's way of flirting. Pescoli hoped so as she winced against the bitter cold, plopping a couple candy-coated chocolate peanuts into her mouth. Together, she and Alvarez half-sprinted past the gas pumps, where two cars were being refueled, to the spot where her Jeep was parked, already collecting snow.

"Want some?" she asked again as they climbed inside and she held the open bag toward her partner where Alvarez was dutifully snapping on her seat belt.

"No."

"God, they're great," Pescoli threw a few more into her mouth, then tossed an empty coffee cup onto the floor in front of the back seat and dropped the open bag into her vacant cup holder.

"Maybe to ten-year-olds or pregnant women."

"*Especially* ten-year-olds and pregnant women. But trust me, they're for everybody." Pescoli jammed her key into the ignition and sent her partner a *don't-even-go-there* stare which Alvarez ignored as her cell phone rang sharply.

Plugging one ear to block out the ambient noise of the Jeep's engine, she answered, "Alvarez."

Pescoli strapped her seat belt into place, cranked the heat to the maximum, then slammed the gearshift into reverse and backed out of the gas station.

"Yeah . . . yeah . . . Okay, I got it," Alvarez said. "We're on our way." She hung up. "Looks like we're going to the River View Motel. One of the deputies on the search found out where Ryder's been staying. The River View is on—"

"I know where it is. Just down the road." Pescoli wouldn't admit it to Alvarez, of course, but a few years earlier when she'd first started her affair with Santana, they'd sometimes stayed in little out of the way no-tell motels where they would have complete privacy. Away from her family. Away from her job. Away from Brady Long, the rich pain in the ass Santana used to work for. The River View, as well as a few other motels scattered around the outskirts of town, had been a great little rendezvous spot.

"We're too late. He's already checked out."

"Damn." Pescoli pulled into traffic which, because of the storm, was light. "Always a day late and a dollar short. But maybe he left something behind."

"Maybe."

Her partner didn't sound too convinced or even hopeful, but surely something would break in the case. It damn well had to.

"It's time to go," Ryder said, packing up the last of the electronic equipment. "We've wasted too much time already."

If Anne-Marie had hoped he would change his mind, that he'd hear her tale of battery and pain and give up the outrageous bounty placed on her head by her family, she'd been sadly mistaken. Yes, his eyes had reflected some empathy and a fierce anger as she'd explained about her husband's abuse, but in the end, once she'd finished talking, he'd said nothing for a second, then had clipped out, "I didn't know what you went through."

She realized that, overall, he didn't sound all that moved by her story. Instead, he was staring at her coolly as if she were some interesting, maybe dangerous, specimen. She suddenly understood that he was second-guessing her, wondering if she were lying again. Of course.

She walked to the window and flipped open the blinds. It was daylight and she saw both vehicles parked outside. Hers with more snow piled upon it near the sagging building she thought had once been used as a garage, his truck parked a few yards back, probably where he'd slid to a stop without headlights so as not to wake her. He'd parked carefully, wedging his pickup between two trees, guarding the lane so that no other vehicle could pass and she couldn't get away.

She didn't bother asking him how he'd sneaked in on her as he'd obviously been in the place once before to plant his electronic equipment, so he'd no doubt used his same breaking-and-entering skills.

Snow was still falling and the tracks of both vehicles were covered, his less so as it was parked beneath a canopy of branches and had been stationary for a shorter amount of time. Was she really trapped? If she couldn't convince him to let her go, would she really be forced to return to New Orleans with him?

Thinking of reuniting with her family, of the disappointment carved on her father's face, the disgrace in her mother's eyes, and the hurt on her grandmother's proud visage, she knew she couldn't return to Louisiana. Ever. Even if she could face the condemnation and shame, there was her husband, who seemed to have vanished, as well. No doubt she would be a suspect in his disappearance, or, worse yet, if he should suddenly show up in New Orleans again, she would have to look him in the eye and see him smirk at her fear.

Her stomach turned over at the thought of him. No. She'd never go back. Ryder wasn't going to take her. He just didn't know it yet. Mind turning with thoughts of escape, she started to close the blinds, then stopped. Had she seen something outside the window, some movement that she'd caught from the corner of her eye? She squinted hard, staring through the shifting veil of flakes, but whatever it was had disappeared.

Another deer perhaps.

Or, more likely, a figment of her imagination.

She told herself it was nothing, but couldn't quite shake the feeling that something outside wasn't right. Then again, nothing inside the dilapidated cabin was right, either.

"You can see why I can't go back," she tried.

"If you're telling the truth."

She knew it. The bastard didn't believe her. "Come on, Ryder. You think I made that story up?"

"What I know is you're a liar, Anne-Marie, and a good one, if I recall."

"Everything I said to you was the God's honest truth. Who would make up something so . . . so brutal?"

"Who would rob their damn grandmother?"

Anne-Marie was dying inside. She'd bared her soul to him. Stupidly.

"You told me how much she meant to you. So, it's not making a whole lot of sense to me that instead of running to her and confiding in her, asking for her help and protection, or insisting she take you to the police, you decided to steal from her. From the one woman you swore you adored."

Anne-Marie's throat clogged and she fought tears. The biggest regret in her life had been sneaking in the back door when she'd known her grandmother was sleeping in the next room and with nervous fingers opening the safe that was hidden behind a shelf in the pantry. But she had. When the safe had opened, she'd scooped up the bills that had been stacked so neatly within, money she'd used to escape, to buy her vehicle, to purchase her new identity, to visit a dentist for appliances and a costume store for the extra padding and wigs. And for the doctor in Oklahoma City. "I can't go back," she said again.

His expression hardened. "Maybe not willingly," he said, crossing the room.

"Not ever." She met his uncompromising glare with one of her own. "You'll have to shoot me. Your gun. My gun. It doesn't matter, but I won't go."

"Fine."

To her horror, he dragged a pair of handcuffs from his pocket and before she could move, he reached her and snapped them over her wrists. "We're goin', darlin', and we're goin' right now."

CHAPTER 26

The wipers weren't keeping up with the falling snow, so Pescoli tried to turn them up, to increase their speed, but they were maxed out. The storm was just that fierce. "Global warming, my ass," she muttered as the sign for the River View appeared through the thick, swirling flakes.

"Actually these storms and all the weird weather patterns we've been experiencing are the direct result of climate change." Sometimes Alvarez could really be a buzz-kill.

Pescoli cranked the wheel and her Jeep slid a bit before they drove into the lot of the motel and parked under the broad portico that was, according to several signs posted near the front doors, reserved for guests of the facility.

Pescoli really didn't give a rat's ass what the protocol was.

Inside the brightly lit reception area of the motel, they waited as a hippy woman in a uniform finished a phone call, her fingers flying over the keys of a computer. The lobby was small and smelled of day-old coffee. One faux leather couch that had seen better days was situated near a stand of brochures describing highlights of the area.

"That does it," the receptionist said with a smile wide enough to show off a gold molar. "So what can I do ya for?"

They introduced themselves, showing badges, and asked about Troy Ryder.

"A deputy was in earlier," said the woman whose name tag read Carla Simms. "I told them everything I knew."

"I know, but we'd like to see for ourselves the room he stayed in," Pescoli said.

"Ooookay." The hippy woman checked her computer monitor again. "As I told the deputy, Mr. Ryder was in a king room with a view for a little over a week and didn't bother anyone. If he had company, I didn't see it. Truthfully, we here at the River View respect our guests' privacy."

"I'm sure," Pescoli said, knowing first-hand about the policy.

"It's already been cleaned. We're quick about that, you know." Carla was obviously proud of her work at the River View, as if this dive of a motel was a five-star hotel. She swept a walkie-talkie off the desk, hit a button, and said, "Can you send someone down to the reception?"

She'd barely hung up when a tiny woman appeared. She wore a puffy coat and a knit cap pulled low enough to brush the top of a red scarf wound around her neck. She couldn't have been five feet tall and even in the heavy coat, she seemed diminutive. Pescoli felt like an Amazon next to her.

"Rhonda," Carla said. "This is Detective Pescoli and . . . wait, I'm sorry—?"

"Alvarez," Pescoli's partner supplied.

"Yes, yes. Detective Alvarez. Would you please show the officers to room thirteen? It's been cleaned, right?"

Rhonda nodded her head and began fiddling with a key ring as she led the officers outside and along a covered walkway to room thirteen, which supposedly had one of the sought-after river views.

To Pescoli's way of thinking, it was all false advertising. The place was known to be clean and reasonable, nothing more. The old carpeting, and drapes that matched the bedspread, had to be from the nineties. Unfortunately, the receptionist hadn't been mistaken and the tacky room had been cleaned, no trash, no bit of visible evidence left behind.

"Clean as a whistle." Disappointed, Pescoli leaned down and looked under the bed while Alvarez checked the adjoining bath, then opened the sliding door to the small patio beyond.

"Same here," Alvarez agreed.

The room looked tired and dated, but there was nothing to indicate that Troy Ryder or any other person had ever resided there.

"We'll need to look through the trash," she said. "It hasn't been picked up yet?"

"Thursday." The maid walked them outside where the snow had covered the parking lot and the few cars parked in front of the motel. The empty spot in front of room thirteen, where Ryder's truck had been parked, had accumulated only a few inches over the asphalt. One other slot had the same level of snow. It had recently been vacated, only a thin layer covering the pavement.

"Mr. Ryder left early this morning," Rhonda said. "I'm on the early shift and he was already gone, so I got the notice to clean his room first thing." She tested the knob to make certain that the room was secure. "The same with his friend."

"Friend?" Alvarez asked, exchanging looks with Pescoli. "What friend?"

"The guest in twenty-five. I don't know his name. But he was always asking about Mr. Ryder." She stopped talking abruptly as if she realized she was giving out too much information about customers who guarded their privacy.

Alvarez clarified, "A single man?"

"Yes. No one was with him," the maid assured them, finding her voice again.

"And he hung out with Ryder?" Alvarez made a swirling motion with her finger. "You saw them together."

Shaking her head, the petite woman wagged her head thoughtfully side to side. "I don't know, but I never saw them together. They were both very private, holed up in their rooms. And the guest in room thirteen? Mr. Ryder? He never asked about the man in twenty-five, or anyone else that I know of." She raised and lowered her shoulders. "I wouldn't know. I was only here during my shifts and I was busy, you know."

"But the other man checked out this morning?" Pescoli said. "What time?"

Rhonda said, "I don't really know. He didn't stop at the desk. Just left."

Room twenty-five was around the corner from room thirteen, and offered a bird's-eye view of Ryder's activity. The parking area for that room had only a little snow in front of it, about the same level as thirteen.

"Has room twenty-five been cleaned yet?" Alvarez asked.

The maid shook her head. "I don't think so."

"Hmph." Alvarez eyed the parking lot. "Mind if we look inside?"

"Okay." The maid led the way along the long concrete porch and unlocked the room that was identical to the one Ryder had occupied.

Whoever had resided there had left in a hurry. The bill was still under the door. The bed was a tumble of blankets, and towels and hangers littered the floor. Trash was still in and around the waste baskets—newspapers and fast food wrappers, water bottles, paper cups, plastic packaging for some kind of headphones, and wadded up receipts from local stores.

"Didn't he ever have the room cleaned?" Alvarez asked.

"No. Both he and the man in number thirteen asked for no service. I talked to each of them and they refused." Rhonda shrugged in a *what're-you-gonna-do* manner. "The management doesn't like it, but the guest's wishes are always granted."

"We're going to want to seal both rooms. We don't want either of them cleaned any more," Pescoli said.

Alvarez was looking at the billing that had been left. "I assume your guests have to register their vehicles at the front desk?"

"Yes. Always."

"Good," Alvarez said. "We need to see the registration for"—she met Pescoli's gaze—"Mr. . . . Bryan Smith. I saw cameras outside. Does the motel keep the tapes?"

Rhonda shook her head. "The outside cameras are all for show. All they are is a red light to make it look like they're filming. Just like the security signs about a company that is monitoring the place. It's all just to make people think twice about stealing or loitering or whatever. The only cameras that work are in the lobby."

Alvarez said, "Then we'll need to see the lobby tapes."

They left the room.

Arms wrapped around her, shoulders hunched against the cold, Rhonda led them toward the main building. "You'll have to talk to Carla about that. She's the manager."

"We will," Pescoli said as she tightened her scarf and wondered about Ryder's "friend" in room twenty-five. She had a bad feeling about Bryan Smith. It didn't make sense. Did the two men know each other? She doubted it. Could the maid have been wrong about a possible connection? Probably not. "Just seal the room, make certain it's not cleaned." She recalled Blackwater's comment about Bruce Calderone, Anne-Marie Calderone, and Troy Ryder being in the plot together. Far-fetched, she'd thought, but maybe some part of it was true?

Rhonda was already on a walkie-talkie, speaking in rapid-fire Spanish.

Alvarez whipped out her cell phone. "I'll get officers over here ASAP," she told Pescoli as they headed back to the reception area.

Looking over the registration information in the River View's lobby, they added a 1998 Ford Explorer with Texas plates to the APB they'd sent out earlier for Ryder's Dodge pickup and asked for any and all security tapes from the motel's archives, which, Carla told them proudly, were kept for a month.

As they walked back to the Jeep, Alvarez's phone rang again

"Do you have those head shots yet?" Blackwater asked, finding Zoller at her desk, her fingers on the keyboard of her computer. As a junior detective, she shared an open space with several other detectives, each desk area divided by half walls to create a cubicle.

"Yes, sir," she said, hitting a few keys. Within seconds, a slide show of images appeared on her monitor, each essentially the same face and expression. The features were different in each, changing as they would look if artificially manipulated or permanently altered with surgery. The hairstyles were different, the cut and color changing, glasses added, contacts used to alter eye color, makeup to change the shadows of the cheekbones, eyebrows plucked or thickened, lips made fuller or thinned out, and the aging process factored in, just in case Anne-Marie Calderone had decided to disappear into middle-age. Twenty-five different shots rolled slowly by and with each one, Blackwater became more frustrated.

He was certain he'd seen her before. Would have sworn to it. Something about her eyes and shape of her face caused a memory to tug at his brain. He was good with faces, to the point that he never forgot one, so why then did he sense he'd met her but couldn't quite recall?

One image swept by and he asked Zoller to freeze it. In the shot, the woman looked a good ten or fifteen years older. Her brown hair was short, her glasses rimless, her lips thin. "Can you make her blond? Not like before." There had been several blondes in the lineup. "But this particular hairstyle."

"Sure." With a keystroke, the head shot was of a woman with pale hair.

Blackwater nodded. That seemed better. "And give this one the full lips."

Again, Zoller altered the shot.

God, he *knew* he'd seen her. But where? He concentrated. It was important on a lot of levels. If Anne-Marie Calderone was found under his watch, and the detectives managed to prove a case against her, his job as sheriff would be secure. Solving the bizarre crime would attract lots of media attention. It was already happening, and it wasn't just the local press. Papers and news agencies from as far away as Spokane and Boise were calling. If Anne-Marie Calderone, involved in bigamy and murder, were captured in Grizzly Falls, he might be hailed as a national hero . . . And if his team stopped a serial killer's rampage? Though that kind of spotlight had never been his goal, he would take any means to become the next sheriff of Pinewood County. Any political ambitions after that would have to wait.

But first things first. They still needed to locate and capture Calderone.

"Anything else?" Zoller asked, looking up at him with her hands poised over the keyboard.

He heard footsteps in the hallway and turned to find the receptionist craning her neck around the corner. "Sheriff," Joelle said with a tentative smile. "I don't want to bother you, but Manny Douglas of the *Mountain Reporter* phoned for the third time this morning and I told him you'd call him back. If he calls again, I could refer him to the public information officer, but I've dealt with him before and he doesn't seem to take the hint, if you know what I mean." Her glossy red lips pursed. "The last time he called, less than two minutes ago, he said he was on his way to the station and was only five minutes away."

Blackwater held back his initial annoyance and said, "I'll phone him as soon as I'm done here. If he's already here, give him coffee and let me know. I'll talk to him. In my office." The last thing he wanted to do at this point in his career was piss off a reporter.

She handed him a WHILE-YOU-WERE OUT memo with Douglas's name and number, then hurried off as a phone started ringing down the hallway.

As he folded the note and tucked it into his pocket, Blackwater swung his attention back to the screen. The break in his attention had given him a fresh perspective. As his eyes narrowed on the image, he felt a little sizzle of anticipation, and realized what was wrong, what had to change. To Zoller, he said, "Is it possible for you to change her teeth? Or her jawline? Give her more jowls?"

Concentrating so hard she bit into her lower lip, Zoller actually was able to draw on the screen with her mouse, the computer filling in the gaps or shaving off what she took off. She was able to change the contour of the face and add in some more crooked teeth so that in a matter of minutes, he was no longer staring at the face of Anne-Marie Calderone as pictured on her driver's license. Instead, he was looking at a much dowdier, older appearing woman that he was certain he'd seen before.

"Darken her eyes." He knew before Zoller had finished the change that he would be staring into the face of the waitress from the Midway Diner. Her name tag had read JESSICA, he remembered, but he would bet his badge she was the missing heiress, Anne-Marie Calderone.

Pescoli had already gotten a text from Bianca that there was no school today and, of course, her daughter was ecstatic, saying she was going back to bed for a while, then hoping to get a ride to a friend's later. Driving back to the station, Pescoli hoped her daughter stayed put. As far as she knew, Jeremy was at home, probably still fast asleep and would be for a while. *Good.* At least for the morning, she needed not to worry about either of them.

She wheeled into the station's parking lot and spied a spot in the thickening snow. "If this keeps up, Blackwater will have us all shoveling," she said, cutting the engine. "I can see it now, part of his new military regimen to keep his officers in shape. Did I tell you I caught him in full uniform doing push-ups in his office? Told me it kept the blood flowing."

"It does," Alvarez said as she unbuckled her seat belt.

"Yeah, well, once up and showered, I'm not interested in getting my blood flowing," Pescoli grumbled, climbing out of the car and spying Cade Grayson just parking his pickup in the visitor's lot not far from the pole where the flag was still positioned at half-mast, Old Glory billowing in the falling snow. "Take a look."

"Let's see what he has to say."

He wasn't alone. As he hopped out of one side of the truck, his brother Zed, several inches taller and at least fifty pounds heavier, stepped his size fourteen boots into six inches of icy powder. Both men were dressed in thick outerwear and cowboy hats, the wide brims collecting a white dusting as they made their way to the officers.

"Got your message," Cade said to Alvarez. "We were already in town, picking up supplies, so I thought it might be best to talk face-to-face."

"Let's go inside." Alvarez led the way, and within minutes, they were seated at the conference table, hats removed, jackets unzipped, faces stern, coffee supplied by Joelle on the table, untouched. Alvarez had taken time to dash into her office to retrieve her files and Pescoli, as was her custom these days, had made a quick trip to the bathroom.

The brothers were obviously uncomfortable, whether it was because Cade was being questioned, or due to the fact that they were seated in the sheriff's department, a door away from what had been Dan's office.

"Is this about Bart?" Zed asked, bushy eyebrows pulling together. "We all know that Hattie won't let that one go." He sent his brother a glance that was unreadable, one that Cade tried to ignore.

"I did look through the case files on your brother's suicide," Pescoli said, taking in both brothers as they were seated across from her. "But I can't find any reason to reopen the case. It looks to me that Bart took his own life. I'm sorry."

"Not unexpected," Zed said, his lips twisting down.

More, Pescoli thought, *in disapproval of his ex-sister-in-law, than in disappointment about his brother's cause of death.*

"Hattie's had a bug up her butt about it from the first but hell . . . we all just have to accept what happened. We may not like it, but it's time to move on." Pointedly, he glanced at the door leading to the office once occupied by his brother.

Cade's gaze zeroed in on Alvarez. "Why did you call? You seemed to think it was pretty damn important."

"It is," she said, her tablet firing up in front of her. "I've been in contact with Detective Montoya of the New Orleans Police Department."

"New Orleans?" Zed said. "What the hell's this all about? We've got a ranch to run and a helluva snowstorm to deal with." He shot a disgusted look at Cade. "I told you we should've just called."

"What about New Orleans?" Cade asked, deathly solemn, but not surprised.

"Montoya says you were involved with a woman from there, a woman by the name of Anne-Marie Calderone, or possibly, at that time she might have told you her name was Anne-Marie Favier, though she was married."

He didn't respond, so Alvarez attempted to jog his memory. "You were in Texas at a rodeo, took a side trip to Louisiana, and met her there?" She slid a copy of the woman in question's driver's license across the table.

The edges of Cade's lips turned white as he let his gaze skate over the image on the license before he found Alvarez's eyes again. "What about her?"

"For the love of Christ," Zed said. "You and your goddamn women!" He snorted through his nose and shook his head.

"We're investigating a couple homicides here in Grizzly Falls. You've no doubt heard of them. We think there's a connection to Ms. Calderone, and we think she's here. Has she contacted you?"

"You think there's a connection between Anne-Marie and those murders?" Cade sounded poleaxed.

"Shit, *that* woman? The waitress?" Zed said in a huff of disgust. "I knew she was trouble."

"Slow down," Pescoli advised. "So, she is here in Grizzly Falls?" Alvarez asked, "A waitress?"

"I don't know all the details, but she admitted she was in trouble, that she thought—" Cade closed his eyes for a second, then clenched his jaw and spit out, "Shit-fire," as if he were on the horns of a dilemma.

"She thought what?" Alvarez pressed.

When Cade remained silent for a few moments, clearly trying to get his head around what he'd just heard, Zed jumped into the fray. "She came to the ranch." He flung an angry glare at his brother. "Whatever you think you're doin' by holdin' back, like you're saving her or something, or keeping some damn confidence, it's over. They're on to her."

A muscle worked in Cade's jaw.

"Mr. Grayson," Alvarez urged.

Cade scowled, angry with his brother and quite possibly himself. "She dropped by a few days ago. Said she was in trouble, that it had something to do with those women who'd been found. I don't know how, but she was afraid."

"About what? Being caught?" Pescoli asked.

"That she was in danger. For her life, or something. She'd wanted to talk to Dan about what was going on, but of course that didn't happen. I turned her away. I thought . . . hell, I'd hoped she was going to talk to you."

"She works down at the Midway Diner," Zed stated flatly.

"Did she say what she was afraid of?" Alvarez was making notes, but Pescoli was ready to shoot out of her chair and drive like a maniac to the diner. It was time to end this.

"Yeah." Cade leaned back in his chair and exhaled heavily. "She did, but I didn't believe her. She . . . well, she has a history of lying."

Zed swore under his breath.

Cade straightened. "The thing is, she told me she was afraid of her own damn husband."

"You can't do this!" Anne-Marie spat, trying to worm her way out of the handcuffs he'd slapped on her wrists.

"You had the option. You wouldn't leave on your own."

"You really are a bastard." She was furious, nearly spitting as, to her horror, he walked unerringly to the area along the baseboard where she'd stashed her important documents, her extra cash, her passports. "Don't! You can't!"

Ignoring her, he withdrew her switchblade from his pocket, clicked it open, and bent down to pry the board off to expose her niche. "We'll have to wait until the fire dies a little for the other spot," he said over his shoulder. He was serious. He was actually going to force her back to New Orleans.

He dug out the baseboard, then pulled her papers from their hiding spot. As he straightened, he snapped the knife closed and looked over the documents. "This must've cost you," he said, opening one passport after another, his eyebrows rising in appreciation. "Or your grandmother."

"I had to do it," Anne-Marie said, desperate to change his mind. "If I went back, he would've killed me."

"The police would have protected you."

She gave a short, dry laugh. "I don't think so."

"You should've—"

"I should've nothing," she cut him off. She'd had enough. Taken enough.

With a sudden yank, she removed the ring she wore, the fat piece of costume jewelry that hid her joint. Then quickly, with little effort, she grabbed her left hand with her right and removed the lifelike prosthesis to reveal the stump of her left ring finger, all that remained after the butcher she'd been married to had cleaved off the very finger on which he'd slipped her engagement ring years earlier.

CHAPTER 27

"The Midway Diner?" Pescoli said after the Grayson brothers had left the sheriff's department. She and Alvarez were still in the conference room, picking up their things. "It's almost lunchtime and maybe we'll get lucky. She'll be there, or we can get information from her boss or coworkers." Pescoli's stomach was rumbling again. *Close enough for a meal,* she decided. Even if it was one on the run. They hadn't learned much from the Grayson brothers.

Zed Grayson had been certain he'd spied Anne Marie Calderone in her job as a waitress at the diner, though the one time Cade had seen her had been at his home when she had come to visit him, desperate, it appeared. He'd suggested she turn herself in and tell her story to the police. So far, she hadn't taken his advice. Pescoli only hoped that Anne-Marie hadn't run again. That woman had about half a million questions to answer, though Pescoli still wasn't convinced she was a killer, fingerprint or no.

During the interview, Alvarez had pulled up the most recent photos of Troy Ryder and Bruce Calderone, sent to her by Montoya in New Orleans. She showed Zed and Cade several shots of the men in question. Besides his Texas driver's license photo, there was another picture of Troy Ryder from his rodeo days. As for Calderone, his driver's license photo issued by the state of Louisiana was tucked between two posed shots, one in a business suit, the other of the man in a lab coat, a stethoscope visible in his pocket. Both men were good-looking and about the same height and weight if the information on their licenses was to be believed. Troy Ryder was a little more rough and tumble looking, an outdoorsy type with tanned skin, light brown hair, and a cocksure grin. Dr. Bruce Calderone, dark hair combed neatly, chin lifted in authority, smile forced, did appear more polished and sophisticated, at least according to the shots, but that was how the photographer had staged the pictures, how the man wanted to be portrayed.

The Grayson brothers hadn't recognized either of the two men who had said "I do" to Anne-Marie.

"Let's go." Alvarez was sliding her iPad into its case. "Maybe one of Anne-Marie's coworkers has gotten close to her and knows where we can find her."

Keys in hand, Pescoli said, "Don't count on it." She was already at the door to the hallway when the other door of the conference room, the one leading directly to the sheriff's office, opened.

Blackwater took one step into the conference room. "Detectives," he said, motioning them into his office. "We need to talk. I want you to bring me up to speed, but before you brief me on what you've learned, I think you should know that Anne-Marie Calderone is in Grizzly Falls."

Alvarez gave a swift nod. "We just heard."

"From Cade Grayson?" Blackwater's eyes narrowed.

"Zed thinks he saw her at the Midway Diner, and she showed up at the ranch to visit Cade," Pescoli said. "Neither of them has any idea where she lives, but Zed said she's driving an older model Chevy Tahoe. Silver or gray or light blue, he thought. Colorado plates. Neither brother got the number."

"They still involved? She and Cade?" Blackwater asked. "Or . . . Zed?"

"They both say not." Pescoli shook her head.

"Come into the office and brief me. I know about the Midway Diner. Already talked to the owner." He stepped out of the doorway and they filed in.

Waving them into chairs, he said, "She's e-mailing me information about Jessica Williams—the alias Anne-Marie Calderone is using— her employment application, tax info, and cell number. I asked Zoller to get in touch with the cell phone company who issued the phone, but of course, it's one of those pre-paid things that requires little or no info." His dark eyes sparked and Pescoli recognized the look—a cop hot on the trail of a suspect. "Still, we don't have a physical address for her. Yet. She did pick up mail at a local postal annex, you know, where the box is the 'suite' number?" He made air quotes and added, "I've already sent deputies over there checking her application."

"You're taking over the case now?" Pescoli asked, trying and failing to mask her irritation. He was the boss, yeah, but this was their case and she was a little bristly about it . . . well, about most things these days.

"No. No way." He held up a hand, fingers splayed. "It's all yours. All yours." He glanced from one detective to the other. "But we're a team here, all work together, and so I want you to report to me. I wanted to get some answers pronto and I didn't want to interrupt your meeting with the Graysons. Time is crucial on this one; I thought it best if we get moving. Anne-Marie Calderone has a history of slipping away."

Bugged, Pescoli, for once, didn't argue. "Okay. Anything else? How did you find her?"

"Computer enhancement of her driver's license photo." He actually smiled a bit. "I had Zoller tweak it because I was certain I recognized her. It's amazing what Photoshop can do."

So he thought he'd broken the case wide open on his own. Pescoli got it. No doubt that bit of information would be leaked to the press.

"Okay, so now," he encouraged, "tell me what you learned from the brothers Grayson."

Pescoli took a back seat while Alvarez summarized their morning. "We think Troy Ryder is a party of interest in this case, as well, though we don't know how he's currently involved with Calderone or the homicides." With that as a lead-in, she launched into what they'd discovered about Ryder, the unknown person of interest in room twenty-five of the River View, and Cade Grayson's admission of actually talking to Anne-Marie Calderone, including her fear of her husband.

Blackwater listened thoughtfully.

Beneath some of his bravado, his eagerness to have things his way, Pescoli saw a glimmer of the lawman who had worked his way through the ranks, a good cop who had inherited Grayson's position through ambition and hard work.

She still didn't like him; didn't care for his style, but she grudgingly accepted that he might not be as bad as he initially seemed. He preened too much to the cameras for her taste, and she wasn't completely convinced his motives were what they should be, but maybe she could work with him.

At least for a while.

Possibly even the length of her pregnancy.

Alvarez was talking about the possibility of Bruce Calderone having landed in Grizzly Falls.

Blackwater was listening, just not convinced. He picked up a pencil from the holder on his too tidy desk. "But he's not with his wife."

"Not according to Grayson. He thinks she's running scared."

Blackwater asked the same damn question that had been plaguing Pescoli, "So where is he?"

"Don't know. But there is a possibility that he stayed at the River View Motel, registered as Bryan Smith. He was either in touch with or observing Troy Ryder. According to the maid, he kept tabs on Ryder. We've got security tapes from the motel for all the dates that Ryder was a guest. Smith should be there too as he showed up the day after Ryder checked in and left soon after Ryder checked out. We've got his vehicle description and plates, this time from Texas. Plates and vehicle don't match. Already issued BOLOs on both Ryder's vehicle and Bryan Smith's."

"Good." Blackwater was nodding, agreeing with his own thoughts as he tapped the eraser end of the pencil on his desk. "The trouble with this is that it's getting more complicated as we get closer. Anne-Marie Calderone sighted," he thought aloud, "now, possibly both husbands." Dropping the pencil into its holder, he looked from Alvarez to Pescoli. "Looks like we're searching for three people instead of just one. Let's do it."

Ryder stared at the stump where Anne-Marie's finger had been. His stomach turned sour, bile rising up his throat as he stood in front of the dying fire. "He did that to you?" A new rage burned through him and he felt his back teeth grind together. Yes, Anne-Marie was a liar. A major liar. The best he'd ever come across and that was saying something, but for the first time, he wondered if she could possibly be telling the truth. He didn't want to believe her, didn't trust her as far as he could throw her, but who would make up such a grotesque story?

"Of course he did!" she said, her teeth drawing back in anger. "Look!" She held up her hand, fingers spread wide. "Do you want to know what he did after? Huh?" She didn't wait for an answer. "He kicked me, Ryder. Like so much trash, he kicked my naked body into the river and hoped to hell that alligators would finish me off, eat me alive, to get rid of the evidence."

Ryder's insides curled in repulsion.

She inched her chin up defiantly. "I'd made the ultimate mistake. Of walking away from him."

As they stood inches apart, she unburdened herself, letting go of her secret. She stood toe-to-toe with him and told him about going to the townhouse to get her things, and being discovered by Calderone. How he'd drugged her and jammed her rings on her finger before taking her somewhere deep into the Louisiana swampland. How, while she was starting to rouse, he'd sliced off her finger, rings and all, with the skill of the surgeon he was. As a final act, he'd kicked her, rolling her into the murky water.

Ryder listened, but didn't say a word.

"So"—she stared up at him with her wide eyes—"just so you understand. I'll never go back." She blinked once, then whispered, "Never. I'd rather die first."

He found his voice and dug deep for his resolve. "If what you're saying is true—"

"If?" she repeated as a blast of wind slammed against the cabin, the walls shuddering. "*If?* Oh, my God, what do you think, Ryder, that I cut off my own damn finger?"

"No." He knew a sane person wouldn't mutilate themselves so. And he didn't think Anne-Marie was insane, just . . . self-serving to the max.

"Then take off these frickin' cuffs!" She glared at him as the fire sizzled, dying in the grate.

He almost reached for the key. He'd told himself that no matter what, he was going to haul her back to New Orleans, that no matter what kind of lies she spun, he was going to stand strong, never believe her. Yet there he was in the dilapidated cabin, his determination crumbling. His faith in her had been destroyed long ago. Her lies; her fault. But he found it impossible to believe that she would go to such incredible, grotesque lengths.

She'd do anything to save her own skin. You know it. You lived it. The woman has no scruples. None. Zero. Zilch. Don't be tricked, Ryder. Yes, she's beautiful and seductive and even charming, but she's a twisting, diabolical snake and you know it. Once bitten, re-member? Twice shy? Twice fucking shy!

Her hands bound together, she brushed her hair out of her eyes and frowned, a bit of pain registering in her green eyes. "You don't believe me."

"I don't know what to believe," he said honestly.

"I hurt you that badly?"

"You're just so into your own lies that you believe them yourself," he said. "You don't seem to know the difference between real truth and your own skewed fantasy."

Sighing, she glanced down at the floor, bit her lip, and shook her head as if finally understanding she couldn't convince him of her twisted reality. "Fine," she whispered under her breath. "As I said, I'd rather die first."

"Not gonna happen," he said as she thrust out her chin. Defiant to the end.

"Then let's go," she bit out, furious. "But give me a moment, okay? I need to use the bathroom."

He wanted to argue, didn't think it was a good idea to let her out of his sight. "Five minutes," he said, feeling like an idiot, telling himself not to give her an inch.

But where could she go? Where could she run? The storm was still raging and it was even doubtful that the two of them in his truck would be able to make it out of the mountains, let alone through Montana and south.

But he didn't chase her all the way up there to give up.

"Leave the door open," he said and turned to the fireplace where he started searching for the niche near the firebox. He'd watched her on the screen he'd set up in his hotel room stash more of her valuables there. He wanted everything with him when he returned to the Crescent City.

"You really are a son of a bitch," she threw at him as she walked to the bathroom and left the door cracked.

He felt a bit of satisfaction that she'd followed his order, but experienced a pang of regret and wondered how hard and callous he'd become.

Because of her, Ryder. This is all her fault. You don't trust her. Of course you don't. And the reason is directly because of her actions.

He heard water running and the shuffle of footsteps.

After tossing the tiny leather pouch of papers he'd found in her hiding spot, he grabbed his cell phone and flipped open the blinds to survey the weather. "Anne-Marie?" he called.

"You said five minutes! It hasn't been two."

So she was inside. Good. He stepped onto the tiny porch, then closed the door and looked back through the window to make certain she didn't try to escape, walk out of the bathroom and take a hard right for the back door.

Everything inside the darkened interior remained the same, the fire offering up enough light that he could make out the door to the bathroom.

Quickly, he dialed the phone and turned up the collar of his jacket as it rang. Once. Twice. The wind rushed across the porch, scattering the few dry leaves that weren't already covered in snow.

"Hello?" A man's voice. Rough. Irritated.

"Yeah, it's me. Ryder."

"I see that. Modern technology you know. Where the hell are you?"

"Still in Montana."

"What? I thought you'd be on your way by now! What the hell's taking so long?"

"I've got her."

"Then why the fuck are you still in Montana?"

"Big storm," Ryder explained.

"Big storm? Big deal. You should have prepared for bad weather. Christ, you knew where you were going, what you were doing."

"I know. I did."

"Then, what's the problem?"

What was the problem? Ryder stared through the window into the darkened interior. He felt the wind battering the tiny, falling-down cabin in the middle of the Bitterroot Mountains, a ramshackle abode no rational person would try to make their home. Unless she was desperate. Unless she didn't want to be found.

He thought about the passports he'd riffled through, remembering the different photographs, the changed names, the altered looks. He considered Anne-Marie Favier Calderone. She was a gorgeous girl who'd grown up in wealth and seemingly a princess-like existence who was frantic enough to change her good looks and adopt different personas to hide herself, a woman on the run who had eventually wound up in the middle of the mountains, isolated and alone, in a damn cabin with thin walls, no heat, and barely running water.

Why? he wondered again.

Why would she go to all the trouble? Why would she willingly propel herself into all this hardship? How desperate was she to try and disappear off the face of the earth? What had been the reason that she would tumble to such depths as to steal from her grandmother, the one woman she'd sworn she adored?

It didn't make sense.

Unless she was scared out of her mind.

Unless her bravado was a mask.

Unless her damnably stubborn attitude was propelled by sheer terror.

"Hello?" called the voice on the phone, but he ignored it.

With snow falling all around him, Ryder remembered her vanity. How she'd known how beautiful she was, how sexy and alluring she could be, and she'd reveled in her good looks and charm, in her sensuality. She would never have sliced off her own finger and no accident would have been so clean. As if it had been cleaved by a butcher. Or a surgeon. Or one man who had been both—the monster that she'd married.

"Shit," he whispered, realizing he was making a huge, irreversible mistake—one it might already be too late to rectify.

"Hello? For Christ's sake, Ryder? Are you there? Fuck!"

His boots ringing, Ryder stepped to the far end of the porch and took a quick look down the side of the cabin to the bathroom window, just to make certain she hadn't done anything foolish like squeezing herself through the tiny window and dropping to the ground to escape. As far as he could see, the window wasn't open and the snow below it was undisturbed.

Still, he was uneasy.

And then he saw a shadow. Just a faint image of something beyond the veil of snow. His gut clenched and he reached into his pocket, his fingers curling over the butt of his gun, but the image vanished as quickly as it had appeared and he told himself it was nothing.

Right?

Squinting, he decided it was a trick of light.

"Hello? Are you there?" demanded the voice on the other end of the line. "I asked you when you will get back here?"

"Never," Ryder replied, finally responding.

"What? I can't hear you. Are you outside? I asked when you were coming back!"

The wind screamed as it raced around the corner of the house and the icy, snow-laden branches of the trees danced, shedding pieces of their white mantles.

"And I said 'never!' " he repeated, a little more loudly. Then added, "Oh, and by the way?"

"Yeah?"

"Go fuck yourself."

CHAPTER 28

"The cell phone company should get back to us soon," Alvarez said as she stood. She and Pescoli were still in Blackwater's office, getting ready to hit the road again. "Hopefully they'll have information on Ryder's position."

"If his phone isn't turned off," Pescoli reminded her.

"My guess is, he's made some calls, and if he has, we'll have a place to start," Alvarez said. "We'll take the position of the last ping, wherever it comes from, and work from there. Maybe we'll get lucky."

"Maybe," Pescoli said, not willing to bet on it as she recognized the quick staccato tap of Joelle's high heels in the hallway. From the sound of it, the receptionist was nearly sprinting and stopped abruptly at Blackwater's office.

"Sorry," she said, sticking her head inside, her heart-shaped earrings still swinging in her earlobes. "But I've got a news crew here from KMJC. And Nia Del Ray, the reporter, is being very insistent that someone make a statement. To her." Clutching the doorframe in one hand, Joelle let her gaze skate over the detectives to land on Blackwater. "Apparently someone over at the station heard that you already talked to the *Mountain Reporter,* and now she wants equal time. At least, I think that's how she put it. Any way around it, she's in the reception area and not budging."

"You talked to Manny Douglas?" Pescoli asked her boss. She had no use for the wormy little reporter for the local newspaper. The guy was always crawling around, poking his pointy nose in where it didn't belong, getting himself and the department into trouble.

"I did. It was a good move." Blackwater was making no apologies. "The public might be able to help us locate Anne-Marie Calderone, and now, the others involved in the case. We can use the press to our advantage."

"Or your advantage," Pescoli said, and caught a warning glare from Alvarez.

Blackwater said softly, "My decision." He looked to Joelle, still waiting in the doorway. "Tell her to hold tight. I'll talk to the public information officer, and we'll organize a press conference later today."

"Today?" Pescoli repeated. "You're not going out with what we've got, are you?" She was horrified. "We have to hold all this close, or we could spook Calderone and Ryder, maybe compromise the case."

"I said, 'later.' " He was firm.

Pescoli said, "This is a bad idea."

"Maybe, but mine." Even seated at his desk while she was standing, Blackwater still held the upper hand, was still in command. "Just wrap it up, Detective."

So there it was. Obviously, he couldn't give up another shot at the spotlight.

Joelle clarified. "You want me to ask Nia Del Ray to wait for the press conference."

"She can damn well cool her jets," Pescoli said.

But Blackwater held up a hand to silence her. "I'll speak to Ms. Del Ray," he said to Joelle. "Give me five minutes, then send her in."

It was all Pescoli could do to hold her tongue.

"I'm not going to tell her anything about the case," Blackwater assured the detectives as he pushed his chair back and stood. "I just want to assure her that we're not holding anything back and, as I said, see if the press can help us." With one eye on the mirror, he reached for his jacket. "Keep me up to the minute, Detectives," he ordered and waited as they walked out of his office.

Pescoli seethed.

"Don't let him get to you," Alvarez whispered. "Don't. It won't end well."

"No?" Pescoli threw back. "You know me. Here I was believing in happy endings."

Something was wrong.

Ryder sensed it the minute he stepped inside the cabin again. It was too quiet. Too damn quiet. "Hey!" he called, crossing the living room. "It's been five minutes."

Still nothing. "Anne-Marie?"

No response, just the soft thunk of one of the blackened logs in the fireplace splitting, causing a few sparks to rise and the reddish embers to glow bright. He told himself to relax, that he was starting to jump at shadows. Hadn't he conjured up someone lurking through the veil of snow around the cabin a few minutes ago? Being cooped up, listening to her lies . . . hell, believing them . . . was making him edgy. "Anne?" he yelled again. "Let's go!"

Nothing.

Not one damn sound.

In a heartbeat, he knew what had happened. "Shit!"

Somehow, though he'd watched the interior during his phone call, even checked the grounds near the little cottage, she'd managed to escape, either by lucking out and running to the back door while he was surveying the snowy landscape near the side of the house, or somehow she'd crawled through that tiny window in the bathroom and dropped outside, hiding her tracks.

He flashed on the shadow he'd witnessed.

Crap! It had been her. Of course!

Damn it all to hell, I've been an idiot, he thought, crossing the small space.

He'd been careless, believing the stupid window was too damn small. But without all the extra padding, Anne-Marie was a slim, athletic woman. And she had a purpose. Hadn't she told him over and over that she wouldn't go back, that she'd rather die than . . .

Jaw clenched, he flung the cracked door open wide. "Anne— Oh, God!"

His voice died in his throat as he looked into the small interior. There, crumpled on the floor, blood pooling beneath her on the dirty old linoleum, she lay.

A pair of long-bladed shears, the kind used by hairdressers, were still clutched in her right hand. Despite her wrists being handcuffed, she'd been able to open the blades and slash at her wrists. Jagged red scratches, blood still oozing, ran lengthwise down the inside of her forearms.

Her eyes were closed.

And she seemed peaceful.

As if she'd accepted death all too willingly.

Pescoli and Alvarez stared at the images Zoller brought up on the computer screen. She had copies of the security tapes from the motel. They'd been on their way to the diner when the junior detective had asked them to step into her cubicle.

"I thought you'd want to see this," Zoller said. "I had the lab send me a digital copy."

"They've already done that?" Alvarez asked.

"I told them it was a rush. I, uh, I might have invoked Sheriff Blackwater's name."

"Better than God's," Pescoli observed, then shut up as Alvarez sent her another sharp look. Her partner was right. If she wanted to keep her job, she needed to keep the peace. You attract more flies with honey than vinegar. Wasn't that the old saying? *Well, it sucks,* she thought.

"So here it is." Zoller freeze-framed the tape. "This is Bryan Smith as he checked in."

Pescoli recognized the registration desk, the same brochures on the stand nearby, the coffeepot, and old couch. Carla, the heavyset manager of the River View Motel was standing on the business side of the counter, her gold tooth catching the light. A tall man stood on the other side, leaning over to fill out the card. He was handsome, fit, with dark hair and the very visage of Dr. Bruce Effin' Calderone.

Heart in his throat, Ryder fell to his knees beside Anne-Marie's pale unmoving body. "Oh, Jesus," he whispered. "Anne, goddamn it, Anne-Marie!" Warm blood seeped through his jeans. "Anne-Marie? Can you hear me? Oh, come on, come on!"

He felt for a pulse and found it, heard the soft sound of her breathing. He felt a bit of relief. It wasn't too late. She was still alive. "Hang in there. You . . . hang in there."

Yanking the phone from his pocket, he dialed 9-1-1, but it was a futile call. They were too far out of town to wait for an ambulance and no helicopter could fly in the storm. "Come on," he said to Anne-Marie as the operator answered.

"9-1-1. What is the nature of—"

"Listen! I have a woman near death. Dying. Her wrists slashed. I need help!" Ryder didn't hesitate.

"Is the woman alive?"

"Yes! Yes! I said so."

"Sir, I need your name and your location."

"We're off a county road in the mountains, twenty miles north of Grizzly Falls, maybe fifteen miles west of Missoula, I'm not sure, but I'm bringing her in. To the hospital in Missoula. Northern General." *God, this is taking too much time.*

All the while Anne-Marie was bleeding out.

He set the phone down and found a roll of gauze in an emergency first aid kit, probably Anne's, and probably where she'd kept the damn scissors she'd used to try and end her life. Heart thudding, operator yelling at him, he quickly unlocked her cuffs, stuffed them into his pocket, then pried her blood-stained hands apart. As he'd learned in the Army, he wrapped the wounds, binding them, hoping to staunch the flow of blood as the 9-1-1 operator still yelled at him, her voice squawking instructions as he worked.

"Sir!" she yelled. "Are you still there? Keep this line open. Officers are dispatched and—"

He ignored her instructions. "Come on, Anne-Marie," he said, forcing himself to remain calm, to go into that zone he'd learned long ago. But it wasn't working. Not with her, the only woman he'd married no matter how false it had been. "Hang in there, honey." His voice cracked a little.

Why hadn't he paid attention to her desperation?

Hadn't she said she'd rather die?

She was on the brink of death by her own hand, her choice, because he'd run her to the ground. Guilt tore at him as he looked at her, the woman who had been so full of life, such a brilliant, careless liar, the only woman he'd ever met who could hold her own with him in a verbal sparring match or while making love. His damn heart wrenched and he realized he'd been kidding himself. It had been a lie when he'd convinced himself that he didn't care for her and never had. She'd gotten to him, burrowed under his skin and into his damn soul.

The reason he'd agreed with her bastard of a father to bring her back to New Orleans wasn't about justice or even money. It was about seeing her again, having his day of reckoning.

Well he was having it.

In spades.

As for her old man, the devil with whom he'd partnered, Talbert was nearly broke. No way would Ryder have gotten paid. He'd known that from the get-go. Had done a little research. The old man had probably hoped that with his notorious daughter's return, he could somehow capitalize on her capture, figure out a way to make some big cash. Maybe a tell-all book? A movie of the week? Or even a reality television series. Who knew? The man had grandiose opinions of himself.

Stupidly, Ryder had wanted to see Anne-Marie again and yes, to take her back to New Orleans to clear up the mystery. He had outwardly been Talbert's willing pawn.

Ryder had told himself he had to be the one to bring Anne-Marie to justice, to make her face her sins. Oh, yes, his own motives had been far from altruistic.

Well, no longer.

That whole returning to New Orleans thing was over. At least for him.

He would take Anne-Marie to the hospital and hope beyond hope that she survived. That was all that mattered. How they dealt with the rest of their lives was of little concern. Once she was healthy again, he would help her prove that she was innocent of any crimes and that her husband, the bastard of a doctor who had severed her finger, was the true ungodly culprit.

What was it she'd said? That she'd worried the women killed recently in Grizzly Falls had been targeted because of her? Killed to terrorize her.

That, of course, had to be her own fears taking flight.

Right?

But the thought gnawed at him as he worked over her, and he wondered if it was possible. Was she crazy? Or singularly perceptive where Bruce Calderone was involved? As he tucked the final end of the gauze strip around her bandaged arm, she moaned. Gently he tried to rouse her. "Anne-Marie? Honey. Anne? Come on. Hang in there. We've got to go now."

The white strips of gauze covering her arms were already turning scarlet.

Time was running out.

And the damn 9-1-1 operator was still yammering, advising him to stay on the line when he slid his arms under Anne-Marie and gently lifted her, his heart hammering at the urgency. Would he make it in time? Or would she die on the way?

Either way, guilt would be his lifelong companion.

"We've got a hit," Alvarez said, checking her phone as they were leaving Zoller's cubicle. "Ryder's cell phone."

"Already?"

"Today's technology."

"Let me get my coat." Pescoli grabbed her jacket, sidearm, purse, and another energy bar as they'd never made it to the diner. Her stomach had started growling again, the hunger pangs only subsiding by the shot of adrenaline that pumped through her bloodstream at the thought of catching one of the key players in the homicide cases.

Once she and Alvarez met in the hall again, walking rapidly to the back door, Alvarez explained. "Not only is Ryder's location being triangulated by the cell phone company and our department, but, get this, he's on the line now with 9-1-1."

"Are you kidding me?"

"Nope. The call is being traced, emergency vehicles dispatched."

"What's the emergency?" It didn't sound good. People on the run didn't tend to call the police unless something unexpected and dire, usually life-threatening, had gone down.

"Don't know for certain. He said something about a possible suicide attempt."

"By whom?"

"A woman."

"Shit. It's Anne-Marie Calderone. Suicide attempt, my ass."

"He claims he's at a cabin in the Bitterroots off the county road. The triangulation confirms the location. A cabin owned by someone who lives out of state."

"He's there? With her? You mean, they're there?"

"It's sketchy. He's not responding to the operator though he hasn't hung up."

"Ominous," Pescoli thought aloud as she scrabbled into the side pocket of her purse for her key ring. Side-stepping around Pete Watershed, who was heading in the opposite direction, Pescoli tried to piece it all together. "Maybe he tracked her down and they got into some kind of lover's quarrel. She did do the bogus marriage thing with him. That's gotta sting. Big rodeo rider. Probably a macho guy. Maybe he tried to kill her and has remorse."

"Who knows?"

"It's just unbelievable that after all this time of chasing shadows, we get a goddamn call for help from one of the suspects."

"Person of interest," Alvarez pointed out. "Not a suspect."

"There you go again, semantics." Pushing open the back door, Pescoli caught a blast as the arctic air slapped her full in the face. "You know, just once, just damn once, it would be nice if one of our local serial killers decided to do his business in the summer." She hit the button on the remote lock, and the Jeep's lights flickered, its horn giving a soft beep. "Yeah, wouldn't that be the ticket."

"Careful what you wish for," Alvarez said. "Summer brings heat, rotting flesh, maggots, flies, stench, you name it."

"Still—" Pescoli's breath formed clouds as she talked.

Alvarez turned the conversation back to the case. "Even though emergency vehicles have been dispatched, Ryder's claiming he's taking the victim to a hospital in Missoula. Northwest General."

Where Dan Grayson had died. Pescoli didn't like the reminder.

At the county vehicle, Alvarez opened the door to the passenger seat. "Oh. I've already advised Blackwater."

Perfect. Pescoli slid behind the wheel and remembered the new sheriff showing up at the O'Halleran ranch where the first victim had been discovered. The two doors closed simultaneously. "Isn't Blackwater already driving to the location? Trying to grab a little glory?"

"You're awful."

"So I've heard." Pescoli started the Jeep, flipped on the wipers, and backed out of the parking spot.

Alvarez actually grinned. "I don't know if the sheriff will show up. He was still eyeball deep in a conversation with Nia Del Ray. I had to text him the info. Didn't want to break up his moment to shine with the press."

"Then, no," Pescoli said, answering her own question. Ramming the Jeep into gear, she nosed out of the lot. "He wouldn't pass up the opportunity for a sound bite."

"Even for capturing a serial killer?"

"Eh." Pescoli tipped a gloved hand up and down. "Maybe. Maybe not." She checked the street, then gunned the engine and cut in front of a slow-moving van of some kind.

Alvarez hung on. "Slow down, Detective. Remember, we don't know that we're going to find Calderone and even if we do and she survives, we still don't have proof other than one lousy fingerprint that she's the killer."

Pescoli flipped on the overhead lights and siren. No time to waste.

Ryder didn't bother gathering his things. He had to get Anne-Marie to the hospital. Nothing else mattered. Though she was a dead weight in his arms, he kicked open the door and carried her to the truck, trying like hell not to jar her, but feeling the clock ticking. Once at the pickup, he set her on the worn cushions then laid the passenger seat back as far into a reclining position as it would go. "Anne," he called to her. "Anne-Marie? Darlin', come on, now. Stay with me."

Her eyes fluttered and he felt hope swell in his heart.

"We're goin' now," he told her but her eyes didn't track. "Hang on." He closed the side door, then rounded the truck and climbed in, his keys already out of his pocket. Double-checking that the rig was in four-wheel drive, he flipped on the starter. The old engine fired. He found reverse and started to back up past the trees that had flanked the lane. The snow was deep, but his Dodge moved easily, cutting tracks through the powder to the wide spot in the lane a little farther back, an open space where he could turn his vehicle around and head to the main road. Hopefully, it had been plowed.

If so, within twenty minutes or so, he would be able to get Anne-Marie to the hospital. "Hang in there," he said again, squinting through the snow. His back window was fogged and it was hard to see. He used his mirrors, trying to keep his truck on track. Almost at the place he hoped to swing the back end around, he caught a glimpse of something that appeared through the veil, a huge shadow looming behind him.

"What the hell?" He looked in the rearview mirror, and God

Almighty, if there wasn't another vehicle behind him, blocking his path. A grayish Ford Explorer. Older model.

Like the one he'd seen at the River View.

His heart nearly stopped. He thought of the shadow he'd seen earlier. Squinting, he didn't see anyone inside the Explorer, but the interior was impossible to clearly discern through the snowfall. He glanced around the area. Was the vehicle there because of them or had it been parked by someone going cross-country skiing or snowshoeing or even poaching?

The hairs on the back of his neck rose and he thought about his pistol, hidden deep in the pocket of his jacket, just behind the passenger seat.

It didn't matter. He just had to get around the thing.

He didn't like it, but he had to deal with it.

He thought he could squeeze around one side, but he'd have to back around the Ford; there just wasn't enough room between the trees to rotate his truck. "Son of a bitch," he muttered, his attention on the Explorer.

He didn't notice her move.

Didn't see it coming.

All of a sudden, quick as a rattler striking, Anne-Marie sat bolt upright, reached forward, and grabbed the handcuffs from his pocket. As he jerked, she managed to click one over his wrist. With a snap, the other was locked over the steering wheel.

"What the hell?" he said, pulling back, trying to release the lock.

As if she'd done it a thousand times, she slid his Glock from his jacket pocket, cut the engine, then opened the side door.

"Hey!"

"I told you I wasn't going back, Ryder."

"Wait! No! Anne-Marie! For the love of God! I was taking you to the frickin' hospital!"

"Sure. Give me a break!" She slammed the door shut and took off running, racing along the tracks he'd just cut, hurrying back to the cabin.

Furious with himself, with his damn gullibility where she was concerned, he pounded the wheel. *Damn.*

He'd been a fool. Not just once, but again! He swore and pulled at the cuffs, but they were locked solid. "Shit!" he yelled. "Shit, shit. Shit! Anne!"

But she was gone. Through the windshield and falling snow, he watched her leap over the step, not slowing an inch, her self-inflicted injuries all part of her disguise. In the blink of an eye, she disappeared into the cabin.

God. Damn. It.

With a sickening sense of what was happening, he realized that he'd been duped. She was never in any real danger of dying. Her whole suicide attempt had been a ruse. And he'd fallen for it, hook, line, and sinker.

CHAPTER 29

Anne-Marie worked fast. There wasn't much time. She found Ryder's phone in the bathroom where the stupid 9-1-1 operator was still bleating out instructions. She turned the phone off, severing the connection, then disabled it completely, ignoring the smeared blood on the bathroom floor—her blood.

Heart thumping, hating herself for her deception, she changed quickly, but didn't remove the damn bandages. She was still bleeding a little bit but wasn't worried. She hadn't cut an artery or even a major vein, just sliced the surface over and over again, a trick, considering the restrictions of those damn handcuffs, but one she'd researched on the Internet long ago. She had become a master of disguise and deception, two traits of which she wasn't all that proud, but sure as hell came in handy.

She thought of Ryder trapped in the truck.

It wouldn't be for long.

The damn cops were on their way.

So she couldn't waste a second. She changed quickly, tucked Ryder's Glock into the back of her jeans, the waistband holding it snug against her back. "Here we go," she said and started loading her SUV.

"Anne!" Ryder yelled. "Anne-Marie!" *Shit! Fuck! Damn!* "Anne! Oh, for the love of . . ." Pissed beyond pissed, he yanked at the handcuffs holding him fast to the steering wheel.

Wait a second!

The key!

"Where the hell is the key for the cuffs?" He'd put it on the ring . . .

then he saw the tiny notched piece of metal dangling from the key ring still in the truck's ignition.

He couldn't believe his good luck. Tantalizingly close, he reached for it, but it hung just out of his reach. No matter how he strained, leaned, and twisted, he just couldn't get it.

His mind started spinning with options, none of them possible. As cold as it was, he started to sweat with his efforts. He'd been such a fool to let her, a known criminal, a major liar, and a master of deception, get the drop on him. Letting his breath out in frustration, he glanced in the rearview again to that damn SUV blocking his escape. No doubt it was part of Anne-Marie's plan.

How had I been so stupid?

How had I let her lie to me?

He took another swipe at the keys and swore when his fingertip brushed the bottom of the ring. But that was it. Not good enough. Too far away by less than an inch. If he could just reach the key ring, if he could slide the handcuffs up the steering wheel to give him just a bit more leeway, then maybe he could . . . *Crap.* The steering wheel wasn't an unbroken circle, of course. The braces holding the wheel to the column prevented him from sliding around it completely. He stretched, trying to reach the keys with his free hand, but the most he could do was tick the key with the tip of his middle finger.

"Son of a bitch." He strained, the cords of his neck distending, his muscles stretching to their limits, but no go. Through the fogging windshield, he watched as she loaded her SUV with essentials and her bag. Even a wig was tossed into the back seat. Swiftly. Efficiently. Something black and bulky was tucked into the belt of her jeans at her back and he realized it was a gun—his damn Glock. She never once looked in his direction, just packed her truck with singular efficiency and climbed behind the wheel.

Damn her.

Where did she think she could go? How could she drive around his truck and that damn vehicle parked behind him? And where was the driver of the truck? The bad feeling that had been with Ryder when he first saw the Explorer blocking the lane burrowed a little deeper in his soul. Though he told himself he was imagining things, that the truck was just a coincidence, he didn't quite believe it.

He felt the weight of her tiny pistol in his pocket, a practically useless weapon, but a weapon nonetheless. Of course, it was lodged deep on the opposite side of his body as his free hand but, just to be on the safe side, he decided it was worth the effort to retrieve it and her damn switchblade. But of course, he was thwarted. The weapons in that pocket, like the keys dangling in the ignition, were just out of reach. No matter how he twisted and contorted his body, he couldn't slide his free hand near the pocket. However, he could, just maybe, shrug out of the coat, at least on the side of his body that wasn't clamped to the wheel. If he got his shoulder free and slid the jacket down his back, partially off his cuffed arm, he might be able to twist the fabric enough to be able to reach the gun. Then, at least, he'd be armed. Trapped, but armed.

But it wasn't going to happen.

Try as he might, all he could do was free up his left arm, the padded sleeve of his jacket no longer binding, which gave him a little more wiggle room. Not much. But he didn't need more than another half an inch. He reached for the keys again, finally able to touch part of his house key.

Maybe he wasn't trapped after all.

Maybe he could—

Through the snow collecting over the windshield, he saw the very same kind of shadow he'd viewed from the porch only minutes earlier. He squinted and his heart stopped.

The shadow was a man. A tall man.

And in his hand, he held a gun.

"We've got a little more info," Alvarez told her partner as Pescoli hit the gas and sped around a dawdling minivan that thankfully pulled to the side of the road. With the Jeep's light bar lit menacingly and the siren screaming a warning for the slow-moving traffic to get out of her way, she was able to push the speed limit despite the storm.

As she drove into the hills, she slid around a flatbed truck that was inching up an incline, her red and blue lights reflecting off the snow.

Alvarez was staring at the small screen of her phone.

"What?" Pescoli asked.

"It's on Ryder's phone. Apparently, he didn't think he was doing anything worrisome, because his last call, the one before the hospital, was to an unlisted number in Louisiana. Private cell. Zoller called

Montoya, who's in the loop, and he was able to come up with the owner of the phone."

"Let me guess. Bruce Calderone."

"Not even close." Alvarez slid a glance at her partner. "The phone is listed to Favier Industries. Specifically Talbert Favier."

"Anne-Marie's father?" Pescoli asked. "He's in cahoots with the illegal second husband?"

"Seems so."

"I wonder what the hell that's all about."

"We should find out soon," Alvarez said, checking her GPS. "We'll be there within ten. Deputies and an ambulance are probably arriving."

"If anyone's still there. By now, Ryder was supposed to be taking her to the hospital, isn't that what you said?"

"Yeah." Alvarez was still staring at the screen. "We've got officers waiting at Northern General?"

"And the other hospitals in the area in case that was a ruse to throw us off."

"Good."

Pescoli smiled as she took a corner a little too fast and the Jeep slid a second before the wheels caught. "This is all going down. Finally."

Anne-Marie stepped onto the porch.

Ryder witnessed the assassin raise his gun and aim. "No!"

Shit! With a supreme effort, Ryder reached for the keys again, his fingers touching the end of his dangling house key. No longer did he care about the handcuffs. No, he had another plan in mind . . . if the bastard would just stay put.

And he had enough time.

God, help him. He felt the cold metal brush against his fingers.

Once.

Twice.

And then he grabbed the truck key, still engaged. All he had to do was throw his weight into it and then . . .

Anne-Marie stopped dead in her tracks.

Her heart hit the ground as she recognized her husband, her first and only legal husband standing behind her SUV, a huge pistol aimed straight at her heart.

"Bruce," she said, going cold inside, her worst fears crystalizing.

"Going somewhere?" he asked in that voice she found so hateful.

"What're you doing here?" she said, trying to stay cool when she was beyond freaked. She needed to buy time. She had a weapon, too, a large pistol, but it would take a second or two to reach behind her.

"You've been hard to find."

She moved to one side, and the muzzle of his huge gun followed her. Sick inside, she realized that once again, she was at his mercy, the little wife of the outwardly handsome, inwardly insidious monster of a husband. Only this time, she knew she was doomed. If he'd gone through all the trouble of tracking her down, he wouldn't just let her be.

"I-I thought you'd disappeared," she said, thinking hard, looking for some means of escape. If she could just buy some time . . .

"Like you."

"You left me for dead."

"I did," he admitted with a mock-disgusted smile. "And damn it, I made a mistake, thinking the alligators would finish you off." All humor faded from his voice. "Trust me, this time I won't."

She didn't doubt it. But the gun. If she could just get to the gun. "How did you find me?" she asked, though it didn't matter. She was just putting off the inevitable.

"Simple. I didn't have to look for you." Again, he was pleased with himself, thought he was so damn clever, was glad to rub her nose in it. "I just followed Ryder."

She felt sick inside at the thought that she, even inadvertently, had dragged Ryder into this.

"He was pretty dogged you know. Seems as if he had as much of a bone to pick with you as I do." Calderone chuckled humorlessly. "Husbands. They can be such a problem. Especially when you have more than one at a time."

"That was a mistake. I know it now," she said, wondering if there was a chance that she could reason with him and desperate enough to try. It wasn't just her skin she had to worry about, but Ryder's as well. Handcuffed as he was, Ryder was a sitting duck.

"Look," she said, inching up slightly to the open door of the cabin but splaying her hands to keep his attention off her feet. She saw him stare at his handiwork. Her stump—the finger he'd cut off as a reminder of how she'd abused her wedding vows. "It's over. You and me. We both know it and we knew it a long time ago. So, don't do anything foolish. You're a doctor for God's sake, you're young. Go and live your life. Leave me alone."

She was rambling, she knew, but still, he hadn't shot her. Not yet. Though she was panicking inside, still intending to shoot him if she had the chance, she forced her voice to remain calm. "Go away, Bruce. So far, you're not a killer and you could leave me . . ." Her voice faded away as reality hit her and she thought of the two women who had been killed recently.

"Too late for that. Sacrifices had to be made."

"Sacrifices? I don't under—" But she did. Her stomach turned over. She thought she might throw up. God, how she hated this man. How, how, how had she ever remotely thought she loved him? Why in the world did she marry him? Because her own home life hadn't been the picture-perfect postcard everyone had believed. And she'd been duped by him. If given the chance, she'd blow him away and not think twice about it.

"They needed to die, so that you would be blamed."

"Me? But how? I had nothing to do with them."

"Didn't you?"

"Of course not." She inched backward, still trying to figure out how to save Ryder, save herself. "I didn't even know them."

"Oh, but Anne-Marie, there's the problem." Calderone wagged the gun a little and her eyes were fixed on the muzzle. Was it her imagination or over the whistle of the wind did she hear the faint shriek of sirens?

The police!

Ryder had called 9-1-1!

Had they come up with the right location?

Hurry, hurry, hurry!

"You can't prove it though, can you? That you'd not met those women," Calderone was saying, so caught up in his own story, in his bragging, that he hadn't heard the sirens as he stood confidently behind her SUV.

He couldn't prove it—yet. But he would. He wouldn't be so outwardly cocky if he hadn't made certain of that fact. Oh, how her fingers itched to grab Ryder's Glock.

"You know, it looks very suspicious that those women happened to die just about the time you arrived in town, don't you think? And then, oh dear, evidence points to you."

'What do you mean?"

"Your fingerprint, Anne-Marie. Your fucking telltale print showed up on the victims' personal effects."

"But I never—"

"I guess you just got careless."

"What? No! You're bluffing," she accused. But she knew him too well to believe her own words.

The glint of satisfaction in his eyes, and his cold, cold smile convinced her he wasn't lying. To prove his point, he kept the gun trained on her with one hand, while with the other, he unzipped his jacket to expose a chain that he lifted and she saw something withered and dark and . . .

Her stomach dropped and she retched, fighting the urge to throw up. "Oh, God."

"That's right. A little keepsake from my dear whore of a wife."

"You shit!"

His eyes flared. "So let's end this," he said harshly.

The sirens were getting closer, but Calderone didn't seem to notice the noise over the wind, so intent was he on killing her. "Go ahead and try for the gun," he said smoothly. Confidently. Always the supercilious egomaniac. "I know you've got one, but, trust me, Annie-girl, you'll never reach it, aim it, and fire before you're dead."

So much for the element of surprise. She saw him level the gun straight at her heart and threw herself backward into the open doorway.

Blam! Calderone fired.

Wood splintered.

She hit the floor, rolled over, reached around her back.

A big engine roared to life.

What the hell?

Blam! Another shot, the bullet whizzing into the cabin.

The engine raced louder, a truck spinning its tires in the snow.

Looking through the doorway, she saw Calderone turn, his face a mask of horror. Suddenly his aim was no longer on her or the open doorway, but on the huge truck, Ryder's Dodge, churning forward, gathering speed, heading straight at him.

Blam! Calderone fired again.

The Dodge's windshield shattered.

Ryder's body jerked.

Blood sprayed.

The horn blared.

"Nooooo!" Anne-Marie screamed, rolling to her feet, yanking out her weapon from the back of her jeans and swinging her arm around. "No! No! No!" She started firing wildly, all of her pent-up rage forced into pulling the trigger.

But the truck didn't stop.

Calderone stepped back, a bullet grazing his shoulder. For a second, he forgot the truck. When he looked up again, it was too late. The Dodge slammed into him, pinning him against the back of her SUV. In a mash of shattering bones and crumpling metal, he howled in agony. His voice rose to the heavens. Writhing. Screaming. To no avail. Calderone dropped the gun and frantically pushed on the hood of Ryder's truck as if he could shove it off him. But the wheels kept grinding, churning in the snow, mangling him, twisting the lower half of his body into a pulp of bone and tissue and blood.

"Oh, God!" Horrified, Anne-Marie threw herself off the porch and ran to the truck. Snow was blowing inside the cab. She yanked open the door as the engine continued to turn over, trying to drive the Dodge's spinning wheels forward, still crushing the man pinned in the contorted metal.

"Troy. Ryder!"

His body spilled into her waiting arms, blood everywhere.

"Don't die," she said to him, though he was obviously unconscious. "Don't you dare die on me!" With all her effort, she reached across him and yanked out the keys. The engine died, the wheels stopping suddenly.

Tears filled her eyes and she didn't bother dashing them, just fumbled with the damn key ring until she found the smallest key and unlocked the cuffs. As the cuff sprang open, he slithered out of the truck and his weight pulled them both onto the frozen ground.

Blood spilled, and she tried frantically to stanch it.

She had done this. It was her fault that he lay dying in her arms.

For a second, everything seemed to go quiet. The engine no longer ground and Calderone's voice had been stilled, probably forever. She felt that in that one suspended second, she and Ryder were alone in the universe.

"Don't you die on me," she said to him again, sobbing, holding him close. Blood covered her hands, smearing on her clothes. So wrapped up in saving him, she barely heard the sirens or the wind or the sound of anxious shouts. "Do you hear me, Ryder? Don't you dare die on me." She heard him expel a rattling breath.

Then he opened one eye. Looking up at her, his lips barely moved as he said, "Wouldn't dream of it, darlin'. Wouldn't dream of . . . it."

Epilogue

Never in her life would Pescoli have dreamed that she would be standing next to Santana, saying "I do" in a tiny chapel in Las Vegas, but here she was, her kids at her side, witnessing their mother getting married again.

Surprisingly, it felt right.

As if she'd been destined for this moment for all of her life.

Okay, she knew that was the stuff of romantic dreams she didn't believe in, but just for the day, wearing an off-white dress that almost touched her knees, Santana looking handsome as as hell in a black suit, she went with the fantasy.

It wasn't February fourteen, but the day after. Bianca and Jeremy, if not thrilled at the hasty marriage, went with it. Santana had promised to take Jeremy target shooting in the next few days and Bianca was able to sunbathe in the bikini she'd received from her father and stepmother last Christmas. So it was a win-win situation, or as much as it could be, considering.

Less than two weeks ago, she and Alvarez had wrapped up the Anne-Marie Calderone case. Bruce Calderone had died at the scene. No big loss there. The finger found dangling from his neck matched the prints they'd found on Calypso Pope's purse and Sheree Cantnor's shoe and was the ring finger he'd sliced off his wife's left hand, the proof of which she bore as a stump on her hand.

Troy Ryder had survived a bullet wound to the neck, though he'd lost enough blood to kill a lesser man. However, he was out of the hospital and in New Orleans where he, Anne-Marie, and Detective Montoya were sorting things out.

The last Pescoli had heard, Anne-Marie's grandmother wasn't pressing charges, but that was just the first and foremost of Anne-Marie's crimes, now that she'd been cleared of murder. She had other nasty details, like false passports and IDs, to deal with.

Again, Pescoli was glad that was all part of the New Orleans Police Department's problems. She had heard that Anne-Marie's parents were filing bankruptcy and had disowned her after being exposed as trying to profit from their daughter's notoriety.

The true killer of Sheree Cantnor and Calypso Pope had been exposed, all part of Calderone's twisted plan to get back at his wife. Sometimes, marriages weren't exactly made in heaven, which was a weird thing to think on her wedding day. Then again, it was her third time down the aisle, so she could be a little cynical.

She wasn't going to think about the whole Calderone mess another minute.

That case was closed.

At least for her.

And from this moment forward, she was a bride. Again. God knew what the future had in store for her. Bianca, in a short pink dress, the maid of honor, blinked back tears. Jeremy stood tall and solemn, a man who had given his mother away to a new man he didn't quite trust. In a suit, he resembled his father on that long ago day when Pescoli had married Joe Strand.

But that was the past. Santana was the future.

As she held Santana's hand and thought of the baby that was growing inside her, the infant her other children knew nothing about, she felt a wellspring of hope that was unlike her. The pseudo clergyman, grinning widely, proclaimed them man and wife and Santana leaned down to kiss her.

"Just one thing," she whispered before his lips met hers. "I'm not changing my name. I've done that enough."

"You think you might have mentioned that a little earlier?"

"Probably."

He winked at her, and she wondered how it was possible to love someone this much, especially a man she'd once considered just a fling. "It's fine," he assured her.

"Really? You don't care?"

"Don't you know me by now?" His dark eyes flashed in that sexy way that always made her throat catch and she couldn't help but grin. "I'll take you any way I can get you, Regan Pescoli. Any damn way you want." And then, to seal the deal, he kissed her so hard, she nearly swooned.

Yes, she thought, *this time I finally got it right.*

HOME

Along the shores of Oregon's wild Columbia River, the Victorian mansion where Sarah McAdams grew up is as foreboding as she remembers. The moment she and her two daughters, Jade and Gracie, pull up the isolated drive, Sarah is beset by uneasy memories—of her cold, distant mother, of the half-sister who vanished without a trace, and of a long-ago night when Sarah was found on the widow's walk, feverish and delirious.

IS WHERE

But Sarah has vowed to make a fresh start and renovate the old place. Between tending to her girls and the rundown property, she has little time to dwell on the past. . . . Until a new, more urgent menace enters the picture.

THE FEAR IS

One by one, teenage girls are disappearing. Frantic for her daughters' safety, Sarah feels the house's walls closing in on her again. Somewhere deep in her memory is the key to a very real and terrifying danger. And only by confronting her most terrifying fears can she stop the nightmare roaring back to life once more . . .

Please turn the page for an exciting sneak peek of
Lisa Jackson's
CLOSE TO HOME

CHAPTER 1

October 15, 2014
Blue Peacock Manor

"God, Mom, you've got to be kidding!" Jade said from the passenger seat of the Explorer as Sarah drove along the once-gravel lane.

"Not kidding," Sarah responded. "You know that." Winding through thick stands of pine, fir, and cedar, the twin ruts were weed-choked and filled with potholes that had become puddles with the recent rain.

"You can't actually think that we can live here!" Catching glimpses of the huge house through the trees, Jade, seventeen, was clearly horrified and, as usual, wasn't afraid to voice her opinion.

"Mom's serious," Gracie said from the backseat, where she was crammed between piles of blankets, and mounds of comforters, sleeping bags, and the other bedding they were moving from Vancouver. "She told us."

Jade shot a glance over her shoulder. "I know. But it's worse than I thought."

"That's impossible," Gracie said.

"No one asked your opinion!"

Sarah's hands tightened over the steering wheel. She'd already heard how she was ruining her kids' lives by packing them up and returning to the old homestead where she'd been born and raised. To hear them tell it, she was the worst mother in the world. The word "hate" had been thrown around, aimed at her, the move, and their miserable lives in general.

Single motherhood. It wasn't for the faint-hearted, she'd decided long ago. So her kids were still angry with her. Too bad. Sarah needed a fresh start.

And though Jade and Gracie didn't know it, they did too.

"It's like we're in another solar system," Jade said as the thickets of trees gave way to a wide clearing high above the Columbia River.

Gracie agreed, "In a land far, far away."

"Oh, stop it. It's not that bad," Sarah said. Her girls had lived most of their lives in Vancouver, Washington, right across the river from Portland, Oregon. Theirs had been a city life. Out here, in Stewart's Crossing, things would be different, and even more so at Sarah's childhood home of Blue Peacock Manor.

Perched high on the cliffs overlooking the Columbia River, the massive house where Sarah had been raised rose in three stories of cedar and stone. Built in the Queen Anne style of a Victorian home, its gables and chimneys knifed upward into a somber gray sky, and from her vantage point Sarah could now see the glass cupola that opened onto the widow's walk. For a second, she felt a frisson of dread slide down her spine, but she pushed it aside.

"Oh. My. God." Jade's jaw dropped open as she stared at the house. "It looks like something straight out of *The Addams Family.*"

"Let me see!" In the backseat, Gracie unhooked her seat belt and leaned forward for a better view. "She's right." For once Gracie agreed with her older sister.

"Oh, come on," Sarah said, but Jade's opinion wasn't that far off. With a broad, sagging porch and crumbling chimneys, the once-grand house that in the past the locals had called the Jewel of the Columbia was in worse shape than she remembered.

"Are you blind? This place is a disaster!" Jade was staring through the windshield and slowly shaking her head, as if she couldn't believe the horrid turn her life had just taken. Driving closer to the garage, they passed another building that was falling into total disrepair. "Mom. Seriously. We can't live here." She turned her wide, mascara-laden eyes on her mother as if Sarah had gone completely out of her mind.

"We can and we will. Eventually." Sarah cranked on the wheel to swing the car around and parked near the walkway leading to the entrance of the main house. The decorative rusted gate was falling off its hinges, the arbor long gone, the roses flanking the flagstone path leggy and gone to seed. "We're going to camp out in the main house until the work on the guesthouse is finished, probably next week. That's where we'll hang out until the house is done, but that will take . . . months, maybe up to a year."

"The guest . . . Oh my God, is that it?" Jade pointed a black-tipped nail at the smaller structure located across a wide stone courtyard from its immense counterpart. The guesthouse was in much the same shape as the main house and outbuildings. Shingles were missing, the gutters were rusted, and most of the downspouts were disconnected or missing altogether. Many of the windows were boarded over as well, and the few that remained were cracked and yellowed.

"Charming." Jade let out a disgusted breath. "I can't wait."

"I thought you'd feel that way," Sarah said with a faint smile.

"Funny," Jade mocked.

"Come on. Buck up. It's just for a little while. Eventually we'll move into the main house for good, if we don't sell it."

Gracie said, "You should sell it now!"

"It's not just mine, remember? My brothers and sister own part of it. What we do with it will be a group decision."

"Doesn't anyone have a lighter?" Jade suggested, almost kidding. "You could burn it down and collect the insurance money."

"How do you know about . . . ?" But she didn't finish the question as she cut the engine. Jade, along with her newfound love of the macabre, was also into every kind of police or detective show that aired on television. Recently she'd discovered true crime as well, the kind of shows in which B-grade actors reenacted grisly murders and the like. Jade's interests, which seemed to coincide with those of her current boyfriend, disturbed Sarah, but she tried to keep from haranguing her daughter about them. In this case, less was more.

"You should sell out your part of it. Leave it to Aunt Dee Linn and Uncle Joe and Jake to renovate," Jade said. "Get out while you can. God, Mom, this is just so nuts that *we're* here. Not only is this house like something out of a bad horror movie, but it's in the middle of nowhere."

She wasn't that far off. The house and grounds were at least five miles from the nearest town of Stewart's Crossing, the surrounding neighbors' farms hidden by stands of fir and cedar. Sarah cut the engine and glanced toward Willow Creek, the natural divide between this property and the next, which had belonged to the Walsh family for more than a hundred years. For a split second she thought about Clint, the last of the Walsh line, who according to Dee Linn and Aunt Marge, was still living in the homestead. She reminded herself sternly that he was not the reason she'd pushed so hard to move back to Stewart's Crossing.

"Why don't you just take me back to get my car?" Jade said as Sarah swung the Explorer around to park near the garage.

"Because it won't be ready for a couple of days. You heard Hal." They'd left Jade's Honda with a mechanic in town; it was scheduled to get a new set of tires and much-needed brakes, and Hal was going to figure out why the Civic was leaking some kind of fluid.

"Oh, right, Hal the master mechanic." Jade was disparaging.

"Best in town," Sarah said, tossing her keys into her bag. "My dad used him."

"Only mechanic in town. And Grandpa's been gone a long time, so it must've been eons ago!"

Sarah actually smiled. "Okay, you got me there. But the place was updated from the last time I was there. Lots of electronic equipment and a couple of new mechanics on staff."

To her amazement, Jade's lips twitched as well, reminding Sarah of the younger, more innocent girl she'd been such a short while ago. "And a lot of customers."

"Must be bad car karma right now," Sarah agreed. There had been an older woman with her little dog and two men, all having problems with their vehicles; the little group had filled the small reception area of the garage.

"Is there ever such a thing as good car karma?" Jade asked, but she seemed resigned to her fate of being without wheels for a while. Good.

Until recently, Jade had been a stellar student. She had a high IQ and had had a keen interest in school; in fact, she had breezed through any number of accelerated classes. Then, about a year ago, she'd discovered boys, and her grades had begun to slip. Now, despite the fact that it might be a bit passé, Jade was into all things Goth and wildly in love with her boyfriend, an older kid who'd barely graduated from high school and didn't seem to give a damn about anything but music, marijuana, and, most likely, sex. A pseudo-intellectual, he'd dropped out of college and loved to argue politics.

Jade thought the sun rose and set on Cody Russell.

Sarah was pretty sure it didn't.

"Come on, let's go," she told her daughters.

Jade wasn't budging. She dragged her cell phone from her purse. "Do I have to?"

"Yes."

"She's such a pain," Gracie said in a whisper. At twelve, she was only starting to show some interest in boys, and still preferred animals, books, and all things paranormal to the opposite sex, so far at least. Blessed with an overactive imagination and, again, keen intelligence, Gracie too was out of step with her peers.

"I heard that." Jade messed with her phone.

"It is kinda creepy, though," Gracie admitted, leaning forward as the first drops of rain splashed against the windshield.

"Beyond creepy!" Jade wasn't one to hold back. "And . . . Oh, God, don't tell me we don't get cell service here." Her face registered complete mortification.

"It's spotty," Sarah said.

"God, Mom, what is this? The Dark Ages? This place is . . . it's horrible. Blue Peacock Manor, my ass."

"Hey!" Sarah reprimanded sharply. "No swearing. Remember? Zero."

"But, Jesus, Mom—"

"Again?" Sarah snapped. "I just said no."

"Okay!" Jade flung back, then added, a little more calmly, "Come on, Mom. Admit it. Blue Peacock is a dumb name. It even sounds kind of dirty."

"Where is this coming from?" Sarah demanded.

"Just sayin'." Jade dropped her phone into her bag. "And Becky told me the house is haunted."

"So now you're listening to Becky?" Sarah set the parking brake and reached for the handle of the door. The day was quickly going from bad to worse. "I didn't think you liked her."

"I don't." Jade sighed theatrically. "I'm just telling you what she said." Becky was Jade's cousin, the daughter of Sarah's older sister, Dee Linn. "But it's not like I have a zillion friends here, is it?"

"Okay. Got it." In Sarah's opinion, Becky wasn't to be trusted; she was one of those teenaged girls who loved to gossip and stir things up a bit, gleeful to cause a little trouble, especially for someone else. Becky cut a wide swath through everyone else's social life. Just like her mother. No doubt Becky'd heard from Dee Linn the tales that Blue Peacock Manor harbored its own special ghosts. That kind of gossip, swirling so close to home, just barely touching her life but not ruining it, was right up Dee Linn's alley.

Gracie said, "I think the house looks kinda cool. Creepy cool."

Jade snorted. "What would you know about cool?"

"Hey . . . ," Sarah warned her oldest.

Used to her older sister's barbs, Gracie pulled the passive-aggressive card and acted as if she hadn't heard the nasty ring to her sister's question. As her seat belt clicked open, she changed the conversation back to her favorite topic. "Can we get a dog, Mom?" Before Sarah could respond, she added quickly, "You said we could. Remember? Once we moved here, you said we'd look for a dog."

"I believe I said 'I'll think about it.' "

"Jade got a car," Gracie pointed out.

From the front seat, Jade said, "That's different."

"No, it's not." To her mother, Gracie threw back Sarah's own words, " 'A promise is a promise.' That's what you always say." Gracie regarded her mother coolly as she clambered out of the backseat.

"I know." How could Sarah possibly forget the argument that had existed since her youngest had turned five? Gracie was nuts about all animals, and she'd been lobbying for a pet forever.

Once her younger daughter was out of earshot, Sarah said to Jade, "It wouldn't kill you to be nice to your sister."

Jade threw her mother a disbelieving look and declared, "This is so gonna suck!"

"Only if you let it." Sarah was tired of the ongoing argument that had started the second she'd announced the move two weeks ago. She'd waited until the real estate deal with her siblings was completed and she had hired a crew to start working before breaking the news to her kids. "This is a chance for all of us to have a new start."

"I don't care. The 'new start' thing? That's on you. For you. And maybe her," she added, hitching her chin toward the windshield

Sarah followed her gaze and watched Gracie hike up the broken flagstone path, where dandelions and moss had replaced the mortar years before. A tangle of leggy, gone-to-seed rosebushes were a reminder of how long the house had been neglected. Once upon a time, Sarah's mother had tended the gardens and orchard to the point of obsession, but that had been years ago. Now a solitary crow flapped to a perch in a skeletal cherry tree near the guesthouse, then pulled its head in tight, against the rain.

"Come on, Jade. Give me a break," Sarah said.

"You give me one." Jade rolled her eyes and unbuckled her seat belt, digging out her cell phone and attempting to text. "Smartphone, my ass—er, butt."

"Again, watch the language." Sarah pocketed her keys and tried not to let her temper get control of her tongue. "Grab your stuff, Jade. Like it or not, we're home."

"I can *not* believe this is my life."

"Believe it." Sarah shoved open the driver's side door, then walked to the rear of the vehicle to pull her computer and suitcase from the cargo area.

Of course, she too had doubts about moving here. The project she planned to tackle—renovating the place to its former grandeur before selling it—was daunting, perhaps impossible. Even when she'd been living here with all her siblings, the huge house had been sinking into disrepair. Since her father had died, things had really gone downhill. Paint was peeling from the siding, and many of the shiplap boards were warped. The wide porch that ran along the front of the house seemed to be listing, rails missing, and there were holes in the roof where there had once been shingles.

"It looks evil, you know," Jade threw over her shoulder before hauling her rolling bag out of the cargo space and reluctantly trudging after her sister. "I've always hated it."

Sarah managed to hold back a hot retort. The last time she'd brought her children here, she and her own mother, Arlene, had gotten into a fight, a blistering battle of words that precipitated their final, painful rift. Though Gracie was probably too small to remember, Jade certainly did.

Gracie was nearly at the steps when she stopped suddenly to stare upward at the house. "What the . . . ?"

"Come on," Jade said to her younger sister, but Gracie didn't move, even when Sarah joined her daughters and a big black crow landed on one of the rusted gutters.

"Something wrong?" Sarah asked.

Jade was quick to say, "Oh, no, Mom, everything's just perfect. You get into a fight with that perv at your job and decide we all have to move." She snapped her fingers. "And bam! It's done. Just like that. You rent out the condo in Vancouver and tell us we have to move here to a falling-down old farm with a grotesque house that looks like Stephen King dreamed it up. Yeah, everything's just cool." Jade reached for her phone again. "And there's got to be some cell phone service here or I'm out, Mom. Really. No service is like . . . archaic and . . . and . . . inhumane!"

"You'll survive."

Gracie whispered, "Someone's in there."

"What?" Sarah said. "No. The house has been empty for years."

Gracie blinked. "But . . . but, I saw her."

"You saw who?" Sarah asked and tried to ignore a tiny flare of fear knotting her stomach.

With one hand still on the handle of her rolling bag, she shrugged. "A girl."

Sarah caught an I-told-you-so look from her older daughter.

"A girl? Where?" Jade demanded.

"She was standing up there." Gracie pointed upward, to the third story and the room at the northwest corner of the house, just under the cupola. "In the window."

Theresa's room. The bedroom that had been off-limits to Sarah as a child. The knot in Sarah's gut tightened. Jade again caught her mother's eyes in a look that silently invoked Sarah to bring Gracie back to reality.

"Maybe it's a ghost," Jade mocked. "I hear there are lots of them around here." She leaned closer to her sister. "And not just from Becky. You told me you'd been doing some 'research' and you found out the first woman who lived here was killed, her body never found, her spirit roaming the hallways of Blue Peacock Manor forever."

Gracie shot her mom a look. "Well . . . yeah . . ."

"Oh, please," Jade snorted. "The second you step foot here, you see a ghost."

"Angelique Le Duc did die here!" Gracie flared.

"You mean, Angelique Stewart," Jade corrected. "She was married to our crazy, homicidal, great-great-great-not-so-great-grandfather or something. That's what you said."

"I read it on the Internet," Gracie responded, her mouth tight at being corrected.

"So then it must be true," Jade said. She turned her attention to her mother. "The minute you told us we were moving, she started in on all this ghost stuff. Checking out books from the library, surfing the Net, chatting with other people who think they see ghosts. And she didn't find out about just Angelique Le Duc—oh, no. There were others too. This place"—she gestured to the house and grounds—"is just littered with the spirits who've come to a bad end at Blue Peacock Manor!" Jade's hair caught in the wind as the rain picked up. "Do you see how ridiculous this all is, Mom? Now she's believing all this paranormal shi . . . stuff and thinking we're going to be living with a bunch of the undead!"

"Jade—" Sarah started.

"Shut up!" Gracie warned.

"You sound like a lunatic," Jade went right on, then turned heatedly to Sarah. "You have to put an end to this, Mom. It's for her own good. If she goes spouting off about ghosts and spirits and demons—"

"Demons!" Gracie snapped in disgust. "Who said anything—"

"It's all a load of crap," Jade declared. "She's going to be laughed out of school!"

"Enough!" Sarah yelled, though for once Jade seemed to be concerned for her sister. But Sarah had enough of their constant bickering. Forcing a calm she didn't feel, she said, "We're going inside now."

"You don't believe me," Gracie said, hurt. She looked up at the window again.

Sarah had already glanced at the window of the room where she knew, deep in her soul, dark deeds had occurred. But no image appeared behind the dirty, cracked glass. No apparition flitted past the panes. No otherworldly figure was evident. There was no "girl" hiding behind the grime, just some tattered curtains that seemed to shift in the dreary afternoon.

"I saw her," Gracie insisted. A line of consternation had formed between her brows.

"It could have been a reflection or a shadow," Sarah said as the crow cawed loudly. Deep inside she knew she was lying.

Gracie turned on Jade. "*You* scared her away!"

"Oh, right. Of course it's my fault. Give me an effing break."

"She'll punish you, you know." Gracie's eyes narrowed. "The woman in the window, she'll get even."

"Gracie!" Sarah's mouth dropped open.

"Then you'll see," Gracie declared, turning to the front entrance and effectively ending the conversation.

"Here's the latest," Rhea announced as she stepped through the door of Clint's cramped office in the small quarters that made up Stewart Crossing's City Hall. As city building inspector, he checked on all the jobs currently being constructed or renovated within the city limits and beyond, and contracted with the county for the outlying areas. "You might find one particularly interesting." She raised her thinly plucked eyebrows high enough that they arched over the frames of her glasses. "A neighbor."

"Don't tell me. The Stewart place."

"The Jewel of the Columbia?" she said dryly, shaking her head, her short, red hair unmoving.

His insides clenched a bit. "Maybe Doug wants to take this one."

"I thought you hated Doug."

"Hate's a strong word," Clint said. "He just wouldn't be my first choice to become my replacement." He wasn't sure why he didn't trust Doug Knowles, but the guy he was training to take over his job seemed too green, too eager, too damned hungry, to give each job its proper attention. There was something a little secretive about him as well, and Clint had a suspicion that Doug would take the easy way out, maybe let some of the little details slide on a job. "On second thought, I'll handle the Stewart project."

"Figured," she said, her red lips twisting a bit. "Oh, and wait!" She hurried out of the room and returned a few seconds later with a candy dish that she set on the corner of his desk. "Halloween candy for your clients with sweet tooths, er, teeth."

"I don't need these."

"Of course you do. It's that time of year. Don't be such a Grinch."

"I believe he's associated with Christmas."

"Or whatever holiday you want. In this case, Halloween." She unwrapped a tiny Three Musketeers bar and plopped it onto her tongue.

"Okay, so I'm a Grinch. Don't hate me."

Laughing, she gave him a wink as she turned and headed through the door to the reception area of the building that housed all the city offices. Built in the middle of the last century, the structure was constructed of glass and narrow, blond bricks; it had a flat roof and half a dozen offices opening into the central reception area. The ceilings were low, of "soundproof" tile, the lights fluorescent, the floors covered in a linoleum that had been popular during the 1960s. Now, it was showing decades of wear. "Just take a look." Rhea clipped away on high heels as a phone started jangling. She leaned over her desk and snagged the receiver before the second ring. She did it on purpose, he suspected, knowing he was still watching her as she gave him a quick glimpse of the skirt tightening over her hips.

"Stewart Crossing City Hall," she answered sweetly. "This is Rhea Hernandez."

She had a nice butt, he'd give her that, but he wasn't interested.

Attractive and smart, Rhea had been married and divorced three times, and was looking for husband number four at the ripe old age of forty-two.

It wasn't going to be Clint, and he suspected she knew it. Rhea's flirting was more out of habit than sincerity.

". . . I'm sorry, the mayor isn't in. Can I take a message, or, if you'd like, you can e-mail her directly," Rhea was saying as she stretched the cord around the desk and took her seat, disappearing from view. He heard her start rattling off Mayor Leslie Imholt's e-mail address.

Clint picked up the stack of papers she'd dropped into his inbox. Plans for the complete renovation of Blue Peacock Manor, the historic home set on property that backed up to his own ranch, was the first request. No surprise there, as he'd heard Sarah was returning to do a complete renovation of the Stewart family home. The preliminary drawings were already with the city engineer for approval; these had to be renovations to the original plans. A helluva job, that, he knew, and to think that Sarah was taking it on and returning to a place she'd wanted so desperately to leave. He eyed the specs and noted that he needed to see what work had already been accomplished on the smaller residence on the property—the guesthouse, as the Stewart family had called it.

Until the mayor had hired Doug Knowles, Clint had been the only inspector in this part of the county and had checked all the work himself. Now he could hand jobs off to Doug if he wanted. Clint had already decided that was generally a bad idea. It certainly would be in this case, he thought.

But if he took on Blue Peacock Manor, no doubt he would see Sarah again.

Frowning, he grabbed one of the damned bits of candy, and unwrapping a tiny Kit Kat bar, leaned back in his chair. He and Sarah hadn't seen each other for years, and if he were honest with himself, he knew that their split hadn't been on the best of terms. He tossed the candy into his mouth, then wadded up the wrapper and threw it at the waste can.

High school romance, he thought. So intense, but in the larger scheme of things, so meaningless, really.

Why, then, did the memory of it seem as fresh now as it had half a lifetime ago?

His desk phone jangled, and he reached for it willingly, pushing thoughts of Sarah Stewart and their ill-fated romance to the far, far corners of his mind.

CHAPTER 2

"That's it. I'm outta here," Rosalie Jamison said as she stripped off her apron and tossed it into a bin with the other soiled towels, aprons, jackets, and rags that would be cleaned overnight, ready for the morning shift at the three-star diner. She slipped her work shoes onto a shelf and laced up her Nikes, new and reflective, for the walk home. "I'll see you all later."

Located a few blocks from the river, the restaurant had been dubbed the Columbia Diner about a million years ago by some hick with no imagination. It was located at one end of the truck stop about a half mile out of Stewart's Crossing. Rosalie had spent the past six months here, waiting tables for the regulars and the customers just passing through. She hated the hours and the smell of grease and spices that clung to her until she spent at least twenty minutes under the shower, but it was a job, one of the few in this useless backwoods town.

For now it would do, until she had enough money saved so she could leave Stewart's Crossing for good. She couldn't wait.

"Wait!" Gloria, a woman who was in her fifties and perpetually smelled of cigarettes, caught up with Rosalie before she got out the door, and Gloria stuffed a few dollars and some change into Rosalie's hand. "Never forget your share of the tips," she said with a wink. She continued, "They keep me in all my diamonds and furs."

"Yeah, right." Rosalie had to smile. Gloria was cool, even if she continually talked about how long it would be before she collected Medicare and Social Security and all that boring stuff. A frustrated hairdresser, she changed her hair color, cut, or style every month or so and had taken Rosalie under her wing when a couple of boys, classmates from high school, had come in and started to hassle her with obscene comments and gestures. Gloria had refused to serve them and sent them out the door with their tails between their legs. The whole scene had only made things ugly at school, but Rosalie had solved that by cutting classes or ditching out completely.

"If you wait a half hour, I'll give you a ride home," Gloria said, sliding a fresh cigarette from her pack as she peered outside and into the darkness. "I just have to clean up a bit."

Rosalie hesitated. It would take her at least twenty minutes to walk home on the service road that ran parallel to the interstate, but Gloria's half hours usually stretched into an hour or two, and Rosalie just wanted to go home, sneak up the stairs, flop on her bed, and catch an episode of *Big Brother* or *Keeping Up with the Kardashians* or whatever else she could find on her crappy little TV. Besides, Gloria always lit up the second she was behind the wheel, and it was too cold to roll down the windows of her old Dodge. "I'd better get going. Thanks."

Gloria frowned. "I don't like you walking home alone in the dark."

"It's just for a little while longer," Rosalie reminded her, holding up her tips before stuffing the cash into the pocket of her jacket, which she'd retrieved from a peg near the open back door. "I'm gonna buy my uncle's Toyota. He's saving it for me. I just need another three hundred."

"It's starting to rain."

"I'm okay. Really."

"You be careful, then." Gloria's brows drew together beneath straw-colored bangs. "I don't like this, y'know."

"It's okay." Rosalie zipped up her jacket and stepped into the night before Gloria could argue with her. As the diner's door shut behind her, she heard Gloria saying to the Barry, the cook, "I don't know *what* her mother is thinking letting that girl walk alone this late at night."

Sharon wasn't thinking. That was the problem. Her mom wasn't thinking of Rosalie at all because of crappy Mel, her current husband, a burly, gruff man Rosalie just thought of as Number Four. He was a loser like the others in her mother's string of husbands. But Sharon, as usual, had deemed Mel "the one" and had referred to him as her soul mate, which was such a pile of crap. No one in her right mind would consider overweight, beer-slogging, TV-watching Mel Updike a soul mate unless they were completely brainless. He owned a kinda cool motorcycle that she could never ride, and that was the only okay thing about him. The fact that Mel leered at Rosalie with a knowing glint in his eye didn't make it any better. He'd already fathered five kids with ex-wives and girlfriends that were scattered from LA to Seattle. Rosalie had experienced the dubious pleasure of meeting most of them and had hated every one on sight. They were all "Little Mels," losers like their big, hairy-bellied father. Geez, didn't the guy know about waxing? Or man-scaping or, for that matter, not belching at the table?

Soul mate? Bull-effin'-shit!

Sharon had to be out of her mind!

Rosalie shoved her hands deep into her pockets and felt the other cash that she'd squirreled away in the lining of her hooded jacket, a gift from her real dad. The jacket was never out of her sight, and she'd tucked nearly nine hundred dollars deep inside it. She had to be careful. Either Mel or one of his sticky-fingered kids might make off with the cash she was saving for a car. Until she could pay for the Toyota outright, as well as license and insure it for six months, she was forbidden to own one.

All around, it sucked.

Her whole damn life *sucked.*

As rain began to pelt, striking her cheeks, splashing in puddles, peppering the gravel crunching beneath her feet, she began to wish she'd waited for Gloria. Putting up with a little cigarette smoke was better than slogging through cold rain.

She couldn't wait to get out of this hole-in-the-wall of a town where her mother, chasing the ever-slippery Mel, had dragged her. Kicking at the pebbles on the shoulder, she envied the people driving the cars that streaked by on the interstate, their headlights cutting through the dark night, their tires humming against the wet pavement, their lives going full throttle while she was stuck in idle.

But once she had her car, look out! She'd turn eighteen and leave Sharon and hairy Mel and head to Denver, where her dad and the boyfriend she'd met on the Internet were waiting.

Three hundred more dollars and five months.

That was all.

A gust of wind blasted her again, and she shuddered. Maybe she should turn back and take Gloria up on that ride. She glanced over her shoulder, but the neon lights of the diner were out of sight. She was nearly halfway home.

She started to jog.

A lone car had turned onto the road and was catching up to her, its headlights glowing bright. She stepped farther off the shoulder, her Nikes slipping a little. The roar of a large engine was audible over the rain, and she realized it wasn't a car, but a truck behind her. No big deal. There were hundreds of them around Stewart's Crossing. She expected the pickup to fly by her with a spray of road wash, but as it passed her, it slowed.

Just go on, she thought. She slowed to a walk, but kept moving until she saw the brake lights glow bright.

Now what?

She kept walking, intent on going around the dark truck, keeping her pace steady, hoping it was only a coincidence that the guy had stopped. No such luck. The window on the passenger side slid down.

"Rosie?" a voice that was vaguely familiar called from the darkened cab. "That you?"

Keep walking.

She didn't look up.

"Hey, it's me." The cab's interior light blinked on, and she recognized the driver, a tall man who was a regular at the diner and who now leaned across the seat to talk to her. "You need a ride?"

"No, it's only a little farther."

"You're soaked to the skin," he said, concerned.

"It's okay."

"Oh, come on. Hop in, I'll drive you." Without waiting for an answer, he opened the door.

"I don't—"

"Your call, but I'm drivin' right by your house."

"You know where I live?" That was weird.

"Only that you said you're on Umpqua."

Had she mentioned it? Maybe. "I don't know." Shaking her head, she felt the cold rain drizzling down her neck. She stared at the open door of the pickup. Clean. Warm. Dry. The strains of some Western song playing softly on the radio.

"You'll be home in three minutes."

Don't do it!

The wind blasted again, and she pushed down her misgivings. She knew the guy, had been waiting on him ever since she took the job. He was one of the better-looking regulars. He always had a compliment and a smile and left a good-sized tip.

"Okay."

"That-a-girl."

Climbing into the truck, she felt the warm air from the heater against her skin and recognized the Randy Travis song wafting through the speakers. She yanked the door shut, but the lock didn't quite latch.

"Here, let me get that," he said. "Damned thing." Leaning across her, he fiddled with the door. "Give it a tug, will ya?"

"Okay." The second she pulled on the door handle, she felt something cold and metallic click around her wrist. "Hey! What the hell do you think you're doing?" she demanded, fear spreading through her bloodstream as she jerked her hand up and realized she'd been cuffed to the door handle.

"Just calm down."

"The hell I will! What is this?" She was furious and scared and tried to open her door, but it was locked. "Let me out, you son of a bitch!"

He slapped her then. Quick and hard, a sharp backhand across her mouth.

She let out a little scream.

"There'll be no swearin'," he warned her.

"What? No what?" She swung her free hand at him, across the cab, but he caught her wrist.

"Ah-ah-ah, honey. You've got a lot to learn." Then, holding her free wrist in one hand, he gunned the engine and drove toward the entrance to the Interstate.

"Let me out!" she screamed, kicking at the dash and throwing her body back and forth, screaming at the top of her lungs. The heel of her shoe hit the preset buttons of the radio and an advertisement filled the interior.

Dear God, what was this? What did he plan to do to her?

Panicked, she tried to think of a way out of this. Any way. "I—I have money," she said, thinking of the cash in her pocket, all the while struggling and twisting, to no avail. His grip was just so damned strong.

"It's not your money I want," he said in that smooth, confident tone she now found absolutely chilling. His smile was as cold as the wind shrieking down the Columbia River Gorge. "It's you."

Karen Kingsbury

Toegift

Roman

Vertaald door Lia van Aken

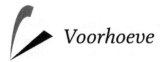 Voorhoeve

Toegift is het vervolg op *Laatste dans.*

© Uitgeverij Voorhoeve – Kampen, 2009
Postbus 5018, 8260 GA Kampen
www.kok.nl

Oorspronkelijk verschenen onder de titel *A Time to Embrace* bij Thomas Nelson, Inc.
P.O. Box 141000, Nashville TN 37214-1000, USA.
© Karen Kingsbury, 2002

Vertaling Lia van Aken
Omslagillustratie istockphoto
Omslagontwerp Bas Mazur
ISBN 978 90 297 1959 9
NUR 302

Voor mijn man, ter ere van zijn veertien jaar als basketbalcoach voor een schoolteam. Ik ben blij dat ik je vrouw mag zijn.

Voor Kelsey, mijn lieve tienertje. Ik ben dankbaar voor de jonge vrouw die je aan het worden bent. Het lijkt wel gisteren dat je over onze keukenvloer waggelde en je fopspeen aan de kat wilde geven.

Voor Tyler, mijn sterke en vastberaden oudste zoon. Altijd ben je bezig ons te vermaken met zang, dans en rare trucs, alles om ons maar aan het lachen te maken. Blijf luisteren naar Gods leiding, jongen.

Voor Sean, mijn gevoelige jongen. Toen we je uit Haïti ophaalden, wist ik dat je God liefhad. Pas later heb ik ontdekt hoezeer.

Voor Joshua, mijn ondernemende kind. Vanaf het moment dat ik je voor het eerst zag, wist ik dat je anders was dan de andere kinderen in het weeshuis. Steeds duidelijker zie ik je vastberadenheid in alle dingen.

Voor EJ, onze uitgekozen zoon. Jouw gezicht was het eerste dat we zagen op de fotolijst op internet toen we voor het eerst nadachten over adoptie uit Haïti. God heeft je in ons leven gebracht.

Voor Austin, mijn wonderkind. Je geeft me zoveel blijdschap, mijn jongste zoon. Ik zal nooit vergeten dat we je bijna kwijt waren geraakt, en hoe dankbaar ik ben dat God je aan ons terug heeft gegeven.

En voor de Almachtige God, de Auteur van het leven, die mij met hen gezegend heeft.

Een

Coach John Reynolds werd zenuwachtig van de jongen. Hij was lang en slungelig en zat al sinds het begin van het lesuur gezondheidsleer op zijn schrijfblok te krabbelen. Nu het uur bijna om was, kon John zien wat de jongen tekende.

Een schedel met gekruiste beenderen.

Het was dezelfde tekening die op zijn zwarte T-shirt stond afgebeeld. En ook op het lapje dat op zijn slobberige zwarte spijkerbroek was genaaid. Zijn haar was gitzwart geverfd en om zijn nek en polsen droeg hij zwarte leren banden met scherpe punten.

Het was overduidelijk dat Nathan Pike geobsedeerd werd door de duisternis. Hij was een *goth*, een van de weinige tieners op Marion High School die een sinistere subcultuur aanhingen.

Dat was niet wat John stoorde.

Wat hem stoorde, was wat de jongen *onder* het duistere symbool had gekrabbeld. Een van de woorden leek op *dood*. John kon het voor in de klas niet goed onderscheiden, daarom begon hij met grote passen heen en weer te lopen.

Zoals hij elke vrijdagavond als footballcoach van het schoolteam deed langs de zijlijn van het stadion, dwaalde John op en neer tussen de rijen leerlingen om hun werk te controleren, om hier en daar een aanwijzing te geven of kritiek als het nodig was.

Toen hij Nathans tafeltje naderde, keek hij weer naar het schrijfblok van de jongen. Van de opgeschreven woorden kreeg John ijskoude rillingen. Meende Nathan dat? Tegenwoordig kon John niet anders dan aannemen dat de leerling meende wat hij

7

schreef. John kneep zijn ogen tot spleetjes om te zien of hij het goed gelezen had.

Inderdaad.

Onder de schedel en de gekruiste beenderen had Nathan geschreven: *Dood aan sporters.*

John stond er nog naar te staren toen Nathan opkeek en zijn blik ontmoette. Die van de jongen was ijskoud en doods, zonder te knipperen. Bedoeld om te intimideren. Nathan was er waarschijnlijk aan gewend dat mensen één blik op hem wierpen en dan hun ogen afwendden, maar John had zijn hele loopbaan jongens als Nathan om zich heen gehad. Hij wendde zich niet af, maar bleef staan en bracht met zijn ogen aan Nathan over wat hij op dat moment onmogelijk kon zeggen. Dat de jongen de weg kwijt was, dat hij een naloper was, dat de dingen die hij had getekend en de woorden die hij had geschreven ongepast waren en niet getolereerd werden.

Maar vooral hoopte John dat zijn ogen overbrachten dat hij er was voor Nathan Pike. Zoals hij er geweest was voor anderen, zoals hij er altijd zou zijn voor zijn leerlingen.

Nathan keek als eerste weg en richtte zijn blik weer op zijn schrijfblok.

John probeerde zijn razende hart tot bedaren te brengen. Hij deed zijn best om onaangedaan te kijken en keerde terug naar de voorkant van het klaslokaal. Zijn leerlingen hadden nog tien minuten voordat hij zijn les zou hervatten.

Hij nam plaats achter zijn bureau, pakte een pen en trok het dichtstbijzijnde schrijfblok naar zich toe.

Dood aan sporters?

Uiteraard moest hij wat hij gezien had melden bij het bestuur, maar wat moest hij er als leraar mee aan? Stel dat het Nathan ernst was?

Sinds de schietincidenten op een aantal scholen in het land, hadden de meeste regio's een soort signaleringsplan opgesteld. Marion High School was geen uitzondering. Volgens het plan moesten alle leraren en personeelsleden een oogje houden op de klassen die ze onder hun hoede hadden. Als een leerling of een situatie zorgen baarde of hun ongewoon voorkwam, moest de leraar of het personeelslid onmiddellijk melding doen. Eens per maand werd er vergaderd om de leerlingen te bespreken die wellicht door de mazen glipten. De tekenen waren duidelijk: een leerling die gepest werd, wanhopig was, zich afgewezen voelde, uitgestoten was, die dwars was of gefascineerd werd door de dood. En in het bijzonder leerlingen die met geweld dreigden.

Nathan Pike voldeed aan alle categorieën.

Maar aan de andere kant, vijf procent van de schoolbevolking voldeed eraan. Zonder specifiek bewijs konden een leraar of bestuurslid weinig doen. Het handboek over moeilijke leerlingen adviseerde onderwijzend personeel om het pesten af te remmen of de leerlingen bij het schoolleven te betrekken.

'Praat met hen, probeer meer over hen te weten te komen, vraag naar hun hobby's en vrije tijd,' had de directeur tegen John en de rest van het personeel gezegd toen ze het handboek bespraken. 'Adviseer eventueel hulpverlening.'

Dat was allemaal leuk en aardig. Het probleem was dat jongens als Nathan Pike niet altijd met hun plannen te koop liepen. Nathan was vierdejaars. John kon zich nog herinneren dat Nathan voor het eerst op Marion High kwam. In zijn eerste en tweede jaar had Nathan behoudende kleding gedragen en was hij op zichzelf geweest.

Pas vorig jaar was hij van uiterlijk veranderd.

Hetzelfde jaar waarin de Marion High Eagles hun tweede regiokampioenschap football wonnen.

John wierp een snelle blik op Nathan. De jongen zat weer te tekenen. *Hij weet niet dat ik zijn schrijfblok heb gezien.* Anders had hij zijn hand toch over de schedel met de gekruiste beenderen gelegd en de verschrikkelijke woorden verborgen? Het was niet voor het eerst dat John dacht dat Nathan een probleem kon worden. Gezien zijn veranderde zelfbeeld had John hem sinds het begin van het schooljaar nauwlettend in de gaten gehouden. Minstens een keer per dag slenterde hij langs Nathans tafel en hij paste goed op om hem gedurende het hele lesuur beurten te geven, met hem te praten of oogcontact met hem te maken. John vermoedde dat er een hartgrondige woede brandde in het hart van de jongen, maar het was vandaag voor het eerst dat er bewijs voor was.

John bleef zwijgen, maar liet zijn blik door de klas dwalen. Wat was er vandaag anders? Waarom schreef Nathan juist nu zoiets hatelijks op?

Toen viel het hem in.

Jake Daniels was er niet.

Ineens klopte het hele scenario. Als Jake er was, vond hij waar hij ook zat altijd wel een manier om zijn klasgenoten tegen Nathan op te zetten.

Engerd... mietje... dokter dood... watje... sukkel.

Al die gefluisterde scheldwoorden werden losjes in Nathans richting gesproken. Als het gefluister doordrong tot voor in de klas, trok John zijn wenkbrauwen op naar Jake en een paar andere footballspelers in de klas.

'Genoeg.' De waarschuwing was gewoonlijk het enige wat John hoefde te zeggen. En dan was het gepest een poosje afgelopen. Maar de achteloze schimpscheuten en de wrede woorden troffen altijd doel. Daar was John zeker van.

Niet dat Nathan ooit zijn pijn toonde aan Jake en de anderen. De jongen negeerde alle sporters en deed alsof ze niet bestonden. Wat waarschijnlijk de beste manier was om de leerlingen die hem treiterden terug te pakken. Niets stoorde Johns huidige football- spelers meer dan over het hoofd te worden gezien.

Dat gold met name voor Jake Daniels.

Ondanks het feit dat het team van dit jaar de lofbetuigingen die hun werden toegezwaaid niet had *verdiend*. Het feit dat de score- stand van het team slechter was dan in welk seizoen dan ook in de recente geschiedenis, deed voor Jake en zijn teamgenoten weinig terzake. Zij geloofden dat ze bijzonder waren en ze waren van plan ervoor te zorgen dat iedereen op school hen ook zo behandelde.

John dacht aan het team van dit jaar. Het was eigenlijk vreemd. Ze waren getalenteerd. Op school werd gezegd dat ze misschien nog wel meer vóór hadden dan het team van vorig jaar, toen Johns eigen zoon Kade de Eagles naar een regiokampioenschap had geleid. Maar ze waren arrogant en verwaand, zonder oog voor omgangsvormen of karakter. In alle jaren dat hij coach was geweest, had John nog nooit zo'n moeilijke groep meegemaakt.

Het was niet vreemd dat ze niet wonnen. In het licht van hun gedrag was hun talent onbruikbaar.

En de ouders van veel van de jongens waren nog erger. Vooral nadat Marion twee van zijn eerste wedstrijden had verloren.

Ouders klaagden voortdurend over speeltijd, trainingsprogramma's en natuurlijk de verliezen. Ze waren vaak onbeschoft en neerbuigend, en dreigden John te laten ontslaan als zijn staat van dienst niet verbeterde.

'Wat is er gebeurd met het onverslaanbare Marion High?' vroegen ze hem. 'Een goede coach had de reeks overwinningen doorgezet.'

'Misschien weet coach Reynolds niet waar hij mee bezig is,' zeiden ze. 'Iedereen kan het talent van Marion High coachen en ongeslagen uit de strijd komen. Maar verliezen?'

Ze vroegen zich hardop af wat voor een kolossale mislukkeling John Reynolds was om een Eagles-team op het veld te zetten en dan te verliezen. Het was ondenkbaar voor de ouders van Marion High. Schandalig. Hoe durfde coach Reynolds zo vroeg in het seizoen twee wedstrijden te verliezen!

En soms waren de overwinningen nog erger.

'Dat was een slapjanus van een tegenstander vorige week, Reynolds,' zeiden de ouders dan. Als ze gewonnen hadden met twee touchdowns, zanikten de ouders dat het er minstens vier hadden moeten zijn. Johns 'lievelingszinnetje' was: 'Tjonge, als *mijn* zoon maar meer speeltijd had gekregen…'

Ouders roddelden achter zijn rug en ondermijnden het gezag dat hij op het veld had. Ongeacht het feit dat de Eagles vorig seizoen kampioen waren geweest. Ongeacht het feit dat John een van de vaakst winnende coaches in de regio was. Ongeacht het feit dat meer dan de helft van de kampioensploeg van vorig jaar hun diploma had gehaald, zodat John dit jaar de boel opnieuw moest opbouwen.

Het draaide er alleen maar om of de zoons van Johns lasteraars wel werden ingezet op wat zij de juiste posities vonden en elke wedstrijd genoeg spelminuten kregen. Of hun nummer wel op het juiste moment werd afgeroepen voor de grote wedstrijden en hoe sterk hun afzonderlijke statistische gegevens in de krant verschenen.

Het was gewoon zwaar pech dat het grootste geschil in het team op een indirecte manier Nathans leven verzuurde. Twee quarterbacks waren naar de zomertraining gekomen, beiden klaar voor de startpositie: Casey Parker en Jake Daniels.

Casey was de gedoodverfde winnaar, de laatstejaars, degene die tot vorig jaar achter Kade op de bank had gezeten. Zijn hele footballloopbaan was hierop neergekomen, zijn laatste seizoen bij de Eagles. In augustus meldde hij dat hij verwachtte de startpositie te bezitten.

Wat de jongen niet had verwacht, was dat Jake Daniels hetzelfde in zijn hoofd had.

Jake was derdejaars, een gewoonlijk brave zoon van een gezin dat vroeger bij John en zijn vrouw Abby in de straat had gewoond. Maar twee jaar geleden waren meneer en mevrouw Daniels uit elkaar gegaan. Jakes moeder was met Jake in een flat getrokken. Zijn vader kreeg in New Jersey een baan als presentator van een sportprogramma op de radio. Het was een akelige scheiding.

Jake was een van de slachtoffers.

John huiverde. Wat waren Abby en hij er dichtbij geweest om hetzelfde te doen! Die tijd lag gelukkig achter hen. Maar Jake Daniels zat er nog midden in die nare periode.

Aanvankelijk had Jake zich tot John gewend, een vaderfiguur die niet aan de andere kant van het land woonde. John zou nooit vergeten wat Jake hem eens had gevraagd.

'Denkt u dat mijn vader nog van me houdt?'

De jongen was ongeveer een meter negentig, bijna een man. Maar op dat moment was hij weer zeven jaar, wanhopig op zoek naar een bewijs dat de vader op wie hij zijn hele leven had vertrouwd, de man die was verhuisd en hem in de steek had gelaten, nog om hem gaf.

John deed alles wat hij kon om Jake gerust te stellen, maar met het verstrijken van de tijd was de jongen zwijgzaam en nors geworden. Hij was vaker alleen in de trainingsruimte en op het veld om zijn werpvaardigheid te scherpen.

Toen de zomertraining aanbrak, bestond er geen twijfel over wie de startende quarterback zou zijn. Jake won de strijd met gemak. Zodra dat gebeurde, had Chuck, de vader van Casey Parker, een gesprek aangevraagd met John.

'Hoor es, coach...' De aderen op zijn slaap puilden uit terwijl hij sprak. 'Ik hoor dat mijn zoon de startpositie kwijt is.'

John moest een zucht onderdrukken. 'Dat klopt.'

De man uitte enkele krachttermen en eiste een verklaring. Johns antwoord was eenvoudig. Casey was een goede quarterback met vervelend gedrag. Jake was jonger, maar had meer talent en luisterde beter, en daarmee de beste keus.

'Mijn zoon kan niet de tweede viool spelen.' Caseys vader sprak luid, met een rood aangelopen gezicht. 'Zijn hele leven zijn we hier mee bezig geweest! Hij is laatstejaars en hij gaat niet op de bank zitten. Als zijn gedrag niet deugt, dan komt dat alleen door zijn gedrevenheid. Daar leer je maar mee leven.'

Gelukkig had John een van zijn assistenten meegenomen naar het gesprek. Hij vond dat hij niet voorzichtig genoeg kon zijn, als je bedacht hoe gemakkelijk de beschuldigingen en loze praatjes over de tafel vlogen. Dus hij had samen met zijn assistent naar Parker zitten luisteren.

'Wat ik bedoel is…' Chuck Parker boog zich naar voren en keek hen fel aan. 'Dat er coaches in mijn nek zitten te hijgen. We overwegen een transfer. Dan krijgt mijn jongen tenminste een eerlijke kans.'

John weerstond de verleiding om met zijn ogen te rollen. 'Je zoon heeft een gedragsprobleem, Chuck. En behoorlijk ook. Als andere schoolcoaches in de buurt hem willen aanwerven, is dat omdat ze niet met hem hebben gewerkt.' John keek de man strak aan. 'Wat is precies je probleem?'

'Ik zal je vertellen wat mijn probleem is, coach.' Chuck stak een opgeheven vinger naar John uit. 'Je bent niet loyaal aan je spelers. Dát is mijn probleem. Loyaliteit is alles in de sport.'

En dat zei een man wiens zoon naar een andere school wilde gaan. Uiteindelijk bleef Casey Parker. Hij nam beginpasses en loste Jake af als quarterback. Maar de kritiek van Caseys vader was elke week doorgegaan. Casey voelde zich in verlegenheid gebracht en deed nog harder zijn best om met zijn rivaal Jake overweg te kunnen. Jake was klaarblijkelijk dankbaar dat hij geaccepteerd werd door een laatstejaars als Casey en algauw brachten die twee het grootste deel van hun vrije tijd samen door. Het duurde niet lang voordat Jake begon te veranderen. De verlegen, ernstige jongen die twee keer per week in Johns klas binnenviel om een praatje te maken, was verdwenen. Verdwenen was de jongen die vroeger aardig was geweest tegen Nathan Pike. Nu was Jake net als de meerderheid van de spelers die over de campus van Marion High paradeerden.

En in die zin had het quarterbackgeschil Nathans leven alleen maar beroerder gemaakt. Terwijl Nathan vroeger door ten minste een van de sporters gerespecteerd werd, had hij nu geen enkele bondgenoot meer in het team.

John had laatst twee leraren met elkaar horen praten.

'Hoeveel footballspelers van Marion High zijn er nodig om een gloeilamp in te draaien?'

'Geen idee.'

'Eentje: hij houdt hem vast terwijl de wereld om hem heen draait.'

Er waren avonden dat John zich afvroeg of het tijdverspilling was. Vooral wanneer het elitaire gedrag van zijn sporters verdeeldheid zaaide op de schoolcampus en leerlingen als Nathan Pike vervreemdde. Leerlingen die soms door het lint gingen en een hele school lieten boeten voor hun lage plaats in de sociale pikorde.

Wat deed het ertoe of Johns sporters een bal konden gooien of de hele lengte van een veld over konden rennen? Als ze het footballprogramma van Marion High verlieten zonder zweempje mededogen of karakter, wat had het dan voor zin?

John ontving een salaris van 3100 dollar per seizoen om te coachen. Hij had eens uitgerekend dat het in een bepaald jaar neerkwam op minder dan twee dollar per uur. Het was duidelijk dat hij het niet voor het geld deed.

Hij keek naar de klok. Nog drie minuten.

Er flitsten beelden van wel tien verschillende seizoenen door zijn hoofd. Waarom deed hij er dan aan mee? Niet om zijn ego te strelen. In zijn tijd als quarterback voor de Universiteit van Michigan had hij meer successen geboekt dan de meeste mannen in een heel leven. Nee, voor zijn trots hoefde hij niet te coachen.

Het was eenvoudigweg omdat er twee dingen waren waar hij kennelijk voor in de wieg was gelegd: football spelen... en tieners onderwijzen.

Coachen was de puurste manier die hij kende om die twee samen te brengen. Seizoen na seizoen na seizoen had het gewerkt. Tot nu. Nu voelde het helemaal niet meer puur. Het voelde belachelijk. Alsof de hele sportwereld van de wijs was.

John haalde diep adem en stond op, de pezen rekkend in zijn slechte knie, de knie met de oude footballblessure. Hij liep naar het bord waar hij de volgende tien minuten een diagram opschreef van een reeks voedingswaarden en die nauwgezet verklaarde. Toen deelde hij huiswerk uit.

Maar hij kon aldoor maar aan één ding denken: Nathan Pike.

Hoe was een keurige leerling als Nathan zo dwars en haatdragend geworden? Allemaal vanwege Jake Daniels? Waren de ego's van Jake en de andere spelers zo opgeblazen dat ze niet samen konden gaan met iemand die anders was dan zij? En wat te zeggen van de woorden die Nathan op zijn schrijfblok had geschreven? *Dood aan sporters.* Meende hij dat?

En zo ja, wat moest er gedaan worden?

Scholen als Marion High ontsproten uit de veilige grond van Midden-Amerika. De meeste hadden geen metaaldetectors of gazen rugzakken of videocamera's die een gestoorde student konden betrappen voordat hij in actie kwam. Ze hadden wel een signaleringsprogramma. Nathan was al gesignaleerd. Iedereen die hem kende, hield hem in de gaten.

Maar als dat niet genoeg was?

John kreeg een knoop in zijn maag en hij slikte moeilijk. Hij wist het antwoord niet. Alleen dat hij vandaag, naast proefwerken nakijken, cijfers in de computer zetten, middagtraining houden en enkele geïrriteerde ouders langs de zijlijn te woord staan, ook met de directeur moest praten over Nathan Pikes opgeschreven verklaring.

Het was acht uur tegen de tijd dat hij in zijn auto stapte en een envelop openmaakte die hij vlak voor de training in zijn postvak had gevonden.

'L.S.,' begon de brief. 'Wij vragen dringend om het ontslag van coach Reynolds…'

John hapte naar adem. *Wat was dit?* Hij kreeg buikpijn toen hij verder las.

Coach Reynolds is niet het morele voorbeeld dat we voor onze jonge mannen moeten hebben. Hij is ervan op de hoogte dat verscheidene spelers van hem drinken en deelnemen aan illegale wegraces. Coach Reynolds weet dit, maar doet er niets aan. Daarom eisen wij zijn ontslag, vrijwillig of onvrijwillig. Als hier niets aan wordt gedaan, zullen we de media op de hoogte stellen van ons verzoek.

John ademde eindelijk uit. De brief was niet ondertekend, maar er waren kopieën gestuurd aan zijn sportcoördinator, zijn directeur en drie regiobeambten.

Wie kon zoiets geschreven hebben? En waar doelden ze op? John greep het stuur met beide handen vast en drukte zijn rug tegen de leuning. Ineens wist hij het weer. Toen in augustus de training weer was begonnen, hadden geruchten de ronde gedaan… geruchten dat enkele spelers hadden gedronken en met hun auto hadden geracet. Maar dat waren het dan ook geweest: geruchten. John had er niets tegen kunnen doen…

Hij leunde met zijn hoofd tegen het autoraampje. Hij was woest geweest toen hij het had gehoord. Hij had de spelers er rechtstreeks naar gevraagd, maar allemaal hadden ze enige wandaad ontkend. Verder kon John er niets meer aan doen. Het was protocol dat er geen geloof aan geruchten werd gehecht tenzij er bewijs was dat er regels overtreden waren.

Geen moreel voorbeeld voor de spelers?

Johns handen begonnen te trillen en hij staarde over zijn rechterschouder naar de deuren van de school. Zijn sportcoördinator zou zo'n laffe, niet ondertekende brief toch niet willen accepteren. Maar aan de andere kant…

De sportcoördinator was nieuw. Een dwarse, prikkelbare man die strijd voerde tegen christenen. Hij was een jaar geleden in dienst genomen om Ray Lemming te vervangen, een formidabele vent die hart had voor coaches en sporters.

Ray was zo bij de schoolsport betrokken, dat hij op school een deel van het meubilair was geworden, maar vorig jaar was hij op de rijpe leeftijd van drieënzestig jaar met pensioen gegaan om meer bij zijn familie te kunnen zijn. De meeste coaches vonden dat het ware hart van de sport op Marion met hem mee gepensioneerd was. Zeker nadat de school Herman Lutz als sportcoördinator had aangenomen.

John zuchtte vermoeid. Hij had al het mogelijke gedaan om de man te steunen, maar na een klacht van ouders had hij de zwemcoach van de jongens al ontslagen. Stel dat hij deze absurde brief serieus nam? De andere coaches zagen Lutz als iemand die verdronk in de complexiteiten van de baan.

'Er is maar één ouder voor nodig,' had een van de coaches die zomer na een vergadering gezegd. 'Eén ouder die dreigt naar Lutz' baas te gaan, en hij geeft hun wat ze willen.'

Ook als hij daarvoor een coach moest ontslaan.

John liet zijn hoofd langzaam op het stuur zakken. Nathan Pike… de doodsdreiging tegen sporters… de verandering in Jake Daniels… het gedrag van zijn spelers… de klagende ouders… de onverklaarbare verliezen dit seizoen…

En nu dit.

John voelde zich tachtig. Hoe had Abby's vader zich staande gehouden tijdens een leven lang coachen? Die vraag verzette zijn gedachten en hij liet alles van de dag even vervagen. Dertien uur geleden was hij op school aangekomen en pas nu kon hij doen wat hij liever deed dan wat ook. Datgene waar hij zich elke dag meer op verheugde.

Hij zou naar huis rijden, de deur openen van het huis dat hij bijna kwijt was geweest, en de vrouw van wie hij meer hield dan van het leven zelf in zijn armen nemen. De vrouw van wie de blauwe ogen tegenwoordig meer twinkelden en van wie iedere warme omhelzing een stukje meer uitwiste van hun pijnlijke verleden. De vrouw die hem elke ochtend aanmoedigde en zijn hart vulde als hij het coachen en lesgeven geen minuut langer kon verdragen.

De vrouw die hij bijna had verlaten.

Zijn geliefde Abby.

Twee

Abby zat de openingsalinea voor haar nieuwste tijdschriftartikel te schrijven toen het gebeurde.

Tussen de derde en vierde zin verstarden haar vingers op het toetsenbord en begonnen de vragen te komen. Was het waar? Waren ze echt weer bij elkaar? Waren ze echt aan een echtscheiding ontkomen, terwijl zelfs hun kinderen niet wisten hoe dichtbij ze waren geweest?

Langzaam gingen Abby's ogen omhoog van het computerscherm naar een plank boven haar bureau, naar een recente foto van John en haar. Hun pasgetrouwde dochter Nicole had de foto genomen op een familiesoftbalwedstrijd tijdens het eerste weekend van september. Daar stonden ze, Abby en John, naast elkaar op de tribune achter de thuisplaat, met de armen om elkaar heen. Alsof ze nooit anders dan gelukkig getrouwd waren geweest.

'Jullie zijn zo schattig,' had Nicole destijds gezegd. 'Met het jaar verliefder op elkaar.'

Abby staarde naar de foto, de stem van haar dochter weerklonk als een windklokkenspel in haar hoofd. Er waren geen uiterlijke tekenen, niemand had kunnen zien hoe na ze eraan toe waren geweest het kwijt te raken. Hoe ze bijna tweeëntwintig jaar huwelijk hadden weggegooid.

Maar Abby wist het toen ze naar de foto keek.

Het stond in hun ogen te lezen, zo diep dat niemand anders dan John en zij het opmerkten. Een glinstering van doorleefde liefde, een liefde die beproefd was en daar des te sterker uit was gekomen. Een liefde die op de rand had gestaan van een koude, donkere kloof, zich schrap had gezet tegen de pijn en was gesprongen. Een liefde die pas op het laatste moment in zijn nekvel was gepakt en meegesleurd was naar veiliger grond.

Nicole wist het natuurlijk niet. Geen van hun kinderen eigenlijk. Kade niet, die nu achttien was en eerstejaarsstudent. En Sean, hun jongste, zeker niet. Met zijn elf jaar had hij er geen idee van dat John en zij bijna uit elkaar waren gegaan.

Ze keek naar de kalender. Vorig jaar om deze tijd waren ze plannen aan het maken om te gaan scheiden. Toen hadden Nicole en Matt hun verloving aangekondigd, en dat had de plannen uitgesteld. Maar Abby en John hadden de bedoeling gehad om het aan de kinderen vertellen als Nicole en Matt terug waren van hun huwelijksreis.

Abby huiverde. Als John en zij gescheiden waren, waren de kinderen er misschien nooit meer bovenop gekomen. Vooral Nicole, die zo idealistisch was en vol vertrouwen in de liefde.

Kind, als je eens wist…

En toch waren ze nog samen, zij en John, precies zoals Nicole geloofde.

Abby moest zichzelf vaak knijpen om te geloven dat het waar was, dat John en zij geen echtscheiding hadden aangevraagd en gezocht hadden naar een manier om het aan de kinderen te vertellen. Ze maakten geen ruzie, ze negeerden elkaar niet en ze stonden niet op het punt een verhouding te beginnen.

Ze hadden het overleefd. En dat niet alleen, maar ze waren zelfs gelukkig. Gelukkiger dan toen ze hun huwelijksbeloften hadden uitgesproken. De dingen die zo veel echtparen uit elkaar hadden gedreven, hadden hen door Gods genade sterker gemaakt. Eens, op het juiste moment, zouden ze de kinderen vertellen wat er bijna was gebeurd. Misschien zou het ook hen sterker maken.

Abby richtte haar aandacht weer op het computerscherm.

Het artikel was voortgekomen uit het diepst van haar hart: *Jongerencoaches in Amerika: een uitstervend ras.* Ze had een nieuwe redacteur bij het nationale tijdschrift dat het meeste van haar werk kocht. Een vrouw met een scherp gevoel voor de hartslag en het geweten van Amerikaanse gezinnen. In september hadden Abby en zij mogelijke artikelen besproken. Een exposé over coachen was het idee van de redacteur geweest.

'Het hele land sport als een gek,' zei de vrouw. 'Maar om de haverklap houdt weer een kwaliteitscoach het voor gezien. Misschien wordt het tijd dat we eens kijken waarom.'

Abby moest bijna hardop lachen. Als iemand eerlijk kon schrijven over de pijn en passie van het coachen van jeugdsport, dan was zij het wel. Ze was per slot van rekening de dochter van een coach. Haar vader en de vader van John waren teamgenoten aan de Universiteit van Michigan, de school waar John speelde voordat hij zijn graad haalde en het enige deed wat voor de hand lag: football coachen.

Haar hele leven had zich afgespeeld rondom de seizoenen van het spel.

Maar nadat ze de afgelopen twintig jaar met John Reynolds had doorgebracht, kon Abby meer dan een tijdschriftartikel schrijven over coachen. Ze kon er een boek over schrijven. En ze zou het er allemaal in zetten: ouders die klaagden over speeltijd, spelers die geen karakter toonden en geen verantwoordelijkheid namen, onrealistische verwachtingen, twijfels en gejoel van de tribunes.

Verzonnen beschuldigingen die in roddelkringen achter de schermen werden geuit om een coach onder druk te zetten om het veld te ruimen. Ondanks de teambarbecues in de achtertuin of het feit dat John tientallen keren na de zondagse training van zijn eigen geld een ontbijt voor de jongens had betaald.

Het kwam altijd hierop neer: win meer wedstrijden, en anders…

Was het een wonder dat coaches ermee ophielden?

Abby's hart verzachtte. Er waren nog steeds spelers die het spel tot een vreugde maakten, nog steeds ouders die John na een zware wedstrijd bedankten of hem een kaart stuurden om hun dankbaarheid te tonen. Anders was er geen man zoals John meer over in de coachgelederen. Een handvol spelers op Marion High deed nog steeds goed zijn best in de klas en op het veld, toonde nog steeds respect en verdiende het door hard te werken en ijver. Spelers die de barbecues bij de Reynolds thuis op prijs stelden, en de tijd en liefde die John in elk seizoen, in elke speler stak. Jongemannen die verder gingen studeren en een goede baan hadden gekregen, die jaren na hun afstuderen nog bij de Reynolds aanbelden en vroegen: 'Is de coach thuis?'

Die spelers waren vroeger de norm. Hoe kwam het dat ze nu voor coaches door heel Amerika de uitzondering waren?

'Ja,' had Abby tegen haar redacteur gezegd. 'Ik wil het verhaal graag schrijven.'

In de afgelopen weken had ze coaches van langlopende, succesvolle programma's geïnterviewd. Coaches die er in de laatste jaren mee opgehouden waren vanwege dezelfde moeilijkheden waar John mee kampte, om dezelfde redenen waarom hij steeds vaker vermoeid en terneergeslagen thuiskwam.

De voordeur ging open en Abby hoorde hoe haar man hem zuchtend achter zich sloot. Zijn voetstappen klonken op de tegels in de hal. Niet de ferme, energieke stappen van het voorjaar of de zomer, maar de droevige, schuifelende stappen van een misgelopen footballseizoen.

'Ik ben hier.' Ze wendde zich van haar computer af en wachtte.

John sleepte zich de kamer in en leunde tegen de deurpost. Zijn blik vond de hare en hij stak een opgevouwen stuk papier naar haar uit.

Ze stond op en pakte het van hem aan. 'Lange dag gehad?'

'Lees maar.'

Abby ging weer zitten, maakte de brief open en begon te lezen. Het werd haar benauwd te moede. Ze wilden Johns ontslag. Waren ze gek geworden? Was het niet genoeg dat ze hem dagelijks lastigvielen? Wat wilden die ouders? Ze vouwde de brief op en gooide hem op haar bureau. Toen liep ze naar John toe en liet haar armen om zijn middel glijden. 'Wat erg.'

Hij trok haar dicht tegen zich aan en omhelsde haar zoals vroeger toen ze pas getrouwd waren. Abby genoot van het gevoel. Johns sterke armen, de geur van zijn aftershave, de manier waarop ze kracht putten uit elkaar...

Dit was de man op wie ze verliefd was geworden, de man die ze bijna had laten gaan.

John richtte zich op en keek haar onderzoekend aan. 'Het is niets om je zorgen over te maken.' Hij boog dicht naar haar toe en kuste haar.

Abby voelde een spoortje van twijfel. 'Er staat dat Herman Lutz een kopie heeft gekregen. Sportcoördinators ontslaan coaches als ouders klagen.'

'Dit keer niet.' John haalde zijn schouders op. 'Daar kent Lutz me te goed voor.'

'Ray Lemming kende je het best van allemaal.' Abby bewaarde een vriendelijke toon. 'Ik heb een vervelend gevoel bij Herman Lutz.'

'Lutz zal me steunen.' Hij lachte even. 'Iedereen weet dat ik mijn spelers nooit laat drinken of laat meedoen aan... wat was het ook alweer?'

'Straatraces.'

'Precies. Straatraces. Ik bedoel, kom op zeg.' Hij hield zijn hoofd schuin. 'Er zullen altijd wel een paar ouders klagen. Ook al winnen we elke wedstrijd.'

Abby wilde er niet op doorgaan. 'God heeft de leiding.'

John knipperde met zijn ogen. 'Wat bedoel je daarmee?'

'Dat God je zal steunen. Ongeacht wie je verder al dan niet steunt.'

'Je klinkt ongerust.'

'Niet ongerust. Alleen bezorgd om de brief.'

John leunde tegen de muur, zette zijn honkbalpet af en gooide hem op de bank. 'Waar is Sean?'

'Op zijn kamer.' Hun jongste zoon zat in de zesde klas. De laatste tijd belden er af en toe meisjes op. 'Door zijn sociale leven is hij een beetje achter met school. Hij zal er goed aan doen om tegen tien uur te stoppen.'

'Geen wonder dat het zo stil is.' Hij liet zijn greep om Abby's middel verslappen en bracht zijn hand naar haar gezicht om met zijn vingertoppen haar jukbeenderen na te trekken. 'Zo hoort het niet.'

Het gevoel van zijn handen tegen haar gezicht deed een rilling over haar rug lopen. 'Coachen?'

Hij knikte. 'Vorig jaar hebben we het regiokampioenschap gewonnen.' Zijn toon was vermoeid, zijn ogen waren donkerder dan ze in tijden had gezien. 'Wat willen ze van me?'

'Ik weet het niet.' Abby keek hem een ogenblik onderzoekend aan en boog toen haar hoofd. 'Maar ik weet wel wat je nodig hebt.'

Johns gezichtsuitdrukking verzachtte. 'Wat dan?'

'Dansles.' Abby voelde haast de glinstering in haar ogen.

'Dansles? Zodat we aanstaande vrijdagavond de foxtrot kunnen dansen bij Jefferson?'

'Nee, rare.' Ze gaf hem een duwtje. 'Houd eens op met alleen maar aan football te denken.' Ze vlocht haar vingers door de zijne en walste één stap met hem van de muur af en weer terug. 'Ik heb het over *ons*.'

Een zacht gekerm steeg op uit Johns borst. 'Kom, Abby. Geen dansles. Ik heb geen muzikaal gehoor, weet je nog? En geen steek ritmegevoel.'

Met haar lichaam dicht tegen het zijne, leidde ze hem nog een paar passen verder de kamer in. 'Dans met me op de aanlegsteiger.' Haar toon was smekend en ze pruilde opzettelijk. Ze klonk als Nicole als die haar zin niet kreeg.

'Ach, Abby… nee.' Zijn schouders zakten een beetje af, maar er danste een licht in zijn ogen dat er eerder niet was geweest. 'Dansen op de aanlegsteiger is wat anders. Krekels en krakende planken… de wind op het meer. Op *die* muziek kan ik best dansen.' Hij kromde zijn arm en liet haar een wervelende beweging maken. 'Alsjeblieft, Abby. Dwing me niet om dansles te nemen.'

Ze had al gewonnen. Zwijgend keek ze hem grinnikend aan en stak een vinger op. 'Wacht even.' In een flits vloog ze naar haar bureau en griste het krantenartikel op dat ze eerder die dag had uitgeknipt. 'Kijk. Ze zitten in de school.'

Hij rolde met zijn ogen en las de kop. 'Ballroom dansen voor *volwassen* paren?' Hij zette zijn handen in zijn zij en trok zijn wenkbrauwen op. 'Leuk, hoor. Niet alleen zal ik voor het eerst van mijn leven rond hopsen, maar ook nog eens in het gezelschap van mensen die twee keer zo oud zijn als ik.' Hij legde zijn hoofd in zijn nek. 'Abby... alsjeblieft.'

Ze wees naar de kleine lettertjes. 'Veertig jaar en ouder, John. Dat staat in het artikel.'

'Zo oud zijn we niet.' Nu bespeelde hij haar, haar plagend zoals vroeger toen ze in haar laatste jaar zat, en stomverbaasd was dat deze oudere sterquarterback die altijd al een vriend van de familie was geweest, met haar uit wilde. Met háár, nota bene.

Ze giechelde en drukte zich weer dicht tegen hem aan. 'Ja, zo oud zijn we.'

'Nee.' Hij liet zijn mond openhangen en wees eerst naar haar en toen naar zichzelf. '*Hoe* oud zijn we?'

'Ik ben eenenveertig en jij vijfenveertig.'

'Vijfenveertig?' Geluidloos vormde hij het woord met zijn mond, zogenaamd vol afgrijzen.

'Ja, vijfenveertig.'

'Echt waar?' Hij nam het krantenknipsel van haar aan en bestudeerde het nogmaals.

'Echt waar.'

'Nou, dan...' Het artikel zweefde naar de vloer. Dit keer nam hij haar hand in de zijne en walste met haar naar de deur. 'Dan is het tijd voor dansles.'

Met John leidend dansten ze van het midden van haar werkkamer de gang in. 'Volwassen, hè?'

'Ja.' Ze hield van zulke momenten, waarop het leek of John en zij één van hart waren. Ze walsten door de gang naar de keuken.

'Maar *jij* denkt toch niet dat ik volwassen ben?' Terwijl hij het zei, raakten zijn voeten verstrikt met de hare en hij viel achterover, Abby in zijn vaart meeslepend. Met een smak landden ze boven op elkaar tegen de muur.

De schok duurde maar even.

Toen duidelijk was dat ze allebei niets mankeerden, barstten ze samen in lachen uit. 'Nee, John…' Schaterend rolde Abby naast hem op de grond. 'Wees maar niet bang, ik denk niet dat je volwassen bent.'

'Mooi.' Hij lachte nog harder dan zij. Zo hard dat hij tranen in zijn ogen kreeg. 'Dat zou ik ook niet willen.'

'Maar je hebt wel dansles nodig.'

'Kennelijk.' Hij schaterde. 'Het doet me denken… aan die keer dat jij…' Hij probeerde op adem te komen. 'Die keer dat jij in Sea World van de trap viel.'

'Dat is waar ook.' Haar ribben deden pijn van het lachen. 'Ik moest die plaats hebben.'

'Ik vergeet die zeeleeuwen nooit.' John imiteerde hoe de dieren die dag hun hoofd met een ruk naar Abby hadden omgedraaid.

'Niet doen…' Abby hijgde. 'Ik houd het niet meer.'

'Mensen die armen en benen uitstaken om je val te stoppen.' John ging rechtop zitten en liet zijn ellebogen op zijn knieën rusten.

Ze zuchtte, eindelijk op adem gekomen. 'We zijn me een stelletje.'

John krabbelde overeind en leunde tegen de muur. 'Het heeft wel gewerkt.' Hij stak zijn hand uit en hielp Abby overeind.

'Wat?' Abby's hart was licht als een zomerbries. Wat lekker om zo te lachen, over de vloer te rollen en gek te doen met John.

'Nu weet ik dat je niet denkt dat ik volwassen ben.' Ze haakten hun armen in elkaar en gingen de keuken binnen.

'Beslist niet.'

'Uitgehongerd, misschien.' Hij wreef over zijn achterwerk. 'Maar nooit volwassen.'

Drie

Het diner was in volle gang. Het was woensdag en elke plaats aan tafel was bezet. John en Abby en Sean aan de ene kant, terwijl Nicole en Matt en Matts ouders Jo en Denny Conley aan de andere kant zaten.

Abby hield van zulke avonden, als de familiekring zich bij de Reynolds thuis verzamelde om samen te lachen en bij te praten over hun leven. Abby keek bewonderend naar de gloed op Nicoles gezicht tegenover haar. *Dank U, God, dat U Matt in haar leven hebt gebracht. Laat hen nooit hoeven doorstaan wat John en ik hebben doorstaan...*

De groep zat ergens om te lachen. Denny had iets gezegd over een vishaak die het afgelopen weekend vastgeraakt was in het haarstuk van de dominee.

'Het punt is...' Jo legde met een rood gezicht van het lachen haar vork neer. 'Dat niemand van ons van dat haargevalletje afwist. Ik bedoel, de dominee staat daar elke zondag zo eerlijk als een forel in de zomer op die preekstoel.' Ze gebaarde de tafel rond. 'Jullie snappen wel wat ik bedoel... het is niet zo'n vent met een grote haardos zoals je op tv ziet. Hij is het echte werk. Authentiek.'

Abby kende de man niet, maar ze voelde niettemin met hem mee. 'Hij moet diep gekwetst zijn geweest.'

Denny haalde zijn schouders op, maar voordat hij antwoord kon geven, boog Jo zich naar voren en stak haar vinger op. 'Weet je wat hij tegen mij zei? Hij zei: "Jo, vertel niemand in de kerk hierover. God heeft mijn haar weggenomen, maar dat wil niet zeggen dat ik geen hoed mag dragen."' Jo sloeg hard op tafel en het water in haar glas klotste over de rand. 'Een hoed! Heb je ooit zoiets grappigs gehoord?'

Abby bestudeerde de roodharige vrouw, tenger en vol vuur, een vrouw die Abby nooit had uitgekozen als schoonmoeder voor haar dochter. Maar Abby en Nicole waren gewend geraakt aan Jo en nu vonden ze haar charmant. Een beetje praatziek en misschien een beetje al te geïnteresseerd in vissen, maar heerlijk oprecht en vol liefde. Hun familiebijeenkomsten waren niet hetzelfde zonder haar.

Nicole veegde haar mond af en keek naar John. 'Heb je nog iets van Kade gehoord?'

'Niets nieuws.' John haalde zijn schouders op. 'Op school ging het goed, met football ook.'

'Hij is dit jaar toch vrijgesteld van competitie voor training?' Denny zette zijn ellebogen op tafel.

'Inderdaad. Daarmee wint hij een extra jaar.'

'Die hele vrijstelling vind ik maar niks.' Jo trok een gezicht. 'Net een emmer met slecht aas.'

Abby glimlachte. 'Het is een beslissing van de coach. Er zit een hoop talent voor Kade uit op de reservebank. Hij vindt het prima om vrijgesteld te zijn.'

'Kan me niet schelen.' Jo verhief haar stem en sprak hartstochtelijk. 'Kade is per slot van rekening goed genoeg om te starten en als ik het nummer van de coach had, zou ik hem dat zelf wel eens even in zijn oor fluisteren.' Ze hield haar hoofd schuin naar John. 'Heb jij het toevallig?'

Iedereen lachte behalve Jo, die de kring rondkeek alsof ze allemaal gek waren geworden. 'Ik meen het in diepe ernst. Die jongen is goed.'

'Het geeft niet, Jo.' John keek de vrouw grinnikend aan en Abby genoot van het effect. Johns glimlach deed de laatste tijd heerlijke dingen met Abby's hart. Met vriendelijke stem deed hij zijn best het Jo uit te leggen. 'Kade heeft er zelf mee ingestemd. Hij heeft nog veel te leren voordat hij het veld op gaat.'

'Ja.' Nicole keek Abby aan. 'En hij komt toch binnenkort thuis?'

Abby bewonderde haar dochter om de manier waarop ze met Jo omging. In de paar maanden dat ze met Matt was getrouwd, was Nicole er een expert in geworden de conversatie te sturen en Jo af te leiden als ze al te opgewonden werd.

'Inderdaad.' Abby knikte. 'Iowa speelt op twintig oktober in Indiana. Het is maar vier uur rijden hiervandaan. Er is die maandag geen school, dus Kade komt naar ons toe, blijft zondag slapen en vliegt maandag weer naar school terug.'

'Ja.' Sean keek op van zijn bord. 'Over tien dagen en we tellen de tijd af.'

'Nou, je weet toch zeker wel dat ik daar bij wil zijn. Denny en ik gaan gewoon met jullie mee…' Ineens hapte Jo naar adem. 'Wacht eens even.' Ze gaf Denny met haar elleboog een por tussen zijn ribben, zodat de man opschrok. 'Dat is toch het weekend dat wij dat zendingsding hebben?'

Denny dacht even na. 'Ik geloof van wel.'

Matt keek op, zijn vork bleef in de lucht hangen. 'Zendingsding?' Hij was dol op Abby's kookkunst en onder het eten liet hij de anderen meestal maar praten terwijl hij zijn bord leegat. Abby had gevulde varkenskarbonaadjes en geglaceerde aardappelen gemaakt en Matt had al voor de derde keer opgeschept. Met twinkelende ogen keek hij zijn moeder aan. 'Wat voor zendingsding?'

'Hè, bah.' Jo wisselde een blik met Denny en blies hard uit. 'We wilden het nog niet aan de jongelui vertellen. Het moest een verrassing zijn.'

Nicole boog zich naar haar schoonfamilie toe. 'Gaan jullie een zendingsreis maken?'

Denny pakte Jo's hand vast. 'Eigenlijk komt er nog wel wat meer aan te pas.'

Abby voelde hoe iedereen aan tafel gespannen afwachtte. Matts ouders waren per slot van rekening gescheiden toen Matt nog klein was. Ze hadden apart van elkaar gewoond totdat Matt en

Nicole zich verloofden. Na een reeks wonderlijke gebeurtenissen was toen eerst Denny en later Jo gelovig geworden. Twee maanden geleden waren ze hertrouwd en lid van de kerk geworden. Nu gingen ze 's zaterdags vissen met hun dominee.

'Mam.' Matt legde zijn vork neer en leunde met zijn onderarmen op tafel. 'Waar hebben jullie het over?'

'Lieve help.' Jo wierp Denny een verontschuldigende blik toe. 'Ik en mijn grote mond.' Toen keek ze haar zoon aan. 'Je vader en ik overwegen om een jaar naar Mexico te gaan. Om in een weeshuis te werken en…'

Misschien wel voor de eerste keer sinds Abby Jo kende, zweeg de vrouw. Het was zulk verbazingwekkend nieuws, zoiets heel anders dan Jo ooit had gedaan, dat zelfs zij er niets aan toe te voegen wist.

Nicole gilde: 'Dat is *fantastisch*!' Ze sprong op van haar stoel, stelde zich op tussen Jo en Denny in en legde een arm om elk van hen heen. 'Wat zullen jullie daarvan genieten.'

Jo haalde haar schouders op, haar wangen waren ineens rood. 'Nou ja, niet dat we veel voor ze kunnen doen, hoor. Maar we zijn bereid. Volgens de dominee is dat het belangrijkste.'

Denny schraapte zijn keel. 'We gaan helpen een tweede babyruimte te bouwen en algemeen onderhoud te doen. Als een soort huismeesters.'

'Pap, wat geweldig.' Matt drukte zijn vader de hand. 'Niet te geloven. Ik had nooit gedacht dat mijn ouders nog eens een jaar zendingswerk zouden gaan doen.'

John wierp Abby een snelle blik toe. 'We dienen toch wel een God van wonderen, hoor!'

Abby sloeg haar ogen neer naar haar bord. Ze begreep de geheime betekenis in Johns woorden, en op ogenblikken als deze verlangde ze er wanhopig naar de kinderen over hun eigen wonder te vertellen. Dat ze bijna gescheiden waren en toen op de een of andere manier de weg hadden gevonden naar de oude aanlegsteiger achter hun huis. Hoe God daar in de uren na Nicoles bruiloft hun oren had geopend voor de muziek van hun leven, en ze weer wisten hoe ze dansen moesten.

Het wonder was dit: ze waren samen gebleven en hadden iets moois van hun huwelijk gemaakt. Dat zou niet gebeurd zijn zonder Gods hand en als zodanig was het een vermeldenswaardig wonder.

Maar het mocht niet. Abby en John hadden niemand ooit verteld wat er bijna was gebeurd. De kinderen zouden te geschokt zijn geweest, vooral Nicole. Nee, de kinderen wisten van niets. Ze betwijfelde of ze het ooit zouden weten.

Abby keek op en liet de gedachte varen. Om de tafel werd druk gefeliciteerd en Jo en Denny beantwoordden een spervuur van vragen. Als alles goed ging, zouden ze in juli naar Mexico vertrekken en een jaar later terugkomen.

'Ze hebben ons gevraagd of we de kinderen iets konden leren als we er waren.' Denny gaf Jo een knipoog. 'Ik heb gezegd dat ze die kinderen in minder dan geen tijd een hengel in de hand zal stoppen.'

Matt schonk zijn moeder een hartelijke glimlach en zei luchtig op plagerige toon: 'Jou kennende, breng je vast een paar kleine vissertjes mee terug.'

'Inderdaad.' Jo's mondhoeken zakten langzaam naar beneden en haar lach klonk ineens gedwongen.

De verandering was niet zo groot dat iedereen aan tafel het merkte, maar Abby wel. Iets in Matts opmerking over de weeskinderen had Jo geschokt. In de komende maanden moest Abby uitzien naar een gelegenheid om met Jo te praten. Ze was er haast zeker van dat de vrouw diepe gevoelens over het onderwerp koesterde, gevoelens die ze misschien niet met Matt of Nicole had gedeeld.

'Wacht eens even.' Denny knikte in Matts richting. 'Je moeder en ik zitten er niet op te wachten weer ouders te worden.'

'Wat hij bedoelt is dat ik grootmoeder wil worden. Hoe eerder, hoe beter.'

'Grootmoeder?' Nicoles mond viel zogenaamd geschokt open. 'Sorry, Jo. Die wens zal nog in geen jaren uitkomen.'

'Mijn idee.' Matt sloeg zijn arm om Nicoles schouders. 'Over een jaar of vier is het plan, hè?'

'Precies.'

Abby moest op haar lippen bijten om niet hardop te lachen. 'Werkte het maar zo.'

'Ja.' John kneep zijn ogen tot spleetjes. 'Wij trouwden op 14 juli 1979. En wanneer hadden we kinderen gepland?'

'Na een jaar of vijf, geloof ik.'

'En wanneer is Nicole geboren?'

'16 april 1980.' Abby wierp Nicole een snelle glimlach toe. 'Maar dat geeft niet, kind. Je kunt best doen of je een plan hebt. Dat geeft minder spanning.'

Aan de overkant van de tafel zat Jo nog te rekenen. Ze telde op haar vingers af en hield abrupt stil. 'Wil je zeggen dat Nicole negen maanden en twee dagen na de bruiloft is geboren?' Haar ogen straalden weer als tevoren. Ze boog zich over Matts bord heen en klopte Nicole op de hand. 'Geen wonder dat je zo'n schat bent. Ik dacht altijd dat het door je opvoeding kwam.' Ze wierp een snelle blik naar John. 'En dat is het natuurlijk óók.' Ze keek weer naar Nicole. 'Maar ik had geen idee dat je een wittebroods- baby was. Wittebroodsbaby's zijn supermakkelijk. Ze geloven in het geluk.'

Jo haalde diep adem en verplaatste haar blik naar Matt. 'Zorg maar goed voor haar, jongen. Het is geen gewoon meisje. Ze is een wittebroodsbaby.' Ze dempte haar stem en de anderen moes- ten zich inspannen om haar te verstaan. 'Je boft, jongen. Je hebt een betere vangst te pakken dan je ooit met een hengel binnen had kunnen halen. Bovendien brengen wittebroodsbaby's witte- broodsbaby's voort. Dat heb ik tenminste altijd gehoord.'

'Pardon.' Nicole stak oprecht glimlachend haar hand op. '*Deze* wittebroodsbaby brengt de eerste vier jaar nog helemaal niets voort.' Ze leunde tegen Matt aan en keek hem in de ogen. 'Mijn geniale echtgenoot moet zich eerst op zijn rechterlijke loopbaan storten.'

Pas toen zag Abby Johns ogen. Ze waren in de afgelopen paar minuten afstandelijk geworden, alsof hij al naar bed was gegaan en zijn lichaam uit beleefdheid had achtergelaten.

Abby keek nog eens beter. Nee, het was geen afstandelijkheid. Het was diepte... diepte en pijn. Toen begreep ze het. Hij zat weer aan football te denken. Het onderwerp was de hele avond niet ter tafel geweest en daar was Abby blij om. Beiden hadden ze de laatste dagen gestreden met de vragen die alle coaches zich moeten stellen als ze lang genoeg in het vak blijven: Waar doe ik het allemaal voor? Waarom ben ik hiermee bezig? Is er niet méér in het leven?

De maaltijd was voorbij en Nicole en Matt vertrokken met Denny en Jo achter zich aan. Sean ging naar boven en beloofde zijn wiskundehuiswerk af te maken. Abby volgde John naar hun slaapkamer.

'Waar denk je aan?'

Pas toen ze eindelijk alleen waren, vond hij de woorden voor zijn gevoelens. Het waren woorden die ze nooit had verwacht te horen uit de mond van John Reynolds. Hij wreef over zijn achterhoofd en keek haar indringend aan. Toen zei hij het, vol overtuiging en met een vermoeide stem.

'Ik stop met football, Abby. Dit is mijn laatste jaar.'

Het schokte haar tot in haar diepste wezen. Ze had altijd geweten dat deze dag zou komen. Maar niet op dit moment. Niet vlak na een kampioensseizoen. Tja, dit seizoen was natuurlijk zwaarder dan andere. Maar John had wel vaker met klagende ouders, slecht gedrag en onverklaarbare verliezen te stellen gehad. Die dingen overkwamen elke coach. Maar het idee dat hij nu zijn fluit in de wilgen zou hangen, nu hij nog zoveel onderwijsjaren voor zich had, was verrassender dan alles wat John had kunnen zeggen.

Bijna even verrassend als de gevoelens die in haar opkwamen.

Haar leven lang had Abby in het diepst van haar hart opgezien tegen de dag dat football niet langer deel van haar dagelijks leven zou uitmaken. Maar hier en nu… met haar ogen vast in die van John, zag ze nergens tegenop.

Ze voelde zich verlicht.

Vier

Zelfs geparkeerd zag hij eruit als een snelle auto.

Jake Daniels en een stel teamgenoten kwamen zaterdagochtend uit de training toen ze hem zagen staan. Een rode Acura Integra NSX. Misschien uit '91 of '92.

De groep bleef met open mond stilstaan. Casey Parker was de eerste die zich herstelde. Het was de mooiste auto die Jake ooit had gezien.

'Gaaf, man.' Casey slingerde zijn sporttas over zijn schouder. 'Reken maar dat dat ding kan scheuren.'

De auto glom zo dat Jake zijn ogen een beetje dicht moest knijpen. Hij had twee portieren, een spoiler aan de voorkant en langs de achterkant. De carrosserie lag vlak boven de grond, gezellig tegen een schitterend stel Momowielen.

Ineens zakte het zwartgetinte passagiersraampje naar beneden en een man zwaaide in hun richting. Jake vernauwde zijn ogen nog meer. *Wat ter…?*

'Zeg, Daniels, is dat je vader niet?' Casey gaf Jake een stomp tegen zijn arm. 'Waar is dat blondje?'

Jake hapte naar adem. Het was inderdaad zijn vader. Hij was gisteravond bij de wedstrijd verschenen; de eerste wedstrijd die hij sinds zijn verhuizing naar New Jersey had bijgewoond. Naast hem had een of andere blond meisje gezeten in uitdagende kleding. Ze kon niet ouder zijn dan vijfentwintig. Een enorm dom blondje, met een prop kauwgom in haar mond en wapperende wimpers. Tijdens de zaterdagse training hadden de andere jongens Jake de hele ochtend met haar zitten stangen.

Na het eerste uur waren de opmerkingen oudbakken geworden, maar de jongens bleven aan de gang. Maar wie de blondine ook mocht zijn, ze zat niet in de Integra. Jake knikte zijn teamgenoten toe, zwaaide zijn tas over zijn schouders en zette koers naar de auto. Normaal gesproken haalde zijn moeder hem na de training altijd trouw op tijd op in hun oude busje.

Maar vandaag niet.

'Hoi…' Zijn vader wachtte tot Jake dichterbij was voordat hij iets zei. 'Stap in.'

Jake deed wat hem gezegd werd. Het moest een huurauto zijn. Kennelijk verdiende zijn vader flink geld bij de radiozender. Toen hij voor de scheiding nog bij de krant van Marion werkte, zou hij nooit een Acura NSX hebben gehuurd. Maar goed, toen had hij ook geen leeghoofd als vriendin. Er was veel veranderd.

'En… wat vind je ervan?' Zijn vader grijnsde van oor tot oor.

'Waar is ze?'

Zijn gezichtsuitdrukking werd neutraal. 'Wie?'

'Dat meisje. Bambi. Blondie… hoe ze ook heten mag.'

'Bonnie.' Er viel een schaduw over zijn ogen en hij zag er ouder uit dan mam. Ze waren van dezelfde leeftijd, maar pap had nu meer rimpels in zijn voorhoofd. Hij bewerkte ze met zijn duim en wijsvinger en schraapte zijn keel. 'Ze krijgt een massage.'

'O.' Jake wist niet wat hij moest zeggen. 'Bedankt voor het ophalen.' Hij klopte op het dashboard. 'Leuke huurauto.'

Zijn vader boog zich naar voren met zijn zonnebril in zijn hand en liet zijn arm op het stuur rusten. Hij leek op iemand uit een sportadvertentie. 'Als ik je nou eens vertelde dat het geen huurauto is?'

Het duurde even voordat Jake er weer aan dacht om adem te halen. 'Geen huurauto?'

De grijns keerde terug op het gezicht van zijn vader. 'Weet je nog dat we het van de zomer over auto's hadden?'

'Auto's?'

'Ja.' Er rolde een vreemd lachje uit zijn vaders mond. Het gaf

Jake het gevoel dat hij de man niet kende. Haast alsof hij te hard zijn best deed om *cool* te zijn.

'Eh…' Jake probeerde zich niet te ergeren. Waar leidden al die vragen naartoe? 'Toen je me vroeg welke auto's op dit moment populair zijn?'

'Precies. Je zei dat de populairste auto een tweedehands Acura NSX was… uit '91 misschien. Weet je nog?'

'Oké…' Jakes hart begon te bonzen. Het kon toch niet waar zijn? Hij werd per slot van rekening volgende week zeventien. Maar kwam zijn vader echt helemaal uit New Jersey om hem een…

Hij slikte moeilijk. 'Pap… van wie is deze auto?'

Zijn vader haalde met een weids gebaar zijn arm van het stuur, zette de motor af, haalde de sleutel uit het contact en overhandigde hem aan Jake. 'Van jou, jongen. Gefeliciteerd met je verjaardag.'

Jakes mond viel open. 'Echt niet.'

'Jazeker.' Zijn vader begon weer te grijnzen en zette zijn zonnebril op. 'Volgend weekend heb ik het druk, daarom heb ik hem nu maar gebracht. Dan heb je hem tenminste op je verjaardag.'

In Jakes hoofd buitelden de gedachten over elkaar. Meende zijn vader het echt? Zo'n auto moest wel veertig mille kosten! Man, je zat waarschijnlijk binnen vijf seconden van nul op honderd. Bij een straatrace kon hij vast wel tweehonderdtwintig, tweehonderddertig halen.

Jake hapte naar adem. Wat zou mam ervan vinden? Ze wilde niet dat hij al een auto bezat, laat staan het gaafste racemonster van Illinois.

Zijn vader zat hem grijnzend aan te kijken. 'Nou…'

'Pap, het is supergaaf. Ik ben sprakeloos.'

'Tja, ach… het is het minste wat ik kan doen.' Hij zette de zonnebril weer af, zijn ogen stonden ernstig. 'Ik heb veel gemist doordat ik weg was, jongen. Misschien dat dit het een beetje goedmaakt voor je.'

'Een beetje? Wat zou je zeggen van heel veel.' Jakes vingers en tenen tintelden en het vlees op zijn armen en benen jeukte van opwinding. Hij kon wel op het dak gaan staan en het uitschreeuwen naar de wereld: *Ik heb een Acura NSX!* Zijn vader mocht dan veranderd zijn, maar de man hield toch nog van hem. Dat moest wel. En Jake hield ook van hem. Zeker nu.

Zijn vader zat hem afwachtend aan te kijken. Maar wat kon Jake zeggen? Hoe bedankte een jongen zijn vader voor zoiets als dit? Hij haalde een paar keer zijn schouders op. 'Ik weet niet wat ik zeggen moet, pap. Bedankt. Het is geweldig. Ik… ik kan niet geloven dat-ie van mij is.'

Zijn vader lachte weer, het gladde lachje dat hij waarschijnlijk vaak in zijn radioprogramma gebruikte. 'Ik geloof dat je op mijn plaats zit, jongen.' Zijn vader trok aan de motorkaphendel en stapte uit. Jake volgde zijn voorbeeld. Aan de voorkant van de auto kwamen ze elkaar tegen en Jake kon de verleiding niet weerstaan. Hij liet zijn vingers onder de motorkap glijden en maakte hem open. Jakes adem stokte. Wat nou? Hij wierp een snelle blik over zijn schouder. Wist zijn vader dat dit geen standaardmotor was? *Normaal doen*, zei hij tegen zichzelf. *Verraad het niet.*

Het motorblok was verhoogd, met een omgevormde verbrandingskamer en een speciaal gemaakt inlaatspruitstuk. Hoezo snel. Deze auto kon vliegen.

'Goed spul, hè?' Zijn vader klopte hem op de schouder en liet zijn hand daar liggen. Dat gevoel maakte dat Jake de oude tijd miste. Toen dat… dat pijnlijke gedoe nog niet tussen hen was.

'Ja… mooi.'

Zijn vader hoestte zacht. 'Het is een snelle auto, jongen.'

Jake draaide zich om en keek zijn vader in de ogen. Hij was waarschijnlijk van plan de motor volgende week meteen standaard te laten maken. 'Ja.'

'Laten we dat kleine detail maar voor je moeder verzwijgen, hè?'

'Echt waar?' Jakes mond was droog. Wat zouden de jongens

hiervan zeggen? Ze zouden natuurlijk elk weekend met hem op willen trekken. Hij werd de meest gewilde jongen van Marion High. Mam zou woest zijn als ze wist hoe snel hij was... of hoeveel hij kostte. Maar pap had gelijk. Het had geen zin om haar met de details lastig te vallen. 'Ik zeg geen woord.'

Pap stak zijn vinger op en hield hem onder Jakes neus. 'Maar geen bekeuringen, begrepen?'

'Niet één.' Jake knikte ernstig en overtuigd. Dit was een auto waar hij plezier mee kon maken, maar hij zou voorzichtig zijn. Geen risico's nemen. Geen straatraces. Nou ja... misschien een enkel keertje, maar niets gevaarlijks. Een paar jongens van het team waren de laatste tijd begonnen met straatraces. Maar goed, hij ging het in elk geval niet váák doen. Eén keertje per maand misschien. Bovendien stond hij bekend als een van de veiligste bestuurders van de school. 'Je kunt me vertrouwen, pap.'

'Mooi.' Zijn vader zette de zonnebril weer op zijn plaats en keek op zijn horloge. 'Dan moest je maar naar huis gaan. Je moeder zal niet weten waar je blijft.'

Bovendien staat Bunny, of hoe ze ook heten mag, te wachten. Jake verwierp die gedachte. Hij liep langs zijn vader heen naar de passagierskant. Het was een moment waarop Jake in vroeger jaren zijn vader stevig had omhelsd, of met zijn elleboog om zijn nek een paar zachte, speelse stompjes in zijn maag had gegeven.

Maar nu niet.

Sinds de scheiding van zijn ouders was alles veranderd. Eerst het woonadres en de baan van zijn vader, toen zijn kleren en de manier waarop hij de zaterdagavond doorbracht. Meisjes zoals hoe-heet-ze waren lopendebandwerk voor zijn vader. En waarom niet? Zijn vader was een knappe vent. Sterk, atletisch, diepe stem...

Meisjes waren gek op mannen zoals zijn vader.

Maar wat Jake niet snapte, was wat zijn vader in die meisjes zag. Vooral omdat een fantastisch mens als zijn moeder alleen thuis zat.

Met elke seconde die verstreek werd het ogenblik pijnlijker, en ten slotte stak Jake zijn hand maar uit. Zijn vader deed hetzelfde en ze drukten elkaar stevig de hand. 'Nogmaals bedankt, pap. Hij is supergaaf.'

Jake liep om de auto heen, stapte in en startte de motor. Terwijl hij naar huis reed, en erop lette dat hij zich aan de maximumsnelheid hield, voelde de auto aan als een racepaard dat vlak voor de grote race stond te popelen. Iets vertelde hem dat zijn Integra pas op dreef kwam als hij ruim boven de honderdzestig reed.

Dat vertelde hij natuurlijk niet aan zijn vader. Hij betwijfelde zelfs of hij het aan de jongens zou vertellen. Deze auto blies alles waar zij in reden van de weg, dus wat had het voor zin? Racen zou hem alleen maar moeilijkheden brengen. Het bezit van zo'n auto was genoeg. Hij glimlachte. Zijn vader had niets te vrezen. Hij werd de voorzichtigste Integra NSX bestuurder aller tijden.

Op het moment dat zijn moeder naar buiten kwam, waren haar gevoelens duidelijk. Eerst schrik, dan ontzag, dan een woeste en scherpe woede rechtstreeks tegen zijn vader gericht. Ze keek Jake amper aan toen ze met z'n tweeën uitstapten en zich aan weerskanten van de auto schrap zetten.

'Wat heeft dit te betekenen?' Ze gebaarde naar de auto zoals ze naar zijn wiskundeproefwerk had gewezen toen hij een onvoldoende had gehaald.

'Dit?' Pap keek van de auto naar mam. 'Een verjaardagscadeau voor Jake. Ik ben volgende week de stad uit, dus ik heb hem een paar dagen eerder gebracht.'

'Bedoel je die cruise die je met *Bonnie* gaat maken?' De glimlach van zijn moeder gaf Jake kippenvel... zo boosaardig was hij. 'Je vriendinnetje heeft gepraat, Tim. De geruchtenmolen draait wel.'

Jake huiverde van de pijn die hem diep vanbinnen raakte. *Dat komt door mams toon*, hield hij tegenover zichzelf vol. Niet doordat zijn vader liever een cruise ging maken met een blondje dan bij de verjaardag van zijn eigen zoon te zijn. Hij sloeg zijn ogen op naar zijn vader.

Paps mond hing open en hij scheen naar woorden te zoeken. 'Hoe weet je…' Hij sloeg zijn armen over elkaar. 'Hoor es, wat ik in mijn eigen tijd doe zijn mijn zaken, ja?'

'Dus vandaar.'

'Wat?'

'Die dure sportwagen.' Jakes moeder lachte één keer vreugdeloos. Jakes buikpijn werd erger en hij dacht dat hij moest overgeven. Hij haatte het als ze zo deed. Zijn moeder maakte een wegwerpend gebaar naar de auto en vervolgde: 'Ik snap het, Tim. Het is een soort boetedoening voor alles wat je dit jaar niet voor Jake doet. Een goedmakertje voor alle uren die je met de dames doorbrengt.'

'Je hebt het recht niet dat te zeggen waar…'

'Waar wie bij is? Jake? Net of jou dat wat kan schelen.' Ze snoof. 'Een jongen van Jakes leeftijd hoort niet in zo'n auto te rijden.'

Wacht eens even… Jake wilde tussenbeide komen, maar één blik op zijn moeders woedende gezicht deed hem anders besluiten.

'Je bent gek, Tara. Die auto is perfect.'

'Denk je soms dat ik achterlijk ben? Dat is een *Integra*.' Haar stem werd luider. Jake greep zijn maag vast. Zijn ouders ruzieden als kinderen om een dom stuk speelgoed. Alleen was *hij* het speelgoed. En het was eigenlijk niet zozeer dat ze hem wilden hebben, maar dat ze van elkaar wilden winnen.

'Nou en?'

'Hij is te snel!' Ze deed een paar stappen in de richting van het appartement en draaide zich toen met een ruk om. 'Als je wilt dat hij vervoer heeft, Tim, koop dan een Bronco voor hem of een truck.' Ze vernauwde haar ogen. 'Maar een Integra?'

Jake had genoeg gehoord. Hij zwaaide zijn sporttas over zijn schouder en glipte langs zijn ouders heen zonder dat een van beiden het leek op te merken. Daarom waren ze gescheiden. Dat ruziemaken en schreeuwen. Het schelden. Jake haatte het, en zeker vandaag. Hij haatte de pijltjes die daarmee naar zijn prettige gevoelens geworpen werden.

Hij liet zich op zijn bed vallen en begroef zijn gezicht in het kussen. Waarom konden ze niet net als vroeger van elkaar houden? En waarom moesten ze aldoor ruziemaken? Wisten ze niet hoeveel pijn hem dat deed? Andere tieners hadden gescheiden ouders, maar die probeerden tenminste goed met elkaar op te schieten. Maar zijn ouders niet, hoor. Elke keer als ze samen waren leek het alsof ze elkaar haatten.

Jake draaide zich om en staarde naar het plafond. Waarom liet hij de dag verknoeien door hun problemen? Niets kon verandering brengen in de spannende gebeurtenis van daarstraks. De auto was van hem en het was een droom. Stukken beter dan die roestbak waarin die halvegare Nathan Pike reed.

De ruzies van zijn ouders waren hun probleem. Hoe vastbesloten ze ook waren het weekend te bederven, maandag werd om één eenvoudige reden de geweldigste dag van Jakes leven.

Hij was de trotse eigenaar van een glanzend rode Integra NSX, een auto die sneller was dan wat dan ook in Illinois.

Vijf

Het had weinig met volwassenheid van doen.

De dansles in de gymzaal van het Marion High was een halfuur aan de gang en John voelde zich een brugklasser die zich door
de gymles heen worstelt, met zijn twee linkervoeten en onzeker
van zijn volgende stap.

De instructrice was een vrouw van achter in de vijftig met wit
haar die Paula heette. Ze had een microfoontje om en was
gekleed in een gympakje met een dikke maillot. Ze sloeg een
neerbuigende toon aan, met een gedwongen vrolijkheid waardoor
John zich allesbehalve volwassen voelde. Bovendien klapte ze vaak
in haar handen. 'Goed, klas.' Ze liet haar ogen over de rij van vijftien paren heen dwalen.

Twee, misschien drie koppen koffie te veel. John trok een grimas.

Paula klapte weer in haar handen. 'In de rij.' Haar wenkbrauwen leken permanent opgetrokken. 'Dat proberen we nog eens.'

Abby stond haar mannetje, behalve toen hij op haar voet trapte. Dat deed hij zo vaak dat het leek of het bij de danspassen hoorde. Hij keek Abby grijnzend aan. 'Daar gaan we weer. Ik hoop dat
je voeten ertegen kunnen.'

'Houd op, John.' Ze giechelde. 'Straks hoort de juf het.'

'Parmantige Paula, bedoel je.' De muziek was begonnen en ze
hadden al meteen moeite om de andere paren bij te houden. John
fluisterde: 'Ze heeft het te druk met de maat te tellen.'

John liet Abby een rondje draaien en ze knikte hem toe. 'Heel
goed.'

'Tuurlijk, nog even en ik sta vooraan met Paula.' John danste wat rechter en probeerde de volgende reeks passen zonder naar beneden te kijken. Daarbij kwam hij op Abby's voet terecht, zodat haar schoen over de vloer van de gymzaal vloog.

Paula wierp hun een strenge blik toe van het soort waarmee ondeugende leerlingen berispt worden. Ze klakte met haar tong. 'Alstublieft… Vlug weer in de rij.'

Abby perste haar lippen op elkaar, haar laatste verdediging voordat ze in lachen uitbarstte. Ze rende op haar tenen achter haar schoen aan, naar beneden gedoken alsof ze daardoor minder zouden opvallen. Toen de schoen weer aan haar voet zat, keerde ze terug naar John en ze deden hun best om zich weer bij de anderen in de rij te voegen.

Het was geen wonder dat John zich niet op de danspassen kon concentreren. Abby zag er eenvoudigweg schitterend uit. Ze had makkelijk tien jaar jonger kunnen zijn en de vonk in haar ogen gaf hem hetzelfde lichtzinnige gevoel als toen ze nog verkering hadden. Waarom had hij verleden jaar of het jaar daarvoor haar schoonheid niet gezien? Of het jaar dáárvoor? Hoe was het toch mogelijk dat hij zich door een andere vrouw had laten afleiden?

'Waar denk je aan?' Ze fluisterde de woorden die rechtstreeks de weg naar zijn hart vonden.

Het was niet meer belangrijk dat hun danspassen niet volkomen in de maat waren met de andere paren om hen heen. 'Dat je mooi bent. Dat je altijd de mooiste vrouw van de wereld bent geweest.'

Abby bloosde. 'Ik houd van je, John Reynolds.'

Zijn voeten hielden stil en Abby danste tegen hem op. Hij boog zich over haar heen en kuste haar. 'Dank je, Abby… voor je liefde.'

Het paar één plaats achter hen in de rij botste tegen hen op en danste om hen heen.

'In beweging blijven, mensen.' Paula klapte in haar handen, met haar ogen strak op John en Abby gericht. 'Dit is dansles… geen schoolbal.'

Ze voegden zich weer bij de anderen in de rij. Maar geen standje van de instructrice kon Abby en hem ervan weerhouden elkaar diep in de ogen te kijken en de rest van de wereld te laten vervagen terwijl ze dansten zoals ze altijd al hadden gewild. Maar waar waren ze zonder de genade van God nu geweest? En met wie zou John nu zijn bed gedeeld hebben?

Hij huiverde.

God… dank U dat ik niet zo gevallen ben als ik had kunnen vallen. Laat me altijd van Abby blijven houden zoals nu. Laat ons nooit meer van elkaar afdwalen. Of van U… alstublieft.

EEN KOORD DAT UIT DRIE STRENGEN IS GEVLOCHTEN, IS NIET SNEL STUK TE TREKKEN, MIJN ZOON.

De stille fluistering in zijn ziel, de herinnering aan een Bijbeltekst die Abby en hij op hun bruiloft hadden gebruikt, was genoeg om Johns concentratie te verbreken. Haast precies op de maat van de muziek stapte hij weer op Abby's voet.

Dit keer gaf ze een gilletje en sprong op. Achter hen in de rij maakten twee andere vrouwen ook een sprongetje, kennelijk denkend dat het bij de dans hoorde. Toen Abby besefte wat er gebeurde, was ze verloren.

Ze lachte geluidloos, maar zonder ophouden. En John kon niet anders dan met haar meedoen. Een paar keer wierp Paula hun een gefrustreerde blik toe en ze schudde haar hoofd alsof ze zeggen wilde dat Abby en John nooit volwassen dansers zouden worden. In geen honderd jaar.

Tegen de tijd dat de les voorbij was, hinkte Abby.

Ze waren halverwege de auto toen John voor haar zijn rug aanbood. 'Uw rijtuig, mevrouw.'

Haar lach klonk als het windklokkenspel op hun zonneterras in de lente. John genoot van het geluid. Ze trommelde zachtjes op zijn rug. 'Dat hoeft niet, John. Ik kan wel lopen.'

'Nee, kom op. Ik heb je tenen beschadigd. Ik geef je een lift.' Hij reikte achterom naar haar benen en meteen sprong ze op zijn rug. Hij begon te lopen, maar hoe harder ze lachte, hoe harder hij begon te rennen tot hij galoppeerde. Hij rende langs de auto heen en draaide een rondje om het parkeerterrein. Het was een ogenblik van vrijheid en leven. Alsof de tijd had stilgestaan zodat zij hun blijdschap dat ze weer samen waren konden vieren. Hij uitte een kreet die weerkaatste tegen de muur van de school. 'Joeeehieeee!!'

'Ik vraag me af…' Abby's woorden werden onderbroken door het hobbelen. 'Wat die ouwe Paula van *deze* danspassen zou vinden?'

Eindelijk rende hij naar hun auto en zette Abby neer naast het passagiersportier. Het parkeerterrein was leeg, alle volwassen dansers waren naar huis gegaan om kamillethee te drinken en vroeg naar bed te gaan. Abby leunde ademloos van de lift en het lachen tegen het portier. 'Wat een avond.'

John werd stil; hij kwam voor haar staan en drukte zich dicht tegen haar aan zodat hun lichamen zich naar elkaar vormden. Het was een hartstochtelijk moment en hij bestudeerde haar zwijgend. De enige geluiden waren nu en dan het ronken van een auto op de weg in de verte en de bedwelmende fluistering van Abby's hartslag tegen de zijne. Hij streek langs haar kin, de delicate lijn van haar kaak. 'Ik voel me net een verliefde tiener.'

'Tja…' Ze boog haar hoofd achterover, haar hals was slank en gebogen in het maanlicht. Haar stem was hees van verlangen, zoals John de afgelopen maanden vaak had gehoord. 'Misschien komt dat doordat we op het parkeerterrein van een school staan.'

'Nee.' Hij hield zijn hoofd zo dat hij het licht niet blokkeerde. Hij wilde haar gezicht zien… helemaal… om alles van haar in zich op te nemen. 'Niet daarom.'

'Nee?'

'Nee.' Hij streelde met zijn vingers licht over de lengte van haar armen. 'Het komt door jou, Abby. Jij geeft me dat gevoel.'

Ze zwegen een ogenblik, hun lichamen bewogen subtiel tot ze nog dichter bij elkaar waren dan eerst. John wreef met zijn neus over haar gezicht en snoof de geur van haar parfum op terwijl hij met zijn lippen de zijkant van haar hals streelde.

Toen hij opkeek, zag hij dat haar ogen vochtig waren. Hij voelde een steek van angst. Hij had zich vast voorgenomen haar nooit meer aan het huilen te maken. 'Waar denk je aan, schat?'

Er rolde een traan over haar wang. 'Het is een wonder, John. Wat ik voel... wat we voor elkaar voelen. Zes maanden geleden...'

Ze maakte de zin niet af en daar was John blij om. Hij legde zijn vinger op haar lippen. 'Heb ik je pas nog gezegd hoe mooi je bent?'

'Ja.' Ze boog haar hoofd en knipperde langzaam met haar ogen. Haar blik was zowel verlegen als flirtend, een blik die hem gek had gemaakt vanaf dat hij een schooljongen was.

'Wanneer dan?'

'Onder het dansen, weet je nog?' Abby's mondhoeken gingen omhoog en haar ogen schitterden.

'Dat is een hele tijd geleden.' Hij kuste zacht haar beide ogen om beurten. 'Ik bedoel pas nog. Heb ik *pas nog* tegen je gezegd hoe mooi je bent?'

Er viel nog een traan en ze maakte een geluid dat meer op lachen leek dan op huilen. 'Ik geloof van niet.'

'Nou... je bent mooier dan een zonsopgang, Abby Reynolds. Mooier dan de lente. Dat moet je weten, voor het geval ik het niet vaak genoeg zeg. Ik kon tijdens die dansles aan niets anders denken.' Hij schonk haar een scheve grijns. 'En het enige wat ik wilde doen was...'

Ineens kon hij geen woorden meer vinden. Hij drukte zich tegen haar aan en kuste haar zoals hij al een uur had willen doen.

Toen ze naar lucht hapten, was hun hartslag versneld. 'Zeg...' Hij kuste haar nog twee keer en hield haar blik vast. 'Zin om met mij mee naar huis te gaan?'

'Niet om te dansen, hoop ik.' Een van haar wenkbrauwen ging een klein stukje omhoog, zoals altijd als ze hem plaagde. 'Mijn voeten doen al zo'n pijn.'

'Nee.' Hij legde zijn handen om haar gezicht en er kroop een trage glimlach om zijn mond. 'Geen ballroomdansen tenminste.'

'Hmmm.' Zacht streek ze met haar lippen tegen de zijne, legde haar handen op zijn schouders en duwde hem naar zijn kant van de auto. 'Gaat u voor, meneer Reynolds. Gaat u voor.'

Eenmaal thuis slopen ze naar binnen als een stel delinquenten dat te laat is voor de avondklok. Niet dat het belangrijk was. Sean logeerde bij een vriendje, dus ze hadden het huis voor zichzelf.

Abby voelde zich beter dan in jaren toen ze achter John aan de woonkamer binnenliep. 'Goed, waar is de balzaal voor deze dans?'

'Ik zal het u laten zien, mevrouw Reynolds.' Hij pakte haar hand en nam haar mee de trap op naar hun kamer. 'Komt u maar.'

★

Het uur dat volgde, was heerlijker dan Abby had durven dromen. Ze had van andere vrouwen gehoord dat de lichamelijke intimiteit nooit meer helemaal hetzelfde werd na wankele tijden in hun huwelijk. Vooral als er een andere vrouw in het spel was geweest.

Maar vanaf het moment dat John en zij in de uren na de bruiloft van Nicole op de aanlegsteiger achter hun huis hadden gestaan en erkend hadden dat het onmogelijk was om bij elkaar weg te gaan, was Abby weer helemaal opnieuw verliefd geworden op haar man. Het was echt een wonder. Hun relatie was nu een intense, passionele bevrijding van alle gevoelens die ze die drie vreselijke jaren begraven hadden.

Nu gebruikten ze hun intieme momenten om het met elkaar goed te maken. De blijdschap te vieren om de herontdekking van iets wat bijna voorgoed verloren was gegaan. Ondanks de conventionele opvatting dat ze op dit gebied van hun relatie moeite zouden hebben en dat er een jaar of meer voor nodig was om weer op te bouwen wat die slechte jaren hun hadden gekost.

Abby vertrouwde John volkomen. En hij vertrouwde haar.

Voordat ze in slaap vielen, rolde John op zijn zij en keek haar aan. 'Heb ik je pas nog verteld...'

Het maanlicht speelde op zijn gezicht en hij glimlachte. 'Ja... je hebt het me verteld.'

'Weet je wat ik vanavond het leukste vond?'

Ze kroop op haar zij zodat ze met hun gezichten naar elkaar toe lagen. 'Het dansen?'

Hij lachte zachtjes. 'Tuurlijk. Maar weet je wat nog meer?'

'Nee?'

'Ik heb helemaal niet meer aan coachen gedacht. Al was het maar een avondje.'

Ze voelde een steek van pijn in haar hart. 'Is het zo erg?'

'Erger.' Zijn glimlach stierf weg. Daarvoor in de plaats kwam een blik die eerder bedroefd was dan gefrustreerd. 'Weet je wat ik gisteren in de krant heb gelezen?'

'Wat dan?'

'De ouders van een basketbalspeler op een middelbare school eisen zeven miljoen dollar schadevergoeding van zijn coach.'

'Zeven miljoen?' Abby steunde met haar ellebogen in het kussen. 'Waarvóór?'

'Omdat hij die jongen de kans ontnomen heeft op een professionele basketballoopbaan.'

'Wat?' Ze begreep het verhaal niet. 'Hoezo is dat de schuld van de coach?'

John zuchtte. 'Omdat de coach hem bij de junioren liet zitten in plaats van in het schoolteam.'

Abby hapte naar adem. 'Dat meen je toch niet?'

'Jawel.' John lachte zo droevig dat het Abby's hart haast brak. 'Ik meen het. Zo ver is het gekomen, Abby. Soms denk ik dat ik het seizoen niet zal overleven.'

'Wat erg.' Ze verschoof haar elleboog en liet haar wang op het kussen rusten. 'Ik wou dat ik iets kon doen.'

'Ik moet aldoor aan die brief denken. Dat de ouders van een van mijn spelers me zo graag ontslagen willen zien dat ze tot regioniveau gaan om het gedaan te krijgen.' Hij rolde zich weer op zijn rug. 'Zou ik spelers laten drinken en straatracen? Kennen ze me dan helemaal niet? Stellen ze het niet op prijs wat ik voor die school heb gedaan sinds ik er werk?'

De pijn in Abby's hart strekte zich uit tot haar ziel. Hoe haalden ze het toch in hun hoofd om het karakter van deze man aan te vallen? Als het kon, zou ze de school binnenwandelen, het openbare omroepsysteem in handen nemen en de hele school vertellen dat coach Reynolds nooit iets onwettigs zou doen als het om zijn spelers ging. Ze zou eisen dat ze zijn inspanningen erkenden en hem behandelden met het respect en de dankbaarheid die hij verdiende.

Maar dat kon ze niet doen.

Ze kon niet eens een brief schrijven namens hem, al zou ze dat nog zo graag willen. 'Ik kan maar één ding doen, John. Maar dat is meteen het belangrijkste van alles.'

'Bidden?' Hij draaide zijn hoofd weer naar haar toe.

'Precies.' Ze haalde haar vingertoppen door zijn haar. 'Bidden dat God laat zien hoeveel de kinderen nog van je houden, de kinderen die voor geen enkele andere coach wilden spelen.'

'Goed.' Hij glimlachte en voor het eerst sinds hij het onderwerp aangesneden had, ontspanden zijn trekken. 'Bid jij maar. Alleen door jouw gebeden heb ik hier nog zo lang gecoacht.'

'Weet je wat ik denk?' Ze legde haar hoofd op Johns schouder en kroop lekker dicht tegen hem aan.

'Dat mijn seizoen mislukt?'

'Nee.' Ze legde haar hand op zijn hart. 'Ik denk dat er iets heel groots staat te gebeuren.'

'Zoals drie wedstrijden achter elkaar winnen?'

'Nee, ook niet.' Abby lachte gesmoord. 'Iets spiritueels. Dat God een grote daad zal doen. Misschien is het seizoen daarom zo slecht begonnen. Misschien zien we op dit moment niet hoe alle stukjes in elkaar passen. Maar binnenkort misschien wel. Snap je?'

John zweeg.

'Ben je nog wakker?'

'Ja. Ik lag alleen te denken.' Zijn borst ging omhoog toen hij diep ademhaalde. 'Dat was ik vergeten.'

'Dat God een plan heeft?'

'Hmm.' Hij aarzelde. 'Dat moet het zijn.'

'Ja. En wat het ook is, het wordt reusachtig.'

'Hoe weet je dat?'

'Ik voel het gewoon.'

'O. Goed.' John begon langzamer te ademen en zijn woorden liepen in elkaar over zoals zo vaak vlak voordat hij in slaap viel. 'Het spijt me.'

'Wat?'

'Dat ik vanavond op je voeten heb getrapt.'

'Dat geeft niet. Volgende week hebben we weer les.'

'Ik houd van je, Abby. Trusten.'

'Welterusten… Ik houd ook van jou.'

Ze viel in slaap met haar hoofd op Johns schouder en haar geest gevuld met prettige herinneringen aan de avond.

En met het toenemende gevoel dat God iets groots van plan was op Marion High School. Iets wat met football te maken had en met ouders en heel in het bijzonder met haar fantastische echtgenoot.

Coach John Reynolds.

Zes

Nicole was bang.

Er was geen ander woord voor. Na het wervelwindweekend met Kade thuis was ze niet gewoon moe; ze was uitgeput. Te uitgeput. Nu was het woensdag en Matt en zij waren van plan om uit eten te gaan. Maar toen Nicole een spijkerbroek en een trui had aangetrokken, voelden haar armen en benen zwaar als lood. Elke beweging was een kolossale inspanning.

Griep kon het niet zijn. Ze had geen koorts, ze hoestte niet en haar ingewanden waren niet van streek. Ze trok de rits omhoog en bestudeerde zichzelf in de badkamerspiegel. Bleek… asgrauw, zelfs. Haar zomerse bruine kleur was weliswaar vervaagd, maar Nicole kon zich niet herinneren dat haar gezicht ooit zo wit had gezien.

Ze zuchtte. Misschien begonnen de gebeurtenissen van de afgelopen maanden eindelijk hun tol te eisen. Na de huwelijksreis waren ze thuisgekomen en had Matt meteen gesolliciteerd naar een functie bij het Openbaar Ministerie. Nu hij aangenomen was, zat Nicole tot over haar hoofd in de studie en probeerde ze een evenwicht te vinden tussen het huishouden en de eisen die aan een afstudeerder werden gesteld.

Daarbovenop kwamen de voortdurende discussies met Matt over de ophanden zijnde zendingsreis van een jaar die zijn ouders gingen maken. En dan was er nog haar jongere broer Kade.

Toen hij vorige week thuis was, was hij anders geweest. Ouder misschien, stiller. Hij hoopte speeltijd te krijgen aan de Universiteit van Iowa en hij had veel aan zijn hoofd. Die zondagavond was hij bij Matt en Nicole in de flat langsgekomen. Ze hadden er tot drie uur 's nachts over zitten praten of het een vergissing van hem was geweest om de beurs in Iowa aan te nemen terwijl hij liever dichter bij huis in Illinois zou spelen.

'Het is te ver weg,' had Kade gezegd toen ze al een uur zaten te praten. Matt was al vroeg naar bed gegaan en had Nicole en Kade in de woonkamer achtergelaten. Kade had zijn handen omhoog gegooid. 'Ik heb het gevoel of ik op een andere planeet leef.' Hij zat op de grond met zijn rug tegen de muur.

'Het is maar een dag rijden hiervandaan.' Nicole wilde niet dat hij uit Iowa vertrok alleen omdat hij heimwee had. 'Het eerste semester is altijd moeilijk.'

'Ja, maar pap is altijd mijn coach geweest, Nick.' Hij had zijn knieën opgetrokken en zijn benen gespreid, zoals hij altijd zat als ze door de jaren heen dit soort gesprekken hadden gevoerd. 'Ik zou hem graag op de tribune willen zien zitten, snap je?' Hij liet zijn onderarmen rusten op zijn knieën. 'Dit was het eerste weekend dat mam en hij naar een wedstrijd zijn geweest.'

Nicole begreep het. 'Waarom heb je Illinois niet eerder overwogen? Ze hebben je toch een brief gestuurd?'

'Ja.' Kade fronste. 'Een heleboel brieven. Ik dacht dat het leuk was om van huis te zijn.'

'Dat komt misschien nog. Je bent er pas twee maanden.'

'Weet ik… maar nu wil ik hier zijn. Snap je dat nou?'

Zo draaide het gesprek in kringetjes rond tot Nicole alleen nog maar kon zeggen wat hij wilde horen. 'Overplaatsing aanvragen dan.' Ze lachte vermoeid. 'We zouden je graag dichterbij hebben, maatje. Dan konden we elk weekend zulke gesprekken voeren.'

Kade grinnikte. 'Net als vroeger.'

'Precies. Net als vroeger.'

Herinneringen aan die avond vervaagden en Nicole keek nog eens in de spiegel. De ochtend na hun late gesprek had ze om acht uur college gehad. Sindsdien was elk uur van de dag en de avond vol gepland. Geen wonder dat ze moe was. Haar lichaam had moeite om het bij te houden.

Tenzij…

Nicole slikte moeilijk en wendde zich van de spiegel af. Ze spoot parfum in haar hals. *Niet aan denken… het kan niet.* Maar haar hersenen weigerden van onderwerp te veranderen. Vooral in het licht van één herinnering die niet wilde wijken.

Het was drie weken na hun huwelijksreis gebeurd. Ze hadden afgesproken drie of vier jaar te wachten met kinderen, dus anticonceptie was noodzakelijk. Door te wachten kon Nicole haar studie afmaken en een baan zoeken in het onderwijs. Ze zou twee jaar voor de klas staan en dan tien jaar ophouden met werken om kinderen te krijgen. Als de kinderen op school zaten, zou ze weer les gaan geven. Dan kon ze na school bij hen zijn en hoefde ze niets te missen van de tijd dat ze thuis waren.

Dat was tenminste het tienjarenplan. En ze waren van plan geweest het tot op de letter te volgen. Wat betekende dat ze heel voorzichtig moesten zijn. Niet alleen vanwege het tienjarenplan, maar vanwege iets anders. Iets wat ze aan niemand had willen vertellen. Iets wat ze zelfs voor zichzelf niet onder woorden kon brengen.

Ze hadden het over de pil gehad, maar Nicole was ongerust over de bijwerkingen. Uiteindelijk hadden ze besloten dan maar condooms te gebruiken.

'Op school heb je natuurlijk over condooms gehoord,' zei de dokter tegen Nicole toen ze vlak voor haar trouwdag voor onderzoek bij hem was.

'Inderdaad. Het is toch een van de veiligste manieren om zwangerschap te voorkomen?'

De dokter lachte. 'Niet bepaald.' Hij gaf haar een scheef lachje. 'Elke maand komt er wel iemand zwanger op mijn spreekuur van wie de partner een condoom heeft gebruikt.'

Het had Nicole verbaasd, maar ze had gedacht dat de dokter overdreef. Natuurlijk werkten condooms, anders werden ze niet verkocht.

Maar er was die ene keer…

Een paar weken na hun huwelijksreis was Matt 's avonds laat na een vrijpartij uit de badkamer gekomen met een vreemde blik op zijn gezicht.

'Wat is er?' Nicole had rechtop in bed gezeten, met het laken over zich heen getrokken.

'Ik geloof dat het gescheurd is.' Matt haalde zijn vingers door zijn haar en schudde zijn hoofd. 'Ik dacht dat dat alleen in de film gebeurde.'

Er spoelde een golf van ontzetting over Nicole heen, die weer verdween. Het kon niet gescheurd zijn. 'Misschien leek het alleen maar zo.'

Matt stapte weer in bed. 'Laten we het hopen.'

Het was nu tien weken later en om de paar uur moest Nicole aan dat gesprek denken. Niet alleen omdat ze vermoeider was dan anders, maar omdat ze na haar bruiloft niet meer ongesteld was geweest.

Ze had haar moeder wel eens horen zeggen dat ze het vanaf het moment van de conceptie had geweten, zonder enige twijfel, dat een nieuw leven in haar was beginnen te groeien.

Nicole had naar zulke tekenen uitgekeken, maar er was niets geweest. Haar menstruatiecyclus was altijd al onregelmatig. Soms had ze drie maanden achter elkaar overgeslagen voordat het weer kwam. Dus er was eigenlijk geen reden om te denken dat ze in verwachting zou kunnen zijn.

Toch...?

De slaapkamerdeur ging open en Nicole schrok op. Matt stak zijn hoofd om de hoek. 'Klaar?'

'Ja, hoor.' Ze glimlachte gedwongen. 'Ik kom eraan.'

Ze was zwijgzaam onder het eten en toen Matt klaar was, schoof hij zijn bord opzij en keek haar aan. 'Goed, Nick. Wat is er aan de hand?'

'Niks.' Haar antwoord kwam te snel. Ze staarde naar haar bord. Haar cheeseburger was nog voor meer dan de helft onaangeroerd. Ze keek op. 'Alles is in orde.'

'Niet waar. Je slaapt 's morgens uit en je gaat vroeg naar bed. Je geeuwt aldoor en je hebt amper eetlust.' Matts stem klonk vriendelijk, maar bezorgd. 'Ik maak me zorgen over je.'

Ze sloeg haar ogen weer neer. Ze stak haar vork in het bergje bonen naast de burger. Het eten zag er oudbakken en onaantrekkelijk uit. Ze zuchtte. Het was tijd. Als ze een huwelijk wilden opbouwen met vertrouwen en intimiteit, mocht ze haar vrees geen minuut langer voor hem verzwijgen.

'Goed.' Ze haalde diep adem en keek hem aan. 'Ik denk dat ik misschien zwanger ben.'

Ze had verwacht dat hij geschokt en ontstemd zou zijn. Een baby betekende per slot van rekening een streep door hun plannen.

Maar Matts gezicht lichtte vrolijk op. 'Nicole? Meen je dat?'

'Matt.' Ze boog haar hoofd zodat de mensen aan de andere tafels haar niet konden verstaan. 'Het is te snel. Je *kunt* er niet blij mee zijn.'

Even bleef zijn gezicht zonder uitdrukking, toen lachte hij zacht. 'Ja, hoor. Baby's zijn een wonder, schat. Wanneer ze ook komen.'

De moed zonk haar in de schoenen. Zijn enthousiasme maakte de mogelijkheid ineens een stuk reëler. Stel dat ze echt zwanger was? Hoe kon ze moeder zijn als ze haar studie niet had afgemaakt? En haar ergste angsten durfde ze niet eens aan zichzelf toe te geven. Ze werd overspoeld door de vragen die op haar afkwamen, tot ze Matts handen op de hare voelden.

'Lieverd, ik snap het niet. Ben je van streek omdat je denkt dat je misschien zwanger bent?'

'Ja!' Nicole voelde de tranen prikken. 'We wilden vier jaar wachten, weet je nog?'

'Tja.' Hij leunde achterover. 'Maar als je nu zwanger bent, heeft het geen zin om van streek te zijn. God zal ons helpen.' Hij nam haar hand in de zijne. 'Bovendien, misschien is het niet zo. We hebben opgepast.'

'Ja, maar weet je nog die ene avond? Toen je dacht dat het gescheurd was?'

Er verscheen een veelzeggende blik in Matts ogen. 'Denk je dat het toen...'

'Misschien. De dokter vertelde dat het zo vaak gebeurt.' Ze liet haar hoofd even achterover hangen en keek hem toen weer aan. Er gleden twee tranen over haar wangen. 'Ik geloofde hem niet.'

'Oké.' Matt pakte haar hand. 'Maar schat, je hebt altijd gezegd dat je popelt om moeder te worden. Dus waarom... huil je nou? Ik bedoel, we kunnen de plannen toch aanpassen?'

'Het zal wel.'

'Nou... waarom dan die tranen, schat? Ik snap het niet.'

Nicole kon wel over de tafel klimmen om hem te knuffelen. Hij was zo'n goeie vent, zo vol liefde voor haar en het toekomstige gezin. Ze zette zich schrap en besloot hem te vertellen waar ze bang voor was. De angst die haar 's nachts wakker hield, al had ze haar slaap hard nodig. 'Ik denk dat ik bang ben.'

'Waarvoor?'

Nicole leunde achterover en nam een slok water. 'Weet je nog, toen we plannen aan het maken waren voor de bruiloft?'

'Natuurlijk.' Matt keek haar onderzoekend aan, met zijn lichaam half over de tafel geleund om zich naar haar toe te buigen.

'Er was iets mis met het huwelijk van mijn ouders.' Nicole gaf Matts vingers een zacht kneepje. 'Ik geloof dat ik je verteld heb dat ik me zorgen over hen maakte.'

'Ja. Je hebt voor hen gebeden en toen we ons op de avond van onze bruiloft bij het hotel inschreven, voelde je dat God je gebeden had verhoord. Dat alles goed zou komen.'

Nicole knikte. 'Ik heb er sindsdien veel aan gedacht en ik heb vastgesteld dat... hun huwelijk misschien wel niet is wat het lijkt. Snap je?'

'Oké.' Matt zag er zo verloren uit als een kind alleen in de dierentuin. 'Dus...'

'Dus ik denk dat ik het weet.'

'Wat weet?'

Nicole staarde hem aan. 'De reden waarom mijn ouders niet zo gelukkig zijn als ik wel dacht.'

Matt knipperde met zijn ogen. 'Een maand geleden zei je nog tegen hen dat ze een pasgetrouwd stel leken.'

'Dat was voordat ik de puzzel in elkaar gezet had. Het was iets wat je moeder op een avond onder het eten zei.' Nicole liet zijn vingers los en leunde achterover. Alsof hij het kon begrijpen. 'Ik denk dat ik nu weet wat het probleem is.'

'En…?'

'Ik was een wittebroodsbaby, weet je nog?' Kon Matt het niet begrijpen? Met moeite bewaarde ze haar geduld. 'Ze hebben te vroeg kinderen gekregen.'

'Sorry, Nick.' Nu ging Matt achterover zitten en hij sloeg zijn armen over elkaar. 'Ik snap het niet.'

'Wat valt er nou aan te snappen?' Nicole stak vragend haar handen op. 'Mijn ouders hebben nooit die cruciale jaren gehad, de jaren waarin ze samen een band hadden kunnen smeden en bouwen aan hun liefde.'

Matt bleef haar even aankijken. Toen stond hij op, liep om de tafel heen en gleed naast haar op de bank. Hij legde zijn arm om haar schouders en trok haar tegen zich aan. 'Ik heb sterk het gevoel dat je het mis hebt, Nicole. Je ouders houden heel veel van elkaar. Dat ze vroeg in hun huwelijk kinderen hebben gekregen, heeft hun geen kwaad gedaan. Toen niet en nu niet.'

De nabijheid van haar echtgenoot, de warme beschutting van zijn arm om haar heen, maakte alles beter. Haar afweer viel als herfstbladeren van haar af. Misschien had Matt gelijk, maar Nicole had er aldoor aan moeten denken sinds ze terug waren van hun huwelijksreis. 'Dus jij denkt niet dat het hen kwaad heeft gedaan?'

'Nee.' Hij gaf haar een kus op haar wang en streek haar haar glad achter haar oren. 'Maar als je er ongerust over bent, waarom vraag je het dan niet aan je moeder? Ze zal het je echt wel vertellen.'

Aan haar moeder vragen? Waarom had Nicole daar niet aan gedacht? Het kon geen kwaad om er rechtuit naar te vragen, in plaats van te speculeren over de problemen waarmee haar ouders vorig jaar hadden getobd. Ze verschoof op haar plaats om Matt in de ogen te kijken. 'Goed. Dat zal ik doen.'

'Zullen we dan nu de rekening betalen en een beetje gaan winkelen voordat we naar huis gaan? Volgens mij moeten we een kleinigheid kopen die niet tot morgen kan wachten.'

Nicoles hart was lichter dan in weken. Met God aan haar zijde en een echtgenoot als Matt kwam het allemaal goed.

'Wat dan?'

Hij grinnikte. 'Een zwangerschapstest.'

Zeven

De informatie was overal op internet te vinden.

Het onderzoek dat Abby voor haar artikel had gedaan, kon ze daarmee makkelijk aanvullen. Ze meldde zich aan en wachtte op de verbinding. Na het weekend met Kade had ze het zo druk gehad met het inhalen van haar achterstand dat ze pas laat die avond tijd had gehad om aan haar coachartikel te werken. Gisteravond had ze misschien een paar uur gehad, maar John had de computer nodig. Hij moest een nieuwe internetsite opzoeken waarop coaches tips en verdedigingstechnieken konden vinden. John had er van een van de andere coaches over gehoord.

Abby had geen bezwaar gehad. Ze had tijd in overvloed om het artikel in elkaar te zetten.

Het scherm kwam tot leven en een digitale stem kondigde aan: 'U hebt een nieuw e-mailbericht.'

Heel even dacht ze er weer aan hoe ze een jaar geleden naar die woorden had uitgekeken. Toen John en zij met grote snelheid recht op een echtscheiding afstevenden. Ze had toen bijna dagelijks e-mailcontact met een redacteur, een man die omgang met haar wilde hebben.

Als ze na Nicoles bruiloft Johns dagboek niet had gevonden, het niet had gelezen en te weten was gekomen hoe hij dacht over hun huwelijk en de fouten die hij had gemaakt, had ze hem misschien nooit vergeven. Dan had ze wellicht op ditzelfde moment een hevige relatie met de redacteur gehad.

Abby's maag draaide om als ze eraan dacht. Vlug zette ze de gedachte opzij. Tegenwoordig was haar e-mailverkeer bijna alleen zakelijk. Ze werkte voor verscheidene nieuwe tijdschriften en hield de relaties met redacteuren strikt zakelijk. Nu en dan was er een e-mail van een vriendin of iets wat een van de vrouwen van de kerk had doorgestuurd.

Maar dat was het wel zo'n beetje.

En hoewel John meer tijd achter de computer doorbracht, kreeg hij nooit e-mail. Hij surfte slechts over het net op zoek naar footballstrategieën en manoeuvres waar hij nog niet aan gedacht had. Nu en dan bekeek hij een site met te koop staande boerderijen en meldde hij Abby dat ze in het noorden van Montana een stuk land van veertig hectare konden kopen. Maar dat was maar een grapje, een manier om de spanning van het footballseizoen te verlichten.

Abby klikte de mailbox open en er verscheen onmiddellijk een lijst met mails. Er was meer dan anders en ze had even tijd nodig om de lijst door te nemen. Iets van een nieuw tijdschrift, drie van haar huidige redacteuren, en toen…

Haar hart stond stil.

De volgende e-mail op de lijst had als onderwerp: *Meer opwinding dan je je kunt voorstellen!* Hij was van iemand genaamd *Candy* op een website die *Sexyfun* heette.

Abby's hart gaf een harde bons en begon twee keer zo snel te slaan als anders. Haar ogen gleden snel over de lijst naar beneden en er waren nog vijf van zulke e-mails. Allemaal van meisjes op websites met soortgelijke namen als de eerste.

Haar hersenen schreeuwden dat het niet waar was. Het kon niet. Overal om je heen hoorde je over internetpornografie. John en zij hadden het fenomeen besproken, maar geen van beiden had precies begrepen wat er zo boeiend aan was. Het kon toch niet waar zijn dat John pornosites had bezocht? Hij had vaak op internet gezeten. Maar toch alleen om coachsites op te zoeken?

Er was maar één manier om erachter te komen.

Abby manoeuvreerde haar muis door een reeks klikken tot een lijst van websites op haar scherm verscheen. De laatste vijftig sites die op hun computer waren bezocht. De laatste drie hadden duidelijk met football te maken. Maar verder was de lijst afgrijselijk.

Namen van websites die Abby amper kon lezen, laat staan hardop uitspreken. Ze sloot haar ogen. *God, nee... Laat dit niet waar zijn. Alstublieft.* Na alles wat John en zij hadden meegemaakt, zo veel als hij van haar scheen te houden... kon hij toch niet aan porno beginnen. Het was onmogelijk.

Maar wat voor andere verklaring was er? Zij waren de enige twee mensen die internet gebruikten op deze computer, afgezien van Sean. En die gebruikte hem alleen voor zijn huiswerk. Abby ging terug in haar herinnering. Het was minstens een maand geleden dat Sean in de buurt van de computer was geweest.

Dus dat wilde zeggen...

'Nee, God! Ik kan het niet aan.' Ze sloeg haar handen voor haar gezicht. Het was al moeilijk genoeg geweest om met de fascinatie van haar man voor een andere vrouw af te rekenen. Maar dit?

U hebt ons door die tijd heen geholpen, God... dus waarom dit? Waarom nu?

Ze wachtte, maar er kwam geen geruststelling in haar ziel en er vielen haar geen teksten in. Alleen een afschuwelijk leeg gat in haar maag, een gat dat steeds groter werd.

Ze deed haar ogen open en keek naar de lijst. Misschien waren het geen pornosites. Misschien waren het coachsites met stomme namen. Ja, dat zou het zijn. Een dun waasje van transpiratie brak uit op Abby's neus en voorhoofd. Ze voelde zich licht in haar hoofd, wanhopig, met angst vervuld. Haar hart kon de schok niet aan, kon de lijst met websitenamen die haar aanstaarde niet verwerken.

Opnieuw was er was maar één manier om erachter te komen.

Ze koos de eerste, iets over naakte meisjes, en klikte op de link. *Laat het coachinformatie zijn... verdedigingsmanoeuvres... alles behalve...*

Een foto begon vorm te krijgen en Abby hapte naar adem. Ze vond direct het kruisje in de rechterbovenhoek en sloot het venster. Het waren geen speltechnieken, het was precies wat je op een website met die naam verwachtte te zien.

Porno.

In zijn verslagenheid en verdriet had John de late uurtjes op het internet gebruikt om zich een weg te klikken in een ranzige onderwereld van zonde. Boosheid bubbelde in Abby omhoog en vulde haar met een razende woede. *Hoe durft hij…*

Ze sloot de computer af en draaide haar computerstoel naar het donkere raam. De maan was die avond maar een schijfje, maar Abby staarde toch naar buiten. Wat dacht hij wel? Het was zo goed tussen hen gegaan, ze genoten van elkaar als vrienden en als minnaars. Hoe kon hij…

Toen viel haar een nieuwe gedachte in.

Misschien had hij daarom de laatste tijd zo genoten van hun lichamelijke liefde… misschien dacht hij helemaal niet aan Abby, maar aan die… die…

Een golf van misselijkheid kwam in haar omhoog en ze dacht dat ze moest overgeven. Hoe durfde hij boven te slapen alsof er niets aan de hand was, terwijl hij al die tijd dit vreselijke geheim voor haar verborg? En hoe kon haar lijf, haar liefde ooit de vergelijking doorstaan met de beelden op zijn computerscherm?

Het scala van emoties dat op haar afkwam, was haast te veel om te dragen. Verdriet… boosheid… spijt. Zij had hem per slot van rekening vertrouwd. Hem geloofd dat hij wilde zijn als de adelaar: sterk aan haar zijde tot de dood hen scheidde. Waarom ter wereld begon hij dan met pornosites te experimenteren? Vooral als hij van vrienden van hen wist hoe verslavend en verwoestend dat kon zijn?

Meer dan een uur bleef Abby daar zitten, met een knoop in haar maag, tot ze eindelijk naar boven ging en haar man bekeek. Vorig jaar had ze moeiteloos vastgesteld dat John belangstelling had voor een andere vrouw. Zijn afstandelijkheid, de uren dat hij weg was van huis, de vreemde telefoontjes. Alle tekenen waren aanwezig geweest. Maar dit… dit pornogedoe? Hij had het meesterlijk verborgen. Abby knipperde in het donker met haar ogen, misselijk van de onschuld op zijn gezicht.

Ze ging op de uiterste rand van het bed liggen, draaide haar rug naar hem toe en viel in slaap. Maar niet voordat twee simpele gedachten haar hoofd vulden…

Hoe was het nu mogelijk om bij elkaar te blijven?

En vooral, waarom was zij niet genoeg voor hem geweest?

★

Vrijdag was er een uitwedstrijd en Johns Eagles wonnen met een fieldgoal in de laatste minuut. Er gingen geruchten rond over de spelers die dronken en deelnamen aan straatraces. Het was zo erg dat John de ouders bijna over hem kon horen fluisteren.

'Coach Reynolds is niet de man die we dachten…'

'We moeten een man hebben met meer moraal en karakter dan hij…'

Natuurlijk was volkomen duidelijk wat de echte reden was. De Eagles hadden maar drie wedstrijden gewonnen. Een armzalige prestatie, gezien de hoop die iedereen voor dit team had gehad. Winnen snoerde de mond van de critici. Verliezen maakte dat je mocht schieten op de coach.

De tribunes zaten stampvol met ouders die heel andere beslissingen genomen zouden hebben. Mensen van wie de zoons niet veel speelden, waren het ergst. De meesten dachten dat het team zou winnen als hun zoons maar meededen. Degenen van wie de zoons wel speelden, hadden een ander antwoord klaar: een slechte coach.

Hoe dan ook, de slechte start van dit seizoen kwam op Johns bordje te liggen.

Toen John die avond in de teambus stapte om terug te gaan naar Marion voelde hij zich maar weinig opgelucht door de overwinning. Jake Daniels had zijn hoofd niet bij de wedstrijd gehad, hoe John ook probeerde om hem te inspireren. John had Jakes nieuwe Integra NSX gezien. De hele school praatte erover.

Het gerucht ging dat Jake de bedoeling had om ermee te gaan racen zodra het footballseizoen afgelopen was.

John staarde knarsetandend uit het vuile raam van de bus. Wat bezielde Jakes vader om zo'n auto voor die jongen te kopen? Hoe moest een tiener zich concentreren op zijn studie en zijn rol als quarterback als er een raceauto op het parkeerterrein stond?

Bovendien waren Jake en Casey en nog enkele spelers Nathan Pike en zijn *gothic* vrienden erger gaan pesten. John had het bestuur verteld over Nathans afschuwelijke woorden: *dood aan sporters.* Kennelijk had de directeur Nathan bij zich laten komen om hem te ondervragen. Nathan had zich kalm en onverschillig gedragen.

'Dat is een liedje, man,' had hij hoofdschuddend tegen de directeur gezegd. 'Jullie snappen er ook niks van.'

De directeur kon niet anders doen dan Nathan geloven en hem een waarschuwing geven. Liedje of niet, hij hoorde geen doodsbedreigingen op zijn schrijfblok te noteren. Nathan stemde in en het voorval was gepasseerd. Wat het bestuur betreft tenminste.

De werkelijkheid was een heel ander verhaal. Nathan en zijn duistere vrienden waren nog haatdragender geworden en hadden nog meer afstand genomen. Tegelijkertijd waren de wrede, arrogante opmerkingen van Jake en Casey juist frequenter voorgekomen. Soms was er zoveel spanning tussen de groepen dat John er zeker van was dat de situatie tot een uitbarsting zou komen.

Hij had hij Jake en Casey verscheidene keren apart genomen en er iets van gezegd, maar het antwoord was altijd hetzelfde: 'Het was maar een geintje, coach.'

Hun ouders schenen zich er niet om te bekommeren dat hun zoons jongens als Nathan Pike treiterden. Die hadden het te druk met de winst-verliessituatie van de Eagles, en met fluisteren en roddelen en Johns ontslag te eisen, en ze vulden de tribunes met genoeg negatieve energie om de rest van het seizoen om zeep te helpen.

Geen wonder dat Abby vanavond niet mee had gewild.

Tot nu toe had ze sinds het begin van het seizoen geen wedstrijd overgeslagen. John was haastig naar huis gesjeesd, had zijn sporttas gepakt en was op weg gegaan naar de wedstrijd.

'Je gaat toch mee?' Hij wilde haar een snelle kus op de lippen drukken, maar op het laatste moment wendde ze haar gezicht af en de kus kwam op haar wang terecht. John had het een vreemd gebaar gevonden, maar geen tijd om erbij stil te staan. Hij moest de bus halen.

'Vanavond niet.' Ze was afwezig geweest. Eigenlijk al sinds donderdagochtend. Niet bepaald boos. Maar... afstandelijk.

De busrit leek langer te duren dan anders en John leunde achterover in zijn stoel. Wat zat haar eigenlijk dwars? Hij dacht een poosje na en ineens viel het hem in. Het moest haar tijdschriftartikel zijn. Soms werd ze zwijgzaam vlak voor de deadline voor een groot stuk. Hij had ontdekt dat de beste oplossing was om haar met rust te laten. Als hij haar zoveel mogelijk tijd en ruimte gaf om haar werk klaar te krijgen, kwam het goed.

Toch had hij haar vanavond gemist. Het was altijd prettiger coachen langs de zijlijn als Abby ergens achter hem op de tribune zat. Iedereen mocht over hem klagen, maar Abby zou juichen. En zeker vanavond, nu ze een overwinning hadden behaald.

John rekte zich uit. Genoeg negatieve gedachten. Jake Daniels... Nathan Pike... de klagende ouders. Het hoorde slechts bij een voorbijgaand seizoen. Hij zou bidden voor de jongens en uitkijken naar gelegenheden om hen te bereiken. Maar hij leerde onderhand wel om alles van Marion High achter zich te laten als zijn werk voor de dag er opzat.

Het leven was te kort om je problemen mee naar huis te nemen. Vooral nu het zo ongelooflijk goed ging met Abby.

Het was bijna elf uur toen hij het huis binnenkwam. Er brandde geen licht. Abby was zeker klaar met schrijven en naar bed gegaan. John deed de deur achter zich dicht en zette drie stappen. Toen hoorde hij haar stem.

'John… ik zit in de kamer.'

Hij tuurde in het donker en knipte het licht in de hal aan. 'Abby? Wat doe je?'

'Ik bid.' Ze zweeg even. 'Kom je even hier? We moeten praten.'

Hij wist niet of hij vereerd of ongerust moest zijn. Ze had kennelijk zitten wachten tot hij thuiskwam, met de bedoeling met hem te praten. Maar er was niets luchtigs in haar toon. Hij zette zijn tas neer en ging in de stoel tegenover haar zitten. 'Wat is er?'

'Dit.' Met de bewegingen van een oude vrouw raapte Abby een stuk papier op van de vloer. 'Ik heb het een paar dagen geleden gevonden, maar ik had tijd nodig om te bedenken hoe ik erover moest beginnen.'

Waarover beginnen? Waar had ze het over? Hij nam het papier aan en staarde er bij het schemerige licht vanuit de hal naar. Onmiddellijk zag hij wat het was en zijn maag draaide om.

'Waar komt dit vandaan?' Hij bracht het vel papier dichter naar zijn gezicht zodat hij het goed kon lezen.

Het was een lijst van pornografische websites. De ene na de andere, wel zo'n twintig in totaal. Bovenaan het blad stond hun e-mailadres. Ineens begreep hij het. Abby zat hier in het donker te wachten omdat ze deze lijst op het internetlog van hun computer had gevonden en een verklaring wenste.

De hele tijd dat hij de lijst had zitten bekijken, had Abby niets gezegd. Nu keek John met bonzend hart naar haar op. 'Heb je dit van *onze* computer gehaald?'

'Ja.' Ze had haar armen strak om haar middel geslagen. 'Naast mij ben jij de enige die de computer gebruikt, John.' Haar stem begaf het. 'Het is duidelijk dat we moeten praten.'

Hij had zin om tegen haar te schreeuwen. Dacht ze nu echt dat hij in zijn vrije tijd pornosites bezocht? Dat hij, met alles wat er op school en met het team aan de hand was, zo stom zou zijn om zich met internetvuiligheid bezig te houden? Terwijl hij was getrouwd met de enige vrouw van wie hij ooit had gehouden?

Het was een ongehoord idee.

'Denk je dat *ik* die sites heb bezocht?' Hij plantte zijn vingertoppen tegen zijn borst.

'Wat moet ik anders denken?'

John verfrommelde het papier en gooide het tegen de muur. Toen stond hij op en liep met grote stappen heen en weer. 'Abby, ben je helemaal *gek* geworden? Ik heb van mijn leven nog nooit een pornosite bekeken.' Zijn toon was scherper dan zijn woorden. 'Hoe kun je zoiets denken?'

'Lieg niet tegen me, John.' Ze was duidelijk net zo boos als hij, maar ze bleef in haar stoel zitten. 'Je hebt vaker dan anders op internet gezeten en altijd 's avonds laat. Waarom?'

Hij staarde haar verbijsterd aan. 'Je twijfelt echt aan me, hè? Na alles wat we hebben meegemaakt, vertrouw je me nog steeds niet.'

'Ik vertrouwde je *wel*.' Ze dempte haar stem, maar haar felheid bleef. 'Maar drie jaar geleden vertrouwde ik je ook. Toen Charlene en jij elke ochtend samen doorbrachten.'

Hij voelde het bloed uit zijn gezicht wegtrekken. 'Dat is niet eerlijk, Abby, dat weet je best.' VooROvergebogen vuurde John de woorden op haar af. 'Toen zaten we *allebei* fout, maar die tijd ligt achter ons. Weet je nog?'

'Dat dacht ik ook.' De vechtlust was uit haar stem verdwenen. 'Totdat ik die lijst vond.'

Ze had hem evengoed een klap in zijn gezicht kunnen geven. Bezeerd en boos en niet zeker over wat hij moest zeggen, viel John achterover in de stoel en stopte zijn hoofd in zijn handen. 'Je kent me niets beter dan de ouders van mijn spelers.'

Abby zweeg en een ogenblik zei geen van beiden iets.

Er moest een verklaring zijn voor de sites. Abby had ze duidelijk niet opgezocht, maar hij evenmin. En hoe durfde ze hem te beschuldigen, nadat hij ontkend had er iets mee te maken te hebben.

God, geef me de juiste woorden… hoe kan Abby hierin aan me twijfelen?

DE LIEFDE LAAT ZICH NIET BOOS MAKEN…

68

Het heilige antwoord flitste door zijn geest en nam de scherpte van zijn woede weg. Zijn schouders zakten af en hij schudde zijn hoofd. Natuurlijk geloofde Abby hem niet. Na wat hij met Charlene had gehad… de leugens die hij Abby op de mouw had gespeld toen hun huwelijk dreigde te mislukken…

Voor het eerst sinds hun verzoening besefte John iets wat hij nog niet begrepen had.

Het zou jaren duren voordat ze zich allebei weer volkomen veilig voelden. Hoe goed het tussen hen ook ging. De zonde had altijd gevolgen. Abby's twijfels over hem op dit moment hoorden daarbij.

Zij verbrak als eerste de stilte. 'Ga je nog iets zeggen? Ik loop hier al twee dagen mee rond en ik vraag me af waarom ik niet genoeg voor je ben.' Ze begon te huilen. Geen boze snikken of onbeheerst jammeren, maar kleine, geluidloze kreetjes die zijn hart beklemden.

John liet zich op de grond vallen en kroop op zijn knieën naar haar toe. 'Abby…' Zijn stem klonk kalm en rustig nu. Hij tilde haar kin op zodat ze hem aan moest kijken. 'Ik beloof je met alles wat ik in me heb, dat ik dit niet heb gedaan. Ik heb nog nooit een pornosite bekeken. Nog nooit.'

Ze snufte en veegde met de rug van haar hand over haar wangen. Ze zei niets, maar John zag het in haar ogen. Twijfel… angst… ongerustheid. Ze dacht dat het opnieuw ging gebeuren, dat hun huwelijk uit elkaar viel.

God… geef me alstublieft wijsheid. Er moet een antwoord zijn.

Er gingen twee seconden voorbij en nog één, en ineens wist hij het antwoord. De verklaring gaf hem evenveel pijn als opluchting. De verklaring zou Abby tevredenstellen, maar liet hen achter met een probleem dat geen van beiden had voorzien.

'Weet je het niet meer?' Ze keken elkaar recht in de ogen. 'Kade is hier vorig weekend geweest. Hij is tot en met maandagmiddag gebleven.'

Het duurde even voordat het tot haar doordrong.

John zag haar gezichtsuitdrukking veranderen. Als smeltende was verzachtte haar gezicht en haar boosheid viel weg. Daarvoor in de plaats kwam droefheid en schuldgevoel, zo rauw dat het pijnlijk was om naar te kijken. Er ging bijna een minuut voorbij voordat Abby haar mond opendeed. 'Kade?'

'Hij was hier. Ik weet niet zeker of hij op de computer heeft gezeten, maar het moet wel. Want…' hij keek haar recht aan, 'ik heb alleen coachsites bezocht. Ik heb er drie gevonden.'

Abby staarde afwezig voor zich uit in het donker. Na lange tijd richtte ze haar blik weer op John. 'Zondagavond was hij bij Nicole. Maar zaterdag… zaterdag was hij hier. Hij is pas na enen gaan slapen, want ik ben opgestaan en…'

John nam haar handen in de zijne. 'En wat?'

'Ik kwam naar beneden om water te drinken.' De tranen sprongen haar in de ogen. 'Hij zat achter de computer. Het… het drong pas tot me door toen ik halverwege de trap was en de klikgeluiden hoorde. Dat was ik helemaal vergeten.'

John had niets te zeggen. Abby's twijfel had hem in de kern geraakt, maar hij kon niet ontkennen dat hij die verdiend had. Gelukkig was de gedachte aan internetporno nog nooit bij hem opgekomen. Toch kon hij moeilijk boos op Abby zijn omdat ze het voor mogelijk had gehouden.

'John…' Ze nam zijn gezicht in haar handen en keek hem onderzoekend in de ogen. 'Het spijt me zo. Hoe kon ik denken dat…'

'Stil maar, Abby. Niet doen.' Hij legde zijn hoofd tegen het hare en streelde haar haar. 'Het is mijn schuld. Als ik je in het verleden niet in de steek had gelaten, was het nooit in je opgekomen.'

'Maar het is zo gemeen van me.' Haar tranen werden snikken en ze klampte zich aan John vast alsof haar leven ervan afhing. 'Waarom heb ik het je niet eerst gevráágd? In plaats van je te beschuldigen?'

'Het is goed.' Zijn hart stroomde vol vrede. Dit was zijn Abby, vechtend voor hun huwelijk, vastbesloten het verleden los te laten. Wat hij had gezien toen hij thuiskwam, was simpelweg een tijdelijke vertrouwensbreuk, wat je kon verwachten in het licht van de beproevingen die ze hadden doorstaan. 'Natuurlijk zul je je twijfels hebben, schat. Het is voorbij. Laat het los.'

Abby ging rechtop zitten, haar ogen waren rood en haar ademhaling ging snel en stotend. 'Ik wil nooit meer aan je twijfelen, John Reynolds.' Ze snufte en schudde haar hoofd. Haar stem was nauwelijks meer dan een fluistering. 'Het geeft *wel*. Wat wij hebben is te kostbaar om te laten verknoeien door twijfels aan elkaar.'

Ze had gelijk. Zonder vertrouwen konden ze niet bouwen aan de liefde en blijdschap van de afgelopen maanden. Ineens vroeg hij zich af of dit de eerste keer was. 'Heb je al eerder twijfels gehad? Over mij, bedoel ik?'

'Nee, ik…' Ze begon haar hoofd te schudden, maar onderbrak zichzelf. 'Nou ja… soms.' Lange tijd zei ze niets. 'Ik vraag me denk ik wel af of er op een keer een nieuwe Charlene in beeld zal komen, of ik genoeg voor je zal zijn. Knap genoeg… slim genoeg. Jong genoeg.'

Als hij niet al op zijn knieën had gelegen, had haar bekentenis hem daar gebracht. 'Je bent *altijd* genoeg geweest. Het lag niet aan jou, het lag aan het leven. Tijd. Drukte. We hebben te veel tussen ons laten komen.'

'Weet ik.' Haar stem was nu kalmer en beheerster. 'Maar de Charlenes van deze wereld zullen er altijd blijven.'

'Nooit meer, Abby. Weet je nog van de adelaar?'

Abby hield haar hoofd schuin. 'Kades werkstuk voor Engels. Hij beschreef hoe de adelaar zijn hele leven bij zijn vrouwtje blijft… zich aan zijn partner vastklampt en zelfs liever met haar zijn dood tegemoet valt dan haar los te laten.'

'Precies.' John liet zijn vingers langs haar armen omhoog glijden naar haar wangen. 'Ik klamp me vast als nooit tevoren.' Hij boog zich naar haar toe en kuste haar voorhoofd. 'Ik laat je nooit los, niets kan daarvoor zorgen. Niets.'

Ze gleed naar het puntje van haar stoel en omhelsde hem. 'Ik geloof je. Sinds Nicoles bruiloft heb ik je geloofd. Die twijfels zijn gewoon... Ik weet niet, stom denk ik.'

Hij keek naar binnen in zijn eigen hart en wist dat er nog iets was. Als hij volkomen eerlijk wilde zijn, moest hij haar ook zijn gedachten vertellen. 'Je bent niet de enige.'

Ze maakte zich los om hem in de ogen te kijken. 'Niet de enige?'

'Met stomme twijfels.'

Er verscheen iets zachts in haar ogen. 'Echt waar?'

'Echt waar.' John sloeg zijn ogen even neer voordat hij weer opkeek. Het ging zo goed tussen Abby en hem, dat hij zijn vluchtige gedachten niet had willen opbiechten. Niet eens aan zichzelf. 'Ik vraag me wel eens af wat er gebeurd zou zijn als ik die avond van Nicoles bruiloft niet terug was gekomen. Ik bedoel, ik stond op het punt om voorgoed te vertrekken. Alleen God kon me de auto laten omdraaien en terugkomen.' Hij beet op zijn lip. 'Maar als ik niet was gekomen? Zou je dan met die redacteur uit zijn gegaan of een soort internetrelatie met hem hebben gehad?'

'Ik had je nooit moeten laten gaan.' Ze streelde met haar vingers door zijn haar, haar ogen straalden. 'Dan hoefde je je dat niet af te vragen.'

'Nu maak ik me geen zorgen over je. Alleen over het verleden en hoe het was gelopen als ik niet was teruggekomen.'

Abby liet haar hoofd tegen het zijne rusten en ze hielden elkaar vast. Een hele tijd later liet Abby zich weer achterover in haar stoel vallen. 'Maar we zitten nog steeds met een probleem, hè?'

John kon haar gedachten nog net zo makkelijk lezen als toen ze tieners waren. 'Kade?'

'Kade.' Ze vernauwde haar ogen, niet zozeer boos als wel verward. 'Waarom doet hij zoiets, John? Zo hebben we hem niet opgevoed. Die vuiligheid zal het leven uit hem knijpen.'

'Ik zal met hem praten.'

'Door de telefoon? En als hij het ontkent?'

Ze had gelijk. Dit vroeg om meer dan een telefoongesprek. 'De tweede week van november hebben ze vrij. Laten we hem naar huis laten vliegen. Dan zal ik met hem praten.'

'En als hij verslaafd is? Dat gebeurt zo vaak.' Abby aarzelde. 'Ik wou dat we niet hoefden te wachten.'

'Hoeft ook niet.' John nam haar handen weer in de zijne en vouwde ze. 'We kunnen op dit moment iets doen.'

Met hun harten en handen verbonden, bogen ze hun hoofd en baden voor hun oudste zoon. Dat hij eerlijk zou zijn over de internetsites die hij had bekeken. Dat hij bereid zou zijn om het onderwerp met John te bespreken.

En dat ze samen het probleem uit de wereld konden helpen. Voordat het te laat was.

Acht

Parmantige Paula schopte hen er vast en zeker uit.

Abby zag het op het moment dat ze Jo en Denny op de drempel van de gymzaal zag staan. Het was de eerste zaterdag van november en Abby had Nicoles schoonfamilie uitgenodigd, alsof het voorlopig niet hilarisch genoeg was dat John op haar voeten danste. Ze hadden bij de ingang afgesproken.

Abby had een jurk aan en John een nette broek en een kaki overhemd. Zondagse kleren. Het was tenslotte *ballroom*dansen. Voor Abby stond dat gelijk aan elegantie en goede smaak. Zelfs als haar echtgenoot op haar tenen trapte.

Jo en Denny daarentegen waren uitgedost voor een cowboydansfeest.

Abby zou medelijden met hen hebben gehad als Matts ouders zich er niet om schenen te bekommeren hoe ze gekleed waren. *Misschien hebben ze nooit ballroomdansen gezien.* Het was trouwens heel goed mogelijk dat ze nog nooit een danszaal vanbinnen hadden gezien.

Denny droeg puntige cowboylaarzen en een grote zwarte hoed. Jo had zich in een roze met zwarte minirok geperst met een bijpassende blouse met roze franje en roze laarzen.

Toen ze dichterbij kwamen, fluisterde John in Abby's oor: 'Heb je niet gezegd wat ze aan moesten trekken?'

Abby zwaaide naar Jo en fluisterde terug: 'Ik dacht dat ze dat wel wisten.'

Beide paren schreven zich in en namen hun plaatsen in.

Jo kwam naast Abby lopen. 'Weet je zeker dat de juf het niet erg vindt dat we er zomaar bij komen?'

'Ja, hoor.' John en Denny gingen voorop. 'Het is een doorgaande klas.'

John wierp Denny een snelle blik toe. 'Heb je er zin in?'

Denny schonk hem een scheve grijns en draaide met zijn vinger in de lucht. 'Het wordt vast lachen.'

'O, hou op.' Jo gaf haar man een stomp tegen zijn arm. 'Je vindt het heerlijk om met me te dansen.'

Paula had heen en weer gefladderd om met verscheidene paren een praatje te maken. Nu kwam ze met een haastige glimlach op Abby en John af. 'Welkom, ik zie dat u uw…' Meteen werd de glimlach een frons en Paula nam Jo en Denny van top tot teen op. 'Lieve help…' Ze mompelde het juist luid genoeg om te worden verstaan. 'Volkomen ongepast.' Ze schudde haar hoofd en ging naar de voorkant van de gymzaal.

Abby voelde Jo's boosheid van twee meter afstand. *Daar gaan we.* Abby pakte John bij de hand en wachtte.

Jo draaide zich met een ruk om, haar wenkbrauwen donker gefronst. 'Die vrouw heeft lef! Wat mankeert haar?'

'Niks.' John klopte Jo op de rug. 'Ze neemt haar dansles heel serieus.'

Abby zag Jo's nekhaartjes haast rechtop gaan staan toen ze haar handen in haar zij zette. 'Ik neem vissen ook heel serieus, maar je zult mij geen vishaken zien slaan in beginnelingen.'

De paren gingen in de rij staan terwijl Paula met de muziekband in de weer was. Abby en John stelden zich op naast Jo en Denny. Jo siste in Abby's richting.

'Trouwens, moet je háár zien! Op haar leeftijd in een maillot en een gympakje!'

Denny stootte haar discreet aan. 'Jo…'

'Wat nou? Ze ziet er bespottelijk uit.'

Jo wierp een blik als een laserstraal op Paula's rug. 'Laat ze me niet meer zo aankijken, anders…!' Jo ving Denny's blik op en ontspande enigszins. 'Laat maar. Sorry.' Ze schonk Abby en John een zwak lachje. 'Ik laat me een beetje meeslepen.'

'Precies.' Verontschuldigend keek Denny John en Abby aan. 'Jo laat niet met zich sollen.'

Abby grinnikte en gaf een kneepje in Johns hand. 'Zit er maar niet over in, Jo.' Ze schonk de vrouw een liefdevolle glimlach en probeerde zich voor te stellen wat Nicole in deze situatie zou doen. Abby haalde diep adem. 'Zeg, hoe gaat het met de zendings- reis? Zijn jullie nog steeds van plan om een jaar naar Mexico te gaan?'

'Absoluut.' Jo liet haar boosheid varen. 'We popelen. Die kleine kindjes hebben mensen nodig die van hen houden en Denny en ik zijn er precies geknipt voor.' Ze gaf haar man een knipoog. 'Bovendien schijn je daar fantastisch te kunnen vissen.'

Een van de paren was met Paula in gesprek, zodat ze nog even de tijd hadden voordat de les begon. John gaf Denny een por met zijn elleboog. 'Pas op haar voeten. Na onze eerste les heb ik Abby naar buiten moeten dragen.'

'Nee!' Jo gaf John een klapje op zijn arm. 'De sierlijke sterquar- terback van de Universiteit van Michigan? Niet te geloven.'

'Het is waar.' Abby huiverde en lachte tegelijk. 'Mijn tenen zijn nog bont en blauw.'

'Zeg, hebben jullie de kinderen onlangs nog gezien?' Jo haalde overdreven haar schouders op en rekte zich uit met haar handen boven haar hoofd. Zoals meestal op aerobicles wordt gedaan. Twee paren vooraan merkten haar op en begonnen te fluisteren.

'Eh…' Abby probeerde te bedenken wat Jo had gevraagd. 'Ja. Nicole is gisteren langs geweest.'

'En… wat denk je?'

Denny wisselde een verwilderde blik met John, alsof hij wilde zeggen dat hij zoals gewoonlijk geen idee had waar zijn vrouw op doelde.

'Wat ik denk?'

Jo snoof. 'Van Nicole. Ze straalt, hè?'

Abby dacht even na. 'Het is me niet opgevallen.'

'Goed, klas.' Paula klapte in haar handen. 'Iedereen op zijn plaats, alstublieft. We zullen even snel de passen doornemen die we vorige week hebben geleerd. Klaar? En één en twee en…' De muziek begon.

Abby en John kwamen op gang en waren halverwege de gymzaal voordat John op haar voeten walste. 'Au!' Abby struikelde even en was weer in de pas. Dit keer cirkelden ze zonder problemen de zaal door. 'Niet slecht.' Ze glimlachte naar hem. 'Je begint al aardig volwassen te worden.'

John knikte over haar schouder. 'Dat kan ik niet van Jo en Denny zeggen.'

Abby keek over haar schouder en struikelde haast.

Jo en Denny negeerden volledig wat Paula voordeed. In plaats daarvan hadden ze hun armen in elkaar gehaakt en dansten naast elkaar met hoog opgetrokken benen een boerenlijndans, zonder oog voor de walsende paren om hen heen.

Abby keek John met grote ogen aan. 'Paula schopt ze eruit!'

'Ik denk het niet.' Johns ogen schitterden. 'Ze heeft hen de hele tijd gadegeslagen. Ze is te geschokt om er iets van te zeggen.'

Het bleek dat Paula geen woord zei tot halverwege de les. Op dat moment schreeuwde Jo hard: 'Joeeeehieeee!!' midden in een stemmig klassiek stuk.

Daarop zette Paula haar hoofdband met oortje en microfoon recht en klapte opnieuw in haar handen. 'Geen geschreeuw van de leerlingen. Volg het paar voor u of ik zal u moeten vragen te vertrekken.'

Jo wierp Paula een boze blik toe, deed haar mond open en schreeuwde nog een keer: 'Joeeeehi…'

Denny legde zijn hand stevig op haar mond voordat ze haar kreet af kon maken.

Abby gluurde over Johns schouder. 'Wauw.' Ze deed haar best om zachtjes te lachen. 'Dat mens is ongelooflijk.'

'Jij hebt haar uitgenodigd.' John liet speels zijn ogen rollen. 'Ik had het kunnen voorspellen.'

'Ach, kom... ze is gewoon een beetje enthousiaster dan de meeste mensen.'

'Zoals een tornado enthousiaster is dan een windvlaag.'

Jo en Denny deden nu de two-step en Denny fluisterde tegen haar. Jo kreeg een berouwvolle blik in haar ogen en daarna werd ze kalmer. Abby keek vol ontzag toe. Kennelijk was Denny's invloed op Jo behoorlijk groot.

De rest van het uur ging het paar op in hun eigen wereld van de two-step en lijndansen. Geen van beiden deed ook maar één keer een poging tot een ballroompas.

Toen de les voorbij was, stonden de paren voor de gymzaal op adem te komen. 'Ik denk dat de juf iets tegen me had.'

'Nee... Denk je dat echt?' Denny sloeg zijn arm om Jo's hals en trok haar dicht tegen zich aan. Hij lachte naar Abby en John.

'En waarom leerde ze ons die ouderwetse stijldans? Ze moesten haar eens meenemen naar een countrydanszaal om haar te laten zien dat ze het leven een beetje luchtiger op moet nemen voordat ze te veel in zichzelf opgaat en...'

Denny legde zijn hand weer over Jo's mond. 'Wat ze wil zeggen is, bedankt voor de uitnodiging. We hebben het erg naar ons zin gehad.'

Abby smoorde een giechel. Opeens bedacht ze iets. 'Zeg, wat zei je daarstraks eigenlijk over Nicole?'

Jo deed haar mond open, maar Denny's hand smoorde haar. Hij lachte en liet zijn hand vallen. Ze trok haar wenkbrauwen op. 'Dank je.' Toen wendde ze zich tot Abby. 'Alleen dat ze straalt als een regenboogforel, mocht het je niet zijn opgevallen.'

Stralen? Wat bedoelde ze daarmee? 'Die pasgetrouwde blik?'

John en Denny wisselden een nieuwsgierige blik.

'Nee...' Jo boog zich naar haar toe alsof ze topgeheime informatie had. 'Die *stralende* blik.'

'Je bedoelt...' Abby popelde tot Jo zich nader verklaarde. Ze wilde toch niet zeggen...

'Goed.' Jo richtte zich weer op. 'Nicole is een wittebroodsbaby, hè?'

John verplaatste zijn gewicht en keek op zijn horloge. Het teken voor Abby dat het gesprek kon wachten.

'Ja, en?' Abby kon de woorden wel uit haar mond trekken.

'Dus…' Jo grinnikte. 'Wittebroodsbaby's brengen wittebroodsbaby's voort. Zo werkt dat.'

'Jo, kom op.' John lachte. 'Je denkt toch niet dat Nicole zwanger is?'

'Ho, even.' Jo stak haar hand op en hief haar kin. 'Dat heb je mij niet horen zeggen.'

Abby kreeg een knoop in haar maag. Als Nicole inderdaad zwanger was, zou ze het toch niet eerst aan Jo en Denny hebben verteld? Maar aan de andere kant, misschien had Nicole niets gezegd. Misschien… 'Heeft Matt dat gezegd?'

'Nee, hoor. Niks van dat al. De kinderen hebben geen woord gezegd.' Jo tikte met een vinger tegen haar slaap. 'Gewoon intuïtie. En dat Nicole zo straalt.'

John gaf een rukje aan Abby's arm. Ze reageerde met een paar subtiele stapjes achterwaarts. 'Nou, we moeten gauw gaan. Ik zou er niet te lang over nadenken dat Nicole zwanger zou zijn. De kinderen zijn van plan om een poosje te wachten.'

'We weten allemaal wat er van zulke plannen komt, hè?' Jo keek Denny aan. Maar nu was er niets grappigs in haar toon. Als Abby niet zo'n haast had gehad, had ze meer tijd genomen om met Jo te praten. Want de blik die Denny en zij wisselden, was haast droevig.

De paren namen afscheid van elkaar, maar later die avond kon Abby niet van zich afzetten wat Jo had gezegd. Samen met John had ze Sean met zijn huiswerk geholpen. Toen ze klaar waren, had ze John mee naar buiten gewenkt.

Zonder een woord te zeggen, slenterden ze hand in hand naar de aanlegsteiger. Als een van beiden iets op zijn hart had, wist hij even instinctief als ademhalen wat hij moest doen.

Toen ze het eind van de steiger bereikten, gingen ze op het bankje zitten dat John daar een maand geleden had neergezet. Abby wachtte even voordat ze iets zei en staarde naar het lint van licht aan de overkant van het water. Ze hield van dit meer en vond het heerlijk dat ze hier al woonden sinds de kinderen klein waren. Sinds hun dochtertje Haley Ann als baby plotseling in haar slaap gestorven was.

Altijd als ze hier samen zaten, dacht Abby wel even aan hun tweede dochter, van wie ze de as op ditzelfde water hadden uitgestrooid. Door de jaren heen hadden ze dit plekje bezocht om de hoogte- en dieptepunten van het leven te delen. Toen Abby's moeder omkwam bij de tornado in Barneveld, Wisconsin… toen Johns vader stierf aan een hartaanval… toen John de Eagles naar hun eerste kampioenstitel had geleid… en toen hij diep geraakt was door de klachten van de ouders.

Ze zaten bij elkaar tot de woorden als vanzelf kwamen. En als ze dan uitgepraat waren, pakte John haar bij de hand en wiegde met haar heen en weer. Niet het soort dansen waar je les voor moest hebben. Maar het soort waar je voor moest luisteren. Blaadjes die ruisten in de bomen achter de steiger, krekels en krakende planken. Het fluisteren van de wind. Het zwakke refrein van verre herinneringen.

'Hoor je dat?' vroeg hij dan.

'Mmm.' Ze lag met haar hoofd tegen zijn borst. 'De muziek van ons leven.'

'Dans met me, Abby… nooit ophouden.'

Abby ademde de koele avondlucht diep in. Hij smaakte naar de komende winter, koud en vochtig. Het zou niet lang meer duren voordat ze zich op zulke avonden warm moesten aankleden. En Abby had het gevoel dat er meerdere zouden komen, met Johns coachproblemen en hun zorgen over Kade.

Ze wendde zich tot John en pakte zijn hand. Hij zat naar haar te kijken. Abby hield zijn blik even vast. 'Ik vraag me af of hij het toegeeft.'

'Vast wel.' John keek uit over het water. 'Meestal heeft hij geen geheimen voor me.'

'Ja, maar…'

'Ik denk dat hij het me zal vertellen.'

'Ik ben er zenuwachtig over.'

Hun vingers waren door elkaar gevlochten en John streek met zijn duim over de rug van haar hand. 'Ik niet. Het is een beste knul, Abby. Wat hij ook doet op internet… ik betwijfel het of hij eraan verslaafd is.'

'Weet ik. Maar als hij boos wordt omdat we het weten?' Ze probeerde de knoop in haar maag weg te duwen. 'Zulke dingen kunnen een kloof tussen hem en ons veroorzaken. Een kloof die hem zelfs van God af zou kunnen trekken.'

'Abby…' John keek haar aan op dezelfde manier als hij de kinderen aankeek als er een zwaar onweer dreigde. Kalm en vol vertrouwen, vol vriendelijk begrip. 'We hebben sinds zijn geboorte voor die jongen gebeden. God zal hem niet zomaar loslaten.'

Ze knikte en er ontspande iets in haar maag. 'Je hebt gelijk.'

'Wat nog meer?'

'Je kent me te goed.'

'Ja.' Hij grijnsde. 'Dus wat nog meer?'

'Weet je nog dat je me over die jongen vertelde? Nathan Pike?' Ze sprong wel van de hak op de tak vanavond, maar John had er geen bezwaar tegen. Hij was aan zulke gesprekken gewend. Onbestemde losse flodders, noemde hij het.

'Hoe kan ik hem vergeten? Hij zit elke dag bij me in de klas.'

'Het bevalt me niet.' Abby's hartslag versnelde. 'Ik maak me ongerust over hem, John. Stel dat hij gekke dingen gaat doen?'

'Dat gebeurt niet. Zulke jongens zijn niet degenen die een wapen kopen en gestoord gaan lopen doen.' John liet haar hand los en vouwde zijn handen achter zijn hoofd. 'Nathan wil aandacht, dat is alles. Dat *gothic* uiterlijk, de bedreigingen; dat is zijn manier om iemand te dwingen hem eindelijk op te merken.'

'Het bevalt me niet.'

Ze zwegen weer en boven hun hoofd dook een adelaar laag over het water, kreeg een vis te pakken en scheerde over een groepje bomen. John keek hem na tot hij verdwenen was. 'Hij neemt eten mee naar het nest.'

'Dat denk ik ook.' Abby liet haar hoofd achterover leunen. Het was vanavond volle maan, zodat het licht van de sterren gedempt werd. Abby ontspande zich. John had gelijk. Alles kwam goed met Kade… en met Nathan Pike. Zelfs met het footballteam. God zou een oplossing brengen.

'Je denkt toch niet dat Nicole zwanger is?'

John stond op en rekte zich uit, hij draaide eerst naar rechts en toen naar links. Toen hij klaar was, zuchtte hij diep en stak een hand naar Abby uit. 'Nee, ik denk niet dat Nicole zwanger is. Ze wilden toch een poosje wachten met kinderen?'

'Weet ik.' Abby klemde zijn vingers stevig vast toen hij haar overeind trok. 'Maar stel dat Jo gelijk heeft? Nu ik erover nadenk, had ze inderdaad iets stralends over zich.'

'Geloof me, Abby.' John nam haar in zijn armen. 'Als onze dochter zwanger was, zou ze het eerst aan Matt vertellen en dan aan jou. Ze is gewoon gelukkig. Waarom zou ze niet stralen?'

'Je hebt gelijk.' Abby aarzelde. 'Maar als het wel zo was… dat zou me toch wat wezen? Jij en ik, *opa en oma*!'

John lachte. 'Dan *moet* ik wel volwassen worden.'

Abby bestudeerde Johns trekken, de subtiele rimpels in zijn voorhoofd, de grijze sporen in zijn bakkebaardjes. 'Raar om te bedenken dat we oud worden.'

'Raar?' John trok haar dichter tegen zich aan. 'Ik weet het niet; ik vind het fijn.'

'Ja.' Abby zag hen zo voor zich, dansend op de steiger, lachend en vol liefde, en kracht vindend bij elkaar. 'Het lijkt me leuk om oud te worden met jou, John Reynolds.'

'Later zetten we hier schommelstoelen neer.'

'Zodat we even kunnen schommelen als we te moe zijn om te dansen?'

'Precies.' Zijn mondhoeken gingen omhoog en Abby voelde haar ruggengraat tintelen. 'Weet je nog ons eerste afspraakje?'

'Jij kwam met je familie naar een footballwedstrijd in Michigan.' Hij trok zijn wenkbrauwen op. 'Eindelijk.'

'Ik was zeventien, John.' Ze boog haar hoofd en dacht aan het verlegen meisje dat ze was geweest. Hun families kenden elkaar al heel lang, maar John was ouder dan zij. Tot die cruciale football-wedstrijd had Abby niet gedacht dat ze een kans bij hem maakte. 'Hoe kon ik denken dat John Reynolds, sterquarterback van de Wolverines, met me uit wilde?'

'Ik was het al twee jaar van plan.' Hij trok haar kaaklijn na, met zijn ogen vast in de hare. 'Ik wachtte gewoon tot je oud genoeg was.'

'En nu zijn de rollen omgedraaid.'

'O ja?'

'Hmmmm. Nu wacht ik tot jij groot genoeg bent.' Abby gaf een speels schopje tegen Johns voet. 'Op de dansvloer tenminste.'

'Ik kan dansen als het belangrijk is.' Hij keek uit over het meer en dronk de schoonheid in van zijn lievelingsplek. Toen begon hij heel langzaam te wiegen. Zijn blik vond de hare, zoals door de jaren heen zo vaak was gebeurd. 'Dans met me, Abby.'

Zijn tedere woorden deden haar hart smelten. 'Altijd, John.' Ze bewoog met hem mee. 'Voor altijd en altijd.'

Ze nestelde haar hoofd tegen zijn schouder en ontleende kracht uit elke slag van zijn hart. Ze bewogen samen op de verre kreet van een havik en het kabbelen van het meer op hun privé-oever. Abby sloot haar ogen. Hoe zou het leven zijn zonder haar man? Een leven waarin ze niet hierheen konden, deze aanlegstei-ger waarvan ze allebei hielden, de plek waar de as van hun dochter rustte en waar ze elkaar zoveel hadden verteld? Een leven waarin ze geen avonden zoals deze hadden?

Onmogelijk voor te stellen.

Toch viel niet te ontkennen dat ze ouder werden. En eens, als de jaren van grootouders en overgrootouders zijn voorbij waren, hield de muziek op. Was de dans afgelopen. Dat was onvermijdelijk.

Abby drukte haar wang nog eens tegen Johns borst en genoot van zijn nabijheid. *Dank U, God... Dank U dat U ons van onszelf gered hebt.*

Voordat ze later die avond in slaap viel, sprak Abby nog een gebed uit. Een gebed dat ze in de afgelopen maanden vaker had gebeden.

God, nooit heb ik méér van John gehouden. Alstublieft... geef ons nog duizend avonden zoals deze. Alstublieft.

Negen

Het gesprek zou zaterdagmiddag plaatsvinden.

Kade wist het natuurlijk niet, maar John had de dag allang uitgestippeld. De avond tevoren hadden de Eagles hun footballwedstrijd gewonnen, dus er was die zaterdagochtend een lichte training. Kade was meegegaan, om eens lekker bij te kletsen met tientallen voormalige teamgenoten.

'Zeg, pap, ik denk dat ik een paar balletjes ga gooien voor de eerstejaars.' Kade wees naar het aangrenzende veld, waar de jongere Eagles aan het trainen waren.

John keek toe vanaf zijn plaats in de buurt van de schoolploeg. Zodra Kade in hun midden verscheen, verzamelden de eerstejaars zich om hem heen, drukten hem de hand en keken hem vol ontzag aan. De grote quarterback Kade Reynolds terug op school. Het was genoeg om hun hele week goed te maken.

John verplaatste zijn blik naar zijn oudere spelers. 'Oké. In de rij, we gaan weer beginnen. Nu wil ik de lijnmannen schouder aan schouder. Jullie zijn een muur, geen tuinhekje. Denk erom!'

Toen de oefening halverwege was, wierp John nog een blik op het andere veld. Kade gooide passes voor de jonge receivers, op een manier waarvan zelfs Johns mond openviel. De jongen had beslist talent. John was apetrots op hem.

Later die dag zou Kade niet langer meneer de grote atleet zijn, maar simpelweg Johns Reynolds' zoon. En het vader-zoongesprek zou niet over Kades talenten gaan.

Geef me de woorden, God... hoe ik hiermee omga kan op de rest van zijn leven van invloed zijn.

Twee uur later waren ze thuis en hadden ze geluncht. Sean had nieuwe voetbalschoenen nodig en Abby had afgesproken met hem naar de winkel te gaan. Dan konden John en Kade alleen zijn.

Toen ze onder elkaar waren, liep Kade op de televisie af. 'Ha… zaterdags football. Tijd om de competitie te zien.'

Voordat hij de afstandsbediening kon pakken, schraapte John zijn keel. 'Laten we een eindje gaan varen. Wij samen.'

Kade aarzelde even en haalde toen zijn schouders op. 'Goed, hoor. Waarom niet? Ik zie de hoogtepunten straks wel op de sportzender.'

Het was een ongewoon warme dag, alsof de herfst zijn uiterste best deed om een paar uur te stelen van de ophanden zijnde winter. Een lichte bewolking dempte de felle zon, maar er was geen regen voorspeld. Het was de perfecte middag voor een paar uur op het meer.

Eerst praatten ze over koetjes en kalfjes en maakten grapjes over de tijd dat Sean vier jaar was. Abby was naar de supermarkt gegaan en John zou op de kinderen passen. Hij had met Nicole en Kade gefrisbeed op de grazige heuvel achter hun huis, toen Sean stiekem weg was geglipt, een zwemvest aan had getrokken, in de roeiboot van hun gezin was geklommen en de meertrossen los had gemaakt. Tegen de tijd dat John merkte dat Sean weg was, dreef het kind al honderd meter verder op het meer. Hij stond rechtop in de boot om hulp te schreeuwen.

'Ik was vreselijk bang.' John liet de roeispanen hun werk doen terwijl ze samen lachten om de herinnering.

'Dacht je dat Sean zou verdrinken?'

'Ben je gek?' John snoof. 'Hij had een zwemvest aan. Bovendien kon hij zwemmen.' Hij knipoogde naar Kade. 'Ik was bang voor je moeder. Ze had me vermoord als ze thuis was gekomen en Sean midden op het water had betrapt!'

Het was een privémeer, dat voornamelijk werd bezocht door de huiseigenaren van wie de huizen langs de vijf kilometer lange oever stonden. Vandaag waren er maar enkele bootjes helemaal aan de andere kant. John roeide nog een eindje en haalde toen de roeispanen binnenboord.

Kade leunde achterover en draaide zijn gezicht naar de dun gesluierde zon. 'Ik was vergeten hoe lekker het is. Rustig. Vredig.' Hij grinnikte naar John. 'Goed idee, pap.'

'Hier op het meer kan ik nadenken.' John aarzelde. 'Of een echt gesprek voeren.'

Het duurde even, maar Kade ging weer rechtop zitten en keek John aan. 'Wil je ergens over praten, pap?'

'Inderdaad.'

'Oké, brand los.'

John keek zijn zoon onderzoekend aan op zoek naar een teken… een flits van bezorgdheid of schuld. Maar Kades gezichtsuitdrukking was het toonbeeld van vertrouwende onschuld. Het werd John benauwd te moede. Was Kade hier al zo in verwikkeld dat hij zelfs geen spoor van schuldgevoel had?

Daar gaat-ie. God… geef me de juiste woorden. John liet zijn ellebogen op zijn knieën rusten en keek Kade diep in de ogen. 'Na je vorige bezoek hebben je moeder en ik een paar twijfelachtige webadressen in haar internetgeschiedenis gevonden.'

Kade keek hem neutraal aan. 'Twijfelachtig?'

'Nou, erger dan twijfelachtig, eigenlijk.' John vocht tegen zijn verlegenheid. 'Wat ik bedoel is dat we een lijst met pornosites hebben gevonden, Kade.'

'Porno?' Zijn wenkbrauwen schoten verbaasd omhoog. 'Beschuldig je me van het bekijken van pornosites?'

John werd overvallen door twijfel. 'Hoor es, jongen. Je moeder dacht dat *ik* ze had bekeken. En ik weet dat ik het niet was. En mam duidelijk ook niet. Sean had al een maand niet op de computer gezeten en hij heeft trouwens een eigen gebruikersnaam waarmee hij niet op zulke sites kan.' John wees naar zichzelf. 'Wat moet ik anders denken?'

Kades mond was opengevallen en John zag de strijd in zijn

ogen. Hij wilde het ontkennen, hij wilde schreeuwen dat John zich niet met zijn zaken moest bemoeien en moest ophouden met snuffelen. Maar langzaam verdween de boosheid van zijn gezicht. Daarvoor in de plaats kwam een mengeling van emoties, aangevoerd door een onmiskenbare schaduw van schuldgevoel. John kon het makkelijk herkennen, want zo had hijzelf nog niet zo lang geleden gekeken.

Toen Kade niets zei, dempte John zijn stem tot normaal. 'Ik heb gelijk, hè?'

Kade zuchtte vermoeid. Hij sloeg zijn ogen neer.

'We moeten erover praten, jongen. Wanneer ben je ermee begonnen?'

De jongen liet zijn schouders zakken en hij hief zijn hoofd op. 'Ik ben niet de enige.' Hij sloeg zijn armen over elkaar. 'Alle jongens doen het.'

Kades trekken werden hard en opstandig. Dat had John nog nooit bij een van zijn kinderen gezien, en het maakte hem bang. 'Dat kan wel waar zijn, maar het is verkeerd, Kade. Dat weet jij beter dan de anderen in je team.'

Kade wierp zijn handen in de lucht. 'Het is net een virtueel vriendinnetje, pap. Snap je het niet?' Zijn toon was gespannen en hij keek om zich heen alsof hij zocht naar een manier om het John duidelijk te maken. 'Je zit er niet aan vast en je hebt geen seks.' Zijn wangen werden warm. 'Nou ja... niet echt tenminste.'

'Toch blijft het immoreel, jongen. En voor een hoop mensen wordt het een obsessie.'

'Vertel jij me dan maar eens wat ik moet doen! Ik ben christen, en ik mag geen seks hebben voordat ik getrouwd ben. Weet je hoelang *dat* nog kan duren. Ik ben footballspeler, dus ik heb geen tijd voor een vriendin. En ik heb geen geld, al had ik er tijd voor.' Hij snoof. 'Snap je het niet? Internet lost al die problemen met een paar klikken op. Het is er wanneer ik er zin in heb. Bovendien is het beter dan zomaar een meisje zwanger maken.'

John had zin om te schreeuwen. 'Er is niks beters aan.' Dacht Kade echt dat porno niets bijzonders was? Had de universiteitscultuur zo snel alles wat ze hem geleerd hadden ondermijnd? 'In Gods ogen is porno net zo verkeerd als ongeoorloofde seks, Kade. Het is hetzelfde.'

'Het is *niet* hetzelfde.' Kade was boos. 'Er zijn geen mensen bij betrokken, pap. Alleen plaatjes.'

'Ja.' John leunde met zwaar bonzend hart achterover. 'Plaatjes van mensen.'

Kade zweeg. De spanning in zijn trekken werd enigszins verlicht. 'Ze worden betaald voor wat ze doen. Het is hun keus.'

'Moet je jezelf es horen, jongen. Denk je dat die vrouwen het *leuk* vinden om op die manier geld te verdienen? Sommigen zijn slaven van de handel, ze worden geboeid, bedreigd en onder schot gedwongen om afgrijselijke dingen te doen. Anderen zijn weggelopen tieners die amper oud genoeg zijn om auto te rijden, wanhopig op zoek naar een manier om op straat te leven. Sommigen zijn drugsgebruikers, die zo om hun volgende shot zitten te springen dat ze er alles voor over hebben.' John zweeg even en zijn toon werd zachter. Bedroefder. 'Is dat een bedrijfstak die je wilt ondersteunen?'

'De jongens praten erover alsof het prima is, alsof er niks mis mee is.' Kade wrong zijn handen en staarde naar de vloer van de boot. 'En meestal... leek het alsof ze gelijk hadden.'

'Natuurlijk leek het zo.' John keek zijn zoon onderzoekend aan, hevig wensend dat hij het begreep. 'Dat is wat de duivel wil dat je denkt. Ach, het zijn maar plaatjes, niks bijzonders. Maar zulke plaatjes leiden ergens toe, Kade. Heb je daaraan gedacht?'

Hij keek op. 'Wat bedoel je?'

'Plaatjes leiden tot video's... en al gauw is zelfs dat niet genoeg.' Kade kromp ineen en de moed zonk John in de schoenen. 'Kijk je ook naar video's?'

Kade keek van de ene kant van het meer naar de andere en toen naar John. 'Een paar keer maar. Na de training komen de jongens soms bij elkaar in een van de studentenhuizen. Ze hebben een heel stel films en tja…'

John had het gevoel dat de boot onder hem verdween en dat hij verdronk, begraven werd in een soort water waaruit hij niet kon ontsnappen. 'Het duurt niet lang voordat video's ook niet meer genoeg zijn. Dan wordt het prostitutie.'

'Nee!' haastte Kade zich te antwoorden. 'Dat heb ik nooit gedaan.'

'En de jongens?'

Kade aarzelde. 'Een paar… een of twee keer. Voordat het seizoen begon.' Zweetdruppels parelden op Kades voorhoofd. 'Maar ik niet, pap. Echt niet!'

Het probleem was erger dan John had durven denken. *Kom nu, God… geef me wijze woorden.* 'Porno is een leugen, jongen.'

'Een leugen?' Ondanks Kades nederige toon vertelde zijn gezichtsuitdrukking John dat hij de ernst van het probleem nog steeds niet inzag.

'Ja, een leugen. Het stelt vrouwen voor als niets meer dan seksobjecten met geen ander doel dan mannen te behagen.' John hield zijn hoofd schuin. 'Dat is toch een leugen?'

'Ja, ik denk van wel.'

'Je *denkt* van wel?' Johns kaakspieren trokken krampachtig samen. 'Denk eens aan je zus… of de meisjes met wie je uit bent geweest. Hoe zou je het vinden als je na een reeks computerklikken *hun* naakte lijf op internet aantrof?'

'Pap!' Kade kneep zijn ogen tot spleetjes. 'Hoe kun je zoiets zeggen?'

'Tja… de meisjes naar wie jij kijkt horen ook bij iemand. Ze zijn iemands zus, iemands dochter. Iemands moeder, in veel gevallen. Iemands toekomstige vrouw. Waarom is het niet verkeerd om hen zo te behandelen?' John haalde snel adem. 'Dat is de eerste leugen: dat een vrouw slechts een lichaam is.'

Kade keek op. Luisterde hij met meer aandacht of was het verbeelding van John?

'De tweede leugen is deze: dat er echte seksuele bevrediging kan voortkomen uit zondig gedrag.' John staarde een ogenblik naar de lucht. De wolken begonnen op te klaren en ineens wist hij precies wat hij moest zeggen. Hij ontmoette opnieuw Kades blik. 'Het kan prettig voelen voor je lichaam, maar niet voor je ziel. En echte bevrediging kan nooit zonder intimiteit.'

'Zoals wanneer je echt seks hebt, bedoel je?'

'Nee. Intimiteit en seks zijn totaal verschillende dingen, jongen. Intimiteit is de band die God bewerkstelligt tussen twee getrouwde mensen. Het komt voort uit jaren van toewijding, van samenleven en praten en problemen uitwerken. Jaren waarin je die persoon beter leert kennen dan wie dan ook in het leven. Een lichamelijke relatie met zo iemand, dat is intimiteit. En al wat minder is, is een leugen.'

Kade keek John strak aan. 'Je bedoelt zoals jij en mevrouw Denton?'

Johns adem stokte. Was het mogelijk? Wist Kade dat John bijna een verhouding had gehad met Charlene Denton? Ze had samen met John op school lesgegeven. Jarenlang had Charlene genadeloos met hem geflirt, al waren ze beiden getrouwd. Nadat ze van haar man was gescheiden, had Charlene vaak haar weg naar Johns lokaal gevonden.

In het jaar voordat ze ergens anders naartoe was verhuisd, had Kade haar meer dan eens bij hem aangetroffen als hij de klas van zijn vader binnenliep, maar John had zich er altijd uit weten te praten. Eén keer had Kade hen betrapt toen ze elkaars hand vasthielden… John had gelogen en gezegd dat hij met haar had gebeden. Hoe verkeerd dat destijds ook was geweest, John had altijd gedacht dat Kade hem had geloofd.

Tot nu toe tenminste.

'Wat is er met mij en mevrouw Denton?' John was radeloos en probeerde tijd te winnen. De blik op Kades gezicht vertelde John dat zijn zoon van begin af aan zijn twijfels had gehad over de verkeerde relatie van zijn vader.

'Kom op, pap. Ze was altijd bij je. De jongens in het team praatten er zelfs over. Mevrouw Denton kwam altijd naar de training en dan stond ze naast je, of ze hing in je lokaal rond… Ik ben niet achterlijk.'

John voelde zich een stervende. 'Waarom heb je er tot nu toe nooit iets over gezegd?'

'Je zei dat ze gewoon een vriendin was. Dat ze je gebed nodig had.' Kade haalde zijn schouders op. 'Ik wilde het graag geloven, denk ik.'

Er waaide een bries over het meer die iedere valse schijn die John nog over had, wegspoelde. 'Alles aan mijn vriendschap met mevrouw Denton was verkeerd. Het was een leugen, net zoals porno een leugen is.'

'Dus je bent met haar naar bed geweest?' Kade leek op het punt van tranen.

'Nee.' John overwoog Kade te vertellen over de twee keer dat Charlene en hij hadden gekust. Maar het had geen zin. Dat lag nu achter hem. 'Ik heb dingen gedaan waar ik niet trots op ben, jongen. Maar die grens heb ik nooit overschreden.'

'Dus het is waar.' Kade schudde zijn hoofd. Zijn schouders zakten af en John kon niet onderscheiden of zijn betrokken gezicht afkeer of wanhoop uitdrukte. 'De jongens zaten me aldoor te narren en ik zei dan dat ze de pot op konden. Mijn ouders waren anders. Ze hielden van elkaar. En nu… al die tijd… wat een aanfluiting.'

'Wacht even, Kade. Dat is niet eerlijk.'

'Jawel. Porno is niet de enige leugen. Mam en jij ook, alles is een leugen. Dus wat heeft het voor zin om…'

'Stop!' John boog zich naar voren tot zijn knieën die van Kade raakten. 'Wat je moeder en ik hebben, is geen leugen. We hebben het moeilijk gehad, inderdaad. En we zijn er samen sterker uitgekomen.' Hij keek Kade recht in de ogen, als om bij hem naar binnen te kijken. 'Weet je waarom we uit elkaar gegroeid waren?'

Kade zei niets, zijn lippen waren strak op elkaar geperst.

'Omdat we de intimiteit vergeten waren. We praatten niet meer en deelden onze gevoelens niet meer met elkaar. We lieten onze relatie regeren door het leven en onze drukke agenda's, en daardoor hadden we bijna een liefde achter ons gelaten die afgezien van de liefde van God de grootste is die ik ken.' Hij lachte kort. 'Nee, jongen, wat je moeder en ik hebben is zo eerlijk als goud. Charlene Denton: dat was een leugen. En elke dag dank ik God dat Hij me dat heeft laten inzien voordat het te laat was. Dat Hij je moeder en mij het belang van intimiteit opnieuw heeft laten zien.'

Kade richtte zich enigszins op, zijn wenkbrauwen waren nog vol twijfel gefronst. 'Dus… alles is in orde? Met jou en mam?'

'Veel meer dan in orde. Ik denk dat we nu meer van elkaar houden dan ooit tevoren.' John pakte Kades schouder vast. 'Maar we maken ons zorgen over jou.'

'Met mij is niks aan de hand.'

'Jawel. Als je nu in de leugen gelooft, als je jezelf ervan overtuigt dat bevrediging te vinden is in visuele onwerkelijkheden, hoe moet je dan ooit intimiteit delen met een echte vrouw?'

'Dat is iets anders.'

'Eens zul je iemand ontmoeten en zij zal alles van je willen weten. Als ze ontdekt dat je gek op pornosites bent geweest, zal ze je vast en zeker laten vallen als een baksteen. Welk meisje wil zich meten met zulke beelden? Bovendien zou ze geen respect voor je hebben als je vrouwen ziet als niets meer dan objecten, seksslaven.'

Kades gezichtsuitdrukking veranderde. Nu was John er zeker van. Eindelijk luisterde de jongen.

'Aan relaties moet je werken, jongen. Uren en dagen en jaren om dichter bij elkaar te komen. Dat is echte liefde, echte intimiteit. Als je jezelf voorhoudt dat werken niet belangrijk is, ga je niet alleen in tegen ieder plan dat God voor je leven heeft… je ontneemt jezelf ook de kans om het grootste geschenk te ervaren dat Hij ons heeft gegeven. Het geschenk van ware liefde.'

'Dus je denkt echt dat het zonde is?'

'Ja,' zei John op kalme, redelijke toon. 'Absoluut.'

Kade wendde zijn blik af. 'Daar hebben we het over gehad, een paar jongens en ik. Zij zeiden dat het niet erg was omdat die meisjes het goedvonden dat de foto's gemaakt werden en dat we eigenlijk niks verkeerds deden.' Kades gezicht betrok. 'Maar van-binnen... wist ik denk ik aldoor dat het niet goed kon zijn.'

'En nog een probleem is de verleiding om er weer mee te beginnen als het je in het echt eens tegenvalt.'

Kade zuchtte.

'De kwestie is...' John leunde achterover tegen de rand van de boot, 'hoe moeilijk wordt het om te stoppen?'

Kade tuurde naar een rij bomen in de verte. 'Moeilijk.'

Het was of John een stomp in zijn maag kreeg. 'Heb... heb je al eerder geprobeerd te stoppen?'

'Eén keer.' Kade leek weer acht jaar oud. 'Maar mijn computer staat daar in het studentenhuis en... ik weet niet... je went er-aan.'

Voor het eerst ving John een glimp op van waarom internet-porno zo verslavend was. Overal waren computers, toegang tot het web was even eenvoudig als een telefoontje plegen. Als iemand één keer op die sites kwam en er plezier aan beleefde, schreeuwde het lichaam om meer.

'Je kunt er filters voor kopen. Misschien dat dat helpt.'

'Ja. Dat heeft een van de jongens gedaan. Hij moest ook hulp-verlening hebben. Misschien kunnen hij en ik elkaar helpen.'

'Wij kunnen hulp voor je zoeken, jongen. Het kan me niet schelen wat het kost. Je moet van me geloven dat het slecht voor je is. Als je het laat voortbestaan, ga je er kapot aan.'

Kade knikte langzaam. 'Ik geloof dat ik het nooit zo gezien heb. Zoals waar het toe kan leiden en zo.'

'Die keer... toen je probeerde op te houden...' John liet zijn hand op zijn knieën vallen. 'Heb je God toen om hulp gevraagd?'

'Niet echt. Ik dacht niet dat het zo moeilijk zou zijn.'

'Je moet je ervan afwenden, jongen, en nooit meer omkijken. Nooit meer.'

'Weet ik.' Kade keek neer op zijn handen, waarmee hij zenuwachtig friemelde. 'Ik heb een boek gekocht over stoppen. Voordat ik naar huis kwam. Het zit in mijn tas.'

'Een boek?' John was mateloos opgelucht. 'Waarom sprak je me dan tegen, Kade? Je deed net alsof pornosites een goede zaak waren.'

'Ik voelde me in een hoek gedreven. Van alle kanten wordt me verteld dat het slecht is.' Hij keek op, zijn ogen waren vochtig. 'En als... als ik nou niet kan stoppen?'

John gleed dichter naar Kade toe en omhelsde hem. 'Je zult echt wel stoppen, maat. God zal je de kracht geven.' Hij dacht weer aan Charlene. 'Hij kan je de kracht geven om slechte dingen achter je te laten, hoe gevangen je je ook voelt.'

Kade snufte en sloeg zijn arm om Johns nek. Er klonken tranen in zijn stem. 'Bid voor me, pap. Wil je dat doen?'

Het duurde even voordat de brok in Johns keel afnam.

Toen liet hij zijn voorhoofd tegen Kades voorhoofd vallen en daar in de roeiboot, midden op het meer, bad hij voor zijn zoon met een intensiteit die hij nooit eerder had gekend. Hij vroeg of God Kade de kracht wilde geven om afstand te nemen van de smerige, zondige wereld van de pornografie. Of hij de juiste vriendschappen en hulpverlening en steun mocht krijgen om zijn ogen te openen voor de gruwel van die wereld. Of God de beelden wilde wissen die in Kades geest gevangen zaten en hem daarvoor in de plaats een juist begrip wilde geven van de schoonheid van een vrouw. En of Kade echte intimiteit mocht zien in het voorbeeld dat John en Abby gaven. Of Kade net als zij mocht leren van zijn fouten.

En ten slotte of hij een sterkere, godvrezende man mocht worden.

Tien

De anonieme brieven kwamen nu regelmatiger.

John werd er niet alleen van beschuldigd een slecht moreel voorbeeld voor de jongemannen van Marion High te zijn, maar hij werd onbeschaamd afgeschilderd als 'een coach die zijn tijd heeft gehad'. Het bestuur, dat John er aanvankelijk van verzekerd had dat het volkomen achter hem stond, begon te kletsen.

'De mensen maken zich ongerust over het programma,' vertelde Herman Lutz hem die week. 'Als sportcoördinator van de school baart me dat zorgen. Je kunt je mijn positie wel voorstellen.'

Hoewel het een jaar geleden ondenkbaar was geweest, droeg John nu het weeë gevoel mee dat hij ontslagen zou worden voordat hij zijn ontslag kon indienen. Dat Lutz hem door de ouders zou laten dwingen tot een beslissing die het makkelijkst voor hem was. John probeerde er niet aan te denken. Als hij het uit kon zitten, zou hij na de laatste fluit van het seizoen ontslag nemen.

Het punt was dat de prestaties van het team waren gekeerd.

John pakte zijn sporttas en liep naar de teambus. Ze hadden hun laatste vier wedstrijden gewonnen en na een overwinning vanavond op de ongelukkige Bulldogs in North County konden de Eagles naar de regiokampioenschappen.

Wat alles met elkaar betekende dat het seizoen nog niet bepaald voorbij was.

Maar die middag haalden football en fanatieke ouders niet eens de lijst van Johns grootste zorgen. Hij stond op het punt iets te doen wat hij niet meer had gedaan sinds hij met coachen was begonnen. Het sportkantoor van de jongens was open en John stapte naar binnen. Hij had nog maar een paar minuten voordat de bus vertrok.

De telefoon ging drie keer over voordat ze opnam. 'Hallo?'

'Abby, met mij.'

'John?' Ze aarzelde. 'Hoor je niet in de bus te zitten?'

'Ja. Hé, even vlug. Ga vanavond niet naar de wedstrijd.'

Het bleef even stil en John hoopte dat ze het begreep. Hij had niet genoeg tijd om uitgebreid op de details in te gaan. Eindelijk herstelde ze zich. 'Waarom niet?'

'Er is vandaag een bedreiging binnengekomen op kantoor. Iets over de wedstrijd.' John zocht steun bij het bureau. 'De politie denkt dat het vals alarm is, maar je weet nooit… Ik wil niet dat je erbij bent. Voor de zekerheid.'

'Zit Nathan Pike erachter?'

'Weten ze niet. Misschien.' Hij keek op zijn horloge. 'Hoor es, ik moet rennen. Ik houd van je. En kom alsjeblieft niet naar de wedstrijd.'

'Maar John…'

'Niet komen, Abby. Ik moet gaan.'

'Goed.' Er klonk bezorgdheid in Abby's stem. 'Ik kom niet. Ik houd ook van jou.'

'Tot over een paar uur.'

'Wacht…' Ze aarzelde. 'Wees voorzichtig, John.'

'Goed.'

Hij hing op en holde naar de bus. Hij stapte als laatste in. Het was een kwartier rijden naar North County en hoewel het team uitgelaten was, staarde John uit het raam naar het landschap en vroeg zich af hoe het zover had kunnen komen. Hij had Abby niet alle details verteld. Ze zou zich kapot geschrokken zijn.

Klaarblijkelijk was het telefoontje rond één uur die middag binnengekomen. Een hese stem had de schoolsecretaresse verteld dat er vanavond tijdens de wedstrijd een zelfmoordaanslag zou worden gepleegd.

'Het wordt gigantisch, dame.' De beller had gelachen. 'Let op mijn woorden.'

De secretaresse gebaarde naar de directeur dat hij de lijn op moest nemen, maar hij stond bij de balie druk met een ouder te praten. 'Met… met wie spreek ik?'

'Ja, hoor!' De beller lachte weer. 'Dat weten jullie gauw genoeg. Zeg maar tegen de coach dat het nu te laat is om me te helpen. Vanavond is de grote avond.'

'Als dit een grap is, kunt u het beter zeggen.' De secretaresse zocht vlug pen en papier. 'Het is een misdrijf om zulke bedreigingen te uiten.'

'Dit is geen bedreiging, dame. Er gaan vanavond mensen dood. Ik heb het je gezegd.'

Toen hing hij op.

Bleek en geschokt trok de secretaresse de directeur mee naar een lege kamer en vertelde hem wat er gebeurd was. Binnen vijftien minuten was de politie op de campus om vragen te stellen. Was er op school al eerder met de dood gedreigd? Hoe werden zulke voorvallen afgehandeld? Wist iemand of een leerling toegang had tot explosieven? Waar werd de wedstrijd van vanavond gehouden? En hoeveel ingangen waren er tot het stadion? Had iemand iets tegen het footballteam?

Steeds weer wezen de antwoorden op Nathan Pike, maar de politie kon niets doen. Ze konden niet eens met de jongen praten over het telefoontje.

Nathan Pike was die dag ziek thuis.

Vastbesloten om hem te ondervragen, was de politie naar Nathans huis gegaan. Klaarblijkelijk had zijn moeder met een verwilderd gezicht opengedaan. Voor zover zij wist, was haar zoon op school. Ze had hem sinds die ochtend niet meer gezien.

Al met al had John er maagpijn van gekregen. Goed, de politie zou bij de wedstrijd aanwezig zijn, geposteerd bij alle ingangen en verspreid tussen de menigte. Maar wat had je daaraan? Zelfmoordenaars liepen niet bepaald met hun plannen te koop.

Ze liepen gewoon naar binnen waar het stampvol was en bliezen zichzelf en iedereen om hen heen naar de maan. Tegen de tijd dat de politie Nathan Pike in het oog kreeg, was hij een lichaam in een rij doden.

Het was geen troost dat John en het team op het veld op veilige afstand van de tribunes waren. Er kwamen vanavond honderden tieners naar de wedstrijd. Misschien zelfs duizenden. Als er temidden van die menigte een bom afging... John kon zich er niet toe zetten erover na te denken. Natuurlijk kon de zelfmoordenaar wachten tot na de wedstrijd, als de tribunes leegstroomden op het veld. Dan kon de politie niets doen om een tiener ervan te weerhouden om...

'Coach?'

Zijn angst verdween toen hij omkeek. Het was Jake Daniels.

De jongen was in de afgelopen weken een lichtpuntje geweest. Hij was een stuk milder voor Nathan geweest. Drie keer was hij zelfs bij John langsgekomen om te praten over de spanningen op school en zijn bezorgdheid over zijn moeder. Kennelijk was ze woedend op zijn vader. Die twee maakten ruzie elke keer als ze gedwongen waren met elkaar te praten en Jake zat tussen twee vuren. Na een half uurtje praten met John over levensvragen leek Jake altijd minder gespannen.

Dat was de reden dat John nog steeds coachte, om jongemannen zoals Jake te helpen. En sinds ze weer met elkaar praatten, leek Jake gelukkiger en meer op zijn gemak. Minder geneigd om mee te doen met Casey Parker en de anderen die dachten dat zij op school de dienst uitmaakten.

John had zich zelfs afgevraagd of ze daardoor beter presteerden op het veld. Er was geen twijfel aan dat Jakes cijfers hen naar de recente overwinningen hadden geleid. Maar nu keek Jake ongerust.

John bracht een glimlach op. 'Ha, Jake.'

De jongen keek rond alsof hij zeker wilde weten dat niemand hen tweeën zag praten. 'Eh... mag ik hier even zitten?'

'Tuurlijk.' John schoof op. 'Wat heb je op je hart?'

'Het gerucht gaat dat… nou ja, dat Nathan Pike vanavond bij de wedstrijd mensen dood gaat schieten.'

John hield zijn adem in. Als de media ooit met tieners moesten wedijveren om een nieuwsflits openbaar te maken, zouden de tieners altijd winnen. Hij blies hard uit. 'Er is een bedreiging binnengekomen op kantoor. Ja. De politie heeft het nagetrokken. Ze maken zich er geen zorgen over.'

'Serieus? Is er echt een bedreiging binnengekomen?' Jake zette grote ogen op. 'Coach, maar als de politie het mis heeft? Nathan Pike is gestoord, weten ze dat dan niet?'

'De politie is op de hoogte van Nathan.' John deed zijn best om kalm te schijnen, maar vanbinnen was hij net zo ongerust als Jake. Wat hadden ze te maken bij een wedstrijd waarbij gedreigd was met moord en ellende? Welke footballwedstrijd kon daar belangrijk genoeg voor zijn?

'Dus er wordt niks aan gedaan?'

'De politie zal aanwezig zijn bij de wedstrijd.'

'Ja, maar dat houdt hem niet tegen. Ik bedoel, stel dat het hem niet kan schelen om dood te gaan?'

'De politie is er redelijk zeker van dat het geen serieuze bedreiging is, Jake. Anders hadden ze de wedstrijd wel afgelast.'

'Dat betwijfel ik.' Jake hield zijn helm op schoot en drukte hem tegen zijn buik. 'Iedereen maakt zich alleen maar druk over winnen. Zodat we naar de regiokampioenschappen kunnen, hè.'

Jake was dichter bij de waarheid dan hij wist. 'Daar heb je gelijk in.'

'Coach.' Jake keek even naar John op. 'Ik weet wie die brieven schrijft.'

'Brieven?'

'Ja, die brieven dat u ontslagen moet worden.'

De schrik sloeg John om het hart. Het was erg genoeg dat *hij* afwist van de boze zwerm ouderlijke protesten tegen hem, zonder dat zijn spelers het ook wisten. Zeker een jongen zoals Jake, die altijd naar John had opgekeken. Hij wilde weten wat de jongen wist, maar hij wilde het niet vragen. Hij klopte Jake op zijn knie. 'Een coach krijgt nou eenmaal altijd kritiek.'

'Casey Parker had het er laatst over in de kleedkamer. Hij zei dat zijn vader het helemaal met u gehad had. Ze hebben vergaderingen gehouden.'

'Zijn vader en hij?'

'Zijn vader en een paar andere ouders. Eerst wilden de andere mensen niet komen, maar… nou ja, nadat we een paar keer verloren hadden, kwamen er meer mensen. Ze hebben met meneer Lutz gepraat.'

'Dat is hun goed recht, denk ik.' John plooide zijn mond in een glimlach. 'Meer dan mijn best kan ik niet doen.'

'Maar u gaat toch niet weg?' Jake had zijn ogen wijd opengesperd en John wenste dat hij iets bemoedigends kon zeggen. 'U laat ons toch niet in de steek? Ik heb nog een jaar te gaan.'

'Ik zou er volgend jaar graag bij willen zijn, Jake.'

'Dus u doet het?'

'We zullen zien.' John wilde niet te veel informatie geven, maar hij wilde ook niet liegen. De kans dat hij nog een seizoen coach bleef op Marion High werd almaar kleiner.

'Bedoelt u dat u misschien gaat stoppen?'

John zuchtte. 'Misschien hoef ik niet te stoppen, als meneer Lutz me voor die tijd ontslaat.'

'Hij ontslaat u niet! Kijk eens wat u allemaal gedaan hebt voor het football op Marion High.'

'Zo zien mensen het niet. Ze zien dat hun zoons geen speeltijd krijgen, dat het team niet genoeg wedstrijden wint. Als je de verkeerde ouder tegen je krijgt, tja… soms valt er gewoon niets aan te doen.'

John zag er vanaf meer te zeggen over Herman Lutz. Het was niet aan hem om het gezag van de man bij een leerling te ondermijnen. Maar uiteindelijk lag Johns professionele lot in Lutz' handen, en hij stond erom bekend dat hij ouders hun zin gaf. Als de vader van Casey Parker hem eruit wilde hebben, zou Lutz de man waarschijnlijk tegemoetkomen in zijn wens.

Als John voor die tijd geen ontslag nam.

'Als het helpt, coach, ik zal vanavond de wedstrijd voor u winnen.'

John glimlachte. Was het maar zo eenvoudig. 'Bedankt, Jake. Dat betekent veel voor me.'

Jake speelde met de kinriem van zijn helm. 'Wat kan ik doen aan Nathan Pike en die bedreigingen?'

'Bidden.'

Jake zette grote ogen op en zijn mond viel open. 'Ik?'

'Niet alleen jij… het hele team.' John fronste zijn wenkbrauwen, maar hield zijn ogen op Jake gericht. 'Jullie zijn dit jaar niet bepaald aardig voor Nathan geweest. De bedreiging verbaast me eigenlijk niets.'

Jake slikte moeilijk en staarde naar de zitplaats voor hem. 'Dus u wilt dat ik samen met de jongens bid?'

'Je vroeg ernaar.'

Jake zweeg een ogenblik. 'Coach, ik denk dat hij jaloers is op mijn auto.'

'De Integra?'

'Ja. Een paar dagen nadat ik hem had gekregen, zag ik dat Nathans moeder hem bij school afzette. Ze heeft zo'n afgereden ouwe stationwagen met een deuk aan de zijkant. Op dat moment keek hij naar mijn auto en toen naar mij. Meestal kijkt hij naar me alsof hij me haat, maar die keer meer alsof hij mij wilde *zijn*. Alsof hij er alles voor over had om met me te ruilen.'

'Heb je hem daarom de afgelopen weken met rust gelaten?'

Jake knikte. 'Het was niet goed. Ik heb me beroerd gedragen.'

'Klopt.'

'Maar nu… Stel dat het te laat is? Als hij iemand echt iets aandoet?'

John keek de jongen onderzoekend in de ogen. 'Ik heb je gezegd wat ik zou doen.'

'Goed, coach.' Jake verstevigde zijn greep op de helm. 'We zullen bidden. Ik zal ervoor zorgen.'

★

Niets ter wereld had Abby die avond bij de wedstrijd weg kunnen houden.

Jazeker, John zou boos op haar zijn. Dat zag ze later wel. Maar als iemand leerlingen of spelers of zelfs haar man kwaad wilde doen, wilde Abby erbij zijn. Misschien kon ze iets doen, een leerling helpen, of een leven redden. Het kon wel de laatste keer zijn dat ze haar man in leven zag.

Die gedachten schoten in een ogenblik door haar hoofd op het moment dat John haar vertelde wat er die dag op school was gebeurd. Hij was laat voor de bus, dus ze kon hem niet tegenspreken. Maar er was geen sprake van dat ze thuisbleef.

Ze liep in de rij naar de tribunes en nam haar plaats in aan de verste kant, in de buurt van de ouders van de andere school. Bommelding of niet, ze zat niet graag bij de ouders van Johns spelers. Dit jaar niet tenminste. Zelden, eigenlijk. Het was gewoon niet goed om er zo bij betrokken te raken.

Nadat John de baan op Marion High had aangenomen, had Abby genoten van haar rol als vrouw van de hoofdcoach. Ze had het idyllische idee dat ze bij de ouders zou zitten om met hen te kletsen en vriendschap te sluiten. En aanvankelijk deed ze dat ook. Dat waren de jaren dat ze ouders uitnodigde voor het diner op Thanksgiving en een borrel op zaterdagavond.

'Wees voorzichtig, Abby,' waarschuwde John haar. 'Je denkt dat ze nu je vrienden zijn, maar wacht maar af. Soms houden mensen er bijbedoelingen op na.'

Abby had een afschuw gehad van zijn insinuatie dat de geweldige mensen naast wie ze tijdens wedstrijden zat alleen maar aardig deden om een wit voetje voor hun zoon te halen bij coach Reynolds. Ze was het keer op keer met hem oneens geweest en had volgehouden dat mensen niet zo oppervlakkig waren en dat football niet *zo* belangrijk was.

Maar uiteindelijk had John volkomen gelijk gehad.

Eén echtpaar, mensen die christen waren en vaak bij de Reynolds hadden gegeten, kwam als eerste op kantoor klagen over John toen hun zoon niet genoeg speeltijd kreeg. Andere ouders bleken net zo huichelachtig te zijn. Ze praatten over Abby achter haar rug en stonden met een brede glimlach vrolijk gedag te zeggen als ze er aankwam.

Ze waren natuurlijk niet allemaal zo, maar ze had haar lesje over spelersouders geleerd en nam het risico niet meer. Al jarenlang zat ze alleen of bij de vrouw van een van de andere coaches.

Maar vanavond was ze niet van plan om bij iemand anders te gaan zitten. Ze wilde zich aan de verste kant van de tribunes ophouden en de boel gadeslaan. Niet de wedstrijd, maar de tribunes, of er leerlingen waren die zich ongewoon gedroegen, op zoek naar een spoor van Nathan Pike. Ze had Nathan vaak genoeg op de campus gezien om hem te herkennen. Nathan en zijn kornuiten vielen met hun zwarte kleren en puntige halsbanden natuurlijk makkelijk in het oog. Vanavond wilde Abby de eerste zijn die hem zag, de eerste die een aanwijzing opmerkte als een van hen het stadion op wilde blazen.

De klok tikte de minuten af en het werd rust, alles zonder incidenten. Door het hele stadion was politie opgesteld, sommigen in burgerkleding. Maar tot dusver was het opmerkelijkste wat er in de hele wedstrijd was gebeurd de vijf touchdowns van Jake Daniels. Volgens Abby was het een klasserecord. Kade was een van de beste quarterbacks in de streek geweest, en hij was zelfs nooit in de buurt gekomen van vijf touchdowns in één speelhelft.

De tweede helft verliep net zo kalm. In het derde kwart werd Jake uit de wedstrijd gehaald en vervangen door Casey Parker, die twee passes liet onderscheppen. Ondanks dat wonnen de Eagles met dertig punten. Toen de zoemer voor het einde klonk, stroomde de menigte het veld op en omhelsde de Eagles alsof er geen seizoen vol controverse en klachten van ouders was geweest.

Wat deed het er nog toe? De Eagles gingen naar de regiokampioenschappen.

Abby stond op en daalde af naar het veld. *Waar is hij, God? Waar is Nathan Pike? Als hij er is, laat het me dan alstublieft zien, Vader.* Ze speurde de menigte af... en aarzelde. Bewoog daar iets langs het hek van het stadion? Het reusachtige bouwwerk werd aan drie kanten omringd door maïsvelden. Aan de vierde kant was een parkeerterrein.

Abby staarde met haar ogen half dichtgeknepen... Ja. Temidden van de hoge maïs... Abby wist zeker dat ze beweging zag.

Als in trance daalde Abby de trap af, liep langs de onoverdekte tribunes naar de plaats waar John en zijn spelers felicitaties in ontvangst namen van honderden leerlingen en de hele muziekkapel. Aldoor hield ze haar ogen strak gericht op die plek in het maïsveld.

Ineens verscheen een gestalte; een gestalte in het zwart.

Voordat Abby iets kon doen – voordat ze zo dichtbij kon komen dat John en de anderen haar konden horen, kon wegrennen of duiken of een politieagent aanklampen – glipte de gestalte door een gat in het hek en draafde door de menigte op haar man toe.

'John, pas op!' schreeuwde Abby en om haar heen staakte een stel ouders hun gesprekken en staarde haar aan.

Abby sloeg geen acht op hen en zette het op een rennen, zo snel als ze kon de trappen af. *Alstublieft, God... bespaar hun dit. Alstublieft, God. In Jezus' naam smeek ik U...*

Ze was nu op het veld, maar de gestalte was John dicht genaderd en stelde zich op in het midden van de menigte leerlingen en spelers. Van vijftig meter afstand kon Abby het gezicht van de jongen zien.

Het was Nathan Pike.

Hij was zoals gewoonlijk in het zwart gekleed, maar dit keer droeg hij een nieuw kledingstuk. Een uitpuilend jack.

'John… rennen!' Abby schreeuwde de waarschuwing en trok de aandacht van tientallen leerlingen. 'Jullie allemaal, rennen! Vlug!'

Een paar leerlingen deden wat ze had gezegd, maar de meesten bleven roerloos op hun plaats staan en staarden Abby aan alsof ze krankzinnig was geworden.

Ze was nog tien meter van John af toen Nathan op hem afliep en zijn hand op Johns schouder legde. Op hetzelfde moment schoten vier agenten door de menigte en haalden Nathan onderuit.

'John!' Hijgend bereikte Abby haar echtgenoot. Haar maag zat in de knoop en ze haalde moeizaam adem. 'Kom mee.' Ze pakte hem bij de arm. 'Wegwezen hier.'

'Wat krijgen we nou…?' John was bleek en hij sperde zijn ogen wijdopen.

De cirkel van leerlingen was gegroeid en schaarde zich om de plek waar de politie Nathan tegen de grond had vastgepind. De jongen scheen mee te werken. Van alle kanten liepen agenten te hoop en binnen een paar minuten hadden ze de leerlingen van de plaats van actie weggestuurd naar het parkeerterrein. John gaf zijn assistenten opdracht om met de teambus mee terug naar school te rijden.

'Vals alarm,' kondigde een agent aan. 'Geen bommen.'

Elke spier in Abby's lijf werd slap van opluchting. Ze greep de mouwen van Johns jasje en begroef haar gezicht tegen zijn borst. 'Ik dacht dat hij je ging vermoorden, John. Ik… ik was zo bang.'

Ze sprak fluisterend, zodat de andere coaches het niet konden horen. Het hele personeel was op de hoogte van de bomdreiging, dus niemand verbaasde zich over wat er gebeurde.

'Het is goed, Abby. Het is allemaal voorbij.' John streek met zijn hand over haar rug en pakte haar hand. Toen liepen ze naar de plek waar Nathan nog geboeid op de grond lag.

De politie knikte toestemmend en John liep naar de jongen toe. 'Heb jij het gedaan, Nathan? Heb jij dat telefoontje gepleegd?'

Nathan schudde zijn hoofd, zijn ogen waren groot en angstig. 'Dat blijven ze maar vragen.' Hij hapte naar adem, de woorden bleven steken in zijn keel. 'Ik weet niet waar ze het over hebben.'

Abby klampte zich aan Johns arm vast, haar lichaam sidderde van de adrenalinegolf. De jongen loog. Dat moest wel.

John probeerde het nog eens. 'Je was vandaag niet op school.'

Nathan knipperde met zijn ogen. 'Ik… ik ben naar de bibliotheek geweest. Ik moest een werkstuk voor Engels inleveren en daar zat ik lekker rustig. Echt waar, meneer Reynolds, ik weet niet waar ze het over hebben.'

Er stond een agent vlak naast Nathans hoofd. 'Waarom ben je stiekem binnengekomen door het gat in het hek?'

'Ik kwam van… van de bieb en ik wilde even langs gaan. Ik zag de score en wilde… meneer Reynolds feliciteren. Het was een belangrijke wedstrijd.'

Het verhaal was zo lek als een zeef, maar dat was niet Abby's probleem. Het belangrijkste was dat John ongedeerd was. John en de leerlingen en de spelers. Ze deed haar ogen dicht en leunde met haar hoofd tegen John aan. *Dank U, God… dank U…*

De politie trok Nathan overeind en voerde hem mee naar een wachtende politieauto. Voordat ze vertrokken, kwam er een agent naar John toe. 'Denkt u dat hij de waarheid spreekt?'

'Dat is moeilijk te zeggen bij Nathan.' John dacht even na. 'Maar één ding wil ik toch zeggen. In al de tijd dat ik die jongen ken, heb ik hem tot op de dag van vandaag nog nooit bang gezien. Als ik zijn verleden niet kende, zou ik zeker zeggen dat hij de waarheid sprak.'

De agent krabbelde iets op zijn schrijfblok. 'Dank u. Dat zullen we in de overwegingen meenemen.'

Het duurde niet lang of John en Abby waren als enigen over in het stadion. Hij sloeg zijn armen om haar heen en hield haar dicht tegen zich aan. 'Je trilt helemaal.'

'Ik dacht… ik dacht dat hij je zo op zou blazen. Voordat ik iets kon doen om je te helpen.'

'Ik had gezegd dat je niet moest komen.' Ondanks het standje klonk zijn stem vriendelijk en daar was Abby blij om. Hij was niet boos op haar.

'Ja, dag. Alsof ik thuis kan blijven zitten terwijl iemand het misschien op jou had voorzien.' Ze maakte zich los en keek hem recht in de ogen. 'Ik moest komen, John. Niets had me tegen kunnen houden.'

'Waarom verbaast me dat niet?'

Ze grinnikte. 'Raad eens?'

'Wat?'

'Je hebt gewonnen!'

'Ja, we hebben gewonnen.'

'Gefeliciteerd.'

'Dank je.' Het scorebord was nog verlicht en de stadionverlichting brandde nog. Terreinpersoneel zou nog een paar uur bezig zijn met opruimen voordat het stadion gesloten werd. 'Nu gaan we naar de regiokampioenschappen.'

'Je klinkt niet blij.' Ze legde haar handen om zijn gezicht.

'Ben ik ook niet. De ouders haten me, weet je nog?'

'Niet als je wint.' Abby streek licht met haar vinger over zijn wenkbrauwen.

'Deze ouders zijn anders. Jake Daniels vertelde me wie de brieven schrijft. Het is de vader van Casey Parker.'

'Verbaast me niks.'

Hij bracht zijn gezicht dicht bij het hare en kuste haar. 'Bedankt dat je er vanavond was. Al had ik je gevraagd om niet te komen. Het betekent veel voor me.'

'Graag gedaan.' Ze kuste hem terug en ademde zijn geur in, terwijl ze er niet aan probeerde te denken hoe anders de avond had kunnen aflopen als...

'Je ziet er moe uit.'

'Ik ben ook moe. Ik ben nog nooit van mijn leven zo bang geweest.'

'Ach, Abby.' Hij streek met zijn wang langs de hare en klampte zich aan haar vast zoals zij aan hem. 'Lieve Abby. Wat erg. Ik wil niet dat je zo bang bent. Waarom ga je niet naar huis om een beetje uit te rusten?'

'En jij dan?'

'Daar ben ik te gespannen voor.' Hij trok zijn sporttas over zijn schouder en voerde haar mee naar het parkeerterrein. 'Ik ga terug naar school om werkstukken te corrigeren. Ik loop een week of twee achter. Kun je me een lift geven?'

Ze grinnikte. 'Maar al te graag.'

'Mijn auto staat bij school.'

Onderweg naar huis praatten ze over de wedstrijd en toen Abby voor de school stopte, draaide ze zich geeuwend naar John toe. 'Maak je het laat?'

'Misschien. Het kan wel tot één of twee uur duren als ik genoeg energie heb.'

'Vergeet niet dat we morgen dansles hebben.' Ze gaf hem een kus op zijn wang en hij stapte uit.

'Zo laat wordt het niet, wees maar niet bang.'

'Nee, maar ik wil dat je genoeg energie hebt. Paula is behoorlijk veeleisend, hoor.'

John lachte. 'Tot straks, Abby. Ik houd van je.'

'Ik ook van jou.'

Nu meer dan ooit, dacht Abby terwijl ze wegreed.

Elf

Het feest was afgeladen vol met tieners en Jake Daniels was geweldig in zijn sas. Op één ding na.

Hij moest almaar aan Nathan Pike en Casey Parker denken.

Aan Nathan, omdat Jake de hele arrestatie had gadegeslagen. Hij had zelfs het beste uitzicht gehad van iedereen, want hij had een meter van coach Reynolds af gestaan toen het gebeurde. Eerst was hij doodsbenauwd geweest dat Nathan plotseling een pistool tevoorschijn zou halen en hun laatste uur geslagen had.

Maar toen zag hij Nathans ogen.

Jake en Nathan waren nooit goede vrienden geweest, maar een paar jaar geleden waren ze goede bekenden. Ze kenden elkaar goed genoeg om gedag te zeggen en elkaar nu en dan te helpen met een huiswerkopdracht. Toen Jakes atletische eigenschappen en populariteit waren toegenomen, was het met Nathan bergafwaarts gegaan.

Jake had het oprecht gemeend toen hij zei dat Nathan gestoord was. Dat was er van de jongen geworden. Maar toen hij die avond op het veld Nathans ogen zag, had hij diep vanbinnen geweten dat Nathan niets van doen had met de dreiging van die dag. Hij was verschrikkelijk bang.

En dat zat Jake om twee redenen dwars. Ten eerste, omdat het niet juist was dat Nathan gearresteerd werd voor iets wat hij misschien niet had gedaan. En ten tweede, als Nathan het niet had gedaan, wie dan wel? Wie het ook was, hij liep nog rond en maakte plannen.

En dan had je nog Casey Parker.

Die avond was Jake voor de wedstrijd de kleedkamer binnen-gekomen en had iedereen meteen verteld dat de geruchten klop-ten. Iemand had de school opgebeld en gedreigd om die avond bij de wedstrijd mensen te vermoorden.

Toen de commotie bedaarde, vertelde Jake dat ze maar één ding konden doen aan de dreiging. Ze konden bidden. Met twee of drie tegelijk hadden de jongens hun uitrusting laten vallen en waren ze naar Jake toegekomen. Binnen een minuut stond het hele team bij elkaar in een groepje… behalve Casey Parker.

'Dit is een openbare school,' snauwde Casey. 'Bidden is tegen de wet.'

In de afgelopen drie weken, nadat Jake weer bij coach Reynolds was geweest en aardiger was voor jongens zoals Nathan Pike, was de vriendschap met Casey bekoeld. Daarstraks in de kleedkamer had Jake Casey wel willen tegenspreken, maar een van de andere spelers was hem voor. 'Je mag bidden wanneer je wilt.'

Enkele anderen beaamden dit.

Casey hield zich afzijdig terwijl de rest bad om Gods bescher-ming, niet alleen voor de wedstrijd, maar voor iedereen die aan-wezig was. Toen het gebed afgelopen was, vormde het team een strakke cirkel en ze zongen en riepen hun gewone kreet om zich op te warmen voor de wedstrijd.

Casey deed niet mee.

Hij zat de hele avond in zijn eentje. De coach riep zijn num-mer pas af toen Jake zes touchdowns had gemaakt. Het was voor de andere Eagles geen verrassing toen Casey het veld inkwam en prompt vier incomplete passes en twee intercepties gooide.

In de bus terug naar school zei Casey geen woord tegen de rest. Toen er over het feest werd gepraat, smeerde hij 'm zonder gedag te zeggen. Jake probeerde het te vergeten. Het was per slot van rekening *zijn* avond. Zijn team had een enge doodsdreiging over-leefd *en* de wedstrijd gewonnen. Met afstand. Ze gingen zelfs naar de regiokampioenschappen.

Het was tijd om feest te vieren. Groot feest.

Hij keek om zich heen. Het feest was bij een meisje thuis, een eerstejaars cheerleader, dacht Jake. Het meisje had een reusachtig huis, veel lekker eten en ouders die geen bezwaar hadden dat ze daar bij elkaar kwamen. De meeste teamleden waren op komen dagen, maar Casey niet. Een groep jongens die Jake niet goed kende, kwam naar hem toe.

'Goeie wedstrijd, Jake… goed gespeeld.'

'Ja, was het een record of niet? Zes touchdowns?'

Dat was Jake tot nu toe al honderd keer gevraagd, maar hij antwoordde beleefd: 'Een schoolrecord. Gelijk aan een competitierecord.'

'Wat gaaf. Top, man.'

De jongens vertrokken en Jake leunde tegen het aanrecht. Buiten hadden sommige jongens bier in hun auto. Ze dwaalden in en uit, sloegen een paar biertjes achterover en keerden terug in huis. De ouders van het meisje hadden geen bezwaar dat er gedronken werd, zolang het maar niet op hun terrein was.

Dat was prima voor hen, maar niet voor Jake. Vanavond niet. Hij had zijn vader beloofd dat hij niet met drank op achter het stuur zou gaan zitten en sinds hij de nieuwe auto had gekregen, had hij woord gehouden. Hij pakte een plastic bekertje en vulde het met ijswater. Bovendien, hij wilde van de avond genieten en niet opgaan in een nevel van drank. Dat had hij in de zomer te vaak gedaan. Nu was hij wel wijzer.

Het feest was al twee uur gaande en het was na middernacht. Jake wilde fris zijn voor de training in de ochtend. Nog een paar minuten en hij ging er een eind aan maken.

Op dat moment ging de voordeur open. Casey Parker kwam binnen met zijn arm om Darla Brubaker heen geslagen, het meisje dat Jake mee had willen vragen naar het schoolbal. Jake zette zijn bekertje neer en knarsetandde. Wat voor stunt Casey ook uit wilde halen, het zou hem niet lukken. Casey keek zoekend rond tot zijn ogen op Jake bleven rusten. Toen draaide hij zich om naar Darla en kuste haar op de wang.

Jake wendde zijn blik af. Wat mankeerde Casey eigenlijk? Hij gedroeg zich als een echte sukkel. Als Darla met zo'n hufter om wilde gaan, moest ze haar gang maar gaan. Toch kon hij het niet helpen dat hij omkeek naar het stel, dat nog bij de voordeur stond.

Casey fluisterde iets in Darla's oor en het meisje giechelde en nam plaats in de hoek van de kamer. Toen ze weg was, slenterde Casey de keuken binnen. Hij had een hatelijke uitdrukking op zijn gezicht.

'Jake.' Hij knikte één keer en leunde tegen het aanrecht aan de andere kant. 'Mooie wedstrijd vanavond.'

'Bedankt.' Jake pakte zijn bekertje weer en nam nog een slok water. 'Zeg, waar heb jij last van? Je was jezelf niet daarstraks.'

'Laten we maar zeggen dat ik baalde van dat bidden, ja?'

Jake lachte kort. 'Het heeft wel gewerkt, hè? We zijn niet dood-geschoten onder het spelen.'

Casey sloeg met zijn vuist op het aanrecht. 'Houd op over bid-den, ja? Als je geen derdejaars was, zou ik je op je gezicht slaan voor het uithalen van zo'n stunt voor de wedstrijd.'

'Stunt?' Jake fronste. Caseys insinuatie beviel hem niet.

'Ik heb wel gezien dat je tijdens de hele rit naar North County met de coach zat te praten.' Casey sloeg zijn armen over elkaar. 'Wat ik niet snap is dit: jij bent al zijn lievelingetje. Moest je je echt laten overhalen om te bidden? Je hebt toch de afgelopen weken wel genoeg geslijmd? Elke keer bij de coach binnenvallen en ouwe-jongens-krentenbrood spelen.'

Jake zette zijn bekertje neer en deed drie stappen naar Casey toe. 'Wat bedoel je daarmee?'

'Ach, kom. Je hoort bij de C-selectie van de coach. Jongens zoals ik maken geen kans.'

'C-selectie?' vroeg Jake verward. Wat bedoelde Casey toch? Wat ter wereld was een C-selectie?'

'Je weet het best, Jake. De *christelijke* selectie. De coach geeft de christelijke jongens altijd de beste plaatsen. Dat weet iedereen.'

Jake voelde zijn gezicht warm en toen koud worden. 'Je bent gek, Parker. Dat is een leugen en dat kan iedereen in het team je vertellen.'

Casey greep Jake bij zijn T-shirt en rukte hem naar zich toe zodat hun gezichten nog maar centimeters uit elkaar waren. 'Ik ben de beste quarterback van het team.' Hij siste de woorden en gaf nog een ruk aan Jake om het accent te leggen. 'Vertel me dan eens waarom ik op de bank zit en jij alle speeltijd krijgt.'

'Speeltijd *verdien* je.' Jake legde zijn handen op Casey Parkers schouders en duwde hem weg. 'Dat weet iedereen die voor coach Reynolds heeft gespeeld.'

'O ja?' Casey gaf Jake een duw, nu tegen het aanrecht aan.

Voordat Jake wraak kon nemen, stroomde er een troep gillende meisjes de keuken binnen.

'Ophouden, jongens.'

'Ja, kom op… laat los.'

Jake trok zijn shirt recht en keek Casey dreigend aan. Toen de meisjes weg waren, wierp Casey Jake een woeste blik toe. 'Het wordt tijd dat we dit uitvechten.'

'Buiten.'

'Best. Maar niet op het gras.'

'Waar dan?'

'Op straat.' Hij grijnsde spottend naar Jake. 'Jij denkt dat je de enige bent met een snelle auto?' snauwde hij. 'Nou, dat heb je mis.'

'Heb je het over een race?' Er liep een rilling over Jakes rug. Niemand luisterde naar hun gesprek. Het had niet veel te betekenen. Gewoon een simpele race tussen hen tweeën. Dan wist Casey voor eens en voor altijd dat er met Jake Daniels niet te spotten viel. 'Wanneer je maar wilt, Parker. Naast de mijne lijkt jouw auto geparkeerd te staan.'

'Er is maar één manier om erachter te komen.'

'Waar wil je het doen?'

Casey kneep zijn ogen halfdicht, zijn stem klonk hees van boosheid. 'Haynes Street… dat stuk van anderhalve kilometer voor de school.'

'Afgesproken.'

'Ik zie je over een halfuur op Haynes en Jefferson.' Casey draaide zich om en liep terug naar Darla.

Jake had nog maar één ding te zeggen en hij zei het zo hard dat Darla het kon horen. 'Vergeet de winnaarstrofee niet mee te nemen.'

★

De late avonduren na een wedstrijd vond John de prettigste tijd om zijn schoolwerk in te halen. Hij gaf elke dag zes uur gezondheidsleer en hij kon makkelijk achter raken. Vooral gedurende het seizoen. Maar goed dat hij vanavond meer energie had dan anders.

Meestal ging hij naar zijn kantoor, nam een aantal werkstukken door en begon zich vermoeid te voelen. Dan ging hij naar huis en kroop rond elf uur met Abby in bed. Maar vanavond had hij genoeg uithoudingsvermogen om tot de ochtend door te werken. Maar dat deed hij niet. Hij had Abby beloofd dat hij het niet te laat zou maken. Bovendien had ze gelijk. Hij had zijn energie nodig voor hun dansles van zaterdagavond.

John keek een aantal werkstukken na en schreef de cijfers in zijn boek.

Hij was nooit een coach geweest die op vrijdagavond wedstrijdfilms bekijkt. Hoeveel energie het ook kostte om een footballwedstrijd te coachen, hij wilde zijn hoofd vullen met iets volkomen anders. Corrigeren was precies wat hij nodig had. Hij had die avond al heel wat werkstukken nagekeken.

En aldoor moest hij denken aan Nathan Pike.

Diep vanbinnen voelde hij dat Nathan om geen andere reden naar het stadion was gekomen dan hij had opgegeven: om John te feliciteren met de overwinning. Even zat hij na te denken over de gebeurtenis na de wedstrijd. Ongetwijfeld zaten er haken en ogen aan. Waarom was Nathan niet net als iedereen door de hoofdingang het stadion binnengekomen? En waarom had hij de hele dag in de bibliotheek gezeten om daarna vijftien kilometer om te rijden naar een footballwedstrijd? John kon zich niet herinneren dat hij hem in het seizoen bij enige andere wedstrijd had gezien.

Maar John was er een expert in tieners in hun ogen te kijken en de waarheid te vinden. En iets in Nathans verhaal klonk oprechter dan alles wat de jongen ooit eerder had gezegd.

John corrigeerde nog een stel werkstukken en rekte zich uit. Zijn oog viel op de ingelijste foto op de rand van zijn bureau. Abby en hij op Nicoles bruiloft. Abby had het een vreemde keuze gevonden. Er was per slot van rekening meer dan een halve meter ruimte tussen hen en zelfs een vreemde kon de spanning op hun gezicht zien. Het was geen blije foto.

Maar hij was eerlijk.

Ze hadden het besluit genomen om te scheiden en die avond, als de kinderen op huwelijksreis waren gegaan, had John zijn spullen willen pakken om bij een collega in te trekken, een man die een jaar eerder van zijn vrouw gescheiden was. Toen de foto werd genomen, stond Johns auto zelfs al volgepakt met zijn bezittingen.

Hun huwelijk was op een haar na gevild.

Kade en Sean hadden die week bij vrienden gelogeerd en Abby was van plan om naar New York te vliegen en haar redacteur te ontmoeten. Hun levens vielen uit elkaar en de kinderen hadden er niets van geweten.

Die avond was John na de bruiloft al halverwege de weg toen hij stopte. Hij wist niet hoe hij om moest draaien, wist niet hoe hij de fouten die ze hadden gemaakt moest uitwissen… maar hij wist dat hij geen meter verder weg kon rijden van de enige vrouw van wie hij ooit had gehouden. De vrouw die God voor hem bestemd had om voor altijd lief te hebben. Op dat moment waren de scheidingsplannen keurig netjes vastgelegd, de afspraken die ze gemaakt hadden over hoe ze het aan de kinderen zouden vertellen en hoe ze de tijd zouden verdelen… alles was geregeld. Alles, behalve één zorgwekkende kleinigheid.

Hij hield nog van Abby. Hij hield van haar met hart en ziel.

Dus hij stapte uit de auto en liep terug naar huis. Hij vond haar buiten, waar hij had geweten dat hij haar zou vinden. Op de aanlegsteiger, hun eigen plekje. En in het uur dat volgde, waren de muren die ze om hun hart hadden gebouwd afgebrokkeld tot er alleen nog twee mensen over waren die een leven en een gezin en een liefde hadden geschapen die ze niet af konden danken.

John zuchtte.

Wat hield hij veel van Abby… nu nog meer dan ooit.

In gedachten hoorde hij haar stem, de laatste keer dat ze bij hem in het lokaal was geweest. 'Haal die foto weg, John.' Ze had er vol afkeer naar gekeken. 'Hij is afschuwelijk. Ik lijk een oude, verbitterde vrouw.'

'Nee. Het is een aandenken.'

'Waaraan?'

'Aan hoe we op het punt stonden om alles kwijt te raken.'

Bovendien was het niet de enige foto op zijn bureau. Er stond nog een andere vlak naast. Een kleinere foto van John en Abby, lachend op een familiefeestje een paar maanden geleden. Abby had gelijk. Op de laatste foto leek ze tien jaar jonger. Het was verbazingwekkend wat geluk kon doen voor je gezicht.

Hij keek op naar de klok aan de muur van het klaslokaal. Half één. Abby zou onderhand slapen. Die gedachte maakte hem ineens vermoeid. Hij wierp een blik op de werkstukken op zijn bureau. De stapel was tot de helft geminderd, maar de rest kon wachten. Als het moest, kon hij maandagavond ook overwerken.

De rusteloosheid van daarstraks was afgenomen. Als hij nu naar huis ging, zou hij niet wakker liggen om te tobben. Hij zou naast Abby kruipen, haar geur inademen en binnen een paar minuten in slaap vallen.

Dat gaf de doorslag.

Hij raapte de werkstukken bij elkaar, maakte er een nette stapel van en stopte ze in de juiste mappen. Toen pakte hij zijn sleutels, sloot zijn klaslokaal af en liep naar het parkeerterrein.

Terwijl hij de oprit van de school uitreed, bewerkte hij de spieren in zijn benen. Hij was vermoeider dan hij had gedacht. De straten waren allang verlaten en omdat John en Abby maar een paar minuten van de school woonden, kon hij er bijna zeker van zijn binnen vijf minuten naast Abby in bed te liggen.

Hij keek beide kanten uit, begon zijn veiligheidsgordel vast te maken en draaide zijn auto Haynes Street op.

Achter hem klonk een geluid als een naderende goederentrein. In een oogwenk bedacht John dat er geen spoorweg liep in dat deel van Marion. Hij keek in zijn achteruitkijkspiegel en werd verblind door een reeks lichten achter zich.

Wat was dit? Hij ging geraakt worden. *O, God... help me!*

Er was geen tijd om te reageren... geen tijd om na te denken of hij moest remmen of gas geven. Het brullen achter hem werd oorverdovend en toen was er een verschrikkelijke klap. John werd gewaar van gierende banden en brekend glas; samen met iets anders.

Een verblindende pijn brandde door Johns rug, een onbeschrijfelijke pijn zoals hij nog nooit in zijn leven had gevoeld.

Zijn zicht werd wazig en hij zat in volkomen duisternis naar adem te snakken. Hij vond zijn stem terug en gilde het enige wat hij onder woorden kon brengen.

'Aaaabby!'

Zijn stem echode een hele tijd in zijn hoofd. Het was onmogelijk om nog adem te halen.

Toen was er niets meer dan stilte.

Twaalf

De airbag blies onmiddellijk op.

Het ene moment scheurde Jake over Haynes Street, stomverbaasd over de snelheid die Casey Parker uit zijn Honda haalde. Het volgende ogenblik was er de meest afgrijselijke botsing die Jake ooit voor mogelijk had gehouden.

Zijn auto stond nu stil, maar de airbag verstikte zijn gezicht. Hij stompte er naar adem snakkend in. Wat was er gebeurd? Had hij een klapband of was hij de macht over het stuur verloren? Jake probeerde de duizeligheid van zich af te schudden. Nee, dat was het niet. Hij was aan het racen geweest… tegen Casey Parker.

Jake lag voor, maar niet veel. Hij had het gas ingetrapt en de kilometerteller naar de 160 zien klimmen. Dat was sneller dan hij ooit van plan was geweest te gaan rijden, maar nog een paar honderd meter en de race was gereden. Toen had hij beweging gezien, een truck of een auto die vlak voor hem de weg opdraaide.

Was dat wat er gebeurd was? Had hij iemand aangereden? Zijn mond was droog en hij kon niet goed ademhalen. *O, God… dat niet.* Jake schopte tegen de airbag en vocht zich zo ver vrij dat hij zijn portier kon openen. Hij zette zijn voeten op het wegdek en hapte naar lucht. Waarom kon hij niet voluit ademen?

Sta op, sukkel! Maar zijn lichaam wilde niet meewerken. Zijn spieren waren als slappe spaghetti en konden niet bewegen. Er gingen een paar seconden voorbij tot zijn longen langzaam volliepen en de zuurstof weer in zijn systeem terecht kwam. Daarbij kwamen zijn benen met een ruk in beweging. Hij stond op en keek om zich heen. Casey Parker was weg. *God, nee…*

Zijn hart bonsde wild tegen zijn borstkas toen hij zich omdraaide en naar de weg voor zijn auto keek. Een meter of twintig verder lagen de verfrommelde restanten van een pick-up truck. Het was onmogelijk te zeggen wat voor kleur hij had. Jake had zin om over te geven, maar in plaats daarvan begon hij te huilen. Hij had geen mobiele telefoon, dus hij kon niet om hulp bellen. De hele school was omringd door open velden, dus er waren geen omwonenden die de klap gehoord hadden.

Hij staarde naar het verwrongen metaal en wist zonder enige twijfel dat de bestuurder dood was. De passagiers ook, als die erin zaten. Bij autorijles had hij geleerd dat je je veiligheidsgordel moest dragen omdat er in een volledig vernielde auto bijna altijd ruimte was om in leven te blijven.

Maar in deze niet. Alleen de voorkant was nog over. De achterkant was verfrommeld als aluminiumfolie en de bestuurdersplaats... tja, de bestuurdersplaats leek opgeslokt door de andere stukken.

Hij voelde aandrang om weg te rennen, zo snel als hij kon te vluchten. Als hij zojuist iemand had gedood, ging hij voor jaren de gevangenis in. Hij keek om naar zijn auto. De voorkant lag in puin, maar de kans bestond dat hij nog rijden kon.

Hij schudde zijn hoofd en de gedachte verdween.

Wat bezielde hem? Hoe onmogelijk het ook leek, er kon iemand in leven zijn in het wrak! Hij liep wat dichterbij. Wat... wie er ook in de vernielde pick-up lag, hij wilde het echt niet zien.

Zijn hart bonsde nu zo snel dat hij bang was flauw te vallen. Het trillen van daarstraks was sidderen geworden. Luid klappertandend naderde hij de achterkant van het voertuig.

Ineens viel zijn oog ergens op.

Hij keek naar de grond en in de drie meter die hem nog scheidde van de vernielde pick-up lag een kentekenplaat. Jake liep erheen en zijn hart stond stil.

GO EAGLES.

Go Eagles? Nee, God… alstublieft… het kan niet waar zijn. Slechts één persoon had zo'n kentekenplaat. En hij reed in een pick-up truck.

'Coach!' Met wijd opengesperde ogen rende Jake de laatste stappen naar de zijkant van het wrak.

Binnen hoorde hij gekreun, maar de portieren waren zo gemangeld dat Jake niets kon zien, laat staan helpen. 'Coach, bent u dat?'

Natuurlijk was hij het. Waarom kwam er niemand langs? Waar was Casey Parker? Hij trok aan zijn haren en schreeuwde weer. 'Coach! Ik ga hulp halen. Houd vol!'

Met alle kracht die Jake kon vinden, trok hij aan een stuk van het portier. *Open, stom ding… open. Kom op.*

'Coach, volhouden.'

Hij werd overspoeld door paniek. Wat had hij gedaan? Hij had meer dan 160 gereden en coach Reynolds geraakt… Hoe kon dat gebeurd zijn? De coach had al uren thuis moeten zijn. En nu? De coach lag tussen het verwrongen metaal te sterven en hij kon er niets aan doen. 'Coach… kunt u me horen?'

Niets.

'God…' Jake gooide zijn hoofd in zijn nek en stak zijn armen in de lucht. Hij huilde en schreeuwde als een waanzinnige. 'Alstublieft, God, help me! Laat de coach niet doodgaan!'

Op dat moment hoorde Jake achter zich een auto aankomen. *Dank U, God… wat er ook met mij gebeurt, laat de coach alstublieft leven.*

Hij ging midden op de weg staan en zwaaide vertwijfeld met zijn armen. Bijna onmiddellijk herkende hij de auto. Casey Parker. De Honda kwam met gierende banden tot stilstand en Casey sprong eruit.

'Ik geloof dat het de truck van de coach is.' Casey was lijkbleek en trilde diep geschokt. 'Ik… moest terugkomen.' Hij hield een mobiele telefoon omhoog. 'Ik heb het alarmnummer al gebeld.'

'Hij is… hij is…' Jake schokte hevig, te angstig om te spreken.

Casey rende naar het wrak toe. 'Help me, Jake. We moeten hem er uithalen.'

De twee jongens probeerden met verwoede vastberadenheid een manier te vinden om in de pick-up te komen. Maar het lukte niet. Ze gaven niet op, ook niet toen ze sirenes hoorden. Pas toen de hulpverleningsvoertuigen stopten en ambulancepersoneel hen bij de auto wegstuurde.

'Het is… mijn coach die erin ligt!' Jake kon niet helder denken en zijn mond weigerde dienst. '*Help* hem!'

Casey nam het over. 'Onze coach zit in de auto vast. We weten zeker dat hij het is.'

Een van de broeders aarzelde. 'Coach John Reynolds?'

'Ja.' Casey knikte en likte zijn lippen. Hij leek elk moment flauw te kunnen vallen, maar hij kon tenminste praten. Jake stopte zijn handen in zijn zakken en staarde naar de grond. Hij had zin om in een gat te kruipen en er nooit meer uit te komen, of in slaap te vallen met zijn moeder naast zich, die over hem waakte en hem beloofde dat het allemaal maar een nare droom was geweest.

Maar in plaats daarvan stopte er een politieauto.

Jake en Casey stonden drie meter van het wrak en sloegen het reddingswerk gade of staarden naar de grond. Jake had nog niet echt aan de politie gedacht. Daarvoor had hij het te druk met kijken of het ambulancepersoneel coach Reynolds kon bereiken en of ze hem konden redden of niet.

Hij was zo afgeleid dat hij, toen de agenten zich voor Casey en hem opstelden, een stap opzij deed om beter zicht te hebben.

'Bestuurder van de rode Integra?' De agent scheen met een zaklamp in zijn gezicht.

Jakes hart sloeg een slag over en hij kneep zijn ogen tot spleetjes. *O, God… help…* 'Ja… ja, agent.'

'Gewond?'

'Nee, agent.' Jakes keel zat zo dicht dat hij de woorden naar buiten moest persen. 'Ik had een airbag.'

De andere agent scheen met een zaklamp in Caseys gezicht. 'Bestuurder van de Honda?'

Caseys tanden klapperden. 'Ja.'

'We kregen een tip van een bestuurder anderhalve kilometer verderop. Ze had een gele Honda en een rode Integra gezien die als een stel snelheidsduivels door Haynes Street scheurden.' De eerste agent deed een stap dichter naar Jake toe. 'Klopt dat?'

Jake wierp een blik op Casey. Dit was een nachtmerrie. Wat deden ze hier? Waarom had hij er ooit mee ingestemd tegen Casey te racen? Hij had toch naar huis willen gaan? Nog een paar minuten en dan ging hij er een eind aan maken, dat had hij zich toch voorgenomen?

'Pak je rijbewijs.' De agent wees naar Jakes auto. Toen gebaarde hij naar Caseys Honda. 'Jij ook.'

Jake en Casey deden wat hun was opgedragen. De eerste agent overhandigde de rijbewijzen aan de tweede. 'Trek ze even na, wil je?' Toen wendde hij zich weer tot Jake. 'Hoor es, vriend. Maak het jezelf maar gemakkelijk. De technische recherche kan ons tot op de kilometer nauwkeurig vertellen hoe hard jullie reden. Als jullie nu niet meewerken, maken we er voor jullie *en* jullie ouders een beroerd proces van.'

Het geluid van een elektrisch stuk gereedschap klonk op. *Alstublieft, God… laten ze hem eruit kunnen halen.*

Jake probeerde te slikken, maar het ging niet. Zijn tong kleefde vast aan zijn gehemelte. Nu keek hij Casey niet aan. 'Ja, agent… we… we waren aan het racen, meneer.'

'Je weet dat dat bij de wet verboden is?'

Jake en Casey knikten eensgezind. De andere agent kwam weer bij hen staan. 'Allebei een schoon strafblad.'

'Na vanavond niet meer.' Hij knikte naar zijn partner. 'Handboeien om. En bel hun ouders.'

Jake kreeg het ijskoud, niet omdat hij de cel inging, maar omdat ze hem weghaalden bij zijn coach. Hij had zin om te schreeuwen, tegen iedereen te brullen dat ze hem los moesten laten en hier laten blijven tot hij wist dat alles in orde was. Zijn hart werd zwaarder dan cement toen het tot hem doordrong. De coach kon sterven… misschien was hij al dood. En al was hij niet dood, niets kwam ooit meer goed. Jake was een verschrikkelijke ellendeling en wat er hierna ook met hem ging gebeuren, hij verdiende het volkomen.

De eerste agent greep Jakes polsen en hield ze achter zijn rug strak bij elkaar. Het metaal klemde in zijn huid en daar was hij bijna blij om. Binnen een paar seconden zaten de handboeien om en de agent liep terug naar zijn auto. De andere agent deed hetzelfde bij Casey en vertrok, dus daar stonden ze met z'n tweeën alleen op de weg met handboeien om naar de vernielde auto van coach Reynolds te kijken.

De reddingswerkers waren nog steeds hard aan het werk rondom de restanten van de auto om de coach eruit te krijgen. Jake deed zijn ogen dicht en dwong hen met zijn gedachten op te schieten. *God, hoe kon U dit laten gebeuren? Ik had erin moeten zitten, niet de coach. Hij heeft niets verkeerds gedaan. Haal hem er alstublieft uit…*

'Ik heb hem!' schreeuwde een van de ambulancebroeders. Hij gooide een gemangeld portier achter zich. Het kwam terecht op het keurig verzorgde gazon dat het parkeerterrein van Marion High omzoomde. 'Ik moet een rugplank hebben. En een luchtbrug. Over de grond gaat-ie het niet halen.'

Ze kregen hem eruit! Jakes knieën bibberden en weer kon hij haast niet ademhalen. Hoop laaide wild in hem op en Jake vocht tegen de aandrang om boven het kabaal uit de naam van de coach te schreeuwen.

De ambulancebroeder begon bevelen te roepen en schreeuwde woorden die Jake nog nooit had gehoord. Wat hij wel oppikte was dat coach Reynolds nog in leven was! Dat betekende dat er een kans was… dat hij kon bidden dat de coach het mocht halen! Jakes benen konden hem niet langer houden en hij viel met bonzend hart op zijn knieën. *Volhouden, coach… kom op. God, laat hem niet sterven.*

Jake had geen idee hoe lang Casey en hij daar stokstijf naar het reddingswerk stonden te kijken. Eindelijk verscheen er boven hun hoofd een helikopter, die landde in de lege straat. Ongeveer op hetzelfde moment wuifde een van de broeders met zijn hand naar de anderen. 'Hij wordt slechter.'

'Nee!' Niemand hoorde Jake boven het geluid van de heli uit. Hij krabbelde overeind, deed drie stappen in de richting van de kring verplegers en keerde terug naar zijn plaats.

Naast hem begon Casey te snikken.

Er was een golf van hevige activiteit en iemand begon te reanimeren. 'Hij moet hier weg!'

Een team van verplegers tilde een plank omhoog en voor het eerst kon Jake de man zien met wie ze bezig waren. Het was zonder enige twijfel coach Reynolds. Hij had zijn Marion Eagles jack nog aan.

Jake begon te snikken. Wat voor een monster was hij, om zo door een stadswijk te racen? En dan de coach, de man die in de afgelopen jaren meer een vader voor hem was geweest dan zijn eigen vader.

'Laat hem alsjeblieft niet doodgaan!' Weer werd Jakes wanhoopskreet overstemd door de snorrende helikopterpropeller en het lawaai van de motor.

Ze laadden coach Reynolds in de heli, die opsteeg en in de lucht verdween. Jake keek hem na tot hij de motor niet meer kon horen. Toen de heli weg was, viel er een griezelige, doodse stilte in de straat. Hij keek om zich heen en werd zich ineens bewust van de bedrijvigheid in de buurt van de beschadigde auto's. Er was nog meer politie gearriveerd en ze namen maten op en markeerden de plaats van Jakes auto tot het wrak van de truck van de coach. Toen de ambulancebroeders vertrokken, stopten er twee takelwagens. De bestuurders klommen eruit en wachtten naast hun combinatie.

Jake begon weer te trillen en zijn armen achter zijn rug deden pijn. 'We gaan eraan,' fluisterde Casey naast hem. 'We zijn er geweest, Jake. Dat weet je toch? Het seizoen is voorbij.'

Het seizoen? Jake werd misselijk. Wat voor een vent was Casey eigenlijk? Het *seizoen?* Wie kon dat rotseizoen wat schelen? Hij draaide zich naar Casey om, zijn ogen waren zo gezwollen van het huilen dat hij haast niet kon zien. 'Is dat het enige waar je aan kunt denken?'

Casey huilde niet meer, maar hij sidderde alsof hij een insult had. 'Na… natuurlijk niet. Ik ben bezorgd over de coach. Maar… dit zal ons… de rest van ons leven bijblijven.'

Jake werd boos en zijn tranen droogden op. 'Ja, en dat hebben we *verdiend* ook.'

Casey deed zijn mond open en even leek het alsof hij hem wilde tegenspreken. Toen boog hij zijn hoofd en eindelijk kwamen de tranen ook bij hem weer. 'Ja… dat weet ik.'

Jake voelde afkeer van hen allebei. De politie had gelijk. Een stel rijke jochies die in veel te snelle auto's reden. Hij knarsetandde tot zijn kaken pijn deden. Het was niet belangrijk welke moeilijkheden hen te wachten stonden. Wat hem betrof kon de politie kon hem in de cel smijten en de sleutel weggooien. Jake zou zelfs met plezier zijn leven hebben gegeven voor het enige wat nog belangrijk was.

Dat coach Reynolds de nacht doorkwam.

Want als de coach niet bleef leven, kon Jake ook niet meer leven, daar was hij zeker van.

Dertien

Het was een nachtmerrie.

Dat moest het zijn. Abby tuurde naar de wekker en zag dat het even na twee uur 's nachts was. Er was geen sprake van dat John zo laat nog op straat was geweest. Mannen zoals hij kregen geen auto-ongeluk.... Mannen die op dit moment thuis hadden moeten liggen slapen.

Ja, het was gewoon een nachtmerrie. Abby had zichzelf bijna overtuigd, op één zorgwekkend detail na: Johns plaats in bed was leeg en onbeslapen. Ze probeerde te slikken, maar haar keel was te dik. Waarom probeerde ze zichzelf bang te maken? Het was niet zo ongewoon dat John op dit uur niet in bed lag. Niet na een footballwedstrijd. Hij kon beneden zitten televisie te kijken of een kom cornflakes te eten. Dat deed hij zo vaak.

Maar hoe overtuigd ze ook was, ze moest toch iets tegen de beller zeggen.

'Hebt u me gehoord, mevrouw Reynolds? Bent u wakker?' De stem klonk kalm en vriendelijk. Maar de aandrang was onmiskenbaar. 'Ik zei dat u naar het ziekenhuis moet komen. Uw man heeft een ongeluk gehad.'

De man hield aan. 'Ja.' Abby zuchtte het antwoord. 'Ik ben wakker. Ik ben er over tien minuten.'

Ze belde Nicole. Als de droom hardnekkig was, moest ze het spelletje maar meespelen en de rol vervullen die van haar verwacht werd.

'Je vader heeft een ongeluk gehad.'

'*Wat*?' Nicoles stem klonk half gillend, half huilend. 'Is hij

127

gewond? Wat… wat is er precies gebeurd?'

Abby dwong zich om kalm te blijven. Als ze nu instortte, kwam ze nooit in het ziekenhuis terecht. En alleen door mee te werken kon ze zich ooit losmaken van de vreselijke nachtmerrie. 'Dat hebben ze niet gezegd. Alleen dat we moeten komen.' Haar ogen gingen dicht en ze wist dat ze gelijk had. Het moest een nachtmerrie zijn. En geen wonder, zeker na de bomdreiging van daarstraks. Natuurlijk droomde ze akelig.

'Mam, ben je daar nog?'

'Ja.' Met moeite concentreerde ze zich. 'Is Matt thuis?'

'Natuurlijk.'

'Laat hij je brengen. Ik wil niet dat je 's nachts alleen de straat op gaat.'

'En jij dan? Misschien moeten we je ophalen.'

'Sean staat al aangekleed op me te wachten.'

'Gaat het met hem?'

'Best, zodra deze nachtmerrie voorbij is.'

Tijdens de hele rit naar het ziekenhuis schrok Abby ervan hoe werkelijk alles was. De koele wind op haar gezicht, het stuur in haar handen, de weg onder de wielen. Nooit in haar leven had een droom zo echt aangevoeld.

Maar toch moest het een droom zijn.

John had vanavond niets gevaarlijks gedaan. Het gevaar was in het footballstadion geweest, toen hij aan flarden had kunnen worden geblazen. Maar van school naar huis rijden? Er kon geen kip op de weg zijn geweest.

Abby draaide de auto het parkeerterrein van het ziekenhuis op en zag Matt en Nicole voor zich rijden. Met elkaar kwamen ze de spoedeisende hulp binnen en werden meteen meegenomen naar een klein kamertje achter de dubbele deuren, uit het zicht van de rest van het publiek.

'Wat is er aan de hand?' Nicole begon te huilen en Matt sloeg zijn arm om haar heen. 'Waarom brengen ze ons hierheen?'

Abby klemde haar handen tot vuisten toen het besef met kracht tot haar doordrong. Ze had geen enkele informatie. Niet over het soort ongeluk en of er een andere auto bij betrokken was. Niet over de omvang van Johns verwondingen en hoe hij in het ziekenhuis was gekomen. Ze tastte volkomen in het duister en in zekere zin was dat een troost. Zo ging dat in dromen: vreemde, ontbrekende details, onsamenhangend...

Naast haar begon Sean ook te huilen.

'Ssht.' Abby drukte hem tegen zich aan en streelde zijn rug. 'Het komt goed.'

Er kwam een dokter binnen, hij deed de deur achter zich dicht. Het eerste wat Abby opviel, was zijn gezicht. Het stond gespannen en treurig. *Nee, God... laat dit niet gebeuren. Niet in het echt. Maak me wakker. Ik kan het niet meer verdragen...*

STEUN NIET OP JE EIGEN INZICHT, DOCHTER... ZELFS NU BEN IK HIER BIJ JE.

De woorden kwamen uit het niets en spraken rechtstreeks tot haar hart. Ze gaven Abby de kracht om de arts recht aan te kijken en de moeilijkste vraag van haar leven te stellen. 'Hoe is het met hem?'

'Hij leeft.'

Alle vier richtten ze zich een beetje op bij de woorden van de arts. 'Mogen we bij hem?' Abby wilde opstaan, maar de dokter schudde zijn hoofd.

'Hij ligt op de intensive care aan de beademing.' De arts fronste zijn voorhoofd. 'De komende dagen zal het kantje boord zijn. Er is nog steeds een aanzienlijke kans dat we hem kwijtraken.'

'Nee!' Nicole schreeuwde het uit en drukte haar gezicht tegen Matts borst. 'Nee, God... niet mijn papa. Nee!'

Abby sloot haar ogen en drukte Sean steviger tegen zich aan. Ze bedacht ineens dat ze Kade niet gebeld had. Nu zat hij achthonderd kilometer bij hen vandaag en wist niet dat zijn vader vocht voor zijn leven. Weer zo'n onsamenhangend stukje van de nachtmerrie.

Maar de droom werd met de minuut afschrikwekkend echter.

Eindelijk bedaarde Nicole, haar gezicht nog steeds gesmoord in Matts geruite flanellen overhemd.

Het was verstandig om kalm te blijven. Abby sloeg haar ogen neer en zag dat haar handen trilden, maar ze slaagde erin de dokter aan te kijken. 'Wat... wat voor verwondingen heeft hij?'

'Hij heeft een doorgesneden luchtpijp, mevrouw Reynolds. Zo'n verwonding is in de meeste gevallen fataal. Ik denk dat de manier waarop zijn lichaam na het ongeluk gedraaid zat, de luchtpijp lang genoeg op zijn plaats heeft gehouden om zijn leven te redden. Zodra ze hem verplaatsten, hield hij op met ademhalen. Ze hebben zijn levensfuncties kunstmatig in stand gehouden tot hij per helikopter hierheen was gebracht.'

'Helikopter?' Abby zag vlekken voor haar ogen, cirkelende vlekken die haar hele gezichtsveld dreigden in te nemen. Ze schudde haar hoofd. Nee, ze mocht niet flauwvallen. Niet nu. 'Wat... wat is er gebeurd?'

De dokter sloeg zijn ogen neer op zijn klembord en trok een grimas. 'Kennelijk is hij het slachtoffer geworden van een stel straatracers, middelbare scholieren.'

'Straat...' De wereld draaide om Abby heen. 'Een straatrace?'

Geen twijfel aan, het was gewoon een nachtmerrie. In het echte leven gebeurden zulke toevalligheden niet. John Reynolds, de coach die ervan beschuldigd werd door de vingers te zien dat zijn spelers meededen aan straatraces... aangereden door tieners die precies dat deden? Het was zo bespottelijk, het kon onmogelijk waar zijn.

'De jongens reden waarschijnlijk ongeveer 160 toen uw man het parkeerterrein van de school afdraaide. Hij werd van achteren geraakt.'

'Dus...' Abby drukte haar vingers hard tegen haar slapen. Opnieuw wilde haar lichaam flauwvallen, maar ze liet het niet toe. Niet voordat ze alles had gehoord. 'Dus zijn luchtpijp? Dat is het probleem?'

Het gezicht van de arts betrok nog verder. 'Dat is op dit

moment het meest kritieke probleem.'

'Is er nog meer?'

Nicole kermde en klemde zich vast aan Matt. Abby keek naar Sean en merkte dat hij snikte tegen haar mouw. Arme kinderen. Dit moesten ze niet hoeven horen. Maar als het slechts een akelige droom was, kon het geen kwaad. Bovendien, hoe sneller ze zich erdoorheen werkte, hoe sneller ze wakker werd.

De arts raadpleegde opnieuw zijn aantekeningen. 'Het ziet ernaaruit dat hij zijn nek gebroken heeft, mevrouw Reynolds. We kunnen er op dit moment niet helemaal zeker van zijn, maar we denken dat hij verlamd is. Minstens vanaf zijn middel naar beneden.'

'*Neeeee!*' Nicole gilde het weer uit en nu wierp Matt Abby een smekende blik toe.

Maar ze kon niets doen. Het woord was nog bezig tot haar bewustzijn door te dringen. Verlamd? *Verlamd!* Het was totaal onmogelijk. John Reynolds had net de Eagles naar de overwinning gecoacht. Hij was met haar naar haar auto gelopen en was de trap van de school opgegaan naar zijn lokaal. Vanavond moesten ze naar dansles.

Verlamd?

'Ik vind het heel erg.' De arts schudde zijn hoofd. 'Ik weet dat dit heel moeilijk voor u is. Kan ik iemand voor u bellen?'

Abby wilde zeggen dat hij Kade moest bellen. Maar ze stond op en trok Sean naast zich. 'Waar is hij? We moeten naar hem toe.'

De arts keek het groepje onderzoekend aan en knikte. Hij deed de deur open en wenkte hen. 'Kom maar.'

Als een stel zombies liepen ze achter de dokter aan door de ene gang naar de volgende. Het klikken van zijn hakken op de tegelvloer deed Abby denken aan een macabere klok die de uren aftelde die John nog te leven had. Ze wilde tegen hem schreeuwen dat hij zachter moest lopen, maar het sloeg nergens op. Zelfs niet in een droom.

Eindelijk stond de dokter stil en opende een deur. 'Als groep mogen jullie maar een paar minuten blijven.' Hij keek Abby aan. 'Mevrouw Reynolds, u mag de hele nacht bij hem blijven als u wilt.'

Met Abby voorop slopen ze naar binnen en pas toen begaf het laagje van schrik en ongeloof het. Ze stortte met tollend hoofd neer aan het voeteneind van zijn bed.

Het was echt. *O, God… het gebeurt echt.*

Het licht versmalde en ze werd omhuld door duisternis. 'Ik val fl…'

Dat was het laatste wat Abby zich herinnerde.

Toen ze bijkwam, zat ze in een stoel naast Johns bed. Nicole, Matt en Sean stonden om haar heen. Aan haar voeten zat een verpleegkundige met reukzout. 'U bent flauwgevallen, mevrouw Reynolds.'

Abby keek langs hen heen naar het bed, waar haar geliefde John lag. Uit zijn mond, hals, armen en benen liepen slangen zijn lichaam in en uit. Zijn hoofd en nek waren vastgezet met braces, zodat het leek of John gevangen zat. Abby wilde ze losmaken en hem weghalen.

Maar dat kon niet.

Het enige wat ze de rest van de nacht kon doen, was naast John blijven zitten en proberen niet te hard te huilen. Want als hij hier was, dan was hij niet thuis. Hij zat geen tv te kijken, geen cornflakes te eten en geen werkstukken te corrigeren tot in de vroege ochtenduren. Hij lag vastgesnoerd in een ziekenhuisbed en zijn leven hing aan een zijden draad.

En dat kon maar één ding betekenen.

Ze droomde helemaal niet.

Haar lieve man, de man die gerend had als de wind over het footballveld van de Universiteit van Michigan… de man die met haar tenniste en hardliep en patronen voor zijn spelers rende als een diagram niet duidelijk genoeg was… de man die wel honderd keer met haar gedanst had op de aanlegsteiger achter hun huis… danste wellicht nooit meer.

Dit was niet het soort nachtmerrie waaruit je wakker werd.
Maar het soort dat een leven lang duurde.

★

De uren liepen wazig in elkaar over.

Zaterdagmiddag had Kade zich in het ziekenhuis bij hen gevoegd. Hij arriveerde ergens tussen het middag- en avondeten, Abby wist het niet precies. Maar ze zaten allemaal om Johns bed geschaard voor hem te bidden. Jo en Denny waren gekomen en met hen een tiental mensen van de kerk en van school.

Het nieuws had zich verspreid.

Coach Reynolds had een ongeluk gehad en hij kon misschien nooit meer lopen. Betraande footballspelers waakten in de wachtkamer bij de anderen. Alleen directe familie mocht bij hem, Abby en de kinderen en Matt. Abby week niet van Johns zijde, behalve om naar het toilet te gaan. Ze ontweek de gesprekken in de wachtkamer over wie er gearresteerd waren en welke straf ze konden krijgen. Het kon haar op dit moment niets schelen. Het enige belangrijke was dat John bleef leven.

Tot nu toe was hij nog niet bijgekomen, maar de artsen verwachtten dat het elk moment kon gebeuren.

Abby had het idee dat het maar een droom was allang laten varen. Het was werkelijkheid. Maar ze bad dat de werkelijkheid anders bleek af te lopen dan de artsen zich voorstelden. Vanavond zou John wakker worden, de kamer rondkijken en zijn malle grijns lachen.

Dan zou hij met zijn vingers en tenen wiebelen en de eerste de beste langslopende verpleegkundige vragen de nekbrace af te doen. Hij zou natuurlijk wel keelpijn hebben, dat moest wel als je luchtpijp doorgesneden was, maar afgezien daarvan was hij ongedeerd. Een paar dagen in het ziekenhuis en dan konden ze bijkomen van de schrik van het ongeluk en doorgaan met leven en liefhebben en dansles bij Parmantige Paula.

Zo zou het gaan. Abby was er zeker van.

Voorlopig zaten ze met z'n allen te zwijgen. Kade stond als aan de grond genageld tegen de muur, zijn blik vast op zijn vader gericht. Met droge ogen en een bleek gezicht was Kade twee uur lang niet van zijn plaats gekomen. Naast hem zat Sean op de grond, met zijn knieën opgetrokken tot zijn kin, zijn gezicht in zijn handen. Het grootste deel van de tijd zat Sean zachtjes te huilen. Als hij soms ophield met huilen, zag Abby dat zijn droefheid niet voorbij was. Hij hield op met huilen omdat hij zelfs te bang was voor tranen.

Matt en Nicole hadden hun plaats ingenomen aan de tegenoverliggende muur. Nicole zat in een stoel, Matt stond naast haar. De arts had hen aangemoedigd om te praten, omdat John meer kans had om wakker te worden als hij hun stemmen hoorde. Nu en dan zeiden Abby en de jongens een paar woorden, maar Nicole was het spraakzaamst. Om de tien minuten liep ze door de kamer om naast het hoofdeinde van Johns bed te gaan staan.

'Papa, ik ben het.' Dan begon ze te huilen. 'Wakker worden, pap. We zitten hier allemaal op je te wachten en voor je te bidden. Je wordt beter, dat weet ik zeker.'

Na een paar zinnen stroomden haar tranen te hard om erdoorheen te praten, dan liep ze om het bed heen om Abby lange tijd te omhelzen. Dan keerde ze terug naar haar plaats naast Matt. Nu en dan ging er één of meer de kamer uit om iets te eten of te drinken.

Het enige goede nieuws van de dag was die ochtend gekomen toen de arts Johns toestand opvijzelde van kritiek naar ernstig. 'Hij heeft een goede nacht gehad. Volgens mij heeft hij grote kans om in leven te blijven.'

Abby had geen idee hoelang dat geleden was en of het weer nacht geworden was of niet. Ze wist alleen dat ze niet weg durfde te gaan, omdat ze de kamer niet uit wilde zijn als John voor het eerst zijn ogen opendeed en hun allen de waarheid vertelde: dat het helemaal niet zo ernstig met hem was.

Toen de zusters etenskarretjes door de gang duwden, uitte John eindelijk een zacht gekreun.

'John!' Abby schoof dichter naar het bed en pakte zijn hand vast, de hand zonder slangen en draden. 'We zijn allemaal hier, schat. Kun je me horen?'

De kinderen schaarden zich dichter om het bed en keken verwachtingsvol naar hem. Maar hij antwoordde niet. Abby keek naar zijn gezicht. Het was bont en blauw en gezwollen, maar ze was er haast zeker van dat zijn ogen onder de leden heen en weer gingen. Dat was niet gebeurd sinds Abby's komst in het ziekenhuis.

Nicole streek met haar vingers licht over Johns andere hand, voorzichtig om niet tegen de slangen te stoten. 'Papa, ik ben het…' Ze haalde twee keer snel adem en vocht tegen haar tranen. 'Ben je wakker?'

John knipperde heel licht met zijn ogen, zodat Sean zachtjes 'Ja!' fluisterde. Dat John gewond was en een leven tegemoet zag dat misschien nooit meer hetzelfde werd, was één ding. Maar hem te verliezen… dat was voor hen allen een ondraaglijke gedachte.

Zelfs de subtielste beweging was nu als een teken van God dat wat er ook mocht gebeuren, John zou blijven leven.

Er ontsnapte weer een kreun uit zijn keel en zijn lippen bewogen. Er kwam een zuster binnen die zag wat er gebeurde. 'Achteruit. Alstublieft. Hij mag nu niet te veel gestimuleerd worden, nu hij geïntubeerd is.'

Ze bekeek zijn monitors en bracht haar hoofd bij zijn gezicht. 'Meneer Reynolds, u moet heel stil blijven liggen. Kunt u me verstaan?'

Weer ging zijn hoofd op en neer, niet meer dan anderhalve centimeter, maar genoeg om te laten zien dat hij de verpleegster had gehoord. Abby's hart nam een hoge vlucht. Ze had al die tijd gelijk gehad. Hij werd beter. Ze moesten hem alleen helpen van zijn verwondingen te herstellen en dan was alles in orde.

De verpleegster hield haar hand nog achter zich om aan te geven dat de rest afstand moest bewaren tot ze klaar met hem was.

'Hebt u pijn, meneer Reynolds?'

Dit keer bewoog hij zijn hoofd van links naar rechts. Opnieuw was de beweging nauwelijks merkbaar, maar niettemin aanwezig.

'Meneer Reynolds, u hebt een ongeluk gehad. Weet u dat?'

Zijn hoofd lag stil. Abby kon zien dat hij moeite deed om zijn ogen open te doen. Eindelijk gingen zijn ogen haast pijnlijk open en hij tuurde door een kiertje. Bijna tegelijk bewogen zijn armen en hij bracht een hand naar zijn keel.

Hier! Zien jullie nou! wilde Abby schreeuwen. Hij kon bewegen! Als hij zijn handen op kon tillen, dan was hij toch niet verlamd? Ze knipperde met haar ogen en het werd haar benauwd te moede. Ook als hij niet verlamd was, moest hij zich ellendig voelen. Er staken slangen in zijn keel, zijn hoofd en nek zaten vast in een brace, hij kon niet praten. John had er al een hekel aan als zijn temperatuur werd opgenomen, laat staan dit. Voordat hij de slangen eruit kon trekken, pakte de zuster zijn hand en legde hem terug langs zijn zij. 'U moet uw keel met rust laten, meneer Reynolds. U bent gewond en de slangen moeten op hun plaats blijven. Begrijpt u me?'

De stem van de zuster klonk luid en afgemeten, alsof hij een dom kind was. Vanaf zijn plaats tegen de muur wierp Kade woeste blikken naar haar, maar Abby was blij dat ze zo direct was. Anders kon haar man zichzelf kwaad doen en dat moesten ze niet hebben.

'Begrijpt u me, meneer Reynolds? U moet geen plotselinge bewegingen maken en niet proberen uw slangen eruit te halen. Goed?'

John knipperde met zijn ogen en opende ze wat wijder. Voor het eerst leek het of hij kon zien. Hij ontmoette de blik van de zuster en knikte wat beslister. Toen bewoog hij zonder af te wachten of de zuster nog iets te zeggen had heel licht zijn hoofd en vond elk van hen met zijn ogen. Eerst Kade, toen Sean, Nicole en Matt. En ten slotte Abby.

Ze had er geen idee van wat de kinderen in Johns zoekende

ogen zagen, maar wat zij zag, zei meer dan woorden konden zeggen. Zijn ogen zeiden dat ze vol moest houden, dat hij beter werd en dat alles goed kwam. Maar er was ook iets anders in. Een liefde zo diep en sterk en echt dat John het zelfs als hij kon praten niet met woorden had kunnen zeggen.

De zuster deed een stap naar achteren. 'Uw familie mag een paar minuten bij u blijven, meneer Reynolds, maar daarna moet u gaan slapen. U moet heel stil liggen. We doen ons uiterste best om u beter te maken.'

Ze vroeg hem niet naar zijn benen, of hij ze kon bewegen of voelen. Omdat de dokter niet langer dacht dat er een probleem was? Of omdat het geen zin had om hem zo'n emotionele schok te bezorgen vlak nadat hij bij bewustzijn was gekomen? Abby probeerde er niet aan te denken.

In plaats daarvan schoof ze dichter naar het bed, met haar ogen nog vast in de zijne. *Niet instorten, Abby. Laat hem je tranen niet zien. Niet nu.* Ze hield haar adem in en dwong haar mondhoeken omhoog, waar ze hoorden. 'John…'

Hij tilde zijn vingers op van het ziekenhuislaken en ze nam zijn hand in de hare. Hij kon niet praten, maar hij kneep zachtjes in haar vingers. Abby weigerde op te merken dat zijn voeten en benen nog steeds niet hadden bewogen.

Ze ademde oppervlakkig, om niet in snikken uit te barsten. 'God is zo goed voor ons, John. Alles komt goed met je.'

Er veranderde iets in zijn gezicht en ze wist instinctief wat er door zijn hoofd heen ging. Wat was er gebeurd? Wie had hem aangereden? Waar was de andere bestuurder en was die ongedeerd? Abby wist zelf weinig bijzonderheden, dus ze schudde haar hoofd. 'Het doet er niet toe wat er precies heeft plaatsgevonden. Het was jouw schuld niet, John. Het belangrijkste is dat je wakker bent en dat je nu hier bij ons bent. Je krijgt de allerbeste zorg, hoor.'

De spieren in zijn gezicht ontspanden een beetje en hij knikte.

Aan het voeteneind pakte Nicole Johns tenen vast. Maar pas

toen ze zijn naam zei, keek hij haar aan. 'Pap, Matt en ik hebben je iets te vertellen.'

Matt legde zijn hand op Nicoles schouder. 'Hoi.' Hij klonk geforceerd vrolijk. 'Fijn dat je wakker bent.'

Nicole bracht haar vingers naar haar keel. Na een paar keer pijnlijk slikken, schudde ze haar hoofd. 'We hadden het jullie van-avond willen vertellen, voordat mam en jij naar dans…' Haar stem begaf het en even boog ze haar hoofd.

Matt nam het over. 'We hadden nieuws dat we aan de familie wilden vertellen. Toen we hoorden van je ongeluk wilden we wachten, maar Nicole…'

'Ik wil dat je het weet, pap. Want je moet alles doen wat je kunt om beter te worden.' Ze streelde zijn voet en haar ogen lieten John geen moment los. 'We krijgen een baby, pap. Het was niet de bedoeling, maar toch is het een wonder.' Ze snufte twee keer. 'We… we wilden dat jij het als eerste wist, want we hebben je nodig, pap. Ik heb je nodig. Onze baby heeft je nodig.'

John kreeg tranen in zijn ogen die over zijn wangen liepen. Toen knikte hij één keer weloverwogen en zijn mondhoeken gin-gen zo ver omhoog dat ze wisten wat hij voelde. Ondanks dat hij vastgesnoerd in een ziekenhuisbed lag… ondanks wat hem wachtte op de weg naar herstel, John werd grootvader. En hij was opgetogen over het nieuws.

Abby wist niet of ze moest lachen of huilen. Jo had uiteindelijk nog gelijk gehad ook. Nicoles stralende uiterlijk was precies waar haar schoonmoeder het voor aangezien had. Ze was zwanger! Midden in Abby's ergste nachtmerrie was een straaltje hoop, een reden om feest te vieren.

De tegenstrijdige emoties vochten om de voorrang in haar. Ze week van Johns zijde en sloeg haar armen om Matt en Nicole heen. 'Niet te geloven. Hoelang weten jullie het al?'

'Een paar weken. We wilden het eerst zelf zeker weten.'

Sean en Kade feliciteerden hen, al klonken hun stemmen wei-nig enthousiast. Abby liet haar hoofd op Nicoles schouder rusten.

Ze was te uitgeput om iets anders te doen dan bewegingloos staan. John en zij werden grootouders. Ze hadden het er sinds hun trouwen al over gehad, maar het had altijd ver weg geleken. Iets wat andere, oude mensen overkwam. Toen Nicole trouwde, wisten ze dat de mogelijkheid dichter bij was dan ooit, maar toch…

Niemand had verwacht dat Nicole zo snel zwanger zou worden. Behalve Jo.

Abby werd verstikt door een oceaan van verdriet toen ze overvallen werd door vreselijke gedachten. Zou John ooit met zijn eerste kleinkind kunnen rennen en spelen? Zou hij een ommetje kunnen maken met het kind, of het op zijn knie laten paardjerijden?

Alstublieft, God… laat de artsen het mis hebben over zijn benen. Alstublieft…

JULLIE ZULLEN HET ZWAAR TE VERDUREN KRIJGEN IN DE WERELD, MAAR HOUD MOED: IK HEB DE WERELD OVERWONNEN.

Een maand geleden hadden John en zij die tekst gelezen, toen de problemen op Marion High waren toegenomen. De woorden uit het boek Johannes hadden haar niet vaak in het leven getroost, maar juist angst aangejaagd. *Jullie zullen het zwaar te verduren krijgen in de wereld?* Wat voor troost kon je daaraan ontlenen?

Maar door de jaren heen was ze het beter gaan begrijpen.

Problemen waren een deel van het leven… zelfs gebeurtenissen als het verlies van hun geliefde tweede dochtertje aan wiegendood, en de tornado in Barneveld waarbij haar moeder was omgekomen. Sommige problemen haalde je door je eigen daden over je heen. Zoals de jaren die John en zij door hun eigen egoïsme waren kwijtgeraakt. Andere moeilijkheden hoorden bij een geestelijke aanval. Zoals wat dit jaar op school was gebeurd.

Maar soms zat je gewoon tot laat in de avond op school werkstukken na te kijken, je reed van het parkeerterrein af om naar huis te gaan en je leven veranderde in één ogenblik.

Je kreeg het zwaar te verduren. Na meer dan twintig jaar samen wisten Abby en John dat wel. De bedoeling van de tekst was niet om te blijven stilstaan bij de zekerheid van moeilijke tijden, maar om verzekerd te zijn van Gods overwinning door alles heen. Als God op dit moment Johns ziekenhuiskamer binnenwandelde, zou Hij met hen meehuilen en medelijden hebben.

Maar voordat Hij vertrok, zou Hij hun een bemoedigende glimlach schenken en de afscheidswoorden spreken: 'Houd moed! Ik heb het allemaal overwonnen!'

Het was waar.

Het nieuwe leven dat in het lichaam van haar dochter groeide, was het bewijs.

Veertien

Het was ijskoud in de cel.

Jake lag opgerold op een veldbed in de hoek. Hij had één cel-
genoot, een verslaafde tiener die naar hij had begrepen was opge-
pakt voor een mislukte roofoverval. Jake had hem aangekeken
toen hij de cel werd binnengebracht, maar sindsdien had geen van
beiden een woord gezegd.

De afgelopen vierentwintig uur waren net een enge film
geweest.

Casey en hij waren snel onderzocht door ambulancepersoneel
en de politie had hen tweeën meegenomen naar het bureau. Daar
waren ze verschillende kanten opgestuurd. Casey was al achttien,
en volwassen. Jake was met zijn zeventien jaar nog minderjarig.
Dat betekende dat hij de eerste nacht moest doorbrengen in een
cel vol chagrijnige tieners.

De celbeheerder vertelde Jake dat zijn moeder in de hal zat,
maar hij werd aangeklaagd voor een ernstig misdrijf. Hij mocht
geen bezoek hebben voordat er proces-verbaal was opgemaakt en
hij in zijn eigen cel zat, wat zaterdagmiddag allemaal gebeurd was.

Zijn moeder had hij nog steeds niet mogen zien.

Alles waarvoor ze hem gewaarschuwd had, was gebeurd. Hij
was een keer of tien met vrienden uitgegaan sinds hij de auto had,
en elke keer had hij in gedachten haar stem gehoord.

'Blijf thuis, Jake. De verleiding is te groot. Met zo'n auto kun je
iemand doden…'

Het was de hoofdoorzaak geweest van de laatste onenigheden
tussen zijn ouders. Mam vond dat zijn vader de auto gebruikte om

zijn afwezigheid goed te maken, een verontschuldiging omdat hij vertrokken was naar een andere staat en het leven leidde van een ongebonden vrijgezel.

Meer dan eens had zijn moeder door de telefoon tegen zijn vader geschreeuwd, als ze hem ervan probeerde te overtuigen dat Jake te jong was om een auto als de rode Integra aan te kunnen. 'Je bent een vader van niks. Als je van hem hield, was je hier in Illinois. Dan was je niet op stap met een of ander... sletje aan de Oostkust.'

Het laatste wat Jake had gewild, was zijn moeders gelijk te bewijzen en daarmee de kloof tussen zijn ouders te verdiepen. Tja, ach... en dat was precies wat hij nu had gedaan.

Hij rolde op zijn zij en trok zijn benen op. Hij was eenzaam en bang en misselijk. Stel dat de coach gestorven was? En als hij nog leefde, waar was hij en hoe ging het met hem? Wat voor verwondingen had hij? Jake zag er hevig tegenop om zijn moeder onder ogen te komen, maar zij zou hem tenminste kunnen vertellen hoe het met de coach ging.

Om die reden schoot Jake overeind toen de celbeheerder aan de tralies van de cel rammelde.

'Jake Daniels.' De man ontsloot de celdeur met een sleutel. Tegenover Jake fixeerde de sjofele tiener de kale muur met zijn blik. De man met de sleutel blafte tegen hem. 'Bezoek voor je.'

Jake voelde zich ellendig. Zijn eigen kleren waren hem afgenomen en hij droeg een simpele blauwkatoenen overall, zoals misdadigers aan hadden als ze getuigden voor de rechtbank en hun foto in de krant kwam.

'Deze kant op,' zei de man kortaf. Hij voerde Jake mee door een gang met kleine cellen naar een ruimte. Er stonden twaalf stoelen die uitkeken op een stevige glazen muur, elk met afscheidingen die een reeks hokjes vormden. Bij elke stoel stond een telefoon. De agent wees naar de laatste aan het achterste eind van de rij. 'Daar.'

Jakes stappen klonken hol toen hij naar de laatste stoel liep en ging zitten. Pas toen zag hij haar. Zijn moeder zat aan de andere kant van het glas met een telefoon in haar hand. Haar gezicht was gezwollen, haar ogen rood. *Kijk eens wat ik haar heb aangedaan.* Jake greep naar zijn zijden, zijn hart sloeg in een vreemd, angstig ritme dat hij niet herkende.

Ik heb haar leven verwoest. Ik heb iedereens leven verwoest.

Zijn moeder wees naar de telefoon en Jake pakte de hoorn op. Zweet parelde op zijn voorhoofd en zijn handpalmen waren nat. Zijn gevangenisontbijt zat ergens onder in zijn keel vast. 'Hallo?'

Ze begon te praten, toen liet ze haar hoofd zakken in haar vrije hand en huilde.

'Mam… het spijt me.' Jake wilde zijn armen om haar heen slaan en haar omhelzen, maar het glas zat in de weg. Kon hij erdoorheen stormen? Misschien sneed het glas dan zijn polsen door en stierf hij, zoals hij verdiende. Hij schraapte zijn keel. 'Ik… het spijt me zo.'

Eindelijk keek ze op en streek met haar vingertoppen onder haar ogen. Er zaten zwarte vegen, resten van haar mascara van gisteren. 'Wat is er gebeurd, Jake? De politie zegt dat je aan het racen was.'

Het vluchtgevoel kwam terug. Misschien kon hij ergens een deur uit glippen en alles van Jake Daniels achter zich laten…

Maar de deuren aan weerszijden zaten op slot en de berg van ellende die voor hem opees, ging niet weg. Jake wreef zijn slapen. 'Dat klopt. We waren aan het racen.'

Er veranderde iets in het gezicht van zijn moeder en Jakes adem stokte in zijn keel. In zijn hele leven zou hij nooit de schrik, het verdriet en de teleurstelling vergeten die het gezicht van zijn moeder op dit moment tekenden. Ze deed haar mond open, maar lange tijd kwam er niets uit. Toen zei ze maar één gepijnigd woord. '*Waarom?*'

Jake boog zijn hoofd. Er was geen goed antwoord, helemaal geen antwoord. Hij keek op, zijn moeder keek hem afwachtend aan. 'Ik… eh… Casey daagde me uit.' Ineens wilde hij zich radeloos graag nader verklaren. 'Er had om die tijd niemand op de weg moeten zitten, mam. Toen de coach de weg opdraaide, was er geen tijd meer om...' Zijn stem brak af.

Door het beduimelde glas zag hij zijn moeders ogen langzaam sluiten. 'O, Jake... ik kan het niet verdragen.'

'Komt... komt pap?'

Ze beet op haar lip en knikte. 'Morgenmiddag is hij er.'

De vraag lag als een steen op zijn hart. De hele dag had hij naar de coach willen vragen, maar nu zijn moeder er was, zag Jake het met angst en beven tegemoet. Eindelijk kon hij er niet meer onderuit zijn gedachten onder woorden te brengen. 'Hoe is het met de coach?'

'Hij...' Zijn moeder snufte, haar ogen liepen weer vol tranen. 'Hij heeft de nacht doorstaan.'

Een golf van opluchting sloeg door Jake heen. Hij was blij dat hij zat, anders zou hij door zijn knieën zijn gezakt. De coach leefde! Ze mochten Jake voor de rest van zijn leven opsluiten en hij zou er geen bezwaar tegen hebben. Zo lang coach Reynolds maar in orde was. Hij ontmoette zijn moeders blik opnieuw en fronste.

Ze leek overstuur, alsof er iets was wat ze hem nog niet had verteld.

'Jake, ik heb mevrouw Parker gesproken. Zij kent een familie uit de kerk van de Reynolds.' Zijn moeder boog haar hoofd even voordat ze opkeek. 'De coach is er slecht aan toe, jongen. Als hij in leven blijft... zal hij zo goed als zeker vanaf zijn middel verlamd blijven.'

Verlamd? De coach? Verlamd... Vanaf zijn middel? Kan niet... niet de coach! Jake voelde zich wegzakken in drijfzand. De coach kon niet verlamd zijn. Hij was zo sterk als een os. De jongens plaagden hem dat hij beter in vorm was dan de rest van het team. 'Misschien had mevrouw Parker het mis. Wat zeggen ze op het nieuws?'

'Het is nog niet gepubliceerd. Het ongeluk is te laat gebeurd om de krant van gisteren te halen.'

Jake begon weer te beven. Hij streek met zijn hand over zijn kruin en zijn nek. 'Mam, je kunt me hier niet zo laten zitten. Ik moet weten hoe het met hem gaat. Het is allemaal mijn schuld!'

Ze kneep haar ogen dicht en zat volkomen stil. Dat had hij haar maar één keer eerder zien doen, toen zijn vader een paar jaar geleden het huis verlaten had. Jake wist het niet zeker, maar hij dacht dat het betekende dat ze op instorten stond. Opnieuw wilde hij een gat in het glas stompen, erdoorheen klimmen en haar omhelzen, maar zelfs dat kon hij niet. In één ogenblik waren zoveel levens ingestort, en allemaal door hem.

'Mam, houd op. Ik heb je nodig. Die vent zit naar me te kijken en hij kan me elk ogenblik terugbrengen naar de cel.' Op Jakes dringende toon deed zijn moeder haar ogen weer open. 'Ik moet weten hoe de coach eraan toe is.'

'De agent vertelde me dat je hier tot maandag, misschien dinsdag blijft. Hangt ervan af wanneer ze je voor de rechter kunnen krijgen. Ze willen je vervolgen voor…' Haar stem begaf het en nieuwe tranen stroomden over haar wangen. 'Voor een zwaar verkeersmisdrijf. Ook iets over straatracen en het gebruik van een auto als dodelijk wapen. Ze willen je als volwassene berechten, Jake. Dat kan betekenen…' Haar stem stierf weg.

'Dat ik hier nog een poosje moet blijven.' Jake klemde de telefoon vast. 'Dat geeft niet, mam. Ik heb het verdiend.'

'Meer dan een poosje, Jake. De agent zei dat je van geluk mag spreken als je over vijf jaar vrij bent.'

Zijn moeder begreep het niet. Ze had kunnen zeggen dat hij dertig jaar moest zitten en het zou hem niet kunnen schelen. Wat moest hij anders doen? Zijn footballdagen waren geteld, en achter het stuur kwam hij ook niet meer. Hij kon moeilijk terug naar Marion High, waar iedereen zou weten dat hij degene was die coach Reynolds' leven had verwoest. Maar hij was pas derdejaars, zonder diploma of opleiding, en hij had geen idee hoe hij zichzelf moest onderhouden. Hij kon slechts naar een andere stad verhuizen om opnieuw te beginnen.

Nee, hij zat in de val, en dat kwam hem voorlopig goed uit. Hier hoorde hij. En zelfs hier kon hij nog steeds door de gang lopen of door zijn cel heen en weer benen.

Als het waar was wat zijn moeder zei, was dat meer dan coach Reynolds kon.

★

De telefoon ophangen en bij Jake vandaan lopen die middag was het moeilijkste wat Tara Daniels ooit had meegemaakt. Maar de volgende middag Tim ontmoeten in de hal van het huis van bewaring kwam er dicht in de buurt.

Hij kwam binnen en zag haar meteen. Zijn das zat scheef en zijn ogen stonden groot en verwilderd. Toen hij het nieuws had vernomen, had hij de eerste vlucht genomen die hij kon krijgen. Sneller had hij er niet kunnen zijn.

Tara kon wel honderd dingen bedenken die ze tegen hem wilde zeggen. Toen de politie belde om te vertellen dat Jake was gearresteerd voor een verkeersmisdrijf en dat hij op het moment van het ongeluk aan het racen was geweest, wilde ze dat Tim ook gearresteerd was. Had ze het niet gezegd? Had ze hen beiden niet gewaarschuwd dat zo'n snelle auto gevaarlijk was voor een tienerjongen? Net zoals ze tegen Tim had gezegd dat hun huwelijk het waard was om voor te vechten, dat hij door naar New Jersey te vertrekken slechts alles verloor wat het belangrijkste was: de liefde die ze eens hadden gedeeld, de zoon die ze hadden grootgebracht en de eenheid in geloof die eens zo belangrijk voor hen was geweest.

Toen had ze gelijk gehad en nu had ze ook gelijk.

Maar toen Tim met een masker van gekweldheid en verdriet op haar toe kwam, was het niet belangrijk meer dat ze gelijk had en Tim ongelijk. Het enige wat terzake deed, was dat hun zoon bijna iemand had gedood, mogelijk had verlamd. En het leven nooit meer hetzelfde zou zijn.

Het was niet bepaald het ogenblik om verwijten te maken. In de hele wereld was er op dat moment maar één ander mens die de pijn kon begrijpen van wat Tara Daniels doorstond. En die mens was de man die voor haar stond. De man van wie ze nog steeds hield, al was het jaren geleden dat ze hem graag had gemogen.

'Tim…' Ze breidde haar armen uit en langzaam kwam hij naar haar toe, als een stervende. Zijn armen kwamen om haar middel en zij sloeg de hare om zijn hals. En daar, te midden van rondlopende kleine misdadigers en zwervers met lege blikken, met een verscheidenheid aan agenten en beambten die hun werk deden, deden Tara en Tim iets wat ze in geen jaren hadden gedaan.

Ze klemden elkaar stevig vast en huilden.

Vijftien

Twee dagen later begon de zwelling langs Johns ruggengraat af te nemen.

De arts had uitgelegd dat ze pas konden weten of Johns verlamming permanent was nadat de zwelling verdwenen was. Tot nu toe was John niet op de hoogte geweest van de mogelijkheid. Hoewel er sinds zaterdag vierentwintig uur per dag bezoek zijn kamer in en uit was gelopen, was hij voornamelijk in slaap gehouden. Te veel wakker zijn betekende te veel beweging en dat kon de slangen van de beademing en de luchtpijp hinderen.

Het was maandag, vroeg in de middag, en Nicole en Abby zaten alleen in een rustig hoekje achter in de wachtkamer. John sliep, dus ze waren van plan geweest om zelf ook even wat slaap in te halen. Maar ze zaten uitgeput en klaarwakker samen uit het ziekenhuisraam te kijken naar de verkleurende bladeren in de bomen langs het parkeerterrein.

Ze zaten er nog geen tien minuten toen dokter Robert Furin verscheen. Abby en Nicole gingen rechtop zitten. Abby's hart nam een hoge vlucht. De glimlach van de dokter kon maar één ding betekenen. John had zijn voeten bewogen!

Haar mondhoeken gingen omhoog, ondanks de uitputting die als een dubbele zwaartekracht aan haar trok. 'Heeft hij beweging in zijn benen?'

'Eh…' Het gezicht van de arts veranderde. 'Nee, mevrouw Reynolds. Dat hebben we nog niet kunnen bepalen. Misschien over een uurtje.' Hij tikte met de zijkant van zijn pen tegen zijn broekspijp. 'Maar ik heb wel goed nieuws.'

Abby voelde Nicoles reactie op de tegenvaller. Ze moest ook aan Johns benen hebben gedacht. 'Fijn. Dat kunnen we wel gebruiken.'

'Het ziet ernaaruit dat de luchtpijp niet doorgesneden is, zoals we aanvankelijk dachten. We hebben vanmorgen een betere foto kunnen maken en hij schijnt intact te zijn. Dat gebeurt soms als iemand een zwakke klap tegen de keel krijgt.' De dokter zweeg even. 'Het goede nieuws is dat hij van de beademing af kan. Daar zijn ze op dit moment mee bezig. Dus als u hem straks ziet, moet hij weer kunnen praten.' Hij schudde zijn hoofd. 'Het is echt een wonder dat hij nog leeft, nadat hij met zo'n snelheid is geraakt.'

Abby was blij met het goede nieuws. Het was niet wat ze gehoopt had te horen, maar de dokter had gelijk. God had John van een wisse dood gered. Ze had veel om dankbaar voor te zijn.

'Wanneer weten we het van zijn benen?'

'We willen nog een paar foto's maken voordat de verdoving is uitgewerkt. Binnen een uur, zou ik zeggen.'

Binnen een uur.

Nieuws dat hun leven hoe dan ook zou veranderen zou binnenkomen als alle andere stukjes informatie die in de afgelopen dagen hun bestaan op zijn kop hadden gezet. Met één enkele zin, voor een voldongen feit gesteld.

'Dank u, dokter.' Abby glimlachte, maar dat voelde raar aan. 'Wij blijven hier. Laat het ons alstublieft weten zodra u informatie hebt.'

Nicole was zwijgzaam tot de dokter vertrok. 'Heb je het artikel meegebracht?'

'Ja. Ik weet niet wanneer ik het hem zal laten zien, maar op een gegeven moment zal hij het willen weten.'

Matt had gisterochtend de krant meegebracht en hun het verhaal laten zien. Er stond een foto bij van Johns truck, die volkomen onherkenbaar was. Abby had haar handen voor haar mond geslagen toen ze hem zag.

De arts had gelijk. Het was echt een wonder dat John nog leefde.

In het artikel stond dat twee tieners waren gearresteerd voor straatracen, waaronder degene die Johns auto had geraakt toen hij het parkeerterrein van de school af draaide. Die informatie was geen schok voor Abby geweest. Ze had meteen al gehoord dat John slachtoffer was geworden van een illegale straatrace. Maar de namen van de tieners hadden haar diep geschokt.

Jake Daniels en Casey Parker.

Johns quarterbacks. Beste jongens, die een paar foute keuzes hadden gemaakt en de rest van hun leven de prijs zouden betalen. Volgens het artikel werd Casey aangeklaagd voor roekeloos rijden, deelname aan een illegale straatrace en medeplichtigheid aan een verkeersmisdrijf. Hij was onder borgtocht vrijgelaten en zou naar verwachting schuld bekennen aan verscheidene van de aanklachten tijdens een hoorzitting ergens in de volgende maand.

Jakes tenlastelegging was veel ernstiger.

Ten eerste was de officier van justitie vastbesloten hem als volwassene te berechten. Als hij daarin slaagde, en de kans daarop was groot, zou Jake waarschijnlijk voor een jury terechtstaan voor meerdere beschuldigingen, waaronder geweldpleging met een dodelijk wapen. Voor de combinatie van misdrijven kon Jake wel tot tien jaar gevangenisstraf krijgen.

'Deze stad is illegale straatraces beu,' citeerde het stuk de officier van justitie. 'Als de mensen deze jongeman tot voorbeeld willen stellen, kan hij de maximumstraf krijgen.'

Ook Jakes moeder Tara werd aangehaald. 'Jake vindt het afgrijselijk wat er gebeurd is. Hij is bereid elke straf die hij krijgt te aanvaarden.' Vervolgens stond er in het artikel dat mevrouw Daniels hoopte dat de officier van justitie mild voor haar zoon zou zijn, omdat haar zoon geen strafblad had.

Abby wist niet wat ze daarvan moest denken. Als de bestuurder van de racende auto een andere tiener was geweest, eentje die ze niet kende, had Abby zich aan de kant van de officier geschaard en op de allerstrengste straf gehoopt.

Maar… Jake Daniels?

De jongen had een keer of tien bij hen thuis gegeten, had in hun meer gezwommen en was van hun aanlegsteiger afgesprongen. Hoe kon ze hopen dat een jongen als Jake de volgende tien jaar van zijn leven in de gevangenis doorbracht? Abby zag hem er nog geen tien dagen zitten, laat staan jaren.

Ze keek naar Nicole. 'Heb je aan Jakes moeder gedacht? Hoe verschrikkelijk zij zich moet voelen?'

'Ze wil mildheid voor haar zoon.' Nicole sloeg haar armen over elkaar. 'Dat is het enige wat mij is opgevallen.'

De bitterheid in Nicoles stem brak Abby's hart. Nicole was nooit verbitterd. Haar leven lang was Nicole altijd de eerste geweest om ergens voor te bidden en ze had altijd een woord van wijsheid of een Bijbeltekst voor iemand in nood.

Bitterheid stond haar niet.

'Jake is een aardige jongen, Nick.'

Haar dochter zei niets en Abby liet het los. Ze kon zich niet voorstellen hoe vreselijk de beproeving voor Jakes moeder moest zijn. Wat vreemd dat Abby en Tara Daniels nog maar een paar weken geleden juist over de auto hadden gepraat die John bijna had gedood.

'Wat haalt Tim in zijn hoofd om Jake zo'n auto te geven?' had Tara gezegd. 'Weet je wat dat ding *kost*? Bijna veertigduizend dollar. Dat is ongehoord! Daar had hij vier jaar studie van kunnen betalen. En een jongen als Jake wordt er alleen maar door in de verleiding gebracht om verkeerde dingen te doen.'

Profetische woorden, inderdaad. Jake, die pas kortgeleden het besluit had genomen om minder vaak met Casey Parker om te gaan… die was opgehouden de Nathan Pikes van Marion High te pesten en de laatste tijd vaker met John over zijn toekomst sprak. Jake, die een studiebeurs voor football had kunnen krijgen… had een besluit genomen dat al hun levens voor altijd had veranderd.

In plaats van er te zijn om Tara in haar droevigste uur te steunen en bij te staan, beleefde Abby haar eigen nachtmerrie en las de bijzonderheden van het verhaal uit de krant, net als alle andere inwoners van Marion.

Onder een kleinere kop verderop in de krant stond een kort artikel over de vermeende aanslag op Marion High. Er stond dat een leerling na de wedstrijd ondervraagd was en overgegeven aan zijn ouders.

Abby knipte het artikel over het ongeluk uit, vouwde het op en stak het in haar tas. Binnenkort zou John het willen zien. Tot nu toe hadden ze niet gesproken over het ongeluk, omdat John niet kon praten. Nu de slangen uit zijn keel werden gehaald, zou hij vragen gaan stellen.

Abby hoopte dat hij haar antwoorden kon doorstaan.

Nicole draaide zich met een gespannen gezicht naar haar toe. 'Kan ik even met je praten? Niet over het ongeluk, maar over iets anders?'

'Natuurlijk.' Abby pakte Nicoles hand. 'Wat heb je op je hart?'

Nicole had fijne rimpeltjes in haar voorhoofd. Abby voelde de spanning van haar dochter alsof het haar eigen spanning was. 'Het gaat over de baby.'

'Alles is toch in orde?'

Nicole knikte. 'Alleen… nou ja, ik wilde je een paar weken geleden al vertellen dat ik zwanger was, maar ik kon het niet.' Ze aarzelde en sloeg haar ogen op naar Abby. 'Ik was er eerst niet blij mee.'

Arme Nicole. Alsof het niet genoeg was om over Johns toestand te moeten tobben, had ze ook nog haar eigen sores. 'Dat is normaal, lieverd.' Abby verschoof om Nicole recht aan te kunnen kijken. 'Zeker omdat je de eerste jaren niet van plan was om kinderen te krijgen.'

'Vier jaar.'

'Precies.' Abby wachtte af en gaf haar dochter de tijd om haar gedachten onder woorden te brengen.

'Ik ben gek op kinderen, dat is het punt niet.' Nicoles gezicht weerspiegelde de strijd die zich in haar afspeelde. 'Het is alleen… ik wilde niet dat ze tussen Matt en mij zouden komen.' Ze zweeg even. 'Zoals ik tussen pap en jou kwam.'

Abby deinsde een beetje achteruit. Waar had Nicole het nu toch over? 'Lieverd, jij bent nooit tussen je vader en mij gekomen.'

Nicole blies een lokje van haar pony weg en leunde achterover tegen de kunststof ziekenhuisbank. 'Jawel. Misschien zag je het niet zo, maar het is waar. Daarom… daarom was jullie huwelijk niet altijd zoals het had kunnen zijn.'

'Nick, dat is niet…' Abby kon haar gedachten niet onder woorden brengen. Kennelijk had haar dochter beter in de gaten wat er vorig jaar bijna was gebeurd dan Abby had gedacht. Maar wat haalde Nicole zich in haar hoofd? Hun moeilijkheden hadden nooit iets met de kinderen te maken gehad.

'Mam, ik weet dat het raar klinkt, maar het zit in mijn hoofd sinds Matt en ik getrouwd zijn. Ik heb altijd willen geloven dat pap en jij de beste relatie van de wereld hadden. Maar vorig jaar heb ik vele keren gezien dat het niet zo was. Oké, ik zeg altijd dat jullie net een pasgetrouwd stel lijken, maar dat komt alleen doordat ik dat *wil* geloven.' Ze spreidde haar vingers over haar borst. 'Diep vanbinnen weet ik dat jullie niet altijd gelukkig zijn. En ik denk dat het moet komen doordat jullie nooit die jaren samen alleen hebben gehad. Zonder kinderen.'

Er ontsnapte een lachje uit Abby's keel en ze sloeg haar hand voor haar mond. Nicole was opmerkzaam, maar haar redenering klopte totaal niet. Ze sloeg de plank zo ver mis dat het bijna grappig was.

'Mam…' Nicole fronste. 'Hoe kun je nu lachen?'

'Lieverd, ik lach je niet uit. Het is alleen… dat dat het probleem niet was met je vader en mij. Totaal niet.'

Nicole zweeg even. 'Sinds ik ontdekt heb dat ik zwanger ben, ben ik aldoor bang geweest. Diep vanbinnen. Omdat Matt en ik niet genoeg tijd hebben gehad om een band te smeden, om een duurzaam huwelijk op te bouwen.'

'O, Nick.' Abby sloeg haar armen om Nicoles hals en knuffelde haar. 'Kinderen krijgen zal jullie relatie alleen maar sterker maken. Dat was bij je vader en mij ook zo.'

Nicole week een beetje naar achteren en keek Abby in de ogen. 'Wat is er dan gebeurd? Ik weet dat pap en jij moeilijkheden hadden. Je probeert het te verbergen, maar soms is het duidelijk.'

'Heb je de laatste tijd nog problemen opgemerkt? Zeg maar, sinds je bruiloft?'

'Sinds mijn bruiloft?' Nicole maakte zich los uit Abby's omhelzing en keek uit het manshoge raam. 'Ik geloof van niet.' Ze keek om. 'Hoe komt dat?'

Abby stond op en kwam bij Nicole naast het raam staan. Wat moest ze haar geliefde dochter precies vertellen? Hoeveel moest ze zeggen? 'Dat we jou negen maanden na onze trouwdag kregen, is nooit de oorzaak van onze problemen geweest.'

'Wat dan wel?'

'Kort samengevat, we vergaten te dansen.'

Nicole kneep haar ogen samen. 'Wat bedoel je?'

Abby lachte vermoeid. 'Sinds je vader en ik het huis betrokken waarin we nu wonen, gingen we vaak achter buiten op de aanlegsteiger dansen. Niet echt dansen. Gewoon een beetje heen en weer wiegen, luisteren naar de geluiden om ons heen en denken aan wat belangrijk was.'

'Echt waar?'

'Hm-m.' Abby kreeg een brok in haar keel. Hadden ze voor het laatst samen gedanst? Lag John echt verderop in de gang verlamd in een ziekenhuisbed? Ze sloot zich voor die gedachten af en vond haar stem terug. 'Dan praatten we over jou en je broers, over de leuke en nare dingen die je vader in zijn werk als coach meemaakte, over de overwinningen en tragedies die het leven ons door de jaren heen had toebedeeld.'

'Praatten jullie over Haley Ann?'

'Altijd.' De luchtigheid verdween uit Abby's stem. 'Maar een jaar of drie geleden gingen we niet meer naar de steiger en we namen niet meer de tijd om te praten over het leven en onze plaats samen daarin.'

'Is pap toen bevriend geraakt met mevrouw Denton?'

Abby knikte. 'Maar hij was niet de enige die fouten maakte. Ik praatte vaker met een bevriende redacteur van me dan met je vader. Dat hielp ook niet echt. Algauw werden we vreemden voor elkaar.'

'Ik wist niet dat het zo erg was.'

'Het was nog erger.' Abby zweeg even. Als ze Nicole nu het hele verhaal vertelde, schrikte ze haar af voor het huwelijk. Maar als ze het niet deed, nam ze Nicole de kans af om te groeien.

'Hebben jullie nooit overwogen…' Nicoles stem brak af.

'Jawel. Vorig jaar dus.' Abby staarde uit het raam. Buiten in de boom zat een vogelpaartje. 'Weet je nog die dag dat Matt en jij jullie verloving aankondigden?'

'Ja.' Nicole liet haar hoofd achterover vallen. 'We zouden een familiebijeenkomst houden, maar Matt verscheen en we verrasten iedereen.'

'En ons het meest.' Abby keek Nicole aan. 'Wij hadden die dag uitgekozen om jullie te vertellen dat het voorbij was. We zouden gaan scheiden.'

'Mam!' Nicole zette grote ogen op en deed een stap naar achteren. 'Echt niet!'

'Het is waar. Toen jullie je nieuws bekendmaakten, hebben je vader en ik in de keuken afgesproken dat we moesten wachten. We konden het niet doorzetten voordat jullie terug waren van jullie huwelijksreis.'

Nicole greep naar haar hoofd en liep met langzame passen terug naar de bank. 'Nu snap ik het allemaal.'

'Wat?' Abby draaide zich om en leunde tegen het raam.

'Elke keer als ik bad, waar het ook over ging, had ik pap en jou op mijn hart. Ik vertelde het aan Matt. Hij dacht dat het waarschijnlijk kwam omdat jullie onder spanning stonden omdat wij gingen trouwen.' Nicole lachte droevig. 'Ik dacht altijd dat het iets belangrijkers was. Maar dat het zo erg was, had ik niet gedacht.'

'We waren aan het eind van ons Latijn, Nicole. Ik kan alleen maar zeggen dat we je gebeden hebben gevoeld.'

'Dus toen opa die dag stierf en we met z'n allen om zijn ziekenhuisbed heen stonden... waren papa en jij van plan om te gaan scheiden?'

Abby knikte.

'Dat is ongelooflijk. Ik wist het niet.' Ineens verscheen er een ontstelde blik op Nicoles gezicht. 'Had papa een verhouding?'

Maandenlang was ze bezig geweest om die informatie voor Nicole en de jongens verborgen te houden. Nu... nu wist ze dat het verkeerd was geweest om de waarheid te verzwijgen. *God... wilt U dat zij het weet?*

DE WAARHEID ZAL JE VRIJMAKEN...

Abby liet de tekst in het diepst van haar hart rondrollen. Natuurlijk! De waarheid zou niet alleen Abby vrijmaken... maar ook Nicole. Nicole was tenslotte een getrouwde vrouw. Ze kon ooit zelfs zoiets meemaken. Het was cruciaal dat ze de waarheid kende en inzag dat elk huwelijk gered kon worden zolang beide partners bereid waren Gods stem boven hun eigen stem te verstaan.

Ze zuchtte diep. *God, help me het te zeggen zodat ze het kan begrijpen...* 'Het scheelde niet veel. Voor ons allebei.'

Nicole stond op en beende naar het raam en terug. 'Ik geloof het niet.' Ze stond ineens stil en zei boos: 'En toen? Waarom is het niet doorgegaan?'

'Op de avond van je bruiloft... Papa had zijn spullen al ingepakt. Hij zou bij een kennis intrekken als Matt en jij op huwelijksreis waren.'

'Bij mevrouw *Denton*?' Nicole was bleek geworden en de donkere kringen onder haar ogen waren duidelijker zichtbaar.

'Nee, helemaal niet. Toen was mevrouw Denton al verhuisd. Haar vriendschap met je vader was voorbij.'

'Wie dan?'

'Een gescheiden man, een leraar van school.'

'Wat vreselijk.' Nicole zonk weer op de bank neer. 'En toen?'

'Sean en Kade gingen bij vriendjes logeren en toen jij weg was, vertrok je vader ook. Dat wilde hij tenminste. Hij kwam halverwege voordat hij omkeerde en terugkwam. God wilde hem niet weg laten gaan.'

'En jij?' Er klonk twijfel door in Nicoles stem, maar ze keek minder paniekerig dan eerst.

'Ik was boos en van streek. Kapot, eigenlijk. Maar te koppig om hem tegen te houden. Ik ging naar boven en trok een trainingsjack van hem aan. En toen vond ik zijn dagboek.' Abby zag het nog zo duidelijk voor zich alsof het net gebeurd was. 'Tot dat moment wist ik niet eens dat hij een dagboek bijhield.'

'Wat stond erin?'

'Dat het je vader zo speet dat ons huwelijk koud geworden was en hoe fout het was dat hij het met mevrouw Denton had aangelegd. Dat hij graag wilde dat het goed kwam met mij, maar dat hij er zeker van was dat ik het nooit meer zou willen proberen.'

'En kwam papa toen thuis?'

'Nee.' Abby kreeg tranen in haar ogen bij de herinnering. 'Toen ik klaar was met lezen, ging ik naar de steiger, langs de tafels die er nog stonden van je bruiloft, langs de lege glazen en het crêpepapier en de slingers, naar de plek waar je vader en ik altijd samen waren.' Abby keek naar Nicole. 'Een paar minuten later kwam je vader achter me aanlopen. Hij vertelde me iets wat ik nooit zal vergeten.'

'Wat dan?' Er glansde hoop in Nicoles ogen en Abby wist dat ze het juiste had gedaan. Haar dochter moest dit verhaal horen. Zeker gezien alle jaren die Matt en zij nog voor zich hadden.

Abby deed haar ogen even dicht. 'Hij zei dat hij me moest vertellen over de adelaar.'

'De adelaar?'

'Als de adelaar een partner zoekt, is het voor zijn hele leven.'

Abby staarde weer in de verte en zag in gedachten John die avond met uitgestrekte handen op haar toe komen. 'Op een bepaald moment in de balts vliegt de vrouwtjesadelaar zo hoog als ze kan en keert zich op haar rug, in een vrije val. Dan duikt het mannetje naar beneden en pakt haar klauwen met de zijne vast. Daarmee brengt hij de boodschap over dat hij haar toegewijd is.'

'Dat wist ik niet.'

'Je vader pakte mijn handen vast en vertelde me dat hij me nooit meer los wilde laten. Nooit. Dat hij, al werd het zijn dood, van me wilde houden zoals een adelaar van zijn partner houdt. Zoals God wilde dat hij van me hield. Tot de dood ons zou scheiden.'

Abby knipperde met haar ogen en de herinnering vervaagde. Ze keek naar Nicole en zag tranen in haar ogen.

'En... was dat een keerpunt voor jullie?'

'Ja, beslist.' Abby streelde Nicoles hand. 'We zijn nu gelukkiger dan ooit. Het is echt een wonder. Dus je ziet, lieverd. Wees niet bang om de baby. God zal dit net als alle andere dingen in je leven, zelfs de moeilijke, gebruiken om jullie dichter bij elkaar te brengen, en bij Hem.'

Ineens hapte Nicole naar adem. 'Wacht eens even. Er schiet me iets te binnen.' Ze keek Abby aan. 'Toen Matt en ik ons die avond bij ons hotel inschreven, had ik het merkwaardige gevoel dat God tegen me sprak.'

'Waarover?'

'Over papa en jou. Alsof Hij me op mijn schouder tikte en me vertelde dat mijn gebeden voor jullie verhoord waren.' Nicole dacht even na. 'Ik heb het zelfs aan Matt verteld.'

Er liep een rilling over Abby's rug. *Dus U was het echt, God... dank U... dank U.* 'God is zoveel groter dan wij denken. Als wij bijvoorbeeld dit ongeluk zien, dan denken we: *maakte God het allemaal maar beter.* Maar niets gaat langs God heen, helemaal niets. Hij heeft het allemaal uitgedacht en alles wat Hij doet gebeurt hoe dan ook met een reden.'

Er kwam iemand aan en Abby keek om. Het was dokter Furin. Nu glimlachte hij niet. Zijn stappen waren langzaam en afgemeten en hij keek Abby en Nicole aan voordat hij tegenover hen plaatsnam.

'Mevrouw Reynolds, ik heb helaas geen goed nieuws voor u.'

Nicole gleed dichter naar Abby toe en pakte haar hand vast. *Kalm, Abby… wees kalm. Denk aan wat je net zei… God heeft de leiding.* Ze vond haar stem. 'Hebt u… de onderzoeken gedaan?'

'Ja.' Hij fronste. 'Meerdere. Ze wijzen allemaal hetzelfde uit. Door het ongeluk is de ruggengraat van uw man op een heel tere plaats verwond. Met het gevolg waar we van begin af aan bang voor zijn geweest.' Hij zweeg even. 'Mevrouw Reynolds, uw man is vanaf zijn middel naar beneden verlamd. Het spijt me.'

Hoe erg het ongeluk ook was geweest, hoe weinig het ook had gescheeld of ze hadden John verloren, Abby geloofde geen moment dat dit de definitieve diagnose was. Niet voor John Reynolds. De arts zei dat hij er ongedeerd vanaf had kunnen komen als het letsel een centimeter lager had gezeten … maar dat het zijn dood had kunnen worden als het een centimeter hoger had gezeten. En iets over revalidatie en speciale rolstoelen.

Nicole huilde zachtjes en knikte alsof het allemaal volkomen logisch was wat de dokter zei.

Maar Abby hoorde het nauwelijks. Ze zat niet meer in een muffe ziekenhuiswachtkamer het slechtste nieuws van haar leven te krijgen.

Ze was weer veertien en lag uitgestrekt op een deken aan het meer, met een jonge John naast haar die een football in de lucht gooide en naar haar grinnikte, terwijl zijn blauwe ogen straalden van de weerspiegeling van de maan op het water. *Heb je een vriendje, juffie Abby Chapman?* Toen was ze zeventien en zag hem voor de eerste keer in drie jaar, vlak voordat hij in Michigan meespeelde in een footballwedstrijd. *Je bent mooi, Abby. Weet je dat? Ga vanavond na de wedstrijd met me uit…* En ineens was hij op het veld, haalde uit en gooide een football alsof hij ervoor geboren was, hij rende ermee als de wind, groter dan levensgroot. Het beeld verdween en ze was in een kerk. John keek naar haar met alle liefde die hij in zich had. *Ik, John Reynolds, neem jou, Abby Chapman, tot mijn wettige vrouw.* Toen dansten ze, maar het beeld veranderde en ze waren in de gymzaal van het Marion High en Paula zei dat ze in de maat moesten blijven.

'Mevrouw Reynolds?'

Abby knipperde met haar ogen en de herinneringen verdwenen. 'Ja?'

'Ik zei dat u beiden nu naar hem toe mag. Hij weet van de diagnose af. Hij vroeg ernaar en tja… we vonden dat hij het moest weten.'

'Ik wil niet naar hem toe.' De angst stond op Nicoles gezicht geschreven. Ze schudde haar hoofd naar Abby. 'Ik kan hem niet zien. Nog niet.'

'Nu?' Abby keek naar dokter Furin. Ze had het gevoel of ze onder water was, alles om haar heen leek in slowmotion te gebeuren op een niveau dat ze niet goed kon begrijpen.

'Ja. Hij heeft naar u gevraagd.' De dokter stond op. 'Het spijt me voor u, mevrouw Reynolds.'

Abby knikte, maar haar hersenen waren verdoofd en smeekten erom een paar minuten terug te gaan in de tijd. Toen de kans nog bestond dat John weer zou kunnen lopen. Ze hadden zoveel jaren verloren… was dit echt Gods plan? Dat John verlamd raakte, juist nu alles beter ging dan ooit?

Abby's hart bonsde. Hoe kon ze hem onder ogen komen? Wat zou ze zeggen? John had zijn hele leven zijn benen gebruikt. Zelfs nu hij halverwege de veertig was, kon hij nog net zo makkelijk rennen als ademhalen. Op school was hij de actiefste leraar op de campus, hij voerde voor de vuist weg komische nummers op en deed met de basketbalspelers in zijn klas wie het hoogste kon springen om te zien of ze die dag een onverwachte overhoring kregen.

Op een keer waren ze naar Chicago gegaan om Riverdance te

zien. De volgende dag was John alle klassen Iers tapdansend binnengegaan. Het was niet vreemd dat de kinderen gek op hem waren. Diep in zijn hart was hij zelf nog een kind. En zeker nu Abby en hij weer gelukkig waren. Het was alsof ze allebei tien jaar jonger waren geworden.

En nu... *dit?*

Wat moesten ze beginnen nu John nooit meer kon lopen? Misschien nooit meer met haar kon vrijen? De schrik sloeg haar om het hart. Daar had ze niet eerder aan gedacht, dat ze John in die zin misschien nooit meer zou kennen. Het was onvoorstelbaar dat hun lichamelijke liefde tot het verleden zou behoren. Wat moest ze daar in vredesnaam over zeggen?

Abby kon geen antwoorden bedenken. Ze was te ontsteld om te huilen, te geschokt om iets anders te voelen dan de zekerheid van één ding: John had haar nodig. En daarom zou ze naar hem toe gaan. Al had ze niets te bieden, geen troostende woorden of hoop.

Ze zou hem omhelzen en liefhebben en zich aan hem vastklampen, als een adelaar zijn klauwen vastgrijpen, al zou het leven nooit, nooit meer hetzelfde zijn.

Ze ging zonder een woord te zeggen zijn kamer binnen, maar zijn ogen vonden onmiddellijk de hare. Ze liep door de kamer naar hem toe en ging op de rand van het bed zitten.

'John...' Pas toen kwamen de tranen. 'Wat erg.'

Er zat een vers verband om zijn hals, waar ze de slang eruit hadden gehaald. Zijn lichaam leek ouder en kleiner. Alsof hij tien centimeter korter was geworden. Voor het eerst sinds het ongeluk keek hij haar diep in de ogen en sprak.

Zijn stem was het enige wat niet veranderd was.

'Vertel me wat er gebeurd is, Abby.' Zijn woorden kwamen pijnlijk langzaam. Zijn keel moest rauw zijn door de slangen die er de afgelopen dagen in gezeten hadden. 'Vertel. Ik moet het weten.'

En ze vertelde, een halfuur lang.

Hij zei niets toen ze het artikel voorlas en hem nauwkeurig alle bijzonderheden vertelde waarvan ze op de hoogte was. Toen ze klaar was, toen de feiten voor hem waren uitgestald om te aanvaarden of tegen te fulmineren, sprak hij. Wat hij zei vertelde Abby dat de John van wie ze hield er nog was, dat een ongeluk hem zijn benen kon afnemen, maar niet zijn hart. 'Hoe…' Hij aarzelde even en keek haar onderzoekend aan. 'En hoe is het dan nu met Jake?'

Zestien

Chuck Parker kon niet slapen.

Tja, zijn zoon wachtte een boete van honderden dollars en wie weet hoeveel uur dienstverlening voor zijn betrokkenheid bij dat stomme ongeluk. En de jongen had elke kans op een sportbeurs en zelfs toelating aan een van de betere scholen verknoeid.

Maar dat was niet wat Chuck dwarszat. Dat was coach Reynolds.

De man zou blijven leven en dat vond Chuck wel goed, maar er was één bijzonderheid aan het ongeluk dat hem zorgen baarde. Wat deed de coach na middernacht nog op school?

Die bijzonderheid, gecombineerd met andere die in de krant van gisteren aan het licht waren gekomen, hield hem het grootste deel van de nacht uit de slaap. En dat overkwam Chuck nooit. Nooit.

Voor het ongeluk had hij zelfs beter geslapen, voornamelijk omdat hij zo moe was. De lastercampagne die hij sinds het begin van het seizoen tegen de coach voerde, was zwaar werk.

In de afgelopen maanden had Chuck de tribunes bewerkt als een autoverkoper, hij was naast ouders aangeschoven om hen subtiel over te halen tot zijn gedachtegang: coach Reynolds moest opstappen.

'Het is een aardige vent,' zei Chuck tegen wie er naast hem zat. 'Begrijp me niet verkeerd. Maar we hebben hier op Marion High de meest getalenteerde jongens van de hele staat. Onze kinderen hebben iemand nodig met visie, een coach met vuur in zijn bloed. Iemand die de hedendaagse jeugd begrijpt. Bovendien heeft coach Reynolds een poosje rust nodig. Hij moet zich focussen op zijn jongste zoon en meer tijd met zijn gezin doorbrengen.'

In de loop van zijn verhaal glimlachte Chuck vaak en het duurde niet lang, het mislukte bijna nooit, of de ouders knikten instemmend en beloofden naar een van Chucks bijeenkomsten te komen.

Daar werd het menens. Tijdens die bijeenkomsten werden brieven opgesteld en plannen gemaakt. Coach Reynolds werd ontslagen. Het moest. Dat was het voorrecht van de ouders. Ze hadden tot nu toe drie vergaderingen gehouden en na elke vergadering had Chuck Parker ervoor gezorgd dat de sportcoördinator een verslag kreeg.

'Herman, de ouders willen hem weg hebben. De Eagles moeten een nieuwe richting inslaan.'

Meestal zat Lutz achterover in zijn kantoorstoel en hield zijn mond dicht. Om zijn plan te bezegelen, wees Chuck dan op het drinken en straatracen dat de spelers tijdens de zomertraining hadden gedaan...

'Wil je zo'n coach op Marion High hebben?' Chuck verhief zijn stem precies genoeg om Herman zenuwachtig te maken. 'Iemand die door de vingers ziet dat de jongens alle regels aan hun laars lappen? We hebben een coach nodig met lef, een man die het beste van onze jongens eist zonder geschipper met de moraal.'

Het plan werkte ook.

De laatste keer had Lutz hem verzekerd dat hij ermee bezig was. Eindelijk had de man het enige toegegeven wat Parker had willen horen: 'Ik ben niet van plan om zijn contract te verlengen, als je daar wat aan hebt.'

Chuck kon het nauwelijks geloven. Lutz had uitermate slappe knieën. Maar dat was juist het mooie. Herman Lutz was als was in zijn handen en coach Reynolds was nagenoeg ontslagen. Nog een paar wedstrijden en het was een feit.

Natuurlijk geloofde Chuck niet echt dat coach Reynolds van

het drinken en straatracen afwist. Ach wat, hij was niet eens een slechte coach.

Maar Reynolds had een fatale fout gemaakt: hij had Chucks zoon op de bank laten zitten.

Casey was een van de beste quarterbacks van de staat. Goed, hij had een paar onvoldoendes op zijn rapport. En inderdaad, hij kreeg soms moeilijkheden omdat hij een brutale mond had tegen een leraar. Nou en? Casey was een energieke jongen, zeer gedreven, een van die superatleten die – en daarvan was Chuck overtuigd – eens een eerste divisieteam naar een nationaal kampioenschap zouden aanvoeren.

Dat zou althans gebeurd zijn als coach Reynolds niet zo gevoelig had gedaan over zijn spelgedrag. Jake Daniels was geen betere quarterback. Hij kon alleen beter slijmen. En nu was het te laat voor Casey. Zijn hele middelbare school- en studieloopbaan was verknoeid door coach Reynolds' belachelijk hoge normen.

Maar voor Billy was het nog niet te laat.

Chucks jongste zoon had een nog betere arm dan Casey. De jongen zat dit jaar in de derde. Een studiebeurs met volledige onkostenvergoeding was voor een jongen als Billy een vaststaand gegeven en dat was nog maar het begin. Chuck geloofde vast dat Billy op een dag een Super Bowlring zou dragen. Hij zag het al voor zich hoe hij de prijs voor de meest waardevolle speler van de NFL in ontvangst nam.

Jammer dat Billy zich nog beroerder gedroeg dan Casey.

Geen probleem voor Chuck. Maar voor een man als coach Reynolds? Als Chuck niets deed, kwam Billy net als zijn oudste broer op de bank te zitten. En dat kon Chuck simpelweg niet hebben.

Om die reden was de campagne tegen coach Reynolds er toch wel gekomen, ongeacht wat de Eagles dat jaar wonnen of verloren. Het feit dat ze veel te veel wedstrijden hadden verloren, had Chucks werk alleen maar makkelijker gemaakt. Zeker met Herman Lutz aan de leiding. Wat die man wist over opstelling en training en sport in het algemeen paste in een lucifersdoosje. Maar één ding wist Lutz wel: wat het kostte om zijn baan te houden. En aangezien de man al een armzalig figuur had geslagen, stond hij er beslist op dat zijn coaches wonnen.

Alles – de avonden waarin hij de ouders van de spelers bewerkte, de vergaderingen in zijn vrije tijd, de discussies met Herman Lutz – verliep precies zoals Parker had gepland en niet één keer had hij wakker gelegen.

Tot het ongeluk.

Sindsdien hadden er twee artikelen in de krant gestaan. Het eerste was feitelijk. Het vertelde het verhaal van de straatrace en de ernst van coach Reynolds' verwondingen. De kans had bestaan dat hij zou sterven. Natuurlijk hoopte Chuck Parker net als iedereen dat de coach bleef leven. En net als iedereen was hij opgelucht toen in het artikel van maandag stond dat zijn toestand was verbeterd.

Maar dat was niet alles wat in het artikel van maandag had gestaan.

De verslaggever was naar de wachtkamer in het ziekenhuis gegaan en had een heleboel jongeren geïnterviewd. Het was *hun* verhaal en dat vond Chuck, samen met het feit dat de coach die avond zo laat nog op school was geweest, hoogst verontrustend.

Volgens het artikel hielden de scholieren van Marion High net zo veel van coach Reynolds als van football. Eén speler had gezegd dat football en de coach een en hetzelfde waren en voor altijd zouden zijn voor iedereen die zichzelf een Eagle noemde.

Hun woorden vertelden het verhaal.

'Soms komt hij op zaterdagochtend met zakken vol hamburgers aanzetten, genoeg voor het hele team.'

'De coach bekommert zich om meer dan football. Hij is iemand met wie je kunt praten en hij heeft altijd goede raad. Veel van ons zien hem als een tweede vader.'

'Elk seizoen gaan we de avond voor een van de thuiswedstrijden naar zijn huis voor zijn beroemde barbecue in de achtertuin.

Hij behandelt ons allemaal als zoons. De coach houdt van ons.'

De verklaringen van de tieners werden met onuitwisbare inkt geschreven in het steen van Chuck Parkers hart. Als coach Reynolds zo fantastisch was, waarom had Casey het dan niet beter gedaan?

Het antwoord van de coach was steeds hetzelfde geweest: Casey had een gedragsprobleem. Chuck had het altijd weggewuifd. Zijn zoon was gedreven en mat zich graag met anderen.

Maar sinds het ongeluk was Chuck zich gaan afvragen of de coach heel, heel misschien toch gelijk had.

Waarom was Casey tenslotte om te beginnen aan het racen geslagen? Het verhaal luidde dat Casey en Jake op een feestje onenigheid hadden gekregen en dat Casey Jake had uitgedaagd om het buiten uit te vechten. De jongen was tenminste eerlijk geweest tegen de politie. Het was zijn idee geweest om te racen, zijn idee om Jake Daniels op tenminste één punt te verslaan. En als daarvoor de wet moest worden overtreden, jammer dan.

Over slecht gedrag gesproken! Opstandig, eigenmachtig gedrag dat Casey beslist niet zou helpen slagen in het leven.

Door dit alles was Chuck zich gaan afvragen of hij het misschien mis had gehad over coach Reynolds. Chuck kon maar één reden bedenken om op de dag van de wedstrijd 's avonds na middernacht nog op school te zijn. Reynolds had moeten inhalen wat leraren deden als ze niet coachten. Opdrachten schrijven… lessen plannen… werkstukken corrigeren. Dat soort dingen.

Zo had Chuck het nooit bekeken. Coach Reynolds was gewoon een hardwerkende, eerlijke, toegewijde vent… en Chuck was het hele seizoen bezig geweest met pogingen om hem onderuit te halen. Hij wist dat er geen steek van waar was wat hij de mensen over Reynolds op de mouw had gespeld. De waarheid stond in het artikel.

Geen wonder dat hij niet kon slapen.

Het was dinsdagochtend en na een nieuwe slapeloze nacht was Chuck zo vermoeid dat hij zich bedwelmd voelde. Hij strompelde uit bed, plensde koud water in zijn gezicht en daalde omzichtig de trap van de voorveranda af. De krant was tegenwoordig zijn uitkijk op de wereld. Casey was weer naar school, maar hij was uit het footballteam geschopt en mocht niet autorijden. Hij kon Chuck geen informatie over de zaak te verschaffen.

Maar er zou vast wel iets in de krant staan. Het verhaal had de afgelopen twee dagen op de voorpagina gestaan. Er zou vanmorgen ook wel nieuws zijn. Hij pakte de krant, slofte naar de keuken en spreidde hem uit op het aanrecht.

De kop boven aan de pagina overrompelde hem, deed zijn hart meer dan een slag overslaan en zijn maag omdraaien: *Coach Marion High verlamd bij straatrace-ongeluk.*

Het moest een vergissing zijn. Reynolds was lichamelijk fantastisch in vorm. Hij was lang en gespierd, en nu waarschijnlijk nog even sterk als in zijn studietijd. Zo'n man kon niet verlamd zijn.

Chuck las het artikel.

Artsen maakten maandag bekend dat coach John Reynolds van Marion High een permanente ruggengraatbeschadiging heeft opgelopen toen zijn auto zaterdagmorgen vroeg werd aangereden door een jonge straatracer. Door de verwonding zal Reynolds vanaf zijn middel naar beneden verlamd blijven.

Chuck duwde de krant weg. Zijn maag kolkte en hij vloog naar de wc. Daar viel hij op zijn knieën en kokhalsde. Steeds opnieuw trokken zijn ingewanden samen tot hij het gevoel had dat zijn lijf binnenstebuiten keerde.

Kreunend tilde hij zijn hoofd op. Wat was hij voor een hufter om een hetze aan te voeren tegen een man als John Reynolds? De coach had steeds weer gedaan wat het beste was voor zijn jongens. Zelfs voor Chucks eigen zoon.

Zijn maag draaide weer om.

Hij leunde met zijn hoofd op zijn armen en haalde diep adem. Coach Reynolds was het probleem niet. Maar Casey. Casey en Billy... en vooral hijzelf. Hij had zijn charme en invloed bij de ouders gebruikt om hen van leugens te overtuigen, om hen op andere gedachten te brengen en uiteindelijk een man kapot te maken die zestien jaar zijn beste krachten had gegeven aan het footballteam van Marion High. Een man die met niet anders dan hard werken en vastberadenheid het programma had opgebouwd.

Eindelijk kwam zijn maag tot rust en Chuck Parker krabbelde overeind. Toen hij bukte om zijn handen en gezicht te wassen, had hij het gevoel dat er een berg was gegroeid tussen zijn schouderbladen.

In hoeverre was het zijn schuld wat coach Reynolds was overkomen?

Als hij naar de coach had geluisterd, als hij een paar jaar geleden iets had gedaan aan het gedrag van zijn zoon, had Casey Jake misschien niet uitgedaagd tot een race. Dan waren ze vandaag nog gewoon een middelbare school die met hun team naar de regioplay-offs zou gaan, in plaats van voorpaginanieuws met een coach die niet meer kon lopen.

Het was allemaal zijn schuld.

En niet alleen dat, hij was er ook verantwoordelijk voor dat coach Reynolds' laatste seizoen bij de Eagles een nachtmerrie was geweest.

Chuck droogde zijn handen af en wendde zich af van de spiegel. Hij kon de man die hij was geworden niet in de ogen kijken. Maar er was één ding wat hij kon doen, iets wat hij aan het begin van het seizoen had moeten doen. En op dat moment nam hij het besluit om het te doen.

Hij zou zich ziek melden en vandaag nog zorgen dat het gebeurde.

Als hij zich haastte, was het misschien nog niet te laat.

★

Jake Daniels stond voor de kinderrechter. Hij droeg nog steeds zijn blauwe gevangenisoverall en omdat de hoorzitting openbaar was, had de begeleidende agent hem handboeien omgedaan.

Zodra Jake de rechtszaal binnenstapte, wist hij dat er iets mis was. Zijn vader en moeder zaten samen op een bank, maar toen hij binnenkwam, keken ze hem amper aan. Zijn vader had een advocaat betaald, een patserig geklede vent, A.W. Bennington genaamd, die een kantoor in de stad had en de reputatie dat hij zware jongens makkelijk vrij kreeg. Het soort man waar Jake tot nu toe niet mee omgegaan zou zijn.

'De rechter zal de aanklacht voorlezen en je vragen of je schuldig bent,' had A.W. uitgelegd toen ze elkaar maandagmiddag spraken. 'Je zegt niet schuldig. Ik doe de rest.'

'Moet ik hier blijven?' Jake wist niet waarom hij het vroeg. Het kon hem niet echt schelen. Waar moest hij heen als ze hem vrijlieten? Niet naar het ziekenhuis, waar zijn teamgenoten de wacht hielden. Niet naar de kamer van coach Reynolds. Niet bepaald. En niet terug naar school. Hij zou een rariteit zijn, iemand over wie de anderen fluisterden en die gehoond en gehaat werd. Coach Reynolds was met afstand de lievelingsleraar van de school. Onder de Eagle-ouders mocht de loyaliteit aan hem dan wankelen, onder de leerlingen stond die als een huis.

Bovendien hoorde Jake in de gevangenis.

Maar A.W. had zijn hoofd geschud. 'Zodra de hoorzitting voorbij is, word je vrijgelaten.'

Nadat de advocaat gisteren was vertrokken, hadden zijn vader en moeder hem om beurten bezocht. Ze wisten dat hij naar huis zou komen, dus waarom keken ze allebei alsof hij de doodstraf had gekregen?

Jake werd de rechtszaal binnengevoerd en nam plaats aan een lange tafel. A.W. zat er al en was veel chiquer gekleed dan alle andere volwassenen. Wat moest zijn vader de man wel niet betalen? Alles om Jake geen tien jaar in de gevangenis te laten zitten.

A.W. fronste zijn wenkbrauwen naar Jake en boog zich dicht naar hem toe. 'De coach is verlamd. Je ouders zeiden dat het vanmorgen in de krant stond. Dat kan het een beetje lastig maken.'

Jake draaide zich met een ruk om naar zijn moeder. Ze zat naar hem te kijken en toen hun blikken elkaar vonden, zag hij dat ze huilde. Langzaam knikte ze nadrukkelijk met haar hoofd en ze vormde met haar mond woorden die Jake niet kon verstaan. Hij verlegde zijn blik naar zijn vader, die alleen maar op zijn lip beet en naar de grond keek.

Jake draaide zich om. Hij wilde dood, gewoon zijn adem inhouden en zich door God laten wegnemen uit de verschrikking van het leven.

Coach Reynolds was verlamd. Nee, dat was het helemaal niet. Hij had de coach verlamd. Dat was waar het om draaide. Hij had de pick-up truck die avond toch de weg zien opdraaien? Hij had zijn stuur kunnen omgooien. Dan had hij zelf wel kunnen omkomen, maar de coach zou ongedeerd zijn. Hij was een egoïstische hufter geweest om zijn auto recht op die pick-up te zetten. Nu was het leven van de man verwoest. Een man naar wie Jake opkeek en voor wie hij respect had, een man die voor minstens duizend tieners een held was.

Nooit meer zou de coach een baantje met hen kunnen sprinten en spelmanoeuvres voordoen en hen aanvoeren in oefeningen. Nooit meer zouden de jongens de coach met zijn sporttas over zijn schouder en zijn honkbalpet diep over zijn ogen getrokken over het veld naar de training zien lopen. Nooit meer.

En dat was allemaal Jakes schuld. Hij liet zijn hoofd in zijn handen zakken. Wat had A.W. daarstraks ook alweer gezegd? Dat kon het een beetje lastig maken? Hij knarsetandde. Was dat het enige wat die lui belangrijk vonden? Begrepen ze niet wat hij had gedaan? Wat hij coach Reynolds had afgenomen?

'De rechtbank!'

De rechter was een vervaarlijk uitziende vrouw met wit haar en een strak gezicht. *Mooi. Die zal me misschien voor altijd opsluiten.*

A.W. was opgestaan. Hij gebaarde dat Jake hetzelfde moest doen.

'Jake Daniels, je wordt beschuldigd van een reeks misdrijven waaronder de volgende.' Ze las de lijst voor, maar er was niets nieuws bij. Hetzelfde wat de politie had gezegd en zijn moeder, de dingen die A.W. gisteren met hem had doorgenomen. 'Op dit moment word je behandeld als een minderjarige. Wat is je reactie op de beschuldigingen?'

Jake zei het eerste wat er in hem opkwam. 'Schuldig, mevrouw.'

'Een ogenblik, Edelachtbare.' A.W. ging met één reuzenstap voor Jake staan en stak zijn hand op. 'Mag ik mijn cliënt even onder vier ogen spreken?'

De rechter trok haar wenkbrauwen hoog op. 'Snel dan. We hebben het hier druk, raadsman. Uw cliënt had hier vanmorgen voorbereid binnen moeten komen.'

'Ja, Edelachtbare.' A.W. ging zitten en greep de mouw vast van Jakes blauwkatoenen overall, waaraan hij hem mee naar beneden trok. Hij bracht zijn mond bij Jakes oor en siste: 'Wat doe je nou?!'

Jake deed minder moeite om te fluisteren. 'Ze vroeg me wat mijn reactie was.'

'Niet zo hard praten.' A.W. keek hem dreigend aan. Hij was zo dichtbij dat het leek of hij één reusachtige oogbal had. 'Je moest tegen haar zeggen: "Niet schuldig." Weet je nog? Dat hebben we besproken.'

'Maar ik *ben* schuldig. Ik heb het gedaan. Ik heb de auto van de coach aangereden, waarom zou ik daarover liegen?'

Jake kreeg de indruk dat A.W. op het punt stond een zenuwaanval te krijgen. Zweetdruppeltjes parelden op zijn bovenlip. 'Het gaat er niet om of je hem aangereden hebt of niet. Het gaat erom van welk misdrijf je beschuldigd wordt.' A.W.'s handen trilden. 'We zeggen vandaag alleen dat we vinden dat je niet schuldig bent aan geweldpleging met een dodelijk wapen.'

De woorden zwommen zonder bepaalde volgorde in Jakes hoofd. Het leek of alle aanwezigen naar hem staarden, zijn ouders inbegrepen. Wat de hoorzitting ook betekende, hij had geen andere keus dan meewerken. Hij leunde achterover in zijn stoel en sloeg zijn armen over elkaar. 'Mij best.'

A.W. bleef hem nog even aanstaren alsof hij er niet zeker van was dat Jake het goede antwoord zou geven. Toen draaide hij zich langzaam om naar de rechter. 'We zijn klaar, Edelachtbare.'

'Goed.' De rechter keek verveeld. 'Wil de verdachte nogmaals opstaan?'

Jake stond op.

'Wat is je reactie op de beschuldigingen die tegen je zijn uitgesproken?'

Hij wierp A.W. een snelle blik toe. De man had zijn ogen neergeslagen naar zijn schrijfblok en weigerde op te kijken. Jake keek weer naar de rechter. 'Niet schuldig, Edelachtbare.'

'Goed. Je mag gaan zitten.'

Onmiddellijk rees de officier van justitie overeind en liep naar de rechter toe. 'De staat verzoekt Jake Daniels als volwassene te berechten, Edelachtbare. Hij is zeventien jaar oud, over slechts enkele maanden is hij wettelijk meerderjarig.' Even liet de verdediger van de staat zijn hoofd hangen. Toen hij de rechter weer aankeek, leek het alsof hij zou gaan huilen. 'We hebben vanmorgen gehoord dat het slachtoffer in deze zaak door het ongeluk verlamd is. Zijn toestand is blijvend, Edelachtbare. Daarom zijn we er gezien de ernst van het misdrijf van overtuigd dat meneer Daniels als volwassene dient te worden berecht.'

Jake wist niet precies wat het verschil was, alleen dat A.W. niet wilde dat hij als volwassene werd berecht. Het kon Jake niet schelen. De officier had gelijk. Hij was geen klein kind. Hij wist precies hoe gevaarlijk straatracen was, maar hij had het toch gedaan.

De rechter zei dat ze binnen twee weken zou beslissen of Jake als volwassene berecht werd of niet. Toen was A.W. weer aan de beurt. Hij vroeg om Jakes vrijlating omdat hij over het algemeen een goede jongen was. Geen strafblad, geen alcohol in zijn bloed op de avond van het ongeluk. Gewoon een stomme fout met tragische gevolgen.

'Ik wil dat zijn rijbewijs onmiddellijk wordt ingetrokken.' De rechter maakte een aantekening op een schrijfblok. 'Ook wil ik dat hij ingeschreven wordt bij een nascholingsinstituut, zodat hij niet in de klas zit bij de andere jongeman die bij deze zaak betrokken is. Met deze bepalingen wordt uw verzoek toegewezen, raadsman. Meneer Daniels mag hangende de uitkomst van zijn proces worden overgedragen aan zijn ouders.'

De hoorzitting was even snel voorbij als hij begonnen was en er kwam een man in uniform naar Jake toe. 'Omdraaien.'

Hij deed wat hem werd opgedragen en de man haalde de handboeien van Jakes pols.

A.W. keek Jake glimlachend aan. 'Je gaat naar huis, Jake. Je bent een vrij man.'

Maar dat was een leugen.

Coach Reynolds was verlamd.

En zolang Jake leefde, zou hij nooit en te nimmer meer vrij zijn.

Zeventien

Het was alsof je honderd pond dood gewicht met je meesleepte.

Er waren vier weken voorbijgegaan sinds het ongeluk en John was door de artsen overgeplaatst naar een kamer in het revalidatiecentrum. Ze hadden enkele doelen vastgesteld, bepaalde criteria die hij moest bereiken: hij moest zichzelf van een bed naar een rolstoel kunnen verplaatsen, en van een rolstoel naar het toilet en terug. Ze wilden dat hij zichzelf aankleedde en zijn benen en romp leerde onderzoeken op zere plekken.

De les van vandaag was hoe te onderkennen of een open wond medische behandeling nodig had.

'Zere plekken vormen een verraderlijke dreiging, meneer Reynolds.' De fysiotherapeut was een slanke man van achter in de dertig. Het was duidelijk dat hij geestdriftig was over zijn taak om mensen zoals John onafhankelijk te maken.

John hoopte dat de man hem vergaf dat hij weinig enthousiasme kon opbrengen.

'Meneer Reynolds, luistert u?'

'Hmmm?' Vóór zijn opname in het ziekenhuis had John zich niet gerealiseerd hoeveel mensen hem *coach* noemden. Zelfs na vier weken klonk het nog niet goed... *meneer* Reynolds in plaats van *coach* Reynolds. Het was alsof de artsen, verpleegkundigen en fysiotherapeuten heel iemand anders aanspraken dan de man die hij was geweest.

Maar dat was toch eigenlijk ook zo, of niet? Hij was niet de man die hij voor het ongeluk was geweest. 'Sorry. Zeg het nog eens.'

'Zere plekken… ziet u, ontwikkelen zich op plaatsen waar regelmatig wrijving is op uw lichaam. Het probleem is, bij een verlamming kun je dat niet voelen. Het wordt vooral gevaarlijk als je een paar maanden of langer verlamd bent. Dan begint het lichaam tekenen te vertonen van spieratrofie. Zonder de barrière van de spieren kunnen de botten wel dwars door de huid heen dringen. Dus u begrijpt wat het probleem is, meneer Reynolds.'

John had zin om de vent omver te rijden met zijn rolstoel. Of nog liever keihard 'Stop!' te schreeuwen en tien toneelknechten aan zien komen rennen die zeiden dat hij nu mocht opstaan. De filmopname was voorbij.

Natuurlijk kon hij geen van beide doen. Als hij voor Kerst thuis wilde zijn, kon hij hier alleen maar blijven zitten en zich door een onbekende laten vertellen hoe zijn benen zouden wegkwijnen en dat daarbij wonden op zijn lichaam zouden verschijnen. John leunde achterover in de rolstoel en richtte zijn blik op de mond van de man. Die bleef maar bewegen en de realiteit van Johns toestand in geuren en kleuren uiteenzetten.

Maar John luisterde niet meer. Zijn lichaam mocht dan een gevangene zijn, maar zijn gedachten konden gaan waar ze wilden. En op dit moment wilde hij terugdenken aan de afgelopen maand.

Vanaf het moment dat hij die zaterdag na het ongeluk was bijgekomen, had John geweten dat hij in de puree zat. Hij had totaal geen herinnering aan het ongeluk. Het ene moment draaide hij het parkeerterrein van Marion High af, het volgende werd hij wakker in een ziekenhuisbed met het gevoel dat hij stikte. En nog iets, iets wat nog erger was.

Eerst was hij te afgeleid geweest om het op te merken.

Abby was er, en Kade en Sean en Nicole en Matt. Hij wist toen dat wat er ook aan de hand was, het ernstig moest zijn als iedereen om hem heen stond. Hij had naar zijn keel gegrepen, en toen was de zuster gekomen om hem te waarschuwen dat hij stil moest blijven liggen. Hoe stiller, hoe beter.

Maak me rustig, God. En binnen een paar seconden voelde hij zijn lichaam ontspannen. De slangen verstikten hem niet, het leek alleen maar zo. Hoe meer hij zich ontspande, hoe makkelijker ademhalen werd.

Pas toen hij weer normaal kon ademhalen, drong het tot John door. Er was iets verschrikkelijk mis. Zijn lichaam deed pijn van het liggen op één plaats en hij wilde zich uitrekken. Zijn brein stuurde ogenblikkelijk een reeks commando's uit. Tenen: opkrullen... voeten: naar voren wijzen... enkels: omrollen... benen: van plaats wisselen.

Maar zijn lichaam gehoorzaamde er geen een.

In Johns hoofd begonnen alarmbellen af te gaan, maar hij weigerde het te laten merken. Hij moest sterk blijven voor zijn gezin. Bovendien hoopte hij eerst nog dat hij het mis had. Misschien kwam het door de medicijnen die hij had gekregen, iets om hem vermoeid en futloos te maken. Een pijnstiller of zo. Misschien waren zijn benen gewond geraakt bij het ongeluk en waren ze nog onder diepe verdoving.

Zondag sliep hij nog steeds het grootste deel van de tijd, maar hij was helder genoeg om te weten dat die dingen het gevoel in zijn benen niet weg hadden moeten nemen. Die avond begon hij telkens als hij wakker was te experimenteren. In de paar minuten dat er niemand in de kamer was, liet hij zijn hand onder het laken glippen en voelde. Eerst aan zijn buik, dan aan zijn heupen en bovenbenen.

Boven zijn navel kon hij zijn hand gewoon voelen. Hij voelde de koelheid van zijn vingers en pijn als hij kneep. Maar daaronder was er niets. Geen enkele sensatie. Het voelde alsof hij iemand anders aanraakte, alsof iemand zijn onderste helft had weggehaald en vervangen door dat van een vreemde.

Dan keek hij de kamer rond en als er niemand kwam, staarde hij naar een deel van zijn lichaam en gaf het opdracht te bewegen. Zijn bekken of zijn benen. Zelfs zijn tenen.

Het was steeds hetzelfde: niets. Geen beweging.

Dus toen ze de slangen uit zijn keel haalden en een reeks röntgenfoto's maakten en zijn rug onderzochten, wist John waarnaar ze op zoek waren. Hij had hen de tijd kunnen besparen. Eindelijk vroeg John wat er aan de hand was, wat hem was overkomen. Toen dokter Furin de kamer binnenkwam, de deur dicht deed en aankondigde dat hij slecht nieuws had, was John hem een slag voor.

'Ik ben verlamd, hè?'

'Ja.' De arts keek pijnlijk. Alsof hij wenste dat hij loodgieter of advocaat of accountant was geworden. Alles behalve een arts die gedwongen was om een gezonde man als John Reynolds te vertellen dat hij nooit meer zou lopen. 'Helaas wel. We hoopten dat als de zwelling eenmaal afnam…' De arts worstelde om de juiste woorden te vinden. 'We hoopten dat de verlamming tijdelijk zou zijn.'

Zodra John de waarheid wist, had hij maar één zorg. Hoe zou Abby het nieuws opnemen? In het allereerste begin had hij geweigerd er ondersteboven van te zijn. Hij was toch zeker tegen de uitdaging opgewassen? Hij nam een rolstoel en ging gewoon alles doen wat hij altijd had gedaan. En eens leerde hij weer lopen, wat de artsen ook zeiden. Niet alleen lopen, maar rennen. Ja, over een paar maanden of een paar jaar rende hij weer. Wat het ook kostte. Hij zou de dokters eens wat laten zien.

Het enige punt was of Abby de schok wel kon opvangen.

Zodra hij haar zag, wist hij dat hij zich geen zorgen had hoeven maken. Op haar gezicht stond duidelijk te lezen wat er in haar hart leefde en de liefde die ze voor hem voelde. Een liefde die onmogelijk aangetast kon worden door zoiets als een verlamming. In haar ogen stond een kracht te lezen die de zijne weerspiegelde. Ze zouden vechten en strijden. En eens zouden ze samen overwinnen.

Toen ze hem vertelde over het ongeluk, dat hij door niemand anders dan Jake Daniels was aangereden, verlegde hij zijn zorgen geheel naar de jongen. Jake zou er kapot van zijn, te diep terneergeslagen om verder te kunnen. De twee weken daarna over-leefde John door te bidden voor Jake, God te smeken om uit de gebeurtenis iets goeds te laten voortkomen, en Hem te vragen Jake de moed te geven om John te bezoeken. Dan kon de jongen met eigen ogen zien dat John niet van plan was om het loodje te leggen alleen omdat hij zijn benen niet meer voelde.

Niet bepaald.

In die eerste week was Nathan Pike als een van de eersten op bezoek gekomen. De jongen keek ongemakkelijk en was gekleed in zijn gewone zwarte outfit. Maar er was iets veranderd... John had een paar minuten nodig om te ontdekken wat, maar toen was het duidelijk. Zijn opstandigheid was verdwenen.

'Ik heb gehoord wat er gebeurd is.' Nathan schoof met zijn voeten heen en weer en had zijn handen in zijn zakken gestopt. 'Ik moest komen. Gezondheidsleer is niks aan zonder u.'

John lachte. 'Gezondheid is toch al geen lolletje.'

'Ja.' Nathan haalde zijn schouders op. 'U snapt wat ik bedoel.'

Even was het stil en Nathan keek ongemakkelijk.

'Gaat het, Nathan?'

'Nou... toen met die wedstrijd... ik had u de volgende dag willen bellen, maar toen... nou ja...' Hij staarde naar zijn voeten. 'U weet wel. U raakte gewond.'

'Waar had je over willen praten?'

'De dreiging... of wat het ook was.' Hij keek op en zijn ogen stonden oprechter dan John ooit had gezien. 'Meneer Reynolds, ik heb het niet gedaan. Echt niet. Ik heb een hoop stomme din-gen gedaan, maar dat niet. Ik heb de hele dag in de bieb gezeten. Echt waar.'

'Goed.' Het ging tegen alle redelijkheid in, maar John geloofde hem.

'U gelooft me toch, hè?'

John maakte een vuist en duwde zijn knokkels tegen die van Nathan. 'Ik geloof je.'

'Weet u, coach?'

'Wat?'

'U bent de enige.'

Daarna was er nog meer bezoek gekomen, tientallen leerlingen en spelers. Allemaal hielpen ze John af te leiden van de ernst van de toestand. Maar toen John met revalidatie begon, kwam de werkelijkheid met een daverende klap op hem neer.

John had tegen Abby gezegd dat hij er zeker van was dat hij na een paar dagen therapie minstens zijn tenen weer zou kunnen bewegen.

In plaats daarvan was een therapeut bijna twee dagen bezig hem te leren hoe hij uit bed in zijn rolstoel moest glijden. Beweging in zijn tenen of waar dan ook onder zijn middel was even onmogelijk als een lichaamsdeel van iemand anders te dwingen in beweging te komen.

'Hoelang moet ik revalideren voordat ik mijn voeten kan bewegen?' had John op de avond van de tweede dag van therapie aan dokter Furin gevraagd.

De arts had net de kamer uit willen gaan en bleef als aan de grond genageld staan. 'Meneer Reynolds, verlamming is een permanente toestand. Sommige mensen boeken wonderlijke vooruitgang, afhankelijk van hun situatie. Maar op dit moment verwachten we niet dat u ooit weer gevoel in uw benen zult krijgen. Hoeveel tijd we ook aan revalidatie besteden.'

Het was de eerste keer sinds het ongeluk dat John boos was geworden. 'Waarom dan al die moeite?'

'Omdat u anders nooit meer uit bed komt,' had dokter Furin vriendelijk gezegd.

Het antwoord had John razend gemaakt en dat had hij die avond ook tegen Abby gezegd. 'Ze hadden me op z'n minst een beetje hoop kunnen geven.'

Abby was beresterk geweest en huilde zelden, althans niet waar hij bij was. Hij kende haar goed genoeg om te weten dat ze soms wel ergens huilde. Maar hij waardeerde het dat ze zich bij hem flink hield.

Ze was op het ziekenhuisbed gekropen en had zijn vermoeide voorhoofd gestreeld. 'Sinds wanneer vind jij je hoop in wat de dokters zeggen, John Reynolds?'

Zijn boosheid stierf weg. 'Daar had ik niet aan gedacht.'

'Ja.' Ze glimlachte. 'Daar heb je mij voor. Om je op de waarheid te wijzen.'

'Dat mijn hoop alleen in God gevonden kan worden?'

'Precies.'

'Goed, Abby… dan moet je iets voor me doen.'

'Wat dan?'

'Bidden om een wonder.' Zijn ogen waren nat en hij knipperde om haar beter te kunnen zien. 'Bid zonder ophouden.'

In de dagen daarna hadden de Marion Eagles hun footballseizoen afgemaakt met een verlies in de tweede ronde van de play-offs. Johns assistent-coaches hadden na het ongeluk zijn taak overgenomen en er was een quarterback bij de junioren weggehaald om het team aan te voeren. Bijna alle spelers en coaches waren langs geweest, de meesten maar even om John een voetbal met handtekeningen of een kaart of een boeket of ballonnen te brengen.

Toen het seizoen afgelopen was, nam het bezoek geleidelijk af en stopte John al zijn energie in de revalidatie.

Elke dag leerde hij de dingen die zijn therapeuten van hem vroegen. Hij kon zijn romp in evenwicht houden met de kracht van zijn armen en zichzelf in een rolstoel zwaaien. Op het toilet komen was lastiger, maar hij kon het nu zonder hulp. Dokter Furin had hem zelfs verzekerd dat hij misschien over een week al naar huis mocht.

'In elk geval voor Kerst,' had dokter Furin laatst lachend gezegd. 'Dat is vast het beste nieuws dat u in tijden hebt gehoord.'

Dat had het moeten zijn, maar het was niet zo. Na een maand in het ziekenhuis, een maand waarin hij geen centimeter dichter bij beweging in zijn voeten of benen was gekomen, begon Johns gewoonlijk vurige vastberadenheid snel af te koelen.

Kerst? In een rolstoel?

De afgelopen dagen had hij nog gebeden om een wonder, maar zonder er echt in te geloven. Hij dacht er niet meer aan tegen zijn diagnose te vechten en weer te kunnen lopen.

In plaats daarvan dacht hij aan alles wat hij verloren had.

★

Gisteravond was het Abby voor het eerst opgevallen. Ze bracht hem op de hoogte van het laatste nieuws over Jake. De rechter had een beslissing over de vraag of de jongen als volwassene berecht moest worden uitgesteld en tegelijkertijd weigerde de officier van justitie strafvermindering in ruil voor een schuldbekentenis. Over tien dagen zou de hoorzitting over zijn berechting plaatsvinden. Maar het zag er hoe dan ook naaruit dat Jake terecht zou moeten staan.

Toen Abby uitverteld was, zette ze haar handen in haar zij. 'John Reynolds, je luistert niet eens.'

John knipperde met zijn ogen. 'Ik luister wel. Dat is jammer. Voor Jake, bedoel ik.'

'Jammer?' Abby snoof. 'Toen je net in het ziekenhuis lag, vond je het een onverdraaglijke gedachte dat Jake naar de gevangenis zou gaan. En nu is het "jammer"?'

'Het spijt me.'

'Het moet je niet spijten, John, je moet *woest* zijn. Word razend. Word kwaad. Maar lig daar niet zo flauw te zeggen dat het je spijt. Dat is niet de man met wie ik ben getrouwd.'

Johns stem klonk onveranderd. 'Je hebt gelijk.'

'Hoezo?'

'Ik ben niet de man met wie je bent getrouwd, Abby. Ik heb de strijd verloren.'

'*Wat?!*' ziedde Abby. Ze liep met grote passen van de ene kant van de ziekenhuiskamer naar de andere. 'Houd op over de strijd verliezen, John. De strijd is nog niet eens begonnen! Je mag me

niet vragen om voor een wonder te bidden als jij het al opgegeven hebt. Ik bedoel, kom op zeg...'

Zo ging het gesprek een uur door totdat Abby eindelijk begon
te huilen. Ze bood haar verontschuldigingen aan dat ze zo veel
van hem verwacht had en verzekerde hem dat hij het recht had
om ontmoedigd te zijn. Voordat ze wegging, gaf ze toe dat hij niet
de enige was. Ook zij was ontmoedigd.

Geen wonder dat hij zich niet op de therapeut en zere plekken
kon concentreren. Hele uren van de dag, zelfs tijdens de revalidatie, kon John niet anders dan terugdenken. Hoe de aarde onder
zijn voeten aanvoelde als hij over het footballveld vloog; hoe makkelijk hij de afgelopen twintig jaar dag in dag uit voor de klas
heen en weer had geslenterd. Hoe zijn kinderen als baby op zijn
knieën hadden paardjegereden en hoe hij hen op zijn rug had
gedragen als ze door de dierentuin wandelden.

Hoe Abby's benen tegen de zijne aanvoelden als ze dansten op
het eind van de steiger. Hoe haar lichaam onder hem voelde als
ze...

'Meneer Reynolds, ik wil graag dat u het nu aan mij terugver-
telt.' De slanke therapeut tikte op zijn klembord en keek lichtelijk
geïrriteerd.

'Hoe vaak moet u uw lichaam controleren op zere plekken,
vooral nadat de atrofie heeft ingezet? Hebt u wel iets gehoord van
wat ik u verteld heb? Meneer Reynolds?'

John keek de man aan, maar hij kon zich er niet toe zetten om
antwoord te geven. De wonderen die hij had verwacht gebeurden
niet en hij had het volgende stadium bereikt in wat de rest van
zijn leven zou zijn. Het leven zonder dansen of rennen of de liefde bedrijven met Abby. Het was een stadium dat hij niet had
voorzien en waarop hij niet was voorbereid. En om één enkele
reden was het pijnlijker dan zelfs de eerste dagen nadat hij te
horen had gekregen dat hij verlamd was.

De werkelijkheid begon tot hem door te dringen.

Achttien

Abby had nooit in haar leven meer spanning gevoeld.

Voor een deel wenste ze een glorieuze thuiskomst. Het was tenslotte Kerst. Ze hadden de boom moeten opzetten en optuigen en het huis had er zoals altijd feestelijk uit moeten zien. Ze stelde zich een huis vol gasten voor om John te begroeten als hij aankwam en een avond vol gezellige gesprekken.

Maar John wilde niets van dat alles.

'Breng me nou maar naar huis en laat me in de woonkamer zitten met mijn gezin, Abby. Verder niets.'

Ze was voortdurend bezig haar best te doen om te zijn wat John op dit moment nodig had. Als hij bedrukt was, was zij de stille steun. Als hij boos was, de geduldige luisteraar. En als hij tekenen van vastberadenheid vertoonde, van bereidheid om te vechten tegen de vreselijke vloek die hem had getroffen, juichte ze hem toe. Als ze zijn stemming niet kon doorgronden, handhaafde ze een vals gevoel van opgetogenheid. Het was haar manier om hem ervan te overtuigen dat ze overweg kon met zijn verlamming en dat de veranderingen in hun leven niet genoeg waren om haar blijdschap weg te nemen.

Maar het was allemaal een leugen.

Ze was niet gelukkig. Sinds Johns ongeluk was ze niet meer blij geweest. Maar ze was het John verschuldigd om zich vrolijk en positief voor te doen. Dat had hij nodig. De moeilijkheid was dat ze nergens haar masker kon laten vallen, nergens kon huilen en tekeergaan tegen de wending die het leven had genomen.

En zo bewaarde ze het opgekropt in haar hart, waar het alleen

184

maar een zenuwpatiënt van haar maakte. Zorgelijk en gespannen en alleen.

Uiteindelijk deed Abby wat John had gevraagd en beperkte het feestje van zijn thuiskomst tot een minimum. Kade, die weer naar school was gegaan om het footballseizoen en het semester af te maken, was een maand thuis op kerstvakantie. Sean en hij hadden een boom uitgezocht en meegebracht voordat John thuiskwam. Nicole en Matt en Jo en Denny hadden geholpen hem op te tuigen.

Om één uur die middag werd John uit het ziekenhuis ontslagen en een uur later stopten Abby en hij voor hun huis. Ze zette de motor af en even kwam geen van beiden in beweging.

'Kun je het je voorstellen, Abby?' John staarde naar de voordeur van hun huis. 'Ik zal nooit meer autorijden. Heb je daaraan gedacht? Ik bedoel, nooit meer.'

'Je zult heus nog wel autorijden, John. Er zijn auto's met handbediening voor mensen die...'

'Abby, wil je me alsjeblieft even de tijd geven om de waarheid te aanvaarden?' Zijn toon was scherp, maar meteen liet hij zijn hoofd achterover tegen de stoel vallen. 'Bah. Sorry.' Hij keek haar aan en ze zag de zware vermoeidheid in zijn ogen, in zijn trekken. 'Ik wilde niet tegen je snauwen.'

'Ik wilde alleen maar helpen. Er bestaan speciale auto's... liften... dat soort dingen.' Abby's handen trilden en haar keel zat dicht. Hoe zou het zijn om John hun huis binnen te duwen? Te weten dat hij nooit meer naast haar naar de deur zou lopen? Ze klemde haar kiezen op elkaar. Ze hield haar verdriet met geweld van zich af. Dat was het minste wat ze voor John kon doen.

'Weet je wel hoe veel we vanzelfsprekend vinden? De kleine dingen in het leven. Zoals in een auto springen en over het pad naar je voordeur rennen?'

Abby hield haar adem in. 'Ik weet het.' Wilde hij dat ze met hem mee huilde of dat ze een bemoedigende rol speelde? En wat moest er met háár gevoelens? Het verlies dat zij geleden had? Ze ademde beverig uit en vulde haar longen opnieuw. 'Kom, we gaan naar binnen. De kinderen wachten.'

John knikte en deed de deur open. Als de atleet die hij nog steeds was, zwaaide hij zijn benen uit de auto. Abby probeerde niet te zien hoe slap en grotesk ze erbij hingen en op de stoep vielen. Hij deed zijn best om ze recht te leggen, maar het lukte niet.

Hij keek naar haar om en ze kwam met een ruk in beweging. 'Ik pak de stoel.'

John liet zijn hoofd hangen terwijl ze haastig om de auto heen liep, de kofferbak opende en zijn rolstoel op de weg tilde. Abby trok haar jasje recht. Het was koud, maar het sneeuwde tenminste niet. Bijna een minuut lang worstelde ze met de vergrendeling en scheurde daarbij een vingernagel. 'Au!' Ze wapperde met haar hand.

'Wat is er?' John rekte zijn hals, maar hij kon haar bloederige nagel niet zien.

'Niks.' Abby vocht tegen haar tranen. Het voelde vreemd om zo te hannesen zonder hulp te krijgen van John. Hij zat drie meter van haar af. Drie rottige meters maar. Maar hij kon niet opstaan om haar te helpen. 'Ik… ik probeer de stoel open te maken, maar hij zit vast.'

'Er zitten aan beide kanten grendels. Zie je ze?' John deed zijn best om haar te helpen, maar ze had meer nodig dan een suggestie. Ze had zijn kracht nodig.

'Ze willen niet meegeven.' Ze trok weer, nu met meer kracht. *Laat hem niet horen dat ik huil, God…* 'Het gaat niet.'

Abby worstelde nog even door en toen gooide ze de rolstoel in een waas van boze frustratie op het gras naast de stoep. 'Ik háát dat ding!' Ze viel tegen de zijkant van de auto en verborg haar gezicht in haar armen. 'Ik haat hem!'

'Abby, kom hier.' Johns stem klonk vriendelijk.

Ze wilde zich omdraaien en honderdduizend kilometer wegrennen, naar een plaats waar John geen rolstoel nodig had om in huis te komen. Maar dat hielp niet.

God, ik stort in. Vang me op, God… alstublieft, vang me op.

STEUN NIET OP JE EIGEN INZICHT…

Het was dezelfde Bijbeltekst die de vorige keer dat ze zich zo voelde in haar was opgekomen. Maar wat kon het beteken? Niet op haar eigen inzicht steunen? Was er een andere manier om inzicht te krijgen in de dingen die in hun leven waren gebeurd? Kon er een *goed* aspect zijn aan Johns verlamming…?

Abby zag het niet in.

'Heb je me gehoord, Abby? Dit is een rotgevoel.' John sprak nu luider. 'Je huilt en ik kan er niks aan doen. Helemaal niks. Kom hier, dan kan ik je tenminste vasthouden.'

Ze voelde een snijdende pijn. Daar had ze nog niet aan gedacht. Hoe hulpeloos hij zich moest voelen. Als ze van streek was, kwam hij altijd naar haar toe. Nu kon hij zelfs dat niet doen. Ze droogde haar tranen en ging naar hem toe, liet zich voor hem op haar knieën vallen. Zijn benen zaten in de weg, dus ze legde haar handen op zijn bovenbenen en duwde ze uit elkaar. Het was niet voor het eerst dat zij in zijn plaats zijn benen verplaatste, maar ze was er nog steeds niet aan gewend. Ze bewogen niet makkelijk, maar langzaam en zwaar, als de benen van een dode.

Toen de ruimte tussen zijn knieën groot genoeg was, drukte ze zich tegen hem aan en legde haar hoofd op zijn schouder. 'Sorry dat ik huil. Dit hoort een gelukkig moment te zijn.'

'Ach, Abby.' John wreef zijn gezicht tegen het hare. 'Er is niets gelukkigs aan.'

'Jawel.' Ze sprak dicht bij zijn oor. 'Je lééft, John. En je bent op tijd thuis voor Kerst. Dat is meer dan genoeg om gelukkig mee te zijn.'

'Dus dat zijn vreugdetranen?' Hij streek met zijn lippen langs de zijkant van haar hals.

'Ik haat je stoel.'

'Hij is mijn enige middel tot vrijheid. Mijn enige manier om me nog voort te bewegen, Abby.'

'Weet ik. Het spijt me.'

'Geeft niet.' Hij bracht zijn lippen naar de hare en kuste haar zacht en teder. Toen hij zich losmaakte, zag hij haar ogen. 'Ik haat hem ook.'

Er klonk een geluid achter Abby en ze keek over haar schouder. Het was Kade die over het pad aan kwam rennen.

'Zeg, waarom duurt het zo lang? Wij zitten binnen te wachten en jullie zitten hier maar een beetje te knuffelen of zoiets.'

Abby keek hun oudste zoon onderzoekend aan. De pijn in zijn ogen was diep, maar zijn glimlach was oprecht.

Abby stond op en veegde haar handen af aan haar spijkerbroek. Haar ingescheurde nagel deed pijn. 'Ik krijg die stoel niet open.'

'Is dat alles?' Kade controleerde de grendels aan beide kanten en tikte met de neus van zijn schoen een derde vergrendeling onderaan open. Met een enkele draaiing van zijn pols ging de stoel open en Kade klapte hem in positie. Hij maakte een zwierige buiging. 'Uw strijdwagen, heer.'

Abby deed vol ontzag een stap naar achteren. 'Ik bleef maar vechten met die stomme stoel.' Ze schudde haar hoofd. 'Hoe weet jij hoe hij werkt?'

'Ik heb in het ziekenhuis geoefend.' Kade haalde één schouder op. 'Uit verveling, denk ik.'

Abby keek toe hoe Kade de stoel voor John klaarzette, zijn onderarmen onder zijn vaders oksels liet glijden en hem zachtjes neerliet op het kussen van de zitting. Het tafereel deed haar adem stokken. Hoe moest John zich voelen? John, die altijd sterker was geweest dan Kade... John, de mentor en leraar en coach... die nu in een rolstoel getild moest worden? Door zijn zoon? En Kade? De jongen was pas achttien, maar hij wekte de indruk dat het een routineklusje voor hem was om zijn vader op deze manier te helpen.

Toen John in zijn stoel zat vastgegespt, pakte Kade de handvatten en duwde hem over het pad. 'Nou, pap...' Kade opende de voordeur en reed John naar binnen. 'Welkom thuis.'

En daarmee begon een nieuw hoofdstuk van hun leven.

De zwarte wolk die op John was neergedaald, was donkerder dan ooit.

Hij waardeerde de ontvangst en was dankbaar dat hij thuis was en omringd door zijn gezin. Maar waar zijn gedachten ook heen dwaalden, altijd weer kwamen ze op dezelfde ellendige plek terecht: diep in zelfmedelijden en treurnis. Een plek waaruit hij simpelweg niet kon ontsnappen.

Natuurlijk, voor de vorm deed hij mee. Hij nam kaarten en goede wensen en bemoedigende opmerkingen in ontvangst van zijn familie over hoe goed hij eruitzag en hoe fantastisch het was dat hij het overleefd had.

Maar aldoor kon hij maar aan één ding denken: *Waarom ik, God? Waarom nu, nu het net zo goed ging met Abby en mij? Nu we net leerden om weer te dansen?* Sinds zijn thuiskomst was hij kortaf geweest tegen Abby, kortaf tegen iedereen die een oplossing had voor zijn nare gedrag. Hij wilde geen rolstoelbusje, hij wilde geen uitnodiging voor de Special Olympics.

Hij wilde lopen. Al was het nog maar één keer… zodat hij van elke stap kon genieten en blij kon zijn met het gevoel van zijn schoenen aan zijn voeten, zich kon verwonderen over de balans in zijn benen en de sierlijke manier waarop hij het parcours van Marion High rende.

Nog één dag om afscheid te nemen van de benen die hem door elke grote gebeurtenis in zijn leven heen hadden gedragen. Niet dat het zou helpen natuurlijk. Eén dag was niet genoeg. Maar als hij nu zijn voeten en benen weer kon bewegen, zou hij ze voor de rest van zijn leven elke dag waarderen.

Jammer genoeg ging het niet gebeuren. En verder zou er ook niets goeds gebeuren totdat hij in God de kracht kon vinden om de zwarte wolk weg te duwen.

Twee uur nadat hij thuisgekomen was, hadden de kinderen hun gewone bezigheden hervat. Abby was in de keuken, maar John zat nog uit het raam in zijn stoel aan de voorkant te kijken.

God, ik weet dat U er nog bent, dat U naar me kijkt en van me houdt. U hebt een plan voor mijn leven, zelfs nu…

'Maar wat zou het kunnen zijn?' Zijn gekwelde fluistering verbrak de stilte om hem heen. 'Wat heb ik voor nut?'

Er ging nog een uur voorbij. Minstens drie keer dacht John aan iets wat hij ergens in huis wilde pakken of bekijken. Elke keer greep hij de armleuningen van de stoel vast en deed een poging om op te staan.

En elke keer werd zijn lichaam tegen de veiligheidsgordel getrokken en viel terug op zijn plaats. Hij besefte wat het probleem was. Hij dacht nog niet als een verlamde. Zijn hersenen gaven hem nog steeds redenen om in beweging te komen en op te staan en te lopen, maar zijn benen hoorden de discussie niet meer. Hij vroeg zich af of iedereen die aan plotselinge verlamming leed het zo beleefde. En zo ja, hoelang het nog zou duren voordat ook zijn geest het opgaf? Tot zijn brein enkel nog aan zijn benen dacht als dood gewicht?

John had altijd gehouden van het uitzicht door het raam aan de voorkant. De bomen en een kronkelende oprit die zo afkomstig leken uit een schilderij. Maar op dat moment kon hij het niet langer verdragen om op één plek te blijven zitten. Hij trok zijn kaakspieren krampachtig samen en legde zijn handen aan weerskanten van de stoel om de wielen.

De stoel was speciaal ontworpen voor paraplegiepatiënten, mensen die hun armen nog konden gebruiken, en was makkelijker te manoeuvreren dan de meeste andere. John gaf twee harde rukken aan de wielen… en zoefde zo snel naar achteren dat hij tegen de salontafel daverde.

'John?' klonk Abby ontsteld. Ze verscheen in de deuropening en droogde haar handen af aan een handdoek. 'Is alles in orde?'

Hij keek haar aan en liet zijn blik naar zijn knieën afdalen. 'Best, Abby. Niet elke keer dat ik met die stoel ergens tegenaan kletter, is er meteen een noodgeval.'

Hij had meteen spijt van zijn woorden. Waarom moest hij zijn frustratie op haar afreageren?

Langzaam, aarzelend kwam ze naar hem toe. 'Die tafel kan me niet schelen.' Hij rook haar parfum en voelde haar nabijheid naast zich. Normaal zou hij haar op een dag als deze kietelen of speels tegen de muur vastpinnen tot ze om genade smeekte. En als de kinderen het dan druk hadden, konden ze zomaar een uurtje in hun slaapkamer belanden.

Zijn verlangen naar haar was nog even sterk, maar hoe spontaan kon hij nu nog zijn? Ook als ze in staat waren een manier te vinden om lichamelijk intiem te zijn — wat volgens de therapeut absoluut mogelijk was — dan nog kwam er een hoop planning aan te pas, wat ze bij hun vrijpartijen nooit gewend waren geweest.

Ze legde haar hand op zijn schouder. 'Kan ik iets voor je doen?'

'Niks.' Hij reikte omhoog en pakte haar hand, genietend van haar huid tegen de zijne, en hoopte dat ze kon voelen hoe hij naar haar verlangde. 'Sorry, Abby. Ik ben een klier de laatste tijd. Je verdient het niet.'

'Het zal tijd kosten. Dokter Furin... de therapeuten... iedereen zegt het.' Ze bukte en kuste hem op de wang. 'Het zal niet altijd zo blijven.'

'Ik weet het.' Hij nam haar gezicht tussen zijn handen en bracht zijn lippen naar de hare. Ze kusten elkaar weer, langer dan daarstraks buiten. 'Bid dat we een manier vinden om weer te leven, goed?'

'Doe ik, John.' Haar ogen glinsterden en hij begreep haar. Ze had waarschijnlijk zonder ophouden voor hem gebeden. Meer dan hij voor zichzelf gebeden had.

Hij wist ineens waar hij heen wilde. 'Abby, neem me mee naar buiten. Naar de steiger, kun je dat?'

'De steiger?' Ze aarzelde. 'Het is een beetje koud, denk je niet?'

Abby had gelijk. De temperatuur was die dag nauwelijks boven het vriespunt uitgekomen. Maar het kon John niet schelen. Hij wilde daarbuiten op die vertrouwde plek zitten en naar het meer kijken, op zoek naar tekenen dat God luisterde, dat Hij John niet in de steek had gelaten om zijn leven verder te leiden terwijl hij stikte onder een droevige, donkere wolk.

'Ik trek mijn jack aan. Alsjeblieft, Abby. Ik moet naar buiten.'

'Goed.' Ze zuchtte een beetje. Hard genoeg om John duidelijk te maken dat ze het geen goed idee vond. Mensen met een verlamming kregen zelden genoeg lichaamsbeweging om hun longen volledig uit te kunnen zetten. Een verminderde longfunctie betekende een groter risico op longontsteking. Abby kennende had ze liever dat John de hele winter binnen bleef zitten.

Ze zocht zijn jack, het jack met de symbolen van de Marion Eagles op de rug en op het zakje linksvoor. Nadat ze hem erin had geholpen, reed ze hem door de patiodeur de achtertuin in.

Abby had een klusjesman opdracht gegeven om een rolstoeloprit over de rails van de schuifdeuren heen te maken en van het zonnedek af naar de tuin. Toen ze op het gras waren, werd het hobbelig, maar John bekommerde zich er niet om.

Er was nog een oprit naar de steiger en Abby worstelde om hem op het platte oppervlak te krijgen. 'Zo goed?'

'Dichter bij het water.'

'John, denk aan je veiligheid.' Ze ging voor hem staan, zodat hij haar kon zien. 'De steiger helt. Als je rem weigert…'

Als zijn rem weigerde, zou de rolstoel naar voren rollen en in het water vallen, met John erin. Aan het einde van de steiger was het meer zo diep dat John geen schijn van kans had, tenzij iemand het zag gebeuren.

'Die weigert niet.' Hij keek haar recht aan. 'Kom op, Abby. Vanaf hier kan ik niet naar het meer kijken.'

'Goed.' Ze trapte de rem met haar voet los en duwde hem bijna tot de rand. Hij hoorde hoe ze de hendel naar beneden trapte en even probeerde of hij vastzat. 'Zo beter?'

Hij draaide zich om zodat hij haar kon zien. Ze was boos. 'Dank je.'

Ze zette haar handen in haar zij. 'Wanneer wil je weer naar binnen?'

Als er geen rem op de stoel zat, had John zelf naar binnen kunnen rijden. Maar omdat de rem aan de achterkant zat, kon John niet in beweging komen zonder dat iemand hem losmaakte. 'Over een uur.'

Haar handen vielen weer langs haar zijden. 'Sorry, John. We zullen onze weg hierin moeten vinden. Ik... ik zou alleen niet weten wat ik moest beginnen als je erin viel, en...' Ze liet haar hoofd even hangen voordat ze hem weer aankeek. 'Ik kan niet zonder je, John. Ik heb je te hard nodig.'

Zijn nek begon te branden van het omkijken, maar hij knikte. 'Komt goed, Abby. Beloof ik.'

Ze hield zijn blik nog even vast, toen draaide ze zich om en liep terug naar huis.

John ontspande zijn nek en staarde uit over het meer. Zijn andere verwondingen waren nu genezen, zijn keel en wat kneuzingen en blauwe plekken op zijn gezicht en armen. Bij het ongeluk was hij op de vloerplank van de truck gegooid, waarbij zijn nek gebroken was in de klap.

Afgezien daarvan maakte hij het wonderlijk goed. Maar waarom? Wat kon God nog voor hem in petto hebben? De komende maanden zouden op revalidatie zijn gericht, wat betekende dat hij geen les kon geven. In de herfst kon hij terugkomen als hij wilde, maar het zou zwaar zijn. Het medelijden dat hem waarschijnlijk te wachten stond zou na een paar dagen afnemen.

John keek naar een stel dat naar het midden van het meer roeide en een hengel uitwierp. Zijn leven lang had hij zich onderscheiden door sport. Wat voor nut had hij *nu* nog? En wat had het voor zin dat Jake Daniels er de rest van zijn leven voor zou moeten boeten? Ja, Jake had niet moeten afspreken om te gaan racen. Maar zijn vader dan, Tim? Was het niet voor een deel aan hem te wijten omdat hij een auto voor de jongen had gekocht die erom schreeuwde om hard in te rijden?

John had geen idee hoe het met de jongen ging. Jake en zijn ouders hadden John een kaart gestuurd met excuses en de beste wensen voor een snel herstel. Geen van hen was bij hem op bezoek gekomen.

'Dus wat ga ik doen met de rest van mijn leven, God?' De woorden losten op in de koele wind die aan kwam waaien over het meer.

Hij dacht aan de tekst waar hij als jongen veel van gehouden had, een tekst die hem vorig jaar had geholpen toen Abby en hij uit elkaar zouden gaan: Jeremia 29 vers 11. *Mijn plan met jullie staat vast, spreekt de* HEER. *Ik heb jullie geluk voor ogen, niet jullie ongeluk: Ik zal je een hoopvolle toekomst geven.*

Goed, dus wat waren de plannen als dat waar was… en hoe moest hij de komende tientallen jaren doorkomen zonder zich beschadigd te voelen? En vooral, waar was de hoop?

Zijn gedachten werden onderbroken toen de achterdeur openging. Zijn nekspieren deden nog pijn van het geforceerd naar Abby omkijken daarstraks. Hij wachtte tot ze voor hem stond.

'Ik had de officier van justitie aan de telefoon. Morgenochtend is de hoorzitting waarin bepaald wordt of Jake als volwassene zal worden berecht.' Abby's stem klonk neutraal. 'Hij zei dat de rechter meer geneigd zal zijn om in ons voordeel te beslissen als jij er persoonlijk bij aanwezig bent.'

John hield zijn hoofd schuin. 'En wat is ons voordeel?'

'Kennelijk gaat de officier ervan uit dat wij willen dat Jake als volwassene wordt berecht.' Abby zuchtte. 'Dan valt de straf veel hoger uit.'

Het duizelde John. Het zou een zware slag voor hem zijn als Jake als een volwassene gevangenisstraf kreeg opgelegd. 'Je klinkt alsof je het ermee eens bent.'

Ze hurkte neer. 'Ik weet niet wat ik moet vinden.' Haar ogen vielen op zijn rolstoel. 'Mensen moeten geen autoraces houden in stadsstraten.'

'Verandert daar iets aan als Jake de gevangenis indraait?'

Abby's stem was nauwelijks hoorbaar. 'Ik weet het niet.'

John leunde naar voren en pakte Abby's schouder zachtjes vast. 'Denk je niet dat Jake zijn lesje heeft geleerd?'

'Ik weet het niet.' Ze keek weer naar hem op. 'Misschien wel.'

'Ik meen het, Abby. Denk je dat er ooit een dag zal komen dat Jake Daniels weer op die manier gaat racen?'

'Nee.' Ze schudde haar hoofd zonder met haar blik de zijne los te laten. 'Dat doet hij niet, dat weet ik zeker.'

'Dus waarom moet die jongen de gevangenis in?' John was zelf verrast door de plotselinge vurigheid in zijn stem en in zijn hart. 'Stuur hem naar tien middelbare scholen waar hij andere kinderen aan hun verstand kan brengen dat ze niet moeten gaan racen. Stuur hem naar de universiteit en bid dat hij het plezier in football zal doorgeven aan honderden jongens zoals hij.' Hij schudde zijn hoofd en wendde zijn blik even af voordat hij Abby weer aankeek. 'De officier doet wat hij het beste vindt. Dat is zijn werk. Maar ik ken Jake Daniels. De gevangenis zal hem, noch mij, noch iemand anders een dienst bewijzen. En het zal de volgende tiener niet tegenhouden om ja te zeggen tegen een straatrace.'

En vonkte iets in Abby's ogen, iets wat hij sinds zijn ongeluk niet meer had gezien. In een flits begreep John het. Het was een overwinning, een mijlpaal dat ze vastberadenheid in zijn stem hoorde. Haar mondhoeken gingen licht omhoog. 'Wat moet ik tegen de officier zeggen?'

John klemde zijn vingers om de wielen van zijn stoel. Voor het eerst in weken had hij een doel.

'Zeg maar dat ik kom.'

Negentien

Jake Daniels zat tussen zijn ouders en zijn advocaat in toen hij iets zag wat zijn maag deed omdraaien.

Een glimp van een rolstoel.

Voordat hij zich kon verstoppen of zijn handen op zijn ogen kon leggen of op de vlucht kon slaan, verscheen de rest van de rolstoel. En coach Reynolds zat erin, hij werd geduwd door zijn vrouw.

De volwassenen om Jake heen keken om om te zien wat hij zag, en A.W. mompelde fluisterend een krachtterm. 'Als hij getuigt, maken we geen enkele kans.'

Jakes ouders draaiden zich gauw weer om naar de voorkant van de rechtszaal. Maar Jake kon zijn ogen niet van de coach afhouden. Als hij zijn Marion Eagles honkbalpet niet op had gehad, zou Jake hem amper herkend hebben. Hij was flink afgevallen. En hij zag er kleiner en ouder uit.

Eerst zag de coach hem niet, maar toen draaide hij zijn hoofd om voordat Jake zijn blik kon afwenden. Jake bleef hem als gebiologeerd aanstaren, niet in staat met zijn ogen te knipperen of adem te halen of in beweging te komen. Urenlang was hij bezig geweest zich voor te stellen hoe de coach eruitzag in een rolstoel, hoe droevig het zou zijn om zo'n lange, sterke man veroordeeld te zien om de rest van zijn leven te zitten.

Maar dit had Jake nooit verwacht.

Vanaf de andere kant van de rechtszaal glimlachte coach Reynolds naar hem. Niet de brede glimlach van de kleedkamer na een Eagles-overwinning, of de dwaze grijns van als hij een rare streek uithaalde in de klas. Maar een droevig soort lachje dat Jakes verbijsterde hart vertelde dat zijn coach hem niet haatte.

De coach knikte één keer naar Jake en toen reed mevrouw Reynolds hem naar de hoek van de rechtszaal aan het eind van een van de toeschouwersbanken. Ze ging naast hem zitten en ze begonnen samen te fluisteren.

'Jake, je moet weten hoe ernstig dit is.' A.W. leek geïrriteerd door de uitwisseling die zojuist tussen Jake en de coach had plaatsgevonden. 'Als meneer Reynolds getuigt, zal de rechter vrijwel zeker beslissen je als volwassene te berechten.'

'Coach.'

'Wat?' A.W. schoof zijn bril omhoog op zijn neus.

Jake keek zijn advocaat recht aan. '*Coach* Reynolds. Niet *meneer* Reynolds. Oké?'

'Jake, je advocaat wil alleen maar helpen.' Jakes vader legde een arm om zijn schouders en keek A.W. aan. 'Dit is de eerste keer dat hij coach Reynolds ziet na het ongeluk.'

De advocaat wuifde de informatie weg als onbelangrijk. 'Het punt is dat Jake in de puree zit. Als de rechter besluit hem als volwassene te berechten, zullen we om verdaging moeten vragen. Hij kan wel drie tot tien jaar krijgen als hij schuldig wordt bevonden.'

'U denkt toch niet echt dat dat zal gebeuren?' Zijn moeder wreef haar handen. Een gewoonte die ze in de afgelopen zes weken had aangenomen. 'Als hij als volwassene wordt berecht, kan hij toch ook wel worden vrijgesproken?'

'Het is heel ingewikkeld.' A.W. pakte een schrijfblok en een pen en begon een diagram te tekenen. 'De jury kan het op verscheidene manieren bekijken, te beginnen met de aanklacht van zware geweldpleging en…'

Jake sloot zich voor hem af en hield zijn hoofd net ver genoeg opzij om coach Reynolds en zijn vrouw te kunnen zien. Ze zaten nog steeds met hun hoofden naar elkaar toe gebogen te praten. Even later ging de officier van justitie naar hen toe. Het gesprek tussen de drie duurde niet lang en toen nam de officier zijn plaats in aan de andere kant van de tafel.

Het was niet beleefd van Jake, dat wist hij wel. Maar hij kon zijn blik niet afwenden. De coach in een rolstoel was de afschuwelijkste aanblik die hij zich kon voorstellen. *Sta op, coach… ren door de zaal en vertel ons dat het allemaal een grote grap is. Zo'n rare streek die u voor de klas wel eens uithaalt. Alstublieft!*

Maar de man verroerde zich niet.

De hoorzitting kon elk moment beginnen en voor het eerst sinds hij de auto van de coach had aangereden, had Jake geen zin om weg te rennen. Hij had zin om op te staan en naar de coach toe te gaan, om hem te vertellen hoe erg hij hem gemist had en hoe vreselijk hij het vond. Hoeveel berouw hij voor altijd zou hebben.

Toen zag Jake iets wat nog erger was. De voet van de coach gleed van de stoel en bleef los en slap opzij bungelen. En het ergste was nog… dat de coach het niet eens merkte! Zijn vrouw zag het als eerste. Ze bukte en *tilde* zijn voet *op* alsof het een boek was of een plant of zoiets, en zette hem terug op de stoel.

Jake voelde tranen in zijn ogen opwellen. *Coach, nee!* Hoe was het mogelijk? Kon de coach niet eens zijn eigen voeten voelen? Wat het zo erg? Jake veegde een traan van zijn wang. Sinds de scheiding van zijn ouders had hij weinig meer gebeden. Maar één keer. Toen hij radeloos in nood was, vlak nadat hij de truck van de coach had aangereden. Toen had Jake het tot God uitgeschreeuwd om hulp.

En God had hulp gebracht.

Dus waarom zou hij nu niet hetzelfde doen? Jake deed zijn ogen dicht.

God, ik bent het… Jake Daniels. U weet natuurlijk wel dat ik alles verknoeid heb. Mijn hele leven is naar de maan, maar het ergste is, het leven van de coach is ook naar de maan. En hij kon er helemaal niets aan doen. Dus God, daarom wil ik een gunst van U vragen. Ik geloof dat U alles kunt, God. U kunt blinde mensen ziende maken en doven horende… dat zei de zondagsschooljuf tenminste altijd.

De tranen stroomden over zijn gezicht, maar geen van de volwassenen om hem heen scheen het op te merken. *God, ik weet nog een verhaal over een verlamde man. Hij had een mat bij zich, geloof ik. En een stel vrienden. En God, ik weet dat U maakte dat hij weer kon lopen. Volgens mij lag hij het ene moment nog op de grond en het volgende liep hij rond.*

Jake deed zijn ogen open en wierp nog een snelle blik op de coach.

Dus, alstublieft, God... zou U dat voor coach Reynolds ook kunnen doen? Kunt U maken dat hij weer kan lopen en rennen? Doe wat U bij die andere man ook hebt gedaan en geef hem zijn benen terug. Alstublieft, God.

Hoelang was het geleden dat hij op die manier gebeden had? Jake wist het niet, maar het was een heerlijk gevoel. En al hadden zijn ouders hem verteld dat de coach voor altijd verlamd zou blijven, Jake was er zeker van dat God dat kon veranderen als Hij wilde.

De coach ving zijn blik en Jake draaide vlug zijn hoofd om naar zijn ouders. Hij droogde zijn tranen en keek naar zijn vader en moeder. Hij haatte het zoals ze luisterden naar alles wat A.W. zei. De advocaat zag de coach als de vijand... maar zijn ouders toch niet? Een paar jaar geleden nog waren zijn ouders bevriend geweest met de familie Reynolds.

Jake snufte en nam zijn ouders onderzoekend op.

Wat was er eigenlijk met ze aan de hand? Nu het proces zou voorkomen, had zijn vader persoonlijk verlof genomen van zijn werk. Hij logeerde in een hotel niet ver van het huis van Jake en zijn moeder. Jake ging overdag naar een nascholingsinstituut en vroeg zich af waarom hij niet in de gevangenis zat, waar hij thuishoorde.

Maar waar bracht zijn vader de laatste tijd zijn dagen eigenlijk door? Bij zijn moeder thuis? En zo ja, konden ze met elkaar opschieten of probeerden ze alleen te bedenken wat er moest gebeuren als Jake naar de gevangenis ging? Er zat nog steeds een flinke ruimte tussen hun zitplaatsen, dus dat wees nog niet op goed nieuws.

Die tussenruimte was het eerste teken geweest dat er problemen tussen hen waren, voordat het huis vol werd van hun ruzies. Maar de laatste tijd hadden ze niet één keer ruziegemaakt.

De rechter kwam binnen en de hoorzitting begon. De vrouw had al van Jakes ouders gehoord waarom hij als minderjarige moest worden berecht, maar nu keek ze door de rechtszaal naar A.W. en stelde hem een vraag. 'Zijn er nieuwe bewijsstukken die het hof moet overwegen alvorens in deze kwestie een beslissing te nemen?'

Jakes advocaat stond op. 'Nee, Edelachtbare.'

De rechter wendde zich tot de officier. 'Officier?'

De man stond op en richtte zijn blik tot achter in de rechtszaal. 'Ja. De staat roept de heer John Reynolds op als getuige.'

Jake kon amper ademhalen toen mevrouw Reynolds de coach naar voren reed. Nu zou de coach zeggen hoe verkeerd het was om straatraces te houden en dat Jake heus wel geweten had wat hij deed.

Maar het kon Jake niet schelen. Hij verdiende wat er ging gebeuren. Alleen de benen van de coach waren belangrijk en of dit het moment was dat God uitkoos om hem te genezen.

Of dat dat pas later zou komen.

Twintig

Alle ogen waren op John gericht.

Abby wist dat ze naar hem keken en hem pijnlijk mager vonden met onbruikbare benen vastgegespt aan een gevangenis van metaal en wielen, maar dat deed er niet toe. Ze had niet trotser op hem kunnen zijn. Zijn rug deed nog zeer en vanmorgen was de pijn zo erg geweest dat hij amper rechtop kon zitten. Maar toch was hij gekomen.

De officier van justitie wist niet waar hij aan was begonnen.

Abby parkeerde de rolstoel naast de getuigenbank. Ze nam plaats op de voorste rij, niet ver van John. Toen hij zijn naam had genoemd en had verklaard wat zijn rol in de hoorzitting was, gaf de rechter het woord aan de staat. 'Uw getuige.'

'Dank u, Edelachtbare.' De officier van justitie was een saai uitziende man met vierkante kaken, die zijn enige prominente trek waren. Hij droeg een overhemd met korte mouwen en een goedkope pantalon, maar hij zag er vriendelijk uit. Abby hoopte dat hij zou begrijpen wat John op het punt stond te gaan doen.

De officier nam met John een reeks snelle vragen door, die bedoeld waren om hem in het verhaal te laten passen en voor het hof te bekrachtigen dat zijn verlamming in feite het gevolg was van Jake Daniels' straatrace.

'Meneer Reynolds, laten we het even over de verdachte hebben.' De officier hield afstand. Waarschijnlijk om de rechter het zicht op John in zijn rolstoel niet te belemmeren. 'U kent Jake Daniels toch?'

Abby's hart begon te bonzen. Daar had je het.

'Ja, inderdaad.' John wierp een blik op Jake. Abby volgde zijn blik, maar Jake keek naar zijn gevouwen handen. John wendde zich weer tot de officier. 'Ik ken hem al jaren.'

'Kunt u rustig zeggen dat u hem hebt zien opgroeien, meneer Reynolds?'

'Ja.' John liet zijn handen in zijn schoot rusten. 'Ik heb hem zien opgroeien.'

'Nu weet u, meneer Reynolds, dat dit hof op het punt staat om te beslissen of de verdachte als volwassene moet worden berecht, klopt dat?'

'Ja, dat weet ik.'

'U weet dat de verdachte nog maar enkele maanden verwijderd is van zijn achttiende verjaardag, de leeftijd van wettige meerderjarigheid?'

'Ja.'

'Goed dan, meneer Reynolds, bent u van mening dat een jongeman van bijna achttien jaar oud, die instemt met deelname aan een illegale straatrace, als volwassene moet worden berecht?'

Abby ving een glimp op van Jakes ouders. Ze wachtten beiden met gespannen gezichten op Johns veroordeling.

Die niet kwam.

'Nee, meneer, ik vind niet dat Jake Daniels als volwassene moet worden berecht.' John keek Jake aan terwijl hij sprak. 'Jake is eigenlijk een beste jongen. In de maanden voor het ongeluk toonde hij zich opmerkelijk volwassen, hij koos ervoor zijn eigen weg te gaan in plaats van zijn vrienden achterna te lopen.'

John zweeg even en de officier van justitie greep zijn kans. 'Even zien of ik u goed begrijp, meneer Reynolds. In de maanden die voorafgingen aan het ongeluk vond u dat verdachte zich opmerkelijk volwassen toonde, maar u vindt *niet* dat hij als volwassene moet worden berecht. Klopt dat?'

'Precies.' John glimlachte de officier toe. 'Ziet u, het feit dat iemand als Jake naar een feestje kon gaan, niet dronk en in het algemeen een goed voorbeeld was voor de anderen, lijkt te bewijzen dat hij in staat is als volwassene voor het gerecht te staan.'

Abby verplaatste haar blik naar Jakes ouders. Tara zat zacht te huilen met haar hand voor haar mond. Tim had zijn arm om Jake heen geslagen. Er stond ongeloof op hun gezichten te lezen.

John vervolgde: 'Maar wanneer een beste jongen als Jake instemt met zoiets vreselijks als straatracen, kan ik maar één ding veronderstellen.' John aarzelde. 'Dat hij nog een kind is. Een kind dat onoordeelkundig een foute keuze heeft gemaakt.'

Hij keek naar Jake en nu sloeg de jongen zijn ogen op. Hij huilde en op dat moment moest iedereen in de rechtszaal het inzien. Jake was geen man, hij was een jongen. Een bange, met schaamte vervulde, schuldige jongen die zijn leven had willen geven om de gevolgen van zijn fouten op die verschrikkelijke vrijdagavond terug te draaien.

De officier liep leeg als een versleten band. 'Is dat alles, meneer Reynolds?'

'Eigenlijk niet.' John draaide zijn stoel zodat hij de rechter beter kon zien. 'Edelachtbare, ik wil graag genoteerd zien dat ik heb gezegd dat ik niet geloof dat gevangenisstraf het beste is voor een jongen als Jake. Als hij een recidivist was, zou het een ander verhaal zijn. Maar Jake is geen opstandige jongen. Hij verlangt niet zo gauw mogelijk zijn rijbewijs terug zodat hij weer kan gaan racen. Hij heeft geen gevangenisstraf nodig, maar hij moet met zijn verhaal naar de scholen toe om jongeren de waarheid te vertellen over straatracen. Ik weet zeker dat iedereen die hem hoort, zal voelen wat *hij* voelt. En misschien kunnen we dan voorkomen dat dit nog meer mensen overkomt.' Hij knikte één keer. 'Dat is alles, Edelachtbare.'

John reed zelf terug naar Abby. In zijn ogen zag ze hoop. Hoop waarvan ze had gevreesd dat die voor altijd verdwenen was.

'Goed gedaan.'

'Dank je.'

Op de achtergrond hoorde Abby vaag dat de officier om een gesprek met de rechter vroeg. Voordat ze tijd had om erover na te denken, was de hoorzitting voorbij en stond Jakes advocaat naast hen. Hij hiel zijn kin tegen zijn borst gedrukt en zijn handen achter zijn rug gevouwen, een gepast bescheiden houding in het licht van Johns toestand. Maar hij was onmiskenbaar in een jubelstemming.

Abby's maag draaide om. John had zijn toespraak niet gehouden om een advocaat een goed figuur te laten slaan. Maar om Jake te redden, een jongen die hij kende en vertrouwde en in wie hij nog steeds geloofde.

De advocaat vloeide over van lof voor Johns goedgunstigheid, zijn daad van barmhartigheid. Maar voordat John iets terug kon zeggen, riep de rechter de zitting weer tot de orde.

'In het licht van het getuigenis dat vandaag is gegeven door het slachtoffer in deze zaak,' en de rechter keek in Johns richting, 'heb ik besloten de verdachte over te dragen om terecht te staan als minderjarige.'

Achter hen hoorde Abby hoe Jakes moeder een snik binnenhield. Het geroezemoes overstemde de woorden van de rechter en ze roffelde met haar hamer op de rechterstoel. 'Genoeg.' Het werd weer stil en de rechter keek de officier aan. 'De raadsman van de staat heeft om tijd gevraagd om met de advocaat van de verdachte te overleggen over strafvermindering in ruil voor een schuldbekentenis. Over drie weken zullen wij weer samenkomen om vast te stellen of deze zaak een proces vereist of niet.'

Abby wierp een blik op Jakes advocaat. De man grijnsde en drukte eerst Tara en toen Tim en ten slotte Jake de hand. Abby keek geschokt toe, tot ze de uitdrukking op de gezichten van de Daniels zag. Jake en zijn familie lachten niet. Hun advocaat mocht de afloop van vandaag puur als een wettelijke overwinning zien, maar de familie Daniels niet. Ze waren zich er pijnlijk van bewust dat John nog steeds verlamd was.

Welke straf het hof Jake ook toebedeelde, in veel opzichten waren ze allemaal verliezers.

De zitting was afgelopen en Jakes advocaat nam Jake apart.

Abby stond op en draaide Johns rolstoel om. Daarbij viel haar blik recht op Tara en Tim Daniels. Tara verzamelde haar spullen toen haar ogen die van Abby ontmoetten. De twee hadden elkaar sinds het ongeluk niet meer gesproken. Afgezien van hun kaart waren ze op afstand gebleven. Abby begreep het wel. Deze tijd was voor de familie Daniels net zo tumultueus als voor hen.

Abby rolde John dichterbij en manoeuvreerde hem tussen de tafel van de verdediging en de eerste rij toeschouwersbanken. Haar hart bonsde.

Het werd steeds pijnlijker totdat John uiteindelijk de stilte verbrak. 'Tara... hoe gaat het?'

'Ik...' Tara's stem begaf het. Samen met Tim kwam ze dichterbij en met z'n vieren vormden ze een kringetje. Tara kreeg tranen in haar ogen en ze deed nog een stap naar John toe. John stak zijn hand uit en ze drukte hem met trillende vingers. 'Ik vind het zo erg. We hadden langs moeten komen, maar... Ik wist niet wat ik moest zeggen.' Ze keek Abby aan. 'Het spijt me, Abby.'

De tranen vloeiden. Abby kwam achter Johns stoel vandaan en nam Tara in haar armen. 'Jake heeft dit evenmin gewild als wij.' Ze sprak gedempt en snikte onderdrukt. Er kwam een einde aan hun omhelzing en ze stonden ongemakkelijk bij elkaar.

Tim schraapte zijn keel en keek John aan. 'Lang geleden.'

'Ja.' John drukte de man de hand. 'Je hebt nooit afscheid genomen.'

'De situatie was niet...' Tim keek naar Tara. 'Niet goed, John. Het spijt me.'

Hij drukte door. 'Ben je nu hertrouwd?'

'Nee.' Tims wangen werden rood. 'Ik heb verlof genomen. Ik logeer in een hotel in de stad.' Opnieuw keek hij Tara aan en Abby werd nieuwsgierig. Hadden die twee gevoelens voor elkaar? Na jarenlang gescheiden te zijn? Tim verlegde zijn blik weer naar John. 'We hebben over een heleboel dingen gepraat. Waarom ik weg ben gegaan, bijvoorbeeld. En waarom ons huwelijk mislukt is.'

John keek Abby aan en boog zich toen naar Tim toe. 'Zou je erg geschokt zijn als je wist dat Abby en ik vorig jaar zomer bijna uit elkaar zijn gegaan?'

Tara zette grote ogen op. 'Abby? John en jij?'

'We hadden het er al drie jaar over.' Abby wilde Johns lof van de daken schreeuwen. Hij was degene wiens leven door het ongeluk voor altijd was veranderd, maar toch raakte hij nu de kern van een kwestie die hem nog meer aan het hart ging dan zijn benen: het kapotgaan van huwelijken. Vooral de huwelijken van christenen.

Tim stopte zijn handen in zijn broekzak. 'En toen? Ik bedoel… jullie zijn nog bij elkaar.'

'We dachten er weer aan waarom we getrouwd waren en aan alle herinneringen die we hadden opgebouwd. En we dachten er vooral aan hoe troosteloos de toekomst eruitzag als we niet meer samen waren.' John verdraaide zijn hals weer tot zijn ogen die van Abby ontmoetten. Toen richtte hij zijn aandacht weer op Tim. 'Het gaat beter dan ooit.'

Tara veegde een traan weg en snufte. 'Tim wil dat we praten over een nieuwe poging.' Ze schudde haar hoofd. 'Maar ik kan het niet. De eerste keer is die scheiding zowat mijn dood geworden. Een tweede mislukking overleef ik niet.'

'Weet je wat…' John pakte Abby's hand en ze kwam naast hem staan. 'Wat zou je ervan zeggen als Tara en jij een paar avonden in de week bij ons langskomen, nu je toch in de stad bent? Gewoon om er eens over te praten.'

Abby ving Johns blik en haar hart sprong op. 'Misschien kunnen we jullie iets uit ons verhaal vertellen wat kan helpen.'

Tara keek twijfelachtig. 'Ik weet 't niet.'

Ze zwegen even en toen keek Tim rusteloos met zijn voeten schuifelend naar de grond. Toen hij opkeek, had hij tranen in zijn ogen. 'Het spijt me, John. Van je benen.'

John haalde zijn schouders op, hij had meer rust dan hij in weken had gehad. 'Het was jouw schuld niet.'

'Ik heb die auto gekocht.' Tims gezicht was lijkbleek. 'Tara had gelijk. Hij was niet geschikt voor een tiener. Ik… ik zal er de rest van mijn leven mee moeten leven.'

Drie meter verder klopte de advocaat van de verdediging Jake op de schouder en maakte vlug dat hij wegkwam. Toen hij verdwenen was, keek Jake naar de vier mensen en kwam aarzelend naderbij. Abby keek onderzoekend naar hem. Ze wist niet goed wat ze voelde. Soms haatte ze hem. Jakes beslissing had John zijn vermogen om te lopen gekost en hun leven voor altijd veranderd. Maar andere keren…

Ze wist het gewoon niet.

Nu was zo'n andere keer.

Toen Jake bij hen kwam, keek hij naar zijn ouders. 'Mag ik even alleen met de coach praten?'

'Natuurlijk.' Tara zocht haar spullen bij elkaar en liep met Tim naar de deur. 'Als je klaar bent, gaan we weg.'

Abby gaf John een licht kneepje in zijn schouder. 'Zal ik weggaan?'

'Nee,' antwoordde Jake voordat John iets kon zeggen. 'Alstublieft, mevrouw Reynolds… ik wil dat u hoort wat ik te zeggen heb.'

Abby haalde een stoel bij de tafel van de verdediging en zette hem naast John neer. Toen ze zat, sloeg Jake zijn armen over elkaar en haalde diep adem. Abby probeerde zijn ogen te doorgronden. Was dit een danktoespraak die zijn advocaat in elkaar had geflanst? Of had Jake iets echt gemeends op zijn hart? Nog voordat hij sprak, wist Abby dat het het laatste was.

'Coach, mijn advocaat heeft me net verteld dat ik geluk heb gehad.' Jake snufte. 'Dat is toch niet te geloven?'

John zei niets, maar hield zijn blik op Jake gericht en wachtte.

'Ik wil dat mevrouw Reynolds en u weten dat wat er over een paar weken ook gebeurt met de hoorzitting, ik géén geluk heb gehad.' Jake kreeg tranen in zijn ogen, maar hij huilde niet. 'Ik ben stom geweest, en het… het…'

Hij beet op zijn lip en liet zijn hoofd hangen. Lang bleef hij zo staan en Abby begreep het. Zijn emoties waren te dicht aan de oppervlakte om los te laten. Want hij had nog meer te zeggen. Jake hield zijn adem in en keek John weer aan. 'Het was mijn schuld, coach. Ik had nooit met hem moeten gaan racen. Nooit.' Zijn knieën knikten. 'Ik zag uw truck de straat opdraaien, maar ik reed te hard. Ik kon niet stoppen.'

Abby voelde zich beklemd. *God... had U John niet één minuutje kunnen tegenhouden? Genoeg om hem dit te besparen?*

STEUN NIET OP JE EIGEN INZICHT, DOCHTER...

Ze knipperde met haar ogen. De vreemde woorden die in haar hart speelden, voelden haast als een rechtstreeks antwoord van God. Dezelfde Schrifttekst was haar steeds opnieuw te binnen geschoten.

Bent U dat, God?

IK HEB DIT GEZEGD OPDAT JULLIE VREDE VINDEN BIJ MIJ. JULLIE ZULLEN HET ZWAAR TE VERDUREN KRIJGEN IN DE WERELD, MAAR HOUD MOED: IK HEB DE WERELD OVERWONNEN.

Jake vertelde verder hoe snel het ongeluk was gebeurd, maar Abby luisterde niet. Op het moment dat de Schrifttekst in haar hart flitste, liepen de rillingen haar over de rug. Het was een tekst die ze die ochtend tijdens haar stille tijd had gelezen. Een klein poosje geleden hadden John en zij hem samen onder ogen gehad... toen ze na Nicoles bruiloft weer samen de Bijbel waren gaan lezen.

Het was de volmaakte tekst, de tekst die hun situatie precies beschreef. Dat begreep ze nu nog beter dan in het ziekenhuis in de dagen na Johns ongeluk. Het Woord van God, Zijn beloften, de dingen die God tegen hen had gesproken zodat ze vrede kregen. In de wereld hadden ze het zwaar te verduren, dat klopte helemaal. Eerst op het footballveld met ouders en het bestuur. En toen met Johns ongeluk.

Maar uiteindelijk zou God overwinnen, ook al zagen ze dat nu niet. God zou altijd winnen. Hij zou achterbakse ouders overwinnen en zwakke bestuurders. Johns auto-ongeluk zou Hij overwinnen en zelfs zijn verlamming.

Hij zou overwinnen, al zat John de rest van zijn leven in een rolstoel.

Jake zei dat Casey Parker vertrokken was van de plek van het ongeluk en teruggekomen nadat hij om hulp had gebeld. 'We waren zo bang, coach. We dachten dat u doodging.' De jongen kon wel door de grond zakken en eindelijk pletsten zijn tranen op zijn sportschoenen. 'Het spijt me zo.' Jake zonk in een stoel tegenover John en liet zijn hoofd in zijn handen zakken. 'Ik zou er alles voor over hebben om die laatste minuten terug te draaien.'

Casey Parker was ook niet bij John op bezoek geweest. Sinds ze te weten waren gekomen dat de vader van de jongen de brieven over John geschreven had, vroeg Abby zich af of de man soms blij was met wat John was overkomen. Niet dat hij gewond was natuurlijk, maar dat hij niet meer kon coachen. Het was vreselijk om dat te denken, maar Abby kon er niets aan doen. Ze was per slot van rekening met een coach getrouwd. En sommige mensen hadden de neiging om hun grootste minachting en hun slechtste gedrag voor coaches te bewaren. Dat was een onontkoombaar feit in Amerika.

Als John al zoiets dacht, had hij het nooit gezegd.

Hij boog zich nu zo ver mogelijk naar voren en pakte Jakes knieën vast. 'Jake, kijk me aan.' Johns stem klonk vriendelijk, maar streng. Dezelfde toon die Abby hem tegen hun eigen kinderen had horen aanslaan als ze terneergeslagen waren.

'Ik meen het, Jake. Doe die handen naar beneden en kijk me aan.'

Abby keek stil toe vanaf haar plaats naast hem. Dit was de John die ze kende en van wie ze hield, de John die zag wat er mis was en het rechtzette met een onweerstaanbare hartstocht.

Nu vielen Jakes handen in zijn schoot en hij ontmoette Johns blik. De tranen stroomden over zijn wangen. 'Coach, dwing me niet u aan te kijken. Dat is te moeilijk.'

Het verdriet in Jakes ogen verzachtte Abby's hart. Hij *was* ook nog maar een kind, een jongen die verdronk in een rivier van schuld, zonder de andere kant te kunnen bereiken.

John boog zich nog dichter naar Jake toe. 'Jake, ik vergeef je. Het was een ongeluk.'

'Het was *stom*!' Jakes gezicht vertrok en hij uitte een geluidloze kreet. 'U zit in een rolstoel, coach. Door mij! Dat trek ik niet.' Een snik ontsnapte uit Jakes keel. 'Ik *wil* naar de gevangenis. Dan hoef ik niet te doen alsof mijn leven lekker doorgaat terwijl ik het uwe heb verwoest.'

'Je hebt mijn leven niet verwoest. Als ik goed mijn best doe, kan ik alles. En ik ga mijn best doen, Jake, reken daar maar op. Ik heb jullie nooit genoegen laten nemen met een tweede plaats, en nu ga ik zeker geen genoegen nemen met een tweede plaats.'

Abby's hart sloeg een slag over. En dat zei de man die gisteren nog afgezonderd en ontmoedigd in zijn eentje op hun aanlegstei-ger zat? Ze had zin om haar handen op te heffen en een over-winningskreet te uiten, maar ze weerstond de verleiding.

Jake wreef met zijn knokkels over zijn voorhoofd en schudde zijn hoofd. 'Het is niet goed, coach. Wat u vandaag voor me hebt gedaan. Ik verdien het niet.'

'Het is *wel* goed. Niemand heeft iets aan je als je in een gevan-geniscel zit, Jake. Je hebt een fout gemaakt en je leven is binnen een paar seconden veranderd. Mijn leven ook. Maar je zult nie-mand redden door achter de tralies te gaan zitten. Het volgende straatraceslachtoffer niet en jezelf niet. En mij al helemaal niet. Je moet je boodschap naar buiten brengen, andere jongeren vertel-len dat ze nee moeten zeggen als iemand hen wil uitdagen tot een race. Zo red je levens.'

'Coach,' zei Jake gekweld, 'dat is niet genoeg straf. Hoe kan ik in de spiegel kijken? Het is zo gek. U en uw gezin… jullie kun-nen me nooit echt vergeven wat ik heb gedaan. Jullie *horen* me niet te vergeven.'

'Jake…' Johns toon was zachter geworden. 'Ik heb je al vergeven.'

'Niet zeggen.'

Abby deed haar ogen dicht. Ze voelde wat er ging komen. *Dwing me niet hem ook te vergeven, God. Nog niet...*

John leunde een beetje verder naar achteren in zijn stoel. 'Zodra Abby me vertelde wat er gebeurd was... dat jij de bestuurder was van de andere auto... heb ik me diep vanbinnen voorgenomen om je te vergeven.' John lachte droevig. 'Hoe kon ik het je aanrekenen? Het was een ongeluk, Jake. Bovendien ben je als een zoon voor me. Ik vergeef je volkomen.'

Abby verschoof op haar stoel.

Spreek, dochter... vergeef zoals Ik jou vergeven heb...

De aandrang in Abby's hart was onmiskenbaar. *God... alstublieft. Dwing me niet het nu te zeggen. Hij heeft van mij geen vergeving nodig.*

'Abby vergeeft je ook.' John wendde zich tot haar en zijn ogen waren zo transparant dat ze recht in zijn hart kon kijken. Met welke andere gevoelens John in de komende maanden en jaren nog zou worstelen, ze betwijfelde of gebrek aan vergeving erbij zou horen. Hij was oprecht tegen Jake. Hij koesterde geen wrok tegen de jongen. In het geheel niet. John zat haar nog steeds afwachtend aan te kijken. 'Zeg het, Abby. Je vergeeft hem toch?'

'Natuurlijk.' Ze moest het zeggen voor John en later zette ze haar gevoelens wel op een rijtje. 'Wij allemaal.'

Jake boog zijn hoofd weer. 'Ik haat mezelf.'

'Dan is *dat* het echte probleem. Jezelf te vergeven.' John zette zijn ellebogen op zijn knieën en er viel Abby iets in. *Hij kan het niet voelen... het is alsof hij zijn armen op een tafel of een bureau laat rusten.*

Jake zweeg.

'Dan zal ik daarvoor bidden.' John beet op zijn mondhoek. 'Dat God je de genade zal geven om jezelf te vergeven. Zoals *Hij* je vergeeft.'

'God?' Jake keek hem weer aan. 'God gaat me heus niet vergeven. Coach, het was mijn schuld!'

'Heb je tegen Hem gezegd dat het je spijt?'

'Ja!' De pijn werd heviger. 'Die eerste nacht wel twintig keer. Maar toch… moet ik boeten. Ik kan niet verwachten dat God of u of… of mevrouw Reynolds… of iemand anders me vergeeft voordat ik een hele tijd in de gevangenis heb gezeten.'

'Waarom?'

'Zodat ik het goed kan maken.'

'Goedmaken dat mijn benen het niet meer doen?' Er verscheen een glinstering in Johns ogen en zijn mondhoeken gingen omhoog. 'Dan zou je er een hele tijd moeten zitten als dat zo was. Want ik had heel snelle benen, Daniels. Razend snel.'

Weer had Abby zin om in haar handen te klappen of hardop te schreeuwen. John maakte een grapje! Hij plaagde Jake met een oud geintje uit de tijd dat Jake een jaar of twaalf was. De tijd dat zijn ouders nog zo nu en dan op zondag kwamen eten.

Abby hoorde en zag het nog voor zich. Jake betrad met zijn familie het huis en John heette hen welkom. Jake ging teen aan teen staan met John en zette grote ogen op.

Wedstrijdje doen, coach; ik word steeds sneller! En John, die Jake altijd *coach* had genoemd, lachte zacht. *Ik weet het niet, Jake. Ik heb razend snelle benen.* Waarop Jake een wenkbrauw optrok en John zogenaamd een stomp tegen zijn schouder gaf. *Kom op, coach, zo snel zijn ze niet. Lang niet zo snel als de mijne!*

Abby kreeg kippenvel op haar armen toen ze het begreep. John wierp Jake een reddingsboei toe, een kans om zich op te trekken uit de wateren van schuld.

Abby stond stokstijf stil naar de huilende jongen te kijken. Ineens ontspanden de rimpels om zijn ogen en zijn voorhoofd.

'Kom op, coach.' Zijn stem begaf het en er gleed een traan over zijn wang. 'Zo snel waren ze niet. Lang… lang niet zo snel als de mijne.'

'Bravo, Jake.' John gaf hem een klapje op zijn knie. 'Ik mag dan verlamd zijn, maar ik ben niet dood. Ik wil niet dat je elke keer als we elkaar zien je hoofd laat hangen, want dan verlies ik twee keer.'

'Twee keer?'

'Mijn benen… en jou.' John zweeg even. 'Doe me dat niet aan, Jake. Het zal lastig genoeg zijn om de dagelijkse dingen weer onder de knie te krijgen zonder dat ik me af moet vragen of met jou alles wel in orde is.'

Weer liet Jake zijn tranen stromen. Hij leek wel twaalf en Abby's hart smolt voor hem. Misschien kon ze hem toch wel vergeven.

'Maar het spijt me zo. Ik moet iets doen, coach. Iets om het goed te maken.'

'Hoor es, Jake… elke keer als je een stampvolle aula binnenloopt en die jongeren je verhaal vertelt, moet je ergens aan denken.' Hij dempte zijn stem een beetje. 'Ik ben bij je, Daniels. Vlak naast je, stap voor stap. En dat zal alles goed maken.'

Eenentwintig

Nicole was bijna elke dag misselijk.

Het was geen ochtendmisselijkheid. Die was al weken voorbij. Nu ze bijna halverwege haar zwangerschap was, kwam het misselijke gevoel maar door één ding: het was bijna Kerst en haar vader voelde nog steeds niets in zijn benen of voeten.

Zodra Nicole op die vreselijke middag in de ziekenhuiswachtkamer het nieuws over zijn verlamming had gehoord, had ze gebeden. Sindsdien had ze God urenlang gesmeekt en geloofd dat Hij een wonder zou doen bij haar vader. Ze had geen idee hoe dat in zijn werk moest gaan, alleen dat het moest. Elke keer als ze ergens voor bad en dit gevoel had, ging het zoals het moest gaan.

Maar toen de dagen verstreken, namen haar gebeden af en hielden uiteindelijk op. Daarbij had ze geworsteld met een probleem dat haar maag deed omdraaien.

De dingen gingen niet altijd zoals ze moesten gaan.

Want dan zou ze pas over drie jaar zwanger zijn geworden, haar ouders zouden nooit ruzie hebben gehad en nooit een scheiding hebben overwogen. Sterker nog, christenen zouden geen geliefden kwijtraken aan ziekten en ongelukken. Ze zouden nooit aan een depressie lijden of pijn of geldproblemen hebben.

En ze zouden zeker nooit verlamd raken.

Nee, als alles ging zoals het moest, zou hun leven gladjes verlopen tot de dag waarop ze, als stokoude mensjes, 's avonds naar bed gingen en wakker werden in de armen van Jezus.

Maar zo werkte het niet. En die waarheid had haar geloof geschokt.

Misschien was God van plan om het letsel van haar vader te gebruiken om de leerlingen van Marion High School te veranderen. Die optie beviel Nicole niet, maar het was een mogelijkheid. Ze had geruchten gehoord van Kade, die nog steeds contact had met een paar leerlingen van Marion High. Op school werd gezegd dat de leerlingen zich beter gedroegen en vriendelijker waren geworden na het ongeluk van haar vader. Er werd zelfs gesproken over een vergadering over coach Reynolds, maar noch Nicole, noch Kade had daarover iets tegen hun vader gezegd.

Hij had al genoeg aan zijn hoofd nu hij zich in zijn rolstoel moest leren voortbewegen en met zijn letsel moest leren omgaan.

Als dat de reden was dat God de verwonding van haar vader had toegelaten, zou Nicole een zekere rustige vrede moeten voelen, een gevoel dat de Schrift gelijk had in Romeinen, dat alle dingen meewerkten ten goede voor hen die God liefhadden.

Maar dat gevoel had ze helemaal niet.

Ze was alleen maar misselijk.

Haar arts had haar gewaarschuwd dat zich steeds zorgen maken niet goed was voor de baby. Daarna had ze Matt en zichzelf beloofd om meer in de Bijbel te lezen en te bidden, om de stress te verminderen.

Maar elke keer als ze probeerde een lievelingstekst te lezen of te bidden tot God, merkte ze dat ze aan het ongeluk dacht. Waarom had God het toegelaten? Had haar vader niet vijf minuten eerder van school kunnen vertrekken? Vijf *seconden* later? Na alles wat haar ouders hadden meegemaakt, nadat hun harten eindelijk weer voor elkaar klopten? Nadat pap weer met hen mee was gegaan naar de kerk?

De vragen die Nicole aan God wilde stellen, wogen zwaarder dan de dingen waarvoor ze wilde bidden, dus haar zorgelijkheid bleef. Het was eigenlijk niet zo dat ze boos was op God. Ze wist alleen niet of ze Hem kon vertrouwen. Ze deelde deze gevoelens met niemand. Zelfs niet met zichzelf.

Omdat de Nicole Reynolds die ze voor het ongeluk van haar

vader was geweest, nooit aan God zou hebben getwijfeld. Die oude Nicole had Gods fluisterstem beter verstaan, meer op Bijbelteksten en gebed vertrouwd dan wie dan ook in het gezin.

Pas kortgeleden was het eindelijk tot Nicole doorgedrongen wat de reden was voor haar diepe geloof. Het had niets te maken met geloven dat ze beter was dan anderen, of een grotere behoefte dan de anderen had aan Gods vrede en nabijheid. Nee, dat was de reden helemaal niet.

De reden was Haley Ann.

En dat was nog iets wat ze aan niemand had verteld.

Niemand wist dat ze zich het verlies van haar kleine zusje nog kon herinneren. Ze mocht dan nog geen twee jaar zijn geweest, maar bepaalde taferelen van die droevige dag waren haar nog altijd bijgebleven. Haley Ann had in haar wiegje liggen slapen, begreep Nicole nu. De meeste bijzonderheden waren vaag, maar Nicole kon nog steeds haar ogen dichtdoen en grote mannen voor zich zien die Haley Anns kamer binnenstormden en met haar bezig waren om haar weer aan het ademen te krijgen.

Iedereen ging er vanuit dat Nicole, die toen nog klein was, niet getreurd had. Maar Haley Ann was haar zusje! Haar enige zusje. Nicole herinnerde zich een gesprek dat ze met haar moeder had gehad over het verlies van Haley Ann.

'Ze is nu in de hemel lieverd.' Haar moeder had gehuild, zoals ze toen vaak deed. 'Maar zolang je van God houdt, zul je altijd maar een fluistering van haar vandaan zijn. Begrijp je?'

Nicole had het beter begrepen dan Abby zich had kunnen indenken. Als God liefhebben de manier was om dichter bij de herinnering aan Haley Ann te blijven, zou ze dat doen met haar hele hart. En ze had het gedaan. Elke maand, elk jaar... tot nu toe.

Nu was alles veranderd en de reden lag voor de hand. Ze was er gewoon niet zeker van of ze God nog wel kon vertrouwen. Ze had Hem ten slotte de veiligheid van haar hele familie toevertrouwd. Op de ochtend van het ongeluk nog wel. Maar die avond had ze in het ziekenhuis naast haar moeder gezeten en zich afgevraagd wat er mis was gegaan. Zich afgevraagd waar God was geweest toen ze Hem het hardste nodig hadden.

De gevoelens die ze over de hele kwestie had, droegen alleen maar bij aan haar onrust. Het ergste was dat Matt voortdurend praatte over Gods wil zus en Gods wil zo en Gods wonderbare hand die het leven van haar vader had gered. Op de meest ongelegen momenten kon hij haar vinden: als ze aan een huiswerkopdracht werkte; of was opvouwde; of zich klaarmaakte om naar school te gaan.

Twee avonden geleden hadden ze er voor het eerst echt ruzie over gehad. Ze had op internet naar koopjes zitten zoeken op eBay toen hij achter haar kwam staan en haar schouders begon te masseren. Zijn toon was nog zachter dan zijn vingertoppen.

'Nicole, kom eens achter de computer vandaan.'

Ze wierp een snelle blik over haar schouder. 'Waarom?'

'Omdat je aan het vluchten bent.'

'Waarvoor?' Ze richtte haar aandacht weer op het computerscherm en de lijst met artikelen.

Matt zuchtte diep. 'Voor alles. Voor een gesprek met mij… voor de toestand van je vader… voor je zwangerschap.' Hij aarzelde. 'Voor God.'

Nicole snapte niet waarom zijn opmerkingen haar zo boos maakten. Voordat ze het kon tegenhouden, stroomde er een stortvloed van woorden uit haar mond. 'Wie ben jij om mij te vertellen waarvoor ik op de vlucht ben?' Ze draaide de stoel met een ruk om en keek hem woedend aan. 'Dat ik geen zin heb om van elk onderwerp de diepere betekenis op te graven, wil nog niet zeggen dat ik op de vlucht ben.'

'Bidden met je echtgenoot is niet bepaald de diepere betekenis opgraven, Nicole.'

'Oké, best. Je wilt dat ik bid, ik zal wel bidden. Maar vraag me niet mijn hart erin te leggen, want dat kan ik niet. Ik heb op dit moment *even* de tijd nodig voordat ik God aanroep.'

Matt had haar stomverbaasd aangekeken. 'Je klinkt totaal niet als het meisje met wie ik getrouwd ben.'

'En bedankt.'

'Ik meen het. Vroeger praatte je constant over God. Nu zou je liever doen alsof Hij niet bestaat.'

'Dat is het niet.' Ze snoof. 'Ik heb Hem alleen niet meer zoveel te vragen. Laat de benen van mijn vader weer gezond worden? Te laat. Laten we wachten en over een paar jaar pas een baby krijgen? Helaas. Ik ben niet op de vlucht, Matt. Ik zie alleen de zin niet in van bidden.'

Matt wees naar de computer. 'En spelen op eBay geeft je de oplossing?'

'Het is beter dan je tijd verspillen aan bidden als God uiteindelijk toch precies doet wat Hij wil.'

Daarna had Matt haar een lange tijd aangekeken. Toen hij sprak, was zijn stem zachter dan eerst. 'Zolang een van ons tweeën nog in bidden gelooft, wil ik je iets zeggen.'

Nicole zweeg, haar wangen brandden.

'Ik zal voor je bidden, Nicole. Dat God je zal helpen jezelf terug te vinden.'

Sindsdien hadden zijn woorden door haar hoofd gespeeld en zacht hun weg gevonden naar haar hart. Wat was er eigenlijk met haar aan de hand? Ze geloofde toch nog in het gebed? Nadat ze haar leven lang gebedsverhoringen om zich heen had gezien, was de situatie van haar leven nu toch niet erg genoeg om haar geloof te schokken?

Ze trok een zwart truitje aan en een witte zijden blouse. Ze had al een buikje, maar niet zo erg dat ze positiekleding moest dragen. Daar was ze blij om. Het was kerstavond en ze waren samen met Jo en Denny bij haar ouders te eten gevraagd. Matts ouders zaten al beneden bij Matt op haar te wachten.

Nicole pakte een zwarte panty en trok hem aan. Haar oog viel op een bordje met een Bijbeltekst naast hun bed. Het was een tekst uit Hebreeën, en het was altijd een lievelingstekst van Matt geweest.

Laten we daarbij de blik gericht houden op Jezus, de grondlegger en voltooier van ons geloof…

De panty bleef stil in Nicoles handen hangen. Misschien was *dat* haar probleem. Sinds het ongeluk van haar vader had ze haar blik niet veel op Jezus gericht, maar op zijn letsel, haar zwangerschap en het verdriet en de frustraties die met beide gepaard gingen.

Maar niet op Jezus.

Er stond toch ook in de Bijbel dat God de Schepper van alle leven was? En als Hij de Schepper was, dan was het Zijn beslissing of bepaalde personages zonder kleerscheuren door het leven gingen of dat ze slachtoffer werden van een auto-ongeluk.

Die gedachte bracht Nicole geen verlichting. En haar verlangen om te bidden werd er zeker niet groter van. Als God de Schepper was, dan stond alles al vast. Ze konden God liefhebben en Hij kon hen liefhebben. Maar bidden veranderde niets als alles al vaststond.

'Nicole, ben je klaar?' riep Matt onderaan de trap. Na de ruzie van laatst hadden ze allebei hun excuus aangeboden, maar het was niet meer hetzelfde tussen hen. Matt vond dat zij veranderd was en zij vond dat hij ongevoelig was geworden. Dat kon ze ook nog aan de lijst toevoegen.

Ze stak haar hoofd om de hoek van de deur. 'Bijna.'

'Opschieten.' Hij wierp een blik op de klok aan de wand. 'We zijn al laat.'

Nicole ging weer met de panty in de weer. 'Jij ook prettige kerstdagen,' siste ze tussen haar tanden zodat Matt het niet kon horen. Ze ging op de rand van het bed zitten en tilde een voet op. Ze trok de panty over haar enkels omhoog toen het gebeurde.

Diep vanbinnen voelde ze iets trillen.

Alsof iemand haar vanbinnen kietelde. Nicoles hart begon te bonzen en ze bleef stil zitten. Was dat wat ze dacht dat het was? Er ging bijna een minuut voorbij en toen gebeurde het weer. Het voelde als de pootjes van een slapend poesje die haar ergens achter haar onderbuik aantikten.

Toen het een derde keer gebeurde, wist Nicole het zeker. Het was geen poesje.

Het was haar baby. De baby die ze nooit helemaal geaccepteerd had, waar ze nooit helemaal blij mee was geweest. Maar nu meldde dit kindje zich aan, het bewoog gracieus in haar lichaam. Een heldere vreugde explodeerde in Nicoles hart. God weefde een nieuw leven in haar! Hoe kon ze daar niet opgetogen over zijn?

Ze sloeg haar armen om zichzelf heen en vroeg zich voor het eerst af hoe de baby eruit zou zien. Was het een jongen of een meisje? Lang als Kade of zwaargebouwd zoals Matt? Gevoelig als haar moeder of vastberaden als haar vader? De tranen prikten in haar ogen, maar ze wilde niet huilen. Welke andere problemen ze ook nog moest doorwerken, ineens was Nicole klaar om het kind in haar lichaam lief te hebben.

En misschien zou ze een dezer dagen ook weer klaar zijn om met God te praten.

De deur zwaaide open en Matt staarde haar aan. 'Het duurt nou al vijf minuten, Nick. Wat ben je aan het doen?'

Er borrelde een lachje in Nicoles keel omhoog. 'De baby…'

Matt kwam de kamer binnen en deed met een neutraal gezicht een paar stappen naar haar toe. 'Wat is er met de baby?'

'Ik voelde de baby bewegen, Matt.' Weer lachte ze zachtjes. 'Een paar keer licht gefladder, maar ik weet zeker dat het dat was.'

'Echt waar?' Matts gezicht ontspande. Hij kwam naast haar op bed zitten en legde zijn hand op haar buik.

'Je kunt het niet voelen.' Ze legde haar hand op de zijne. 'Het was heel zacht. Ik zou het niet gevoeld hebben als ik hier niet had gezeten.'

Matt keek haar aan. 'Je klinkt blij.'

Was haar teleurstelling zo duidelijk geweest? Het speet Nicole. 'Natuurlijk ben ik blij.' Ze boog zich naar hem toe en kuste hem.

Even keek hij haar aan, zijn ogen vol vragen. Maar net toen ze dacht dat hij weer over bidden en God en haar gedrag zou beginnen, glimlachte hij. 'Kom, dan gaan we gauw naar je ouders om het te vertellen.'

De liefde voor Matt welde in Nicole op zoals in geen maanden. Hij wilde haar zo graag helpen, en maken dat ze weer voelde en dacht en zich gedroeg zoals vroeger. Maar nu hij dit moment had kunnen gebruiken om haar te overtuigen dat God aan het werk was in haar leven, was hij bereid om te wachten.

'Bedankt, Matt. Dat je niet aandringt.'

'Ik houd van je, Nick. Wat je ook voelt of denkt of gelooft.' Hij pakte haar hand. 'Als je klaar bent om te praten, dan ben ik er.'

★

Abby had het moeilijk.

Het was kerstavond en de kinderen zouden er over vijf minuten zijn, maar ze voelde zich ellendig. Ze wierp één laatste blik in de spiegel en haalde diep adem. In deze afgelopen week had John meer goede dagen gehad dan slechte en Abby meende te weten waarom. Het had er alles mee te maken dat hij Jake Daniels had gezien. Dat John die dag met hem in de rechtszaal had kunnen praten en lachen en hem hoop had kunnen bieden, had meer voor John gedaan dan al zijn therapie tot nu toe.

Had zij er ook maar wat aan gehad. Ze kon zich niet over haar woede heen zetten, die ze in zich opkropte en die haar vanbinnen opvrat.

Als vrienden van de kerk belden, kregen ze allemaal hetzelfde te horen: 'Het gaat prima met ons... dank voor jullie gebed... John voelt zich beter... we beginnen te wennen aan de rolstoel.'

Had ze maar de moed om de waarheid te vertellen: 'Ik ben woest... teleurgesteld... kapot. En ik weet niet of ik wel de rest van mijn leven wil toekijken hoe John wegkwijnt in een rolstoel.'

Ze hoorde sterk te zijn, vastberaden, positief. Dat was altijd haar rol geweest, zelfs toen John en zij op het punt van scheiden stonden. Nu leek het wel alsof iedereen die belde, of het nu een oude vriend was of een leerling van John, verlangde dat zij hem of haar bemoedigde en opbeurde.

Waarom rekende iedereen er maar op dat *zij* de juiste houding had tegenover Johns invaliditeit? John… de kinderen… hun familie en vrienden… het was alsof ze allemaal met elkaar afgesproken hadden: 'Nou, met Abby gaat het goed, dus alles is in orde. We kunnen een zucht van verlichting slaken en doorgaan met leven.'

Positief zijn en er vrede mee hebben was de juiste houding, die iedereen van haar verwachtte. Ze zouden niet weten wat ze moesten beginnen als Abby elke keer als iemand naar John vroeg begon te huilen. Of als ze eerlijk vertelde hoe moeilijk ze het vanbinnen had.

Ze keek nog eens onderzoekend naar haar spiegelbeeld.

Wat er ook broeide op de bodem van haar hart, ze zou het nog een poosje langer moeten verbergen. Het was per slot van rekening Kerst. En de hele familie verwachtte een vrolijk gezicht en gezellige praatjes van haar. Vorig jaar had ze haar gevoelens over hun huwelijksproblemen het zwijgen opgelegd, en dat had het alleen maar erger gemaakt…

Maar dit was iets anders. Ze moest zich nu rustig houden, anders kwamen ze geen van allen de dagen door.

Met ingehouden adem liep ze de slaapkamer uit. Haar adem inhouden was een manier om het huilen tegen te houden. *Laat los, Abby… denk niet aan je eigen gevoelens. Denk aan iets anders…* Ze knipperde snel met haar ogen. Kade. Dat was het: ze kon aan Kade denken. Met hem ging het in elk geval beter. Nadat hij thuis was geweest voor de kerstvakantie had hij een paar keer met een hulpverlener van de kerk gepraat. Laatst had Kade aan Abby en John verteld dat hij sinds zijn gesprek met John die dag op het meer niet meer naar porno had gekeken, op internet of anderszins. Kades hulpverlener had hem gevraagd een echtpaar te bestuderen dat het beste echte intimiteit illustreerde.

Kade had Abby en John gekozen.

Ze was onder aan de trap gekomen en hoorde een koor van

stemmen in de kamer. Ze sloeg de hoek om en werd meteen begroet door Jo en Denny.

'Nou, Abby, je lijkt wel een kerstengel.' Jo deed drie reusachtige stappen naar haar toe en sloeg haar armen om Abby heen. 'Ik zeg zo vaak tegen Denny dat je wel een engel lijkt. Je weet wel... met die blonde stralenkrans en zo. Maar nu lijk je er meer op dan ooit.' Ze stootte Denny aan met haar elleboog. 'Vind je niet, Denny?'

De man had zijn handen in zijn zakken en knikte verlegen. 'Ze is heel mooi, dat is waar.'

'Bedankt, jongens. Jullie zien er ook mooi uit.' Abby glimlachte. Complimenten waren fijn. Jammer dat ze zich er niet beter door voelde. 'Het eten staat klaar in de keuken. Laten we de anderen gaan zoeken.'

De maaltijd verliep vrolijk en opgewekt. Aan weerskanten van de tafel brandden kaneelkaarsen en Abby had voor de gelegenheid een kalkoen gebraden. John zat aan het hoofd van de tafel: niet omdat hij daar in het verleden altijd zat, maar omdat het de enige plek was waar de rolstoel paste. Abby probeerde er niet aan te denken.

Kade slikte een hap aardappelpuree door. 'Zeg, pap, een jongen op school vertelde me dat zijn footballcoach de laatste vijf jaar van zijn loopbaan in een rolstoel zat. Hij had een spierstoornis of zoiets.'

Abby wierp een snelle blik op John, maar die zat naar Kade te kijken en knikte peinzend. 'Ik weet het. Het is niet onmogelijk.'

'Nou, dan moet je het doen.' Kade legde zijn vork neer en leunde met zijn ellebogen op tafel.

'Als het anders was, deed ik het misschien.'

Nicole veegde haar mond af. 'Bedoel je de jongens?'

'Ja. En de ouders.' John schudde zijn hoofd. 'Er is op school niets veranderd door mijn letsel. De ouders wilden mijn kop zien rollen, weet je nog? Ik stond op het punt ontslagen te worden toen het ongeluk gebeurde.'

'Ach, pap.' Kade schudde zijn hoofd. 'Ze zouden je nooit ontslaan. Daar ben je veel te goed voor.'

'Dat doet er niet toe.' John nam een grote slok water. 'Als het bestuur niet steunt wat je doet, is het de moeite niet waard.'

'Dus je kapt ermee?' vroeg Kade bedrukt.

John glimlachte droevig. 'Volgende maand schrijf ik mijn ontslagbrief.'

'Nou ja, ik kan alleen maar zeggen: wie ook de hoge piet op die school mag wezen die het voor het zeggen heeft, die moet zich laten nakijken.' Jo had haar eerste bord leeg en schepte zich van alles nog wat op. 'Jou laten gaan is hetzelfde als de grootste regenboogforel aan deze kant van de Mississippi aan de haak slaan en hem loslaten voordat er een foto is gemaakt.' Ze keek de tafel rond. 'Ja, toch?'

Seans vork bleef even in de lucht hangen. 'Wat is een regenboogforel?'

Zelfs Abby lachte, maar Jo stak van wal met een verklaring over de soorten meren waar regenboogforellen voorkwamen en wat voor aas het meest geschikt was om ze mee te vangen.

Toen ze klaar waren met eten, wisselden ze onder de boom in de woonkamer geschenken uit. Ieder één geschenk op kerstavond. Dat was de familieregel. En geen gezoek onder de boom. Het eerste geschenk met je naam erop was het pakje dat je openmaakte.

Volgens de traditie was John de laatste. Hij koos een klein pakje dat toevallig van Jo en Denny afkomstig was. De grond was bezaaid met inpakpapier en iedereen zat naast zijn nieuwe cadeau te kijken hoe John het zijne openmaakte.

Eerst kon Abby niet goed zien wat het was. Maar toen John de verpakking opende, zag ze het duidelijk. Het was een paar handschoenen. Vingerloze handschoenen, zoals sportfietsers dragen.

Of mannen in een rolstoel.

John trok ze aan en maakte de riempjes om zijn polsen vast. 'Geweldig, jongens. Bedankt.'

Maar terwijl hij Matts ouders bedankte, zag Abby tranen in

Nicoles ogen. Jo scheen te bespeuren dat haar geschenk de daarstraks nog zo vrolijke kring een beetje verdrietig maakte. Ze wuifde met haar handen. 'Kijk, Denny en ik zien John altijd als een actief iemand. Hij rent van hot naar her, zodat wij er met z'n allen lui bij lijken, als je snapt wat ik bedoel.' Ze lachte kort, maar het klonk hol.

Denny schoot haar te hulp. 'Wat Jo wil zeggen, is dat we hadden gedacht dat John in de komende weken meer in actie zou komen. Misschien in de rolstoel naar het parcours op school... dat soort dingen.'

'Precies, en die handschoenen... nou ja, het is duidelijk waar ze voor zijn. Anders gaan Johns handen helemaal naar de maan. Dan worden ze eeltig en krijgt hij blaren en worden ze bont en blauw.' Ze keek naar Abby. 'En dat kunnen we niet hebben bij zo'n knappe man als John Reynolds, vind je niet, Abby?'

Daar had je het weer. Iedereen verwachtte van haar dat ze uitkomst bood, dat ze iets bemoedigends en opgewekts zei wat de rest liet herademen. Maar dit keer wist ze niet wat ze moest zeggen. Het was Jo's schuld niet. Denny en zij hadden het goed bedoeld met die handschoenen. Binnenkort kwamen ze waarschijnlijk goed van pas.

Maar op dit moment, nu de Kerst voor de deur stond, wilde Abby niet aan Johns handicap herinnerd worden. Ze wilde pakjes met truien en sjaals en geurtjes. Lievelingsboeken en cd's en snoep.

Geen handschoenen waarmee het makkelijker rondrijden was in een rolstoel.

Toen ze niets kon bedenken om te zeggen, nam Nicole het woord. 'Ze zijn schitterend, Jo.' Ze snufte en veegde een traan weg. 'Ik denk dat we allemaal een beetje droevig zijn omdat papa ze nodig heeft. Maar toch... is het heel attent van jullie.'

'Absoluut.' John keek bewonderend naar zijn opgestoken handen.

'Nou, ik bedoelde er niks mee.' Jo boog haar hoofd. 'Ik vond gewoon dat zijn handen mooi moesten blijven.'

Sean stond op en kwam naast John staan. 'Ze zijn gaaf, pap. Mag ik ze aan als ik ga fietsen?'

Iedereen lachte en de spanning verdween even vlug als hij gekomen was. Abby zuchtte zachtjes. Ze was dankbaar. Ze stond angstaanjagend rood op haar bankrekening met manieren om Johns situatie in een positief licht te bekijken.

En als John in de komende lente over het footballveld hoorde te rennen met zijn spelers, viel er vast helemaal niets positiefs meer te zeggen.

Zelfs niet als iedereen die haar kende op haar rekende.

★

John was als enige wakker. Hij zat aan de voorkant uit het raam te staren en aan kerstfeesten uit het verleden te denken, toen hij een geluid hoorde.

'Pap?' Het was Sean. De zachte voetstappen van de jongen naderden van achteren.

John keek om en zag in het donker de ogen van zijn zoon. 'Ik dacht dat je sliep.' Hij stak een arm uit en Sean kwam naar hem toe.

'Ik kan niet slapen.'

Pas toen zag John dat zijn jongste zoon huilde. 'Wat is er, jongen? Je moet niet huilen op kerstavond.'

'Ik... Alles is zo erg.'

Johns hart brak. Wat hadden ze weinig met elkaar opgetrokken sinds het ongeluk... en toch werd hij natuurlijk ook getroffen door de veranderingen in hun leven. Klaarblijkelijk meer dan John had beseft. 'Bedoel je vanwege mijn benen?'

Sean boog zijn hoofd en perste zijn lippen op elkaar. In het vage maanlicht zag John de boosheid in zijn ogen. 'Het is niet éérlijk, pap!'

John wachtte. Sean had altijd meer tijd nodig dan hun andere kinderen om zijn gevoelens te uiten. Welke kwelling de jongen ook sinds het ongeluk had doorgemaakt, John was blij dat hij eindelijk vertelde wat hij op zijn hart had. 'Ik luister.'

'Ik weet wel dat ik niet aan mezelf moet denken.' Hij haalde zijn schouders op en veegde over zijn ogen. 'Jij bent degene die gewond is. Maar toch…'

'Toch wat?'

Sean sloeg zijn ogen op en keek John recht aan. 'Hoe moet het met *mijn* dromen, pap? Heb je daar wel eens aan gedacht?'

John wist niet goed wat zijn zoon bedoelde. 'Jouw dromen?'

'Ja.' De jongen sloeg zijn armen over elkaar en barstte uit: 'Je hebt Kade gecoacht tot hij naar de derde ging, maar ik? Ik ga over twee jaar naar Marion High, weet je nog? Hoe kan ik voor iemand anders footballen?'

Er ging een wereld voor John open. Natuurlijk… waarom had hij daar niet eerder aan gedacht? Terwijl hij het druk had met revalidatie en wennen aan zijn veranderde leven, had John er niet één keer over nagedacht wat zijn handicap voor Sean betekende. Ze hadden het er vaak over gehad dat John ook Sean zou coachen, zoals hij Kade had gecoacht. Maar tot nu toe had John niet geweten hoezeer de jongen daarop had gerekend. Sean zat pas in de zesde klas. Voor John was de middelbare schooltijd van zijn jongste zoon nog lichtjaren weg.

Maar voor een jongen van elf jaar… stond die vlak voor de deur.

'Sean…' John legde zijn hand om Seans middel en trok hem dichter naar zich toe. 'Het spijt me zo, jochie.'

Sean liet zijn hoofd hangen en huilde. Dit waren tranen die John begreep, tranen van verdriet en frustratie en schuldgevoel om wat hij kennelijk egoïstische gevoelens vond. Hij keek smekend op naar John. 'Hoorde je niet wat Kade vanavond zei? Je kunt coachen in een rolstoel, pap. Dat is niet verboden of zo.'

John schonk de jongen een verdrietig lachje. Het was zoveel ingewikkelder dan dat. Maar zijn zoon had op dit moment geen behoefte aan een lijst met gegevens en bijzonderheden. Hij wilde geloven dat alles goed kwam, dat het leven op de een of andere manier weer prettig zou worden, al zou hij zijn jongensdroom los moeten laten. *Geef me iets om te zeggen, God… iets wat de vrede in zijn hart zal herstellen…*

Toen viel het hem in. Hij schraapte zijn keel. 'Ik zal altijd je coach blijven, Sean. Op het veld of daarbuiten.'

Er veranderde iets in het gezicht van zijn zoon. De boosheid en het verdriet waren nog niet verdwenen, maar er gloorde iets van hoop in zijn blik. 'Echt waar?'

'Natuurlijk. We gaan samen trainen… samen speltechnieken leren.' Johns enthousiasme groeide. Het was waar. Hij mocht zijn Marion High-fluit in de wilgen hangen, maar hij zou nooit ophouden zijn zoons te coachen. Vooral Sean, die nog zoveel footballjaren voor zich had. 'Ik zal je alles leren wat ik Kade heb geleerd.'

Sean richtte zich een beetje op. De zorgelijke rimpels in zijn voorhoofd ontspanden een beetje. 'Zelfs in een rolstoel?'

'Zelfs in een rolstoel.'

Even zeiden ze geen van beiden iets, toen legde Sean zijn hand op Johns schouder en zuchtte. 'Mag ik je iets vertellen, pap?'

John maakte het blonde haar van de jongen in de war. 'Wat je maar wilt.'

'Ik ben zo blij dat je niet dood bent gegaan.'

Tranen prikten in Johns ogen. Opnieuw trof het hem hoe weinig hij de laatste tijd met Sean had gepraat. Dit hadden ze nodig… en nog heel wat vaker. Hij grinnikte. 'Ik ook, jongen.'

Sean boog zich over hem heen en omhelsde hem en ze hielden elkaar een hele tijd vast. Eindelijk stond Sean op en geeuwde. 'Nou… ik ga maar weer naar bed.'

'Ja… straks kom je de kerstman nog tegen als hij stiekem in de kamer komt.'

John was blij toen de jongen lachte. *Dank U, God… Dank U voor deze tijd met mijn zoon.*

'Trusten, pap. Ik houd van je.'

'Ik ook van jou. Tot morgen.'

Sean vertrok en John bleef een lange tijd zitten nadenken over hun gesprek. Het zou heerlijk zijn om Sean te coachen, hij was net zo snel en leergierig als Kade. En John zou zijn belofte nakomen en zo vaak mogelijk met de jongen aan de slag gaan. Niet alleen omdat Sean altijd graag van hem had willen leren, maar omdat hij het eindelijk begreep.

Al stond hij op het punt om ontslag te nemen als coach van de Eagles, zolang hij Sean had, bleef hij coach.

En dat was op zichzelf het mooiste kerstgeschenk dat iemand hem had kunnen geven.

Tweeëntwintig

John had de hele winter tegen dit moment opgezien.

In de eerste week van maart, toen het gras door de smeltende sneeuw heen begon te prikken, wist hij dat het tijd was. Hij had niets gehoord van Herman Lutz of een van de andere bestuursleden, maar het had geen zin om nog langer te wachten. In deze periode werd nieuw personeel voor het volgende schooljaar aangenomen en het schoolbestuur moest het weten. Ze gingen hem niet ontslaan, zoveel had hij wel begrepen na een paar gesprekken met andere leraren. Dit jaar in elk geval niet.

'Ze zijn bang dat het raar overkomt,' had een wiskundeleraar hem verteld. De man had Herman Lutz in januari een keer in het kantoor met de directeur horen praten. 'Ze zeiden dat het publiek woest zou worden als de school je nu ontsloeg. Slechts een paar maanden nadat je verlamd bent geraakt.'

Dus het bestuur was bereid een jaar te wachten, maar ze wilden hem nog steeds weg hebben. Nog steeds hadden ze niet genoeg vertrouwen in hem om te geloven dat hij nooit had goedgevonden dat zijn spelers dronken of straatraces hielden als hij het had geweten. En ze waren nog steeds bereid om te buigen voor de klachten van een paar ouders, in plaats van hem en het werk dat hij op Marion High had gedaan te steunen.

Ja, het was tijd om ontslag te nemen.

John had Abby gevraagd hem te helpen zich die dag warm aan te kleden, met twee hemden en een extra trui. Toen trok hij zijn warmste jack aan en pakte zijn laptop.

'Ik moet een brief schrijven.' Hij knipoogde naar Abby.

Ze wachtte even met haar antwoord. 'Goed. Ik ben hier als je me nodig hebt.'

Hij glimlachte, maar daarmee hield hij haar niet voor de gek. Toen hij de deur uit reed naar de achtertuin, hadden ze allebei tranen in hun ogen. John stond stil en overzag het pad voor hem. Voor de eerste sneeuw was gevallen hadden ze een aannemer in de arm genomen om een cementen pad naar de steiger te gieten. Nu was het geveegd en er was zout gestrooid. Aan weerskanten waren ijsresten opgestapeld.

John vulde zijn longen met de zoete geur van de vroege lente. Zijn therapie had nog steeds niet het resultaat opgeleverd waar hij om gebeden had, maar hij had geleerd om onafhankelijker te zijn. Hij kon nu alleen op de steiger komen. De arts had een nieuwe stoel voorgeschreven, een stoel met een stevige rem binnen handbereik. En zijn bovenlichaam was sterker dan eerst, sterk genoeg om zichzelf heuvels en hellingen op te duwen.

Met zijn laptop op zijn knieën reed hij bijna tot het eind van de steiger, waar hij de rem stevig aantrok. Toen hij de laptop opende, viel zijn blik op zijn benen. Ze waren weggekwijnd, precies zoals de therapeut had gezegd. Voor het ongeluk waren ze twee keer zo stevig als die van Kade geweest. Nu waren ze kleiner en dunner, en John wist dat het niet lang meer zou duren voordat ze weinig meer waren dan huid en botten.

Hij klapte het scherm omhoog, startte de computer op en staarde naar het toetsenbord. Toen het programma klaar was, opende hij een nieuw document en wachtte met zijn vingers boven de toetsen in de aanslag. Wat moest hij zeggen? Hoe kon hij onder woorden brengen dat hij bereid was om zijn levenslange passie op te geven?

Hij begon te typen.

Geachte heer of mevrouw,
Hierbij deel ik u mede dat ik ontslag neem als footballcoach van de schoolploeg op Marion High. Zoals u weet, ben ik sinds de opening

van de school in 1985 coach van de Eagles geweest. In die tijd heb
ik…

Zijn vingers hielden stil.

In die tijd…

Er was zo veel gebeurd sinds hij de baan op Marion had aangenomen. En zelfs al voordien. Wanneer was hij eigenlijk verliefd geworden op het spel? Zijn ogen dwaalden van het scherm naar het meer. Toen hij nog een baby was toch al? Er waren foto's waarop hij een football vasthield voordat hij kon kruipen.

Zijn hoofd stroomde vol met beelden van herinneringen waar hij meer dan tien jaar niet aan had gedacht.

Het leven van zijn vader had om het spel gedraaid, net als het leven van Abby's vader. De twee mannen hadden aan de Universiteit van Michigan gespeeld, waar ze de beste vrienden waren geworden.

Johns vader was na zijn afstuderen bij een bank gaan werken, maar die van Abby niet. Hij was ook football gaan coachen.

'Het zit in mijn bloed.' Hij grijnsde altijd als hij dat zei. 'Ik zou niet weten wat ik moest beginnen als ik niet met football bezig was.'

Zo was het voor John ook geweest. Het was niet belangrijk dat zijn vader zelden praatte over zijn kundigheid op het veld. Toen John oud genoeg was om een uniform te dragen, smeekte hij zijn ouders om hem op te geven. Vanaf het moment dat hij als speler zijn eerste down nam, wist John dat hij het spel zou spelen zolang hij leefde.

Toen zag hij een beeld voor zich… hij was met zijn ouders op bezoek bij Abby en haar ouders in hun huis aan het meer in Lake Geneva, Wisconsin. Hij had Abby al eerder ontmoet, maar dat jaar was hij zeventien geworden en naar de hoogste klas van de middelbare school gegaan. Zij was veertien jaar en zat in de eerste.

Maar ze was de dochter van een footballcoach en dat was te

zien aan alles wat ze deed. Ze kon beter gooien en vangen dan de meeste jongens van haar leeftijd en met z'n tweeën stonden ze uren op het strand over te gooien, met hun blote voeten in het zand.

'Niet slecht voor een meisje,' had John haar geplaagd.

Ze had haar kin in de lucht gestoken. Ze was niet onder de indruk van oudere jongens, want haar vader coachte er elk jaar wel een stuk of zestig op de middelbare school. John wist dat het team vaak bij coach Chapman thuis rondhing om in het meer te zwemmen of kip van de barbecue te eten.

Hij herinnerde zich Abby's antwoord van die middag nog goed. Ze had John met schitterende ogen aangekeken. 'En jij bent niet zo gek voor een *jochie.*'

John had hard gelachen, zo hard dat hij uiteindelijk achter haar aan ging om haar te kietelen en haar in de waan liet dat ze aan hem kon ontsnappen. In werkelijkheid kon hij toen al rennen als de wind. Net als zijn vader was John een beroemde quarterback geworden, die aanbiedingen kreeg van een tiental grote universiteiten, waaronder de universiteit van hun vaders, Michigan.

Op een avond namen de twee gezinnen dekens mee naar het meer en maakte haar vader een kampvuur. Ze zongen liederen over God. Niet de gebruikelijke onzinliedjes van rond het kampvuur, zoals Old MacDonald, maar mooie liederen over vrede, blijdschap en liefde en een God Die veel om hen allemaal gaf. Toen het zingen ophield en de volwassenen in hun eigen gesprekken opgingen, kwam John naast haar zitten en stootte haar met zijn elleboog aan.

'Heb jij een vriendje, juffie Chapman?' Hij grinnikte en stelde zich voor hoe ze er over vijf of tien jaar uit zou zien.

Ze hield zich met gemak staande. 'Ik heb geen vriendje nodig.' Ze tikte met haar blote voet tegen de zijne.

Hij tikte terug. 'Echt waar?' Hij grijnsde breed.

'Ja.' Ze hield haar hoofd iets hoger en keek hem recht in de ogen. 'Jongens kunnen heel onvolwassen doen.' Ze keek hem onderzoekend aan. 'Laat me raden... jij hebt zeker elke week een ander vriendinnetje? Dat is bij de quarterbacks van mijn vader ook zo.'

John lachte hard voordat hij haar weer aankeek en antwoord gaf op haar vraag. 'Dan ben ik zeker anders.'

Abby's ogen werden groot van gespeelde verbazing. 'Wat? Heeft John Reynolds geen vriendin?'

Hij pakte zijn football, die hij de hele zomer onder handbereik hield, en gooide een paar keer losjes op. '*Dit* is mijn vriendin.'

Abby knikte speels. 'Een volmaakte danspartner voor je eindexamenbal.'

Hij gaf haar weer een tik tegen haar voet en keek verontwaardigd. 'Sst, je beledigt haar.'

John knipperde met zijn ogen en de herinnering vervaagde.

Na die zomer was John er zeker van dat hij eens met Abby Chapman zou trouwen. Niet dat hij een bewust besluit had genomen, zoals naar welke universiteit je ging of welk hoofdvak je koos. Het was meer iets wat groeide in zijn hart, gewoon een vaststaande waarheid.

Maar omdat dat nog ver in de toekomst lag, had John zich met hart en ziel op zijn eerste liefde gestort: football. Vooral in het jaar daarop, toen hij een beurs kreeg voor de Universiteit van Michigan.

John stak zijn kin een eindje in de lucht en speurde langs de toppen van de bomen. Hoe ver had hij in die tijd kunnen gooien? Zestig meter? Zeventig? Hij sloot zijn ogen en dacht aan het gevoel van de aarde onder zijn voeten, de explosieve stuwkracht van iedere stap als hij uit de pocket vloog, op zoek naar een receiver verderop in het veld.

Zijn ouders sloegen nooit een wedstrijd over, maar één wedstrijd stond hem nog altijd helder voor de geest. Het was aan het eind van zijn eindexamenjaar, een wedstrijd tegen Michigans grootste rivaal, Ohio. Michigan won die middag met drie touchdowns en na de wedstrijd had John met zijn vader door de buurt gewandeld en waren ze op en oud bankje in Allmendinger Park gaan zitten.

'Het is zo fijn om je op het veld bezig te zien, jongen. Om te zien hoe je dat team leidt zoals ik jaren geleden heb gedaan.'

Johns vader was zelden in een bedachtzame stemming, maar die middag was anders. John zweeg en liet zijn vader het woord doen.

'Soms is het alsof ik naar mezelf kijk, elke stap, elke worp... alsof ik het allemaal nog een keer doe en helemaal opnieuw beleef.'

'Het is het mooiste wat er is.'

'Ja.' Toen was zijn vader volgeschoten, iets wat John maar een paar keer in zijn leven had gezien. 'Beslist. Op het veld... beleef je met je team een toneelstuk, een veldslag, zo rijk en krachtig dat alleen een andere speler het kan begrijpen.'

'Ja.'

'En de tijd is een dief, jongen. Je krijgt maar een bepaald aantal downs, een bepaald aantal fluitsignalen. Een bepaald aantal wedstrijden. Voordat je het weet, ben je volwassen geworden en zie je je eigen zoon spelen. Dan zul je begrijpen wat ik bedoel.'

Natuurlijk had zijn vader uiteindelijk gelijk gehad. Johns jaren als footballer van Michigan vlogen voorbij en aan het eind van zijn laatste wedstrijd als laatstejaars, scheurde hij zijn kniebanden. De scouts die hem eerder dat jaar hadden gebeld, lieten na zijn blessure niets meer van zich horen en niemand hoefde hem te vertellen hoe het ervoor stond. De waarheid was even duidelijk als zijn aanstaande afstuderen.

Zijn dagen als footballspeler waren geteld.

John bewaarde de band van zijn laatste wedstrijd in de archief-kast van zijn hoofd. Hij wist nog hoe hij in de kleedkamer zijn uitrusting had aangetrokken en grappen had gemaakt met zijn teamgenoten alsof ze alle tijd van de wereld hadden.

Vier spelperiodes later zat John op de bank met zijn knie in drie rollen verband toen het eindsignaal klonk. Zelfs nu nog wist hij hoe vreemd dat was. Hoe zijn teamgenoten en hij tot dat fluitsignaal maar één ding in gedachten hadden: Illinois verslaan.

Ze hadden een overwinning nodig om dat jaar mee te kunnen dingen naar de bowl. Maar na Johns blessure kreeg Illinois een punt voor een touchdown en Michigan kwam nooit meer aan de leiding. In de verdrietige stilte die volgde, drong de waarheid tot hem door.

Het was voorbij. De wedstrijd, het seizoen... en John Reynolds' loopbaan.

John had naar de tribunes gekeken, naar de weglopende mensen, en zich afgevraagd wat ze dachten. Volgend jaar beter? Of wat mankeert de Wolverines? Wat ze ook dachten, slechts één man wist hoe John zich die middag voelde... hoe het voelde om zestien seizoenen achter elkaar een wedstrijd te spelen en dat het voorbij was in de tijd die een scheidsrechter nodig had om op een fluitje te blazen. Slechts één man wist hoeveel pijn het John deed, de man die hem een uur later omhelsde nadat hij zijn uniform had ingeleverd, gedoucht had en zich verkleed. Een man die niets zei terwijl hij stil treurde om het feit dat het allemaal definitief en plotseling voorbij was.

Zijn vader.

John slikte en herinnerde zich hoe trots zijn vader was geweest toen hij hem die middag in 1985 opbelde om hem het nieuws te vertellen.

'Ik ben aangenomen, pap! Ik ben hoofdcoach op Marion High.'

'Zo, op Marion?'

'Ja. Het is een splinternieuwe school en ik zit stampvol met ideeën. Ik ga daar een programma opbouwen, pap. Nieuw en anders en beter dan in de hele staat.'

'Nieuwe programma's zijn lastig, jongen. Heb je met Abby's vader gepraat?'

'Nog niet. En je hebt gelijk.' John had zijn enthousiasme amper kunnen intomen. 'Ik weet dat het lastig zal zijn. Maar dat kan me niet schelen. We hebben goeie jongens in deze stad, goeie leraren. Een goed bestuur. We beginnen van onder af aan en over een paar jaar spelen we in de competitie. En daarna, wie weet?'

'Is Abby er blij mee?'

'Nog blijer dan ik. Ze zegt dat ze persberichten over het team gaat schrijven voor de krant en een fanclub gaat oprichten. En als Kade oud genoeg is, neem ik hem mee naar de training.'

Zijn vader had gelachen. 'Kade is nog maar twee jaar, jongen.'

'Maar hij kan al lopen. Dit jaar nog laat ik hem met Abby meekomen naar de training.'

'Goed, maar vergeet niet wat ik gezegd heb.'

'Waarover?'

'Over hoe het voelt als je je zoon ziet spelen. Ik hoop dat ik het nog mag meemaken.' Zijn vader lachte weer. 'Jouw tijd komt nog.'

En die was gekomen... maar niet op tijd voor zijn vader. Vier jaar nadat John de baan op Marion had gekregen, stierf zijn vader aan een hartaanval. Alleen Abby wist hoe groot Johns verlies was. Dat hij niet alleen een vader miste, maar ook een mentor en een coach. En vooral een vriend.

Football coachen was het medicijn voor Johns verdriet. Het bleek haast even opwindend als meespelen in de wedstrijd. Maar er was één heel fijn verschil. De tijd van een speler was beperkt. Een paar jaar op de middelbare school, een paar jaar op de universiteit voor degenen met talent.

Dat gold niet voor een coach.

Elk jaar speelde een groep eindexamenleerlingen met tranen in hun ogen hun laatste wedstrijd voor Marion High. En als het herfst werd, kwam John met zijn personeel terug, heette een nieuwe oogst eerstejaars welkom en maakte plannen voor een nieuw seizoen. John was van plan om coach te blijven tot zijn pensioen. Minstens.

Zelfs in de moeilijke jaren op Marion had hij dat gedacht, de jaren waarin de ouders mopperden dat hij niet snel genoeg wedstrijden won en dat er misschien iemand anders moest worden aangenomen voor de baan. Maar die seizoenen leidden tot Johns eerste regiokampioenschap in 1989.

Toen was iedereen op Marion dol op John. En in 1997 sloot Kade zich aan bij het team. Pas toen begreep John wat zijn vader had bedoeld op die dag in Allmendinger Park.

Als hij Kade zag spelen, speet hem maar één ding: dat zijn vader het niet meer kon meemaken. Kade was alles wat zijn vader en grootvader waren geweest, en meer. Hij was langer en sneller. John kon de keren niet tellen dat hij ademloos had toegekeken hoe Kade zich opstelde, een tactiekwijziging schreeuwde en in de pocket uithaalde om de bal af te vuren naar een receiver.

Zijn vader had gelijk gehad.

Als hij naar Kade keek, voelde hij bijna hoe de stootkussens langs zijn schouders schoven, rook hij het malse gras onder zijn voeten. Het was een bedwelmende ervaring, die alleen overtroffen werd door op het veld te staan en mee te spelen in de wedstrijd.

De huidige problemen op Marion waren die zomer pas begonnen, een paar maanden nadat Kade zijn einddiploma had gehaald.

John verplaatste zijn blik weer naar het water.

Wat zou zijn vader hebben gevonden van het gedrag van zijn spelers en de ouders dit jaar? Zou hij het erg gevonden hebben? Zou het afgedaan hebben aan het spel? En dan was er nog datgene waar John het minst van alles aan wilde denken.

Hoe zou zijn vader met Johns ontslag zijn omgegaan?

Het zou hem verpletterd hebben om John in een rolstoel te zien zitten en te weten dat John nooit meer zou kunnen lopen of rennen. En het zou hem zeker verdriet hebben gedaan dat ouders probeerden John eruit te werken. Maar hoe zou hij het gevonden hebben dat John wilde aftreden als coach? Weg wilde gaan zonder om te kijken?

John haalde diep adem en richtte zijn blik weer op zijn laptop. Zijn vader zou het begrijpen. Omdat hij wist dat John het coachen maar om één reden op zou geven: als het spel veranderd was.

En dat was het.

Ja, zijn vader zou hem volkomen hebben gesteund. Zijn vader

zou begrijpen hoe moeilijk het was om de ontslagbrief te schrijven. En toen John zijn vingers weer op het toetsenbord zette, toen hij de kracht vond om te doen wat hij nooit gedacht had te zullen doen, voelde hij zich van één ding overtuigd.

Zijn vader wist wat er allemaal gebeurd was en zelfs nu, op het moeilijkste moment van Johns footballloopbaan, juichte zijn vader hem toe zoals hij Johns hele leven had gedaan.

Drieëntwintig

John maakte de brief net af toen Abby bij hem kwam staan op de aanlegsteiger.

Haar ogen waren rood, alsof ze had gehuild. Ze slenterde naar hem toe en trok een bankje naast zijn rolstoel. 'Klaar?'

'Ja.' Hij typte zijn naam. 'Net.'

Ze keek uit over het meer. 'Er wordt een hoofdstuk afgesloten.'

'Dat kun je wel zeggen.' Hij pakte haar hand en vlocht zijn vingers door de hare. 'Gaat het?'

Ze hield haar tanden op elkaar geklemd, maar zuchtte vermoeid. Ze wendde zich naar hem toe en hij zag iets wat hij in maanden niet had gezien: pure, onmiskenbare boosheid. Ze deed haar mond open, maar er kwam niet meteen iets uit. Toen vernauwde ze haar ogen. 'Nee, het gaat niet.'

Hij vermoedde al langer dat het met Abby niet zo goed ging als ze voordeed. Hij vroeg nu en dan hoe ze zich voelde, maar ze zei altijd hetzelfde. Het ging best… ze was dankbaar… ze was gelukkiger dan ooit. Zo blij dat hij nog leefde… zo blij dat hun huwelijk weer zo was als toen ze nog jong waren.

Het klonk allemaal mooi, maar niet bepaald oprecht. Niet dat John haar niet geloofde. Ergens diep vanbinnen meende Abby alle positieve dingen die ze zei. Maar ze was gevoelig en John had het vreemd gevonden dat ze in hun grootste lichamelijke uitdaging als echtpaar passief en dociel zou zijn. Hij wachtte tot ze verder ging.

'John, ik heb alles gedaan wat ik kon om dit zo makkelijk mogelijk te maken voor jou en de kinderen en… nou ja, voor zo'n beetje iedereen die we kennen.' Ze haalde haar schouders op en boog zich naar voren, ze zette haar ellebogen op haar bovenbenen. 'Maar ik weet niet of ik het nog wel kan.'

John voelde een flits van paniek door zich heen gaan. Ze kon het niet meer? Waar wilde ze heen? 'Goed. Wil je je nader verklaren?'

Abby klemde haar handen tot vuisten en vervolgde knarsetandend: 'Ik ben zo woest, John! Ik ben zo woest dat ik het niet kan verdragen.' Ze opende haar vuisten en maakte cirkels met haar handen. 'Er wordt een tornado in me opgebouwd. Elke dag ben ik woester dan de vorige.'

John koos zijn woorden zorgvuldig. 'Op wie ben je woest?'

'Ik weet het niet!' zei Abby hard en ziedend. 'Ik ben woest op jou omdat je die avond op school bent gebleven terwijl je thuis had moeten zijn.' Ze stond op en liep met grote stappen naar het einde van de steiger en terug, haar armen strak over elkaar geslagen. 'Ik ben woest op Jake omdat hij je aangereden heeft en op de artsen omdat ze je niet beter hebben kunnen maken. Ik ben woest omdat niemand eraan denkt dat ik hier wel eens woest om zou kunnen zijn.' Ze liet haar handen langs haar zijden vallen. 'En ik ben woest op God omdat Hij het heeft laten gebeuren.'

John beet op zijn lip. 'Ben je woest op mij?'

Zijn vraag overrompelde haar en ongewild ontsnapte er een lachje tussen haar tanden door. Onmiddellijk beheerste ze zich weer. 'John, niet doen.'

'Wat niet doen?'

'Je hoort me naar dat laatste te vragen… dat ik woest ben op God.'

'Ik weet het niet.' John trok één schouder op en leunde achterover in zijn stoel. 'Ik kan begrijpen dat je woest bent op God. Ik ben ook wel eens woest op God.' Hij hield zijn hoofd schuin en kneep zijn ogen halfdicht. 'Maar ik? Kom op, Abby. Wat heb *ik* gedaan?'

Ze blies hard uit. 'Je had met me mee naar huis moeten gaan, *dat* heb je gedaan.' Ze gaf hem een duwtje tegen zijn schouder. 'Dan was dit allemaal niet gebeurd.'

'O ja… nou, dat is waar.'

'Maakt niet uit, snertvent. Nou is het *mijn* beurt om kwaad te zijn.' Abby maakte een geluid dat meer op lachen leek dan huilen, en ze gaf hem nog een duw. Nu ving hij haar hand en trok haar op zijn benen. Ze liet de laptop onder zich uit glijden en zette hem op de steiger. Tegelijkertijd maakte hij de rem van zijn rolstoel los.

'John!' gilde ze. 'Wat doe je? Straks vallen we allebei in het meer.'

Hij greep de wielen vast en draaide de stoel vlak voordat ze over de rand van de steiger doken. 'Wat krijgen we nou? Heeft mijn schone maagd geen vertrouwen in me?'

Ze greep zijn overhemd vast en hij lachte. 'John, houd op! Je bent gek geworden.'

Maar hij reed hen tweeën naar het uiterste puntje van de steiger, draaide weer om en liet de stoel door de zwaartekracht terugrollen over de houten planken naar het water. Abby gilde weer en probeerde zich te bevrijden, maar John hield haar stevig vast, met één hand om haar middel en één hand op het wiel van zijn stoel. 'Neem het terug.'

Ze waren halverwege de steiger en het ging hard. 'Wat?' Abby's stem was een schrille mengeling van afgrijzen en opwinding.

'Zeg dat je niet woest op me bent.'

'Goed!' Het water kwam dichterbij. 'Ik ben niet woest op je.'

In één enkele vloeiende beweging, even sierlijk als hij vroeger een football had gegooid, greep John beide wielen vast en liet de stoel vaart minderen en een beheerste draai maken. Toen ze een hele cirkel hadden gemaakt, zette hij de handrem vast en sloeg beide armen om Abby heen. Haar ogen waren groot en ze hijgde om op adem te komen.

'Dat was het krankzinnigste wat je ooit hebt gedaan, John Reynolds.' Ze duwde weer tegen zijn schouders, nu harder dan daarstraks. 'Als je nou niet op tijd had kunnen stoppen?'

'Ik had het onder controle, Abby.' Hij sprak zacht, de plagerige toon was uit zijn stem verdwenen. 'Net als jij je emoties in de afgelopen maanden.'

Ze verstarde en hij zag tranen in haar ogen opwellen. 'Was het zo duidelijk?'

'Natuurlijk.'

Ze zuchtte vermoeid. 'Ik durfde je niet te vertellen hoe ik me voelde.'

'Waarom niet? Daar heb je nooit eerder last van gehad. Zelfs niet toen we in onmin leefden.'

Ze liet haar hoofd tegen zijn borst vallen. 'Omdat ik bang was dat je niet zou herstellen als je wist hoe van streek ik was.'

'Nee.' Hij wachtte en koos zijn woorden met zorgvuldige precisie. 'Ik zal nooit herstellen als jij jezelf niet kunt zijn, Abby. We mogen niet doen alsof alles in orde is, snap je dat niet? Er zullen dagen zijn dat je het geen minuut langer kunt verdragen dat je me moet helpen met aankleden... dagen waarop je wel uit wilt schreeuwen dat je zo kwaad bent. Maar er zullen ook dagen zijn dat ik me net zo voel. Hoe opgewekt we ons ook voordoen. Alleen als we eerlijk zijn, kunnen we dit doorstaan. Begrijp je?'

'John...' Er biggelden tranen over haar wangen. 'Ik ben zo woest dat dit jou is overkomen. Het is niet eerlijk. Het is gewoon niet eerlijk.'

'Weet ik, schat.' Hij koesterde haar dicht tegen zich aan en streelde haar rug. 'Weet ik.'

Ze bracht haar gezicht naar het zijne en droogde haar tranen af aan zijn wangen. 'Ik wil weer dansen. Heb jij dat gevoel nooit?'

'Voortdurend.' Hij maakte de handrem weer los en rolde weer met haar naar het verste puntje van de steiger.

'John... wat doe je?' Haar lichaam verstrakte in zijn armen. 'Niet weer naar beneden! We vallen erin, hoor!'

'Nee, Abby.' Ze waren boven aan de steiger en hij draaide de rolstoel naar het water. 'Leun maar lekker tegen me aan en ontspan.'

Ze aarzelde en even dacht hij dat ze van zijn schoot zou springen. 'Meen je het echt?'

'Ja.' Hij klopte op zijn borst. 'Kom, leun tegen me aan.'

'Wat gaan we doen?'

'Dit is een soort tangodanspas. Ik heb erop geoefend.' Hij liet Abby tegen zich aan rusten zodat ze allebei naar voren keken. 'Goed… nu moet je alles loslaten… je boosheid, je frustratie… alles. Anders werkt de dans niet.'

Ze giechelde en dat geluid deed wonderen in zijn hart. 'Goed. Ik ben klaar.'

John liet de handrem los en de stoel rolde over de steiger naar het water. Abby begon harder te lachen en ze drukte haar rug tegen hem aan. 'Het is best leuk als je niet bang bent.'

'Dat is altijd zo met de tango.'

'Parmantige Paula zou trots op ons zijn.'

De stoel kreeg vaart en ze begonnen harder te lachen tot John een paar meter van het water inhield en omdraaide voor een laatste werveling. Daarna liet hij hem heen en weer zigzaggen en fluisterde zacht in Abby's oor. 'Hoor je het?'

'Mmmmm.' Haar tevreden gespin klonk diep tegen zijn borst. 'Ik geloof van wel.'

'De danspassen kunnen veranderen, Abby.' Hij kuste haar oorlelletje. 'Maar de muziek blijft spelen.'

Zo bleven ze deinen op de wind en het ruisen van nog kale takken, totdat Abby ten slotte verschoof op een van zijn knieën en hem lang en traag kuste. 'Weet je?'

'Nou?'

'Ik ben niet boos meer. Nu niet in elk geval.'

'Zie je nou… de tango, Abby.' Hij wreef zijn neus tegen de hare. 'Werkt altijd.'

'Nee.' Hun lippen vonden elkaar weer en weer. 'Jouw liefde werkt altijd.'

John wilde haar net nog een zoen geven toen het gebeurde. Het was zo kort en vluchtig dat John aarzelde of het wel iets was. Maar toen... hij bleef doodstil zitten. Waar kon het anders door komen?

Abby ging een beetje achteruit. 'Wat is er, John? Je maakt me bang.'

Hij haalde diep adem en concentreerde zich op de plek waar hij het had gevoeld. En alsof God hem wilde laten weten dat het niet nep was en geen hersenspinsel, voelde hij het nog een keer. Een soort scheut of brandend gevoel in zijn grote teen. Een plek waar hij sinds het ongeluk niets meer had gevoeld.

'Abby, je zult het niet geloven.' Hij keek haar strak aan, door de buitenkant heen naar het hart van deze vrouw die hij liefhad.

'Wat? Zeg het dan.' Abby leunde verder achterover en nam hem van top tot teen op. 'Is er iets?'

'Nee.' Hij wees naar zijn voet, zijn hart bonsde hard tegen de wand van zijn borst. 'Daarnet, een paar seconden geleden... gebeurde er iets. Iets wat ik niet kan verklaren.'

'Wat dan?' Ze klom van hem af en bleef onderzoekend naar zijn benen staan kijken.

Ineens besefte hij dat het belachelijk klonk wat hij op het punt stond te zeggen. Misschien was het maar fantoompijn. Hij had gelezen dat iemand maanden of zelfs jaren na een verlamming de herinnering aan gevoel kon krijgen.

Hij mocht niets zeggen wat haar valse hoop zou geven, die de bodem ingeslagen zou worden als het niets bleek te zijn. Binnenkort vertelde hij het haar, maar nu nog niet. Abby stond hem afwachtend aan te kijken. *Nadenken, John... kom op... verzin iets.*

'Nou...' Hij glimlachte breed naar haar. 'Ik geloof dat we een nieuwe danspas hebben uitgevonden.'

Abby blies hard uit. 'John, ik dacht dat je pijn had... of dat je niet kon ademen of zo.'

Hij lachte en verborg de opwinding die hij vanbinnen voelde. 'Nee, hoor. Dat weet je toch wel, Abby? Dansen is goed voor de longen.' Hij klopte op zijn borst. 'Na zo'n dansje als we net hebben gemaakt, kan ik dagenlang goed doorademen.'

'Wat ben je toch een plaaggeest.' Abby pakte zijn hand en samen begaven ze zich over de steiger naar huis. 'Dat moet je niet doen. Ik dacht echt dat er iets aan de hand was.'

Ze waren halverwege de tuin toen het weer gebeurde. Dit keer had John geen enkele twijfel aan wat hij voelde. Dit was geen fantoompijn, geen herinnering aan vroegere sensatie. Hij voelde een brandende scheut in zijn teen. En dit keer gebeurde er nog iets. Iets wat hij amper voor zich kon houden.

Zijn teen bewoog!

John had geen idee wat dat betekende of waarom het gebeurde. Maar hij had het merkwaardige gevoel dat iets, of Iemand, aan zijn ruggengraat werkte. Het voelde anders dan de handen van een arts of een therapeut.

Het voelde als de vingers van God Zelf.

Vierentwintig

Chuck Parker was net binnen toen de telefoon ging.

Hij was verzekeringsagent en de afgelopen winter had hij het druk gehad: drukker dan ooit in zijn leven. Niet alleen gingen de zaken goed, maar nu Caseys rijbewijs voor een jaar was ingenomen, moest Chuck of zijn vrouw de jongen overal naartoe brengen.

Het ergste van de drukte was dat Chuck geen tijd had gehad om de vergadering te organiseren. Aldoor sinds hij te weten was gekomen dat de coach verlamd was, wilde Chuck een groepsdiscussie op school over de manier waarop ze coach Reynolds dit afgelopen seizoen hadden behandeld. Hij had een paar telefoontjes gepleegd, maar van vergaderen was het nog niet gekomen. Tijd was de moeilijkheid. Hij had zoveel op zijn bordje liggen, dat het hem gewoon was ontschoten.

Maar geen zorgen. Zolang hij en de andere ouders geen druk meer uitoefenden op Herman Lutz, liep de baan van coach Reynolds geen gevaar. Misschien hoefden ze niet eens te vergaderen. Als de coach komende herfst terugkwam, zag hij vanzelf dat iedereen was veranderd na wat er gebeurd was. De spelers, de leerlingen. Zelfs de ouders.

De telefoon ging drie keer over voordat Chuck opnam. 'Hallo?'

'Meneer Parker? Met Sue Diver van Marion High.'

Sue Diver… Chuck pijnigde zijn hersens. O, ja. Sue. De secretaresse van de school. Had in '98 een levensverzekering bij hem afgesloten. Hij keek op zijn horloge. Hij had drie avondafspraken, waarvan de eerste over een halfuur begon. 'Dag Sue… wat is er?'

'Er is vandaag een brief gekomen.' Haar stem klonk zacht en zorgelijk.

'O…'

'Ik weet niet of ik u dit wel mag vertellen.'

'Dat is vast wel in orde, Sue. Anders had je geen behoefte gehad om te bellen.'

Zijn woorden leken te werken. Hij hoorde haar diep ademhalen. 'Het is een ontslagbrief van coach Reynolds. Hij neemt met onmiddellijke ingang ontslag. Hij zegt dat het spel aan hem voorbij is gegaan… en dat de ouders hem niet langer respecteren.'

Wat? Chuck kreeg het gevoel of de grond onder hem het begaf. Waarom had hij de vergadering niet eerder belegd? Nu was het te laat. Als Herman Lutz de brief had gelezen, zette hij de baan van coach Reynolds binnen vierentwintig uur op de vacaturelijst. Hij zou denken dat de mensen dat wilden.

Alleen was dat helemaal niet waar. Nu niet meer.

Hij deed zijn ogen dicht en kneep met duim en wijsvinger in zijn neusbrug. 'Ik moet een paar telefoonnummers van je hebben, Sue. Kun je me de namen en nummers geven van alle teamleden?'

'Ik denk van wel.'

'Mooi.' Hij keek naar de stapel mappen die klaarlagen voor zijn afspraken. 'Ik zal vanavond nog bellen. Wanneer is er plek in de schoolagenda?'

Hij hoorde papieren ritselen. 'Vandaag is het maandag, even kijken…' Nog meer geritsel. 'Donderdagavond?'

Chuck keek in zijn agenda. Hij had die avond vier afspraken staan. 'Prima. Zet maar op zeven uur. In de aula.'

'Goed. Ik zal het even met het bestuur kortsluiten, maar dat moet geen probleem zijn. Ouders mogen het gebouw gebruiken voor vergaderingen die verband houden met de school.'

Sue klonk bezorgd, alsof ze zichzelf probeerde te overtuigen. Maar dat deed niet terzake. Nadat hij het maanden voor zich uitgeschoven had, had Chuck de vergadering gepland. Nu moest hij alleen de telefoonnummers nog hebben. 'Heb je die nummers in de buurt?'

'Eh… zal ik u de lijst even faxen?'

'Graag.' Chuck noemde zijn faxnummer. 'Ik zie het wel. En Sue, bedankt voor de tip. We moeten een dezer dagen een keer afspreken om te kijken of we je polis kunnen opvijzelen.'

'Goed, meneer Parker. Nu moet ik ophangen.'

Zodra Chuck had opgehangen, begon zijn faxmachine te rinkelen. Chuck pleegde vlug drie telefoontjes om zijn afspraken af te zeggen. Met de lijst telefoonnummers in zijn hand, haalde hij diep adem en begon te bellen.

★

John wilde Abby geen hoop geven.

Maar voordat ze die avond naar bed gingen, meldde hij terloops dat hij gauw naar de dokter moest.

'Waarom?' Abby had hem in bed geholpen en was nu bezig zich klaar te maken om naar bed te gaan.

'Ik maak me zorgen over mijn benen.' John probeerde ontspannen te kijken. 'Ze zijn te dun.'

'Schat…' Abby keek hem bedroefd aan. 'De dokter heeft toch gezegd dat dat zou gebeuren. Het is normaal.'

John zocht naar een manier om haar te overtuigen. 'Zo dun toch niet… en niet zo vlug.' Hij drukte de dekens neer op zijn benen. Daarbij bewoog zijn rechterteen een heel klein beetje. 'Ik kwijn weg, Abby. Dat moet de dokter weten.'

'Vind je?' Ze keek verbaasd. 'Nou, als je er zo over denkt. Morgenochtend zal ik dokter Furin bellen.'

De volgende dag zat John na het ontbijt in de keuken koffie te drinken, waar Abby hem vond. 'Hij kan je vandaag om elf uur ontvangen.'

'Mooi.' Hij blies in zijn dampende koffie. 'Hij kan er vast wel iets aan doen.'

'Vind je het goed als ik je afzet?' Abby ruimde als een razende de keuken op en sorteerde een stapel papieren op het aanrecht. 'We moeten een paar boodschappen hebben.'

'Goed. Best... Ik ga wel in de wachtkamer zitten tot je terugkomt.' Wat een geluk! Het laatste wat hij wilde was over zijn tenen praten waar Abby bij was. De afgelopen maanden waren heel moeilijk voor haar geweest en het had geen zin om haar valse hoop te geven.

Twee uur later zat John in de onderzoekkamer toen dokter Furin binnenwandelde. 'Meneer Reynolds... ik heb begrepen dat u bezorgd bent over het slijtageproces van uw benen.'

John lachte kort. 'Dat is het eigenlijk helemaal niet. Ik kon alleen...' Hij toomde zijn enthousiasme in om helderder te kunnen denken. 'Ik kon Abby de echte reden niet vertellen waarom ik u wilde spreken. Ik wilde haar geen valse hoop geven.'

'Goed.' Dokter Furin legde zijn klembord neer naast de wastafel. 'Wat is de echte reden?'

Er brak een glimlach uit op Johns gezicht. 'Ik voel iets in mijn rechterteen.' Hij stak een hand op. 'Niet voortdurend en niet veel. Maar gisteren een paar keer en vandaag weer. Een soort brandend gevoel, een flits van pijn, zoiets. En ik heb de teen een paar keer voelen bewegen.'

Dokter Furins mond hing open. 'Méént u dat?'

'Helemaal. U bent de eerste aan wie ik het vertel.'

De arts stond op en beende naar het raam en terug, met langzame, weloverwogen passen. 'Toen we voor het eerst uw röntgenfoto's bekeken, leek het er even op dat u een van de gelukkigen was. Uw breuk zat in een gebied waarin mensen soms gevoel terugkrijgen. Maar gewoonlijk gebeurt dat binnen een paar dagen, nadat de zwelling afneemt.'

Hij liep nog wat heen en weer, streek over zijn kin en keek met een lege blik naar de grond. 'Bij u kwam het gevoel niet terug, daarom hebben we meer foto's gemaakt en meer onderzoeken gedaan. En daarna zag het ernaaruit dat ik ongelijk had. Dat de breuk misschien maar een haarbreedte in het gebied zat waar verlamming blijvend is.'

John keek de arts nadenkend aan. 'Waarom voel ik dan iets in mijn rechterteen?'

'In alle jaren dat ik werk met mensen met ruggenmergletsel, heb ik nooit een patiënt behandeld van wie de breuk zo dicht bij de scheidslijn zat. Een fractie hoger en een mens loopt weer. Een fractie lager en je zit voor de rest van je leven in een rolstoel. Maar misschien…'

John wachtte tot hij het geen minuut meer uithield. 'Wat?'

'Recent onderzoek heeft uitgewezen dat een breuk in enkele zeldzame gevallen zo dicht bij de scheidslijn zit, dat het ruggenmerg operatief weer verbonden kan worden. Soms kan na een operatie het gevoel worden hersteld. Al scheen iemand voor de rest van zijn leven verlamd te zijn.'

Dit was meer dan John had durven hopen. Met bevende handen keek hij dokter Furin aan. 'En denkt u dat ik misschien een van die mensen ben?'

'We zullen onderzoeken moeten doen, maar als ik me goed herinner is het eerste symptoom gevoel in een of meer tenen. En ik ben er zeker van dat uw breuk zit in het gebied waar wetenschappelijk onderzoek naar wordt gedaan.'

John had zin om zijn vuist in de lucht te steken en het uit te schreeuwen van blijdschap. Maar hij hield zich in en richtte zijn gedachten op God. *God… dank U. Dank U voor deze tweede kans.* Hij popelde om met de onderzoeken te beginnen. Hij wilde alles doen wat nodig was. Want als een operatie het gevoel in zijn benen kon herstellen, wilde hij desnoods diezelfde middag nog onder het mes.

'Kunt u een poosje blijven?'

John lachte. 'Opereer me meteen maar, dokter! Ik ben er klaar voor!'

Dokter Furin fronste. 'U moet wel weten dat er geen garantie is dat de operatie lukt, ook al bent u kandidaat. Het wetenschappelijk onderzoek is nog te nieuw. Tot nu toe ziet het ernaaruit dat slechts ongeveer de helft van de mensen die een operatie ondergaan ooit weer gevoel in de ledematen krijgt.'

'Nou, die kans is heel wat meer dan ik had toen ik hier binnenkwam. Wanneer kunnen we met de onderzoeken beginnen?'

'Ik wil graag meer foto's maken en een paar specifieke onderzoeken doen, die in het ziekenhuis moeten gebeuren. Normaal gesproken duurt het weken voordat je aan de beurt bent, maar er heeft vandaag iemand afgezegd.' Hij aarzelde. 'Ik vind wel dat u uw vrouw moet vertellen wat er aan de hand is. De onderzoeken nemen het grootste deel van de middag in beslag en ze moet u naar het ziekenhuis brengen.'

John knikte. Hoe zou ze reageren? Zou ze bang zijn voor een teleurstelling? Bezorgd? Blij? Hoe dan ook, de arts had gelijk. Het werd tijd dat ze het wist.

Dokter Furin nam een reeks röntgenfoto's en een halfuur later zat John in de onderzoekkamer toen Abby binnenkwam. 'Sorry.' Ze boog zich over hem heen en kuste zijn wang. 'Het duurde langer dan ik dacht.'

'Abby... ga zitten.' Hij wees naar een vouwstoel die tegen de muur stond. 'We moeten praten.'

Haar gezicht vertrok van angst. Maar ze deed wat hij vroeg en toen hun knieën elkaar bijna raakten, slikte ze moeilijk. 'Wat is er? Ga me niet vertellen dat er nog meer is.'

Hij kon haar geen minuut langer laten wachten. 'Abby, weet je nog dat ik gisteren zei dat er iets vreemds gebeurde...'

Ze ging in gedachten terug. 'Toen je die nieuwe dansstap had uitgevonden?'

'Precies.' Hij nam haar hand in de zijne. 'Nou, dat was het niet precies.'

Haar mond viel een beetje open, maar ze zei niets.

'De waarheid is dat ik pijn kreeg in mijn rechterteen.' Zijn stem klonk zacht. 'Ik voelde het, Abby. Ik voelde het echt. En toen we het huis binnengingen, bewoog mijn teen.' Hij keek om zich heen, op zoek naar een manier om het te beschrijven. 'Ik dacht dat ik het me misschien verbeeldde... misschien was het niet echt gebeurd. Maar toen voelde ik het weer voordat we gingen slapen en vanmorgen weer.'

'Wilde je daarom vandaag naar de dokter?'

John knikte. 'Ik moest het hem vertellen. Want iedereen had gezegd dat ik nooit meer zoiets zou voelen. Fantoompijn, misschien. Maar geen echt gevoel. En er was geen twijfel aan dat dit echte pijn was... echte beweging.'

'En?' Abby likte haar onderlip. 'Wat zei dokter Furin?'

John deed zijn best om uit te leggen hoe het ervoor stond, hoe een enkele keer een bepaald type nekletsel geopereerd kon worden en het gevoel mogelijk hersteld. 'Maar het blijft een gok, Abby. Hij wil vanmiddag meer onderzoeken doen. Daarna weet hij of ik kandidaat ben voor een operatie.'

Abby's mond hing open en met grote ogen nam ze het nieuws in zich op. Ze boog zich naar voren en greep zijn stoel met beide handen vast. 'Méén je dat?'

'Helemaal.' John vond het heerlijk om de hoop in Abby's ogen te zien. *Alstublieft, God... help ons hier doorheen. Geef ons een wonder.* Er klonk geen hoorbaar antwoord, zelfs geen stille fluistering in zijn hart, maar John werd ineens overspoeld door een onbeschrijfelijk vredig gevoel.

'Goed, dan. Laten we maar naar het ziekenhuis gaan.'

De onderzoeken duurden vijf uur en waren even uitputtend als langdurig. Halverwege de dag belde Abby Nicole en vroeg haar Sean op te halen als de school uitging.

'Wat is er dan?'

'Vertel ik je later wel.' Abby hing vlug op, verlangend om naar John terug te gaan. 'Beloof ik.'

Aan het eind van de dag arriveerde dokter Furin en met een team ruggenmergspecialisten las hij de uitslagen van de onderzoeken door. Om zes uur die avond ontving Johns arts hen eindelijk in de hal van het ziekenhuis.

John was er trots op dat hij iemands gezichtsuitdrukking kon doorgronden, maar dokter Furin kon de kost verdienen met poker. Het was onmogelijk om aan zijn gezicht te zien wat de uitslag was. Hij wenkte hen mee naar een stille hoek waar ze niet gestoord werden.

Abby hield Johns hand stijf vast, zo stijf dat hij haar hartslag in haar vingertoppen voelde. 'Wat bent u te weten gekomen?'

Er speelde een spoor van een glimlach om dokter Furins mond. 'Uw man is kandidaat voor operatie. Zijn verwonding is haast precies volgens het boekje, van het soort waarnaar ze wetenschappelijk onderzoek hebben gedaan.'

Een ogenblik boog John zijn hoofd. Hij had een tweede kans gekregen! Een gelegenheid, hoe klein ook, om zijn benen terug te krijgen. Het was meer dan hij zich kon voorstellen, meer dan hij kon verdragen.

Toen hij opkeek, zag hij dat Abby haar vrije hand voor haar mond had geslagen. Er kwamen snikkende geluidjes uit haar keel, maar haar ogen waren droog. Ze was net als hij diep geschokt. Wie had ooit gedacht dat dit mogelijk was? Na zoveel maanden verlamd te zijn geweest?

John had nog nooit zoiets gehoord. 'Wanneer kan ik geopereerd worden?'

'Niet binnenkort.' Dokter Furin vouwde zijn handen en boog zich naar voren. 'Ik wil dat de topdeskundigen van het land de operatie uitvoeren. Ik zal assisteren, maar het is hun onderzoek, dus zij doen de operatie.'

'Komen ze hierheen?' John kon het nog steeds niet geloven. 'Ik dacht dat je altijd naar specialisten toe moest gaan.'

'Ze doen het grootste deel van hun werk in Arizona, maar voor een uitzonderlijk geval zijn ze bereid om de reis te maken. Ik zou zeggen dat uw geval uitzonderlijk is.'

'Dus wanneer?' Abby's handpalmen waren nat.

'Ik zou zeggen over een week of vier. Ergens half april. Zo lang hebben we wel nodig om het team samen te stellen.'

'Kunnen we voor die tijd nog iets doen?' John sloeg zijn arm om Abby's schouder en trok haar dicht tegen zich aan. De hoop was zo sterk dat het haast lichamelijk pijn deed. Als de dokter er niet bij was geweest, had John Abby op zijn schoot getrokken en haar vastgehouden tot ze verder over de mogelijkheden konden praten.

'Ja.' Abby klappertandde. 'Kunnen we iets doen om de operatie te laten slagen? Een speciaal dieet volgen of oefeningen doen? Wat dan ook?'

'Ja.' Dokter Furin keek van Abby naar John en terug. 'In een situatie als deze zou ik één ding aanraden.' Hij zweeg even en richtte zijn blik weer op John. 'Ga naar huis en bid. Laat uw kinderen en vrienden en familie bidden. Laat de hele stad bidden. Bid voor ons... bid voor uzelf... bid om een wonder. Daarna nemen we u onder het mes en doen ons best. Het is de enige kans die u hebt.'

Dokter Furin legde nog wat meer uit over de operatie en toen vertrok hij. Zodra hij weg was, stak John zijn armen uit naar Abby. Ze klom op zijn schoot als een kind dat een week verdwaald is geweest. Toen brachten John en Abby zonder acht te slaan op wie er nog meer in de wachtkamer zat of langsliep in de gang hun hoofden bij elkaar en baden. Niet alleen op doktersvoorschrift, maar omdat een wonder op de drempel van hun leven stond. En John was van plan om God dag en nacht te smeken de deur te openen en het binnen te laten.

★

Jake Daniels had een merkwaardig gevoel over zijn vader en moeder.

Over een week was zijn hoorzitting, waar hij en zijn advocaat schuldig zouden pleiten op een lijst met aanklachten, dingen die A.W. en de officier van justitie hadden afgesproken. Zijn vader had zijn verlof verlengd en logeerde nog in het hotel in de stad.

Maar Jake vroeg zich soms af of hij niet eigenlijk beneden op de bank sliep.

Soms zat zijn vader nog lang nadat Jake naar bed was gegaan met zijn moeder te praten. En 's morgens stond zijn vader in de keuken koffie te zetten. Het was een vreemde situatie. Zijn ouders waren per slot van rekening gescheiden. Maar soms, als Jake voor het ontbijt beneden kwam en zijn vader in de keuken aantrof, was het fijn om te doen alsof ze nooit uit elkaar waren gegaan. Of dat ze weer bij elkaar zouden komen.

Het kon toch? Ze waren tenslotte samen uit vanavond.

Jake liet zich net op zijn bed vallen toen de telefoon ging. Hij ving een glimp op van de wekker op zijn ladekast. Bijna negen uur. Maar een paar mensen zouden zo laat nog bellen. Zijn advocaat of zijn moeder.

In feite was Jake er haast zeker van dat het zijn moeder was. Als zijn moeder laat uit was met zijn vader, belde ze vaak om hem een verklaring te geven. Het eten was laat opgediend… of ze waren in een lang gesprek verwikkeld geweest.

Het kon Jake niet schelen.

Zolang ze maar samen waren, bestond de kans dat ze er samen uitkwamen. Hij strekte zich uit op zijn bed en pakte de hoorn.

'Hallo?'

'Jake… met Casey Parker.'

Casey Parker? 'Hoi.' Jake ging rechtop zitten en steunde zijn kin in zijn handen. Hij had Casey sinds het ongeluk niet meer gesproken. 'Hoe gaat het?'

'Ik had je eerder moeten bellen.' Caseys stem stokte, alsof hij zijn best deed om niet te huilen. 'Hoor es, Jake. Het spijt me. Dat ik je gevraagd heb om te racen en zo. Echt, man. Ik… ik weet niet wat ik moet zeggen.'

Jake was benieuwd waarom Casey nu belde. 'Het leven gaat door, hè.'

'Jij zit toch op een nascholingsinstituut?'

'Ja. Het is wel leuk. Ik haal allemaal negens.'

'Kom je in de herfst naar Marion terug?'

Dat vroeg zijn moeder hem ook minstens een keer in de week. De raadsman had gezegd dat het goed was, zolang hij niet in een jeugdgevangenis zat. Tegen die tijd was Jakes verplichte huisarrest afgelopen: de tijd waarin hij nergens anders heen mocht dan naar school en weer naar huis. Als hij niet opgesloten werd, moest hij als taakstraf aan jongeren op andere scholen vertellen waarom ze niet mee moesten doen aan straatraces.

Iedereen scheen te denken dat hij in de herfst beter af was op Marion, om zijn laatste jaar op zijn eigen school door te brengen, als levende herinnering voor zijn klasgenoten dat racen tragische gevolgen kon hebben. Maar Jake wist het nog zo net niet. Met coach Reynolds praten in de rechtszaal was één ding. Om hem in zijn rolstoel door Marion High te zien rijden was een heel ander verhaal.

'Ik weet het nog niet.'

'Nou ja. Ik neem het je niet kwalijk. Het is moeilijk om op school te zijn.' Casey aarzelde. 'De coach is nog thuis. Iedereen zegt dat hij in de herfst terugkomt.'

'Ja.' Jake begon misselijk te worden. Waar leidde het gesprek heen? 'Zeg, bedankt voor het bellen. Ik moet vroeg naar bed voor...'

'Wacht even.' Caseys stem klonk dringend. 'Daarom belde ik niet.'

'Oké.'

'We gaan een vergadering houden voor coach Reynolds.'

'Een vergadering.' Jakes hart sloeg een slag over. 'Wat voor vergadering?'

'Ik geloof dat de coach een ontslagbrief heeft geschreven, dat hij klaar was met football omdat hij...' Caseys stem kraakte een beetje en het duurde even voordat hij weer kon praten. 'Omdat hij de steun niet kreeg die hij nodig had.'

Jakes hart brak. De coach had niet alleen met zijn letsel te stellen, ook moest hij leven met het feit dat de ouders hem vlak voordat hij gewond raakte gezamenlijk hadden aangevallen. 'Waar gaat die vergadering over?'

'Er is veel veranderd sinds de coach gewond raakte, Jake. We hebben de kans gekregen om… Ik weet het niet, misschien een beetje beter naar onszelf te kijken. Ik denk dat we beseft hebben, zelfs de ouders, dat het achteraf niet aan de coach lag. Het lag aan ons. Snap je wat ik bedoel?'

'Ja. Dus het is een goede vergadering?'

'Absoluut. Iedereen die wil dat de coach volgend jaar bij de Eagles blijft, moet komen om te praten. Morgen gaan de jongens het nieuws op school verspreiden. Ik denk dat er een heleboel komen. En ook een heleboel ouders.'

Jake was er zeker van dat hij toestemming van de rechter kon krijgen om te gaan. Hij had maar één vraag. 'Is coach Reynolds ook uitgenodigd?'

'Nou…' Casey zweeg even. 'We hoopten eigenlijk dat jij dat kon doen.'

Na alles wat er gebeurd was, voelde Jake zich alleen maar vereerd met de kans om coach Reynolds te bellen om hem voor de vergadering uit te nodigen. 'Ik doe het meteen.'

'Goed. De vergadering is donderdagavond om zeven uur.'

'Dan zie ik je daar.'

Jake hing op en stelde zich coach Reynolds voor in een enorme ruimte vol mensen die van hem hielden. Die gedachte gaf Jake meer rust dan hij in maanden had gekend. Hij glimlachte in zichzelf en dacht aan wat hij graag zou willen zeggen als hij de moed kon opbrengen. Toen deed hij iets wat hij verwacht had nooit in zijn leven meer te zullen doen.

Hij koos het nummer van coach Reynolds en wachtte.

Vijfentwintig

De aula van Marion High zat vol politieagenten.

Chuck Parker nam de microfoon en begon te praten, maar de agenten gooiden hem dingen naar zijn hoofd en riepen om John. Langzaam en onzeker reed John het podium op, maar de hele aula jouwde hem uit. Zodra hij zijn hand uitstak naar de microfoon, werd het podium bestormd door tien agenten die hem de handboeien omdeden. Een van hen keek naar de menigte en zei: 'Coach Reynolds wist dat zijn spelers dronken... hij wist dat ze straatraces hielden. Nu zal hij ervoor boeten.'

Ze duwden John van het podium af en hij verweerde zich niet één keer.

'John... zeg hun wat er echt gebeurd is!' Abby stond op en schreeuwde hem toe. 'Zeg dat je er niets van afwist!'

Maar John draaide zich alleen maar om en zwaaide naar haar. 'Het is mijn schuld, Abby... het is mijn schuld.'

Ze probeerde achter hem aan te rennen, maar een agent pakte haar bij de arm en zei dat ze het recht had om te zwijgen.

'Rááák me niet aan! Mijn man heeft niets verkeerd gedaan... niets! Die hele vergadering is een val en...'

Ze hoorde iets. Brommen of ronken of zoiets. Het werd almaar harder...

Abby schoot recht overeind in bed en snakte naar adem. Ze keek naar John. Hij was niet weggehaald door de politie. Hij lag naast haar te slapen. Het geluid klonk weer en ineens wist ze wat het was.

John snurkte.

Ze viel achterover tegen het kussen. De reeks emotionele gebeurtenissen van die week werd Abby bijna te veel.

Ten eerste de zekerheid van de arts dat ze Johns rug konden opereren en dat hij heel misschien het gebruik van zijn benen terug zou krijgen. Toen het telefoontje van Jake Daniels. Het team, de ouders... bijna de hele school was van plan om te verschijnen op een vergadering over John.

Maar wat wilden ze precies zeggen? Abby's hartslag werd weer normaal. Kennelijk maakte ze zich er zorgen over. Het idee om te vergaderen met de mensen die geprobeerd hadden John kapot te maken zat haar niet lekker.

De dag ging voorbij met huishoudelijk werk en boodschappen doen tot het eindelijk zes uur was en de vergadering over een uur begon. John was zich boven aan het scheren en Abby staarde naar de telefoon. Het was tijd om Nicole vlug even te bellen. Het arme kind had dolgraag naar de vergadering gewild, maar ze hadden Matts ouders al te eten gevraagd. Bovendien was ze zeven maanden zwanger en vermoeider dan anders.

Noch Nicole, noch de andere kinderen wisten van Johns ophanden zijnde operatie. Abby en John wilden het hun dit weekend vertellen, als ze allemaal thuis waren. Dan konden ze daarna de telefoon op de luidspreker zetten en Kade bellen om het gezamenlijk aan hem te vertellen.

Nicole nam op bij de eerste keer overgaan. 'Hallo?'

'Dag lieverd. Met mama.'

'O, hoi. Moeten jullie niet naar de vergadering?'

'Die begint om zeven uur.' Abby goot een beetje lotion in de palm van haar hand en smeerde haar vingers in. 'Hoe gaat het met je, kind? Ik maak me er zorgen over dat je zo moe bent. Dat is meestal niet in de zevende en achtste maand.'

'Ik weet het niet, mam.' Nicole dempte haar stem. 'Ik wil Matt niet ongerust maken, maar toen ik vanmiddag spaghettisaus aan het maken was, had ik een paar valse weeën. Maar dit keer waren ze behoorlijk sterk.'

'Is de baby lekker aan het bewegen?'

'Vanavond niet zo erg. Maar daarstraks leek het wel of ze een handstand achterover deed.'

'Ze?' vroeg Abby plagend. Matt en Nicole hadden besloten dat ze niet wilden weten of ze een jongen of een meisje kregen. Ze wilden zich laten verrassen. 'Wil je me soms iets vertellen?'

'Ik raad er maar naar. Ik heb zo'n gevoel dat het een meisje is. Matt denkt dat het een jongen is. Dus een van ons zal wel...' Nicole kreunde.

'Nick, wat is er?'

'Ugggh.' Nicole ademde een paar keer vlug achter elkaar. 'Weer zo'n valse wee. Zie je wat ik bedoel? Ze worden almaar sterker.'

Abby deed haar best om de onrust uit haar stem te weren. 'Lieverd, je moet de tijd opschrijven en ze bijhouden. Als ze sterker worden of regelmatiger, moet Matt je naar het ziekenhuis brengen. Alsjeblieft, kind. Hier moet je niet mee spotten.'

Nicole beloofde de tijd tussen de weeën bij te houden en vroeg Abby een boodschap door te geven aan John. 'Zeg tegen papa dat Matt voor hem bidt. Dat deze vergadering bemoedigend zal zijn, wat er ook gezegd zal worden.'

'*Matt* bidt? En j...'

'Houd op, mam.' Ze zuchtte. 'Je weet wat ik ervan denk.'

Abby wist het en ze vond het nog steeds ongelooflijk. Het leven was al tragisch genoeg nu haar man niet meer kon lopen. Maar dat Nicole niet meer kon bidden? Ze praatten nog een poosje en Abby paste op om geen kritiek te leveren. Nicole had liefde van Abby nodig, geen veroordeling. Abby maakte een eind aan het telefoongesprek en sloot haar ogen.

God... werk in haar hart. Alstublieft...

HEB VREDE, DOCHTER... NIEMAND ZAL HAAR UIT MIJN HAND ROVEN...

De woorden waren als balsem voor haar ziel en vervulden haar met vrede. *Niemand zal ze uit Mijn hand roven.* Het was een Bijbeltekst uit Abby's studietijd. Ze had hem uit haar hoofd geleerd na een discussie met een jeugdpredikant over verlossing.

Nicole wees haar geloof niet af. Ze worstelde ermee. Ze dacht aan de weeën van haar dochter. God zou bij haar zijn en haar hier doorheen helpen. En Abby geloofde met haar hele hart dat Nicole binnenkort weer bidden zou.

Misschien diezelfde avond nog.

★

De vergadering was al begonnen toen John en Abby stiekem door een achterdeur de aula binnenkwamen. De verlichting was gedempt en John was er zeker van dat alles stil zou vallen zodra zij arriveerden.

Maar Abby deed de deur open en glipte eerst naar binnen, terwijl John geluidloos achter haar aan de zaal in rolde. Abby vond een stoel tegen de achterwand en John stelde zich naast haar op. Ze bleven achterin en in de schaduw terwijl Herman Lutz het podium beklom.

'U bent hier vanavond aanwezig voor een door de ouders bijeengeroepen vergadering. Zoals u weet, staat ons schoolgebouw open voor dergelijke besprekingen.' Hij stak een stuk papier omhoog en las langzaam en ongeoefend voor wat erop stond. 'Als sportcoördinator van Marion High wil ik de regels duidelijk maken. Houd uw opmerkingen alstublieft zo positief mogelijk en laat ons scheldpartijen vermijden. Bovendien moet u weten dat de meningen die hier vanavond worden geuit, niet de meningen zijn van bestuur of personeel.'

De man deed verveeld en neerbuigend. Zoals hij zich ook gedroeg tegenover de coaches en leerlingen op Marion. John probeerde zich er niet aan te storen.

Lutz legde zijn hand boven zijn ogen en keek naar de voorste rij zitplaatsen. 'Meneer Chuck Parker, u hebt deze vergadering bijeengeroepen, dus ik zou u willen vragen de discussie te openen.'

Dus het was waar. Chuck Parker had de vergadering bijeengeroepen. Dezelfde man die er voor het seizoen met John over had getwist of zijn zoon quarterback moest spelen en, volgens Jake althans, degene die de aanval tegen zijn persoon had aangevoerd. John leunde achterover in zijn rolstoel. Daarbij voelde hij Abby's hand naast de zijne. Hij hield hem vast, blij dat ze er was, en nog blijer dat ze niet gezien waren.

Nu zijn ogen aan het licht gewend waren, kon hij de aula duidelijker zien. Hij was stampvol. Er waren honderden mensen gekomen. Wat konden al die mensen in vredesnaam te zeggen hebben?

Chuck Parker liep naar de microfoon en zei lange tijd helemaal niets. Hij schraapte zijn keel en keek naar de grond. Toen hij opkeek, waren zijn wangen dieprood. 'Ik heb deze vergadering bijeengeroepen om één reden. Om in het openbaar mijn excuses aan te bieden aan coach John Reynolds.'

Abby kneep in zijn hand en zei nauwelijks hoorbaar: 'Het werd tijd.'

John spande zich in om alles te horen. Hij wilde geen woord missen.

'Velen van u herinneren zich mijn gedrag van vorig seizoen. Omwille van mijn eigen doeleinden probeerde ik u ervan te overtuigen dat coach Reynolds niet de man was die onze Eagles nodig hadden op het footballveld.' Hij keek weer naar de grond. 'Maar sindsdien heb ik veel nagedacht.'

Chuck keek op en liep een paar passen naar links en naar rechts. 'Wat er dit afgelopen seizoen met onze jongens is gebeurd, is *mijn* schuld.' Hij wees naar het publiek. 'En de schuld van diegenen onder u die hun kind tegen coach Reynolds hebben opgezet.' Hij aarzelde. 'Waar kon mijn jongen als Eagle op hopen als hij van mij alleen maar hatelijkheden te horen kreeg over zijn coach? Hoe harder ik de man aanviel, hoe minder respect Casey voor hem kreeg. Als spelers eenmaal het respect verliezen voor de coach, is het niet belangrijk meer wat de man doet of hoeveel talent het team heeft. Daar verliest iedereen bij, zo simpel is het.' Hij zweeg even. 'Maar er was een tragedie voor nodig voordat ik dat inzag.'

John dacht dat hij droomde. In zijn wildste fantasie had hij niet gedacht dat Chuck Parker voor de volgelingen van Marion zou toegeven dat hij Johns gezag had ondermijnd. Hij wierp een snelle blik op Abby. Ze had tranen op haar wangen, maar ze zat stil te luisteren naar wat er werd gezegd.

'Ik probeerde coach Reynolds te laten ontslaan. Maar ik had het mis.' Parker haalde zijn schouders op en stond met zijn mond vol tanden. 'De coach heeft deze week zijn ontslagbrief gestuurd. Dat was nog een reden om deze vergadering bij elkaar te roepen, om de coach ervan te overtuigen dat we hem terug willen op Marion High. De school is niet hetzelfde zonder hem.'

Chuck stelde de vergadering open voor wie het woord wilde voeren. Verscheidene ouders namen de gelegenheid te baat en Johns verbazing nam toe. Dit waren mensen van wie hij altijd had aangenomen dat ze hem gesteund hadden. Maar een voor een verontschuldigden ze zich ervoor dat ze de kant hadden gekozen van een handjevol ouders die hem weg wilden hebben.

Een vader zei: 'Wat we coach Reynolds vorig jaar hebben aangedaan maakt verliezers van ons, en van onze zoons. Ik schaam me diep en ik ben blij met de kans om u allen te vertellen hoe ik me voel.'

John verschoof in zijn stoel. Geen wonder dat hij zo onder druk had gestaan. Zelfs ouders die in zijn gezicht glimlachten hadden achter zijn rug gepraat. Abby en hij wisselden een blik. Kennelijk dacht zij hetzelfde.

Nu stroomden er ouders naar het podium die zich publiekelijk tegen John hadden gekeerd. Ook zij uitten hun spijt van wat ze hadden gedaan.

'Niet alleen omdat hij nu invalide is,' zei een vader. 'We zijn hier vandaag niet omdat we medelijden hebben met coach Reynolds. Maar omdat we ons schamen voor de manier waarop we hem behandeld hebben.'

Na een halfuur stond de eerste speler op om te spreken. Het was een lijnman, een zachtaardige sporter die Buck heette, wiens heftigheid alleen op het veld naar buiten kwam.

Tot nu.

'Coach Reynolds was geen gewone coach, geen man die je niet ziet staan.' Buck leek zich niet op zijn gemak te voelen op het kleine podium, maar hij zette door en er klonk hartstocht in zijn stem. 'De coach liet ons bij hem thuis komen om een filmpje te kijken of lekker te eten. We konden altijd bij hem terecht.' Buck begon luider te praten. 'Zoveel hield hij van ons. En ik wil dat de ouders dat weten. Jullie hebben stelling genomen tegen een man die zich meer om ons bekommerde dan alle andere coaches van wie ik ooit heb gehoord. Wij waren de grootste geluksvogels van Illinois. Omdat de coach van ons hield.' Even liet hij zijn hoofd hangen. 'Ik wil maar zeggen dat het tijd wordt om de coach de boodschap terug te geven… dat wij ook van hem houden.'

John kreeg een brok in zijn keel. Hij slikte zijn tranen in en luisterde hoe zijn spelers de een na de ander het podium beklommen en Bucks gedachten herhaalden. Dus ze gaven toch om hem. Het was meer waard dan John zich had kunnen voorstellen. Hij bracht Abby's hand naar zijn lippen en kuste hem teder.

Ze glimlachte naar hem en zei geluidloos: 'Ze houden van je, John.'

Eindelijk viel er een korte stilte en er werd druk gefluisterd tussen de toeschouwers. Alle ogen waren op iemand gericht, maar John kon niet zien wie. Eindelijk kwam de jongen in het zicht.

Jake Daniels.

John had hem sinds die dag in de rechtszaal niet meer gezien en hij zag er nu anders uit. Ouder, volwassener. Hij was niet langer de zorgeloze topspeler die hij in november was geweest.

Abby leunde naar voren. 'Vanwaar die drukte?'

'Jake is sinds het ongeluk niet meer op Marion geweest.'

'O.' Haar ogen werden groot. 'Dat wist ik niet.'

'Dit moet moeilijk voor hem zijn.'

Jake was verlegen noch gegeneerd. Hij hanteerde de microfoon alsof hij nooit anders had gedaan en maakte oogcontact met de verschillende delen van het publiek.

'Ik ben hier om u de waarheid te vertellen over enkele geruchten over coach Reynolds die vorig jaar de ronde deden.' Hij zweeg even, zijn ogen gloeiden. 'Ten eerste klopt het dat enkele jongens van het team op het zomerkamp in augustus hebben gedronken. Ik was een van hen. En een paar jongens hebben geracet.'

John wisselde een blik met Abby. Dus Jake was een van de drinkers geweest. Maar John was er haast zeker van dat de jongen niet had geracet. Toen niet, althans. Pas toen zijn vader die Integra voor hem had gekocht, was hij in de verleiding gekomen. En zelfs toen had hij het maar één tragische keer gedaan. Toch beweerde hij niet dat hij onschuldig was, noch wees hij aan welke spelers de regels hadden overtreden.

Jake stopte een hand in zijn zak. 'Als ik kijk naar ons team van vorig jaar, dan weet ik dat het waar is wat een van jullie daarstraks zei. We waren verliezers. Niet alleen op het veld, maar ook buiten het veld. De meesten hebben de regels overtreden. Drinken, racen, porno kijken.'

Abby wierp John een ontstelde blik toe. Ze fluisterde: 'Op de middelbare school?'

'Blijkbaar.'

'Deed Kade daar vorig jaar ook aan mee?'

'Nee.' John dempte zorgvuldig zijn stem. Zijn gesprek met Kade die dag in de boot lag nog vers in zijn geheugen. 'Pas toen hij ging studeren.'

'Gebeurt het zo veel?'

John knikte. 'En het wordt steeds erger.' Toen viel hem iets in… Hij kon Kade vragen om aan het team te vertellen dat porno verslavend kan zijn, dat je je ervan los moet maken en hulp moet zoeken. Dat zou nou echt…

Toen wist hij het weer. Hij was geen coach meer. Misschien had de nieuwe coach geen belangstelling om de jongens uit de buurt van pornomateriaal te houden. En het was aan hem om sprekers voor het team te regelen.

Jake was nog steeds aan het woord. 'Alsof dat nog niet erg genoeg was, liepen we over de campus rond met het idee dat wij de school regeerden en we behandelden andere mensen als oud vuil. We maakten iedereen op Marion High die niet footballde het leven zuur.' Jake zweeg en stond met gebalde vuisten op de rand van het podium. Zijn ogen dwaalden over het publiek. 'We dachten dat we beter waren dan iedereen. Zelfs coach Reynolds.'

Jake zweeg. Zelfs achterin kon John zien dat hij vocht tegen zijn tranen. Eindelijk schraapte hij zijn keel en vond zijn stem terug. 'De coach wilde dat wij eerlijke, nette jongemannen waren. Mannen met karakter. Iedereen die voor hem heeft gespeeld, heeft hem dat wel honderd keer horen zeggen. Hij gaf ons het goede voorbeeld.'

John dacht aan Charlene en voelde zich diep schuldig. Hij was niet altijd netjes geweest. Maar door zijn geloof, door Gods kracht en niet door zijn eigen, had hij zich van die situatie afgewend en was hij uit de buurt gebleven van anderen die hem op de verkeerde weg zouden hebben geleid. Alleen door Gods genade zagen Jake en de anderen in hem het karakter dat ze als voorbeeld zagen.

'Wij hadden de beste coach van de staat. Een coach die van ons hield, zoals Buck zei. En we hebben hem weg laten gaan.' Jake snufte en moest opnieuw vechten om zich niet door zijn emoties te laten overmannen. 'Ik geloof nog steeds dat God coach Reynolds zal genezen, maar misschien ook niet. Door te racen kan ik de benen van de coach voor altijd verwoest hebben.' Er ontsnapte een snik uit Jakes keel en hij drukte zijn vuist op zijn mond tot hij zich weer in bedwang had. 'Maar wat ons team vorig seizoen heeft gedaan door tegen hem in opstand te komen is erger, want we hebben zijn verlangen om te coachen verwoest.' Jake schudde zijn hoofd. 'Ik kan alleen maar bidden dat de coach op een dag terugkomt en dat de groep die hij dan krijgt slim genoeg is om te snappen hoe goed ze het hebben. Slim genoeg om naar hem te luisteren, hem na te doen en met hun hele hart voor hem te spelen. Hadden wij dat maar gedaan.'

John knipperde zijn tranen weg en keek Abby aan.

'Hij is volwassen geworden.' Ze had tranen in haar ogen.

'Ja.' John keek toe hoe Jake het podium verliet. 'Inderdaad.'

Een tijdlang bleef het stil en ten slotte beklom Chuck Parker het podium. 'Ik had gehoopt dat coach Reynolds vanavond hier zou zijn, maar het is begrijpelijk waarom hij er niet is. Niet alleen vanwege zijn letsel, maar vanwege de manier waarop we hem het afgelopen seizoen behandeld hebben. Waarom zou hij komen?'

Abby stootte hem aan. 'Zeg iets.'

'Nog niet.' John vond het pijnlijk om hardop te schreeuwen terwijl Chuck aan het woord was. 'Wacht tot hij klaar is.'

Chuck schermde zijn ogen weer af met zijn hand en keek speurend de zaal in. 'Als niemand meer iets wil zeggen, ik heb een petitie meegebracht waarin we coach Reynolds vragen zijn beslissing te herroepen en terug te komen als coach voor de Eagles. Als iedereen die wil ondertekenen voordat…'

'Wacht!' Door een zijdeur betrad een lange gestalte de aula en beende naar het podium.

Chuck keek verrast en nerveus. De leerling slenterde naar voren en toen hij op het podium stond begreep John het.

De jongen was Nathan Pike.

Johns ogen puilden uit. Het was Nathan, maar hij was niet in het zwart gekleed en er zaten geen puntige leren banden om zijn armen en hals. Hij zag eruit als alle andere leerlingen van Marion High en er was nog iets. Zijn gezichtsuitdrukking was zachter. Zo zacht dat John hem haast niet herkende.

Nathan keek naar Parker op en stak zijn hand uit. 'Sorry dat ik te laat ben. Ik heb iets te zeggen. Zou dat mogen?'

Chuck keek opgelucht. John was er zeker van dat iedereen op school de geruchten over Nathan had gehoord. Hoe kon dat anders, na de footballwedstrijd waar de jongen was gearresteerd? Later was gebleken dat een jongen uit het team van de tegenstander de bommelding op zijn geweten had, maar het voorval had Nathans reputatie geen goed gedaan, en John had gehoord dat sommigen nog steeds bang waren dat hij iets gestoords zou doen.

Maar Chuck aarzelde niet. Hij overhandigde Nathan de microfoon en deed een stap naar achteren. Nathan wierp een blik achter in de zaal. 'Ten eerste, coach Reynolds is er wel. Hij zit achterin met zijn vrouw. Ik zag hen toen ik binnenkwam.'

Iedereen begon door elkaar te praten en de mensen keken reikhalzend en wijzend naar de plek waar John en Abby zaten.

'Daar gaat je anonimiteit.' Abby dook dieper in haar stoel.

'Coach?' Nathan tuurde in het donker. 'Wilt u hierheen komen?'

John voelde vlinders in zijn maag en zijn handen waren klam.

'Ik bid voor je,' fluisterde Abby.

'Dank je.' John rolde langs de achterwand en door het gangpad naar voren. Hij voelde alle ogen op zich gericht toen hij de helling van het podium opreed.

Aanvankelijk konden ouders en spelers alleen maar naar hem staren. De laatste keer dat ze hem zagen, had hij met zijn een meter vijfennegentig levensgroot rechtop gestaan, een wandelende illustratie van de lichamelijke kracht die nodig is voor football.

Nu was hij op een rolstoel aangewezen, twintig kilo lichter en zijn benen waren raar dun.

Even later stond Jake Daniels op en begon te klappen. Geen beleefd applaus, maar luide klappen die aanstekelijk werkten. Voordat Nathan nog een woord kon zeggen, stond Casey Parker op en toen Buck. Eindelijk rees het hele publiek overeind en klapte voor John zoals ze nog nooit hadden geklapt.

Het was een applaus dat John binnen een minuut een heel seizoen van kritiek en klachten deed vergeten. Een applaus dat hem vertelde dat zijn spelers en hun ouders hem inderdaad onrecht hadden aangedaan, maar dat ze wisten dat ze fout waren geweest en er spijt van hadden. Niet omdat ze medelijden met hem hadden, hoewel dat natuurlijk ook waar was. Maar spijt dat ze hem vorig seizoen niet hadden gesteund en een kans hadden gegeven.

Toen iedereen weer zat en het stil was geworden, sprak Nathan.

'Ik denk dat we vanavond iets over vergeving hebben geleerd. Mensen zoals ik moeten mensen zoals jullie vergeven.' Hij keek naar de plek waar de spelers zaten. 'En mensen zoals jullie moeten mensen zoals mij vergeven. Dat heeft de coach me geleerd en het zijn dingen die me voor altijd zullen bijblijven.' Hij zweeg even. 'Maar vooral moet coach Reynolds ons allemaal vergeven.'

John was te verbijsterd om iets anders te kunnen doen dan luisteren.

Nathan kwam dichterbij en pakte Johns rolstoel vast. 'Ik zou graag willen dat iedereen op het podium om de coach heen komt staan en dat we bidden om twee wonderen.'

Wat nou? Wilde Nathan dat de mensen gingen bidden? Het hele tafereel was zo vreemd dat het ongelooflijk was. Maar het gebeurde echt.

'Het eerste wonder dat we nodig hebben ligt voor de hand: dat de coach weer zal kunnen lopen. Het tweede is ook niet moeilijk te bedenken. Dat de coach zijn ontslag bij de Eagles intrekt. Omdat we hem nodig hebben. We hebben hem allemaal nodig.'

Een voor een kwamen ze: spelers en ouders en leerlingen, veel die niet hadden gesproken, maar niettemin hun steun wilden betonen. De groep mensen op het podium groeide tot iedereen in een kring om John heen stond. Iedereen behalve Herman Lutz en een conciërge achterin.

John zag Abby door het middenpad aan komen lopen. Op het podium legde ze haar handen op Johns schouders en terwijl om hem heen werd gebeden, voelde John beweging in zijn voeten. Dit keer vanuit allebei zijn grote tenen.

In het stilste hoekje van zijn hart hoorde hij de stem van God.

STEUN NIET OP JE EIGEN INZICHT...

Terwijl John zijn ogen sloot en in stilte zijn stem bij die van de anderen voegde en besefte dat God de ramp van het afgelopen jaar oploste, wist hij zeker dat hij nooit meer op zijn eigen inzicht steunen zou.

Zesentwintig

Om elf uur die avond leerde Nicole weer bidden.

Toen had ze het grootste deel van de avond de tijd tussen de weeën bijgehouden en hoewel ze niet regelmatig kwamen, werden ze beslist sterker.

Tegenover Matt en zijn ouders had ze het afgezwakt, om niemand lastig te vallen voor het geval dat het valse weeën waren. Dat had ze ook gedaan toen haar moeder om negen uur belde om haar te vertellen over de vergadering op school.

'Hoe gaat het met de weeën, Nick?' Er klonk bezorgdheid in haar stem.

'Best. Niets ongewoons.'

Nu waren er twee uur voorbijgegaan en ze had zoveel pijn dat ze naar de bank beneden was verhuisd om Matt niet uit zijn slaap te houden en om de tussentijd bij te houden. Maar er was nog iets wat haar dwarszat, bijna nog meer dan de pijn. Iets wat haar moeder eerder die avond aan de telefoon had gevraagd.

Bewoog de baby nog?

Eerst had Nicole ja gezegd. Er was nog beweging, al was het minder dan tevoren. Maar daarna had ze er beter op gelet. En nu, een uur nadat Matts ouders waren vertrokken, begon ze in paniek te raken. Na het eten had ze de baby niet één keer meer voelen bewegen.

En dat had ertoe geleid dat Nicole voor het eerst sinds het ongeluk van haar vader weer had gebeden.

Om elf uur, toen ze door vreselijke pijn werd overvallen zodat ze van de bank op haar knieën viel, begon ze vanzelf te bidden.

God, wat gebeurt er met me? Help me, God… Het is te vroeg, de baby mag nog niet komen!

Stilte.

Toen de wee voorbij was, begon Nicole te huilen. Ze kon niet beschrijven hoe ze zich voelde: afgrijselijk en heerlijk tegelijk. Afgrijselijk vanwege de weeën, maar heerlijk rustig omdat ze voor het eerst in veel te lange tijd tot God had gesproken.

Wat had haar de afgelopen maanden bezield? Waarom had ze zichzelf ervan overtuigd dat bidden geen zin had? God had haar gebeden voor haar ouders trouw verhoord. En voor talloze andere dingen elke dag van haar leven.

Toen viel het haar in. Wat de reden was dat ze was opgehouden met bidden.

Ze had God alleen trouw gevonden als haar gebeden verhoord werden zoals *zij* wilde dat ze verhoord werden. Wat stond er in de Bijbel over bidden? Dat Hij de gebeden hoorde.

Niet noodzakelijk dat Hij aan het verzoek voldeed, maar dat Hij trouw ingreep naar Zijn welbehagen.

Ze herinnerde zich nog iets. Niet alle gebeden werden onmiddellijk verhoord. Anders hoefde je niet te bidden zonder ophouden, zoals de Schrift opdroeg.

Nicole klom weer op de bank. Haar buik was nog strak van de laatste samentrekking. Waarom had ze daar niet eerder aan gedacht? En hoe had ze het al die maanden zonder bidden kunnen stellen?

Wat was ze dwaas geweest…

Ze kreeg tranen in haar ogen en werd overmand door verdriet. Had ze werkelijk gedacht dat ze door het leven kwam zonder een relatie met haar Schepper? Een zo levende relatie dat ze haar leven eromheen kon bouwen? Het antwoord klonk in haar hart. Nee, ze had God nooit voor altijd de rug toe kunnen keren. Ze was alleen boos op Hem omdat Hij haar vader verlamd had laten raken.

Maar God had nooit beloofd dat het leven probleemloos zou verlopen. Dat had Nicole altijd geweten, ze had het haar hele leven gehoord, maar ze had het nog nooit onder ogen hoeven zien. Nooit had ze hoeven worstelen met de tweedeling van een liefdevolle, barmhartige God Die niet voorkwam dat er vreselijke dingen gebeurden.

En toch… terwijl ze daar lag, dacht ze terug aan alle jaren van haar leven waarin God haar had aangeraakt en gezegend. Hij had Zichzelf keer op keer bewezen. En Zijn Woord bewees nog meer. Het vertelde haar de waarheid: God beloofde vrede te midden van pijn en Hij beloofde eeuwig leven. Was dat niet meer dan waarop iemand kon hopen? Vooral in dit leven, dat zo vluchtig en onvoorspelbaar was.

Een nieuwe kramp kreeg haar buik in zijn greep en nu schreeuwde ze het uit. 'Matt! Help me!'

Terwijl de wee in hevigheid toenam, keek ze naar het papiertje op de armleuning van de bank. De vorige wee was om 10.58 geweest. Ze keek op haar horloge, perste haar lippen op elkaar en blies haar adem uit zoals ze op zwangerschapsgym had geleerd.

Het was 11.04. Maar zes minuten waren voorbijgegaan en maar zeven tussen die en de vorige. Ze werden sterker en kwamen korter op elkaar. *God… wat moet ik doen?*

Als antwoord kreeg ze een overweldigend gevoel om Matt weer te roepen. En terwijl de pijn wegebde, riep ze hem harder dan eerst. 'Matt! Ik heb je nodig!'

Boven haar hoofd hoorde ze zijn voeten op de grond belanden. De trap kraakte toen hij met twee treden tegelijk naar beneden stormde. Buiten adem kwam hij binnen en zag haar zitten, met een betraand gezicht weggekropen in een hoekje van de bank. 'Schat, wat is er?'

'De baby komt, Matt.' Ze snikte, nog moe van de laatste kramp. 'Ik heb om de zes of zeven minuten weeën en ze worden almaar erger.'

Matt werd bleek en hij deed een stap in de richting van de trap. 'Ik kleed me aan en we gaan naar het ziekenhuis. Wacht hier, goed?'

Hoewel Matt maar een paar minuten nodig had en ondanks het

feit dat hij de hele weg naar het ziekenhuis hard reed, was het bijna middernacht toen ze opgenomen werd. Toen had ze al een injectie gekregen om de weeën te stoppen, maar ze was er alleen maar zenuwachtig en huilerig van geworden.

'Ik moet mijn ouders bellen.' Ze pakte Matts hand. 'Wat als de baby vannacht komt?'

'Zo gauw je op een kamer ligt, zal ik ze bellen.'

Een arts reed haar in een rolstoel van de spoedeisende hulp naar de lift. Ze gingen twee verdiepingen omhoog naar de verloskamers. 'We doen wat we kunnen om uw weeën te stoppen, mevrouw, maar u hebt vijf centimeter ontsluiting en de weeën blijven komen.'

Vijf centimeter? Nicole had gelezen dat de bevalling zelden tegen te houden was als een vrouw al zoveel ontsluiting had. De arts reed haar een fel verlichte kamer binnen met een tafel van glanzend staal. 'We blijven proberen de weeën te stoppen, maar ik moet eerlijk zijn. U kunt ook binnen een uur bevallen.'

Nicole deed haar mond open om iets te zeggen, maar er kwam weer een wee. Ze zat hem uit terwijl Matt vragen stelde. 'Mijn vrouw is pas zeven maanden zwanger, dokter. Wat betekent dat voor de baby?'

De dokter fronste. 'Dat zullen we moeten afwachten. Baby's die zo vroeg geboren worden, kunnen in leven blijven. Het probleem is dat de longen van zo'n klein kindje niet uit zichzelf werken. We zullen het per geval moeten bekijken.'

Per geval? De woorden kletterden als steentjes in Nicoles hart. Het ging wel over háár kind! De baby waarvan ze het bestaan niet had willen aanvaarden tot die kerstavond in de slaapkamer, toen ze het kind voor het eerst had voelen bewegen. Sindsdien had ze een band gevormd met dit kleintje, een sterkere en diepere band dan ze ooit voor mogelijk had gehouden.

'Mevrouw.' De dokter probeerde haar aandacht te trekken en ze schrok op. 'Wanneer hebt u de baby voor het laatst voelen bewegen?'

'Nou… dat is al even geleden. Meestal is ze actiever.'

'Hmmm.' De dokter bewoog een stethoscoop over Nicoles buik. Het duurde even voordat hij weer sprak. 'De baby vertoont tekenen van nood. Het ziet ernaaruit dat we hem geboren moeten laten worden als we hem een kans willen geven.'

De dokter sloot haar aan op een monitor. 'Ik ben over een paar minuten terug. Blijf zo stil mogelijk liggen.'

Hij verdween en Nicole pakte Matts hand weer. Haar hart bonsde. *Alstublieft, God… red mijn baby. Alstublieft.* 'Matt… bel mijn ouders. Iedereen moet bidden.'

Matt liep naar de telefoon op het tafeltje naast haar bed. Maar toen stond hij stil. 'Zei je nou…?'

'Natuurlijk.' Ze keek hem strak aan, hij zag haar angst. 'Ik was gewoon kwaad. Een paar uur geleden ben ik begonnen te bidden en ik ben niet meer opgehouden.' Ze snikte. 'Ga nu alsjeblieft mijn ouders bellen.'

Matt knikte en pakte de telefoon. Terwijl hij het nummer koos, zag ze een nieuwe emotie bij de angst en onrust en hulpeloosheid die op zijn gezicht geschreven stonden.

Opluchting.

★

Abby werd wakker van het schrille rinkelen van de telefoon.

Ze schoot overeind en hield haar adem in. Wie belde er om deze tijd? Ze pakte de telefoon. 'Hallo?'

'Ma, met Matt.' Hij zweeg lang genoeg om de paniek in zijn stem tot haar te laten doordringen. Een golf adrenaline stroomde door haar aderen. Was er iets mis met Nicole? Ze ging nog rechter zitten toen Matt haastig doorpraatte. 'We zijn in het ziekenhuis en… de artsen kunnen Nicoles weeën niet stoppen. Het ziet ernaaruit dat de baby elk moment geboren kan worden. Ze wil graag dat jullie bidden.'

Abby's hart bonsde in haar borst. Nicole was pas zeven maanden heen. Dat betekende dat de baby niet meer dan een paar pond kon wegen. Ineens dacht ze aan Haley Ann. Zou Nicole ook een kindje moeten verliezen? *God, nee… laat dat niet gebeuren.*

'Mam, ben je er nog?' Matts stem klonk zo gespannen dat Abby hem nauwelijks herkende.

'We zijn onderweg.'

Toen ze opgehangen had, maakte ze John wakker. Twintig minuten later draaiden ze het parkeerterrein van het ziekenhuis op en zochten de kraamafdeling. Matt kwam hen in de gang tegemoet. Hij had een ziekenhuishemd aan en een papieren mondkapje voor.

'Ze hebben alles geprobeerd, maar ze kunnen de bevalling niet tegenhouden.' Zijn ogen waren rood. 'Ze zeggen dat de baby in nood is.'

Abby zette nog twee stappen in de richting van de kamer waar Matt net uit was gekomen. 'Waar is ze?'

'In de verloskamer. Volgens de dokter kan het elk ogenblik geboren worden.'

John rolde zichzelf dichterbij. 'Mogen we bij haar?'

'Nog niet. Ik mag weer naar binnen, maar jullie moeten in de hal wachten. Ik kom jullie halen zodra ik iets weet.'

Matt omhelsde hen beiden. 'Nicole wil dat jullie bidden voor de baby, maar bid ook voor haar. Ze heeft een inwendige bloeding. Haar bloeddruk is veel te laag.'

Abby moest zich bedwingen om niet door de gang naar Nicole toe te rennen. Dat de baby in gevaar was, was één ding… maar Nicole? Die mogelijkheid had Abby niet eens overwogen. God zou toch niet toelaten dat Nicole iets overkwam. Ze hadden al zoveel meegemaakt. Ze hadden al één dochter verloren.

God zou hen toch geen tweede afnemen?

Matt liep weg door de gang en John pakte haar hand. 'Kom.' Hij voerde haar mee naar een leunstoel in een wachtkamer en zette zijn stoel zo dicht mogelijk bij haar. Hij nam haar gezicht zacht tussen zijn handen en dwong haar hem aan te kijken. 'Ik weet wat je denkt, Abby. Maar daar moet je mee ophouden. We moeten geloven dat God hier bij ons is en dat Hij Nicole en de baby hier doorheen zal helpen.'

Abby was te bang om iets anders te doen dan knikken. 'Bid, John. Alsjeblieft.'

Hij boog zijn hoofd dicht naar haar toe en legde Nicole en de baby in Gods handen. 'We vertrouwen U, God. Hoe de situatie er ook voor staat, wat er vroeger ook gebeurd is, we vertrouwen U. En we geloven dat U een wonder zult doen voor onze dochter en haar baby.'

Terwijl John bad, besefte Abby hoe sterk ze nog geloofde. Ondanks alles wat er gebeurd was, waren Gods vingerafdrukken overal zichtbaar. John had het ongeluk toch overleefd? Zij twee-en hielden toch weer van elkaar? En zij had eindelijk eerlijk haar gevoelens kunnen uitspreken.

Haar vredige gevoel werd overschaduwd door een golf van paniek, maar dat duurde maar even. Er was geen tijd voor angst nu Nicole en de baby verderop in de gang vochten voor hun leven. Midden in deze crisis was God aan het werk.

Dat moest Abby geloven.

Anders kwam ze de nacht niet door. Zonder haar geloof zou een nieuw verlies de instorting voor haar betekenen.

Er ging een vol uur voorbij voordat Matt in de wachtkamer verscheen. Hij leek tien jaar ouder, maar Abby zag opgetogen dat hij lachte!

'Met Nicole gaat het goed. De bloeding kwam door een scheur in de placenta, en dat kan fataal zijn.' Hij ademde diep in, zijn ogen waren rood en waterig. 'Ik heb bij haar gewacht tot haar bloeddruk begon te stijgen. Ze is moe, maar volgens de artsen is ze niet in gevaar.'

Abby blies hard uit. 'Gelukkig… Ik weet dat God haar heeft gered.'

'En de baby?' John legde met een gespannen gezicht zijn hand op Abby's knie.

Matts glimlach stierf weg. 'Het is een meisje. Maar het ziet er niet goed uit. Ze weegt amper twee pond en ze heeft moeite met ademen. Ze hebben haar op de intensive care gelegd.'

Dus Nicole had gelijk gehad. Een meisje… maar nu leek het erop dat geen van hen haar zelfs maar zou leren kennen. Arm kleintje, alleen in een couveuse, vechtend voor haar leven. Abby's armen deden pijn van verlangen om haar vast te houden. 'Mogen we een van beiden zien?'

'Nicole ligt weer op haar kamer. Misschien slaapt ze, maar ze wil vast graag dat jullie binnenkomen.' Matt sloeg zijn ogen even neer. 'Van ons kindje weet ik het niet.' Hij keek weer op. 'Ze is zo klein. Ik heb nog nooit zo'n klein baby'tje gezien.'

Ze liepen achter Matt aan naar Nicoles kamer en onderweg tikte John tegen Abby's been. Ze draaide zich naar hem om en hij wees naar zijn voeten. 'Zullen we het haar vertellen?'

Natuurlijk! Het nieuws over Johns operatie, de kans dat hij weer zou kunnen lopen! Dat zou haar vast bemoedigen. 'Vertel jij het maar.'

Ze betraden de kamer en Nicole deed haar ogen open. 'Hoi.' Haar stem klonk versuft. 'Hoe gaat het met de baby?'

'Ze zijn druk met haar bezig, schat.' Matt stond meteen naast haar en streek met zijn hand over haar voorhoofd.

Nicole keek langs hem heen naar Abby en John. 'Ze is gewoon prachtig. Een heel klein beetje donker haar en een prachtig klein gezichtje. Hebben jullie haar gezien?'

'Nog niet.' Abby beet op haar lip. 'Ze is erg klein, Nick.'

'Weet ik, maar het komt goed met haar. Dat voel ik in mijn botten.'

John keek naar Abby op en ze knikte. Afleiding zou haar goed doen. Zeker het soort afleiding dat John haar wilde geven. Hij reed zijn rolstoel naar het voeteneind van haar bed en pakte haar tenen vast. 'Ik moet je wat vertellen, Nick.'

'Goed.' Ze knipperde met zware oogleden en er speelde een lachje om haar mond. 'Klinkt ernstig.'

'Is het ook.' Hij keek nog eens naar Abby. 'Ik ben van de week bij de dokter geweest. Hij heeft een paar onderzoeken gedaan en vastgesteld dat ze me kunnen opereren. De operatie zal over ongeveer een maand plaatsvinden.'

Nicole zette grote ogen op en Matt keek John met open mond aan. Nicole ging rechter op zitten in bed, haar gezicht vertrok van de pijn. 'Waaraan?'

'Nou… ik heb een beetje gevoel in mijn tenen. Nu en dan bewegen ze een beetje.' Johns ogen straalden. Abby was nog nooit zo gelukkig geweest voor hem. 'Ik heb begrepen dat ze in zeldzame gevallen met zo'n operatie de breuk kunnen helen.'

'En je benen dan?' vroeg Matt op eerbiedige toon.

Johns kin beefde en hij worstelde om de woorden te vinden. Abby schraapte haar keel en maakte de zin voor hem af. 'Hij kan het volledige gebruik terugkrijgen.'

Nicole juichte. 'Pap! Dat is fantastisch!'

'Het is maar een kans, maar we bidden erom.' John ging achteruit zitten in zijn stoel en lachte. 'Een poosje geleden dacht je moeder dat God iets groots in ons leven van plan was. Het schijnt dat ze gelijk krijgt.'

'Absoluut. Ik weet het zeker. Jouw benen en dat ons kleine meisje blijft leven.' Nicole sloeg haar armen over elkaar. 'Je moet bij haar gaan kijken, mam. Ze is zo mooi.'

Abby's hart werd vervuld van verdriet, maar ze dwong zich tot een glimlach. 'Dat zal best, lieverd.'

'Jullie zijn opa en oma!' Nicoles stem klonk weer vermoeid, maar haar enthousiasme taande niet. 'Niet te geloven, toch?'

Abby had er nog niet eens aan gedacht. Als Nicole en de baby maar in veiligheid waren. Nu het meisje was geboren, had ze er nog geen gedachte aan gewijd dat John en zij nu grootouders waren. Het was ongelooflijk en even vroeg ze zich af hoe dit tafereel zich af zou hebben gespeeld als ze hun scheidingsplannen hadden doorgezet. Hoogstwaarschijnlijk was hij er dan nu niet bij geweest. Dat was te pijnlijk en te moeilijk geweest.

Wat was God goed voor hen geweest! Ze sloeg haar arm om Johns schouders en keek onderzoekend naar Nicole, die vredig uit haar ogen keek. 'Hebben jullie haar al een naam gegeven?'

Nicole en Matt hadden tientallen namen bedacht, maar er nooit echt een uitgekozen. Maar nu lachten ze naar elkaar en Nicole keek Abby aan. 'Ja. Haley Jo. Naar mijn zusje… en Matts moeder.'

'O, Nick.' Abby kon haar tranen niet tegenhouden. 'Wat mooi.'

Even was het stil. Abby vermoedde dat ze allemaal hetzelfde dachten. De eerste Haley was gestorven en ook deze Haley zou misschien niet blijven leven.

Voordat iemand iets kon zeggen, kwam de dokter binnen. 'Mevrouw, uw baby is ernstig in nood. Ik weet dat u moe bent, maar ik wil u graag in een rolstoel zetten om u naar de neonatale intensive care te brengen. Ik denk dat het goed is als ze uw aanraking voelt en uw stem hoort.'

In een waas werd Nicole van het bed in een stoel getild en Matt en zij gingen de kamer uit met de dokter in hun kielzog. Abby en John bleven alleen. 'Stel dat ze sterft voordat we de kans krijgen om haar te zien?' Abby viel op Johns schoot en sloeg haar armen om zijn hals.

'Dan zullen Haley Ann en zij feestvieren in de hemel.' John kuste haar voorhoofd. 'En eens als wij aan de beurt zijn, zullen ze ons daar ontvangen.'

's Nachts om drie uur kwam Matt bij hen in de wachtkamer. Zijn stem was hees van tranen. 'Jullie mogen naar binnen.' Matt sloeg zijn armen over elkaar. 'Misschien haalt ze het niet. Nicole wil dat jullie haar zien voordat…'

Hij maakte zijn gedachte niet af. John rolde naar Matt toe met Abby achter zich aan. 'We gaan met je mee.'

Matt bracht hen naar een sterilisatieafdeling, waar ze allebei een ziekenhuishemd kregen en hun handen konden wassen. Daarna werden ze bij de ingang van de speciale afdeling ontvangen door een zuster. 'Een vlug bezoekje maar. We zijn hard aan het werk om haar te redden, maar jullie mogen wel even een blik werpen.'

De verpleegster ging voorop, gevolgd door John en Abby en ten slotte Matt. Abby kon niets zeggen toen ze stilstonden voor een couveuse. De zuster legde haar hand op het doorzichtige deksel. 'Dit is Haley.'

Matt bleef een meter achter Abby en John staan zodat ze goed konden kijken. Nicole had gelijk. Het was een prachtig kindje, een miniatuur van Nicole op die leeftijd en zelfs… ja… een sterke gelijkenis met… 'Zie je het, John?'

Zijn ogen glansden van tranen toen hij knikte, zonder zijn blik van het kleine kindje los te maken. 'Ze lijkt op Haley Ann.'

'Echt waar?' Matt stak zijn hoofd tussen hen in en keek naar het kindje. 'Nicole en ik konden niet zeggen op wie ze leek.'

Abby bekeek de baby goed. Haar piepkleine vingertjes waren niet dikker dan spaghettislierten en haar hele lijfje paste makkelijk in één hand van John. Er zaten op verscheidene plaatsen haardunne slangetjes aan haar vast en ze was bijna overdekt met plakkers en bandjes. De huid die wel zichtbaar was, zag er bleek en doorzichtig uit. Geen normale kleur voor een pasgeboren kindje.

Abby legde haar handpalm tegen het warme glas. 'Kom op, kleine Haley, ademhalen. Doorgaan, meisje!'

John gaf een kneepje in haar knie, maar zei niets. Ze had voor hen beiden gesproken. Ineens drong het tot Abby door dat Matts ouders er niet waren. Ze keek over haar schouder naar hem. 'Heb je je vader en moeder gebeld?'

'Hun telefoon ligt van de haak of zo. Ze zijn almaar in gesprek.'

'Op weg naar huis gaan we wel even langs om het te vertellen.' John rolde een eindje achteruit. 'Nicole en jij hebben tijd nodig. Maar we zullen bidden voor Haley. En als er iets verandert, horen we het wel.'

John had gelijk, maar Abby wilde niets anders dan naast de couveuse blijven zitten. Het tafereel deed haar denken aan de laatste ochtend van Haley Ann, toen Abby haar had neergelegd voor een slaapje en haar twee uur later dood in haar wiegje had gevonden.

Was ze maar bij haar gebleven om te kijken hoe ze ademhaalde... om haar aan te stoten om door te ademen als ze ermee ophield. Dan was Haley Ann in leven gebleven. En misschien gold hetzelfde voor deze Haley. Deze kostbare kleindochter.

John wachtte op haar, maar Abby bleef nog even naar kleine Haley staan kijken. *Ik geef haar aan U, God... waak over haar. Houd haar alstublieft in leven.*

Abby kreeg een beeld in haar hoofd van een glimlachende, jeugdige Jezus die Haley Jo in Zijn armen wiegde en dicht tegen Zijn borst aan hield. Daarmee kon Abby zich eindelijk van haar losmaken. De boodschap die ze door het beeld had gekregen, was klaar en helder. Abby kon niets voor Haley doen wat Jezus niet al deed.

Haar leven, haar toekomst... haar volgende ademhaling... waren allemaal in Zijn handen.

Zevenentwintig

Toen er vlak voor het middaguur werd aangebeld, was Abby er zeker van dat het Jo en Denny waren. Nicole had die ochtend opgebeld dat Haley de nacht had overleefd. Nadat Abby en John Matts ouders hadden gewaarschuwd, waren ze rechtstreeks naar het ziekenhuis gegaan. Abby dacht dat ze nu langskwamen om hun bezorgdheid om het piepkleine baby'tje met Abby en John te delen.

Maar toen Abby opendeed, waren het Matts ouders niet.

Het waren de ouders van Jake Daniels.

Tara en Tim stonden op de mat, ze keken eerst elkaar aan als gegeneerde tieners en toen Abby. Tara sprak het eerst. 'Mogen we binnenkomen?'

'Natuurlijk.' Abby deed verrast een stap naar achteren. Sinds die dag in de rechtszaal hadden ze geen van beiden meer contact gezocht met Abby of John. 'Ik verwachtte iemand anders.'

De Daniels kwamen de hal in, maar Tim stond stil. 'Als je bezoek hebt, kunnen we een andere keer terugkomen.'

Abby wuifde met haar hand. 'Nee, niets daarvan.' Ze aarzelde. 'Nicole heeft vanmorgen vroeg haar baby gekregen. Ik verwachtte de ouders van haar man.'

'Is alles goed met de baby?' vroeg Tim bezorgd.

'Nee. Eigenlijk niet.' Abby's stem werd ineens schor. 'Ze is twee maanden te vroeg. We bidden voor haar.'

John had hun stemmen gehoord, want hij kwam door de gang aanrijden en zwaaide. 'Kom binnen.'

Ze gingen de woonkamer in. John zette zijn rolstoel dicht

bij Abby. 'Nog steeds met verlof, Tim?'

'Ja.' Hij wisselde een blik met Tara. 'Donderdag moet Jake voorkomen.'

'Hij krijgt misschien een jaar jeugdgevangenis.' Tara gleed een beetje dichter naar Tim toe. 'Maar erger kan het niet zijn.'

Abby verschoof op haar stoel. Waren ze daarvoor gekomen? Om over Jakes straf te praten?

'Maar daar komen we niet voor.' Tim vouwde zijn handen en zette zijn onderarmen op zijn knieën. 'Weten jullie nog dat jullie ons toen in de rechtszaal vertelden dat jullie vorig jaar bijna gescheiden waren?'

John knikte.

Tara trok een wenkbrauw op. 'Daarna wilden we graag komen, maar… ik kon het niet.' Ze kruiste haar benen en leunde dichter tegen Tim aan. 'Nu is volgende week de zitting en daarna moet Tim weer naar zijn werk. Dat betekent dat onze tijd samen bijna voorbij is en we hebben nog niet gepraat over wat we voelen. En of we het weer samen moeten proberen.'

Abby begreep het. 'Je bent bang.'

'Tim en ik hebben zoveel ruziegemaakt voordat hij vertrok. Toen hij weg was, kon ik alleen maar denken aan wat we hadden weggegooid. De liefde en de lol en de herinneringen. Het was allemaal verdwenen.'

'Zo voelde ik het ook, maar Tara gelooft me niet.' Tim wierp zijn handen omhoog. 'Er is geen twijfel aan dat we samen willen zijn, maar we kunnen ons niet over het verleden heen zetten.'

Dat hadden Abby en John een jaar geleden ook kunnen zeggen, toen Abby's vader stierf. Ze wisten die dag zeker dat ze nog om elkaar gaven en elkaar nog steeds wilden, maar de berg van pijn was gewoon te hoog om te beklimmen.

'Nadat Tim was vertrokken, is hij met vrouwen uitgegaan.' De pijn stond in Tara's ogen te lezen. 'Ik zat te treuren om alles wat we kwijt waren en hij nam in New Jersey een nieuw kapsel, een nieuwe baan en een nieuwe vriendin. Soms om de paar weken.

Hoe kon ik daarmee de strijd aangaan?'

Tim stak zijn hand op. 'Die meisjes hadden niets te betekenen. Ik was op de vlucht voor het verdriet. Alles wat ik deed was mijn manier van vluchten. Zelfs dat ik die auto voor Jake kocht.'

Er viel een stilte tussen hen en Abby haalde diep adem. 'Mag ik iets zeggen?'

'Graag,' zei Tim meteen. 'Daar zijn we voor gekomen.'

Abby keek naar John en vroeg hem zonder woorden of het goed was dat ze hun eigen verhaal vertelden. De rust in zijn ogen vertelde haar dat hij niet anders wilde. Ze glimlachte en richtte haar blik op Tara.

'Toen John en ik problemen hadden, ging hij om met een lerares van school. Ze werkt hier niet meer en haar naam is niet belangrijk. Het gaat erom dat ik er woest om werd. Ik was jaloers. Ze was jonger dan ik en hoger opgeleid. Ik dacht dat ik me niet met haar kon meten, ik *wilde* me niet met haar meten. Ik bleef boos en jaloers, ook nadat John inmiddels alles deed wat hij kon om het goed te maken tussen ons.'

Tara knikte. 'Precies.'

'Wat ik moest leren was dat je, ook al houd je van elkaar, soms een fout maakt. Of een reeks fouten. Toen ik met John trouwde, beloofde ik hem lief te hebben in goede en kwade dagen. Wat er ook gebeurde.' Abby's stem klonk teder, maar er klonk ook hartstocht in door. Ze hoopte dat Tara dat zou horen. 'John wilde het goed maken tussen ons, maar ik was niet bereid hem te vergeven. En weet je wat? Op dat punt was hij niet degene die zijn huwelijksbelofte niet nakwam, maar ik. Ik weigerde hem te vertrouwen, ook nadat hij me keer op keer had verteld dat hij geen verhouding had gehad. Ik wilde hem straffen omdat hij een andere vrouw zelfs maar aantrekkelijk had gevonden, omdat hij vrienden met haar geworden was en verleid werd door haar. En daarom kon ik het rechtvaardigen dat ik hem… wreed behandelde. Omdat mijn gevoelens gekwetst waren en ik vond dat hij het verdiende.'

Het werd weer stil. John keek naar Tim. 'Ik begreep daar

natuurlijk allemaal niks van. Ik dacht dat ze me gewoon niet kon vergeven.'

Tara had tranen in haar ogen en ze veegde ze discreet weg. 'Hoe zijn jullie eroverheen gekomen?'

'Herinneringen.' John leunde achterover en staarde in het verleden. 'Onze scheidingsplannen speelden tegelijk met Nicoles verloving. Het was trouwjurken dit, en kerken dat, en hoe moet het met onze geloften, papa...' Hij schudde zijn hoofd. 'Wat konden we anders doen dan ons herinneren hoe het twintig jaar geleden voor ons was geweest.'

'Hoe we als tieners verliefd werden en hoe fantastisch het was toen we pas getrouwd waren.' Abby glimlachte. 'Ook toen was het niet makkelijk.'

'De herinneringen kwamen bij ieder van ons afzonderlijk boven.' John lachte droevig. 'We wisten geen van beiden hoe we de ander erover moesten benaderen en daarom dachten we dat we onze plannen moesten doorzetten.'

'Wat hield jullie tegen?' Er viel weer een traan op Tara's wang.

'God.' John en Abby zeiden het tegelijk en keken elkaar toen grinnikend aan. John wierp Tim een scherpe blik toe. 'Het was alsof God heel duidelijk tegen ons zei: 'John en Abby Reynolds... ga NIET scheiden. Ik heb jullie voor elkaar gemaakt... vergeef en vergeet... en pak het vreugdevolle leven weer op dat ik voor jullie heb.'

Abby ontmoette Tara's blik. 'Heb je dat gevoel wel eens, Tara? Alsof God wil dat je de pijn en de boosheid loslaat en simpelweg van elkaar houdt?'

'Voortdurend.'

'Waarom heb je het dan niet gedaan?'

'Daarom. Ik ben bang dat het weer gebeurt.' Ze keek naar Tim. 'Jij bent de enige man van wie ik ooit heb gehouden, maar toen je bij me wegging, haatte ik je. En... en ik had me voorgenomen dat je nooit meer mijn hart zou breken. Al smeekte je me om terug te komen.'

John zei zacht: 'Het gaat om een probleem dat de mensheid van het begin van de tijden in moeilijkheden heeft gebracht.'

'*Welk* probleem?' Tim wrong zijn handen.

'Trots.' John glimlachte. 'Daarom namen Adam en Eva de appel, omdat ze dachten dat ze slimmer waren dan God. Ze wilden zijn als God. En dat is de reden waarom goede echtparen, liefdevolle echtparen zoals jullie tweeën en Abby en ik, verschillende kanten opgaan en uiteindelijk geloven dat echtscheiding de beste oplossing is.' Hij pakte Abby's hand. 'Terwijl de enige oplossing is om elkaar stevig vast te pakken, te vergeven en door te gaan.'

Een tijdlang zei niemand iets. Toen stelde John: 'Denk erom, altijd is het de duivel geweest die achter de zonde van trots zit. Hij wil dat we denken dat we niet kunnen vergeven, niet nederig met elkaar kunnen leven. Maar daar heeft de duivel een bedoeling mee. Hij wil dat we ons ellendig voelen.'

Tim staarde John aan. 'En jij denkt dat dat de enige reden is voor een echtscheiding? Twee mensen die naar de leugens van de duivel luisteren?'

'Meestal wel, ja. Wanneer we onze huwelijksbeloften uitspreken, is echtscheiding het laatste waar we aan denken. Toch?'

Tara en Tim knikten.

'Ik wist dat Abby de enige vrouw was van wie ik ooit had gehouden, de enige met wie ik de rest van mijn leven wilde delen.'

'Ik voelde me net zo.' Tim legde zijn hand op Tara's knie en ze liet hem liggen.

'Dus alleen een leugen kan daar verandering in brengen, hè? Anders was de liefde die ik met Abby deelde niet elk jaar beter geworden.' Er klonk spijt in Johns stem. De spijt die Abby en hij samen droegen. Het spijtige besef van al die waardevolle jaren die ze hadden verloren toen ze onder één dak een afzonderlijk leven leidden.

Abby maakte Johns gedachte af. 'Maar in plaats daarvan begonnen we slecht over elkaar te denken. Al gauw luisterden we naar de leugen en geloofden we dat we iets beters verdienden dan een leven samen.'

'Terwijl we moesten ophouden met vluchten, elkaar vergeven en terugdenken aan alle redenen waarom we om te beginnen met elkaar getrouwd waren.'

Tara snufte met droge ogen. 'Het gaat allemaal om vergeving.'

'Ja.' Abby's hart ging naar haar uit. 'Inderdaad.' Ze voelde een steek van spijt. Het was vreselijk geweest om in onverzoenlijkheid te leven. Vast te houden aan bitterheid en de man aan wie ze haar leven had verbonden te haten.

John leunde ontspannen achterover. 'Er staat in de Bijbel een verhaal over een man wie de koning een grote schuld kwijtschold. Zodra hij bevrijd was, rende hij door de straten op zoek naar zijn mededienaar. Toen hij hem vond, greep hij de man bij zijn mantel. "Kom op met dat geld, vriend," zei de man. "Betalen of ik gooi je in de gevangenis."

Toen de koning hoorde wat er gebeurd was, liet hij de man roepen. "De schuld die ik jou heb kwijtgescholden, was veel groter dan de schuld die je mededienaar jou schuldig was. Omdat je het niet over je hart kon verkrijgen om dat kleinere bedrag kwijt te schelden, zal ik je het grote bedrag niet kwijtschelden." En daarop liet hij de man in de gevangenis gooien.'

Abby bewonderde John om zijn illustratie uit de Schrift. Hij was altijd een goed verteller geweest. Dat maakte hem tot een goede leraar. Maar nu hij weer elke week met Abby meeging naar de kerk, kwam hij voortdurend met zulke verhalen aanzetten als hij net had verteld.

Abby keek naar Tim en Tara en zag dat ze het begrepen.

'God heeft ons vergeven.' Tara snufte. 'Veel meer dan wij ooit een ander zullen moeten vergeven.'

'Precies.' Er klonk deernis in Johns stem.

Tara schoof naar het puntje van haar stoel. 'Willen jullie voor me bidden? Dat ik mag leren vergeven.'

Zonder aarzelen deed John het. Toen ze klaar waren, keek hij

Abby aan. 'Lieverd, wil je mijn schoenen even uittrekken?'

Ze wist niet wat hij van plan was, maar zijn grijns beviel haar. Met een licht hart knielde ze voor hem neer en trok zijn schoenen uit. Toen keerde ze terug naar haar stoel en wachtte.

Tim en Tara keken nieuwsgierig naar zijn voeten.

'Kijk.' John wees naar zijn tenen. 'Ik wil jullie iets laten zien om aan jullie zoon te vertellen.'

Zelfs Abby had geen idee wat hij van plan was. Dat Johns tenen nu en dan op willekeurige momenten hadden bewogen was één ding. Maar dit... wat voerde hij in zijn schild?

Toen alle ogen strak op zijn twee grote tenen waren gericht, zag Abby het. De tenen bewogen! Allebei. Een klein beetje wiebelen slechts, maar het was onmiskenbaar. Abby gaf een gil en sloeg haar armen om Johns hals. 'Het gebeurt echt, John. Niet te geloven.'

Aan de andere kant van de kamer keken Tim en Tara sprakeloos toe alsof ze water zagen branden. Tim was de eerste die zich herstelde. 'Wat... hoe deed je... John, weet je arts hiervan?'

'Ja.' John trok Abby op zijn schoot. 'Het is een vorm van spinale shock. Heel zeldzaam. Volgende maand word ik geopereerd. De kans bestaat dat ik mijn benen weer volledig kan gebruiken.'

'O, lieve help!' Tara's handen vlogen naar haar mond. 'Jake vertelde dat hij God om een wonder heeft gevraagd. Dat je... dat je eens weer zou kunnen lopen.'

Tim keek haar aan. 'Dat heeft hij me niet verteld.'

'Het is waar.' Ze bleef met grote ogen naar Johns twee grote tenen zitten kijken. 'Hij dacht dat God hem had verteld dat dit zou gebeuren. Dat coach Reynolds beter zou worden. Maar toen de maand voorbijging, gebeurde er niets. Jake... hield erover op.'

'Nou, zeg maar dat-ie moet blijven bidden.' John grinnikte, met zijn arm strak om Abby's middel. 'Zij die geloven, zullen wonderen zien.'

Lang nadat Tim en Tara vertrokken waren, nadat John naar hun nieuwe slaapkamer op de begane grond was gegaan om een dutje te doen, zat Abby aan de eetkamertafel en keek uit over het meer.

John had gelijk. Zij die geloven, zagen wonderen. Nicole had tenslotte voor Abby en John gebeden. En Jake had gebeden voor Johns beschadigde benen. En nu had de jongen het gevoel dat alles goed kwam met John.

Ze bleef lang zitten en bad voor baby Haley, sprak tot God en verwonderde zich over Zijn plan voor hun leven. Hoe meer ze aan de discussie met Tim en Tara dacht, hoe meer ze ervan overtuigd raakte dat wat er met Johns benen gebeurde maar een deel was van het wonder dat Jake op het punt stond te ontvangen.

Het andere deel, daarvan was Abby vrijwel zeker, kon nu elk moment gebeuren, als een bepaald echtpaar binnenkwam en bekendmaakte dat Jakes vader door Gods genade en vergeving niet meer naar New Jersey terugging.

★

Zondagmiddag was de baby drie dagen in leven gebleven en dat was meer dan de artsen voor mogelijk hadden gehouden. Ze worstelde nog steeds om elke ademhaling, maar Nicole was vlug hersteld en bracht bijna al haar tijd door naast de couveuse waar de baby in lag. Ze mocht haar handen naar binnen steken en met haar vinger Haleys kleine beentje of armpje strelen. De opening was net groot genoeg dat Nicole haar baby kon zien reageren, niet alleen op haar aanraking, maar ook op haar stem.

Ze werd op haar schouder getikt en Nicole keek om. Het was Jo, haar ogen waren rood en gezwollen. 'Hoi.'

'Jo, hoi… ga zitten.'

Jo knikte en schoof een stoel naast die van Nicole. 'Hoe gaat het met haar?'

'Ze houdt vol.' Nicole keek de vrouw onderzoekend aan. Jo was een intens levend mens. Iedere stemming trok ze door tot in het extreme. Maar nu was ze zwijgzaam en melancholisch. Verslagen zelfs. 'Gaat het?'

'Ja, hoor.' Jo's ogen werden vochtig. 'Waar is Matt?'

'Thuis om een beetje bij te slapen. Hij heeft zijn ogen amper dicht gehad na de geboorte van de baby.'

Even bleven ze zo naar kleine Haley zitten kijken. Na vijf minuten haalde Jo diep adem. 'Nicole, ik moet je iets vertellen.'

Ze draaide haar hoofd om naar Jo. 'Ik luister.'

'Och, lieve mensen.' Jo rolde met haar ogen en veegde haar neus af. 'In geen miljoen jaar had ik gedacht dat ik dit ooit aan iemand zou vertellen. Aan jou of Matt het minst van al.'

Nicole keek haar onderzoekend aan. Wat het ook was, de last drukte zwaar op haar. 'Je kunt het me vertellen, Jo.'

Ze wierp Nicole een waakzame blik toe. 'Je moet me niet haten, hoor.'

'Goed.'

'Nou…' Ze snufte hard en zocht naar woorden. 'Het gebeurde lang geleden, toen Denny en ik pas getrouwd waren.' Jo veegde haar handen af aan haar broekspijpen en staarde naar baby Haley. 'We waren jong en dom, en een paar weken na de bruiloft kwamen we erachter dat ik in verwachting was.'

In verwachting? Nicole probeerde niet verbaasd te kijken. Jo had gelijk. Noch Matt, noch zij had dit verhaal ooit gehoord. Ze wachtte tot Jo verderging.

'We waren bang, heel erg bang.' Jo schudde haar hoofd. 'Als vissen die aan de haak geslagen waren. We zagen geen uitweg meer. Snap je?'

'Ja.' Nicole hoopte dat haar gezicht het medeleven weerspiegelde dat ze voelde. Zij had zich precies zo gevoeld toen ze ontdekt had dat ze zwanger was. En als God haar hart niet had veranderd, zou ze zich waarschijnlijk nu nog zo voelen.

'Destijds… tja, Denny en ik kenden God niet. Niemand om ons heen trouwens. Dus…' Haar stem begaf het en ze boog haar hoofd. 'Het spijt me. Ik weet niet of ik mijn verhaal af kan maken.'

In Nicoles hart begon begrip te dagen. Had de vrouw iets gedaan om een einde te maken aan haar zwangerschap? Nicole nam Jo's verweerde hand in de hare. 'Je kunt me niets vertellen waardoor ik minder van je zou houden, Jo. Je hoeft het niet te vertellen… maar dat moet je weten.'

Jo worstelde om haar zelfbeheersing terug te vinden. Toen ze weer kon praten, wierp ze Nicole een snelle blik toe. 'Ik heb een abortus laten doen, Nicole.' Ze knikte en snufte hard. 'Denny bracht me naar de kliniek en wachtte in de hal. En in zo'n smoezelig kamertje kwam er een knappe man naar me toe en zei dat het allemaal goed kwam. Ik hoefde alleen maar heel stil te blijven liggen en het te zeggen als ik pijn voelde. De zwangerschap zou binnen de kortste keren verdwenen zijn.'

Er liepen tranen over Nicoles wangen en haar hart brak voor Jo. Ze wist niet wat ze moest zeggen, dus hield ze haar mond.

'Wat raar, hè? De zwangerschap verdween… alsof het niks met een baby te maken had.' Jo veegde over haar ogen. 'Maar het was meer dan een zwangerschap. Ik was toen vijf maanden heen en een van de zusters heeft het me verteld.' De woorden bleven even in Jo's keel steken. 'Het was een meisje, Nicole. Net zo'n klein meisje als jullie Haley. Alleen heb ik haar in plaats van het leven, de dood geschonken.'

Jo liet haar hoofd in haar handen zakken en smoorde een snik.

'Ach, Jo…' Nicole wreef zachtjes kleine rondjes over haar rug en zocht naar iets om te zeggen. Maar ze kon niets bedenken.

Eindelijk vond Jo haar stem terug. 'Een jaar later werd ik zwanger van Matt. We wilden weer een abortus laten doen, maar iets hield me tegen. Ik weet niet meer wat het was, maar ik wist gewoon dat het niet goed was. Het deed er niet toe dat we jong en arm waren. Het was niet de schuld van de baby en ik wilde niet meer naar die vreselijke kliniek.'

Nicoles hart sloeg een slag over. Als Jo Matt had laten aborteren… Ze moest er niet aan denken. Het deed al genoeg pijn om van Jo's eerste abortus te weten. 'Weet Matt het niet?'

'Hoe had ik het hem kunnen vertellen? Hoe kun je je zoon recht aankijken en hem zeggen dat je zijn zusje hebt gedood?'

'Kom, Jo… niet doen.' Nicole sloeg haar arm om Jo's hals en

drukte haar jonge gezicht tegen Jo's oudere gezicht. 'Jullie wisten niet wat jullie deden.'

'Maar nu weet ik het wel.' Jo begon harder te huilen en Nicole zag een paar verpleegsters naar hen kijken. Jo scheen het ook te merken en ze dempte haar stem. 'Sinds de geboorte van Matt heb ik spijt gehad van wat ik had gedaan. Ik had er alles voor over gehad om die kleine schat terug te krijgen, om het over te kunnen doen.'

Nicole liet Jo los en leunde achterover in haar stoel. 'God vergeeft je, Jo. Dat weet je toch?'

Jo knikte en snufte nog een keer. 'Nadat ik vorig jaar mijn leven aan Jezus had gegeven, heb ik met Denny gepraat. Ik zei tegen hem dat het verkeerd was wat we hadden gedaan en hij was het met me eens. Die avond zijn we helemaal alleen naar de kerk gegaan en hebben we samen de baby aan God opgedragen. We zijn op onze knieën gegaan om God te vertellen hoe erg het ons speet.' Ze hief haar kin een beetje op. 'Ik heb nog nooit een volwassen man zo zien huilen, Nicole. En toen wist ik dat ik niet de enige was die dat kindje miste.'

Nicole was ontroerd door het beeld dat Jo schetste. Beide ouders die verantwoordelijkheid namen voor wat ze hadden gedaan en God om vergeving vroegen. 'Wat mooi, om haar samen zo te gedenken.'

'Nou, het was niet mooi. Het was pijnlijk. Het deed meer pijn dan alles in mijn leven, als je het per se weten wilt. Nadat we God hadden verteld dat het ons speet, vroegen we Hem om in de hemel voor onze baby te zorgen. Je weet wel, haar knuffelen en zoentjes geven en wilde bloemen voor haar plukken op een zomerdag. Haar leren vissen en lachen en haar liefhebben. Over haar waken tot wij dat eens zelf kunnen doen als we boven zijn.'

Jo zweeg weer en nam baby Haley in zich op. 'We stelden ons ons dochtertje zo'n beetje voor als een weeskind. Een hemels weeskind.' Jo wierp Nicole een zijdelingse blik toe. 'En die avond beloofden we God dat als Hij in de hemel voor ons kleine wees-kindje zou zorgen, wij hier op aarde voor Zijn weeskinderen zouden zorgen.'

Ineens viel het allemaal op zijn plaats. 'Jullie reis naar Mexico?'

'Ja.' Jo's lip trilde. 'Daarom gaan we.'

'Wauw…' Nicole hield haar adem in. 'Dat is prachtig, Jo.'

'Ja, nou, wat ik nog meer te zeggen heb, is minder mooi.'

Nicoles hart begon te bonzen, maar ze zweeg.

'Nadat ik het van kleine Haley had gehoord, hebben Denny en ik gebeden tot de blaren ons op de lippen stonden.' Jo legde haar hand op de zijkant van de couveuse. 'Maar elke keer als ik bid, geeft God me een beeld dat me bang maakt.'

Nicole wist niet of ze het wel wilde weten, maar ze kon er niets aan doen. 'Wat voor beeld?'

'Een beeld van drie kleine meisjes die in de hemel arm in arm door de velden rennen.' Jo zweeg en Nicole wilde haar handen over haar oren leggen. 'Een van hen is je zusje Haley Ann, het andere is ons kleine meisje en het derde… het derde is jullie kleine Haley Jo.'

Nicoles adem stokte. Ze glimlachte gedwongen. 'Kom, Jo… is dat wat je dwarszit?'

'Natuurlijk.' Ze keek Nicole verbaasd aan. 'Ik wil dolgraag dat de kleine Haley in leven blijft. Dat wens ik uit het diepst van mijn hart. Maar als God mijn hart kent, waarom zie ik dan steeds dat beeld voor me?'

Nicole deed zich sterker voor dan ze zich voelde. 'Misschien omdat ik ook vroeg zwanger ben geworden. Misschien omdat je weet dat als Haley… als ze het niet haalt gelukkig zal zijn in de hemel bij haar twee tantes.' Nicole hief hulpeloos haar handen op. 'Ik weet het niet, maar dit betekent niet dat God Haley thuis gaat halen. Dat mag je niet denken, Jo.'

Iets in Nicoles woorden of misschien in de klank van haar stem, scheen Jo gerust te stellen. De angstige, gekwelde uitdrukking verdween en er kwam een stil verdriet voor in de plaats. 'Je hebt gelijk. God zal kleine Haley sparen. Dat moet ik geloven.'

Na een tijdje ging Jo weg en Nicole bleef bijna een uur in haar eentje naar Haley zitten kijken terwijl ze haar in stilte aanmoedigde om te blijven ademhalen en te blijven leven. En bad dat als Haley oud genoeg was om door een veld met bloemen te rennen, het in hun eigen achtertuin mocht zijn.

En niet in de hemel.

Achtentwintig

Het was de dag van de zitting en Jake had het gevoel dat hij de afgelopen vier maanden tien jaar ouder was geworden.

Maar dan op een goede manier. Zodat hij zich veel zekerder voelde over zijn geloof en zijn toekomst en zijn plannen om oudere tieners de fouten die hij had gemaakt te helpen vermijden.

Jake was van plan om als hij niet naar een jeugdgevangenis werd gestuurd, in de herfst terug te keren naar Marion High. Iedereen met wie hij had gepraat, was het ermee eens dat het de beste keuze was, de manier om zijn studiegenoten zo duidelijk mogelijk te overtuigen van de gevaren van straatracen. Bovendien kon hij dan weer in de buurt van coach Reynolds zijn. En nadat hij vier maanden weg was geweest, was Jake niet van plan om zijn middelbare-schoolopleiding ergens anders af te maken dan op de campus waar hij les kreeg van de coach. Zo niet op het footballveld, dan toch zeker in de klas. Als de rechter het hem tenminste toestond.

Hij had nog iets besloten. Hij wilde nog een poging doen om te footballen. Niet om zich uit te sloven voor de leerlingen uit de onderbouw of om zich onder zijn vrienden op een voetstuk te zetten, maar om het spel te spelen zoals de coach het hem geleerd had. Met gevoel en klasse en eer.

Natuurlijk was A.W. duidelijk tegen hem geweest. Misschien kreeg hij de kans niet. De rechter kon hem makkelijk veroordelen tot een jaar jeugdgevangenis en als dat gebeurde, zat hij zijn laatste schooljaar opgesloten.

Jake had gebeden voor de afloop van vandaag en als God hem

achter de tralies wilde hebben, dan ging hij daarheen. Er bestond geen twijfel aan dat hij elke straf die hij kreeg, verdiende.

De rechtszaal stroomde vol en Jake keek naar zijn ouders. Ze zaten bij de achterdeur te praten en zagen eruit als goede vrienden. Hij had zijn moeder nu en dan gevraagd wat er gaande was tussen hen, maar ze deed altijd vaag.

'We hebben een hoop te bepraten, Jake. Je vader helpt me gewoon hier doorheen.'

Dan trok Jake een wenkbrauw op en liet het rusten. Maar ze trokken nu zoveel met elkaar op dat hij er een gebedspunt van had gemaakt.

De rechter kwam binnen en onmiddellijk staakten zijn ouders hun gesprek en namen hun plaatsen in aan weerskanten van hem. A.W. legde een stapel papieren recht en fluisterde. 'Daar gaat-ie dan.'

Toen de rechter gezeten was, riep zij de zaal tot de orde. Jakes zaak was als eerste aan de beurt. 'Ik heb begrepen dat de verdachte in de zaak Daniels wil pleiten, klopt dat?'

A.W. stond al. 'Ja, edelachtbare. We hebben een overeenkomst bereikt met de staat over de aanklachten.'

'Heel goed. Wil de verdachte opstaan?'

Jake stond op, verbaasd over de vreemde kalmte die over hem was gekomen. *Het is aan U, God… wat U wilt…*

De rechter keek naar een vel papier dat voor haar lag. 'Meneer Daniels, u wordt beschuldigd van grove onachtzaamheid in het gebruik van een voertuig, roekeloos rijden en illegaal straatracen, allemaal misdrijven.' Ze keek hem aan. 'Hoe pleit u?'

'Schuldig, edelachtbare. Op alle aanklachten.' Het voelde heerlijk om dat te zeggen. Hij *was* schuldig. Het had geen zin om eromheen te draaien. Het kon hem niet schelen wat de rechter nu besloot.

'Meneer Daniels, bent u ervan op de hoogte dat op elk van deze aanklachten een maximumstraf van zes maanden in een jeugdgevangenis staat?'

'Ja, edelachtbare.'

'En dat de combinatie van aanklachten betekent dat u tot achttien maanden in zo'n instelling zou moeten doorbrengen?'

'Ja, edelachtbare.'

De rechter keek in het dossier. 'Ik zie dat uw advocaat mij namens u enkele brieven heeft verschaft. Ik schors de zitting twintig minuten om het dossier te lezen.' Ze keek naar A.W. 'Dan kom ik terug om uw cliënt zijn straf toe te bedelen, is dat begrepen?'

'Ja, edelachtbare.' Zonder overgang zei hij: 'Ik wil ook graag dat u het feit in overweging neemt dat mijn cliënt zich al opgegeven heeft voor dienstverlening. Hij is van plan de komende vijf jaar leerlingen op vier middelbare scholen per jaar toe te spreken om hen te helpen de fouten die hij heeft begaan te vermijden.'

De rechter zweeg een ogenblik. 'Heel goed. Dat zal ik in mijn overwegingen meenemen.'

De zitting werd verdaagd en Jakes ouders omhelsden hem van weerskanten.

'Je bent niet zenuwachtig, hè jongen?' Zijn vader keek hem verbaasd aan.

'Nee. Ik heb het met God uitgepraat. Wat daarna gebeurt, is wat Hij wil. Ik ben niet bang.'

A.W. lachte nerveus. 'Nou, ik wel. Als dat voor u iets uitmaakt.' Hij knikte naar de deur waardoor de rechter was vertrokken. 'Die rechter is een harde. Wat er ook in de brieven staat, ze kan je ten voorbeeld stellen.'

Jake zag hoe zijn moeder ineenkromp bij de gedachte en hij klopte op haar rug. 'Mam, je moet hierin op God vertrouwen. Als Hij wil dat ik naar de gevangenis ga, dan ga ik. En dan komt het helemaal goed.'

'Weet ik. Ik zou je alleen zo graag op Marion terugzien. Je hebt zulke goede ideeën over football en je vrienden helpen.'

'Hoeveel brieven heb je kunnen krijgen?' Jakes vader stelde de vraag aan A.W.

'Vijf. Dat is meer dan genoeg.' De advocaat keek nadenkend op.

'Een van Tara en van jou, een van Jakes reclasseringsambtenaar, een van iemand van de dienstverleningsinstelling met wie hij werkt. En het mooiste van alles: een van John Reynolds.'

Coach Reynolds? Jakes maag draaide om. 'Hebt u coach Reynolds om een brief gevraagd?'

'Ja, hoezo?'

'Niet te geloven dat u dat hebt gedaan... hij heeft al genoeg meegemaakt zonder dat hij een brief voor mij hoefde te schrijven. Wie heeft gezegd dat u dat moest doen, terwijl...'

A.W. stak een hand op en Jake stopte midden in zijn zin. Hij zweeg, maar hij was ziedend. Hij was in lange tijd niet zo boos geweest. Het lef om de coach te vragen om een brief die hem een lichtere straf zou bezorgen.

'Ik heb meneer Reynolds niet om een brief gevraagd.' A.W. hield zijn hoofd schuin. 'Meneer Reynolds bood het aan.'

Jakes maag kwam tot rust. Wat? Had coach Reynolds de tijd genomen om een brief voor hem te schrijven, terwijl zijn kleindochtertje ziek was en hij binnenkort geopereerd werd?

Jake keek zijn ouders aan en zag dat zij hetzelfde voelden. Ze hadden allemaal geweten dat coach Reynolds een geweldige man was. Maar zo geweldig? Zo bezorgd voor een jongen door wie hij in een rolstoel zat? Voor het eerst die dag kreeg Jake een brok in zijn keel.

De rechter verscheen en riep het hof opnieuw tot de orde.

'In de zaak Daniels ben ik tot een besluit gekomen, een besluit waarvan zelfs ik niet zeker ben of het eerlijk is.'

Ze stuurt me naar de gevangenis... Jake knipperde met zijn ogen en probeerde niet bang te worden. *Help me, God... help me.*

De rechter vervolgde: 'Wil de verdachte opstaan?'

Jake stond met knikkende knieën op.

'Zoals ik al zei, heb ik het recht om u, meneer Daniels, een straf op te leggen van achttien maanden in een jeugdgevangenis.' Ze zweeg even en keek naar de officier van justitie. 'Maar in dit geval ben ik overstelpt met verzoeken om anders te handelen.'

Jake zag dat zijn ouders elkaars hand pakten.

'Ik was het meest onder de indruk van de brief die geschreven is door het slachtoffer: de heer John Reynolds.' Ze hield een vel papier omhoog. 'Meneer Reynolds schrijft: *Ik smeek u Jake toe te staan zijn straf af te werken terwijl hij op Marion High zit. Want ziet u, in de herfst kom ik terug naar school en als het ongeluk niet gebeurd was, zou het Jakes eindexamenjaar zijn geweest. Als Jake niet op de campus is, zal ik dagelijks herinnerd worden aan die vreselijke novemberavond. Jake wordt er geen betere autobestuurder of verstandiger jongeman van als hij opgesloten wordt, noch zal het de omvang van mijn letsel verminderen. Maar Jake op de campus van Marion High te zien, lijkt me even fijn als weer te kunnen lopen.*' Ze keek Jake even aan voordat ze eindigde: '*Edelachtbare, ik vraag u mijn herstel te bevorderen door Jake op een andere wijze te straffen. Hij is veranderd sinds het ongeluk en Marion High heeft meer jongens als hij nodig op de campus.*'

In de hele zaal was alleen het zachte snuffen van zijn moeder hoorbaar en het bonzen van zijn eigen hart. Had de coach dat echt gezegd? Dat hem op de campus te zien even fijn was als om weer te kunnen lopen?

De rechter legde de brief neer en keek rond. 'Om die reden, en omdat de verdachte goede cijfers haalt op het nascholingsinstituut, zie ik af van gevangenisstraf. In plaats daarvan leg ik een taakstraf op, waarbij de verdachte de komende vijf jaar vier keer per jaar zal spreken op middelbare scholen.'

Jake was zo blij dat hij de rechtszaal uit had kunnen zweven. Niet omdat hij zijn straf ontging, maar omdat hij terugging naar Marion High, naar dezelfde campus als coach Reynolds! En omdat hij nog een kans kreeg om football te spelen zoals hij het altijd had moeten spelen. *God... ik zal het goed met U maken... dat beloof ik...*

Naast hem leken zijn ouders ineens tien jaar jonger en Jake begreep dat ze zich meer zorgen hadden gemaakt dat hij naar de gevangenis moest dan ze hadden laten merken.

De rechter roffelde met haar hamer op de rechtersstoel. 'Orde!'

Toen het stil was, vervolgde ze: 'Bovendien blijft het rijbewijs van verdachte ingetrokken en mag hij voor zijn eenentwintigste verjaardag geen nieuwe aanvragen. Tot die tijd zal hij een tien weken durende cursus verkeersveiligheid bezoeken, dit jaar en elk jaar totdat hij eenentwintig is geworden.' Ze keek Jake aan. 'Als ik een straf uitdeel, heb ik gewoonlijk het gevoel dat het recht wordt gediend.' Ze hield haar hoofd schuin. 'Dit keer ben ik er niet zeker van.'

'Ja, edelachtbare.'

'Je komt er heel makkelijk vanaf, vriend. Ik wil je gezicht nooit meer in deze rechtzaal zien. Is dat begrepen?'

Jake knikte. 'Maakt u zich geen zorgen, edelachtbare. Ik kom niet terug.'

Ineens was de zitting voorbij en Jake werd gefeliciteerd door A.W. en zijn ouders, en enkele footballspelers van Marion High die achter in de zaal hadden gezeten.

'Jake, fantastisch, man. We hebben je volgend jaar nodig als quarterback.' Dat was Al Hoosey, een receiver. Hij sloeg Jake op de schouder. 'Hartstikke gaaf.'

Jake keek hem recht aan. 'Het wordt volgend jaar anders, Hoosey. Heel anders.'

De jongen knipperde met zijn ogen. 'Dat is toch mooi?'

Nu kon Jake zijn glimlach niet inhouden. 'Héél mooi.'

Er dromden nog meer mensen om hem heen en iemand trok aan zijn elleboog. Hij keek om en zag de officier van justitie staan. 'Hoor es, even over die opmerking van de rechter... dat ze niet zeker wist of het recht was gediend?'

'Ja, meneer?' Jake draaide zich helemaal naar hem om.

'Ik heb ook een gevoel voor zulke dingen. En dit keer weet ik zeker dat het recht gediend was.' Het gezicht van de officier stond ernstig en somber. 'Doe je best en zorg dat die vrienden van je niet met straatraces gaan beginnen, goed? Dat zal mijn werk een stuk makkelijker maken. Afgesproken?'

Jake slikte moeilijk. 'Afgesproken.'

De zaal liep leeg en zijn advocaat zocht zijn spullen bij elkaar en vertrok. Eindelijk bleef Jake alleen over met zijn ouders.

'Verbazingwekkend, hè jongen?' Zijn vader en moeder hielden nog steeds elkaars hand vast. Ze schenen geen haast te hebben om te vertrekken.

'God moet volgend jaar op Marion grote dingen voor me in petto hebben.' Jake wierp een blik op de klok aan de wand. 'Kom, we gaan naar huis. Ik moet een paar bedanktelefoontjes plegen.'

Zijn moeder glimlachte en haalde haar vingertoppen door zijn pony zoals vroeger toen hij nog een klein jongetje was. 'De coach?'

'Ja. Ik popel om het hem te vertellen.'

'Jongen…' Zijn vader ging wat rechter zitten en Jake kreeg het gevoel dat hij iets belangrijks te zeggen had. 'Voordat we gaan, willen je moeder en ik je iets vertellen.'

★

Abby had nooit verwacht dat het op de parkeerplaats van een restaurant zou plaatsvinden.

Ze was er zeker van geweest dat er een moment zou komen dat haar gezin bij elkaar kwam om voor John te bidden. Maar nu Haley nog steeds vocht voor haar leven, glipten de dagen tussen hun vingers door. Eindelijk was het de dag voor Johns operatie.

Kade was thuis voor de voorjaarsvakantie en John en Abby namen het gezin mee uit brunchen. Voordat ze uit elkaar gingen, keek Abby de kring rond. 'We wilden graag met iedereen bidden… voordat John morgenochtend naar het ziekenhuis gaat.'

'Goed idee.' Jo stak haar handen naar beide zijden uit, deed haar ogen dicht en boog haar hoofd. 'Wie begint?'

Ze keken elkaar glimlachend aan. Toen gaf iedereen elkaar een hand en boog zijn hoofd daar op de parkeerplaats. Kade begon als eerste te bidden, en Jo en Denny sloten zich bij hem aan voordat Nicole en Matt en Sean aan de beurt waren.

Abby had moeite met praten. Ze kon alleen een kort woord van dank uitbrengen dat God hun een straaltje hoop had gegeven.

Toen was John aan de beurt.

Hij deed zijn mond open om te bidden, maar er kwam niets. Na een paar tellen begon hij te zingen.

'Groot is Uw trouw, o Heer… mijn God en Vader. Er is geen schaduw van omkeer bij U…'

Het was het lievelingslied van Johns vader, lang voordat John geboren was. Een voor een begonnen de anderen mee te zingen, zonder te letten op de blikken die de langslopende mensen hun toewierpen. In het refrein zongen ze over de grootheid van Gods trouw en de waarheid uit Klaagliederen dat Zijn genade elke morgen nieuw was.

Wat er ook gebeurde.

Abby vond haar stem terug en zong mee, haar hart ging op in de woorden. Dit zou ze nooit vergeten. Toen het lied uit was, keek John naar de gezichten om hem heen. 'Dank jullie wel. God is getrouw, dat geloof ik. Wat er ook gebeurt.'

Enkelen pinkten een traantje weg toen de groep omhelzingen uitwisselde en hun plannen voor de volgende dag besprak. Jo en Denny zouden een tijdje na de operatie naar de anderen in het ziekenhuis komen. Sean en Kade zouden er de hele dag zijn, evenals Nicole en Matt. Nicole zou voornamelijk bij Haley zijn, maar om de zoveel tijd zou ze komen vragen hoe het met John ging.

'Haley ligt op de tweede verdieping en jij komt op de vierde, pap.' Nicole gaf hem een dikke knuffel. 'Dat is toch wat?'

Abby keek naar John. De spanning van wat er de komende dagen stond te gebeuren begon hem eindelijk in zijn greep te krijgen. Hij gaf Nicole een kus op haar wang. 'Zorg goed voor mijn kleindochtertje.'

'Goed.' Ze veegde een traan weg. 'We zullen bidden.'

Sean reed naar huis met Kade, dus toen John in de gordel zat en Abby de bestuurdersplaats innam, waren ze alleen. 'Merkte je dat niemand iets zei over weer kunnen lopen?'

Het was een prachtige aprildag die een voorbode was van de komende zomer. John staarde uit het raam. 'Ik denk dat ze er niet op durven hopen.'

De rest van de weg naar huis zwegen ze, maar toen ze uitstapten, twijfelde Abby er niet aan waar ze terecht zouden komen. Zonder een woord te zeggen, volgde ze John naar de achtertuin, over het cementen pad de steiger op. Ze begaven zich naar het water. Abby ging in de stoel zitten, met John naast zich.

'Wat denk je nu, juffie Abby?' Hij keek haar in de ogen.

'Juffie Abby… zo heb je me sinds onze kindertijd niet meer genoemd.'

'Echt?'

'Echt.'

John lachte. 'Nou, niet omdat ik er niet aan gedacht heb. Jij blijft altijd mijn kleine juffie Abby.' Hij zweeg even en liet de bries van het meer over hen heen blazen voordat hij een nieuwe poging deed. 'Je hebt geen antwoord gegeven.'

'Hmmm.' De zon stond recht boven hun hoofd en veroorzaakte een explosie van licht op het meer. Ze keek uit over het water. 'Nee.'

'Dus… denk je niks bijzonders of wil je het me niet vertellen?'

'Geen van beide.' Ze glimlachte lui.

Hij perste zijn lippen op elkaar en probeerde haar te doorgronden. 'Ik geloof niet dat ik je snap.'

'Ik denk *wel* wat bijzonders,' zei ze speels, 'en ik wil het je *wel* vertellen.'

'Goed.' Hij sloeg zijn armen over elkaar. 'Vertel maar.'

'Ik wachtte op het juiste moment. Omdat ik iets belangrijks te zeggen heb. Ik wil dat je met je hart luistert, John Reynolds.'

Hij verschoof zijn stoel zo dat hij haar goed kon zien. Hun knieën raakten elkaar, maar Abby wist dat John het niet kon voelen. Nog niet, tenminste. 'Ik luister, Abby. Met mijn hele hoofd en hart.'

'Mooi.' Abby haalde diep adem en keek hem recht in de ogen. 'Ik heb veel over je operatie nagedacht, John. Ik heb erover gedroomd hoe het zou zijn als je genezen was.' Ze zweeg even.

'Ik ook.' Hij kneep zijn ogen tot spleetjes. 'Ik denk aan alle manieren waarop ik mijn benen zou gebruiken als ik ze nog één uur had, of één dag.'

'Wat zou je dan doen?' vroeg ze zacht. Boven hun hoofd cirkelde een havik.

'Ik zou 's morgens anderhalve kilometer hardlopen, dan football spelen met Sean en Kade, en dan de hele middag de liefde met je bedrijven, juffie Abby.'

'Fijn.' Ze glimlachte met warme wangen. 'Ik dacht ongeveer ook zoiets.'

'Wilde je me dat vertellen?' Hij boog naar haar toe en greep haar benen vast, wreef met zijn duimen zacht langs de binnenkant van haar knieën.'

'Nee.' Ze keek dieper, naar de kern van zijn wezen. 'Ik wilde je vertellen dat het niet geeft.'

John wachtte tot ze verderging.

'Het geeft niet of je je benen terugkrijgt, John. Er was een tijd dat ik gezegd zou hebben dat alles behalve een compleet herstel tragisch zou zijn voor ons leven en voor onze relatie.' Ze schudde haar hoofd. 'Maar dat zeg ik niet meer. In de afgelopen vijf maanden heb ik geleerd om zo van je te houden. Ik vind het fijn om je in en uit bed te helpen; ik vind het fijn om er te zijn om je broek voor je op te hijsen. Ik vind het zelfs fijn zoals je met dertig kilometer per uur met me over de steiger scheurt in een moderne uitvoering van de tango.'

Ze keek hem onderzoekend aan zonder met haar ogen te knipperen. 'Wat ik probeer te zeggen is: ik wil je benen net zo graag terug als jij, maar als je morgen onveranderd uit de operatie komt, is het ook goed. Ik zou niet méér van je kunnen houden dan nu.'

Lange tijd zei John niets. Hij staarde Abby alleen maar aan terwijl ze gezamenlijk het ogenblik indronken. 'Stel dat we die avond na Nicoles bruiloft niet hadden gepraat?'

'Ik kan het me niet voorstellen.' Abby's stem klonk schor, haar keel was dik van emotie.

'Ik houd zoveel van je, Abby. Gelukkig zijn we verstandig genoeg geweest om naar Gods stem te luisteren en verstandig genoeg om elkaar terug te vinden.' Het meer werd weerspiegeld in zijn ogen. Abby verdronk erin, onbewust van de wereld om haar heen. 'Je bent alles voor me, Abby. Alles.'

'Ik geloof met mijn hele hart dat God er morgen bij zal zijn in de operatiekamer, dat Hij het mes van de chirurg zal leiden en je zal genezen. Maar je moet één ding onthouden, John.'

'Wat dan?'

'Ik zal er ook zijn.' Ze legde haar hand op zijn hart. 'Daar... de hele tijd.'

'Weet je wat we eerst moeten doen?' Johns gezicht klaarde op en zijn ogen schitterden zoals de ogen van zijn zoons schitterden als ze niets goeds in de zin hadden.

'Eerst? Voor de operatie, bedoel je?'

'Ja.'

'Goed... ik geef het op. Wat moeten we eerst doen?'

Hij klopte op zijn schoot.

'O, nee. Niet de tango.'

'Ja, Abby... kom op. We beginnen er net goed in te worden.'

Ze lachte. Ze stond op en liet zich zonder plichtplegingen op zijn schoot vallen. 'Na morgen kan ik dit niet meer doen.'

Hij draaide de rolstoel en begon naar het verste punt van de steiger te rijden. 'Waarom niet?'

'Omdat je me na morgen zult *voelen*, gekkie. Dan ben ik te zwaar voor je.'

'Jij? Te zwaar?' Hij was bovenaan en draaide de stoel rond, om hem met de handrem tot stilstand te brengen. 'Nooit, Abby. We bewaren de stoel en gaan dit één keer in de week voor de lol doen.'

'O, houd op.' Ze gaf hem een duw tegen zijn schouder. Daarbij stootte Johns hand tegen de handrem en de stoel begon over de steiger te rollen.

'Daar gaan we.' Hij leidde de stoel met één hand en hield met de andere de hare tangoachtig voor hen uitgestrekt.

Ze drukte haar wang tegen de zijne toen ze het midden passeerden en steeds harder naar het water doken. Luid en ademloos zei ze: 'Heb ik erbij gezegd dat ik deze dans eng vind?'

'Ach, Abby... kleingelovige... we zullen het net zo vaak moeten doen tot je niet meer bang bent.'

Vlak voordat ze aan het eind waren, liet John de stoel een sierlijke cirkel draaien. Maar dit keer slipten de wielen en de stoel kantelde, zodat John op zijn rug aan het eind van de steiger belandde, en Abby bovenop hem.

Abby smoorde een gil, meer van het lachen dan van angst. Ze hief haar gezicht en hield het vlak bij het zijne. 'Goeie zet, Reynolds.'

'Ik heb er weken op geoefend. Ik dacht wel dat je het prachtig zou vinden.' Hij streelde haar rug en drukte haar tegen zich aan. Ze kusten elkaar, eerst ontmoetten hun lippen elkaar kort, daarna op een manier die de dingen uitsprak die niet in woorden te vangen waren.

Abby begon te lachen.

'Hé, wacht eens even.' John haalde diep adem. 'Je hoort niet te lachen. Dit hoort bij de dans.'

'Ik kan er niets aan doen.' Abby liet haar voorhoofd op zijn schouder rusten tot ze weer kon ademhalen. Ze tilde haar hoofd op en keek hem aan. 'Weet je nog die dag in de gang? Dat je achterover viel toen je me naar de keuken probeerde te leiden?'

John lachte en bleef haar rug strelen. 'Een van mijn betere momenten.'

'Je zei dat je nooit volwassen zou worden, weet je nog?'

John lachte nog harder. 'Zelfs Paula's danslessen konden me niet helpen.'

'Kennelijk niet.'

Ze lachten en kusten en lachten nog meer, tot de geluiden van hun vrolijke geluk over het meer dreven en zich vermengden met de middagwind. Pas toen ze moe waren van het lachen, stond Abby op en zette de rolstoel recht. Ze hielp John er weer in en duwde hem langzaam omhoog over de steiger.

Zo lang ze leefde, zou ze zich deze middag herinneren. De diepte van hun liefde en hun vrolijkheid, de rust en de aanvaarding. Ze had John de waarheid gezegd. Ze kon van haar leven niet meer van hem houden dan nu, en dat gold ook voor morgen.

Wat de dag verder ook nog brengen zou.

Negenentwintig

Jake werd de volgende morgen om zeven uur wakker en keek op zijn kalender.

Dit was de dag. Hij voelde het even duidelijk als zijn eigen hartslag. Hij had gebeden, niet alleen voor coach Reynolds, maar ook voor zijn kleindochtertje. En God had hem laten weten dat er die ochtend voor beiden een ingrijpend wonder zou plaatsvinden.

Het was zijn taak om te blijven bidden.

Dus voordat hij uit bed stapte, voordat hij zich aankleedde of ontbeet of wat dan ook deed, rolde hij op zijn buik, begroef zijn gezicht in zijn kussen en bad. Niet zoals hij bad toen hij nog een kind was, voor het ongeluk.

Maar als een man.

Alsof zijn leven ervan afhing.

*

Het was druk rond Haleys couveuse.

Nicole had verderop in de gang in dezelfde kamer geslapen als waar Matt en zij na Haleys geboorte soms gelogeerd hadden. Het meisje was vier weken in leven gebleven, langer dan de artsen hadden durven hopen. Maar haar longactiviteit was nog steeds zwak. Als de situatie niet verbeterde, liep ze grote kans op longontsteking, wat in haar broze toestand bijna zeker fataal zou blijken.

Zoals altijd had Nicole de zusters gevraagd om haar te halen als er iets in Haleys toestand veranderde. Maar er was niemand naar haar toegekomen en haar hart begon te bonzen toen ze een stuk of zes verpleegkundigen om haar baby heen zag staan. Vlug liep ze langs de andere couveuses tot ze zo dicht mogelijk bij die van Haley was.

'Pardon...' Nicole gluurde om de verpleegkundigen heen. 'Wat is er aan de hand? Mijn baby ligt daar.'

Een zuster die Nicole kende, draaide zich met een ruk om en sloeg haar armen om haar heen. 'Het is een wonder!' Ze trok Nicole een eindje van de couveuse weg. 'Vanmorgen waren de waarden van je kind slechter geworden. We wilden je wakker maken, maar iets na zeven uur is alles veranderd.'

Nicole wist niet wat haar overkwam. 'Veranderd? Wat bedoel je?'

'Haar longen. Het is alsof ze voor het eerst volledig hebben kunnen doorademen. Meteen steeg het zuurstofgehalte in haar bloed naar een gezonde hoogte.'

'Dus... dus het gaat beter met haar?' Nicole keek reikhalzend naar Haley, blij dat de andere verpleegkundigen weer hun normale gang gingen.

'Niet zomaar een beetje beter.' De zuster straalde. 'Ze heeft een mijlpaal bereikt. De dokter is net geweest en hij heeft haar toestand opgevijzeld van kritiek naar ernstig. Als het zo goed blijft gaan, mag ze naar huis zodra ze op gewicht is. Het is ongelooflijk. Daarom stonden we met z'n allen naar haar te kijken. Zulke dingen gebeuren niet zomaar met zulke zieke kindjes.'

Eindelijk was er een open plek aan de couveuse gekomen en Nicole perste zich erin. 'Mag ik haar aanraken?'

De zuster grinnikte. 'Absoluut.'

Nicole werkte haar hand door de steriele opening en aaide met haar vinger over Haleys armpjes en beentjes. 'Schatje, ik ben het, mama.' Nicole lachte en huilde tegelijk. 'God heeft je gespaard, Haley. Hij laat je in leven.'

Ze dacht aan het beeld dat Jo zo vaak voor zich had gezien.

Drie kleine meisjes die in de hemel door de velden huppelden. Nicole huiverde. Wat waren ze daar dichtbij geweest.

Haley strekte haar beentjes en zwaaide met haar handjes als reactie op Nicoles aanraking. Nicole keek om naar de zuster. 'Ze wil dat ik haar vasthoud.'

'O ja?' De zuster trok een wenkbrauw op. 'Later op de dag zullen we haar wegen en als haar ademhaling zo goed blijft, moet je haar vanmiddag wel kunnen vasthouden.'

Nicole had zin om te juichen. Haley bleef leven! Snel bedacht ze wat ze verder moest doen. Ze moest het Matt en zijn ouders vertellen, en haar ouders...

Haar ouders!

Het was even over achten en haar vader kon elk ogenblik de operatiekamer binnen worden gereden. Maar eerst moest hij het nieuws horen. Nicole fluisterde bij het gat in de couveuse. 'Haley, liefje, ga maar even slapen. Ik ben zo terug.' Toen draaide ze zich om naar de zuster. 'Pas jij even op haar? Ik moet het de anderen gaan vertellen.'

Nicole had in tijden niet meer zo hard gerend. Ze vloog door de gang naar de lift en schoot er weer uit zodra hij de vierde verdieping had bereikt. Zo vlug als haar voeten haar wilden dragen, begaf ze zich naar de verpleegpost. 'Ik zoek mijn vader, John Reynolds.'

De zuster wees. 'Hij is op weg naar de operatiekamer.'

'Bedankt.' Nicole rende door de gang. *O, nog niet... alstublieft, God, laat me op tijd bij hem zijn.*

Vlakbij de lift sloeg ze de bocht om en knalde op Kade. Samen belandden ze met verstrengelde armen en benen op de vloer. Vanaf de grond riep ze naar haar vader. 'Niet weggaan, pap. Ik moet je iets vertellen.'

Haar moeder hielp haar overeind, terwijl Kade op zijn achterwerk plofte en moeizaam overeind krabbelde. 'Goeie tackle.' Hij zette zijn honkbalpetje recht. 'Je bent je roeping misgelopen, Nicole. Je had lijnman moeten worden in plaats van schooljuf.'

'Sorry.' Nicole veegde het stof van Kades spijkerbroek en toen van haar eigen. 'Ik moet pap hebben voordat hij naar de operatie-kamer gaat.'

Haar vader lag vlak voor de liftdeuren op een brancard. Hij lachte zacht en vroeg met opgetrokken wenkbrauwen: 'Wat het ook is, het moet goed nieuws zijn.'

Nicole knikte naar Sean en kwam dichter bij haar vader staan. Aan het voeteneind van de brancard stond een ziekenverzorger die haar aankeek alsof ze krankzinnig was. Ze wuifde naar hem. 'Hoi... sorry voor de opwinding.'

De liftdeuren gingen open en Nicole schudde haar hoofd. 'Nog niet. Eén minuutje, oké?'

'Nicole, wat is er toch aan de hand?' Haar moeder kwam naast haar staan en keek haar vragend aan.

'Wacht even. Pap, Haley heeft een mijlpaal bereikt. Ze ademt als een gewone baby en...' Nicole was buiten adem van het rennen en van de opgetogenheid over het wonder dat was gebeurd. 'De dokter zei dat ze een mijlpaal heeft bereikt. Ze is buiten gevaar, pap. Is dat niet *fantastisch*?'

Nu was het Kades beurt om haar te tackelen. Hij tilde haar op in een woeste omhelzing terwijl Sean en haar moeder hun armen om haar heen sloegen. Haar vader pakte haar hand en gaf hem een kneepje. 'Meen je dat echt, lieverd?'

Nicole bevrijdde zich. 'Ja, papa.' Ze boog zich over hem heen en keek in zijn ogen. 'En God is nog niet klaar. Ik kon je niet naar de operatiekamer laten gaan zonder dat je wist wat God heeft gedaan. Wat Hij nog voor jou gaat doen voordat deze dag voorbij is.'

'Hoe is het dan gegaan? Is ze gewoon zomaar uit zichzelf gaan ademen?'

De liftdeuren gingen weer open en Nicole lachte naar de ver-zorger. 'Nog één minuutje? Alstublieft?'

Hij haalde zijn schouders op. 'Zonder je vader kunnen ze niet beginnen.'

Nicole keek haar moeder aan. 'Niemand weet wat er gebeurd is. Rond zeven uur zoog ze een volle hap lucht in. De monitors gingen uit, waardoor het personeel wist dat ze eindelijk uit zichzelf ademhaalde. Sindsdien gaat het geweldig.'

'Yes!' Sean stak zijn vuist in de lucht. 'Mijn nichtje blijft leven!'

Nicoles stem werd zacht. 'Dus, pap… nu ben jij aan de beurt, hè.'

Haar vader glimlachte met droge ogen. 'Zeg maar tegen dat kleine meisje van je dat haar opa binnenkort een eindje met haar gaat wandelen.'

'Goed.' Nicole deed een stap naar achteren en knikte naar de verpleger toen de liftdeuren weer opengingen. 'Zet hem op.'

Ze haakten hun armen in elkaar en het laatste wat ze van John zagen toen hij de lift in werd gereden, was een glimlach. En zijn opgeheven duim.

Nicole kreeg tranen in haar ogen. Het was het teken dat haar vader op het footballveld gaf, maar niet voor elke wedstrijd.

Alleen als hij zeker wist dat ze gingen winnen.

★

Abby had in haar hele leven nog nooit geijsbeerd, maar nu ijsbeerde ze. Niet op de trage, peinzende manier die bestemd was voor meditatieve momenten. Maar met snelle stappen door de wachtkamer naar het raam en nog sneller terug.

Nicole en Matt waren beneden bij Haley, de jongens waren naar het restaurant gegaan om een hapje te eten, en Jo en Denny waren er nog niet. Dus Abby was alleen. De operatie was bijna een uur aan de gang en Abby kon haar energie niet kwijt.

Jazeker, ze zou evenveel van John blijven houden als door de operatie het gevoel in zijn benen niet herstelde. Maar als het wel lukte en hij weer kon lopen en rennen en autorijden? Hoe fantastisch zou dat zijn? Dan was hun liefde niet alleen verdiept door het ongeluk, maar ze kregen ook nog een nieuwe kans om ervan te genieten.

De mogelijkheden deden Abby's hart bonzen en door met grote passen heen en weer te lopen, kon ze zich afreageren. Hard en snel, zodat ze haar nerveuze energie kwijt kon.

Dokter Furin had gezegd dat de operatie vier uur in beslag kon nemen. Ze moesten elk strengetje van Johns beschadigde ruggenmerg identificeren en nauwgezet repareren. Als ze gelijk hadden, als hij ooit nog een kans had om weer te lopen, zouden ze enkele strengetjes intact vinden. Dat verklaarde het gevoel en de beweging in zijn tenen.

Maar dat was maar de helft van de strijd.

De andere helft was te zorgen dat de reparatie helemaal goed verliep. Streng voor streng, uur na uur onverdroten doorwerken.

Abby begon nog sneller te ijsberen.

Ze was er nog steeds mee bezig toen Jo en Denny door de gang aan kwamen lopen en stilstonden bij de ingang van de wachtkamer. 'Goeie help, Abby, wat spook jij nou uit?' Jo kwam naast haar staan en pakte haar arm. 'Probeer je een gat in de vloer te slijten?'

Voor de eerste keer in een halfuur stond Abby stil. 'Ik weet niks anders te doen.'

'Nou, dat is zo makkelijk als vliegenaas.' Jo nam Abby mee naar de bank, terwijl Denny vanuit de deuropening toekeek. 'Je gaat daar zitten en je bidt.' Ze wenkte Denny naderbij.

Hij haalde een krantenkatern achter zijn rug vandaan en overhandigde het aan Abby.

Jo keek haar stralend aan. 'En als je klaar bent met bidden, kun je dit lezen. Daarna zul je niet veel zin meer hebben om te ijsberen.'

Abby nam de krant aan en knikte. Ze deed haar ogen dicht en Denny bad of God de handen van de chirurgen wilde leiden met Zijn machtige greep. Toen ze klaar waren, keek Abby naar de krant. Even wist ze niet wat ze zag. De hele pagina stond vol met kolommen met namen. Toen ze zag wat er bovenaan stond, snakte ze hoorbaar naar adem.

Het was een paginagrote advertentie en de kop luidde: *We bidden voor u, coach!*

Daaronder stond in kleinere letters: *Wij, leerlingen en leraren van Marion High, willen coach John Reynolds publiekelijk bedanken voor alles wat hij heeft gedaan om ons tot winnaars te maken. Nu hij vandaag een operatie ondergaat, zullen wij bidden voor zijn volkomen herstel. En dat hij volgend jaar nog steeds hoofdcoach mag zijn van de sterke Eagles.*

De wens was ondertekend door een lijst namen die te groot was om in één keer te lezen. Honderden namen, namen van leraren en leerlingen en spelers, waarvan Abby er veel niet eens kende.

'Zie je wel.' Jo knikte ferm. 'Ik wist wel dat het je rust zou geven.'

De krant trilde in Abby's hand. 'John zal het niet geloven.'

Jo had gelijk. Nadat ze de advertentie van Marion High had gezien, voelde Abby zich merkwaardig vredig. De drie uur daarna bracht ze afwisselend door met bidden en spelletjes doen met Jo en Denny.

Als ze niet in het restaurant zaten te eten, hielden Kade en Sean zich bezig met Seans spelcomputer. Nu en dan kwamen Nicole en Matt nieuwsgierig vragen of er al bericht was.

Dat was er niet.

Abby wilde het niet als een slecht teken zien. Dokter Furin had gezegd dat hij zijn best zou doen om de familie gedurende de operatie op de hoogte te houden. Er was bijna vier uur voorbijgegaan en nog steeds hadden ze niets gehoord.

'Zouden we het onderhand niet moeten weten?' Denny gluurde over de kaarten in zijn hand naar Abby.

'Ik dacht het ook.' Ze haalde diep adem. *Kom op, hart. Rustig blijven.* 'We zullen gewoon moeten afwachten.'

'Een goede visser weet alles van wachten.' Jo legde een kaart op. Ze zag er volkomen onaangedaan uit, alsof ze gezellig in een zonnige woonkamer zaten en niet in de wachtkamer van een ziekenhuis. 'In plaats van een hengel uit te werpen, werpen we vandaag onze zorgen uit.' Ze grijnsde naar Abby. 'Beter dan ijsberen, hè?'

Er ging nog een halfuur voorbij en het kon Abby niet meer schelen of Jo gelijk had. In het afgelopen uur had ze haar zorgen wel honderd keer uitgeworpen voor God, en de onrust was teruggekomen. 'Goed, jongens.' Ze keek naar Jo en Denny en wenkte dat de jongens mee moesten doen. 'Tijd om weer te bidden.'

Maar voordat ze een woord kon uitbrengen, verscheen dokter Furin. Abby keek gretig naar zijn gezicht. Eerder had ze wel eens een spoor van een glimlach om zijn mond zien spelen, maar ze had hem nooit breed zien grijnzen.

Tot nu toe.

Abby schoot overeind. 'Hoe is het met hem?' De anderen hielden zich stil en keken de arts afwachtend aan.

'Hij is schitterend door de operatie heen gekomen.' Dokter Furin nam een stoel tegenover hen. 'Zijn breuk was precies zoals we gehoopt hadden. We hadden nauwelijks genoeg streng om mee aan de slag te gaan.'

Abby's hele lijf trilde. 'Kunt u al iets zeggen? Of het gelukt is?'

De dokter grijnsde nog breder. 'Hij begint al bij te komen en al zijn belangrijke reflexen reageren.' Hij breidde zijn handen uit. 'De operatie is volkomen geslaagd. Hij moet natuurlijk therapie hebben, om de kracht in zijn benen terug te krijgen. Maar ik verwacht dat hij volledig zal herstellen.'

Jo stond op en keek met haar handen in haar zij op de arts neer. 'Ik ben een stuk simpeler dan de meeste lui, dokter. Ik moet dat gepraat niet over volledig herstel en therapie. De vraag is: zal de man weer kunnen lopen?'

'Ja.' Dokter Furin lachte hardop. 'Voordat het zomer is verslaat hij u met hardlopen.'

'Joechei!' Jo stak haar vuist recht in de lucht. 'Dank U, Jezus!'

Kade en Sean kwamen naast Abby zitten en omhelsden haar. Ze huilden. 'Ik had niet gedacht…' Kades stem ging verloren in tranen.

Sean veegde zijn tranen af. 'Wat hij wil zeggen is dat wij geen van beiden geloofden dat het echt zou gebeuren. We dachten… we vonden het stom van jullie om te denken dat pap door een operatie weer zou kunnen lopen.'

'Ik voel me zo schuldig.' Kade snufte met zijn gezicht tegen Abby's schouder.

Dokter Furin knikte haar toe en stond op om te vertrekken. Later konden ze de bijzonderheden bespreken. Voorlopig zat ze met twee jongens die troost nodig hadden.

Jo pakte Denny bij de hand en fluisterde tegen Abby: 'Ik ga het aan Nicole vertellen.'

Abby knikte en wachtte tot ze weg waren. Toen aaide ze over de ruggen van haar zoons. 'Het geeft niet… jullie hoeven je niet schuldig te voelen. Papa wordt beter.' Ze mochten dan tieners zijn, maar vanbinnen waren ze nog kinderen die troost nodig hadden. Zeker na alles wat er dit afgelopen jaar in hun leven was gebeurd.

Kade hoestte en keek op zodat Abby zijn gezwollen ogen zag. 'Ik geloofde het niet, mam. Nou ben ik al die jaren christen… en Matts ouders hadden meer geloof.' Boos vertrok hij zijn gezicht. 'Wat zegt dat over mij?'

'En over mij.' Sean snufte. 'Ik wist dat iedereen bad om een wonder. Ik heb wel gebeden of papa beter mocht worden, maar ik geloofde niet echt dat hij weer zou kunnen lopen.'

'Jullie zijn niet de enigen, jongens. Er zijn momenten geweest dat ik me ook zo voelde. Ik moest geloven dat de operatie niet zou lukken en zo mijn leven voor me zien. Vandaag nog vond ik het moeilijk te geloven dat het echt zou gebeuren.'

'Echt waar?' Kade ging wat rechter zitten. Hij droogde zijn tranen met de rug van zijn hand. 'Ik dacht dat mensen van jullie leeftijd daar geen last van hadden.'

Abby lachte en stompte Kade zachtjes in zijn buik. 'Mensen van mijn leeftijd?' Ze trok haar wenkbrauwen op. 'Ik denk dat mensen van mijn leeftijd er meer last van hebben.' Ze dacht aan Haley

Ann en haar lach vervaagde. 'Omdat we in ons leven gezien hebben dat God ons soms niet verhoort zoals we willen.'

'Dus papa kan straks echt weer lopen?' De werkelijkheid begon door te dringen en Sean kon zich niet inhouden. Hij sprong op en neer op de bank. 'Misschien kan ik van de zomer met papa gaan hardlopen. Elke dag een paar kilometer of zo.'

Kade lachte. 'Geef hem even de tijd, man. Eerst moeten zijn benen sterk genoeg worden.'

Ze zaten net het proces van spieratrofie te bespreken toen Nicole en Matt om de hoek kwamen rennen. 'Is het waar?' Nicole greep Abby's handen vast. Haar ogen waren groot en vol tranen.

'Mijn ouders vertelden dat de operatie geslaagd is. Zij zijn even bij Haley gebleven, maar wij moesten gewoon naar boven om het zelf te vragen. Heeft de dokter dat echt gezegd?' barstte Matt uit.

Abby grinnikte. 'Hij zei letterlijk dat papa voor de zomer de eerste wordt met hardlopen.'

'*Yes!*' Nicole vloog in Matts armen en maakte toen een rondje om Abby en haar broers te omhelzen. 'Ik wist dat het een dag van wonderen ging worden. Ik *wist* het gewoon.'

Terwijl haar kinderen allemaal tegelijk begonnen te praten en lachen, vervuld van nieuwe hoop, voelde Abby de ongedurigheid terugkomen. Niet omdat ze ongerust was, maar omdat ze iets te doen had. Abby stond op en liep weg door de gang.

'Wacht,' riep Nicole haar na. 'Waar ga je heen?'

Abby grijnsde alleen maar.

'Dat is niet eerlijk. Ik wil ook naar hem toe.'

'Ik eerst. Als hij wakker is, kom ik jullie halen.' Abby wierp hen een blik toe die zei dat ze haar beter niet achterna konden komen. Toen rende ze bijna naar Johns kamer om te doen waar ze vanaf het begin van de operatie al zin in had.

Naar hem toe lopen, hem een kus geven en uitdagen voor een hardloopwedstrijd in juni.

Ze vertraagde haar pas toen ze zijn kamer naderde. Ze wilde hem niet wakker maken als hij sliep. Hij zou wel uitgeput zijn en waarschijnlijk nog onder verdoving. Er kwam geen geluid uit zijn bed toen ze haar hoofd om de hoek van de deur stak en ze liep langzaam naar hem toe.

'John, het is gelukt, schat!' Haar stem was een tedere fluistering en ze hoopte dat hij haar in zijn dromen kon horen.

Even bleef hij stil liggen, maar toen kreunde hij zacht. Zijn nek was vastgezet, zodat hij zijn hoofd niet kon draaien. Maar zijn ogen bewogen onder de leden. Na een paar seconden knipperde hij en Abby zag de paniek in zijn gezicht.

'Lieverd, het is goed. De operatie is voorbij.'

Hij wendde zijn ogen in de richting van haar stem. Zodra hij haar zag, verdween de paniek. 'Hoi.'

Ze streek met haar vingers over zijn arm op en neer en kuste hem op zijn voorhoofd. 'Hoi.'

'Hoelang lig ik hier al?' Hij huiverde van pijn.

'Niet lang. Een uur misschien.'

De verdovende mist leek op te klaren en zijn blik werd gerichter. 'Zeg het, Abby... is het gelukt?'

'O, lieverd, ja!' Er ontsnapte een lach uit Abby's mond en ze smoorde hem met haar hand. Haar ogen vulden zich met tranen. 'Het is volkomen geslaagd. Dokter Furin zei dat je beenreflexen allemaal normaal zijn.'

'Dus...' Hij slikte moeilijk en ze hoorde hoe droog zijn mond was. 'Dus... ik zal weer kunnen lopen?'

Abby knikte. 'Probeer het eens, John. Probeer je benen te bewegen.'

Zijn hoofd was vastgemaakt aan het bed, maar hij staarde langs de lengte van zijn lichaam. Abby keek toe hoe zijn beide benen trilden onder de lakens. Als hij niet net uit de operatiekamer was gekomen, had Abby gedacht dat de beweging een onwillekeurige rilling was.

Maar nu niet.

John vond haar blik weer. 'Zag je dat?'

'Ja!' Ze bracht haar gezicht dicht bij het zijne, ze wist niet of ze moest lachen of huilen. 'Voelde je het?'

'Ja.'

Abby stond op en zag iets wat ze nadat John gewond was geraakt niet meer had gezien. Hij huilde. Niet zoals hun zoons daarstraks hadden gehuild, maar op een stille manier die helemaal niet op huilen leek. Het zag er eerder uit alsof John aan weerskanten van zijn gezicht een lekkage had.

Ze kuste hem op de wang en proefde het zout van zijn tranen. 'Het is een wonder, John.'

Hij snufte en lachte tegelijk. 'Hoelang duurt het nog voordat ik kan lopen?'

'De dokter zei dat je tegen de zomer iedereen er weer uitloopt.' Ze kuste hem weer. 'Maar ik heb gezegd dat hij gek was. Ik ren harder. Ik versla je. Je bent geen partij voor me.'

'O, nee?' Johns stem klonk opnieuw vermoeid en er zweefde een slaperige glimlach om zijn mond. 'Is dat een uitdaging?'

'Absoluut.' Ze giechelde, verlangend om de dagen en weken te zien voorbijgaan. Ze wilde hem dolgraag volledig hersteld zien.

'Goed, afgesproken.' Zijn oogleden werden zwaar en zakten bijna dicht. 'Juni.'

Abby deed een stap naar achteren en leunde tegen de muur. 'Welterusten, John.'

Hij sliep al, met de glimlach nog om zijn mond. Ze wist dat de anderen wachtten om bij hem te mogen, maar ze kon zich niet losmaken, kon niet ophouden naar hem te kijken en zichzelf te vertellen dat het echt gebeurd was. Johns benen waren operatief hersteld!

Ze deed haar ogen dicht en hief haar gezicht naar de hemel.

God... met alleen maar dank U wel kan ik U niet half vertellen hoe ik me voel. Eerst Haley... nu John. U bent zo goed, God. Wat er ook gebeurt, U bent er. U geeft ons vrede... U leert ons lief te hebben... U verkwikt ons met een leven vol hoop. Dank U, God.

Ze dacht aan enkele teksten die haar door de donkere dagen van Johns verlamming heen hadden getrokken: *Jullie zullen het zwaar te verduren krijgen in de wereld, maar houd moed: Ik heb de wereld overwonnen... Steun niet op eigen inzicht, denk aan Hem bij alles wat je doet, dan baant Hij voor jou de weg...*

Abby verwonderde zich over de beloften. God had beslist verlost – en lang voor Johns geslaagde operatie.

Tientallen beelden flitsten door haar hoofd. De dag dat John zijn eerste stappen zou zetten, de ochtend dat hij eindelijk thuiskwam, het moment dat hij voor het eerst het wagentje van de kleine Haley zou duwen... het moment waarop hij weer zou rennen.

En op een junimiddag in de toekomst zouden ze zich aan de ene kant van hun tuin opstellen om een wedstrijdje te doen. Van alle atletische prestaties die John had bereikt, zou die ene run de mooiste van zijn leven zijn.

Dertig

De beweging was nog niet veel.

Ze moesten dicht om Johns bed heen staan, met hun gezicht centimeters van zijn bedekte benen, om het te kunnen zien. Maar Abby had niet gelukkiger kunnen zijn als John op bed had staan springen en op de ziekenhuisdeken de horlepiep had gedanst.

John wees naar zijn benen. 'Kijk dan, ik zal het nog een keer doen.'

Kade en Sean en Nicole en Matt stonden met hun neus op Johns benen. Zijn linkerknie ging een centimeter omhoog, en toen zijn rechter, gevolgd door het ritselen van alle tien zijn tenen onder de deken. 'Het is verbazingwekkend, pap.' Nicole pakte zijn hand. 'Jij en Haley… op dezelfde dag. Dat had alleen God kunnen doen.'

Het was woensdagavond, drie dagen na de operatie, en dokter Furin was dik tevreden. John had in bijna alle delen van zijn onderste ledematen gevoel in huid en spieren. De huid van zijn kuiten was nog een beetje verdoofd, maar daar maakte de arts zich geen zorgen over. In de weinige gevallen waarbij ruggenmergletsel hersteld was, keerde het complete gevoel zelden in de dagen vlak na de operatie terug.

'U bent een uitzonderlijk geval,' had dokter Furin eerder op de dag gezegd. 'U moet mijn advies hebben opgevolgd.'

John gaf de arts een knipoog. 'Absoluut.' Hij wees naar de paginagrote advertentie die aan de muur boven zijn bed hing. 'Zowat heel Marion heeft voor me gebeden.'

Abby stapte naar achteren en liet de kinderen *ooh* en *aah* roepen over Johns vermogen om zijn benen te bewegen. De afgelopen dagen waren onvergetelijk geweest. Het was prachtig om de gezichten van de kinderen te zien toen ze met eigen ogen zagen dat John inderdaad weer gevoel in zijn benen had.

En vooral om hem de krantenadvertentie te overhandigen.

Ze had hem de ochtend na de operatie gegeven en eerst kon hij het evenmin begrijpen als Abby. Toen las hij de kop en de tekst eronder en staarde haar sprakeloos aan.

'Ze houden van je, John.' Ze haalde haar schouders op en zei schor: 'Ze hebben al die tijd van je gehouden.'

'Dus ze hebben...' Hij keek naar de lijst met honderden namen. 'Die hebben allemaal voor me gebeden?'

Abby knikte. 'Kennelijk heeft Kade aan een paar jongens van het team verteld dat iedereen moest bidden van dokter Furin.' Ze glimlachte. 'Een paar hebben het bevel letterlijk genomen en die hebben handtekeningen ingezameld. Iedereen die beloofde te bidden, iedereen die je wilde bedanken voor wat je voor de school hebt gedaan, zette zijn naam op de lijst.'

John keek een hele tijd naar de namen. 'Het is niet te geloven.'

'Dat niet alleen, maar wij en Jo en Denny hebben ook gebeden.'

Een lach kwam omhoog door Johns stijve hals en ontsnapte tussen zijn tanden. 'Ik zou wel willen dat Jo altijd voor me bad.'

'Ze vráágt niet zozeer aan God, ze eist. Alsof ze al weet dat het gaat gebeuren, dus laten we een beetje opschieten.'

'Precies.'

In de dagen na zijn operatie hadden ze vele kostbare uren gedeeld. Tot nu toe was er alleen familie op bezoek geweest. En Jake Daniels. Niets had de jongen kunnen tegenhouden. Abby vermoedde dat hij later op de avond terug zou komen. Maar nu was John ook klaar voor andere bezoekers.

John voelde zich zo goed dat Abby groen licht had gegeven aan verscheidene mensen die langs wilden komen. Er waren al drie spelers met hun ouders geweest en nu waren de kinderen er. John werd het nooit moe zijn benen op commando te bewegen, al was het maar een beetje. Er hing een feestelijke sfeer in zijn kamer.

'Ha, pap. Waarom kun je je knieën nog niet optrekken of uit bed stappen?' Sean streek met zijn vinger over Johns knie. 'Ik dacht dat je benen beter waren.'

'Ach, malloot.' Kade gaf zijn broertje een por met zijn elleboog. 'Zijn beenspieren zijn weg. Dat heb ik je toch verteld? Hij heeft helemaal geen kracht. Hij zal hard moeten werken om ze weer in beweging te krijgen.'

John grinnikte. 'Ja, je vader is net zo zwak als de kleine Haley.'

Abby keek naar Nicole. 'Hoe gaat het met haar, liever?'

'Geweldig. Ik mag haar vasthouden zo vaak als ik wil.' Nicole zag er beter uit dan sinds de geboorte van de baby het geval was geweest. Gelukkig, tevreden en uitgerust. 'Ze weegt drie pond en elke dag wordt ze een beetje zwaarder. Haar ademhaling is normaal en ze heeft geen hersenverlamming van de vroege geboorte.' Nicole klemde Matts hand vast. 'Als alles goed blijft gaan, mag ze over drie weken naar huis.'

De deur ging open en Jo en Denny kwamen binnen. Jo droeg een grote ingepakte doos waaraan een reusachtige visballon zweefde met de tekst *Wat een vangst!* erop. Breed glimlachend overhandigde ze hem aan John.

Hij keek ernaar en beet op zijn lip. 'Bedankt, Jo… Denny. Dat hadden jullie niet hoeven doen.'

'Dat is toch de mooiste ballon die je ooit hebt gezien?' Jo keek recht omhoog naar de groen met gouden vis van folie die boven Johns bed danste. 'Denny vond het een ongepast cadeau, maar volgens mij werkt het.' Ze keek John ernstig aan. 'Kijk, als je eenmaal weer op de been bent, wil je eropuit met die boot van je om te gaan vissen. Ik zou dat tenminste willen. En zodra je weer een hengel in je hand hebt, zul je de vis van je leven vangen, dat voel ik in mijn botten. Dus de ballon werkt. Wat een vangst!'

Abby en de anderen hadden moeite om niet te lachen.

Denny rolde met zijn ogen en knikte met zijn hoofd naar

Jo. 'Dat mens lijdt aan hersenschimmen.'

Jo draaide zich om en schopte Denny zacht tegen zijn schenen. 'Niet waar.' Ze wendde zich weer tot John. 'Hij werkt ook op een andere manier. Als je weer op bent en je voelt je beter, nemen je flinke zoons je binnen de kortste keren mee naar het footballveld. Nou zal je wel een beetje aan je benen moeten wennen, dat weet ik, maar die arm heeft nergens last van.' Jo bracht haar hand omhoog en naar achteren alsof ze op het punt stond een bal te gooien. 'En dan haal je uit, en je gooit uit alle macht... en een van die jongens vangt de bal. En dan zeg je...'

'Wat een vangst!' John gaf Denny een knipoog. 'Ik snap het helemaal.'

John kon nu rechtop zitten en hij hees zich wat hoger op het bed. Hij droeg nog steeds de nekbrace en dat zou nog een paar weken zo blijven. Maar dat weerhield hem er niet van mee te doen met de feestelijkheden. Hij haalde het papier van de geschenkdoos, maakte hem open en haalde er een paar versleten sportschoenen uit. Ze waren vies, er zat amper nog een zool onder en bij de neuzen zaten twee grote gaten.

Jo wees ernaar. 'Ik zal het uitleggen.'

Sean en Kade begonnen te lachen, maar Jo zwaaide met haar vinger. 'Ho, ho... niet lachen. Er zit een verhaal aan die schoenen vast.'

'Daar gaan we weer.' Denny schudde zijn hoofd. 'Ik heb gezegd dat ze net als een gewoon mens bloemen of snoep moest geven, maar... nou ja, je weet 't.'

'Hou op.' Jo knipte met haar vingers. Ze keek naar Abby en toen weer naar John. Abby kon alleen maar raden wat voor verhaal er ging komen. 'Ik heb horen vertellen dat Abby en jij in juni een hardloopwedstrijd gaan houden.' Ze wierp een snelle blik op Abby. 'Niet dan?'

Abby boog haar hoofd en deed haar best om een ernstig gezicht te bewaren. 'Ja, dat is zo.'

'Nou dan.' Ze keek weer naar John. 'Toen ik laatst naar je voeten keek, kwam ik op het idee. Ik zei bij mezelf: "Jo… die voeten hebben haast dezelfde maat als die van mijn Denny."' Ze legde haar handen om haar mond en fluisterde: 'Denny heeft grote voeten voor zo'n klein mannetje.'

'Dank je, lieverd.'

'Graag gedaan.' Jo glimlachte en ging door: 'En toen dacht ik aan het hoogtepunt van Denny's vistijd. De ene dag ving hij drie prijsbeestjes en de andere dag vier. En dat ging wekenlang zo door. En dit…' Ze griste de oude schoenen uit Johns handen en hield ze omhoog zodat iedereen ze kon bewonderen. '… dit waren de schoenen die Denny toen droeg.' Ze knikte krachtig. 'Hij heeft ze al die jaren bewaard voor het geval we nog es een paar geluksschoenen nodig hadden.'

'Dus…' John pakte de schoenen weer aan en grinnikte. 'Je wilt dat ik die aantrek als ik een wedstrijdje doe met Abby?'

'Natuurlijk.' Ze schudde haar hoofd en wierp Abby en Nicole een blik toe. 'Wat zijn mannen toch traag van begrip, hè?'

Abby deed haar mond open om antwoord te geven, maar Jo was haar voor. 'Goed, mensen, luister. Denny en ik willen iets bekendmaken.'

Abby en Nicole lachten vlug naar elkaar voordat ze hun hand voor hun mond sloegen en Jo hun aandacht weer schonken.

'Jo… we hebben het toch al verteld.' Denny's wangen werden rood en hij keek verontschuldigend. 'Haar geheugen is de laatste tijd een beetje vaag.'

Ze zette haar handen in haar zij. 'Helemaal niet. Bovendien heb ik ze de feiten nog niet verteld.' Ze wendde zich weer tot de anderen. 'Denny en ik hebben onze tickets voor Mexico gekocht.' Jo knipoogde naar Nicole, die veelbetekenend keek. Wat Jo ook wilde gaan zeggen, ze had het Nicole kennelijk al toevertrouwd.

Jo haalde twee kleine mapjes uit haar tas en hield ze omhoog. 'Deze zijn gestempeld en gedateerd. Goed voor twee enkeltjes naar Mexico op drie juni.'

'Enkeltjes?' Matt deed een stap dichterbij en bekeek de tickets.

'Jullie komen toch zeker wel terug!'

'Ja. Over zes maanden… een jaar misschien.' Jo stopte de tickets weer in haar tas. 'Wees maar niet bang, ik wil die kleine Haley zien opgroeien.'

'We komen om de paar maanden op bezoek.' Denny sloeg zijn arm om Jo heen. 'Maar we moeten gaan.' Jo en hij wisselden een tedere blik. 'Dat hebben we aan God beloofd.'

Jo tikte Kade op de schouder. 'Denny zegt trouwens dat je met de dominee van de kerk hebt gepraat.'

Kade keek geschrokken. 'Eh… ja.' Hij keek onzeker naar John en Abby. 'We hebben elkaar een paar keer gesproken.'

'Nou ja, daar gaat het niet om.' Jo wuifde met haar hand in de lucht. 'Het gaat erom dat je erover denkt om dominee te worden. Is dat zo?'

'Nee…' Kade zette grote ogen op. 'Niet echt.'

'Zendeling dan?'

'Tot nu toe niet.'

'Nou ja, dat geeft niet.' Jo wapperde met haar vingers boven haar hoofd alsof ze een vlieg wegjoeg. 'Het gaat erom dat we in de maand juli een flinke jongen als jij wel een paar weken kunnen gebruiken in Mexico.' Ze keek naar Denny. 'Hè, lieverd?'

Denny knikte, kennelijk in verlegenheid met Jo's aanpak. 'Dat zei de dominee. Ze willen een team vrijwilligers samenstellen om een nieuw dak op het weeshuis te zetten.'

Abby keek Kade onderzoekend aan en zag hoe zijn verwarring in nieuwsgierigheid veranderde. 'Echt waar?'

'Ja.' Jo gaf Kade een klap op zijn rug. 'En het is maar voor een paar weken. Je footballteam zal je een paar weken in juli niet missen.'

Kade stelde enkele vragen over de reis. Wanneer was het precies… en of er een paar footballmaten van hem mee mochten komen.

Abby keek zwijgend toe. Een jaar geleden zat Kade tot over zijn oren in de ban van smerige porno… en nu overwoog hij een verblijf in Mexico om een onderdak te bouwen voor weeskinderen. Als hij thuis was, praatte hij met hun dominee en er had een verbazingwekkende verandering plaatsgevonden. Kade was vriendelijk en zacht, bewuster van geestelijke zaken. Hij had eelt op zijn ziel gekregen toen hij dagelijks buiten Gods plan voor zijn leven wandelde, maar dat was nu allemaal verdwenen. God Zelf had de ban verwijderd.

Nicole en Sean deden mee aan het gesprek en stelde meer vragen over het weeshuis en het type kinderen dat daar woonde. John pakte Abby's hand. 'Misschien moesten wij ook maar gaan.'

Abby trok een wenkbrauw op. 'Een hardloopwedstrijd is één ding, John Reynolds. Dakdekken in Mexico is een ander verhaal.' Ze keek Jo aan. 'Vraag ons volgend jaar maar.'

'Misschien is het wel een goede therapie als…'

De deur ging open en Tim en Tara Daniels kwamen binnen. Jake liep met een brede grijns op zijn gezicht achter hen aan. Hij keek naar John en samen wisselden ze een veelbetekenende blik. Abby wist het onmiddellijk. Die twee voerden iets in hun schild.

'Komt het goed uit, coach?' Jake ging voor zijn ouders staan en stelde zich op voor het voeteneind van Johns bed.

John keek vlug de kamer rond. 'Ik geloof van wel.'

'Hoi, allemaal.' Jake zwaaide naar de aanwezigen.

Abby voelde een lichte aarzeling bij Nicole, maar de rest van de groep zei de jongen glimlachend gedag.

'Het duurt niet lang. We wilden hier alleen maar even zijn voor een paar bekendmakingen.' Jake knikte naar zijn ouders. 'Mijn ouders mogen eerst.'

Tim deed een stap naar voren en keek van Abby naar John. 'Tara en ik…' Hij reikte achter zich naar haar hand. 'We wilden jullie bedanken voor je gebed voor ons. We… we hebben er uitgebreid over gepraat en besloten dat we nooit hadden moeten scheiden.'

Tara giechelde. 'We wilden het jullie als eerste laten weten.'

'Afgezien van mij natuurlijk.' Jake kwam tussen zijn ouders in staan en sloeg zijn armen om hun schouders.

'Natuurlijk.' Tara glimlachte naar Jake en draaide zich om naar de anderen. 'Tim en ik gaan de eerste zaterdag van juni trouwen.' Ze keek Abby aan met tranen in haar ogen. 'We willen John en jou graag als getuigen.'

'Precies.' Tim knikte. 'Want zonder jullie tweeën zou het niet gebeurd zijn.'

'Is het niet fantastisch!' Jake gaf Kade en Sean en John en Matt een high-five. 'Mijn ouders gaan trouwen!'

'Ach, jongens.' Abby liep om Johns bed heen en omhelsde hen, eerst Tim, toen Tara en ten slotte Jake. 'Dat is geweldig. Natuurlijk komen we.'

Wie had een jaar geleden toen John en zij vastbesloten waren om te scheiden, ooit kunnen denken dat God niet alleen hun huwelijk zou redden en hun liefde sterker zou maken dan ooit, maar dat Hij hen ook zou gebruiken om twee mensen als Tim en Tara te helpen.

Johns ogen straalden en hij wees naar de visballon. 'Ter ere van je verloving, Tim, vind ik dat je mijn ballon verdient.' Hij grijnsde naar Tara. 'Ik bedoel maar, wat een vangst!'

Iedereen lachte en toen wuifde Jake met zijn handen. 'Goed… stil allemaal… nu is de coach aan de beurt.'

Abby voelde een vreemde rilling in haar buik. De coach aan de beurt? Wat ging er nu gebeuren? En waarom had John haar niet verteld dat hij iets te zeggen had?

'Pap?' Kade wierp John een nieuwsgierige blik toe. 'Heb jij iets bekend te maken?'

John haalde zijn schouders op, voor zover dat lukte met zijn brace. Zijn scheve grijns vertelde Abby genoeg. Wat hij ook wilde gaan zeggen, Jake en hij hadden zijn deel voorbereid. 'Ja, ik denk van wel.'

'Kom op, coach. Vertellen.'

'Goed.' John richtte zich een beetje hoger op. 'Jake en ik hebben laatst een beetje gepraat en hij vertelde me dat volgend jaar zijn beste seizoen wordt. Ik bedoel…' John hield zijn hoofd schuin en er speelde een grijns om zijn mondhoeken. 'Dan zit hij in de eindexamenklas en zo.'

'En voor het eerst zal ik naar de coach luisteren… en alles doen wat hij van me vraagt…'

Abby hield haar adem in. Ging hij soms zeggen…?

'Daarom heb ik besloten mijn ontslag in te trekken.' John hief zijn handen en liet ze in zijn schoot vallen. 'Ik ga volgend jaar toch nog coachen!'

Er barstte een koor los van felicitaties en omhelzingen, high-fives en gelach. Jo sloeg op haar been. 'Dat geeft de doorslag. De sportcoördinator van Marion High… hoe heet-ie?'

'Herman Lutz,' grinnikte John.

'Precies, Lutz. Nou, *die* krijgt de visballon. Ik zal hem persoonlijk naar zijn kantoor brengen om hem te overhandigen. "Wat een vangst, vriend!" zal ik zeggen, "Je hebt geluk dat je John Reynolds als coach terug hebt gekregen!"'

Weer begon iedereen door elkaar te praten en te gokken op de kansen van het team van volgend jaar en voorspellingen te doen over Jakes prestaties. Abby sloot zich er grotendeels voor af en leunde tegen de muur. Haar ogen vonden John en ze zag dat hij ook niet luisterde.

In plaats daarvan voerden ze een privégesprek met hun ogen. Een dialoog waarin Abby John vertelde hoe trots ze was dat hij zijn mannetje had gestaan en had gewonnen, dat hij zich bedacht had over zijn baan als coach op Marion en besefte dat hij daar hoorde. En John bedankte haar in stilte dat ze hem had bijgestaan. Niet alleen in de moeilijke dagen van het afgelopen seizoen en in de verschrikking van het ongeluk, maar ook toen hij in een rolstoel zat en ook toen ze zijn operatie afwachtten. En zelfs nu, nu hij ervoor koos om zijn tijd zonder haar door te brengen met datgene waarvan hij hield.

'Ik kan haast niet wachten.' Ze vormde de woorden in stilte met haar mond, genietend van dit ogenblik in afzondering terwijl de anderen om hen heen luidruchtig feestten.

'Ik ook niet.' Hij stak zijn hand naar haar uit en ze kwam bij hem, vlocht haar vingers door de zijne en voelde zijn liefde met elke vezel van haar wezen. 'Weet je, Abby?'

'Wat?' Ze fluisterden nog steeds.

'Dit wordt het mooiste seizoen aller tijden.'

Abby glimlachte en gaf een kneepje in zijn hand. Ze hadden zo'n lange weg afgelegd en samen zoveel meegemaakt. Maar nu was ze terug waar ze zoveel jaren geleden begonnen was. Toen ze zich verheugde op september en de warme gloed van de stadion-verlichting op het gezicht van de man die haar grote liefde was. Opgaand in een reeks vrijdagavondwedstrijden, zoals altijd sinds ze een klein meisje was.

De zomer lag voor hen en daarmee zonder twijfel tientallen kleine wonderen. Haley zou thuiskomen en John zou weer op de been zijn. Maar op dit moment werd Abby in beslag genomen door één tintelende gedachte.

John Reynolds ging weer coachen.

Abby keek reikhalzend uit naar het begin van het nieuwe seizoen in hun leven samen. John had gelijk... het werd het mooiste seizoen aller tijden.

Van de auteur

Verlamming is een uiterst beroerde toestand. De hoofdoorzaak van een plotselinge verlamming is vandaag de dag in Amerika een schotwond in nek of rug. Auto-ongelukken volgen als tweede meest voorkomende oorzaak. De technologie en behandelingen die in *Toegift* worden beschreven, zijn futuristisch en nog niet in gebruik. Niettemin vindt er op dit moment volgens de *American Association of Neurological Surgeons* en het *Congress of Neurological Surgeons* een 'explosie van nieuwe chirurgische technieken' plaats die bedacht zijn om ruggenmergletsel te verminderen of ongedaan te maken.

In veel gevallen zijn voor deze nieuwe chirurgische technieken nog financiële steun en proeven nodig voordat ze ingezet kunnen worden. Sommige zullen pas over jaren of tientallen jaren gebruikt kunnen worden zoals bij John Reynolds. Ik heb coach Reynolds vervroegd van deze nieuwe chirurgische technieken laten profiteren, om te laten zien wat ik hoop en bid dat eens werkelijkheid zal worden voor iedereen die slachtoffer is geworden van dit verwoestende type letsel.

Nawoord

Bedankt voor het lezen van Abby en Johns verhaal. Dit is mijn tweede boek over deze hoofdpersonen en ik ben erg op hen gesteld geraakt. En ik heb veel lessen van hen geleerd. De belangrijkste is wel deze: het leven bestaat uit seizoenen. Er zijn tijden van blijdschap en tijden van pijn, tijden van verdriet en tijden van groei.

Nadat ze bijna gescheiden waren, hebben John en Abby zich door God laten redden. Ik heb tientallen echtparen gesproken die hebben meegemaakt wat John en Abby meemaakten. Echtparen die van elkaar hielden en hun leven lang bij elkaar wilden blijven, om te ontdekken dat hun eenheid ergens onderweg verstoord werd.

God leert ons in de Bijbel dat Hij ons nooit boven onze draagkracht in verzoeking zal brengen, maar dat Hij een uitweg verschaft als we verzocht worden. Vaak is een van de echtelieden niet bereid die uitweg te zoeken, niet bereid de stem van God te horen boven de stem van hun eigen verlangens. Maar als beiden Gods uitweg volgen en hun geschillen opzij zetten, is het resultaat onvoorstelbaar mooi.

De meeste relaties maken trauma's mee. Onenigheid, geschillen, ruzies. Soms zelfs verraad. God wist dat we onderweg zouden struikelen, daarom heeft Hij ons Zijn Woord gegeven met daarin adviezen hoe we daarmee om moeten gaan. En er sterker uit kunnen komen.

Vergeef zoals God u vergeven heeft.
De liefde is geduldig en vol goedheid.
Ze laat zich niet boos maken.
De liefde bedekt tal van zonden.
Verdraag elkaar. Bemoedig elkaar.

Wat deden Jezus' trouwe volgelingen in de hof toen plotseling een troep soldaten verscheen? Ze sloegen op de vlucht. Daar zijn wij ook toe geneigd als ons huwelijk niet gaat zoals wij verwachtten, maar we doen er goed aan Christus' voorbeeld te volgen. Hij vergaf Zijn vrienden en troostte hen na Zijn opstanding zonder nog te denken aan het onrecht dat ze Hem hadden aangedaan.

Als we in een beproefd huwelijk samen naar God opzien, zal onze band er uiteindelijk sterker van worden. Zoek hier alstublieft geen ongevoeligheid in jegens mensen die gescheiden zijn. Het is een zeldzame uitzondering als twee mensen die vastbesloten zijn om uit elkaar te gaan in plaats daarvan naar God opzien.

Als u een scheiding overweegt, houd er dan mee op elkaar aan te vallen en besef in plaats daarvan dat de vijand van onze zielen degene is die verwoest wat God geschapen heeft. En de eenheid in het huwelijk is beslist een door God gegeven geschenk.

Zoek hulp... bid samen... bid voor elkaar... zoek naar wegen om uw echtgenoot te eren. En zoek vooral naar de uitweg. Vaak is een verontschuldiging al genoeg. En laat God uw gebroken liefde helen. U zult zien dat de band die u heeft daar sterker van wordt.

Ook wij hebben moeilijke perioden meegemaakt. Na veertien jaar basketbal coachen, neemt mijn echtgenoot een paar jaar vrij. Enkele zaken die John Reynolds voor zijn ongeluk meemaakte, kennen wij van zeer nabij.

Als uw kind aan een teamsport meedoet, zou ik u willen vragen: bedank de coach. Wees dankbaar als hij of zij om uw kind geeft, geen vuile taal gebruikt of uw kind misbruikt omwille van een overwinning. Maak er een gewoonte van na elke training of wedstrijd de coach, die het werk in zijn vrije tijd doet en er weinig voor betaald krijgt, te bedanken. Een goede coach is moeilijk te vinden.

Ik hoop dat u dit in goede gezondheid leest en geniet van de rijke beloften van onze God.

In Zijn liefde,
Karen Kingsbury

PS Zoals altijd kunt u mij e-mailen op rtnbykk@aol.com of contact opnemen via mijn website www.karenkingsbury.com.

Dankwoord

In de eerste plaats dank aan mijn man en kinderen voor hun begrip als ik me opsluit als de deadline nadert.

Ook dank aan mijn ouders en de rest van de familie die mijn boeken lezen en waardevolle inzichten bieden. Speciale dank aan mijn nicht Shannon.

Ondersteuning met gebed is van essentieel belang als ik aan het schrijven ben. Zonder de gebeden van mijn man en kinderen, mijn familie en vrienden zou ik deze verhalen niet kunnen schrijven. Ook dank aan Sylvia en Walt Wallgren, Ann Hudson en vele trouwe lezers die voortdurend voor me bidden.

Ook speciale dank aan mijn assistente Amber Santiago, die er voor mijn gezin is als ik aan het schrijven ben.

Dank aan Louise en Warren, die een pension hebben waar ik een paar dagen achter elkaar rustig kon schrijven. Ik kom beslist bij jullie terug.

Dank aan de mensen die de drukproeven voor mij lezen: Melinda Chapman, Joan Westphal, Kathy Santschi en de Wallgrens.

Zakelijk wil ik Ami McConnell, Debbie Wickwire en de beste mensen van Thomas Nelson bedanken voor hun toewijding.

Ik had het voorrecht te werken met mijn lievelingsredacteur Karen Book, terwijl ze het moeilijk had met het verlies van haar moeder, enkele dagen voor het redigeren van mijn manuscript.

Ik ben God dankbaar dat Hij Greg Johnson in mijn leven bracht. Greg is als agent voor elke auteur een droom die werkelijkheid wordt.